MW00988423

THE PRAIRIE ROMANCE

COLLECTION

THE PRAIRIE ROMANCE
COLLECTION

12
Complete
STORIES

BARBOUR
PUBLISHING

After the Harvest © 2002 by Lynn A. Coleman
Love Notes © 2007 by Mary Davis
Mother's Old Quilt © 2004 by Lena Nelson Dooley
The Tie That Binds © 2000 by Susan K. Downs
A Heart's Dream © 2001 by Birdie L. Etchison
The Bride's Song © 2000 by Linda Ford
The Barefoot Bride © 2000 by Linda Goodnight
Prairie Schoolmarm © 2005 by JoAnn A. Grote
The Provider © 2000 by Cathy Marie Hake
Freedom's Ring © 2000 by Judith McCoy Miller
Returning Amanda © 2000 by Kathleen Paul
Only Believe © 2000 by Janet Spaeth

ISBN 978-1-60260-435-3

All scripture quotations are taken from the King James Version of the Bible.

This book is a work of fiction. Names, characters, places, and incidents are either products of the author's imagination or used fictitiously. Any similarity to actual people, organizations, and/or events is purely coincidental.

Published by Barbour Publishing, Inc., P.O. Box 719, Uhrichsville, Ohio 44683, www.barbourbooks.com

Our mission is to publish and distribute inspirational products offering exceptional value and biblical encouragement to the masses.

 Member of the
Evangelical Christian
Publishers Association

Printed in the United States of America.

Contents

AFTER THE HARVEST

by Lynn A. Coleman

Dedication

To my granddaughter Leanna.
May you grow up to be strong in the faith of our Lord Jesus.
All my love, Grandma.

Chapter 1

September 1857

A gentle breeze stirred the white tips of rye and barley stalks. Rylan's face creased with a satisfied grin. The bountiful harvest testified of God's good grace.

Tall stalks continued to dance and play like carefree children. Children! The next step in Rylan's plan—a wife and a pack of children. He shifted his weight on his chestnut sorrel, the creak of the leather protesting the sudden change.

Months had passed since his last letter to Margaret. Three years he'd worked to develop the land enough to support her and the children they would have one day. Five months and not a word.

Truth be told, he hadn't had an encouraging word from Margaret in more than a year. The first year he'd come and settled on his land in Kansas and received regular letters. The second, they came less and less. But he refused to believe her love for him had dwindled. No, theirs was a strong one, a divine one. God had placed her in his life. Their love would withstand the hardship of separation. Yet her constant praise of Jackson Pearle, his best friend, made Rylan wonder. . . .

Rylan reached down and pulled the grain from a stalk. The seed rolled in his palm. A farmer with land to work. What could be more exciting than that?

Margaret's fine features glowed in his memory. "Ah yes, Lord, she is a fine one."

Tomorrow the harvesting would begin. Today he would go to town and hire a few extra hands for the harvest. Rylan shifted in his saddle and nudged the horse forward. Perhaps Margaret's letter had arrived, telling him when to expect her and her family. A man could hope.

He rode toward the dozen or so buildings that made up Prairie Center, the seat of Prairie County. This new territory of Kansas represented the hope and future of overpopulated Massachusetts and the rest of the North. Rylan had come and staked his claim, yielding to the enticement of free land. Margaret had agreed to postpone their wedding for a couple years to allow him to get the farm established. The fact that it had taken him a third year to build a suitable house and raise the funds for her ticket shouldn't have been a problem.

Admittedly, her letters came less frequently after he wrote her of the need for yet another year of separation. Rylan shook his head. No, he wasn't going to entertain those dark thoughts again. She was coming; he could feel it in his bones. It was just the knot in his stomach that didn't seem to share the same conviction.

Rylan hitched his horse outside the general store and ambled inside. "Hello, Pete."

"Afternoon, Rylan." Pete Anderson stood behind a counter with a white apron spread across his broad belly.

"Know of anyone needing a couple days' work?"

"Crops ready?" Pete placed a pencil down on the counter.

"Yup, and it's a good one."

"Glad to hear it. How many men do you need?"

Rylan removed his hat and wiped the inside brim with his red handkerchief. "Six is a good start, but I'll go as high as a dozen if there're enough men looking for work."

"Usually are. A day or two's work before a man continues west isn't bad to line his pockets a tad bit more."

Rylan grinned. Hiring extra men at harvesttime wasn't difficult in Prairie County. Keeping men to stay and work the season. . .that was another matter. "Spread the word. Tell 'em to be at my place by sunup, and we'll work 'til sundown."

Pete picked up his pencil. "Can I get you anything else today?"

Rylan didn't want to ask if he had a letter. He'd been asking every time he'd come to town for the past two months. "Think I'll just browse and see what's new."

"There are some newspapers from back east, Boston, in fact. Didn't you tell me you came from there?"

"Yup."

"Set and read a spell."

"Thanks. Don't mind if I do." Newspapers were like gold, and once in a while someone would leave a previously read paper at the store, with a little prompting from Pete, of course. Occasionally Pete would pull them out of the trash and save them.

Beside the front window of the store, Pete had set a table and a couple of chairs. A man could grab a cup of coffee and read to his heart's content. Rylan searched through the papers and found the one from Boston. He placed his hat on the table and sat down in the chair, spreading open the paper. Pete brought over a mug of coffee. Old names, familiar streets... Rylan journeyed back to Boston, to his family home, to a life he'd left behind.

An hour passed before he turned the final page. His heart stopped. He jumped up. The half-full mug of coffee toppled over. The table wobbled. "No!" he moaned.

Randolph and Wilma Cousins are proud to announce the betrothal of their daughter, Margaret Elizabeth, to Jackson Pearle. . . .

Rylan couldn't believe his eyes. He blinked and read the malicious lines again and again. Why? All the work. . .all the planning. . .for what?

❧

Judith leaped out of the way as a man barreled out of Pete Anderson's store. She brushed the skirt of her dress to remove any vestiges of the dust and dirt he kicked up. "How rude," she mumbled under her breath.

Singularly focused and driven were the best ways to describe the human train pushing his way out of the store and to his horse. She opened the basket carrying the few tomatoes she hoped Pete could sell. They weren't much, but they were something to help ease the burden of her father's debt.

Her father wasn't a farmer. He should have stayed in Worcester. Coming to Kansas to start over again seemed impossible. And having looked over the fields her father had planted in the spring compared to the other farmers in the area, it was painfully obvious he should have stayed back east.

"Hi, Pete. Who was that?"

Pete's generous smile warmed his full face. "Rylan Gaines owns the spread west of your father's."

"Oh." The farmer whose fields shouted her father's ineptitude. "I brought some tomatoes. I'm hoping you can sell them and put the money towards my father's debt."

"Sure," Pete said, reaching for the bundle of tomatoes. "Fine-looking vegetables. They'll sell."

Judith smiled. She didn't know if Pete was being truthful or simply generous. It didn't matter. What her father owed for seed, a few tomatoes wouldn't make a dent in.

"There's a paper from Boston over there." Pete pointed to the small wooden table and chairs. Over the summer it had been her only hiatus in this horrible place her parents now called home. They had let her stay in Worcester the first year while they settled.

Judith examined the soiled newspaper, an overturned cup, and a wet brown substance she assumed was coffee. The newsprint bled. The paper bubbled. "Pete, do you have anything to clean up this mess?" she called out.

"What mess?"

"Appears to be coffee."

"Well, I'll be. Something must have rattled Rylan." Pete sauntered over with a dry rag.

Judith scanned what she could of the obituaries, birth announcements, and wedding announcements. "Perhaps someone he knew passed away."

"Always possible. Rylan was one of the first to arrive. He came in fifty-four. Far as I can tell, he hasn't been back east since." Pete sopped up the coffee the paper hadn't. His hand paused in midair.

"What?"

"Uhh, nothing." Pete finished his work and hurried back behind the counter.

Whatever bothered Rylan Gaines had hit Pete with nearly as much force. Judith scanned the paper again. No one named Gaines had passed away, married, or had a baby. Of course, she had no idea who his maternal grandparents were. It was always possible one of these names represented someone from that side of his family. But if someone had died, wouldn't Pete have said?

Pete wasn't a true gossip, but the man openly shared the comings and goings of most folks. He was Prairie County's newspaper. No, it was something worse than death—and something more personal, she assessed. *"Mind your concerns, Judith,"* she heard her mother's voice chide her. Ever since childhood Judith had felt the urge to butt in and know why so-and-so did this and so-and-so did that. Gossip was the hardest sin she fought. Her natural curiosity craved finding out information. Truly this wasn't her concern. If so, Pete would have said what was wrong. But he hadn't, and she needed to leave it at that.

Judith tore the damp page from the rest of the paper and placed it over the other chair to dry. She settled down and read about life back east, the life she'd left behind. The life she desperately wanted to return to.

"Excuse me, Judith," Pete called over to her.

Judith popped her head up over the edge of the newspaper. She'd been reading nonstop.

"Are you aware of the county fair coming up?"

"County fair?"

"Yeah, we hold it once a year. The farmers bring their crops, and the women—what few we have—bake pies. There are horse pulls, judging contests. . . . It's a lot of fun."

"No, I guess I hadn't heard about it." Even if she had, she knew her father wouldn't be bringing his crops to show off.

"Reason I mention it is there's some prize money for the best foods, and I thought you and your mother might like to enter." Pete continued to count his stock.

Prize money. Could she and her mom possibly win?

"There's a flyer hanging in my window. You know, on your father's land there's the best batch of wild black raspberries. They'd make some mighty fine jam."

"If one had the sugar," she mumbled.

"They're so sweet, hardly need to add sugar."

Had he heard her? She really did need to stop mumbling to herself.

"So you hold this fair every year?"

"It's a grand time. Helps bring the folks in the county together. We're spread so far apart."

She'd seen enough of the county to know how true a statement that was. Eighty acres were given to each man and woman who set up their claim, but they needed to stay on the land for five years before the property actually became theirs.

Five years. She closed her eyes as if to shut out the knowledge of how much time stretched out before her until her parents would own their claim. Why did it bother her so much to be here? Nothing remained of the family home or her father's bank back east. Her parents were here. Folks seemed friendly enough. She hadn't left an admirer behind, so why her discontent?

"Where did you say these berries were?"

Pete rubbed his well-shaved chin. "I'd say on the hill behind where they built the house. There's a line of trees that form a *V* and point right to it. You can't miss 'em."

"Thanks. Don't know if I'll be making any jam, but the berries would be a nice treat for the folks." Judith headed toward the door.

"Don't have to make jam—that was just a suggestion. You can make anything and enter it," Pete encouraged.

Judith turned and waved. "Thanks, Pete."

Something for Momma's sweet tooth to get her through the winter would be worth the effort to find those berries. She hadn't searched the land much. She'd been so busy tending the garden and livestock, who had time for exploring?

On the other hand, the money would be a blessing if she should win. Who was she kidding? She held her own in the kitchen, but she was certain she couldn't compete with the other women who lived in this territory.

Of course, there weren't all that many women living in the county. Judith's father had had more offers for her hand in marriage since she'd arrived in Prairie Center than during her entire eighteen years in Worcester. Some men who hadn't even seen her came proposing. She climbed up on the buckboard and headed home.

"Howdy, Miss Timmons, may I escort you home?" Brian Flannery tipped his hat and rode proud in his saddle. He wasn't an unhandsome man, but the lack of a front tooth gave him a less-than-intelligent appearance.

"Thank you, Mr. Flannery, but it isn't necessary."

"Nonsense. A pretty woman like you shouldn't be alone."

Alone? How could she be? If Brian hadn't shown up, there was a list of at least a dozen other men who would. She'd never made a trip back from town without an escort.

"Thank you," she said with a smile. Inwardly she sighed, praying just once an opportunity would arise for her to go home in peaceful solitude.

Rylan stormed home, pushing Max as fast as the workhorse could run. Back in the barn, he brushed the animal down with care. The poor beast wasn't the problem. Margaret and Jackson, they were his problem. How long had they been seeing each other behind his back? The newspaper was nearly a month old, and he'd not even received a sorry-but-I-fell-in-love-with-another-man letter.

"Nothing. Not one single word," he huffed. "Why, Lord?" He threw the brush against the shelf and left Max with a bag of oats in payment for the hard ride home.

He'd trusted her. He'd worked himself weary preparing this place for her and their children. He looked over the barn. A barn, a house, and a root cellar. How much more did a woman need? And what was so great about Jackson?

Rylan didn't consider himself a vain man, but he beat Jackson hands down in the looks department. Jackson barely had a chin to speak of. The poor guy was all neck.

"Jackson, thanks—friend." The bile in his stomach boiled. He kicked a small stone with his boot.

He looked up at the house built for Margaret, a labor of love, now an empty tomb of disappointment and despair. "Why, Margaret? Didn't I give you everything I promised I would? And why Jackson?"

Rylan turned his back to the house. He couldn't sleep in there tonight. Not tonight. He needed to get a handle on his emotions. The temptation to tear the place apart board by board burned at him. Thankfully, something held him back. Perhaps it was all the hours he'd put into it, or hopefully it was God's grace giving him some good common sense.

Every instinct he had urged him to storm home to Massachusetts and demand some answers. His head throbbed from the war being fought within. He needed time. Time to absorb. And time to decide what to do with his future.

He pulled a wool blanket from the barn, tucked a knife in his boot, and grabbed his rifle. Tonight he would camp in the small woods bordering his land and Oscar Timmons's. Oscar wasn't much of a farmer, but you only had to farm ten acres of the eighty to earn your land. The fact that he still lived in a dugout only proved how poorly the man was doing. Oscar once had told Rylan he was a banker. But his bank went bust when some investments he'd made hadn't panned out. In the end, he ended up selling all he had to pay off the debts the bank had accumulated before he sold it off for pennies on the dollar. Whatever Oscar's ability with numbers, he certainly didn't have a hand for growing.

The brisk pace Rylan took as he headed toward the woods raised a sweat. A refreshing swim in the small pond on his property would help chill his burning temper. Most days it took Rylan quite a bit to lose his temper. Today was not most days.

He stripped to the waist and dove in. His long frame sluiced through the water as he swam deeper and deeper under the surface. No sound penetrated under the water. His lungs burned for oxygen. How long did he dare stay below the surface?

Rylan scanned the murky bottom and spun around, looking toward the sky. The water was so clear above him. Below him it was dark, murky, full of decaying leaves and matter. Above, the pure, clean water fed by a small stream.

He pushed his arms upward and kicked his legs with all his strength. He was a man brought to this earth by God for a purpose. He needed to look up to find his direction in life, not down in the pit of darkness and despair. Another strong kick and pull with his arms and Rylan's head broke the surface, his lungs sucking in the precious oxygen that gave him life. "Lord, show me what to do," he gasped.

Chapter 2

Judith stretched her back, placing the heavily laden baskets of fruit on the rustic wooden table.

"Goodness, dear, where did you get these?" Her mother's pale blue eyes widened.

"Pete Anderson told me there were some wild berries on our land. And, Mother, you won't believe how thick those bushes are. I hardly made a dent."

"Mercy, what are we going to do with all these?" Judith's mother, Riaxa, wiped her hands on a small hand towel.

"Enter the Prairie County Fair. Pete said you can win prize money for the best—"

"Judith, sit down," her mother interrupted. Her once-thin frame now seemed to be more rugged and definitely wider in the hips. Back home, she never would have allowed those extra pounds to take over.

Judith obediently sat down. Her mother sat across from her at the small pine kitchen table.

"The fair is a lot of fun but hardly the place to make a lot of money. Yes, there is a contest, and some prize money is handed out, but it's not much. Mostly, it is a place for everyone to gather together and have a good time. The farmers discuss farming, tools, seed, everything under the sun. The women talk about quilting, canning, children, and how to make do with what you have."

"But—"

"Honey, I know you're having a rough adjustment, and yes, money is tight, but we will survive. We may not have the wealth we had back in New England but. . ."

"Don't you miss it?" Judith couldn't believe her mother didn't miss her silk dresses, fancy evening apparel, and the rest. They used to dine out three or four times a week.

"Actually, not too much. Oh sure, I wouldn't mind having servants take care of all the housework, but your father and I have rediscovered ourselves, our relationship to each other, and to God."

"You both do seem happier." Judith realized there had been a change in her parents' behavior. They seemed closer. They talked more often to each other. Many times back home they seemed to simply exist in the same house, each with their own life to live. Here, well, here things were definitely different.

"We are, dear. Extremely," she added, leaning slightly toward Judith.

"I'm happy for you. But we are in need of money. The seed bill alone will bury us. What's Father going to do when it comes time for planting next year if he hasn't paid off this year's debt?"

Her mother's shoulders slumped.

"Don't you see? We need to at least try to win. Even if we don't, perhaps we can sell some of the jam to those heading west."

Raixa Timmons had once reigned as a paragon of proper posture and manners in Worcester. That woman and the woman before Judith now were scarcely the same. Her once finely groomed eyebrows had grown thick. "I suppose you're right. It couldn't hurt to at least try."

Judith jumped up and embraced her mother. Perhaps they could earn enough to return to Worcester. She let that thought exit her head as fast as it entered. A few berries and a few pies wouldn't provide one so much as the cost of meals on the return trip.

"I'll go pick some more. I think there's enough time before sunset."

The older woman chuckled. "Be careful of those briars."

"Yes, Mother."

Judith lit through the door with renewed purpose. Her heart hadn't felt this gay since leaving Worcester.

Bending over in the bushes, Judith realized the only thing she and her mother could make at this point would be jam. The pies and tarts would spoil. She'd have to pick again in a few days. Her picking done, she headed for home. In the distance she spied a man heading toward the grove of trees that ran along their property and her neighbor's. Rylan Gaines. She guessed he was still in an ugly disposition. Perhaps he always walked around with a chip on his shoulder. "Curious," she mumbled.

Back at the house after dinner was served, she asked, "Mother, have you ever met our neighbor?"

"Rylan?"

"Yes."

"Sweet young man." Judith's mother crushed another handful of berries. "Why do you ask, dear?"

"He nearly plowed me over in town today. He didn't seem the friendly sort."

"That is odd. I've never known Rylan to be anything less than a perfect gentleman." She paused in her crushing of the berries and looked toward Rylan's home.

"I think he read something in a paper from Boston," Judith persisted. "I couldn't figure out who died or what bothered him. His surname wasn't listed in the paper."

Her mother turned her gaze back to Judith with a look that was all too familiar. "There you go again, Daughter. You must stop this unbridled curiosity of yours. Every man is entitled to some privacy."

"I know, I know, but—"

"Judith Joy."

Her mother had scolded her on more than one occasion in that tone. "Sorry," she replied sheepishly and looked down at her berries. What was it with this place? Everyone seemed to be overly sensitive about knowing what was going on with others. *I was just being curious, trying to relate in some small way. . . . Stop lying to yourself, Judith. You know you're just curious about why he was so upset. A mystery you haven't been unable to unlock.* She sighed.

Her mother laughed. Judith could hear her father snicker in the other room.

❧

The next morning, Rylan fought the demons that had kept him awake all night. Sleeping in the woods hadn't helped. Nightmares of seeing Margaret and Jackson arm and arm. . . He tossed a pitchfork into the wagon.

"Whoa, you trying to kill someone?" Ed Randolph asked as he walked up to the wagon.

"Guess I wasn't thinking," Rylan mumbled. If he wanted the men to work for him, he'd better rein in his emotions. He'd need the money from harvesting the rye and barley in order to pay for his trip back to Massachusetts. He'd decided he'd have to go back and confront them. Even just for his own peace of mind.

"Pete says you could use some help." Ed's thin frame hid the man's strength. He didn't bulge in the muscle department, but he held his own. Enough so that Rylan wouldn't want to cross him.

"Sure could. Hoped more would be coming, though."

"Ah, not to worry. I saw some headed here. I cut across Timmons's place. That man can't farm for anything. The ground is so rich here all you have to do is drop the seed, but. . ."

"Now don't go pickin' on the man. Seems to me I had to show you a thing or two." Rylan winked.

"Yeah, yeah. But even at my worst, I wasn't as bad as Timmons."

"He's not a farmer."

"What ever gave you that idea?" Ed asked in a sarcastic tone.

"Told me he's a banker."

"Why ain't he being a banker then?"

"That's for him to say, not me. But he has his reasons."

"He couldn't have robbed the bank. He wouldn't have ended up here if he had."

"No, he didn't rob the bank."

"Who robbed the bank?" George Steadman sneezed into his handkerchief and deposited the folded cloth into the back pocket of his overalls.

21

"No one. You guys are worse than women," Rylan teased.

"No worse than anyone else." George set his hands on his hips. "Didn't know if you'd need my wagon, so I have the youngin' bringing it over later, after the missus uses it to buy her supplies."

"Thanks, George. Of course we'll use it."

George nodded.

Half a dozen others showed up, and Rylan put them all to work. The sweat beaded on his back. It felt good to work. Healthy, even. *Perhaps a trip to Boston isn't worth the effort. The damage is done; they're married. What could I do anyway?*

By nightfall they'd cleared a good third of the fields. Rylan paid each man and encouraged him to bring others the next day. As the workers departed, he finished bagging the grain that a couple of the men had threshed. He sewed up each fifty-pound burlap sack after filling it. Dried, the stalks would be used to feed his horses through the winter.

Stretching his back, he realized he'd sleep tonight. He smelled worse than the pigs after a fresh roll in the mud. Pumping out some fresh water, he stripped and bathed in the yard.

"Hello," a male voice called from the darkness.

Rylan grabbed his trousers and pulled them on. "Who's there?" he called. A light swayed in the distance.

"Oscar Timmons."

"What brings you out so late?"

"I need a favor." Oscar's shadowed image came into view.

"What can I do for you?"

The pencil-thin man with his freshly tanned face seemed much older this year than last.

"I need your honest opinion."

Rylan leaned against a fence rail. "I'll be as honest as I can. What's up?"

"Me, I'm no farmer. The second season is in, and I've barely anything to harvest."

"True, but do you have enough to feed your family?"

"I imagine so, if we're careful. Judith has tried to help. She has more of a green thumb than either her mother or I, but—"

"Say no more. Look, the deal with the New England Emigrant Aid Society that helped us get out here is that we live on the land for five years. There's no conditional clause about us having to make a profit. The thing you need to worry about the most is feeding your family. That's all. If you can do that, in three more years the land is yours, free and clear."

A slight grin rose on his cheek. "Thank you for the reminder."

"Don't fuss about it. I might be needing your encouragement soon."

"What's the trouble? I heard you barreled out of town yesterday."

How'd he know that? Of course, everyone knew everything about everybody. But this tidbit was his. No one else needed to know his shame. "Just in a hurry."

"Oh."

Oscar wouldn't ask. Rylan knew he wasn't that kind of man. Being a banker, he was used to keeping other men's secrets. If Rylan could confide in anyone, it would be Oscar.

"Are you entering the fair?" A change in subject was necessary.

Oscar laughed. "Are you serious? Is there a category for the smallest tomatoes?"

Rylan chuckled. "I'm entering the team pull. My team seemed to finally get their act together this year."

"I don't have a team. I have a single mule that's more stubborn than Judith." Oscar's smile slipped.

The man certainly had his problems.

"Don't think they have a 'most stubborn mule' category, but if I hear of one, I'll let you know."

Oscar chuckled. "Good night, Rylan, and thanks again."

"Good night." Rylan watched the light grow dim as Oscar headed across the fields. If Oscar could stick it out, he'd be happy to purchase some of the land from him. He'd even considered farming a section of Oscar's land on a rental basis but hadn't checked the agreement to see if that was allowable or not.

Inside the house, he fought the memories of Margaret's promises. He'd made the furnishings for her. Even the house had been for her. He'd be just as comfortable in the barn. Well, perhaps not as comfortable as the feather bed he'd put together. "Lord, why? Why'd she do it? Why Jackson?" He fell to his knees, covering his anguished face with his rough hands. Tears fell for the first time. The only time. He was a man. He couldn't allow this. He sniffed and straightened himself up. No, with God's grace, he'd get through this, just like every other bad moment of his life.

He wiped the tears from his face with his red handkerchief. *I'll place an ad in a New York paper for a wife. Any woman would do now, since his one true love had deceived him so. Yes, I'll place an ad tomorrow. Tonight I'll sleep outdoors again. The air is fresher,* he reasoned. He lied. He knew it.

🌿

Thursday, the day before the fair, Judith marched out to the berry patch early. The sun rose slowly over the hills as she worked her way toward the plentiful harvest. Getting an early start would allow time for possible failures. The jam she and her mother had made had turned out extremely well. Little sugar had been used. Instead, because of the bounty of the berries, they were able to thicken it with the fruit. The family had tried it last evening on warm bread fresh from the oven. Judith had never tasted anything better.

In the distance she saw a man heading toward Rylan Gaines's place. *All right, Lord, I know I'm not supposed to be so curious, but even You have to admit this is very strange behavior. The man has a huge house. Two stories, clapboard, with a wide front porch. Why on earth is he spending the nights in the woods?*

A bird cawed. The world seemed to be waking up. Was it possible that Rylan Gaines had been hunting? Judith squinted her eyes for a better glance. He didn't appear to be carrying a rifle. But he was carrying something. "Humph." She wouldn't be finding out today what her strange neighbor was up to. Everyone seemed to think rather highly of him, yet there was something about him, something Judith couldn't put her finger on, something she knew wasn't right. Perhaps she was here in Prairie County to discover the truth about a certain Rylan Gaines. *Perhaps he has a secret past no one knows about. Eww, could he be running from the law?*

It wasn't unheard of for criminals to head west hoping to get lost in the crowds. No laws existed. The lands were uncharted. A shiver rolled down Judith's back. She'd given herself enough reasons to stay away and watch him like a hawk. After all, her parents thought the world of him. Yes, she had a purpose for coming to Prairie County. Once that purpose had been fulfilled, she could encourage her parents to move back home.

Judith bent down and picked with renewed vigor. Today she'd discovered the real reason God had seen fit to send her to this godforsaken land.

"Hello."

Judith shrieked.

Chapter 3

Rylan stepped back.

"Get away from me," Judith screamed.

Rylan raised his hands. "Sorry, I didn't mean to scare you. I saw you over here and assumed you were Oscar Timmons's daughter, Judith. I'm Rylan Gaines, your neighbor."

She patted her heart. He squelched a chuckle, seeing her berry-stained hand leave its indelible mark on the white bib of her dress.

"Yes, I'm Judith."

"I won't intrude any longer. I just thought I'd come by and say hello. Good day, Miss Timmons." He nodded and headed home. Rylan searched his memory. He couldn't remember a single time he'd scared someone so badly in all his life. Not even the time he scared his six-year-old sister when she'd been sneaking a pickle out of the pickle barrel. She'd jumped, knocked the barrel over, and sent pickles flying everywhere. The cellar reeked of vinegar for years.

"Pickles, nice big sour ones." His stomach grumbled. Yes, a wife would be a good thing. Pete had thought it foolish to advertise for a wife. Pete being Pete, he only said, "You're wasting your money." Then silently he wrote out the ad to be wired to New York later in the day.

Rylan shot back a glance at the berry-stained woman with a set of lungs that could deafen a man.... *It's all your fault, Pete.* Rylan stuffed his hands in his trousers and headed back toward his farm.

If Pete hadn't gone on and on about how pretty the Timmons's daughter was, Rylan wouldn't have taken the time to say hello. Granted, Pete was right. The woman was a real looker. But she seemed. . .what? *More afraid than scared of me? Maybe I just scare women off, Lord.*

With the rye and barley shipped off to market, Rylan began work for the winter. The seeds needed to be dried and bagged. The hay needed to be bundled for the livestock. And wood needed to be split for the cold winter months. The harvesting might be over, but there was plenty of work to be done. Plus, he'd be helping his neighbors pull in their harvests. Rylan's crop choices were rye and wheat. But he'd planted a couple acres of corn, too. It made for variety over the winter months.

Most of the area farmers planted corn. Many had trouble with the lack of rainfall for their crops during the summer. Having come to this land earlier, Rylan had been blessed with prime property. Two streams ran through the land, a river to his south, and the pond northeast that abutted the Timmons's property.

His mind drifted back to Judith Timmons and the blackberry stains on her white apron. Rylan chuckled. "She's an odd one, Lord."

❦

The next day he found himself at the Prairie County Fair. This year the number of people seemed double over the previous. The place buzzed with activity. Children ran from one event to another. The women huddled near their wares, and the men gathered around their livestock.

"Morning, George." Rylan held back his team.

"You entering in the pull?" asked a man Rylan didn't recognize.

"Yes, sir. My team's ready this year."

"Take a look at McCoy over there. He's really been working his team. Seems mighty impressive," George added.

Rylan watched for a few moments. No question about it, McCoy would offer serious competition. "Just means we'll be putting on a better show."

The men roared and continued to talk about their harvests. Several of the farmers who were raising corn had had a bad go of it.

"I'm hoping some of your wives will trade some of their canned vegetables for some of my rye," Rylan offered.

"Hazel should be willing. She's rather fond of rye bread."

"Wonderful. You're wife packs away some of the finest vegetables I've ever had. Afraid most of my summer vegetable crop will go to feed the pigs. I don't know how to can. Not that I have the time to do it."

Ralph Davis scratched his chest. "Seems to me you might be able to bring some of your vegetables to some of the womenfolk, and they might can some for you."

"I couldn't impose. Besides, they're a might busy taking care of their own."

"Hey, there," Josh Williams called, striding over with a bushel basket of apples. "Look at these fine apples. Hard to believe I got such a fine crop from those wee trees this year."

Everyone admired the beautiful apples Josh brought over. A row of apple trees would be nice around the house, Rylan thought. But his thoughts darkened. When would he have time to care for them? Perhaps a single tree was all he could handle. *A wife, I definitely need a wife.* "Excuse me, gentlemen, I need to take care of my team."

He brought his team over to the corral and noticed Judith Timmons sitting at a table. "Blackberries," he murmured, chuckling, then brought the horses into the corral.

⚘

Judith couldn't ignore Rylan Gaines. He stood tall, and he smiled a warm, genuine smile. Perhaps she'd been wrong in thinking he was a criminal, she reflected as she watched him work. He walked his team of horses into the corral. The way he treated his animals spoke volumes of the man's character. He placed some feedbags on their snouts and brushed them down.

Judith scanned the fairgrounds. So many people she didn't know. Yet they all knew her. At least, they all knew who she was. She hadn't seen her father this proud in all his life, introducing her to everyone he met. Men were plentiful. They came over to her table in a steady stream. Everyone bought something, whether a piece of pie, a tart, or some jam, it didn't matter. They were there not to purchase goods but to try and purchase her, she supposed. Three marriage proposals this morning alone. And ages varied from a young boy of sixteen to an old man of sixty. She certainly had plenty to pick from. But if she picked one, she wouldn't be returning to Worcester, and Worcester was the only place she wanted to be. Not that she was looking for a husband.

"Good morning." Rylan's distinguished voice drew her from her musings. "I see you've made good use of those berries." His smile was disarming.

A capricious smile rose up her cheeks. "Yes, Mother and I worked hard."

"It shows. How do you like Kansas?"

"Not much." She snapped her mouth shut and placed her hand over it. "I'm sorry," she mumbled.

Rylan's rich laughter eased her troubled state. A woman of society would not have spoken her mind so. "It's quite all right. Nothing wrong with being honest."

His eyelids closed over the most vibrant brown eyes she'd ever seen. Brown eyes never appealed to her. They seemed to just be dark orbs that blended into the background of one's soul. Blue eyes, now those were eyes that attracted her. So why was she so taken in by Rylan Gaines's brown eyes?

He opened them slowly; his posture stiffened. "Truth comes in short supply these days. Good day, Miss Timmons, and keep being honest."

He left as silently as he'd appeared. Was the man half fox? Another gentleman appeared in front of her table. "May I help you?"

"That ya can, lass. I'm looking for a wife. . . ."

Here we go again. Judith put on her pleasant "but I don't want to be here" smile. When would these men get the message? "I'm sorry. I'm not available."

"Oh, I apologize, lass. I heard ya were single."

She had to admit she loved his Irish accent. "I am single, so you didn't hear wrong. However, I'm not available."

He knitted his red eyebrows then released them. "Many pardons, lass. You'd best tell your husband-to-be to put a ring on your finger, and do it soon, or they'll be no end to the proposals."

Judith chuckled.

The poor man's face reddened even more.

"I'm sorry," she replied.

He scurried off before she could explain. Perhaps she shouldn't clarify the issue. Perhaps it would be best to let the entire town think she was engaged to be married. Of course, Mother and Father won't appreciate the deception. But what's a poor girl to do in a county where men out-number the women twenty to one?

The day continued with plenty of sales and far fewer proposals. They had actually stopped. Word must have gotten around. Her mother was working the table, which gave Judith her first real opportunity to peruse the fairgrounds. A crowd gathered at the corral; cheers and whistles filled the air. Judith worked her way toward the front. Inside the corral she saw Rylan working his team. "Oh my," she gasped.

"They're a pretty sight, aren't they, miss?" a man next to her observed.

Pretty wasn't exactly the word she had in mind. Muscles bulged on the horses. . .and on Rylan. They worked in unison, pulling the heavy load.

"What are they doing?" she asked the stranger.

"The goal is to have your team pull in unison as heavy a load as pos-sible and work them around those posts without losing your load."

"Oh my."

"Rylan did well last year, but I think he's going to beat McCoy this year. He's got a fine team. They were just too young last year."

Rylan's broad shoulders were straining the seams of his perspiration-soaked shirt. Was it that hard to keep a team working? Shouldn't the team work with ease? "Why is he working so hard?"

"His team wants to move faster than Rylan is allowing them to, but he knows they can't make the turn if they move faster. It's the difference between man and beast. The animal has learned how to haul but doesn't have the wisdom to analyze. On the other hand, in the wild these animals wouldn't be hauling this amount of weight, either."

Judith clenched the rail as Rylan worked his team around the first post. The crowd roared with excitement. Her informative new companion whispered, "This is where he lost his load last year."

Lord, help him, she silently prayed. Why was she so concerned about Rylan Gaines? It didn't make sense, but something deep inside of her wanted, no, needed him to succeed.

The horses pulled together. The load wobbled but stayed on the flat. They strained forward and twisted around the second post. Sweat beaded down Rylan's forehead. His grin was infectious. "Excellent job, Rylan!" she heard herself scream. He turned toward the crowd.

The crowd turned their attention on Judith. She felt her cheeks flame.

Rylan nodded.

Judith escaped from the probing eyes of the crowd. She heard murmurings but didn't care to listen. The safest place for her was back behind the table.

As Judith approached their stand, her mother asked, "Did you have fun, dear?"

"I found it quite interesting, Mother."

Her mother stood and straightened the skirt of her dress. "I'm glad. We've just about sold out. The raspberry tea is chilled, and your father insists we simply give it out as a gesture of friendship to our neighbors."

"Yes, Mother."

"They're about to judge the jams. Do you want to watch?"

"No, thank you." Judith sat down behind the table.

Her mother took two steps back toward her. "Is everything all right, dear?" she whispered.

Judith startled back to her senses. "Just fine, Mother. I think I'll have some of that tea myself."

"Great. Don't forget there's a sandwich in the basket also. Oh, and your father had me make one for Rylan if he should ever come around."

Judith swallowed and waved her mother off. The mere thought of meeting up with Rylan after such an outburst. . .

Her cheeks heated up again. *Lord, what's happening to me? I've been here for all of four months, and I'm forgetting all the social graces I've learned. Why?*

She poured herself a tall glass of tea and grabbed the smaller sandwich in the basket. Why had her father asked her mother to make a sandwich for Rylan?

"Congratulations, Miss Timmons." Pete waved as he walked past.

"Congratulations? What for?" she mumbled. Had they won the contest? Her spirit brightened. The sales and the prize money would make a good dent on the debt with Pete's store. But Mother just left to go to the judging. Could it be over that quickly?

❧

"Congratulations, Rylan, excellent job."

"Thanks, Jim." Rylan took McCoy's hand and pumped it.

Jim smiled. "I'll have to see what I can do to beat you next year."

Rylan chuckled. "Good idea. I worked hard on my team this past year."

"It shows. Excellent job, just excellent. By the way, when'd you have time to get yourself engaged to Judith Timmons?"

"What?"

"Everyone's talking about it. I didn't even know you were courting her. I thought you had a gal back east."

"I thought I did, too. I don't know about being engaged to Miss Timmons, though. When did this happen?"

Jim McCoy chuckled. "Well, if you're not the reason she's unavailable, who is?"

"I wouldn't have a clue. I've barely spoken with the gal. Who told you I was engaged?"

"Everyone. . .and no one in particular. Seems Michael O'Hara asked her earlier, and she told him she was unavailable. Seems he wasn't the only one asking, either. Anyway, when she burst out at the pull, I guess everyone assumed you were her beau."

"Hmm, don't suppose it occurred to anyone that we're just neighbors."

Jim chuckled. "What would be the fun in gossiping about that?"

Rylan wagged his head. "None, I suppose. I'm hunting for a wife, but I want one who wants to live here, not back east."

"Oscar said she wasn't too fond of the area." Jim leaned against a rail.

"He said the same to me. They gave up a lot to live out here." Rylan continued to brush down his horses.

"Can't understand why society folks would come back to the land. Wouldn't it be easier to hire folks to work your land instead?"

"If Oscar could afford that, I'm sure he would."

"I heard he ran into some financial troubles back east. Guess we all came for various reasons. But free land is free land and worth the work."

"Amen," Rylan added. He finished brushing down the horses after allowing them to walk off the heavy labor from moments before.

"Well, I won't be keeping you. Just wanted to congratulate you. And warn ya that I'll be winning next year." Jim smiled.

"If you can." Rylan winked.

As Jim took off, Rylan turned to his team. "Engaged! Can you imagine?" he muttered.

"I heard it too," Pete said with a wink as he walked over. "Congratulations."

"Don't tell me the entire town. . . ?" Rylan asked.

"Just about. Probably the entire county will have heard by the end of the day."

"Wonderful," Rylan moaned.

Pete took a step closer. "You mean, it's not true?"

"Not in the slightest."

"Oh, but I thought. . ." Pete rubbed his chin with his right hand.

"I have no idea why she cheered me on, but we are just neighbors."

"True, she doesn't know many."

"No, I can't imagine that she does. I've barely seen her all summer."

"That explains how she didn't know you when you nearly toppled her over a few days ago."

"What are you talking about?"

Pete reached over, placing his hand on Rylan's shoulder. "I read the announcement in the paper. I'm sorry."

"Thanks, but what does that have to do with me practically running over Miss Timmons?"

"Oh, well the day you read the announcement, she came into the store as you were departing."

"I wasn't in a good mood."

"No, I suspect not. She asked who you were, seemed to recognize your name, but I gathered she hadn't met you."

"No, I've been too busy working on the house in the evening after a full day of working the farm. I suppose I should have introduced myself to my neighbor sooner, but I was preoccupied."

"Doesn't matter. I'll start letting folks know it's not true." Pete took a step back.

"Thanks, Pete."

"No trouble at all. I don't mind being the man in the know." He wiggled his eyebrows.

Rylan chuckled. Then his mind sobered. Perhaps others would be congratulating Miss Timmons as well. He worked his way to her table. *She's a pretty thing, Lord,* he realized as the distance between them disappeared.

"Good afternoon, Miss Timmons," he said with a smile.

"Mr. Gaines, I—I . . ."

"Shh. I thank you for your praise."

She teased golden hair back and forth. Her yellowish brown eyes captivated him. "I'm so flustered. It's not right for a lady to speak so openly."

"Is it wrong for a woman to speak such to her fiancé?" he teased.

"What?"

Chapter 4

W hat on earth are you talking about?" She planted her hands on her hips. These backwoods yokels weren't going to mess up her reputation.

Rylan grinned. The dimple on his right cheek eased her tension. He reached for her hand. The warmth of his fingers made her breath catch in her throat. "Rumors have us engaged."

"How?...When?...Why?"

"Apparently you told Michael O'Hara you were unavailable."

"Michael?"

"Red-headed Irishman."

"Oh." *Lord, what have I done?* she silently petitioned.

"And when you spoke up after the pull. . ." His grin broadened.

"Oh, no."

"Oh, yes. When shall we set the date for our marriage?"

"You can't be serious," she hissed. Only a fool would propose something so preposterous on the basis of rumors and gossip.

Rylan released a deep barrel laugh. "No, Miss Timmons, I'm not serious, but the reaction on your face was worth the trouble."

"Oh, you! What is it with folks around here? Don't they have an ounce of proper manners and respect?"

Rylan's gaze narrowed. "Look, we may not be fancy here like Boston. And we don't have the high society balls, but we are honest folk. Which is more than I can say about your high society. Here, if a man gives his word, it is his word. He doesn't change his mind and back down."

"Huh?"

"Sorry, that has nothing to do with you. Or perhaps in some small way it does. Oscar never said you were engaged."

"I never said I was. I simply said I was unavailable. And I am. I have no interest in courting anyone." She held back her tongue, not wanting to anger the man any further. "What has you all fired up about high society?"

"You wouldn't understand." Rylan's shoulders slumped, and he looked down at his feet.

"Try me."

"All right, Miss Timmons. Here's the situation. If you pledged yourself to a man, and he went off to build your future together, would you wait for him?"

"Of course. That is what making a pledge is all about."

"Well, some don't."

Her curious nature piqued, she reached for the cask of black raspberry iced tea and poured him a glass. "Here, drink this. Tell me what happened."

"Maybe some other time." Rylan gulped down the tea. "Excellent tea."

"Thank you. I have a good ear if you decide you need to talk with someone."

Rylan chuckled. "I lived in the East, Judith. I know how society women gossip."

"I don't. All right, maybe I do sometimes. But who do I know here to gossip to? Besides, I never said a word to anyone that someone shared confidentially. I do have my morals."

Rylan leaned toward her, his gaze so beguiling she rapidly blinked, trying to break the connection she felt. "I do need a wife. Perhaps we should get engaged."

"Did you fall off your horse?" Judith stepped back. She needed air. For a fleeting moment she actually considered his absurd proposal.

"No, I'm just being practical. I need a wife; you need a husband. I've got a good farm, a house; I can provide nicely. Why not?"

"If you didn't just fall off your horse, he must have stomped on your pretty little head."

"You think I'm pretty?" he asked with a wink.

She was dying here. What kind of a man could be so forward and so intoxicating at the same time? "It's just not done that way!"

"In Boston, perhaps. But you're in the wilds now, remember?"

"Don't even get me started on that. I'm not available for the same reasons I told the young Irishman earlier, because I'm moving back east. I don't want to live here. I wouldn't make anyone a good wife. Not here."

"Perhaps, Miss Timmons. On the other hand, a woman with as much spirit as you possess is born for life in the untamed country of this land. Think about it."

Rylan placed his hat on his head and worked his way back into the crowd.

Judith collapsed in the chair behind her.

"Judith." Her mother came running. "I just heard the news. Honey, I'm so happy for you. I didn't even know you and Mr. Gaines had met each other."

Judith groaned and buried her face in her hands.

"Stupid, stupid, stupid, Gaines. Why'd you do something so foolish?" he chided himself and headed back to the corral. The safest place was home. He'd gather his horses and be gone. The sooner, the better.

"Rylan!" Oscar called.

Rylan took a deep breath and eased it out slowly. "I'm sorry."

"What are you sorry for?" Oscar's face filled with complete puzzlement.

Perhaps he didn't know. "Rumors have your daughter and I engaged. There's no truth to the rumor, but I found myself teasing your daughter, and I probably went too far."

"Oh. Well, she needs a good shaking. The girl's got her mind so muddled with what she thinks life is all about, she's forgotten what matters most."

"Money?"

"That and social standing. It's all rubbish, you know. Once you're in trouble, your so-called friends leave you faster than a hot coal cools in water."

"It was pretty rough, huh?"

"We had our moments. We sheltered Judith from the worst of it, and that quite possibly was a tragic mistake. She doesn't understand the difference living out here makes on a person's soul. You know?"

"Yeah, I know. My fiancée married another. She won't be coming. Guess I was feeling the sting when I teased your daughter."

"What did you do?" Oscar's voice lowered.

"I told her we ought to get married anyway. I needed a wife; she needs a husband. . . ."

Oscar roared. "And you're still standing?" Oscar slapped him on the back. "My boy, you just might be what the good Lord has in mind to tame that one."

Rylan guffawed. "The good Lord better not."

Oscar sobered. "The reason I came over to see you was, I'm. . .I'm. . ."

"What's the matter, Oscar?"

"My bills—I don't know if I'm going to meet them. The women gave it a good-hearted try, and they raised some funds, but it won't meet my debt at Pete's store for the seed I ordered last year. Do you have any ideas how I can raise some cash and still live on the land?"

Rylan scratched the day's growth on his chin. "Not at the moment, but I'm certain the Lord will help us out here. You know the men made a suggestion to me earlier. I have vegetables that need canning, and I have no wife to can them. I don't have the time to do it, either. I'd hate to see the food spoil. Do you think your wife and daughter might come over and do some canning for me?"

"I'm sure they'd lend a hand, but how's that going to help with my debt?"

"It won't, really. However, whatever they harvest and can that I don't need, you and your family can have for payment. You might not have any cash, but your bellies will be full."

"I'll speak to Raixa. Thank you."

"My pleasure. I've tasted your wife's cooking. Having her put up vegetables for the winter will be a blessing for me."

After exchanging a brief handshake and good-byes, Rylan gathered his horses. The sassy smile of Judith Timmons shot back into his mind's eye. *Lord, she is beautiful. And what's with those eyes? Yellow and brown. . . I've never seen anything like them. I could possibly find myself. . . Nope, I won't go there. Sorry I teased her, Lord.*

He guided his buckboard out of the fairgrounds. A woman with slumped shoulders walked by the side of the road. "Whoa, boys, who's that?"

He paused before asking hesitantly, "Judith?"

She turned, her eyes damp. His heart sank. "Judith, I'm sorry. Please forgive me."

"You don't understand. My mother heard the rumors. She thinks it's just wonderful. She didn't believe me when I told her it wasn't true."

"What? I spoke with your father. He knows I was just teasing you."

"Father knows?" She nibbled her lower lip.

"Yes." He leaned over the edge of the wagon. "Judith, are you heading home?"

She nodded.

"May I give you a lift?"

"But it isn't—"

"Proper. I know. But everyone thinks we're engaged anyway. You can end our engagement tomorrow, and no one will think the worse of you. Of course, you'll have to contend with the others who are standing in line to propose to you."

She audibly sighed.

"Please, let me make amends for teasing you."

She looked to her left and to her right. Rylan fought the desire to check if others were watching him, too.

"All right."

She placed her slender hand in his. How can a woman's hand be so small? Shifting, he made room for her on the seat of his buckboard.

He sucked in the hot afternoon air, making the clicking sound that told his team to move forward.

"I was fascinated with how well you worked your team," Judith said. "I've never seen anything like that before."

"I've been practicing all year. I lost to Jim McCoy last time, and I was determined not to lose to him this year. Consequently, Jim is determined to beat me next year."

"Healthy competition?"

"But of course, miss. A man has few things to compete with."

Judith giggled. The purr of her laughter set his insides doing flip-flops. What was it about this woman? He stared into her eyes.

"What? Do I have dirt on my face?"

"No, a little dust maybe. I'm just fascinated with your eyes. I've never seen any others quite like them."

She smiled. "They're rare, but I'm told they are a family trait. My grandmother on my mother's side is said to have had them, as well as my mother's great-aunt Ruth."

"Interesting."

"When I was young I was teased by the other children. But when boys started noticing girls, things changed. Some were attracted because they were so different; others were afraid of them. One boy said they reminded him of tigers' eyes. Not that the boy ever saw a real live tiger, but that's how he described them."

"Fascinating. Truthfully, I think they are beautiful. They remind me of golden wheat when the sun is setting on the grains at harvesttime."

Judith blinked and turned her head, looking to their right.

"I'm sorry, did I offend you again?" Rylan sighed.

She placed her hand on his forearm. "Who hurt you?"

"Her name is Margaret. She married my best friend. They didn't have the decency to tell me they'd married. I read it in the newspaper the other day."

"I'm so sorry. No wonder you were in such a bad mood that afternoon."

"Pete said I nearly knocked you down. I'm sorry. I didn't even know I banged into anyone."

"All is forgiven. You had reason to be upset."

"I reckon I did, but it doesn't excuse my rude behavior to you. I guess

I was feeling pretty sorry for myself. I've spent the last three years building up the farm, building the barn and house, all for Margaret, and now she's not coming."

"I guess I've been feeling rather sorry for myself, too. I don't want to be here. I want to be back home with my friends. Mother and Father are happier here, but I miss the evening socials."

"Is there a gentleman waiting for you?"

"No. I have a bit of a sharp tongue, as you have seen."

Rylan chuckled. "But it comes with such a pretty face. Those men in Worcester must be fools."

"I thank you for saying so, but I've been hard on them. Especially when they'd talk about Daddy and the bank. So many lies were being said."

Her face whitened. "Oh, no!" She cupped her hand over her mouth.

"Your father told me of his business troubles back east. I know what happened."

"Phew, I thought I'd blown it again. You're right when you pegged me for having trouble with my tongue."

"Everyone has faults, Judith. I can't imagine yours being so difficult a man couldn't look past them."

"It's like I was saying—it had more to do with Daddy's business misfortune. Once people knew I was the daughter of Oscar Timmons, the invitations ceased. I guess that's why I want to go back. To prove to everyone they were wrong."

"Why? What would it matter? I wanted to go back and see Jackson and Margaret, but then I realized it wouldn't change anything. They would still be married. They still had betrayed me. It wouldn't have made any difference, except for the possibility of me sinning with my fist."

"Ouch. Jackson better stay in Boston."

Rylan's spirit lifted. "Thanks."

He eased the buckboard to a halt at the corner of the path to her home. "You're easy to talk with, Judith. Thank you."

"You're not so bad yourself. I suppose there really isn't anything for me back east."

"Wanna reconsider my offer?"

Chapter 5

"I should probably scare the pants off you and accept your foolish invitation."

Rylan chuckled.

Just how forward should she be with this man? Judith wondered. He did fascinate her, and not just on the curiosity level. The man had genuine appeal, and she felt irresistibly drawn to him in a way she'd never before experienced. "You did say you needed a wife." She wiggled her eyebrows.

"And you need a husband."

"Why?"

His smile slipped. "Uh, uh."

"Seriously, why? Why do people think a woman needs a husband? I can cook, clean, take care of my house. I can even make an income for myself. Admittedly, it isn't as much as a man could make but. . ."

He placed his finger to her lips. "Shh. Save your passion."

Judith didn't dare move. His finger seared her lips. Her insides felt like jelly.

"I used to believe a man and woman should have a passion for one another. I loved Margaret, but apparently it wasn't enough."

Judith cleared her throat. "Is it possible she wasn't the right one? I used to believe that God designed the perfect spouse for me, and I simply hadn't found him yet. But as time went by, that belief has dwindled. However, seeing my parents now, the love they have for each other, I've been wondering again if perhaps God may still have a perfect spouse for me."

Rylan leaned back and knitted his fingers behind his head. "I used to believe Margaret was the one. I did until a few days ago. But now, I don't know. I just don't know what to think anymore."

"Tell me, Rylan, what would you have done if Margaret came out here, saw the farm, married you, then left in less than a year? If she couldn't live without proper society, things might have turned out that way."

"I don't know. The thought never crossed my mind. I assumed she'd be happy here with me. Isn't that what true love is—to be happy when you're with the other person?"

"You're probably right. I haven't experienced it yet. And while I'm getting older by social standards back east, living here doesn't mean I'm at a loss for possible husbands."

Rylan chuckled. "No, I'd say you're the prime choice for wife this year. How many proposals have you had? Not counting mine, of course."

"Ha, you're not getting off that easy. Last count was around ten, I think. It might be closer to fifteen. It's hard to keep track."

Rylan let out a slow, lazy whistle. "Someone better knock you off your feet soon, or you might hit the world record. You could be an attraction at the county fairs—the woman with the most proposals."

"Thanks a lot," she huffed.

He held his hands up in the air. "Just teasing."

Judith stood to get down from the buckboard. "Thank you for the ride home. Our engagement is officially over."

He gave an exaggerated sigh. "This one was shorter than the last. I didn't even make it to a full three hours."

"At least you didn't have to build me a house." She jumped down.

"Ouch! You're a vexing woman. Beautiful, but vexing." Rylan smiled.

She reached up and touched his hand. "Rylan, pray about whether or not she was the right one. God will help settle it for you."

"I will. And Judith—" He paused. "Pray about your new home. Ask the Lord to show you the beauty of the area. We're good, hardworking people here. All of us are trying to make a better life for our families."

"I will. And thank you, Rylan."

He tipped his hat and snapped the reins.

"Lord, have mercy he's a handsome man," she mumbled.

"I heard that."

Judith's cheeks flamed.

Rylan avoided Judith for days. Every time he saw her in the meadow, he'd steer clear of her. Every time he saw her in town, he'd cross the street and wave from a distance. The woman was not good for his system. She brought up feelings he hadn't sensed in years. Feelings he'd had for Margaret and more. He'd tried to pray about Margaret and whether or not he'd made the wrong decision three years ago. He couldn't help but wonder what life would have been like if he'd not moved west. If he'd stayed in Boston and married her. Would they have moved to New York, where his parents lived? Would they have stayed in Boston? Would he have been happy there? He felt so much pleasure working the land, digging his hands deep in the soil. Had it been best that he'd been delayed a year in bringing Margaret to Kansas? Was it what was best in the long run?

He didn't have an answer, and every time he thought about it, his head pounded.

Then memories of Judith and their conversation would flood his mind. She would be a woman to wrestle with, so forward and open, yet also sensitive. She didn't know it, but she was perfect for living in an untamed area. Her stubborn, defiant way fought well the hardships of nature. Unfortunately, those thoughts went on to suggest how perfect she'd be as his wife. He wanted a wife, needed a wife, but was he just grasping at the only available woman in the area? Or was the Lord above opening his eyes to another?

It was futile. All this thinking was going nowhere. Unable to sleep in the farmhouse, he knew it was another matter to take to the Lord in prayer. Indian summer had set in across the region. The days were uncommonly warm, and the nights pleasantly cool. Rylan stripped to the waist and dove into the pond.

The cool water washed away the day's heat. He floated on the surface and allowed the warmth of the sun to warm his face and torso.

"Caught ya."

Rylan splashed the water, rousing himself from his peaceful slumber. "What are you doing here?"

"I followed you," Judith answered.

"You followed me?" Rylan treaded water and stared at his unexpected visitor.

"I need to know why you're avoiding me."

"I'm not. . ."

She placed her hands on her hips. "You know and I know you've been avoiding me. So 'fess up. What did I do wrong?"

"Nothing."

"Then why? I thought we'd become friends after sharing such intimate conversation with one another."

With a hard kick, Rylan swam toward shore. He didn't want to hurt Judith. She turned her head and looked toward the thick forest as he stepped out of the lake. Quickly he gathered his tossed shirt and covered himself. "Judith, my avoidance had nothing to do with you."

Golden eyes searched his own. Perhaps it had everything to do with her. He squashed the thought. "I'm sorry, I didn't mean to hurt you."

"Rylan, I don't understand. You're the only friend—or almost friend—I have in these parts and—"

"Shh. I'm sorry. It has nothing to do with you and everything to do with me and my feelings for Margaret. I need to get a handle on them."

"But what does that have to do with your avoidance of me?"

Because you are threatening my sanity, he wanted to shout. "I need time. Time to work through my hurt emotions before. . ." He let his words trail off. Did he want to label his feelings for Judith? No, it wouldn't be right.

"Before?"

Rylan drew in a deep breath and expelled it slowly. "Come over here and sit down." He pointed to a fallen tree that made a perfect bench at the pond's edge. He combed the wet strands of his hair back with his fingers.

Rylan paced back and forth in front of the log bench, then stopped and faced Judith. "I hadn't told anyone until that day of the fair about Margaret and Jackson, and you know more than most. It's hard for a man to admit he's no good at love, and that something he's been working for, planning for, and praying about for the past three years burned up as fast as grass in a prairie fire."

"Which is why I thought we had developed a friendship."

"Yes, but it wasn't just friendship, was it?"

"Of course it was."

Rylan came to her and sat down beside her on the log. "Judith, I'm attracted to you, and you're attracted to me. We can't deny that."

"I'm not. . .well, maybe a little."

He knitted his eyebrows and locked his gaze with hers.

"All right, maybe more than a little." She looked away. A soft glow of pink rose on her cheeks.

"I can't, Judith. Not until I'm over Margaret. I can't even sleep in my own house yet."

"What?"

Judith couldn't believe her ears. The man hadn't slept in his house since the day he'd nearly run her over, the day he'd learned of Margaret's betrayal.

"The house was my wedding gift to her."

"What makes the house so specifically for Margaret?"

"You mean besides the fact that I built it for her?"

"Let's do this. Let's remove Margaret from the picture. A man builds a house for shelter for himself and his family, correct?"

"Of course, that's what I just told you."

"No, you said you built it as a wedding gift for Margaret. Are you telling me you never slept in the house before you got the news?"

"Don't be ridiculous. Of course I slept in it, ate in it; it's my house."

"Exactly. It's your house, Rylan, not Margaret's. You may have built it with her in mind, but you also built it for yourself."

He folded his hands in his lap. "True. But so much of the house is her."

"How so?" She fought the desire to reach out and touch him.

"The wallpaper in my bedroom is covered with her favorite flowers, lilacs."

"You wallpapered?" *And with my favorite flower. I wonder if he has some more?*

He jerked his head up and probed her with his glance. "Only the one bedroom. I wanted one room of the house feminine for her. Most of the house would be a working farmhouse and the children's rooms, of course."

She smiled. "How many children were you hoping for?"

"A dozen, but I'd settle for six."

"A dozen! Are you raising children or farmhands?"

Rylan grinned. "Both."

Judith couldn't resist a chuckle. "What else in the house is specifically for Margaret? Is it something that can be removed? Wouldn't that be easier for you than sleeping in the woods?"

Rylan was silent for a moment then got up to pace again.

Judith knew her attraction to him was strong, but more than her feelings had created her desire to see Rylan through this problem. She wanted to help him work this out. He'd helped her so much with his admonition to give this wilderness a chance. She still didn't want to give up her longing to live back east, but an overall appreciation for the area and its people daily grew within her. But the idea of her and Rylan having a personal relationship deeper than friendship was one idea she buried deep. He wasn't ready, and she wasn't ready. The mere thought of being that close with this man kept her awake to the wee hours of the night.

"Rylan?" He stood there motionless, staring in the direction of the pond but not really focusing on it. "Rylan?" she called again.

"Huh? Oh, sorry, I guess I got to thinking."

"I guess," she grinned.

"I was pondering your questions. I'm not really sure what in the house is Margaret and what is me. To me it's more of a sense of her in every room, in every nail I put into the place. I probably should just take it down and build again."

"Are you a glutton for punishment?"

47

"No, I . . ."

She marched over to him, grabbed his forearm, and yanked. He stood firmly planted. She released her grasp. "Come on, show me this shrine. I can't believe it's as bad as you say it is."

"It's not bad. It's a beautiful home," he protested.

"I didn't mean bad in the sense that you didn't do a good job. I meant bad in the sense of the overwhelming feelings you have when you're in the place. Let's go confront this demon before it takes the last bit of common sense you have out of your head."

She yanked his arm again.

"Can I at least put my socks and shoes on?" he muttered.

"If you must." She winked. *Watch your step, Judith, or you'll be encouraging that personal relationship that neither one of you are ready for.*

They walked in silence across the field and down the pasture toward his home. Judith gasped as the wonderful structure came into view. "You built this?"

"Yes." He beamed.

"Are you sure you should be a farmer? A woodworker or carpenter seems more in order." She wagged her head. It was a real house, a grand house with a large front porch and beautifully paned windows.

"The house is built for additional rooms in the back. I did start with three children's bedrooms and one large bedroom for me—and Margaret."

"Lead on, oh master of wood. I'm impressed."

"Thank you."

He opened the front door, and the well-polished hardwood floors reflected the fading sunlight. Rylan had spared no expense on the house. It had large, nine-over-six paned windows, which Judith imagined would be hung with heavy drapes for the winter. A hearth stood between the kitchen and the living room.

"I put the fireplace here for warmth in the front parlor, as well as a working fireplace and bread oven over on the other side in the kitchen."

"It's lovely. Did you use stones from your field?" She reached up and touched the rough-hewn stones held in place with gray mortar.

His grin widened. "Yes. Growing up in the North, I have a healthy sense of being frugal."

"I don't think you were tightfisted here. The hardwood floors, the large windows. . ."

"I purchased the glass, but the wood is lumber I cut and milled from my land. It's one of the reasons I had to delay Margaret's coming for a year."

"The house is beautiful, but we're here to have you point out what you put in for Margaret."

"Come into the kitchen."

She followed behind, looking over the tall ceilings and the mixture of wood and plaster walls. He might think he was being frugal, but she was convinced he'd spent a bundle on the place. Inside the kitchen he pointed out the cabinets for canning, the woodstove, and the sink with a pump.

"I'm sorry, Rylan. I see a functional kitchen here. Well designed, but still it's simply a kitchen. Nothing that shouts Margaret to me."

He scanned the room slowly.

Father, help me get through to him. I know he's hurting, and the loss is great, but help me show him that there's room for him and another in this house. He's too fine of a man not to have a wife, Lord, she prayed.

Rylan continued the tour. With the exception of the flowered wallpaper in the master bedroom, Judith didn't find anything that shouted Margaret. She tried to gently point this out, a real exercise in controlling her tongue. She didn't need to bait the man. He needed to allow the reality to sink home.

"You can change the wallpaper, Rylan. It's beautiful, but if it reminds you too much of Margaret. . ." She let her words trail off. She wanted to ask if he had more rolls of the paper for her own family, but she couldn't see putting wallpaper up on the dugout's walls.

"I suppose I could do that. I don't have the heart right now. I'm afraid my anger may take over, and I'd be replacing more than wallpaper. Perhaps a wall or two."

"You don't seem like the kind of man who can lose his temper."

"Normally, I'd agree with you, but this hurt went deeper than any other I've ever experienced."

"You mean more than the hurt God felt when your sins kept you from Him?"

He groaned. "You don't play fair."

"Am I supposed to?" She quirked a smile.

"Well, you should at least give me a chance."

"Never. I take all the advantages I can."

"I can tell." Rylan reached for her hand and caressed the top of it with his thumb. "Thank you, Judith. I don't know if I can sleep in here, but. . ."

"Give yourself time. Sleep in one of the children's rooms. You know those aren't going to be used for a while," she teased.

"You are vexing."

"I try," she chuckled.

"As a woman, do you approve of the house?"

"Do you have to ask? I've been drooling since I saw it in the distance. You've done a wonderful job. And that kitchen is so workable."

"Good, because I wanted to hire you and your mom to come do my canning. I have some tomatoes, corn, and squash that need to be canned soon or they'll spoil. The winter squash, turnips, carrots, potatoes, and other hard vegetables can go in the root cellar."

"Father mentioned you would like us to can. It would be a dream to work in this kitchen after working in my parents'."

"When can you start?"

"Tomorrow morning. Mother might not be able to right away, but I can."

"Thank you. You don't know how much of a blessing that will be for me."

"I can guess."

He released her hand. "Don't misunderstand me; I love my meat, but I also love vegetables."

"Guess that's a good thing for a farmer, huh?"

"Judith, I promise not to avoid you again."

She gave him a soft punch in the shoulder. "You'd better not, or I'll come after you again."

"Is that a promise?" He wiggled his thick reddish brown eyebrows. Judith's stomach fluttered.

The sun had set, and it was getting darker inside the house.

"Rylan!" A panicked cry came from outside.

Chapter 6

"Father, what's the matter?" Judith ran toward her father.

"What's the trouble, Oscar? How can I help?" Oscar wrapped his arms around his daughter and pulled her close.

After a few awkward moments, Rylan cleared his throat.

"Sorry," Oscar offered. "I came running over for your help to find Judith. Her mother and I feared she'd gotten lost in the woods."

"I'm sorry, Father. I should have told you where I was off to." Crimson-stained cheeks and pleading eyes implored Rylan to explain.

"I was showing her the house and the kitchen. She's agreed to can what's left of my vegetables for the winter season."

Oscar grinned. "Wonderful. She's nearly as good a cook as her mother."

A few pleasantries exchanged, then Oscar and Judith departed for their home. Rylan gazed up at the farmhouse. He'd painted it white. No curtains hung in the windows, and bits of colored sunlight played off the glass. He'd spent a small fortune in glass to bring in the sun. He'd even positioned the house at the right direction for the breezes to blow through and cool the house during hot summer days.

Judith's words about it being his house played back in his mind. "Father God, can I start looking at this place as my house and not Margaret's?"

He fought his legs and forced himself up the porch stairs. Each step closer to the front door became more difficult. He placed his hand on the wrought-iron latch. Broken promises, betrayal, stormed his mind. He released the latch. Perhaps tomorrow he could tackle those demons. He turned to leave. At the base of the stairs he stopped. The empty house seemed to reach out to him and envelop him in its presence.

Rylan squared his shoulders and marched back into the house. Tonight he would slay these dragons. Tonight, with God's grace, he would begin to move forward with his life.

The next morning Rylan woke in one of the children's bedrooms. The cock's crow and the glorious sunrise gave him a new outlook on the day. He hadn't slept much, but when he finally did fade off, his sleep was deep.

Day after day Rylan found himself getting stronger. The pain of Margaret's betrayal wore less on him. The house began to smell alive, and Judith's canning every day helped tremendously. The smell of new wood was mixed with wonderful aromas. Several evenings he even arrived to find home-made meals, thanks to Judith.

Oddly enough, he and Judith spent little time with each other. She'd leave him a message of what she'd accomplished each day and what she planned to do the following day. Only once had he managed to get home early enough from the fields to find her cleaning up.

Today would be different. He needed to see her. He needed to thank her, he continually told himself. He caught a whiff of. . .of. . .roast beef? Rylan took the front steps two at a time.

"What smells so heavenly?" He tossed his hat on the old rocker and rounded the corner into the kitchen.

"Rylan!" She jumped. "I wasn't expecting you."

"Sorry to startle you. What smells so good?"

"Beef brisket."

"Judith, you don't have to cook my meals for me. But thank you; they are most enjoyable."

She smiled. "I know, but I'm here cooking anyway. Besides, I figured it would help you feel more at home in your own house."

He pulled out a chair and sat at the table. "It does, and I'm doing better on that score. Thank you very much. You were right. There's more in this house that is a part of me than Margaret."

"Oh, Rylan, I've prayed for you every day. I'm so glad to hear the Lord is answering our prayers."

"I hope you don't run out of vegetables to can. My stomach will never forgive me if I make it go back to my own cooking."

She giggled. "Better prepare your stomach. One more day, and I'll be done."

Rylan didn't know what to say. He searched his mind for any other possible vegetables needing canning. "Did you get the vegetables out of the root cellar?"

"All that needed canning, yes. We don't need to can the potatoes, carrots, or hard squashes."

"I wouldn't want to have them spoil." He knew she'd see through this ruse but. . .

She slapped him on the shoulder. "You can hire me as your cook."

"Now that's a thought. How much?"

"Hmm." She tapped his shoulder. "How much is it worth?"

Judith chuckled as she left Rylan's house. She hadn't meant to work herself into a permanent job, but it looked promising. The extra income would be helpful, and the change of scenery a blessing. The dugout, while functional, depressed her. Its dark interior didn't compare to Rylan's light-filled home. She enjoyed her time there, perhaps too much.

The next day she found Rylan in the kitchen when she arrived. "Good morning, Rylan. Are you feeling ill?"

"No, I'm fine. I've been waiting for you."

Why? Was he regretting his decision to hire her to cook his meals? She poured herself a cup of coffee, added some cream and sugar, and sat down beside him. "What's the matter?"

"Nothing." He looked down at his hands then back at her. "Everything."

"I don't understand."

"We need to talk."

"All right." She sipped the bitter coffee and added more cream and sugar.

"I've had a response to my ad."

"What ad?" She sat down at the table with him.

"For a wife."

A wife? He advertised for a wife? Why would he do such a thing? He's a handsome, caring man. Any woman would love to have him as a husband.

"After I read the marriage announcement in the paper, I decided I had little choice. I need a wife, Judith." His gaze pierced her soul. "Do you know why I've been working late every night?"

"Avoiding me."

"Yes, but do you know why?"

What could she say? He was afraid of his feelings. She was avoiding her own as well. They had connected at the fair, a real connection. She'd been dreaming about Rylan every night. She'd been wondering if she could be happy as his wife. She knew she loved his house, but that wasn't the reason a woman should marry a man. It should be for love. Something both of them avoided, and something that each of them was too afraid to talk about.

"Judith." His voice softened. He reached for her hand. "Am I just fooling myself, or do you care about me, even a little?"

Her mouth went dry. Did she want this much honesty? Could she afford to? "I care, Rylan, but we don't know each other. Do I care only because of your house?" She slipped her hand over her mouth. She hadn't intended to be that open.

Rylan grinned then relaxed. "I hadn't thought of that."

"I understand your desire for a wife, but I'd be lying to you if I said I was in love with you. I love your house, I love the way the light streams through the windows, and I enjoy speaking with you. But are we right for each other? Do we. . .can we have a love for one another?"

Rylan pushed himself from the table, scraping the chair across the hardwood floor. He paced for a moment then stopped and kept his back to her, looking out the back door. "I've given up on love, Judith. I need a wife to have my children, to care for my house."

Judith's heart sank. She wouldn't marry a man without love. She understood his anger and hurt to some extent, but he hadn't seen the woman in three years. And he'd confessed Margaret hadn't written to him in well over a year, and the year before that had brought only occasional letters. Quietly Judith got up from the table and walked over to him. She placed her hand on his shoulder. Warmth radiated from the gentle contact. She cared for Rylan more than she wanted to admit. "Rylan?"

He turned and faced her. Hurt, anger, confusion swirled in his rich orbs. She wanted to tell him there was more to love than what they'd both experienced, but what could she say? She'd avoided relationships. She'd kept men at a distance, not wanting to be dragged into a life of social commitments and a house empty of love. Then reality hit. She didn't like the lifestyle she'd been raised in, she hated its false pretense, and she yearned for a real and honest relationship. One like her parents now had. One she could have with Rylan if he could open himself to love.

She reached up and touched his cleanly shaved face.

He placed his hands on her shoulders, holding her but keeping her at a distance. "Please, don't give up on love," she whispered. "God can heal all our wounds."

His grip softened.

Words unspoken played between them for what seemed like an eternity. Unspoken and yet heard, the language of lovers. She knew then that she loved this man, not for his house, not for his land, but because of him. Just him. It wouldn't matter if he owned nothing, if they lived in a simple dugout. She'd love him until she breathed her last breath. But should she marry him when he was still hurting?

"Judith, should I answer the letter?"

"Do you care at all for me, Rylan?"

"Yes, I care. But I can't. . ."

She placed her finger to his lips. "Don't say it. Just promise me one thing, and I'll marry you."

"What do you need me to promise?" His stance became more rigid.

"That you will continue to pray and ask God to heal the hurt Margaret has caused you."

"But..."

"I'm asking little, Rylan. I'm not asking you to declare your love for me. I'm not asking for anything more than a promise to allow God to do what we are all asked to do in the Scriptures. I realized something just a moment ago. I never got involved with the men back home because I didn't like the shallowness of their lives. I didn't like how people lived for recognition in society and not for one another in their homes. Marriages were unions that bettered one in business and in social standing. I didn't want that in my life."

"Why were you all set to go back?"

She moved from his arms and walked back toward the table.

"Because I didn't recognize the truth about my life back there. I also now realize that I love you for who you are and not your beautiful house. I'll accept your marriage proposal."

"But I don't love..."

She held back the hurt.

"I'm sorry. That is unkind. I care for you, Judith, truly I do." He came up beside her and wrapped his arms around her. "I would never do anything to hurt you intentionally. At least I will try not to do that. But..."

She turned in his arms. "Stop talking and kiss me," she said, wiggling her eyebrows.

Rylan had not been prepared for the heat of passion that filled him when he'd kissed Judith. It pretty near stole his breath away. They decided to wait a couple days before they told anyone the news of their engagement. But Rylan couldn't wait. He'd gone straight to town and sent word for a preacher. He'd also sent off a letter to the woman who'd answered his ad, gently declining her offer.

What he didn't expect was to find Judith on his doorstep later that evening. "Judith!" Her name brought a smile to his face.

He came closer. Red eyes...

"Rylan, we need to talk."

"What's the matter?" He came and sat beside her.

"My parents and I are moving home by the end of this week."

"What?"

"They need me, Rylan. They can't afford to make it on their own. They can't pay the debt for the seed, which means they can't plant next year. . . ." She burst into another round of tears. He held her close to his chest. He wasn't going to lose her. There had to be a way to keep Oscar and his family in the area.

"Did you tell them we're getting married?" He stroked her head.

"No, we agreed to wait."

"But, for pity's sake, woman. I can afford to have your parents live with us. They don't need to move."

She pushed herself from his embrace and placed her hands on her hips. "My father has some pride, Rylan. He can't accept a handout like that. Besides, I can't leave them. I don't want to leave you, but. . ."

He'd grown to appreciate Judith. *She'd make a perfect wife. But I'm not about to lose another one to the call of the East.* "I thought you said you loved me?" he challenged.

"I do, but they. . ."

"They need you, and I need you. What's it going to be, Judith, me or your parents?"

"Don't."

Why did I send that letter off to the woman who answered my ad? Rylan's anger bubbled to the surface. "Go, Go! I don't need you. I can get along just fine."

She wiped the tears from her eyes and punched him in the chest. "You stupid oaf." She stomped off and headed toward her home.

"I still have that woman's letter," he mumbled to himself. "I could write to her again." A bitter knot rose in his stomach at the very thought of someone other than Judith as his wife.

He marched into his house, a house filled with Judith's presence. She'd left a bouquet of flowers on the table and a note. His hand trembled as he reached for the paper.

Dear Rylan,
As you look at these golden mums, think of me, and know that
I love you and look forward to our life together.

Love,
Judith

Rylan closed his eyes and swallowed back the bile. He'd hurt her. His chest still smarted from the solid punch she'd landed on him. "Of course you hurt her. You are an oaf," he chided himself.

He crumpled down in a chair. "And now you've lost her."

Chapter 7

Judith wiped her tears away and washed her face by the well before coming into the house. Her parents didn't need to know her heart was breaking. She'd given them months of grief, telling them how much she wanted to go back home, and now that they'd decided to go...

No, don't think about it. Don't even trek down the path where those foolish thoughts will lead. Who got engaged without a courtship anyway?

She'd been affected by the constant marriage proposals, forgetting her good social graces and openly discussing matters of the heart that were best left in private.

In her room, if the small section of the house could be called a room, she began packing her trunk.

"Judith," her mother called.

"I'm in my room, Mother. Packing."

"Goodness, child, we have a few days."

She kept her back to her mother. She could still feel the swelling of her eyes.

"We aren't moving back to Worcester."

Judith turned. "We're staying?" she said a bit too brightly.

"No, what I meant to say was that we were going to Springfield, to stay with your father's cousin. But what's going on, Judith? You look like you've been crying."

"Must be the dust," she said evasively.

"The dust, my foot. Sit down, Daughter, and tell me what's going on."

"There's nothing to tell, Mother."

"Judith Joy Timmons."

Judith cringed. It didn't matter that she was twenty-two years old. She still felt as if she were five years old and had been caught doing something wrong.

"Please, Mother, don't ask."

"All right. But if someone's— No, I won't finish that thought." She bit her lower lip and lines of worry etched across her forehead.

"Oh no, Mother. Nothing like that." Judith drew in a deep breath. "All right, I'll tell you. But promise me you won't tell Father."

"I'm not promising anything. 'Fess up, child. What has happened?"

Judith filled her mother in on the details of her short-lived engagement with Rylan and his insistence for her to choose between her parents and he.

Her mother held Judith's hand. "He is right, you know. A woman needs to go with her husband."

"But he isn't my husband yet, and. . ."

"No, Daughter. If you consented to marry him, then he had the right to want you to stay and be with him."

"But you need me."

"Truthfully, dear, we can get along quite well without another mouth to feed and body to clothe. I would miss you terribly, and I would miss seeing my grandchildren. You say he wants a dozen?"

Judith chuckled. "Yes. I do love him, Mother. And I think he loves me more than he realizes."

"Then go back to him and work this out."

"But what of you and Father? I don't want you so far away."

"Leave it in the Lord's hands, Judith. He'll work everything out. Even with you and Rylan."

Judith got up to leave. "You're sure?"

"Positive. Now shoo."

She practically ran to Rylan's, her third trip in one day. The small path between their two farms was getting well worn.

"Rylan," she called. No answer. She called again. She entered each room. Nothing. "Where are you?" She placed her hands on her hips and sighed. Then it hit her. He spent so much time in the woods, perhaps he was there.

The sun was setting by the time she made it to the edge of the tree line. She could smell a small campfire and headed toward it. "Rylan," she called.

"Judith, what are you doing out here?"

"Looking for you."

He came to her and held her to himself. "I'm sorry, Judith. I didn't mean to speak so sharply."

"I'm sorry, too. I want to be your wife, but I don't want my parents to move back to Massachusetts. Mother said they would move back to Springfield and work in the mills or factories."

"There's got to be an answer." Rylan held her close. "Judith, I don't want to lose you. I—I. . ." He bent down and kissed her again. She wrapped her arms around the back of his neck and savored the sweet kiss. A lifetime of his kisses would keep her satisfied, she mused.

Rylan cleared his throat. "I sent for a preacher."

"Already? I thought we were going to wait. Oh, I did tell my mother."

Rylan chuckled. "When the preacher comes, we'll marry. He should be here by the end of the week."

"You give a girl a long time to make her wedding dress," she said with a smile. In all honesty, she didn't want to wait, either.

"Come sit by the fire. The air is starting to cool."

She looked around at the canopy the trees made. "It's beautiful in here."

"I find solace here—the gentle lull of the brook, the way the trees circle and make this an outdoor cathedral."

"It's beautiful."

"You're right, you know. I am an oaf. Just this morning I promised not to hurt you; then I did. I am sorry."

"It's. . ."

He placed his finger to her lips. "Shh. I have more to say. I found your note and flowers. Thank you. But more importantly, when I walked into the house, I couldn't imagine anyone but you as my wife. I don't want anyone else. I want you, Judith, only you."

Her smile brightened.

"I only want you for a husband, Rylan. Tell me about yourself as a boy. What do I have to look forward to when raising our sons?"

Rylan roared. "A handful. I wore my mother out. I brought home more critters in my pockets—toads, snakes. The spiders had a way of getting out long before she found them, though."

"Oh dear, maybe I ought to reconsider."

"For better or worse, you're promised to me." Rylan grinned and kissed her again.

Under the sparkle of the stars, they talked for an hour, maybe longer. "I'd better take you home," Rylan finally said, regret tingeing his words.

"Yes, Father will be worried."

"Do you need anything to prepare for our wedding?"

To hear those three special words, she thought. But she held back her tongue and decided not to push. He'd almost said he loved her when he'd said he didn't want anyone else as a wife. For now, she'd have to settle for that. "No, I couldn't possibly sew a new dress by week's end."

He nodded and held her elbow as he escorted her out of the woods and toward her home. "Careful, there are some gopher and prairie dog holes around the area."

"Rylan, would you pray with me about my parents?"

"I have been, but sure, I'll pray with you." They stopped in the field under the black velvet sky. He took her hands. "Father, we don't know the answer here, but we're trusting you to work out the details in the Timmonses' lives. You know their financial needs, and you know where they should live. We trust them into Your care. Amen."

As they prayed together for the first time, Judith's heart warmed hearing Rylan's words. She cleared her throat. "Father, we also ask that You would help lead us in making the right decisions, and I thank You for someone as wonderful as Rylan for a husband. In Jesus' name, amen."

"Judith, how can you pray that way? You don't know me."

"But I do. I know you by the character you've expressed to me and to others. How you care for your animals. The details you put into the house when building it. And I now know that you kept your mother hopping as a boy. I do look forward to getting to know you better, though."

He wrapped his arm around her shoulders and pulled her toward himself. "You're too good for me, Judith."

"Perhaps you don't know me all that well, either."

Rylan chuckled.

※

What a day! Rylan pulled the covers up over his weary body. First he got engaged, then not, then engaged again, and now he was lying here wondering why she loved him. It wasn't as if he'd given her many reasons. The memory of their shared kisses brought assurance that he would be happy with this woman by his side the rest of his life. But there was still the issue of love. Could he really love her? A part of him ached to love her. Another part of him refused to open his heart.

The words of Proverbs 24:27 circled around and around in his head. For three years he'd lived by that Scripture. Every decision he'd made about the farm, the house, Margaret, and himself revolved around that verse: "Prepare thy work without, and make it fit for thyself in the field; and afterwards build thine house."

First he'd prepared the fields. Then he'd built the house. Preparing the fields had taken him the extra year. He couldn't develop the land and build the house as fast as he'd hoped. But now, with Judith, the fields were prepared and so was the house. She didn't have to wait. He didn't have to wait. They could, and would, be married by the end of the week.

But he knew she loved him, and he couldn't say the words to her. "Father, am I so hard-hearted that I can't receive the love she's giving me? I want her love in return. I crave her love. But shouldn't I be giving her that same love? Doesn't she deserve that from the man she loves? Is it really fair to her to go into a marriage when I don't know if I love her?"

Rylan rolled to his side and pulled the covers higher. The heat of Indian summer had passed. Kansas was now experiencing much cooler temperatures. He glanced out the window to the wooded area between his land and Oscar's. He'd cleared most of the trees from his land for farming. Those trees gave him the wood to build the barn and the house, and have many winters of heat from the cords of logs stored behind the barn.

"The trees!" Rylan jumped up out of bed. "That's it."

He hustled into his pants and shoes. Oscar could cut and sell the wood from the trees on his property.

Rylan stopped buckling his trousers. It was late, real late. The news could wait until morning. He reversed his actions and went back to bed. Proceeds from the sale of the trees would clear up Oscar's debt, but it wouldn't solve the problem of his needing to live on the land for three additional years. It would only be a temporary fix.

He took in a deep breath and sighed. Oscar and Raixa would still end up leaving the area. But it would help with the debt, he reasoned.

Late into the night he considered Oscar's problems. Even later into the night he thought about bringing Judith into his home as his wife. A smile crept across his face. Yes, God had blessed him. The woman with golden eyes weaved through his dreams.

※

The next morning Rylan found himself studying his bedroom. "Should I tear down the wallpaper, Lord?"

"Only if you must," Judith whispered from behind him.

"Judith, when did you arrive?"

"A minute ago."

He reached for her and held her close. "Do you mind that the flowers are purple lilacs?"

"No, they are one of my favorite flowers, too. And look here—they've put the pink and white lilacs in the design as well."

She traced the floral pattern. He'd noticed it. He thought he remembered them being there. Guess I didn't pay too close attention to them. "You don't mind?"

"No, but if it's too hard of a memory for you. . ."

"I don't believe it's a problem."

She smiled. "Great, because I think this has to be one of the prettiest rooms I've ever seen. Come here." She grabbed his hand and brought him to the bay window facing the east. "The room fills with the morning sunlight. It's wonderful."

"Do you. . .would you want to make curtains?"

"Yes, I'm thinking some light sheers under some nice thick colonial off-white. What do you think?"

"I'm thinking I don't know the first thing about curtains, as you can tell, because there isn't one in the house. Just tell me what you need, and I'll purchase it."

"You'll spoil me, Rylan. I haven't had spending money in a few years."

Rylan smiled. There were things he could do to let her know she was special. "I'm not rich, but I have some set aside for the house."

"All right then, if you don't mind, I think we should put heavy curtains up before winter sets in. I'll measure the windows and tell you what I need."

"Excellent. Now, I need to speak with your father. I think I found a way for him to pay off his debts."

"Really?" Judith jumped into his arms. "Tell me."

❧

Everything was fitting into place, Judith decided. Rylan's news about the trees answered her parents' needs. Rylan and her father went to work on cutting the trees the next day. The goal was to cut only what was needed. The wooded cathedral area would stay intact. Her parents would try and stay another year but knew they would need help with the planting. Rylan couldn't work both farms, but he'd given his word to help them with a small section.

In the past two days, she'd seen Rylan increase in his comments of appreciation, complimenting her beauty and repeating how happy he was that she'd agreed to be his wife.

Judith scanned the cleaned kitchen. Satisfaction flooded her soul. Tomorrow the preacher was due in. The house sparkled. The wedding was to be held in the house at two in the afternoon. She went to Rylan's room and made the bed and dusted. Her mother had helped her move her clothing in earlier in the day. Tomorrow she'd be spending her first night with her husband. . . . Judith trembled at the thought. "Husband," she whispered.

"Judith," Rylan called from downstairs.

"I'm upstairs." She wanted to add "in our room."

"Judith!" Panic filled his voice.

Judith ran down the stairs. She didn't know what to expect. To see him lying in a pool of blood or what? Relief washed over her when she found him sitting in the rocker with a crumpled paper in his hands. "What's the matter?"

"Margaret is arriving tomorrow."

"What?" Couldn't this woman have picked a better time to ruin this man's life again?

"Here." He handed her the paper from the telegraph office.

She plopped onto the floor.

"Does she not know you read about her marriage to Jackson?"

"I didn't tell her. But look, they're both arriving. Why?"

"I don't know, but can't you have someone meet them at the stage and tell them not to bother to get off?" She knew he still loved Margaret. Was she so afraid of Rylan seeing his first love that their marriage would end before it began?

"I thought of that, but it doesn't seem right somehow."

"And you think it's right that they should be arriving on our wedding day." Her voice rose.

He jumped up from the rocker. "Of course I don't think it's right, but what can we do? I have to see them. I have to postpone our wedding."

"No, you don't."

"It's the Christian thing to do, don't you think?"

"That's not fair."

"Look." He knelt beside her. "I know this isn't fair. It's not fair to you, and it's horrible timing. But I do feel I need to speak to them. Especially when she wires that she's here to discuss our marriage. Don't you think that's a bit odd?"

"It's more than odd; it's deceitful." She could taste the bile in her words.

He knit his reddish brown eyebrows together. "I want to find out what's going on. I need to know, Judith. Can you understand that?"

"Yes and no. Oh, Rylan, I don't want to lose you."

"You won't. I'm not a foolish man. They can't deceive me."

He pushed back the strands of her hair that had fallen in her face. "I promise we'll marry."

"But. . ." The tears came. She couldn't hold them back. He'd never declared his love to her, and now on their wedding day, he was going to meet the woman he loved. It was horribly unfair and dreadfully painful.

"Oh, sweet Judith. Come here, my sweet golden eyes. I give you my word we shall marry. I promise."

"Marry me now, Rylan. Let's not wait. The parson is in town tonight. Can't we call upon him?"

She leaned forward to kiss him.

He placed his finger upon her lips. "Trust me," he whispered and left.

Left her alone, sitting on the floor of the room that moments before had held so much promise.

"Oh, God, no," she cried.

Chapter 8

C ongratulations, Rylan, I'll see you at the wedding," Dick Morgan called out from across the street the next morning. Rylan had left a note on the door of the house explaining that the wedding had been postponed. He'd even filled Pete Anderson in and asked him to spread the word. Apparently it hadn't spread as quickly as he'd hoped. Thankfully, the parson understood the situation and agreed to stay another day. The town needed to hear a gospel message on Sunday, anyway, Rylan reasoned. He avoided Judith. He'd promised not to hurt her, and that's all he'd been doing.

The stage was late.

Rylan felt the pulse on his neck throb. "Get control," he reminded himself.

He released his clenched fist.

The noise of creaking leather, clinking chains, and horses working their way down Main Street indicated the stage was rounding the bend into town. Rylan placed his hat on his head and waited.

The door of the stagecoach opened slowly.

Rylan's breath caught in his throat.

Margaret emerged from the carriage. He'd always thought her beautiful, but her looks paled in comparison to Judith's.

"Rylan!" She waved and smiled, her hands gloved in white.

He gave a slight nod.

Jackson emerged, a bit thinner than in years past. "Hello, Rylan, it's good to see you." He reached out his hand.

Rylan accepted the gesture.

"He knows," Margaret whispered.

Jackson eyed him slowly. "Yes, I believe he does. Sorry, Rylan. We'd like to talk with you if you wouldn't mind."

"There's not much to say, is there?"

Jackson put his arm around his wife. "Actually, I believe there is. If I didn't, I wouldn't have wasted our time coming out here. I. . .we need a favor."

"You two are really something." Judith's voice rang through the air.

"Pardon me, miss, but this is a private conversation." Jackson bowed slightly.

Rylan caught his voice and his temper. "Judith, not here. Jackson, Margaret, you can come to my home and discuss the matter. And Jackson, this does involve my future wife." He held out his hand and grasped Judith's. "You shouldn't have come," he whispered.

"I know, but I was going stir-crazy in the house."

"I'm glad you're here." He held her closer.

Rylan made arrangements for Jackson and Margaret to be transported to his home and returned with Judith in his wagon. "They're in trouble, Judith. I don't know what the problem is, but I can see it in their eyes. Something is terribly wrong."

"Why would they come to you?"

"Other than the fact that Jackson and I have been through thick and thin together as young men, I wouldn't know."

"She's in a family way," Judith offered.

"Are you sure?"

"Fairly. I'm not certain, but she looks to be."

Rylan felt his jaw tighten. "I'll. . .no, we'll need to help them. I don't know how, but. . ."

Judith reached over and took his hand. "The Lord will show us what to do." She paused, then hoping to break the tension, teasingly added, "You sure you don't want to swing by the parson's and get hitched before we go back to the house?"

Rylan chuckled. "I'd love to, but you deserve better, Judith. I'll not be a party to giving you less than you deserve on your wedding day."

"On our wedding day," she corrected.

"On our wedding day." He reached his arm around her and pulled her close. "I love you, Judith. I love you more than I've loved anyone else. I didn't want to admit it. I didn't want to admit that I'd been wrong for three years. But seeing Margaret"—he paused and eased out his breath— "I know I never loved her the way I love you. What I feel for you is so much more than what I ever felt for Margaret."

"Oh, Rylan, hearing those words, I can wait as long as it takes."

Rylan grinned. "Not too long, I hope. Do you know how hard it was to sleep in that house last night, knowing your belongings are all in there and that I shouldn't have postponed the wedding?"

"We could still call on the parson." She winked.

"Come here, golden eyes."

She snuggled closer. He leaned over and kissed her. "Soon, my love. Soon."

❧

Rylan could take all the time he wanted. She'd heard the words she'd been longing for. He loved her; he truly loved her. She could wait. But she prayed it wouldn't be too long.

By the time they all gathered at Rylan's house, it was time to start cooking dinner. Rylan and Jackson went for a walk to speak privately with each other while Margaret stood in the kitchen and observed Judith's preparations for the noon meal.

"How far along are you?" Judith asked.

Margaret paled. "Five months."

"Oh." Judith flinched. Only one interpretation could be given to Margaret's answer. The woman had been expecting before she married Jackson.

"My father is furious. He's ruined Jackson's chances of employment. We came here because. . ."

"Because you hoped Rylan could help."

Margaret nodded.

"Why didn't you write him, tell him the truth? You hurt him." Judith clamped her mouth shut.

"How do you tell a man who writes you faithfully that you've fallen for his best friend, and worse yet, how do you tell him you've, you've. . ."

"Got your point there. But still. . ."

"I should have written him. I know there's no excuse."

"Sit down, Margaret. Can I get you anything?"

"Some tea would be nice."

Judith poured boiling water into a china teapot.

"That's beautiful. Is it yours?" Margaret asked.

"Yes, it was my mother's. She gave it to me for our wedding."

"When is your wedding?"

"It's been postponed."

"Why?" Margaret's gaze met Judith's. "I'm sorry," she offered. "I didn't know."

"Your timing could use some work."

Margaret plopped her swollen feet up on the chair next to her. "You are so right. Seriously, I am sorry to have ruined your plans. Jackson says we can go west and build a home."

"Plenty of land around here." Judith clamped her mouth shut again. Why did she offer that?

"Jackson is hoping to find work in the area and move west after the baby is born. I don't mind telling you, I'm frightened. I know what we did was wrong, and we're paying for that, but I feel it would have been just as wrong to marry Rylan. He's a good man, but. . ."

Judith grinned. "What you feel for Jackson isn't the same as what you felt for Rylan."

"Exactly. It didn't start out that way. The first year Jackson would just check in on me, see how I was faring, that kind of thing. But then we started to talk and talk, and things just escalated from there. For a year I've been trying to write Rylan and tell him what happened. For a year, Jackson refused to marry me until I told Rylan about us. Then it happened. We announced our engagement and married before my parents

72

could notice my condition. When they found out. . ." She shook her head and buried her face in her hands.

"Judith," Rylan called.

She handed Margaret a cool, damp cloth. "In the kitchen."

"Judith, Jackson and Margaret will be staying with us for a little while." *Us.* Her heart raced.

"All right. Dinner is just about ready. I'll see you later." Judith stepped toward the door to leave.

"Hang on, Judith, we need to talk. Excuse us, Jackson, Margaret." Rylan gently grabbed Judith's elbow, led her up the stairs to one of the spare rooms, and closed the door. "I'm sorry, this isn't the way a newly married couple should live, but they're in trouble."

"Real trouble." She sighed.

"What did she tell you?" he asked, sitting on a chair.

"That she's with child."

"Yeah, Jackson told me about their relationship before and after they married. I'd like to wring the man's neck, but he's done enough of that to himself. He's skin and bones from worry."

"I imagine so. Is her father that cruel of a man?"

"I've heard rumors to that effect. I know some fathers do it, but I can't imagine throwing out your own child like that."

"Me, either."

"Judith?" He captured her hand and pulled her toward himself. "We can do a couple of different things here. We could get the parson to come over after the service tomorrow. Or we could go and see him tonight. In either case, I want to take you away from here. For a day or two, I want it to be just you and me. Helping Jackson and Margaret is going to take a lot of patience and a whole lot of God's grace, but I want us to start our marriage on our own. Just you and me. What do you say?"

"I say you're the most wonderful man in the world, and I'll follow you anywhere."

He pulled her into his embrace. "Marry me, Judith, and make me the happiest man alive."

"You silly oaf, of course I'll marry you. How about tonight?"

Rylan groaned and captured her lips. "Tonight's just fine, my love. Let's get word to your parents, the parson, the entire town!"

Judith chuckled. "In a minute. I'd like another moment with you all to myself."

Rylan picked her up and carried her down the stairs.

"Don't you have this wrong?"

"No, ma'am, we're doing it right. First the marriage, then the threshold. I'm just practicing the carrying part." He kissed the top of her head.

Epilogue

September 1856

C ome on, honey, the fair is going to start without us," Rylan called up to his wife.

"Hold your horses."

He roared. "That's the problem—they want to win again."

"Tell them to behave themselves or I won't be giving them sugar tomorrow."

Rylan smiled as he watched his wife descend their stairway. "I hope you and your mom made the black raspberry tea again. I know I'll have a powerful thirst today."

"More than you know. Sit down, Rylan. I need to make a cup of tea."

"Are you feeling all right?"

"I'm fine—nothing a few months won't take care of."

Rylan gazed down toward his wife's stomach. "You mean?"

"Yes."

"Ye-ha!" He grabbed her into his arms and twirled her around. She paled. "Oh, sorry. Can I get you anything? Sit down. Honey, are you all right?"

"I'm fine." Judith smiled. "Crackers, dry crackers would be nice. At least that's what Mother said would help."

"Honey, we can stay home if you're not up to it," Rylan offered.

"No, you've been working that team too hard not to let them compete. Besides, I like watching the way your muscles play on your back. It was the first thing that attracted me to you."

"It wasn't my winning personality, huh?"

"Nope, pure physical attraction."

Rylan roared again. "Don't ever change, my love. I love you just the way you are. Pure, honest, and straight to the point. God's blessed us."

"Yes, and I'm so glad Jackson and Margaret are in their own place now."

"Me, too. Your father is amazing with numbers. The town will benefit from the new bank he's organizing."

"I pray it remains stable."

"It will; he won't make the same mistakes."

Rylan pulled her into his arms.

"I love you, Judith. Thank you for becoming my wife and the mother of our children."

"I love you, too, Rylan. You're right, I fit into life here much better than I ever did back east."

He kissed her, a kiss that spoke volumes in commitment and love. Life was definitely better. . .after the harvest.

A pastor's wife from North Miami Beach, Florida, LYNN A. COLEMAN is the president of the American Christian Romance Writers and enjoys helping authors achieve their writing goals.

Love Notes

by Mary Davis

Dedication

To my hubby, Chip, who has given me
a greater appreciation for the musical note.
And to JoDee for sparking an idea in me.

*And the King shall answer and say unto them,
Verily I say unto you, Inasmuch as ye have done it
unto one of the least of these my brethren,
ye have done it unto me.*
MATTHEW 25:40

Chapter 1

Texas, 1910

Bang! Bang!
Laurel jumped up from the edge of the hotel bed and rushed to the open window.

Several people ran in the dusty street toward the bank next door. "Jonathan Rivers tried to rob the bank!" one of them shouted.

"Pa?" She gasped and stumbled over the packed carpetbags at the end of the bed on her way to the door. Holding up her skirt, she ran out of the hotel and to the bank. The crowd packed outside made it impossible to see inside. "Excuse me." She wedged her way between shoulders, excusing herself repeatedly, then finally spilling inside the bank entrance.

A man lay stretched out on the floor, his head covered with a gray coat, his clothes familiar. "Pa." Someone touched her arm, and she spun, looking into the sheriff's ruddy face.

"I'm sorry, miss."

"No, no." Tears fell as she dropped to her knees and reached a shaky hand toward the coat that covered the dead man.

"Laurel, don't." Ethan sat against the counter, Doc Benson tending to his bloody arm.

She lifted the wool fabric from the face. "Oh, Pa."

He'd said to pack and wait for him. They were leaving today. She smoothed the hair off his forehead. The worry lines that had deepened the longer Pa had stayed in Hollow Springs were all but erased.

She had prayed for Pa to turn back to the love and acceptance the Lord Jesus was waiting to give him and to find peace in Ma's death. Had he died before he found it?

Covering her face, she wept.

The strain of the past two days lay heavy on Laurel's shoulders as the pungent smell of the disturbed earth filled her nostrils. She stood with only the minister and the sheriff for company beside Pa's freshly turned grave, tears cascading down her cheeks. She dabbed them away with Ma's lavender embroidered handkerchief, but they were quickly replaced. The sheriff brooded under his bushy red eyebrows, his squinting eyes almost hidden. Had he come to see for himself that Pa was no longer trouble for him? Or did he wonder if she would be trouble, as well?

She turned the events of what must have happened that day over in her mind as she had done many times in the past forty-eight hours. Pa had told her to pack, knowing what he was about to do. He'd gone to the bank and pulled out a gun. Where in the world had Pa gotten a gun? She shook her head. Then the sheriff must have shot him, but not before Pa had wounded Ethan.

The breeze tousled Minister Howard's sandy hair as he spoke his final words and closed his Bible. "I'm terribly sorry for your loss." He hesitated as though he wanted to say more, then gave her a nod and left with the sheriff.

She didn't blame the residents of Hollow Springs for not wanting to share her sorrow. Why would they want to show support to the daughter of a bank robber?

I'm just seventeen. What am I to do? She dropped to her knees, sobbing. "Why, Pa?" He'd caused a great deal of trouble for a lot of people and now left her alone. She set a small bouquet of blue wildflowers on top of the raw dirt then looked away.

Ethan Burke, in a suit and bowler, stood outside the cemetery's low, wooden border fence, one arm cradled in a sling. Even he didn't want to be near her. She averted her gaze, too ashamed to look at him after what Pa had done. She used to steal glances and catch him looking back. He would give her a smile or tip his hat, and when Pa wasn't looking, she would smile back.

Since Pa had given up going to church after they'd left Maryland, Laurel went by herself with Pa's blessing, because Ma would have wanted her to continue attending church. Pa felt that if one of them went, it was as good as both.

From the first Sunday, Ethan Burke took to walking her back to the hotel. They walked slowly. And last Sunday, he'd been waiting for her outside the hotel before church. Pa didn't know until three days ago when Ethan insisted on asking Pa to court her. Pa wouldn't talk about their conversation, but the next day. . . She closed her eyes in regret. Now all she saw when she looked at Ethan were the glaring results of Pa's bad judgment. She peeked again, but Ethan was gone. She stood and looked around. He was nowhere to be seen.

What had Pa been thinking? Robbing a bank? She shouldn't have asked to stay in Hollow Springs; Pa had been agitated by her request. But she'd felt comfortable in this rustic little town—she hadn't wanted to leave and had hoped hard to stay. Now she had no hope. And no choice. People in town wouldn't talk to her or even look at her, yet she had no means to leave or live.

She still didn't understand Pa's drive to get to California. Ma had wanted to live there, and Pa had kept promising, but they'd never made the move. Not until after Ma died did he get a bee in his britches about it. She'd lost Pa, too, the day Ma died. Her true Pa. He'd become a stranger almost overnight. The day after Ma's funeral, he'd started selling everything they owned, then bought a broken-down Ford. It hadn't even made it to the first town on their trek to the opposite coast. Pa hadn't been the same since.

Now she was left to wrestle with her own conflicting emotions. She was sad that Pa was gone but also happy his suffering was over. Did that make her a terrible daughter? She hoped not. Maybe *happy* wasn't the right word. Content? She'd wanted to stay in Hollow Springs; now she longed for California. If the anguish and pity in Ethan's cobalt blue eyes were any indication, there was nothing left for her here.

She trudged along the boardwalk to the hotel where she and Pa had been staying. She pulled out her room key as she headed for the staircase.

"Miss Rivers?"

She turned to the desk clerk. "Yes."

"May I speak with you a minute?"

All she wanted to do was collapse on her bed and cry, but she walked to the desk.

Mr. Gonzales dipped his head, and she could see his balding crown. "I hate to do this in your time of sorrow, but unless you can pay your father's outstanding bill, I'm going to need your key back."

Outstanding bill? She set her handbag on the counter. "How much?"

"Fifteen dollars."

She gasped. "I don't have that much money."

"I'm really sorry, miss. I can't let you stay unless you can pay."

"Of course not." She pulled three dollars and six bits from her handbag. "This is all I have."

He held out a hand. "I'll take what you've got."

She set the money on the guest registry. "I'll pay you the rest of what my pa owes, Mr. Gonzales, somehow. Do you happen to have any positions open? I could work in the dining room or clean rooms."

"I'm sorry. I don't need a girl right now."

She nodded. "Do you know of any jobs in town?"

He shook his head. "Sorry."

"When I find work, I'll pay the rest of my pa's debt."

He gave her a sad smile and tipped his head to her.

She kept her back straight as she ascended the stairs. When she reached the room, the carpetbags she'd packed the day Pa had robbed the bank were waiting for her by the bed. Two days they'd sat untouched. Pa had said he'd be back soon.

Tears coursed down her face, and she fell to her knees. "Sweet Lord Jesus, what am I to do? I have nowhere to go."

She couldn't remain here at the hotel, so where was she to go? She could sleep outside. The late-spring Texas nights weren't nearly as cool as they had been when they'd arrived in town a month ago. She did not relish the thought of sleeping outdoors, but she and Pa had done it a few times since they'd left Maryland.

Poor Pa. This past year, it was as though he'd been looking out of a dark cave and all he could see was California, as though making it to California would somehow make Ma less dead. Now he was dead, too— and in debt. As his heir, she was responsible for clearing his accounts. That meant she needed to find employment.

Ethan Burke adjusted the sling on his left arm as he stood in front of the barbershop across the street from the Starlight Hotel. Laurel had seemed so alone at her pa's grave site. Even the way she'd walked, slowly and wearily, showed her lonesomeness. He ached for her. Not one soul from town had shown up at the funeral. How could the whole town blame her for what her father had done? He would have been right next to her if it weren't for what he'd done; at twenty-three, he'd killed a man. Ethan shook his head. It was an awful feeling deep in the pit of his stomach, like a burning coal.

He kicked the post holding up the awning, but instead of the satisfaction he expected, all he got was a bruised toe. If he'd learned how to shoot a gun, Laurel wouldn't have a reason for her tears. He'd only aimed to wound the man. But he was a bad aim, really bad.

In church, Laurel would close her eyes and raise her voice up in song. The serene, ethereal look on her face as she sang to the Lord told him all he needed to know about her faith. And his heart had gone out to her. Now his heart lay battered in the corner of his soul, fearful to make any attempt at contact.

Though Laurel and her father were drifters heading west, he had hoped they would make Hollow Springs their home, but Mr. Rivers had been dead set on California. So Ethan, too, had begun to set his heart on California, if Laurel would be a part of it for him.

The day before the robbery, he'd asked Mr. Rivers if he could court

THE PRAIRIE ROMANCE COLLECTION

Laurel. Mr. Rivers had given him a gruff no and walked away. Laurel had been right when she said her pa wouldn't take it well. He should have suggested that he could help with travel expenses. Had he pushed Mr. Rivers into making that fatal decision?

Ethan jerked forward at the familiar slap on his back, though not as hard as usual. He had his wounded arm to thank for that. "*Hola*, Alonzo."

"*Mi amigo*, looking tired. You rest."

He tore his gaze from the hotel. "I'm fine."

Alonzo's dark eyes widened. "To the funeral, you went?"

He'd wanted to. He'd wanted to be right beside Laurel to comfort her in her grief. "I kept my distance."

"You no talk to her? And your *grande* shoulder, you didn't give it to her?"

He looked up at his six-foot friend. "Mine is the last shoulder she'd want for comfort."

"She not give you smiles like honey when her *padre* not look?"

His mouth pulled up at the thought. How could one young lady so captivate him with her guileless smile and soft, quiet voice that caressed his heart like a gentle melody? "She does have a nice smile."

"And eyes that sparkle like green cactus, and hair that is silky and the color of cinnamon, and all perfect things about her," Alonzo recited like a child mimicking a parent. "I know sure she likes you."

"Maybe. Before I killed her pa."

"So on purpose you shot him?"

"No."

"And the padre of the woman you love, why you shot him?"

"Because he was trying to rob the bank."

"The money, you let him take it, not yours anyway."

He pictured Mr. Rivers's shaking hand and the way his gaze had darted about the room. "He was edgy. I was afraid any little thing would spook him. I didn't want him to hurt an innocent person."

"So an accident it was."

"No. I killed her pa."

86

"She can see that not on purpose you did it."

He had made a grave miscalculation that morning. If he could go back, he would have aimed for the man's shoulder instead of his hand. Or his leg. No. He wouldn't have reached into the drawer for the bank's gun at all. Then maybe no one would have gotten hurt. But then what? Mr. Rivers would have just given up? Not likely. Let Mr. Rivers get away with the robbery? Then Laurel would be a fugitive on the run. What if Mr. Rivers were subdued and went to jail? He shook his head. Once Jonathan Rivers decided to rob the bank and pulled out his gun, there could be no good outcome.

He shrugged. "It doesn't change anything."

"I *comprendo* why you be here in this place to breathe air that is fresh for your *pulmones*." Alonzo pointed across the street. "Your *señorita* of perfection."

He stood up straighter. What was Laurel doing coming back out of the hotel? And with her luggage?

"You will talk to her, yes?"

He wanted to. "It's too soon."

"I talk to her for you?"

"No. Promise you won't say anything to her about me. I'll talk to her when I'm ready. And when I think she's ready."

Alonzo put his hand over his heart and gave a quick nod. "No wait very long." He stepped off the boardwalk.

"Where are you going?"

"I think to talk to a beautiful señorita."

"Alonzo, no. You promised."

Alonzo turned around and walked backward. "I no mention you."

Ethan doubted that. How could he pull him back? "What about Rosita?"

"You no talk to her about this."

Alonzo disappeared into the mercantile after Laurel. He should go, too—accidentally bump into Alonzo, then he could see for himself how she was. He stepped off the boardwalk.

"*Señor* Burke."

He turned. Rosita Menendez sashayed toward him in a brightly colored dress. He glanced at the mercantile then back to Rosita. "Señorita Menendez."

"Hola. I. . .look. . .for Alonzo." Rosita's English wasn't nearly as good as Alonzo's, but she worked hard at it.

If Ethan told her where he was, Alonzo could be in trouble if he was talking to Laurel. Rosita had a fiery jealous streak where Alonzo was concerned. Alonzo wasn't ready to settle down, but when he did, it would be with Rosita. Until then he'd keep Rosita just interested enough that she didn't go off and marry someone else, but not so close she was begging to set a wedding date. If he were Alonzo and had a chance to marry the woman he loved, he wouldn't waste a day. Not one day.

Chapter 2

Laurel looked around the inside of the mercantile. Mrs. Jones stood behind the counter ringing up a man's purchase. She looked at a rack of ready-made dresses while she waited. She'd never had a ready-made dress. Ma had made all her clothes. She hadn't had a new dress since Ma died. Pa had told her to pack light for quick travel. They'd get new things in California. But she'd packed a few small keepsakes—and Ma's wedding dress.

The man at the counter left, and she walked up. "I'm looking for employment and was wondering if you could use a salesgirl."

Mrs. Jones's gray topknot wobbled as she shook her head. "I'm sorry. Some days we barely have enough business for the two of us."

Laurel nodded, and her stomach growled. It had been two days since she'd eaten. "I'd like to get a pickle." She dug in her handbag and then remembered she'd given all she had to Mr. Gonzales.

"I'm sorry. I can't add any more to your pa's bill."

She looked up sharply. "Pa owed money here, too? How much?" She sighed at the amount. "When I find work, I'll pay my pa's outstanding debt."

"Señorita Rivers." Alonzo Chavez filled the doorway. As he came forward, he doffed his hat and put it over his heart, bowing slightly. "Very sorry about the death."

Tears welled in her eyes. He was the first person besides the minister to offer condolences. The surprising thing was, Alonzo was Ethan's best friend. She wouldn't think he would want to talk to her. "Thank you." She blinked back the blur.

"You are doing well, yes?"

How was she supposed to respond to that? *I have no place to live, no family, no money, but I'm well.* "I'll make do."

Ethan Burke was suddenly at Alonzo's side. She froze and stared at his sling. She was not ready to speak to him yet. It was too much for one day.

"Excuse me, Miss Rivers. I need to speak to Alonzo."

She nodded and looked at the floor. She didn't want to see the pity in his blue eyes.

Ethan and Alonzo moved to the corner of the store, spoke a few words, then hurried out the door. Her gaze followed them. She should have at least inquired about his arm. Said hello. Or something. But she was too raw from Pa's death and the current trouble that he had caused. She was not up for a confrontation with the man who obviously didn't want to speak to her. The way he'd hurried Alonzo out of there told her all she needed to know about how he felt. He didn't even want his friend to speak to her.

She picked up her carpetbags and walked outside, where Mr. Jones stood stacking produce.

"Miss Rivers." Mr. Jones plucked an orange from one of the produce boxes in front of the store and held it out to her. "Got some in fresh."

She shook her head. "I can't pay for it."

He took the orange back. "Sorry."

As the sun began its western descent, she was still without a job. She walked past the bank as one of the employees flipped the closed sign and latched the door. She gazed a moment through the window where Pa had fallen from grace. *Oh, Pa. Why couldn't you have been happy here? What was so almighty important in California?*

She had wanted to stay in Hollow Springs. She'd dreamed of Ethan Burke courting her and asking her to marry him, making a home here. Now she just wanted to leave this town as soon as she was able. And now she, too, could feel the pull of California. Was it her duty to finish the trip her parents had begun?

She noticed Ethan looking at her from behind the bank counter and quickly hurried on her way—then stopped. On her way to where? She had nowhere to go. *Lord?* Fresh tears threatened to spill. She blinked them back. People would hardly look her in the eyes. She sensed that people had positions but didn't want her to fill them. Everyone was ashamed of her. And instead of finding a job, she'd discovered outstanding bills Pa owed.

She must leave town as soon as she was able and start fresh somewhere else, someplace where no one knew what Pa had done. California was as good a place as any. But she would need money to get there. And first she needed employment to pay Pa's debts.

"Miss Rivers."

She turned at her name.

Minister Thomas Howard crossed the rutted dirt road toward her. "Again, I'm sorry for your loss. Have you thought about what you are going to do?"

She tucked her chin. "I've just learned my pa owed money all over town. I had to move out of the hotel, and I must find a job to pay his debts."

"You could go back to family."

"Except for the Lord, I am alone in the world." She felt the loneliness deep within.

"Fortunate for me." He stepped up onto the boardwalk. "My wife needs help around the house and with the little one. Doc Benson has told her to rest more or she could lose the baby. I can only offer you a place to stay and three meals a day for your assistance."

A roof over her head and food in her stomach. It would keep her from sleeping under the starry sky tonight. "I'd be glad to do it, but I'll also need to find a paying position to take care of Pa's accounts."

"If my memory serves me right, when you first came to town, you offered to play piano for Sunday services."

"That's right."

"With Mrs. Howard having a difficult time with this baby, I don't want her overexerting herself. Would you be willing to play for us?"

"Most certainly." Her fingers were aching for the ivory keys.

"The church can only pay a small stipend."

She wanted to tell him she would do it for free, but she needed the money. "I'd be most grateful." The Lord was supplying a roof, food, *and* a way to pay off Pa's debts. *Thank You, Lord, for Your abundant provisions.*

❧

Laurel stood in the doorway of the Howards' bedroom. Mrs. Howard looked half asleep while her two-year-old son sat next to her lifting her hand and letting it fall. Mrs. Howard tucked her arm under the double wedding ring quilt. When the boy dug it out, she moaned.

Minister Howard held out his arms to his son. Little Tommy dropped his ma's arm again and stepped on her leg to get to his pa.

Mrs. Howard rolled her head and sighed. "You're back."

"I'm sorry I took so long." The minister leaned over and kissed her forehead.

Mrs. Howard's gaze darted to Laurel, her eyes widening before looking back to her husband. "What is she doing here?"

The minister adjusted his son in his arms. "Miss Rivers is going to help you with the house and look after Tommy so you can rest."

"I don't need help."

"Doc said for you to rest. We don't want to lose this one, too."

She sighed and nodded.

Laurel swallowed hard. "Mrs. Howard, I appreciate you taking me in like this. Anything I can do to make you more comfortable, just let me know."

Mrs. Howard turned away. "I'm tired."

Minister Howard turned to her. "Maybe you could start supper."

❧

After supper, Laurel bathed Tommy and carried him upstairs to say good night to his ma. At the voices coming through the Howards' open bedroom door, she stopped.

"I just don't trust someone whose parent could do such a thing," Mrs.

Howard said. "She has bad blood in her."

Laurel caught her breath.

"Miss Rivers is no more a threat to you or Tommy than I am. Mr. Rivers made some bad choices, but they have no reflection on her. The Good Book tells us to care for those in need. 'But whoso hath this world's good, and seeth his brother have need, and shutteth up his bowels *of compassion* from him, how dwelleth the love of God in him?'"

The minister was giving her charity. She wished she weren't in such desperate need of it.

"I wish I had your confidence," Mrs. Howard said.

"Should I not trust you because of your brother's behavior?"

Tommy wiggled out of her arms, and before she could catch him, he ran into his parents' bedroom. She stepped to the doorway. "Tommy wanted to say good night before I put him to bed."

Minister Howard scooped him up. "Thank you, Miss Rivers. I'll tuck him in."

She nodded, hoping they couldn't see her distress. "I'll straighten up the kitchen."

As she wiped crumbs from the table, Minister Howard entered the room. "Please don't take my wife's words to heart."

"Pardon?"

"By the look on your face, I guess you were standing out in the hall just long enough."

She felt the blood drain from her face. "I never meant to listen in. I promise."

He smiled a sad sort of smile. "I know. I'm just sorry you had to hear anything at all. My wife has lost seven babies early on. She's afraid to lose this one now that her time is so close. So please don't fret over her words, Miss Rivers. She gets cross with me, too, these days." He sighed. "You should know that something happens in her mind when she is pregnant. She's not herself. Her condition will only get worse the closer her time gets. All we can do is make her as comfortable as possible and ride out the storm."

Poor Mrs. Howard—to lose so many children before they even had a chance in this world. And then to have her mental condition on top of that. She understood all too well about a loved one no longer being the person he or she once was. Such a cross to bear. "How long until the baby is due?"

"About eight weeks or so. I've been praying powerfully hard for this child. I fear Mrs. Howard might not be able to handle losing another." He turned and left the room.

But she'd caught the sheen in his eyes that he'd tried to blink away. A loss would likely be as hard on him. She sat down at the table and prayed for grace and mercy to blanket the minister, Mrs. Howard, the unborn babe, and little Tommy.

Once she finished in the kitchen, Laurel climbed the stairs to the room she would be sharing with little Tommy. Her heart ached for family, but she'd lost everyone. She desperately wanted to belong but had no one. The loneliness seeped deep inside as she unpacked her traveling bag. She opened Pa's pocket watch, and the photograph of Ma and Pa on their wedding day blurred before her. Once she cleared her vision, she pulled the picture free. A small lock of Pa's ashen hair lay with Ma's cinnamon curl. "I'll take you both to California. It's where you wanted to be."

She dressed and curled up in bed, wishing she were seven again in Pa's lap, crying into his chest over the cruel words of the other schoolchildren. He would stroke her long cinnamon hair and promise her that everything was going to be all right, that Jesus would make everything better. That was the pa she lost the day Ma died. Then it was no longer Pa she imagined holding her, comforting her, but Jesus. She sobbed silently in the darkness until she fell asleep in her Savior's arms.

Chapter 3

Laurel confiscated the last piece of bread and jam with which Tommy was painting the table—and himself. "I think you're done with that." She ruffled the boy's hair, then dumped the mashed bread into the slop pail. As she came back with a cloth to wipe Tommy's face, Minister Howard entered the kitchen.

"Mrs. Howard hasn't finished with the tray you brought up, so I left it. I'll be out all day but back for supper."

"I'll have it ready."

"Thank you. Could you choose four hymns, three for the beginning of the service and one to close? Mrs. Howard always did that. Whatever you pick will be fine. I'll be speaking on forgiveness." He kissed Tommy on the top of his head and walked to the doorway, then turned. "I can't tell you the amount of comfort it gives me knowing you are here for my wife."

She wished poor Mrs. Howard could feel the same.

"She's just going through a difficult time right now."

Mrs. Howard wasn't the only one. But Laurel couldn't dwell on her own hardships, or she'd be stuck in that muddy place Pa had been for nearly a year. She couldn't think too long on being orphaned in an unwelcoming town in a strange part of the country where she knew next to no one and had no place to go, no home.

"In every thing give thanks: for this is the will of God in Christ Jesus concerning you."

She had to focus on her blessings, though she couldn't think of any at the moment. But then she looked up and saw the roof over her head, felt the food in her stomach and the clothes on her back. Next to the Lord, wasn't that all she really *needed*?

She cleaned up Tommy, set him on the floor with his blocks, and headed up the stairs to retrieve the tray. She had put off long enough facing Mrs. Howard without the minister there. Knocking softly on the door, she opened it. Mrs. Howard lay on her side with her back to the door. *Please let her be asleep.*

Laurel tiptoed in and took the teacup off the nightstand, setting it on the tray on the floor, but left the glass of water. She lifted the tray. On top was a sheet of paper labeled HYMNS FOR SUNDAY. How thoughtful. Maybe Mrs. Howard was warming to her after all.

Laurel finished up her chores in the kitchen then took little Tommy for a walk to tire him out before she stopped at the church to practice for Sunday service, two days away. The songs Mrs. Howard had chosen were some of the hardest she'd ever tried; she must be far more proficient. Not having played in a long time, Laurel chose easier, more familiar hymns, hoping Mrs. Howard wouldn't mind.

When she finished, she still felt alone and wrapped her arms around herself. She needed a great big bear hug from Pa, but the closest she could hope for was a hug from Tommy. She went over to where he lay sleeping on her ma's granny square shawl and scooped him up. "Time to go," she whispered. She dreaded returning to a place she wasn't completely welcome, but she had nowhere else to go. Even so, she really was grateful for the Howards' generosity.

❧

Laurel's stomach was all aflutter as she sat on the piano bench. The small rustic clapboard church was so different from the church with stained-glass windows and padded pews she'd come from in Maryland. She waited for the minister's signal to start. She hadn't played in front of anyone in so long and with so little practice. She had wanted to come over early and practice before anyone arrived, but taking care of Tommy and making sure Minister Howard had a filling breakfast had consumed all her time. Now she had to make do and trust in the Lord.

Shoe soles scuffled on the worn wood floor. People looked her way then whispered to those close to them. They would be scrutinizing everything she did, every mistake she made. She knew they could pressure the minister to have her removed. But she needed this job. She would show them that God could still use her. *Dear Lord, help me play for You and to forget about all these people waiting for me to make a mistake.*

She swung her gaze to the minister, who was talking to Mr. Jones at the side of the pews. She let her gaze travel the room, and it froze on Ethan Burke. When he looked at her, she looked away. He was the reason she'd wanted to stay in town. Now she couldn't even look at him for the shame she harbored inside. She needed to ask his forgiveness on behalf of Pa, but how could she if she couldn't bring herself to face him?

Had someone just spoken to her? She turned and found Minister Howard staring at her.

"You may begin."

"Oh." She put her fingers to the keys and took a deep breath. *Please let me play well.*

She made it through the first line but stumbled over a note in the second. People were singing, so she hoped no one noticed. Being in front of the town was harder than she'd thought. She usually loved being in church, but today she couldn't wait for it to be over so she could leave.

Ethan ached for Laurel as she missed another note. She was so tense. It didn't help that people had come in whispering behind her back like circling vultures. He hadn't expected to see her here today. Her presence here took all the courage and inner strength that he heard in her playing.

She played the notes with all her heart and soul. The music had emotion. Mrs. Howard's playing was technically perfect, but there was no life in it. Laurel put her whole being into it.

Minister Howard spoke on forgiveness. Ethan could tell that the minister was wanting the people of Hollow Springs to forgive Mr. Rivers for what he'd done and, in kind, forgive Laurel. He noticed a great deal of shifting and slouching in the congregation as the minister spoke about removing the log from your own eye before removing the speck in your brother's, and about forgiving others so God can forgive you. But forgiveness was slow in coming in this town—if it came at all. Like the time Kenneth Kline was drunk and accidentally shot Widow Olson's goat, thinking it was a deer. Kenneth eventually moved away.

Then the minister seemed to speak to him, though he never looked directly at him, and discussed forgiving oneself. How could he do that? He'd killed a man, and the townspeople hailed him as a hero. He was no hero, just the unfortunate soul who'd had the misfortune to pull the trigger.

After the service while the congregation filed out the door, Laurel played softly through the final hymn again. He let the melody wash over him. He would wait until she was finished to approach her.

As the last note hung in the air, Laurel closed the lid to the keys. Here was his chance. He headed toward the front, but she scooped up her shawl and slipped out the side door at the back.

He scrambled to the front and followed her out, but she was already almost to the minister's house. He watched her long hair pat her back as she hurried away. It was clear that she hated him. He'd suspected it, but now he knew.

⚘

After preaching on Sunday, Minister Howard took Monday off, leaving Laurel free to run her errands without little Tommy along. With her handbag clutched tightly, she hurried to the hotel. At the door she stopped and took a deep breath. She hoped Mr. Gonzales wouldn't be offended at her small offering toward Pa's account. She opened the door and walked to the counter. Mr. Gonzales was registering a man and his young daughter. She stared at the little girl clinging to her pa's side. Sorrow lodged in Laurel's throat. The man handed the room key to his daughter and picked up the two larger suitcases. He looked down proudly at his daughter taking charge of the smaller bag and headed up the stairs. Longing ached deep inside Laurel.

"Miss Rivers, is there something I can do for you?"

She took a small amount of money from her handbag. "I've come to make a payment on my pa's bill. I know it's not much. I can even pay a little more if you need me to." She'd wanted to make a small payment on each of Pa's debts, but if Mr. Gonzales wanted more, she'd give him the whole sum and pay on the others next week.

He pushed her money back across the counter to her. "You don't owe me anything."

"But my pa did."

He shook his head. "You don't understand. Your bill has been cleared."

Cleared? "Someone paid it for me?"

"Yes, miss."

"Who?"

"I can't rightly say."

"I want to thank them. Let them know I'll pay them back."

"The person doesn't want to be paid back. And I think he knows you are grateful."

"But who would do such a thing for me?"

He just shook his head.

Obviously Mr. Gonzales had been sworn to secrecy, and she wouldn't push him any further. "Mr. Gonzales, the next time you see my benefactor, would you tell him thank you from me?" She turned to leave but stopped. "And tell him I'd like to meet him and thank him in person."

Well, that would make paying off her other two obligations go faster. She walked to the mercantile. Mrs. Jones looked down her long, narrow nose at the money Laurel set on the counter. "I know it's not much, but—"

Mr. Jones stepped over. "You don't owe us anything. Your account here has been settled."

Again? "By whom?"

"We are not at liberty to say."

Who was clearing her debts? "Will you tell the kind person thank you for me? And that if I knew who he was, I'd thank him in person?" In spite of their frowns, her spirit buoyed. She couldn't think of one person in town who would do this for her. Everyone avoided her and looked away as though ashamed and appalled. Just as the Lord Jesus had paid the price for her sins, someone was paying Pa's. *Thank You, Lord, for the kindness of a stranger.*

She headed across the street to the barbershop and bathhouse. "Mr. Adams, do I still have a bill here?"

He ran the straight edge of the razor up Mayor Vance's neck then wiped it on a towel before looking up at her. "Four bucks."

So her benefactor hadn't found her last debt. She was glad in a way. It would give her a chance to show the citizens of Hollow Springs that she was not the bad person they thought she was. And maybe a certain bank clerk would see it, too. "Here is a small part of what my pa owed you. As I earn it, I'll pay the rest." It shouldn't take her more than a month to settle this account. Then she could start saving to purchase a stagecoach ticket and move on to a town where the people didn't know her story. There she could earn money for a train ticket to the West Coast.

Mr. Adams took her coins and put them in his pocket. "I appreciate that."

"I hear Hank over at the saloon is always looking for pretty girls," Mr. Toole said, waiting for his turn for a shave.

She felt her cheeks warm. She would let them lock her up in jail before she'd work there.

"We don't need any of that, Silas." Mayor Vance shot him a stern look.

She didn't know what to say after that, so she hurried out the open door and crashed into Ethan Burke.

Ethan gripped his wounded arm and sucked in a breath through his teeth.

Laurel gasped, her eyes widening. "I'm so sorry."

He nodded.

"Are you hurt?"

He straightened and took his hand from his arm. "I'm fine."

His hard-set jaw told her he was trying to hide the pain she'd inflicted. Or was he still angry with her over what Pa had done to him? "I didn't mean to hurt you."

"I said I'm fine," he hissed through gritted teeth, a grimace on his face.

She backed away. "I'm really sorry." It was bad enough that Pa had shot him; she didn't have to hurt him, too.

※

Ethan held his breath as Laurel walked away at a brisk pace. He wanted to call her back and tell her he was fine, but the truth of the matter was, he wasn't fine. The pain that shot through his arm had caused sweat to bead on his lip and forehead. He'd probably popped stitches again. It had happened the second night when he had the nightmare that had haunted him every night since.

He walked to Doc Benson's office and slumped into a chair.

Doc came out of the examination room and shook his head. "What happened this time? You didn't roll over on that arm again, did you?"

"No. Just a little accident. I got clumsy. I may have pulled a few stitches out." He took his hand from his arm. Crimson tinged his shirt.

"That you did. Come on in."

The pungent medicinal odors in the room stung his nostrils. He held his breath for a moment but was then forced to breathe in the smells.

"Sit."

He sat on the table.

Doc helped him remove the sling, rolled up his sleeve, and slowly unwound the dressing. "Looks like all you did was tear her open. I don't see any signs of infection."

The bullet had barely missed the bone but had ripped his flesh wide open. He thanked God again that his wound was minor and that there was still no infection. Mr. Rivers hadn't been so fortunate.

"Is the laudanum helping with the pain?"

He hesitated. "I haven't been taking it."

"Why on earth not? Do you miraculously have no pain?"

"No. It makes me lethargic." He didn't like feeling tired and in a semi–dream state. The stuff tasted awful, to boot. And what ached more than his arm, the laudanum wouldn't help.

"Well, I'll offer it anyway. You want laudanum before I clean this and stitch you back up?"

"I'll pass."

Laurel fell to her knees at the front pew. "Please, Lord, heal Ethan's arm. Don't let him be in much pain. And please let him know I didn't mean to run into him and hurt him." She knelt there for a long while pleading for Ethan Burke and crying.

When she'd exhausted her heart, soul, and mind, she stood and walked to the piano bench. A single sheet of music stood on the music stand, a carefully hand-drawn staff, with notes only on the first line. She picked out the tune in her head then opened the lid to the keys and played the notes. She played it again and let it wash over her until it was embedded in her heart. The notes caressed her and wrapped around her like a toasty warm hug on a chilly night. It was a natural tune, flowing and simple but with a depth in the chords. The piece, however short, ministered to her soul, as well as to her aching heart.

She looked for an author, but there was no signature.

"Thank You, Lord, for this small blessing in the midst of my trials."

Chapter 4

Ethan saw the glint of the Colt .45 and pulled the bank's .45 out of the drawer behind the counter, coiling his finger around the trigger. He raised it up and fired a moment after a flash exploded from the end of the other gun. Burned gunpowder accosted his nostrils. Through the haze of smoke he could see red soak through the front of the bank robber's shirt as he fell to the ground. He wanted to go to the man, but his legs wouldn't take him there. Then suddenly he was at the dying man's side and putting his hand on his chest. The bleeding wouldn't stop.

Mr. Rivers grasped Ethan's shirtfront with a bloodstained hand. "Laurel will never love you now."

He sat up with a start and moaned, tossing back the covers with his right arm, the sling holding his left arm to his chest. A cold sweat dampened his body. *Oh, Laurel.* He scrubbed his face then stared at his free hand. He rubbed it down the side of his nightshirt then went to the washbasin and poured some water. Though the only physical blood on his hands that day was his own, he could feel Jonathan Rivers's blood in every line and crack. He'd scrubbed and scrubbed, but the feeling would never go away.

His nightmare was different in another way. In reality, Mr. Rivers hadn't mentioned love. He'd looked at the hole in his tan shirt grow red with blood; then he'd looked at Ethan with the utmost sorrow, as though he'd come back to his senses, out of some crazed delusion, and realized what he'd done. He'd looked directly at Ethan and said, "I'm sorry," then dropped to his knees.

Ethan had dropped his gun and come out from behind the caged counter, gripping his left arm and kneeling beside him. "I only meant to shoot the gun out of your hand."

Pain contorted the dying man's face as someone eased him to the floor. His gaze locked with Ethan's. "Tell. . .Laurel. . ."

He waited. "Tell Laurel what?" He wanted to tell Mr. Rivers not to die but knew the request would be futile. "Tell Laurel what?" Tears pooled.

The pain seemed to leave, and a smile touched Jonathan Rivers's mouth. A peace settled on his face as he whispered, "Katherine," then closed his eyes.

In life, he had never looked as peaceful as he did at the moment of his death.

Ethan splashed cool water on his face and stared into the mirror on the wall even though he could see only a dim outline of who he was in the dark. It was better that way. He didn't want to look a killer in the eyes. He put his wet hand on his aching left arm and looked down at the bottle of laudanum the doctor had given him. He'd stopped taking it, so if his recurring nightmare didn't disturb his sleep, the persistent ache in his arm did.

Would it comfort Laurel to know that at the end her pa was at peace? Would she want to hear it from him? Or had Ethan imagined the peace to ease his own conscience? If death brought peace to Mr. Rivers, did that make his own misdeed less atrocious?

He'd relived that day over and over and always came to the same conclusion. If he hadn't fired, Mr. Rivers might have killed an innocent person in his agitated state before coming to his senses. Mrs. Turner had been in the bank with her three children.

Ethan had done the right thing. He just wished he had been accurate—for the first time in his life. *Lord, help me put this all behind me. Show me I did the right thing. And please help Laurel to see that, too, and to forgive me.*

He sat down at his upright piano, lifted the lid, and caressed the keys.

Did she enjoy her song? He looked up at the blank sheet of paper propped on the piano and freed his left arm. Doc had told him not to use it at all for at least a week, but he couldn't help it. He didn't need the written music. It was committed to heart, so he played the notes softly in the dark. When he got to the last one, he continued playing, adding a new line. He lit a lamp and wrote it down. Why couldn't he have done that before he'd left the song for Laurel? He'd tried to figure out another line, but nothing had come; he'd decided that was all there was and had left the sheet of music for her on the piano in the church.

After writing in the second line, he filled in the first. A drop of ink fell on the edge of the sheet. He blotted it with his finger, smearing it slightly.

Ethan put his fingers to the keys again and played through the first two lines, hoping to continue. He tried several things, but nothing sounded right with the beginning. He tried to force the notes to cooperate. He struggled the remainder of the night to add to the melody. Nothing came. It was done, then.

First thing in the morning, before work, he would rush the new sheet of music over to the church. Hopefully Laurel hadn't seen the other one yet.

At daybreak, he walked to the church and crept inside. He came early to avoid the risk of anyone catching him, especially Laurel. His music was set on top of the piano. Had she seen it? She must have. He'd left it right on the stand. She had to have moved it. Had she bothered to play it? Or had she simply cast it aside as unimportant?

He put the new sheet in the center of the music stand. She couldn't miss it.

Lord, please let this song touch her in some way. Let her know I care.

❦

Laurel hummed the song that had become dear to her heart as she wiped crumbs from the cutting board after supper. Two more lines of music had been added on separate days this week. The song soothed her aching soul and allowed the healing to come gently. She could feel it. *Thank You, Lord.*

"That's a lovely tune." Minister Howard stood in the doorway holding the supper tray. "I don't recognize it. What is it?"

Minister Howard had taken a tray up with plates for his family, since Mrs. Howard missed eating with them. Laurel didn't blame her. If Laurel were her, she would want to eat with her family, too, but she had no family. That left her to eat by herself, but she didn't feel lonely doing so. She had the song playing in her heart for company. It surprised her how comforting it had become. The song was her own special gift from the Lord. "It doesn't have a title yet."

"Did you compose it?"

She shook her head. "It's a tune I committed to memory."

"Who did compose it?" He set the tray on the counter.

Should she tell him that someone was sneaking into the church and leaving it? No harm was being done. "I don't know."

He seemed satisfied with that. "Thank you for supper. It was delicious. You will make someone a fine wife."

Ethan's face immediately popped into her head. She mentally shook it away. "You're welcome." She hoped she got the chance to be someone's wife one day. "Minister Howard, can I ask you something?" He nodded. "The piano at the church—does anyone else play it?"

He squinted his eyes in thought. "Not that I know of. Why do you ask? Is something wrong with it?"

"No, nothing wrong. I was just wondering."

He headed for the door. "Tommy fell asleep, so I put him in bed."

"Thank you."

"No, thank you. Your being here is a godsend."

She didn't want to say it out loud, but she had to. "Minister Howard, you should know that Mrs. Howard still doesn't want me here. If you want me to leave, I will." There. She'd said it.

"Nonsense. I've noticed a marked improvement in Mrs. Howard's health since you arrived. She has more color in her face. She's just not used to sitting back while someone else does her work."

That was a relief. She'd felt like a stowaway all week, knowing how Mrs. Howard felt. But Mrs. Howard's contention toward her was a result of more than just her inability to do her daily chores.

On Pa's grave, a single dried firewheel flower lay next to her own dried bundle of bluebonnets from the funeral a week ago. Who else had been there? And why? She looked around, but she was alone.

She discarded the dry bundle but left the single dried firewheel. Someone had cared enough to leave it. But who? It didn't seem right for her to be the one to take it away, so she laid down her fresh, colorful bouquet of rose vervain, winecup, foxglove, and butterfly weed. The sweet fragrance settled around her.

"Pa, I'm sorry for not coming back sooner. I've been busy since. . .you left. I'm staying with the minister and his wife. Mrs. Howard hasn't been able to keep up with her chores in her condition, so I've been doing a lot of catching up for her. It's awful hard work, but I don't mind so much. It keeps my mind off things." She thought of it as her duty.

"To be honest, Pa, I've been avoiding you because of my guilt, not over your shooting Ethan—I mean Mr. Burke—but over not mourning you as I feel I should." Tears filled her eyes. "I miss you so much it aches, but I'm not sad at your passing." She drew in a shuddered breath. "I know it sounds mixed up, but you went away inside yourself so long ago." She wiped her cheeks with her ma's old embroidered handkerchief. "I'm going to California as soon as I pay the debts just like you promised Ma." She fingered Pa's watch in her pocket. "I love you, Pa."

Pa's struggles in this life were over after nearly a year of fighting with his sorrow, but she would see him again in heaven. Jesus had left the ninety-nine sheep to come rescue her pa from his pain. His suffering was finally over, and he was in a far better place.

She opened the church door, the cool, dark interior a peaceful solace. Propped up on the music stand was the hymn in progress with another line of notes. She rubbed her finger on a smudge of ink on the side and smiled. There were two different sheets of music after all. The one with the smudge and the one without. When the smudged one had disappeared, she'd thought the composer had made a fresh copy and discarded the other. But he was using both.

Whoever was writing this song was writing it at another piano or in his or her head. Should she write something back? *My longing heart has found solace.* As she had hoped Pa had found at last in death. The Lord had given her a measure of serenity in this simple piece of music. But why was the composer adding such small chunks? Why not write the whole thing and then leave it? Why leave it here at all? She didn't really care why. She was just grateful to have it.

Once she had bathed in the song, she turned to the hymnal. The music Mrs. Howard had chosen was once again some of the most difficult she'd tried. Someday she might be as good as Mrs. Howard, but today was not that day.

Laurel hated what she was about to do. But was it any worse than finding out what Pa had done? She took a deep breath and steeled herself as she entered the mercantile.

She stood at the counter with Tommy on her hip. Mrs. Jones eyed her sideways as she measured out red gingham yard goods for a woman. She'd always wanted a dress of red or green gingham. Maybe in California.

She would rather Mr. Jones helped her. He seemed a touch more compassionate toward her plight, but he didn't seem to be nearby. Mrs. Jones was probably hoping she would go away. Well, she wasn't, so she waited.

After helping two other customers, Mrs. Jones turned to her. "You'd best have money if you're wanting something, even a pickle. I don't run a charity."

There would be no pickle today. "I have money."

Mrs. Jones squinted her eyes as though not believing.

"I'm here on Mrs. Howard's behalf."

"How is Roberta doing?" Mrs. Jones's sneer softened.

"As well as can be expected, now that she's able to rest."

"It's a wonder."

Laurel bit her tongue to keep from making a snide remark back. "Mrs. Howard made out a shopping list. She asked if you would mind putting the prices and total on the list for her." She handed the list and money to Mrs. Jones as instructed.

Giving a knowing nod, Mrs. Jones went about filling the order.

Laurel also knew the reason for the prices and total. She hated the distrust. She'd always been an honest person, and she would prove herself trustworthy to the citizens of Hollow Springs. *This is a lot to bear, Lord. How much more before I break?*

Mrs. Jones made the notations on the list then handed it back with the change. "I've noted the money Roberta should receive."

How humiliating. "I'll see that she gets every penny." She grasped the handle of her shopping basket and left.

Ethan stopped her outside. "Laurel."

She liked the way her name sounded on his lips. It soothed her ire. Maybe he didn't hold Pa's actions against her after all, but still she could do little but stare at his arm cradled in the white sling, a stark reminder against his dark suit. "Mr. Burke, I hope you are healing well." It wasn't exactly the apology she knew he deserved, but at least he knew she held concern for him.

"It's feeling better." He touched his arm but didn't linger over it. "I've been meaning to talk to you."

Tommy wiggled out of her arms. She held his hand as he stood next to her.

"Bug." Tommy pulled his hand free and sat on the boardwalk to watch the ant crawling along the wood.

"I was there that day in the bank. . .with your pa."

She riveted her gaze back to Ethan's sling. As if she wasn't already painfully aware of that fact. "Yes, I know."

"I was beside him when he. . .died."

Tears welled in her eyes thinking of Pa and the way he died—from a plan of his own making. Were things so bad he had to resort to robbery and violence?

"Just before. . ." Ethan looked to the ground then back up to her. "The pain. . ." He seemed unsure of what to say.

If tears hadn't closed her throat, she would have spared him from going on.

". . .seemed to disappear, and he had a look of pure peace on his face.

He whispered, 'Katherine,' then just closed his eyes."

Pa had thought of Ma. The thought warmed her. At peace, and with Jesus and Ma. Her prayer answered.

"I just thought you should know."

Tommy screamed.

She spun to see him on his hands and knees in the dirt just off the boardwalk. She set her shopping basket down, lifted him up, and put him on the edge of the boardwalk. Tiny rocks and dirt were embedded in his chubby hands and knees.

Ethan wetted his handkerchief in the watering trough and handed it to her.

She tried to wipe Tommy's small hands, but he just reached out to her and gripped her around the neck. She lifted him, and he whimpered near her ear. His tears and slobber soaked her neck. "I should get him home." She held out the handkerchief to Ethan.

Ethan held up a hand. "You may need it later." He picked up her shopping basket. "Do you need some help?"

She took the basket. "It's not far. I can manage." She'd caused him enough pain and misery, or rather Pa had. Besides, he shouldn't be lifting or carrying things with a bullet wound.

She was halfway to the minister's house when she realized she hadn't thanked Ethan for telling her what he had. *Next time, Lord.*

Chapter 5

Laurel pulled her shawl tighter as the wind whipped her hair around her face. She wouldn't have gone out at all if she hadn't been anxious to see if the mystery composer had added any more to the hymn. Two new lines had been added last week and one on Monday. She also needed to practice more before Sunday.

As she reached for the handle on the church door, someone called her name. Alonzo Chavez came toward her with a brown paper–wrapped bundle under one arm. "Señorita Rivers, these shirts you can fix." He handed her the package.

"You want me to mend some shirts?"

"*Sí*. One shirt needs buttons. One shirt needs new cuffs."

"Shouldn't you have Miss Menendez do that for you?"

"You do this. I pay you." He started to walk away.

"But—"

He held out his hands as he walked backward. "*Por favor.*"

"Are the buttons in here?"

He nodded. "The old shirt there, you use parts of it." He turned and hurried off as the first drops of rain began to splatter; the dry, thirsty earth swallowed them with hardly a trace on the surface.

She scurried inside. That was odd. Was Rosita Menendez not skilled with a needle and thread?

She set her shawl and the package on the front pew and went to the piano, hoping for another line of music. Not one but two lines. Her heart danced then suddenly stopped. Bittersweet. Since the staffs were all full, the melody was finished now; there would be no new lines to look forward to. But still the author had not signed it or titled it.

Would the composer take the music away now that it was complete?

Why would someone write this song elsewhere and leave it here? If the composer didn't play here and no one else played here except her. . . Someone was going to a lot of trouble to make sure she found it. Was the song truly meant for her? Was someone writing her a song? Was it the Lord Himself? She shook her head. He wouldn't need two separate sheets. "Lord, I care not from whence this music comes, but I thank You." She raised her hands to the keys and played the first four lines by heart, then plucked through the last two lines several times until she had them perfect.

Ethan settled into the second pew from the front on the piano side, close to the outside edge. He'd discovered this seat gave him the best view of Laurel without making it obvious that he was watching her. The piano bench sat empty, and the pews were filling. Where was she? It had to be about time.

Laurel walked in the side door. As she took off her shawl, Minister Howard spoke to her. She nodded and sat then stopped suddenly as she looked up at the music stand. She quickly tucked the sheet of music behind the hymnal.

Does she like the new addition? Did she read it? As with the melody, he'd been given only one line of lyrics, but at least he knew others would come. He understood the Lord's pattern now.

He felt the worship to his innermost being with Laurel's playing. Something he'd never felt with Mrs. Howard's. But then, he wasn't in love with Mrs. Howard.

As soon as the opening three hymns were through, Laurel gave a nod to the minister, scooped up her shawl, and slipped back out the door.

She wasn't staying? Disappointment settled in his gut like a hot coal. Mrs. Howard must need her. Would she come back this afternoon to play the song? Did she ever play it? Did she care?

Yes, he believed she did play it; otherwise, why would the Lord be having him write it for her? He was sure she would be back to play it. He waited outside the church all afternoon so that when she did come back and play it, he could hear her.

She never came.

✤

Laurel lay awake, disappointed and exhausted. Tommy had been sick. The poor tyke just wanted the comfort of his ma, but Minister Howard didn't want to risk Mrs. Howard's health or the welfare of the baby. Laurel had had her hands full all day and hadn't been able to go back over to the church to play the piano. She'd desperately wanted to know what the line said. She'd been too stunned to read it and in too much of a rush. At least she knew the music wouldn't be taken away. . .just yet.

The sooner she slept the sooner she could go back to the church, so she let the exhaustion consume her.

In the morning, Tommy behaved as though he hadn't been sick yesterday, running around and eating a larger than normal breakfast. Minister Howard was staying home today, so Laurel left the breakfast tray upstairs. She wanted to run into town before Mrs. Howard started loading her down with additional chores.

She knew she should run her errands first so that she could sit and enjoy the music and study the words, but she couldn't wait that long. She hurried up to the piano. The words were still there. " 'I am here for you through everything,'" she read aloud. She held the sheet to her chest and closed her eyes. No matter her circumstances, the Lord was with her.

Thank You, Lord, for this reminder.

It didn't take much to memorize the words. "I'll be back." She set the music back on the stand and walked into town.

Laurel looked through the bank window. Ethan Burke was talking to the sheriff. She would run her other errand first. She went to the barbershop and paid Mr. Adams what she'd been given from playing piano and went back to the bank. Thankfully, the sheriff was gone. She took a deep breath then opened the door. She hadn't been in the bank since Pa had died there.

She stared at the floor where he'd fallen. Her lungs shrank.

"Miss Rivers, may I help you?"

She looked up at Ethan Burke and scooted around the spot on the floor that was scrubbed cleaner than the rest. "I'm—" She croaked and cleared her throat. "I'm looking for Alonzo Chavez. I have his mending completed." Would he give her the information? She didn't know who else to ask. And Mr. Chavez hadn't told her how to get his shirts back to him.

The bank manager eyed her from the corner. Did he think she, too, was here to rob him?

"He's not in town today. I can give them to him the next time he's in."

She handed him the package. Was the air thinner in here? She imagined Pa pointing a gun at Ethan and the bank manager.

He took out his billfold and handed her three dollars. "To pay for the mending."

"What? No. That's too much." Her shrunken lungs now refused to take in air.

"Take it. I'll settle up with Alonzo."

Her hand reached out and took the money; then her feet expedited her escape. Once outside, she dragged in a gulp of air as though she'd been submerged underwater and had just come up.

I am here for you through everything.

She breathed more easily. "Yes, Lord. Thank You." She looked at the money in her hand. With this she would be able to finish paying off Mr. Adams and have some left over to put toward a stagecoach ticket out of town. She hurried off to the barbershop and bathhouse. "Mr. Adams, here is the rest of what I owe you."

He squinted his bulging brown eyes at the money. "You just gave me all you said you had. Where did you get more?"

"I was just over at the bank—"

"And they just gave you money?"

"No." Was he insinuating she stole it? "Mr. Burke paid me for some mending I did. If you don't believe me, you can ask him yourself."

He took the money. "I might just do that."

California had to be better than this. She didn't want all that Pa had done in trying to get there to be for naught.

She returned to the church and hammered out the song, letting the words soak into her soul. *"I am here for you through everything."* At least the Lord always loved and accepted her.

Chapter 6

Laurel tiptoed into the bedroom to retrieve Mrs. Howard's lunch tray. The cup rattled slightly against the plate as she picked it up. Mrs. Howard rolled over. "I thought you would have been up before now."

"I was dusting the mantel as you asked." *And I was hoping you would be asleep.*

"I need you to mop the kitchen."

"I did that two days ago."

"Well, it needs it again. I used to mop it every day."

Laurel bit back a retort. "I'll mop it before I go to the church to practice."

"I also need you to beat the living room rug."

She had done that three days ago. . .at Mrs. Howard's request. Dare she remind the woman?

"The house has to be clean for the new baby. And I'm in no condition to do it."

"Can I beat the rug tomorrow? I haven't had a chance to practice any hymns yet."

"Fine." Mrs. Howard waved a hand in her direction. "Go practice. You ignore what I tell you anyway. Don't be long."

Ignore? She knew she should hold her tongue, but she just couldn't. She was too tired from the woman's demands. "I have done everything you have asked of me."

Mrs. Howard narrowed her eyes. "You haven't played one hymn I have recommended."

How did she know that? "The hymns you chose were too difficult for me."

"I can play them." Mrs. Howard's mouth turned up in a joyless smile.

Laurel finally got it. Mrs. Howard was trying to make the hymns difficult for her. "If you would choose simpler hymns—"

"It's not so easy replacing me, is it?"

"What?"

"Don't be coy with me." Mrs. Howard adjusted the covers over her swollen belly. "I know what you are up to."

"Exactly what is it you think I'm up to?"

"Taking my place."

"I'm not trying to take your place." Why would she want to?

"I've seen the way you look at Mr. Howard. He'll always love me. He'll never love you."

She never looked at Minister Howard in a *way*. "Mrs. Howard, I am not trying to steal your husband."

"But if I die giving life to this child—"

"Don't even think that way."

"You would be right here to take over. You would have a ready-made family."

"I don't want your family," she shot back. "As soon as I have enough money, I'm heading to California. I don't want to stay in a town where everyone hates me."

"Can you blame them?"

No.

"You are only here by the grace of Mr. Howard."

"I know that. But I only want to help you."

"Humph. Leave Tommy with me."

"You need your rest."

"I'll not have him calling you Mama before you leave this house."

Laurel scurried out of the room as she fought back tears. She had to keep in mind Mrs. Howard's physical and emotional conditions. And her mental one, as well. Still, the words stung. Minister Howard had said it would get worse, but she never imagined such atrocious accusations.

※

Laurel sat on the top step of the front porch in the cool evening air. The Howards were all in bed. This was her time of quiet. She let the hymn drift through her. She'd found another line of lyrics today. *"I am here for you through everything; In the wind and rain, I am here."*

She carried the words in her heart wherever she went, whatever she was doing. The song was her secret. Not even the composer knew what it meant to her. What a treasure it was to her.

She wanted to write a thank-you note, let the composer know how much he had helped her. She ran inside to get pencil and paper and sat back in the moonlight, bright enough to write by. She tapped the pencil on her lips.

Dear Hymn Author. . . No, that sounded too austere. *Dear Sir*—too formal. She felt as though she knew this person's heart, and the author could be a woman. *Dear Person*—too general. *To Whom It May Concern*—too cold.

She would skip the salutation, just get to the heart of the matter.

> *I can't begin to tell you what your hymn has meant to me these past weeks. My life has been fraught with trouble, and your hymn has brought healing to my wounded heart and battered spirit. Thank you for sharing your heart with me even if it was unintentional. I feel as though I know you through your music. Besides God, it has been the one respite in my current difficult circumstances.*

She stopped. *Sincerely, Miss Rivers?* She wanted to give a warmer regard than "Sincerely," but she'd never met this person. And if she signed her name, the person could take offense because of who she was.

Thank you from the bottom of my heart, she wrote, then folded the letter twice.

Laurel stepped out of the mercantile with her shopping basket full. Across the street, Ethan held out a brown paper package to Mr. Chavez. This must be the first chance in four days for Ethan to return Mr. Chavez's shirts. The package seemed a bit larger than she remembered. Mr. Chavez kept his hands in his pockets and shook his head, but eventually he took the package.

"Excuse me, miss," a man said, trying to get past her into the mercantile.

"Pardon me." She moved. How rude of her to be watching them unaware. She hurried on her way.

Once inside the church, she could breathe more easily. She hated going into town. She felt as though people were watching her, scrutinizing her. But Sundays were worse. Even though the whispers had stopped, she knew the citizens of Hollow Springs would never embrace her as one of their own. She had to move on. She wanted to move on.

She set the thank-you note on the piano with the sheet of music, but what if he or she got upset she had been playing the song and took it away? She needed this music right now in her life. She slipped the note back into her pocket. She would leave it when the song had been completed and she had it committed to memory.

A third line of lyrics had been added to the sheet. The sheet with the ink smudge. *"Through good and bad, call on me."* Such a sweet reminder. *Thank You, Lord.* She committed the line to memory and quickly ran through the selections for Sunday. Mrs. Howard was more and more nervous about being alone lately. When she finished and returned to the house, she went straight upstairs to Mrs. Howard. "Is there anything I can get for you?"

"The curtains in the kitchen need to be washed, and the ones in the front room. Beat all of the rugs and clean out the fireplace; don't just sweep it, but give it a good scrubbing. And scrub the kitchen floor—make sure you get all the corners."

She wanted to tell her that the kitchen floor didn't *need* scrubbing again today and that she *had* gotten the corners. But she held her tongue.

The woman must be miserably scared of losing this baby.

Later, on her hands and knees in the fireplace with a scrub brush in hand, Laurel sighed at the knock on the door. The last thing she wanted to do was wash out the fireplace, but she shouldn't complain; it could be worse.

She struggled to her feet and dried her hands on her way to the door. She widened her eyes at the visitor. "Mr. Chavez."

He thrust a brown paper package at her. "They both need hemming and one a torn seam and a button gone." He started to walk away.

"Mr. Chavez?"

He turned around but continued walking backward with his hands out from his sides. "Por favor."

He almost seemed desperate in his plea.

And he walked away.

She finished scrubbing the fireplace and fixed supper. Everyone had gone to bed by the time she could get back to the package Mr. Chavez had dropped off. It appeared to be the same one she'd seen Ethan with earlier. She opened it and found two pair of dress slacks. She'd never seen Mr. Chavez in britches like these. She held them up. A little short for Mr. Chavez, too.

Her hands fisted around the fabric. These weren't Mr. Chavez's clothes, and she guessed the shirts weren't, either. Why was Ethan Burke giving his clothes to someone else for her to mend? Was her guilt not enough? Did he pity her that much? *Poor orphan girl of the bank robber. She has no family or home.* She would rather have the town's hatred than Ethan's pity.

What had she read this morning in Romans 12? She went quietly upstairs, retrieved her mother's worn Bible, and set it on the table in the circle of candlelight. She ran her finger down the page to verses 20 and 21: "Therefore if thine enemy hunger, feed him; if he thirst, give him drink: for in so doing thou shalt heap coals of fire on his head. Be not overcome of evil, but overcome evil with good." Did Ethan think her his enemy? Was he trying to heap coals of guilt on her head? Too late; she'd heaped them on herself. Was he trying to overcome Pa's evil with good deeds toward her?

Or did he think her evil? Either way, there wasn't much hope of forgiveness from him. She would leave town as soon as Mrs. Howard had her baby, even if she had to walk. If she didn't feel the minister's desperation, she'd leave now.

She sat up by candlelight in the kitchen until she'd repaired the pants and pressed them. Right after breakfast in the morning, she would return them.

Laurel had left the house later than she'd intended. The sun was already straight overhead and hot. She walked into the bank, purposely trying to keep what had happened there from her mind. Ethan was not at his window.

"May I help you?" the bank manager asked.

"I'm looking for Mr. Burke."

"He's gone out to lunch. He'll be back soon."

"Thank you." She stepped back outside to think. Maybe he ate his lunch at the hotel restaurant. Or had he gone home? Since she didn't know where he lived, she decided to check the hotel.

"Mr. Gonzales, has Mr. Burke come in for lunch?"

"I'm sorry, no."

She went back outside and looked up the street in both directions. Alonzo Chavez leaned on the awning post outside the mercantile with his long legs stretched out across the opening to the steps. Rosita Menendez was telling him something in Spanish, evidently about his rudeness in blocking her path. He had a cocky grin on his face.

"Mr. Chavez. Miss Menendez."

Mr. Chavez stiffened and stood up straight as a board. "Hola—I mean hello." His jaw was set, and his gaze flickered from her face to the package she clutched to her chest. Miss Menendez looped her hands around his arm.

"I'm looking for Mr. Burke. Do you know where I might find him?"

His Adam's apple bobbed as he swallowed hard. "He was posting a letter."

"Thank you." As she turned to leave, Rosita Menendez gave her a sweet smile, but Mr. Chavez still looked uneasy. Did he think she was going to let his sweetheart know she was mending for him? Even if these were his clothes, she was smarter than that.

※

Ethan stepped out of the small clapboard post office. His brother, Charles, would get the letter soon, and Ethan hoped he would reply quickly. Laurel was striding toward him. "Miss Rivers."

"Mr. Burke." She handed him the package. "These are repaired."

He pulled his brows together. "Shall I give them to Alonzo?"

"Mr. Burke, I saw you give him this package yesterday. These are no more Mr. Chavez's britches than they are mine. They are far too short. No offense."

"No offense taken. Let me pay you." He hadn't thought about how easy it would be for her to discern the difference.

She held up her hand. "You overpaid me for the shirts. We'll call it even."

He was only trying to help.

She lowered her lashes and said something too soft to make out.

"What was that? I couldn't quite hear you."

When she looked back up, tears rimmed her green eyes. "I can't do this anymore. I need to wash you from my heart." She turned to leave.

"Laurel, please wait."

"I have to go. I left Tommy with Mrs. Howard. She gets more and more agitated each day." She hurried away from him as though he'd hurt her.

He wanted to call her back, but it was obvious she didn't want anything to do with him. He looked down at the package. *Lord, how am I to help her if she won't accept my help?* Maybe he shouldn't have done it in secret. Would she also be mad at him for paying the hotel and mercantile bills? He only wanted to help. He would do anything for her.

Chapter 7

Ethan counted the money in his drawer and turned in the cash and receipts to Mr. Yearwood.

Mr. Yearwood took them. "You all healed up?"

He automatically touched his wound. "My arm still aches and is stiff, but I don't have to worry about ripping it open again." And he'd left his sling at home. He didn't like the way Laurel always glared at it. Was it a reminder to her of what he'd done to her pa? If he could help her get past the tragedy, then maybe she could forgive him. He wasn't looking for her sympathy.

"I sent word to the bank's investors about your bravery. Maybe they will give you a small reward for your heroics."

"I wish you hadn't done that. I'm no hero."

Mr. Yearwood clamped his hand on Ethan's shoulder. "It's never easy when you are forced to kill a man. Mr. Rivers was out of control. Think of the lives you saved. I believe he would have killed someone had you not reacted so quickly."

He knew that. But why couldn't someone else have grabbed the gun from the drawer? Anyone else. Then he could have been the one at Laurel's side to comfort her instead of avoiding her. "If you don't need me any longer, I'm going to leave."

"Go. Have a good weekend."

Outside, Alonzo was leaning against the storefront.

He went over to Alonzo and inclined his head down the street. "Starlight Hotel Restaurant?"

Alonzo nodded and pushed away from the building. "Your señorita, she looked for you."

He wished Laurel were his. "Unfortunately, she found me." Not that it would have made any difference if she hadn't found him. She would still hate him.

Alonzo held the door to the hotel open. "You almost put me in big problems with Rosita."

"How? I haven't seen her all day."

"Señorita Rivers, she brought me the mending, and Rosita, she was there."

Oops. "I'll talk to Rosita."

The hostess showed them to a table. "We have a great pot roast tonight with potatoes and carrots."

They both agreed, but he didn't feel much like eating.

Alonzo continued. "No need. Your señorita asked for you; she not give me package."

"I'm glad it all worked out." He'd ruined enough lives. He didn't need to add to the damage.

"This time. I not do it again."

"No need. She knows they were my clothes." He shook his head. "She hates me more now than ever."

"And you love her more, *mucho mas* than before."

He sighed. "I can't control my heart."

A waitress came with coffee for them both.

"Mi amigo, I very afraid for you."

"Why?"

"You fall too hard with love."

Love was the most painful thing he had ever experienced, more painful than a bullet. And he'd do it again for a chance to love Laurel and to have her love him back. "Just as she lost her father, I lost her that day in the bank."

"You not know that. Speak to her. Say everything to her."

He stirred his coffee. "What's there to tell her? She already knows everything."

"Say you are very sorry and you love her. She know that, yes?"

He set the spoon down and took a drink. Too bitter. Hadn't he added sugar? He did so and stirred again. "Why would she listen to me?"

"Maybe she love you also."

He laughed at that. The chances of Laurel loving him were nonexistent.

After supper he walked home and sat at his piano. He played through Laurel's song. The next line came to him as all the others had. One at a time.

⁂

A muzzle flash. Mr. Rivers looked down at his bloodstained shirt. When Mr. Rivers raised his head, Ethan saw Laurel's sorrow-filled face. "Nooo!" Ethan rushed around the counter to where she fell and held her in his arms.

Her gaze found his face. "Why?"

A deep ache ripped him open inside. "I'm sorry. Forgive me." He willed her not to die but could feel her life slipping away.

He sat there for a long time with her lifeless body in his arms. Then he was beside her open grave, still holding her. They wanted to put her in the cold, uncaring earth, but he wouldn't let them.

He woke to find his arms tightly wrapped around his pillow and tears on his face. "Laurel," he whispered in the dark. "Forgive me."

He stayed huddled with the pillow until dawn broke over the horizon and began to light the room. His dream was quite clear. He would never have peace until he asked Laurel's forgiveness for what he had done. He'd told her he was sorry, but forgiveness was different. Anyone could be sorry for her loss, but asking forgiveness acknowledged responsibility. Would she forgive him?

He set his pillow aside and reluctantly climbed out of bed.

Chapter 8

Laurel closed the church door and headed for the cemetery. The fourth line of lyrics had been waiting for her. The second line had been there on Monday when she went to practice and the third on Thursday. It had taken two weeks for the music to appear one line at a time, but four out of the six lines of lyrics had rushed in during one week. The continual anticipation was exciting, but she knew it would soon be over. She both looked forward to the end and dreaded it. She wanted this blessing to last. If she could stop time, she would right now, here, with this song. Would the author title it once he or she was through? She would call it "I Am Here."

She hummed the tune and let the words play in her mind.

> *I am here for you through everything;*
> *In the wind and rain, I am here.*
> *Through good and bad, call on me;*
> *My love for you is true and faithful.*

She stopped at the edge of the cemetery and stared. Ethan Burke was kneeling beside Pa's grave. He was the last person she would expect there. Had he come to unleash pent-up anger on Pa? She wanted to leave but found herself walking closer. It was time she faced up to what Pa had done and begged for Ethan's forgiveness.

As she came to the grave, she could hear Ethan murmuring softly, pleading. But for what? A fresh red and yellow firewheel lay on Pa's grave. It had been Ethan? A twig cracked under her foot. Ethan jerked around then stood. His eyes were red, but no tears streaked his cheeks.

He blinked. "Laurel. I mean Miss Rivers." He seemed flustered. "I'm sorry for intruding." He pointed to Pa's grave.

"I'm glad you're here, Mr. Burke. I've needed to speak to you for a long time now." She took a deep breath.

"Please call me Ethan."

Would it be right to be so familiar? "I wanted to tell you how deeply sorry I am."

He knit his brow. "You have nothing to be sorry for."

"What my pa did to you. . ." She stared at his injured arm now out of the sling. "You are a good and kind man. I beseech you on behalf of my pa to find it in your heart to forgive him."

His eyes widened. "I'm the one who needs to beg your forgiveness. I did far worse to your pa than he did to me."

She couldn't imagine what. "Pa shot you."

"His bullet only injured. Mine. . ." The words choked off, and he stared down at his splayed hands, then back up to her with fresh tears in his cobalt blue eyes.

She stared at him a moment and pictured Ethan with a gun in his hand pointed at Pa, then a flash. She gasped. Pa fell, and then there was red. "You?"

He nodded.

"But the sheriff—I always thought the sheriff. . ."

"The sheriff arrived later. I was only trying to wound your pa. I never meant to—to kill him." He looked down at his shaking hands.

Poor Ethan, forced to kill to protect others. What torment he must be fighting within. She couldn't even imagine. She looked to Pa's grave. Poor Pa. So desperate, and Ethan was unfortunate enough to get in the way.

✳

"If I could go back, I'd change it all. Please forgive me." Ethan blinked to focus his vision, to see Laurel more clearly.

"I am so sorry he put you in that position. Of course I forgive you. For a long time he was not the father who raised me. Believe me, he had been a good Christian man. He changed the day Ma died. He died inside, too."

Her forgiveness washed over him, soothing his soul. "Was your ma's name Katherine?"

She nodded.

"I think he saw her just before he passed on—or thought he saw her."

Tears pooled in her green eyes. "I would like to believe so. He would have liked that."

He reached out and took Laurel's hand. "I'm going to see to it you make it to California."

"What?"

"It's what your pa wanted."

She blinked several times, and the glisten in her eyes receded. "You are a very sweet man, but I don't want to burden you any further."

"You are not a burden. Everything I did was to help you."

"Everything? You mean the mending?"

He stared at her a moment. He already knew that giving her work in secret had been a mistake. How would she feel about the rest? "The mending."

She squinted at him. "Was it you? Did you pay Pa's debts at the hotel and the mercantile?"

He was reluctant to answer, but he knew he couldn't deny it. He nodded.

"Why would you do that for me?"

He saw something in her upturned face. Was it hope? "I feel responsible for you—because I took your pa away."

Laurel's shoulders drooped slightly. "The one responsible is my pa. I absolve you from any responsibility you feel you owe." Her voice had become flat and lifeless. "Please let go of your guilt. I don't hold your actions against you. Thank you for all you have done for me."

He sensed he'd hurt her in some new way but didn't know how. Was she further from his reach than ever?

✿

Laurel wiped the crumbs from the table and dumped them into the slop pail. Everything she thought was good about Hollow Springs wasn't, except the song. She longed to go play its soothing notes.

Ethan didn't think of her as anything more than a burden that needed to be taken care of then forgotten. She didn't want to be anybody's burden. She blinked back tears. *Responsible.* No word could have dashed her hopes faster. She'd cried after her encounter with Ethan yesterday and later cried herself to sleep. She hadn't realized how deep her feelings for Ethan were. Her emotions were all mixed up inside her. She couldn't tell if her tears were because of her poor circumstances or because she now knew that there was no future for her and Ethan.

Minister Howard came into the kitchen with the tray. "Mrs. Howard wasn't hungry this morning." He set the tray on the counter, the food untouched. "I asked her if she wanted you to stay here this morning."

No. She wanted out of this house for a little while.

"She said she's just going to sleep, so you can go, but I'd appreciate it if you would come back as soon as the service is over." His kind eyes looked tired.

Relief washed over her. "I was wondering if I could go over to the church now. I need to practice a little more before the service starts."

He nodded. "I'll be over in a little while."

She escaped out the door before he could change his mind. She breathed in the sweet scent of wildflowers as she walked to the church. She would play the mystery song first then practice the hymns; that way she wouldn't be playing the unnamed hymn when people started arriving. She didn't want the composer catching her. But first. . .

She knelt at the first pew and opened her heart to God. This was what she needed most, to be alone with God. When she had purged and felt cleansed, she moved over to the piano. She noticed that the sheets of music had been switched just since yesterday. She scanned to the bottom. The fifth line of words was there: *"Believe in me; I believe in you."*

Yes, Lord, I do believe.

She put her fingers to the keys and sang the song in her head as she played.

✳

Ethan leaned against the side of the clapboard church. The song he'd written for Laurel drifted out through the open window. She played it beautifully, better than he. She'd almost caught him, but he'd seen her coming and slipped out in time.

After he'd spoken with her yesterday, he'd gone home, and the Lord had given him the new line. And soon He would give him the last. He listened to her play it through three times; then he headed back home with the copy of the music. He'd return for the service in an hour. He needed to add the new line to the second sheet so it would be ready when he finally knew the last.

Later, as he sat in his regular pew, he kept his gaze on Laurel. She didn't once turn his way or anyone else's way. She looked only at the piano and hymnal. After service she left quickly, and he followed. "Miss Rivers."

She stopped and paused a moment before turning his way but kept her gaze down. "Good day, Mr. Burke."

He'd thought they were beyond the formalities. "I would prefer you call me Ethan."

"I really need to be getting back to Mrs. Howard. She's been feeling poorly as of late."

"I wanted to talk to you about the trip to California."

"I do truly appreciate all you have done for me, but I won't be leaving until after Mrs. Howard has her baby. She needs me."

I need you.

"At that time, I'll have my own means to get there. But thank you for your generous offer."

"But I want to help. I feel responsible."

There it was again—her shoulders shifting downward—but why?

"As I told you yesterday, I free you from any obligation you think you have where I am concerned."

But he wanted to be responsible for her.

"Pa did what he did, and you did what you had to do. I don't blame you. Honestly. He was not himself."

"But if I hadn't—if I had only wounded him."

"Then Pa would be in jail, he would still have debts, and my circumstances wouldn't be much different than they are now."

He gripped her shoulders. "But I did kill your pa, and I am responsible."

Tears rimmed her eyes. "I don't want you to feel you owe me a debt. The feeling I want from you is. . ."

"Is what, Laurel?" He searched the depths of her green eyes.

After a moment of silence, her words gushed out. "I want you to care about me, but not because of anything that has happened, not because you feel *responsible*."

"I do care about you."

"Because you feel responsible." She pulled from his grip. "I really do need to go check on Mrs. Howard. Good day, Mr. Burke." She turned and walked away.

When would he ever hear her call him by his given name? Yesterday she said she'd forgiven him, so why did she seem to want to be far away from him? *Lord, what do I do now?*

Chapter 9

Laurel heard a crash. Mrs. Howard cried out. She glanced at Tommy stretched out on the floor asleep and raced upstairs. Mrs. Howard stood with one hand on the foot post of the bed, the other under her belly.

"Let me help you back into bed."

"Stay away from me." A small pool of water gathered at Mrs. Howard's feet.

She halted. The baby was coming. "Mrs. Howard, you must get back into bed."

"Leave. I want you to leave."

She backed up to the doorway. "I'll leave once you are back in bed." She watched Mrs. Howard struggle into the bed. "I'll go get help."

Mrs. Howard gripped her stomach and waved her away.

She was at the bottom of the stairs before she realized she had touched any of them.

Tommy stood there crying. "Mama hurt."

"Mama will be fine." She scooped up the child and headed out the door. "We have to go get the doctor."

Tommy struggled in her arms. "Want Mama."

"Shh. I know. We'll come right back." She hurried into town and turned the knob on the doctor's door, but it was locked. She pounded on it.

"Doc's not there." Mayor Vance stood a few feet away.

That was obvious. "Do you know where he is?"

"I think he's out at the Shepard place."

"How far is that?"

"Too far to help."

"Mrs. Howard is having her baby."

His eyes widened. "Martha Peabody just went over to the bank. She's a midwife."

She ran to the bank. Mrs. Peabody stood at Ethan's window. "Mrs. Peabody, Mrs. Howard needs you. She's having her baby."

"Calm down, child. Roberta's baby isn't due for at least four weeks yet."

"Ma'am, it's coming." She leaned close and whispered about the water on the floor.

Mrs. Peabody straightened. "Is her husband with her?"

"No. No one." She'd hated leaving Mrs. Howard alone in her time of need, but what choice did she have?

"I'll tend to her. You find Preacher." Mrs. Peabody hustled out the door.

Someone else in the bank piped up. "Heard tell he was heading over to the Myers' house."

Ethan appeared at her side. "I'll get the preacher."

❧

Laurel stood at the back of the Howards' bedroom, waiting to help in any way she could.

"I'm not having this baby while she is under my roof!" Mrs. Howard had become feverish and seemed delirious, thrashing her head from side to side.

"She can be of help," Minister Howard said.

"She'll steal the baby!" Then Mrs. Howard hollered in pain.

"If you won't do it, I will," Mrs. Peabody said. "She can't be this agitated."

Minister Howard nodded to her.

Laurel rushed to her room and put her few meager belongings in her carpetbag. As she walked back past the bedroom, she glanced in. Minister Howard gave her a small smile then turned to his wife. "You can have our baby now."

133

She rushed down the stairs. Five ladies from the church stood in the kitchen; one held Tommy on her hip. Rosita and her ma were among them. Rosita's ma was also a midwife and rushed up the stairs with an armful of clean sheets. The three church ladies turned away. Could they really pretend she wasn't there? But Rosita's gaze didn't waver from her. Her big dark eyes filled with sadness as she watched her leave.

She had no place to go. *"When all around my soul gives way, He then is all my hope and stay."* Her only refuge now was God. She would go to His house. He alone was her source of help and hope.

She'd felt that the Lord wanted her to stay until the birth of the Howards' baby. That day was today. She'd thought she'd have a few more weeks, though. The little money she had must be enough to get her to the next place the Lord would have her go. Fear gripped her heart at the thought of traveling alone.

Rosita followed her out to the porch and started speaking to her in Spanish.

Laurel just shook her head. All she caught was Burke and Alonzo. "I don't know what you are trying to tell me."

Rosita pinched her face in frustration then pointed to the church.

"Yes. I'm going to the church. Then I'm going to buy a stagecoach ticket that will take me as far as my small amount of money will let me go." Why was she explaining this to her? Rosita couldn't possibly understand.

But Rosita's eyes widened as though she did; then she stepped off the porch, heading into town, away from the church.

What was all that about? She heard Mrs. Howard scream and hurried on her way. She set down her carpetbags inside the door and knelt in front of the first pew.

"Please, blessed Lord Jesus, be with Mrs. Howard and her baby. Protect them both. It's too early for this baby, but I know that in Your hands the baby can live. Please don't take this little one from her. Please don't let anything I did harm either of them."

She thought she would pray for her own troubles, but the only words that came were for Mrs. Howard. She kept praying until she had nothing left. Then she just sat, exhausted, on the floor. She looked up at the cross hanging on the wall. "What now, Lord?" She supposed the only thing left to do was leave town.

❧

Ethan looked up as the bell above the bank door jingled.

Rosita bustled in and walked right up to his window. She rattled off paragraphs in Spanish.

"Slow down. I need English."

Rosita took a deep breath. "*Señora* Howard—go—Señorita Rivers."

He nodded. "Yes, Mrs. Howard is going to have her baby, and Miss Rivers got help. Everything is going to be fine."

Rosita shook her head and started off in Spanish again.

He shrugged and held up his hands.

Rosita huffed out a breath. "*¿Dónde esta Alonzo?* Where Alonzo?"

"He was getting his hair cut at the barbershop." He started to make scissors with his fingers and bring them up to his hair, but Rosita had turned and was out the door. She understood far more than she could speak. Hopefully, Alonzo could make sense of what was upsetting her.

A few minutes later, Alonzo strode in with Rosita. "Can you come away?"

Ethan looked over at Mr. Yearwood. "Go. It's slow today. I don't expect much business with people distracted over the Howards' impending arrival."

"Thank you." He grabbed his jacket and followed Alonzo and Rosita outside. "What's this all about? Rosita came in upset, looking for you."

"No. She look for you."

Rosita started in rapid Spanish again.

"*¡Silencio!*" Alonzo ordered. "*El gringo no comprendo.*"

He understood that: *The American doesn't understand.* Rosita quieted. "She mentioned Mrs. Howard. I tried to tell her that we already got help."

"Rosita, she was there. She knows. Her *madre* help. Señora Howard has. . ."

Alonzo was searching for an unfamiliar word or phrase, so Ethan thought he'd offer help. "Had her baby?"

135

Alonzo shook his head in frustration. *"Echar a patadas."*

"Rápido, Alonzo." Rosita turned to Ethan. "Go, go."

"Señora Howard told Señorita Rivers to go. Leave," Alonzo finally said.

Ethan furrowed his brow. "She kicked her out?"

"That is not all. Señorita Rivers leaves town. She buys stagecoach ticket."

Ethan's insides twisted. He thought he would have more time to woo her. "I have to find her." He started off for the stagecoach ticket office.

"Rosita, she says Señorita Rivers go to church first."

He spun around and headed for the church.

Chapter 10

Laurel stood by the piano and picked up the sheet of music. She ran her fingers over it. She would never see the piece completed, but she would always carry it in her heart. It was time to continue her journey west. She would miss the song most of all, but she couldn't stay. Pa had ultimately let Ma's dream destroy him. California hadn't been good for either Ma or Pa, but maybe it would be good for her. She pulled out the thank-you note she'd written.

The door at the back creaked, and she heard footsteps. She kept her gaze on the piano. Whoever it was would leave once they saw her.

"Laurel."

She turned. Ethan! Her heart pitter-pattered at the sight of him. She wanted to run into his arms, let him take the undue responsibility he thought he had. But she didn't. She stayed rooted in place. "Mr. Burke." For the first time since Pa shot him, she didn't still see the sling. Forgiveness was a sweet thing.

He walked to the front where she stood. "What am I going to have to do to get you to call me by my given name?"

She lowered her gaze to the floor. "I don't know." She saw his foot take the last step between them and looked up.

His cobalt blue eyes met hers. They were trying to tell her something, but she couldn't figure out what.

"Rosita said that Mrs. Howard put you out. Is it true?" He held his hat in his hand.

"Yes." And there was relief in being put out. Though she didn't know just what she was going to do, she was glad to be out from under the Howards' roof.

"What will you do?"

"I have a little money now. I'll buy a coach ticket to another town where they don't know about Pa and get a job."

"Don't go."

"I must. The people of Hollow Springs don't want me here. It is best for everyone if I go."

"Not for me."

Her heart skipped a beat. Did he truly care? Or did he only feel responsible?

He stepped closer. "From the moment I saw you, the Lord put you in my heart. I don't want you to leave without me. Marry me. I can give you a place to live, provide for you, and I'll take you to California. Unless there is someone else. Someone in California?"

Ethan wanted to marry her? Her heart sang. The paper in her hand called out to her, and she looked down at the sheet of music.

He looked, too. "What do you have there?"

"It's a hymn. I don't know who wrote it, but I've been wondering about this person."

"Would you choose the unknown author over me?"

She stared up at him. Would she? If the composer walked in right now and professed his love for her, which she knew he wouldn't, would she choose him? The composer had only been the Lord's instrument to comfort her. To her, God was the true author of the music.

"It's okay if you would. More than anything, I want the truth."

Ethan was here and real. She'd loved him before she ever discovered the music, but the song had helped heal her. She set the sheet on the bench. "You. I would choose you."

His smile stretched his mouth. "You have made me the happiest man in the world." He picked up the music. "Would you play it for me?"

Glad to finally share it with someone, she sat and put her fingers to the keys. "I don't sing well, so I'll just play it."

"How about if I sing the words?"

She would like that. She hadn't heard both parts together yet. She began, and so did Ethan.

"I am here for you through everything." His voice was smooth and deep. "In the wind and rain, I am here." Deeper than his speaking voice. "Through good and bad, call on me; My love for you is true and faithful." The song fit his voice, seemed to be written for him. "Believe in me; I believe in you."

As she came to the last line, she knew he'd have to stop, but she would play to the end. But he didn't stop. He sang the last line, sure and strong. She stopped in the middle of the line, but he continued.

"No other man will love you more than I do."

She stared at the sheet of music as he finished. Ethan was the author. It wasn't a song about God's love, but a song about a man's love for a woman. She turned slowly on the bench. "You?"

He nodded.

"For me?"

"I wanted to give you something for what I took from you. I couldn't bring your father back, but I could give you my love. I didn't think you would let me in person, so I wrote it down in a language I hoped you wouldn't reject."

Tears filled her eyes. "Thank you."

Ethan took her hand and pulled her to her feet. "I've loved you since the day you came into town."

"I love you, too."

He wrapped her in his arms and kissed her.

The clearing of a throat caused her to push away from him. The minister stood at the back of the church.

"Minister Howard, I'm sorry."

Ethan hooked his arm around her waist. "I'm not. I love her, and she loves me."

Minister Howard smiled back. "You two make a fine couple."

"Minister, has Mrs. Howard had the baby yet?"

He nodded. "Peter Sean Howard."

"Is he healthy?"

Minister Howard nodded. "He's tiny but a fighter like his mother."

"How is Mrs. Howard?"

"Right as rain. She's resting." He smiled at them. "Let me know when you two want to tie the knot."

Ethan stood taller. "Now."

She jerked her gaze up to him. "Now?"

"You need a place to live. I could pay for a room at the hotel, but that would start tongues to wagging. Marry me now? I don't want to wait one day and risk losing you."

She wanted to be Mrs. Ethan Burke right now, today. "I have Ma's wedding dress in my carpetbag. Can I change first?"

Ethan smiled, and the minister said, "I'll go round up a witness or two and meet the two of you back here."

"Alonzo and Rosita are probably not far away," Ethan said. "I'll bring them back with me."

The minister directed his gaze at her. "You can go over to the house to change. Mrs. Howard is asleep and won't even know you are there." He closed the door behind him.

"This is for you." She handed the thank-you letter to Ethan.

He tucked his eyebrows. "What is it?"

"I wrote a letter to the song's composer. That's you."

He unfolded it and read it. "I never knew if you were actually playing it until yesterday morning when you almost caught me here. I'm glad it helped you. I was praying it would."

"Some days, other than the Lord, it was the only good thing I had to look forward to. Do you have a title for it?"

" 'A Song for Laurel.'"

A smile stretched her lips. "I like that."

He took her hands. "So you're really going to marry me today?"

"Yes, Ethan. I'm going to marry you."

He shook his head. "So it took asking you to marry me to get you to call me Ethan. I should have asked you a long time ago, then." He drew her into his arms and kissed her before they went their separate ways to prepare.

Laurel put her carpetbag on the bed she used in Tommy's room and took out everything to get to the bottom, then she pulled out the bedsheet-wrapped dress. It was a simple white dress with a touch of lace at the cuffs and neck and wrinkles galore. Was there even time to iron it? She shook her head. Even if there was time, she would rather wear wrinkles than spend time in the kitchen with the clucking hens.

A light knock sounded at the door. She opened it, and Rosita walked into the room. "I help you." She gingerly touched the dress lying on the bed. *"Muy bonita."* She held the dress up to Laurel. "Bonita, señorita. You… make…beautiful bride."

"Thank you." Tears gathered in her eyes. Was it just because someone gave her a kind word? Or was it because she was getting married? Or was it because Ma and Pa weren't here with her?

Rosita scooped up the dress over both arms. "I go iron."

"You don't have to do that."

Rosita rattled off several sentences in Spanish then swept out the door with the dress.

The tears that had gathered spilled over her cheeks at Rosita's kindness. She pulled out Pa's pocket watch and opened it. Ma and Pa on their wedding day looked up at her. "I wish you both were here." She paced the room until Rosita returned with her pressed dress.

Rosita laid it on the bed.

"Thank you so very much." Laurel gave her darling, black-haired angel a hug.

Rosita hugged her back then helped her dress. "You wait." And Rosita left her again.

She wanted to call her back. Rosita had been so kind to her, she just wanted her to stay. She wasn't sure how long she would need to wait and suddenly grew nervous. She was going to get married today. She was going to be someone's wife. Her life would forever change. *Lord, am I doing the right thing?*

She knelt down beside the bed, careful not to undo Rosita's hard work, and poured out her hopes and fears to the Lord. When the knock came on the door, she was at peace with what her future held.

Minister Howard stood in the hall. "Are you ready?"

"Yes."

"Are you sure this is what you want? I can speak to Mrs. Howard. I can make her understand. Or I can make arrangements for you to stay with another family."

She didn't have to get married out of necessity. She had a choice. Did she want to marry Ethan for no other reason than that she could? *Yes!* her heart cried. From the day she'd first seen him, she'd known. She took a deep breath. "Very sure. I want to be Mrs. Ethan Burke."

"Ethan Burke is a good man." Minister Howard smiled and handed her a bouquet of wildflowers. "These are from Miss Menendez."

That was thoughtful of her. They were tied with a blue ribbon. Her dress was old, the flowers new, the ribbon blue. Rosita probably wasn't even aware of the tradition. The only thing missing was something borrowed. She would borrow Ma's favorite prayer: *Lord, from sunup to sundown, may my actions shine glory to You.*

Minister Howard walked her to the entrance door of the church. "Wait here until you hear the music start." The minister slipped inside.

Music? Who had he found to play the piano—and on such short notice? The music started, and she stepped inside, then stopped and stared. The pews were half full of the townspeople: Mr. Gonzales and his wife, Mr. and Mrs. Jones, the ladies from the Howards' kitchen, as well as a few others. They'd certainly not come for her. They must be here at the minister's request and for Ethan, but their presence gave her a sense of acceptance anyway. The Lord was working extra for her today.

She turned her focus to the front of the church and headed down the aisle. Ethan sat at the piano. Of course it would be him. As she walked down the aisle, she could see Rosita giving Alonzo a look that said she wanted to be getting married next. Alonzo just smiled back at her and winked. When she reached the front, Ethan played the final notes and then joined her.

She was very sure and couldn't wait to become Mrs. Ethan Burke.

After the vows, Minister Howard smiled as he said, "I now pronounce you husband and wife." Then he looked directly at Ethan. "You may kiss your bride."

Ethan cupped Laurel's face in both of his hands and gave her a gentle, lingering kiss.

Very, very sure.

Epilogue

One month later

Laurel stood on the sandy shore and stared out at the Pacific Ocean with the salt breeze caressing her face. "We made it, Ma." She pulled out Pa's pocket watch from her handbag and opened it, Ma and Pa gazing up at her. "We all made it."

She pulled the small photograph free. A cinnamon-colored curl lay beneath along with Pa's ashen one. She took them out. "I love you, Ma and Pa." She separated the hairs between her fingers and let the salt breeze take them away. How apropos to bring Ma to the Pacific Ocean on the anniversary of her death. Now Ma and Pa would forever be a part of California, and she could move on with her life.

She turned to her new husband, took his hand, and folded the watch into it. "My wedding gift to you."

Ethan opened his hand and stared at it. "I can't take this."

"Ma gave it to Pa on their wedding day. I know it's not our wedding day, but I want you to have it."

"Thank you."

She slipped her arms around his waist. "Thank you for bringing us here."

Ethan looped his arms around her. "My pleasure." He kissed the top of her head. "Now that we're here, where do you want to live?"

"Anywhere you are." She turned in his embrace to look up at him. "I love you, Mr. Burke." He didn't seem to mind her calling him Mr. Burke anymore.

He gave her a squeeze. "I love you, too, Mrs. Burke." He kissed her. "I think the Lord has good things planned for us here in California."

She was sure of it.

MARY DAVIS is a full-time fiction writer who enjoys going into schools and talking to kids about writing. Mary lives near Colorado's Rocky Mountains with her husband, three children, and six pets.

Mother's Old Quilt

by Lena Nelson Dooley

Dedication

To my two best friends, Rita Booth and Aleene Harward.
They have prayed for every book I've written,
every proposal I've sent in, and every meeting
at which I was the speaker.
I love you both from the bottom of my heart.
You have added a special dimension to my life.
I'm glad God tied our heartstrings together.
The book is also my small tribute to John Collins,
a wonderful youth minister and strong man of God
who is now at home with the Lord.
As with every book, it is also dedicated to my husband, James,
who has helped our family create a colorful tapestry of love.

Chapter 1

Wayzata, Minnesota—Early March 1905

"If one more thing happens, I think I'll scream."

Maggie Swenson trudged through snowdrifts on the way from her house to the barn. The tops of her boots didn't come above the snow, so the cold stuff spilled over, wetting her thick wool socks. Before she had to come out here again, she needed to borrow some of Valter's trousers. She knew it wouldn't be ladylike to wear her brother's long pants, but it would be better than dragging a woolen skirt that grew heavier and heavier because of the damp snow clinging to it.

It had been so long since she had any time to herself. Only six months ago, both her parents died when the buggy they were riding in smashed against an outcropping of rocks because something startled their horse, making it run away. Maggie and her brother, who at twenty-one was two years older than she, inherited the farm their parents had worked hard to sustain through summer droughts and harsh Minnesota winters. Now Maggie tried to run the farm all by herself. Valter lay in the house with a high fever, growing weaker every day no matter what she did for him. She feared he had the dreaded influenza that was taking such a toll this year.

Just as she reached up to unlatch the door to the barn, Maggie heard a soft moan followed by a pain-filled whine. She glanced around, and the sun glinting off the white world around her stabbed her eyes. As she squinted, her gaze traveled over the landscape around the barn. The few bushes were laden with snow, as were the trees in the pasture and beyond. When she heard the sound again, she determined that it came from the side of the building. Maggie plunged into the drift that had blown against the wall of the secure structure. Now her long underwear was wet up to her knees. If she didn't go inside soon, she might get as sick as Valter.

With her curiosity stronger than the desire to get out of the biting wind, Maggie rounded the corner of the barn in search of the origin of the sound. She almost stumbled over a warm lump in the snow. Horror filled her mind when she realized what it was.

"Rolf!"

She fell to her knees and lifted the head of her beloved dog. His thick, light brown coat was clumped with dampness, and a red stain spread across one shoulder and down his leg. Already his eyes were glassy, and he didn't seem to recognize her.

"Rolf." Ignoring the damp snow, she sat back and pulled his large head into her lap. "What happened?" Maggie whispered against the wet fur and wished her pet could answer. While she held him, crooning encouragement into his ear, his head went limp in her hands and his labored breathing ceased. An icicle fell from the edge of the roof, shattering on the crust of the snow behind her. Silence surrounded her, broken only by the irregular click of icy tree limbs tapping a staccato rhythm in the cold wind.

Maggie looked beyond the lifeless body and noticed a bloody trail in the snow, leading toward the woods that ran from the back of the barn all the way to the creek a couple of miles away. She knew Rolf liked to romp in those woods, and she had allowed him that freedom. After all, it was on their property, so the animal should have been perfectly safe.

What had Maggie been thinking a few minutes ago? *If one more thing happened.* . . Well, it had, and she didn't have the strength to scream, so she dropped her face into both upraised hands and sobbed—deep, wrenching sobs that shook both her body and her soul.

When John Collins emerged from between the trees, he saw a girl or woman hunched over. Although she appeared to be a woman, she was tiny. She looked as though she was crying as she sat in the snow beside a barn, an animal stretched out beside her, half in her lap. John's heart almost stopped beating. He knew he was the reason she cried. Why hadn't he been more careful? He had been so sure that the patch of light brown fur he glimpsed between the trees was a deer or an elk that he had taken aim and pulled the trigger. If only he had waited until he was close enough to be completely certain.

John took pride in the fact that he shot so accurately from a distance. Pride made him risk the shot, knowing he wouldn't hit anything except the patch of brown fur he sighted down the barrel of his rifle. He shifted slightly to allow for the wind and squeezed the trigger. Immediately after the loud boom of the gun stopped echoing in the trees, the animal dropped behind the underbrush.

It had taken John awhile to climb the fence and find a place to cross the creek without getting wet. Then he worked his way to the spot where he was sure he would find the deer or elk to dress. The meat would be a welcome addition to the larder at the boardinghouse where he lived, and he planned to give some of it to the preacher's family. Before he reached the spot, John pulled his hunting knife from its sheath so he could make quick work of field dressing the animal.

Instead of the game he expected, he found an impression in the snow where an animal had fallen, but it couldn't have been a deer. The path through the snow told its own story. Paw prints surrounding the bloody trail where an animal had dragged its body were evidence that John had shot something besides wild game. Probably someone's guard dog or pet—or both. His heart sank. Heaviness fell over him like dusk on a winter evening in North Dakota. He followed the trail to find the heart-breaking sight before him.

Reluctantly, John trudged across the open space between himself and the woman. When he was about three feet from her, he stopped. He knew she wasn't even aware of his presence. Tears ran down his own cheeks as he studied her. Although she was bundled up against the cold, she appeared to be almost as old as he was. Blond curls peeked from the edge of the multicolored knitted cap she wore pulled down around her ears, and tears made streaks on cheeks rosy from the winter wind. John wished he could relive the last half hour. He constantly battled his pride. This time, pride won, and this woman paid the price.

John cleared his throat. "Ma'am, I'm sorry."

He stepped forward, and after sliding the animal to the ground, he pulled her up into his arms. John hadn't held anyone this way except his mother and sisters, but he wanted to comfort this woman. She cried so hard that she didn't seem to be aware of much, but she let him pull her into his embrace. She continued to sob as if her heart had shattered.

He looked down at the lifeless animal, and silently he called himself all kinds of uncomplimentary names. At that moment, he never wanted to shoot his gun again. All the warnings his father had given him while teaching him to hunt ran through his mind in a cycle, the chants magnifying just how far he was from heeding them. John felt helpless. Was there any way he could ever undo the damage?

When Maggie became aware of the warmth surrounding her, she pulled back and looked up into the face of. . .a stranger. The tall man wore a heavy coat with a scarf to ward off the cold, but she noticed dark curls peeking from under the brim of his hat. The clear green eyes that gazed back at her held sympathy and great sorrow, and traces of tears stained his cheeks.

Maggie looked at her gloved hands grasping the front of his coat. Quickly, she let go, and his arms dropped to his side. She stepped back, never taking her gaze off her gloves. They were stained with Rolf's blood. She stared at them before looking down at the lifeless body at their feet.

"I'm really sorry."

Maggie glanced up at the man and realized he had apologized two times to her. What did he have to apologize for? Who was he?

She must have voiced the last question, because he answered it. "I'm John Collins, the new stationmaster in Wayzata."

Maggie continued to stare at him. What was the stationmaster doing beside their barn?

"I was hunting, and. . .I must have shot your dog by mistake." His gaze dropped to where Rolf lay on the cold ground. "I followed his trail through the woods."

Maggie didn't have to look where he gestured to know that he had come from her woods. Why would anyone kill her dog, even by mistake? Rolf was her companion during the long, hard nights. He stayed near her feet while she sat in the rocking chair beside Valter's bed. Just last night, Maggie had tried her best to stay awake, but she had been so tired her head dropped against the high back of the chair. Exhaustion brought a deep sleep. She wasn't even aware when Vally began struggling to breathe. But Rolf knew. He managed to wake her up. Because of their dog, she had been able to keep Vally from dying.

While these thoughts ran through Maggie's head, she became aware of the cold. Realizing she had become chilled to the bone, she stamped her feet, trying to get her blood to circulate in her nearly frostbitten extremities.

"Can we at least go into the barn to get out of this wind?" Mr. Collins's words brought her attention back to him.

She nodded and led the way. Being a well-built barn, it had no cracks where the wind could swirl through. With two workhorses, two riding horses, and three cows inside, the temperature felt almost warm.

After the man latched the door, Maggie turned her fury on him. "What were you doing hunting on our property anyway?"

He took a step back and pulled his hands in front of his chest as if to ward off her attack. "I didn't realize it was anyone's property."

"You won't find many places this close to town that aren't owned by someone." She placed her fisted hands on her hips the way her mother had when she was upset. "We don't mind if people hunt here if they ask permission. . .and as long as they don't kill our animals."

The man stuffed his hands in the pockets of his heavy coat. "I know I made a mistake. What can I do to make it right?"

"You can never make it right!" Maggie knew she shouted at the man, but she didn't care. She was very near losing all control. "Just get off my property and don't ever come back!" She pointed toward the closed door.

The man shifted his weight from one foot to the other. "I want to do something to help you. You're not all alone out here, are you?"

Maggie wondered if the man was some kind of monster who preyed on lonely women. "No! My brother's in the house." She put her shaking hands under her arms. "Now please, leave." She started toward the door.

The man didn't move from his place, blocking her exit. "I'll take care of the dog for you."

Rolf! Maggie hadn't even considered what she would do with his body. The ground was too frozen for her to bury him by herself. Maybe she should let Mr. Collins do it. At least he could do that much.

Maggie slowly nodded. "Okay. Then leave our farm and don't ever come back." She stepped around John Collins and reached for the latch.

"I'll go to town and get a wagon." His baritone voice held sympathy she didn't want to accept. "I won't be long."

Without turning her head, Maggie nodded again then exited the barn.

❦

John's heart broke for the woman he left at the farm. He hadn't even asked her name. When he stepped into the brightness of the wintry sun reflecting off the snow, he squinted to watch her walk toward the house. Her shoulders sagged and shook. She probably sobbed as she went. He wouldn't be surprised if her brother came looking for him after he heard about the fiasco. John hoped he wasn't a violent man.

Because his father was a preacher, John had been taught to be honorable, but he felt anything but honorable right now. He would rent a wagon from the livery and drive back to pick up the dead dog. Perhaps his new pastor would tell him what to do with it. He couldn't just drag it off into the woods where some wild animal would devour it. The dog meant too much to this woman. However, John knew that just disposing of the animal wasn't enough. He had to do something more. Maybe he should go out and talk to her brother. Help him with the chores or something like that. Of course, he could pray and ask God to show him what needed to be done to make up for what he destroyed. John's heart sank within him as he made his way toward his new home.

❦

After Maggie shut the door, she slumped against it. The heaviness of disease hung in the house, filling it with a palpable feeling of misery. Even this room, which had been warm and cheery before her parents died, looked and felt dreary. After a moment, she took off her coat, hat, and gloves and went into Valter's bedroom. She sank into the rocking chair beside his bed. He slept soundly. She pulled her arms tight across her abdomen and gently rocked the chair. What was she going to do if her brother didn't get well soon?

"Please, Valter," Maggie whispered as she leaned close to his ear. "Your name means 'strong fighter.' Live up to that name. Fight this illness."

As the sound of her last word died, his eyes fluttered. Soon they opened, and he looked at her. When he spoke, the words crackled through his dry lips. "Margareta, our pearl, you've been so good to take care of me."

His words scared Maggie. They carried the sound of finality with them. She pushed his hair back from his face. His hot skin felt like delicate parchment, making her afraid she would hurt him just by touching him.

"Vally, dear brother, you're going to be okay." With her words of assurance, his eyes once again closed, and he fell into restless slumber.

Maggie stood and paced around the room. *Oh, God, please don't let Vally die. I need him so much. Our parents are gone, and Thou didst not prevent their accident. Now Rolf is gone. I can't take much more.*

She opened the door to the kitchen and slipped into the other room. The fire in the fireplace burned low, so she went out on the back porch and brought in another armload of wood. The woodpile had really dwindled in the last few weeks. When Vally cut all the wood and loaded it onto the sheltered porch, he told her it should last all winter, but now Maggie feared it wouldn't. She would have a hard time cutting more wood.

After the fireplace once again warmed the room, she went back to get more fuel for the kitchen stove. Mother had been so proud of the new cookstove. Father bought it only a few months before their deaths. Every time Maggie looked at it, she remembered how happy Mother was when he brought it home. When he finished setting it up, Mother grabbed him from behind. He turned around and danced her across the kitchen, and their shared laughter filled the house. At the time, Maggie thought they were crazy. Now she would give anything to have them back, even if they did dance around like children. It had been a long time since she felt happy about anything, and she wasn't sure she ever would again.

Chapter 2

J ohn had left his mare tied in a grove of small trees with plenty of underbrush to protect her from the biting wind. He hurried back there. Quickly he mounted and rode into town. When he reached the livery stable, he found a note tacked to the door. It said that Henry had gone to Rose's Café to have coffee with the preacher. John led his horse into the stable and rubbed her down before going down the street to find the livery owner.

When John stepped out of the stable, the wind had died down, but the air still felt nippy. He blew out a deep breath and watched the cloud it formed dissipate around him. He had lived through many cold winters. In North Dakota where he grew up, the weather was even colder than in central Minnesota. Halfway to the café, John wished he hadn't forgotten the gloves he shoved into his saddlebags before he rubbed down his horse. He stuffed his hands into the pockets of his suede coat. At least it had a warm woolly lining.

More than a block away from the café, the tantalizing aromas of biscuits and bacon met him. His stomach growled. He hadn't taken time for more than a cup of coffee at dawn. Maybe he could eat a quick bite while he talked to Henry and Pastor Martin Hardin.

The preacher was a young man, barely older than John, and they became friends soon after John moved to town. Since John grew up in a parsonage, it helped him understand what a man of the cloth had to contend with.

When John stepped through the door of the eating establishment, warm, moist air made him shed his heavy coat. He hung it on the coat tree by the door, noticing that all the windows were completely steamed up, adding a cozy but cutoff feeling to the room. He leaned across the counter so the cook could hear him.

"Rose, can you scramble me two eggs? And if there are any of your wonderful biscuits left, I'd love to have a couple."

The two men he was looking for sat alone at a table at the far end of the room. They looked up when they heard John. Martin waved him back.

John dropped into a vacant chair at the table. "I wanted to talk to the two of you anyway."

Both men leaned toward him expectantly. "What's on your mind?" the livery owner asked.

John tried not to show how emotional he felt. "A couple of things." He cleared his throat. "I went hunting this morning."

"Did you kill anything?" Henry raised his bushy eyebrows at the end of his question. John noticed he often did that.

"Well, yes. . .and no."

A thoughtful expression covered Martin's face, much like John's father often looked. It must be because they were both preachers. "What exactly do you mean?"

John countered with a question of his own. "Whose farm is directly northwest from the edge of town, about half a mile or so?"

"You mean the Swenson place." Henry shook his hoary head. "It's sad, really."

John's interest piqued. He leaned his arms on the tabletop. "What's sad?"

Henry looked at Martin as if expecting him to answer.

"The farm is owned by Valter Swenson and his sister. Her name is Margareta, but we all call her Maggie."

John couldn't see anything sad about that.

"Last summer their parents died in an accident. It's been hard on Maggie and Vally. Now Vally is very sick, and Maggie is trying to run the farm by herself, as well as take care of her brother."

Can things get any worse? He had added to the pain the woman was already dealing with. A huge lump settled in his chest, right beside his heart, making it hard to breathe.

"Well, I killed her dog this morning." The shocked expressions on the faces of his companions added to John's distress. "It was an accident, but. . ."

"Here's your breakfast, John." The grandmotherly woman who owned the café set a steaming plate in front of him then retreated to wait on another customer.

John looked at the food, and his stomach congealed. He knew he wouldn't be able to eat more than a few bites, if that. He didn't want to offend Rose. She had been good to him since he came to town, so he forced some eggs and a bite of biscuit past the boulder inside him.

Pastor Hardin studied John. "What kind of accident would kill her dog?"

John took another bite before he answered. The food seemed to grow larger in his mouth, so he picked up his glass of water to wash it down. "I thought I was shooting some game."

Henry gave a snort. "That dog is big enough to be a deer or elk, but he didn't look anything like either of them."

John rested his fork on the edge of the plate. "I know it was a stupid mistake, and it's one I'll regret for a long time."

Martin nodded. "I'm sure you will."

"I told Miss Swenson that I would take care of her dog's body." He turned toward the owner of the livery. "It's a pretty big animal, so I want to rent a wagon to pick it up."

The grizzled man shook his head. "Won't need to rent it. Just take what you want. Bring the body back here. I'll start a fire near the stand of trees a ways behind the stable to soften up the ground a little. When you get back, I'll help you dig the grave."

When John stood, so did the pastor. "Would you like me to go with you?"

John nodded, and the two men headed toward the livery stable.

The horses plodded down the rutted road toward the farm. Cottony clouds scudded across the blue-gray sky. A rabbit hopped across the snow-covered meadow beside the road, leaving a thin trail behind it.

John had been silent for a while before he turned to the pastor. "Is anyone helping the Swensons?"

Reverend Hardin, who had been staring at the road ahead, looked at John. "We try, but they're proud people. They think they can do everything by themselves, so we let them. I've been keeping an eye out for any way their neighbors can help, but they've done a good job. . .until the boy got sick."

"Just how old are they, anyway?"

Martin gave a wry laugh. "I guess I shouldn't call them boy and girl. Vally must be at least twenty or twenty-one, and Maggie isn't far behind. They're adults doing an adult job. But she's had her hands full since Vally got sick. At least it's winter, and there isn't so much outside work to do. Doc told me that all their stock is in the barn. Maggie just has to go that far to take care of them. It'll be a different story when spring and summer get here. I hope Vally gets well soon, but Doc doesn't hold out much hope at this time. He tries to go out there every day or two."

❧

Maggie heard the wagon rumbling down the road. She walked to the window and peeked through the curtains while the two men took Rolf away. Maggie almost opened the door and asked where they were taking him, but she wasn't ready to face anyone yet. She had cried so much that her face looked all blotchy, and her eyes were swollen.

After the two men left, Maggie went back into the bedroom to sit beside her brother. Earlier she had spooned broth between his pale lips. She wasn't sure how much he swallowed. It took her awhile to clean him and his bed up from all that spilled. Her strong playmate and protector was now helpless. She spent most of the night with her head leaning against his bed, napping when she could. Two times she had to prop him up so he could just get a breath.

Maggie didn't want to put a name to the icy fear that gripped her heart. She was so tired she could hardly hold her eyes open. She knew she should go out and check on the stock again. First she sat in her mother's rocking chair by the fireplace to rest just a few minutes. Her head nodded, and she sank into the oblivion of slumber.

Thwunk! Maggie jumped awake. How long had she slept, and what was that noise? The clatter of falling wood followed another large thump. She hurried toward the back door. The disturbance came from that direction. Not taking time to put on a wrap, she pulled the door open and peered out. A tall man placed a large piece of wood on the chopping block. Although he looked wiry, he must have been all sinews. When he raised the axe and brought it down on the thick slice of a tree, he made it look easy. With precision and using only one stroke, he placed the blow to split the log into the right size pieces for the fireplace. But why was he cutting wood in her backyard? Didn't the man understand anything about private property? This was the second time today that he had trespassed on her land.

Realizing she felt chilled, Maggie shut the door and went to get her coat from its hook. She quickly threw it on and pulled a warm knitted cap down over her hair and ears. After turning up the collar of her coat, she jerked on gloves before opening the door again.

"Mr. . . . Collins, isn't it?" Maggie tried to rein in her anger.

The man leaned against the handle of the axe. "At your service, Miss Swenson." He removed a handkerchief from his hip pocket and swiped it across his forehead. He must have been working awhile to sweat in this weather. His cavalier behavior reignited her anger.

"What do you think you're doing?" Maggie didn't care that she shouted.

"I thought that was obvious." His smile dampened Maggie's wrath. "I'm chopping wood."

She stomped through the snow toward him. "Why are you doing it *here*. . .in my backyard?" Maggie felt as if her world had tilted and nothing made sense.

"To fill your wood box. It's nearly empty." He reached to place another piece of log on the chopping block. When he lifted the axe, Maggie finally realized that although he wore a heavy woolen shirt, he didn't have a coat on.

"Mr. Collins, I don't need your help." Maggie stomped her foot for emphasis, and pain shot through her foot. Why did she do that? It didn't accomplish anything.

"That's all right, Miss Swenson." He started toward the back porch, his arms loaded with wood. "I need to do this for you."

Maggie didn't know what to reply, so she turned and hurried back inside. Maybe the man would work off his penance with this one good deed and leave her alone after that. This stranger wasn't the answer to her loneliness.

It didn't take long for Maggie to find out that chopping wood wasn't the only thing he planned to do for her. John Collins often came to the farm. No matter how many times she told him she didn't need his help, he kept coming back.

One day when her best friend, Holly Brunson, sat with Valter so Maggie could go to town for supplies, she found John working in the barn when she got home. He must have heard her drive up in the wagon, because he came out and helped carry things into the house. Then he took the wagon to the barn and unhitched her horses. She could talk until she was blue in the face, telling him she didn't need his help, but Mr. Collins didn't listen to a word she said. The man was almost a nuisance. Almost. . .but not quite.

At least his assistance allowed Maggie to spend more time with her brother. Not that it did much good. Each day, she thought he couldn't get any weaker, and every day, he did. The doctor often came out from town to check on Valter. Maggie did everything Dr. Morgan said to do, but she began to think Vally wasn't going to make it. Everything inside her screamed against the idea whenever it dropped into her mind.

One morning in early April, John Collins came out of the barn just as Maggie prepared to check on the stock. She felt bad for always telling him not to come. The pain of losing Rolf was receding, and she had finally forgiven him for shooting the dog. Maggie couldn't remember if she had ever thanked him for all his help. She stepped out on the porch.

"Mr. Collins!"

He untied his horse from the hitching post then looked up at her. "Yes, Miss Swenson?"

Maggie tried to smile, but her lips stayed flat beneath the weight of her fatigue. "I don't think I've thanked you for all you've done."

His eyes narrowed, and he studied her as though trying to figure her out. "That's all right. No thanks are needed."

"Yes, they are. I do appreciate all you've done for me. . .for us."

He tipped his hat and turned back toward his horse. Just as Maggie shut the door, she became aware of a different sound coming from her brother's room. She rushed toward the door. Vally was breathing in a strange rattling way she hadn't heard before. His body made a slight jerky movement with each breath.

Maggie raced out the front door. John Collins was just turning his horse toward town.

"Mr. Collins! Please get the doctor out here right away!"

John rode as fast as he could. It didn't take the doctor long to hitch up his buggy. John followed him as he drove as fast as the buggy would go down the road toward the farm. He wasn't sure Miss Swenson would want him to be there, but he had to know what was happening. He would stay out of the way and pray while the doctor took care of his patient.

No one answered the doctor's rap on the front door, so he opened it and went in. John was right behind him. The cabin's large main room stood empty, so Dr. Morgan headed toward one of the other doors. John followed him, but the doctor stopped in the doorway.

When John saw Maggie, his heart ached. She sat beside the bed, mechanically rocking the chair and staring at some unseen spot across the room. A sheet covered the face of the man in the bed. A man John had never met.

The doctor went to Valter and pulled the sheet back. He listened to the patient's chest with the stethoscope and felt for his pulse. Then he replaced the covering.

John felt helpless. He wanted to do something for the vulnerable young woman who looked to be in shock. Maybe he should have become a minister the way his parents wanted him to. Then he would've learned how to help those in need. Especially Margareta Swenson.

Doc turned toward John. "Please go to town and ask Holly Brunson to come out here. She's Maggie's best friend."

John nodded before he strode through the silent house. Shouldn't Maggie be crying? Maybe she'd already cried before he and Doc arrived. John hoped so.

It didn't take him long to find out that Holly Brunson lived about a mile out of town in the opposite direction. When he inquired at the café, Rose told him that Holly had been married only a few months. He hoped she would be able to come to the Swenson farm with him.

When he knocked on the door to the farmhouse, a young woman about the same age as Maggie answered the door. Her dark blue eyes contained a question as she stared up at him. "My husband has gone over to a neighbor's because his cow is having a hard time birthing a calf. He'll be back later."

John removed his hat and held it with both hands in front of him. "I didn't come to see your husband. Are you Mrs. Brunson?"

She moved a little farther behind the door. "Yes, I am. What can I do for you?"

This wasn't going to be easy. "I'm here to ask if you can come with me." When her eyes widened and a frown veiled her face, John cleared his throat and tried again. "I've just been at the Swenson farm. Margareta's brother passed away, and Dr. Morgan thinks she needs you."

Quickly, Holly wrote a note telling her husband where she was going. She packed a valise while John saddled her horse. Then she rode beside him. They didn't talk. There didn't seem to be anything to say.

When they entered the house, John followed Holly as she went straight to the room where her friend sat.

"I'm here."

Maggie jumped up from her chair and threw her arms around Holly. Then she burst into tears.

John knew they didn't need him, so he went to the woodpile and picked up an armload to feed the fire. It was the only way he could help Maggie right now.

Chapter 3

Maggie couldn't have made it through the last three weeks if it hadn't been for Holly. Even though they hadn't been married very long, Hans Brunson insisted that Holly stay with Maggie. He ate his meals with them, so Maggie didn't feel so bad about taking her best friend away from him.

As soon as the neighbors heard about Valter, they let Maggie know that she wouldn't be alone. Besides providing a big meal the day of the funeral, they made sure food arrived on time for dinner and supper every day for the next two weeks. Maggie told everyone they didn't need to do that, but she was thankful they did. Managing the farm and nursing Valter had drained her more than she realized.

Holly pampered her during those weeks, taking care of the house so Maggie could rest. She was surprised by how much Maggie slept. While Maggie was asleep, Holly searched through the trunk and found the dresses her friend had worn after her parents died. She even hemmed a black dress that had been Maggie's mother's so she would have something new to wear during her mourning.

Now, though, Maggie was ready to do more. After thanking Holly and telling her to go home to her husband, she found herself alone for the first time since her brother died. She tried to turn her thoughts away from all her sorrow. If she ignored it, maybe it would go away. Many of her friends from the church had told her to pray, but Maggie wasn't sure she could trust God anymore. Hadn't He taken away everything dear to her? If He hadn't caused it, at least He had allowed it to happen.

When she went out to the barn, Maggie couldn't believe what she found. Neighbors had come every day to care for the livestock. She assumed they had only fed the animals. But when she entered the stable, it was clean. The stalls had been mucked out and new hay placed down. Maggie had dreaded all the backbreaking work it would entail to get the barn in good shape.

She walked to the stall where her mare, Stormy, stood munching grain. The horse looked up and shuffled over to Maggie, playfully nudging her shoulder. Maggie threw her arms around the mare's neck and crooned words of love into her ear.

"You're all I have now since Vally and Rolf are gone." Maggie had told all her secrets to her dog. Now she would have to talk to her horse instead.

Every few days since Vally had been buried, Maggie had made the trip into town to visit her brother's grave at the cemetery by the church. She wiped off the plain wooden cross that marked his place. Maggie often talked to him while she was there.

That day, she dropped to her knees on the cold ground. "You'll never believe what happened today. I went into the barn, and someone had cleaned it up for me." She rubbed her finger over the carved letters that spelled Valter Swenson. "Vally, why didn't you fight the disease harder?" A sob escaped her throat. "I miss you so much."

When she stood, tears streamed down her face. She wiped them away, but others pooled in her eyes, making it hard for her to see as she turned toward her horse tied outside the cast-iron gate. She almost bumped into someone standing close behind her. Strong hands took her arms to steady her, and she looked up into light green eyes filled with sorrow.

"Mr. Collins?" Maggie pulled away. "What are you doing here?" She straightened her shoulders and stood taller.

"I wanted to make sure you were all right." The sound of his rich baritone voice reached deep inside her, releasing a whisper of something she couldn't define.

"I'm just fine." More tears spilled over as if to deny her claim. She dashed them away with the back of her hands. As she hurried toward her mount, she thought she heard a soft reply.

"I'm sure you are."

Why did the words sound as if he didn't mean them?

❧

John watched Maggie ride away. The more he saw of the petite blond, the more something inside him called out to her. He prayed for her every day. As he prayed, he wondered if she could be the woman God was preparing for him. What else could explain the way he was so drawn to her? But John knew that she wasn't ready for any kind of relationship, and when she was ready, she probably wouldn't look in his direction. He wondered if she would ever forgive him for shooting her dog. They never mentioned it after the day it happened. John expected her to ask him where the grave was, but she never had.

He feared that Maggie was mad at God. The only time he saw her at church was at her brother's funeral. When people consistently stayed away from services, it usually meant they had a problem with God. John talked to Martin about both Valter and Maggie. He found out that their whole family had been active in church for years, so John prayed for her spiritual well-being as well as for comfort from her sorrow.

Not only did John pray for her, but he also got up before dawn every day. That way he could go out to the farm and take care of the chores before he returned to the depot for the first train of the morning. And he kept her wood box filled. If he could think of anything else to do, he would have done it, because his heart broke for Maggie and her grief—and for the fact that the first time they met, he added to her already heavy burdens.

John didn't want to awaken Maggie when he rode up to the farm, so he usually left his horse tied in the woods and walked the rest of the way to the barn. He slipped in the door and went about his work without making any noise that could be heard from the house. It hadn't taken him long to make friends with all the animals. They turned their attention to him as soon as he came through the door, knowing they were about to be fed. When he had time, he even curried the horses, gently talking to them as he did.

One Tuesday, John climbed into the hayloft to throw down enough hay to replace what he had taken out of the stalls. Before he filled the pitchfork, the door opened. He glanced down to see Maggie walking toward her horse. He couldn't decide what to do. He didn't want to startle her. While he was trying to figure out a way to let her know he was there, she started talking to the animal. John didn't plan to eavesdrop, but her sweet voice drifted up toward him.

John peeked over the edge of the hayloft. Maggie's arms were around the horse's neck, and he heard every word she said.

"Oh, Stormy, I wish you could come into the house with me the way Rolf did. He was so much company to me when Vally was sick. I talked to him, and I wasn't as scared. Now I'm alone, and the house feels so empty. Sometimes I just climb into bed and pull the covers over my head and cry."

Her voice became more muted, and John could no longer understand what she said. He thought about what he heard. There must be some way he could help her.

When John got back to town, he took his horse to the livery. The proprietor was raking the hay that covered the floor.

"Henry." John dismounted and walked his horse toward its usual stall. "Have you heard about anyone whose dog has had puppies recently?"

The old man took a minute to answer. He scratched his stubbly chin while he thought about it. "Not right off. I'll ask around, though, if you want me to." He leaned his arm on the handle of the rake. "You want a dog, do you? They're a mite o' trouble to take care of, 'specially since you're living in the boardinghouse."

John chuckled. "It's not for me. I want to give it to someone."

Henry stood looking at John as if he wanted to know who, but he didn't ask, and John didn't tell him.

The next day, Martin came by the Wayzata depot. John was receiving a telegraph message, so the preacher walked around the station, looking at all the information tacked up on the walls. When John finished, he called to his friend.

"Martin, how can I help you? You don't need tickets to go somewhere, do you? It's pretty cold to be traveling."

Martin quickly came to the counter and leaned on its polished surface. "No, but maybe I can help you."

"Help me? I didn't know I needed any."

The preacher smiled. "I heard you were asking about a puppy."

John chuckled. "Oh, that. News travels fast around here. I only asked Henry about it yesterday."

"You know how it is." Martin joined his laughter, his fingers tapping an accompaniment on the polished wood. "He told me over coffee at Rose's Café. Rose heard him, so she asked everyone who came in yesterday and today. It's a good thing she did. There's a family with a farm west of Lake Minnetonka whose dog had puppies a few weeks ago. They were just starting to try to find homes for them. Does it matter what kind of dog it is?"

John hadn't thought about that. "I don't know. What kind are they?"

"Well, the momma is a big, long-haired dog. They aren't sure who the daddy is. Henry said you wanted to give it to someone. Will that person want a big dog?"

John nodded. "A big dog would be just fine." He figured that a large dog would help Maggie feel safer. When it was grown, it could protect her.

Martin pulled a piece of paper out of the inside pocket of his suit coat. "Here are the directions to their house. You can go today if you want to, but you probably should take something to wrap the puppy in. It's only been in the barn with its mama and the other puppies. The wind is still nippy in the evenings. It might be too cold to carry it far without being wrapped up."

John took the proffered paper and unfolded it. He read the words scribbled on it and studied the crude drawing of a map. "Thanks, Martin. I'll go out there after the last train leaves this evening."

It didn't take John long to pick out which puppy he wanted. While he watched them tumble around their mother, one seemed to have more personality. Light tan in color, it sported irregular white patches around each eye, making it look as if it were wearing a mask. When he picked it up, the puppy jumped higher in his arms and licked his face. Then it settled down against his chest as if satisfied. John held the little dog away from him and studied it all over. If this puppy looked anything like his mother when he was grown, he would have long hair.

Now the wiggly ball of fur was wrapped in an old quilt John's mother had given him when he moved from North Dakota. He had used it to wrap some of the things that could break easily. Since he had been at the boardinghouse, it had remained in the corner where he dropped it after unwrapping the framed photos of his family that spread across the top of the bureau in his room. Sometimes when he undressed, his shoes landed on the quilt, transferring dirt and mud to the surface of the coverlet. He was sure this dog didn't care if the quilt wasn't too clean. Besides, by the time they arrived at the farm, the puppy might have soiled it, anyway.

Maggie carried a bowl of stew to the table. After she set it down, she heard a horse ride up. Although she was lonely in the house by herself, she wasn't sure she wanted unannounced company this late in the evening. On most days, she would have already been through eating and washing the dishes by now, but she had spent extra time in the barn with Stormy. It wasn't that she didn't want to come in the house, but she felt less lonely when she could talk to her horse. She set a pan of hot corn bread on the table and covered it with a tea towel to keep it piping hot. Then she went to the door to peek out between the curtains on the window.

It was so dark that she could see only shapes and shadows. A man was having a little trouble dismounting from the horse. He carried some kind of bundle that moved a lot. Finally, both feet were planted on the ground, but he stood there a minute, looking down. From the soft murmur of a masculine voice she could hear through the door, the man was talking to the bundle.

Maggie hoped he wasn't some kind of lunatic. Her door had a lock on it, but she seldom used it. However, she reached for the skeleton key and inserted it into the lock. Before she had time to turn it, the man started toward the house. His gait looked familiar. Just before he stepped up on the porch, Maggie caught a glimpse of his face in the moonlight. It was John Collins!

She placed her hand on her chest to try to quell the rapid beating of her heart. Lately, every time he came near, she went hot all over and her knees felt weak. She tried to convince herself that she was only responding to his kindness, but she knew that didn't completely explain what she felt.

Maggie took the key out of the lock and hung it on the hook between the door and the window before pulling the door open.

"Mr. Collins, what are you doing here this time of night?"

A smile lit his face. "I brought you a present."

Maggie shook her head. "I can't accept anything else from you."

John pulled the edge of the dirty quilt away from a squirmy mass of fur in his arms. The cutest puppy face she had ever seen peeked over the fabric.

"Maggie, I wanted to replace what I took from you. Please don't say no." He was able to get a good hold on the bundle with one arm, so he removed his hat. "I know it won't be the same as the dog you lost, but he could be a real friend to you if you let him."

Maggie opened the door farther and moved back to give him room to enter. "Please, come in." After he stepped through the opening, she shut the door to keep the cool air out.

How did the man know that a puppy was just what she needed? Maggie guessed it had to be John who came to the barn so early every morning. Yesterday she had tried to get there while he was still working, but when she arrived, he was nowhere to be seen.

"Mr. Collins, you do too much for me as it is."

His eyes twinkled before he answered. "I don't know what you're talking about."

No matter how hard he tried to sound sincere, Maggie knew different.

As if he just that moment realized he still held the wiggling puppy, he looked down and pulled the quilt away some more. He held the little animal out to her.

If Maggie hadn't already fallen in love with it, she would have now. The big brown eyes were full of mischief and affection as the puppy squirmed, trying to reach her face with its tongue.

"If you'll hold him for me, I'll get something to make him a bed." She dropped a quick kiss on the furry head before she deposited the warm puppy back into John's arms.

She went into the room that had been Vally's and returned with a wooden crate. She set it near the fireplace and turned to go get something to line the box to keep him warm. All the time, John played with the puppy, talking nonsense to him. She grinned as she looked at them.

"Why don't you use this old quilt in the box?" John pulled the puppy under one arm and reached down to pick up the cover that now lay on the floor.

"I can probably find something. You need to keep that."

John shook his head. "No, I'm not using it anyway. It's just one of Mother's old quilts."

After Maggie finished making the bed, she asked John if he had eaten supper. When he said he hadn't had time, she offered to share her stew and corn bread with him.

After he was seated at the table, John glanced at Maggie. "Would it be all right if I say grace before we eat?"

Maggie liked the way he talked to God as if He were a friend.

John smiled when she passed the hot bread to him. "I really like corn bread with stew. My father says Mother makes the best corn bread in the whole church."

Maggie handed him the butter and watched him slather it on. "Does she?"

He looked up almost as if he didn't know what she meant, then laughed. "She has as long as I remember." He took a bite and smiled while he chewed it. "This is as good as hers is." He reached for his spoon and dipped it into the fragrant broth. "She always laughs when he says she is a good cook. Evidently, she didn't know how when they married."

Maggie liked the way his eyes lit up when he talked about his parents. "Where are you from?"

"North Dakota. My father is a pastor there, but he also lives on the farm that belonged to my grandfather."

Quiet fell around the table as they continued to enjoy the food, and Maggie tried to think of what else to ask him. "Why did you come to Wayzata?"

"I wanted to venture out on my own. The railroad had been looking for men to train as telegraphers. When I became proficient, the position of stationmaster came open here, and they offered it to me." John put his spoon back into his bowl and trained his gaze on Maggie. "I'm really glad they did."

I am, too.

Later as John started to leave, Maggie couldn't believe that they had found so much to talk about. It almost felt as if they were old friends.

John stopped just before he opened the door. "Thank you, Maggie, for the good food. . .and the congenial company."

Maggie glanced at the crate where her puppy snuggled into the quilt fast asleep. "Thank you for the puppy."

John looked toward the box. "What are you going to name him?"

Maggie thought for a minute before answering. "With that mask on his face and his bright eyes, I think I'll call him Rascal."

"Sounds like a good idea to me." John settled his hat on his head and reached for the doorknob.

"John, thank you for all the work you've done for me, too." Maggie clasped her hands in front of her waist and gave him a tentative smile. "But you can stop. I can take care of things now."

She couldn't interpret the expression on John's face, but when he went out and the door shut behind him, she said to herself, "You're a good man, John Collins. A very good man."

Chapter 4

Before she went to bed, Maggie played with the puppy on the rug in front of the fireplace. Then she took him outside until he finally did his business in the yard behind the house. When they came back inside, she sat in the rocker and watched the fire as it died down, all the time rocking the puppy as it snuggled close against her heart. After she put him in the box and covered him with the quilt, Rascal slept.

Maggie was surprised that she slept so peacefully that night. Since Rascal was in a strange place, she had expected him to wake her several times during the night, but it didn't happen. Instead, Maggie woke early and jumped out of bed, looking forward to taking care of her new puppy. He gave her an added purpose in life, a purpose that had been missing since she'd lost her brother a month ago.

John Collins was a good man. But Maggie had already decided that, hadn't she? How could any man understand what she needed and meet that need for her? Yet John had done that very thing. This puppy filled a void in her heart.

Maggie needed to concentrate on something besides the never-ending work. Spring had arrived, and she didn't like to think about what that meant. After growing up on the farm, she understood just how much work it involved. Since she was old enough to know what was going on, she had watched her parents fight the forces of nature to keep their land. Through good seasons and bad, Momma and Daddy had worked, and now the farm was something to be proud of.

If only her parents hadn't met their sad end. They had been traveling to Minneapolis to look at new homes. They planned to get rid of their snug cabin and purchase a two-story house. After the double funeral, it was all she and Vally could do just to keep the farm going. Now it was up to her, and she felt alone in the face of almost insurmountable odds. She didn't want to think about the possibility of having to sell the farm until she tried her best to keep it. Just having Rascal to talk to gave Maggie the feeling that she could make it.

After she took the dog back outside, she fixed breakfast for both of them. She pulled Rolf's tin pans out of the bottom cabinet where she had put them after he died. She filled one with water and the other with bread soaked in milk and set them on the floor near the table. While she ate, she talked to the darling puppy. Every time she spoke, Rascal turned those big brown eyes toward her and looked as if he understood every word she said. By the size of his paws, Maggie knew he was going to be large when he grew up. Although his puppy fur was short, it was thick and wooly. She felt sure he would be a long-haired dog when he was grown.

When she went out to the barn, Rascal darted around her, jumping and nipping playfully at her skirt until she found herself laughing into the fresh spring air. Maggie had forgotten how good it felt to laugh. Because she often went to see about the animals, the path was dry and packed down. At least the little dog wouldn't pick up mud to track into the house.

While Maggie checked on things, Rascal became acquainted with every nook and cranny of the building. He even made friends with all the livestock. She and Rascal didn't stay very long, because, as usual, John must have taken care of the chores. Maggie decided that she would get up really early tomorrow so she could insist that he not come anymore. The thought caused an unhappy catch in her heart. She liked knowing he was around, even when she didn't actually see him, but she felt odd about it. He had more than compensated for Rolf's death. His constant penance made her feel guilty, as though she were taking advantage of his kindness.

Maggie turned the animals out into the pasture to spend part of the day, but she returned before it got too cool and herded them into the shelter. The night wind was still sharp, and she didn't see any reason to make the animals stay out when she had a warm barn for them. Every time she entered the barn, she pictured the man who often worked there. She was sure his dark curls fell across his forehead while he worked. She had seen them there on many occasions. Her hands itched to reach up and push them back so she could see the sparkle in his eyes, which were the color of the leaves on the trees in the pasture.

The next morning, Maggie did awaken before dawn. Quietly, she stoked the fire and dressed in front of it, but Rascal woke anyway. She watched as he rose up on his front legs and stretched his neck. One eye opened and looked at her. Then he hopped up and gave a happy yip. Maggie decided to take him with her to meet John in the barn.

This time she caught him. He didn't hear her come in because he was singing:

What a Friend we have in Jesus, all our sins and griefs to bear!
What a privilege to carry everything to God in prayer!
O what peace we often forfeit, O what needless pain we bear,
All because we do not carry everything to God in prayer.

Have we trials and temptations? Is there trouble anywhere?
We should never be discouraged; take it to the Lord in prayer.
Can we find a friend so faithful who will all our sorrows share?
Jesus knows our every weakness; take it to the Lord in prayer.

The lyrics sung in his strong baritone resonated through the lofty structure. Maggie stood inside the door and listened, enjoying the texture he added to the words. When John paused before going on to the third verse, Rascal yipped and tumbled toward him, stirring up the straw on the floor as he went.

John turned. "Maggie." The sound of her name spoken in such a tender tone made her breath catch.

His gaze sought hers, and they connected for a moment before the little puppy jumped up on his legs, seeking attention. For an instant, Maggie wished she was adorable like the puppy and could snuggle in John's arms. While he knelt and picked up Rascal, Maggie shook her head, trying to clear it of the crazy thoughts.

John stood with the puppy in his arms. Rascal pawed at him and tried to reach John's face with his tongue. "What are you doing out here so early, Maggie?"

She took a step closer. "I wanted to tell you that you don't need to do my chores anymore, John. I appreciate all you've done for me, but you don't owe me anything." She ended on a whisper.

John's gaze never wavered from her face. "I want to come, Maggie. Although my father was a pastor, I grew up on a farm. Since I live at the boardinghouse and work at the depot, I miss the physical labor. It's a blessing for me to have a place to get all this exercise." Rascal succeeded in reaching John's chin with his tongue. John raised his head a little higher. "Besides, I need to check on this little mutt." He gave the puppy a big hug while he scratched it behind the ears.

A week later, the desire to do a thorough spring cleaning filled Maggie with restlessness. After going to the barn and letting the animals out into the sunshine, she headed toward the house. She pulled all the quilts off her bed then went into the room that had been Valter's. There was no need to change his. Evidently Holly had washed the linens during the three weeks when she had stayed at the farm. Maggie hadn't even realized that.

While the water heated on the stove, Maggie glanced toward Rascal. The puppy slept on the rug in front of the fireplace. The quilt John had wrapped around the dog was pretty dirty, so she went to the box and lifted it out. She hadn't paid much attention to it when she made the bed the night John brought Rascal to her. Maggie looked closer at the places on the quilt where it wasn't soiled. This wasn't just some old quilt as John said. Someone had worked hard to piece beautiful fabric together into a lovely pattern.

Maggie spread the large cover on the floor. Running her fingertips over one clean area, she appreciated the predominantly light green pattern that made up the center section of the quilt. The fabric had a fine texture. Many patches were made of this color. The other patches were a variety of lovely hues that coordinated with the green. Strips of creamy fabric surrounded each block, framing it. The small squares on each corner of the frame were flannel with yellow dots. Maggie held up a corner of the coverlet. This quilt was a work of art.

Maggie had learned to sew by helping her mother make many of the quilts her family used over the years. This quilt was not some haphazard job. It had been well planned. Did John realize how much work went into making this coverlet? Maggie hated to see it ruined or mistreated by a rambunctious puppy. She went to the cedar chest and searched for an old quilt that had seen better days. After putting it in the dog's bed, she lovingly washed the one John had brought.

As she finished washing each quilt, she hung it across the clothesline in the backyard to dry. Once John's quilt was spread out in the bright sunlight, Maggie saw the exquisite beauty that had been hidden under all that soil. While she handled it, she noticed several places where the stitches had pulled apart. Maggie decided to restore the quilt and return it to John. It should stay in his family. The idea of doing something nice for him filled her with a sense of excitement. After all he'd done for her, this was the least she could do.

When she went back into the house, Maggie took out the sewing basket. It had been awhile since she'd thought of replenishing these supplies. She needed more thread and needles. After lunch, she put Rascal in his box for a nap. The puppy had worn himself out chasing butterflies and grasshoppers around the yard while Maggie had washed the quilts.

After Rascal fell asleep, Maggie saddled Stormy and headed into Wayzata. Each time she went into town, she noticed many changes. It amazed her how quickly they took place. Because of Lake Minnetonka, people from other places often came to their city. The streets bustled with activity. Today strangers in one of those new motorcars made their way down the main street. Maggie had to keep a tight rein on Stormy. Those noisy contraptions made the horse a little skittish. She tied the animal to a hitching post on a side street and walked to the mercantile. Maggie hoped those people would keep their vehicle on the main thoroughfare and not venture anywhere near her mare.

While Maggie was choosing thread, Holly walked up behind her. "Maggie, it's good to see you in town."

Maggie turned and gave her friend a hug. "I'm glad I ran into you, too."

"I've been planning to go out to the farm to see you." Holly picked up a couple of spools of thread.

"Why don't you come tomorrow?" It would feel good to have company again. "I'll fix lunch, and we can make a day of it. Hans can come over for lunch if he wants to. I'm restoring a quilt John Collins left at the house."

"I would love to help you." A speculative gleam twinkled in Holly's eyes. "You can tell me all about why Mr. Collins would do such a thing."

When Holly arrived the next morning, she carried a basket over her arm. The tantalizing aroma of cinnamon wafted through the room even before she removed the towel covering the food.

"I baked these this morning." Holly went to the cabinet and removed a couple of plates and took them to the table where she forked two of the hot rolls onto them. "Hans likes pastries for breakfast. I thought I'd share them with you. By the way, Hans won't be coming for lunch. He's going to town to have some horseshoes replaced. He's planning on eating at Rose's with Henry."

"My mouth is watering already." Maggie lifted the dish containing her roll and took an appreciative sniff. "I set a pot of tea to steep only a few minutes ago."

After they finished eating, Maggie went to Valter's room and picked up John's quilt, which she had spread across Vally's bed. She brought it out and laid it across the settee. "Isn't this lovely?"

Holly studied the handiwork. "Now tell me why he brought this to you."

When Maggie finished the story about John bringing Rascal wrapped in the quilt, Holly asked where the puppy was.

"I put him in the barn. We wouldn't get much work done without him tearing things up. I'll introduce you to him when we take a break."

Maggie sat at one end of the quilt and Holly at the other. While they talked, they worked their way around the cover, repairing every place that had pulled loose.

"Tell me about Mr. Collins." Holly didn't waste any time getting to the point.

"Well, first he killed my dog."

Holly's eyes widened, and her work dropped into her lap. "I wondered what happened to Rolf. You never did say."

"It was an accident, and John has been coming out and doing chores before I get up in the mornings. Then last week, he showed up with Rascal. What a blessing that little puppy is! I'm not as lonely or as fearful as I was before."

At lunch Maggie brought Rascal in so he could eat at the same time they did. Holly enjoyed the exuberant puppy as much as Maggie did. After they finished their meal, both women sat on the floor and played with him. When Maggie put him in his box for a nap, she and Holly went back to working on the quilt.

"Maggie." Holly looked up from her stitching. "I've been missing you at church. People ask about you all the time."

Maggie had expected this question to come sometime, but she dreaded it. If she had to explain how she felt to anyone, she was glad it was Holly. They had been friends most of their lives, so she should understand.

"I haven't even read the Bible since long before Vally died."

Instead of the shock that Maggie expected, Holly's expression contained only sympathy. "Why not, Maggie?"

"I can't understand how a loving God could let all these things happen to me." There, she had finally said the words out loud. "I'm not sure I even trust Him anymore."

Holly put the edge of the quilt down and stood. She looked around the room. Then she turned to Maggie. "Where's your Bible?"

"It's on a table by my bed."

Holly marched into Maggie's room and returned with the book in her hands. She sat in the rocking chair and leafed through the pages. Finally, she started reading silently. Maggie tried to ignore her, but she was aware of every move her friend made. With renewed vigor, Maggie worked on the quilt, making tiny, almost invisible stitches.

"Here it is."

When Maggie looked up, Holly held the Bible with her finger marking her place.

"I read this chapter just this morning, and I wanted to share a portion with you. It's from Psalm 51: 'Make me to hear joy and gladness; that the bones which thou hast broken may rejoice. Hide thy face from my sins, and blot out all mine iniquities. Create in me a clean heart, O God; and renew a right spirit within me. Cast me not away from thy presence; and take not thy holy spirit from me. Restore unto me the joy of thy salvation; and uphold me with thy free spirit.'"

Maggie listened to the words her friend read. She often felt as if God had broken her bones. That was why she didn't know if she trusted Him or not. But this passage said a lot more. She put the quilt down and went to stand behind Holly so she could read over her shoulder. Holly pointed to verse 8, and Maggie started reading there.

"I really like verse twelve." Holly handed the Bible to Maggie then went over to the quilt and lifted the edge, running her fingers over a place that had been badly torn. "See how we're restoring this. God wants to restore your relationship with Him in the same way...if you'll let Him."

Chapter 5

Finally, summer arrived. John had always thought that North Dakota was lovely in summer, but Wayzata had a special beauty that touched his soul. Working at the train depot added to his blessings. To see the most spectacular panorama, all he had to do was look out the window. The rippling waters of Lake Minnetonka reflected the blue of the clear sky. Tall trees framed the picture postcard scene. Occasionally he would glimpse the *City of St. Louis* as the side-wheeler traversed Minnesota's largest lake, carrying passengers to various towns scattered along its banks. Other times, small fishing boats bobbed like corks on the surface.

Whenever John feasted his gaze on the soothing water, his thoughts returned to Maggie Swenson. Her eyes often flashed the same shade as the deep water outside his window. Of course, lots of things reminded him of Maggie. Since he took Rascal to her, Maggie had changed. Sometimes when John saw her, he detected the remnants of sorrow in her expression, but she was finally moving on from the devastating sadness she had experienced after the death of her brother.

John continued to go to her farm and do chores early in the morning, but he no longer tried to keep from waking Maggie. Often, she and Rascal joined him in the barn. He enjoyed those times with her working beside him. John wondered what it would be like if he had her waiting at home when he finished work every day. John knew that he wanted her always to be a part of his life. If she had some family left, John would ask her father or brother if he could court her. He wasn't sure what the proper move would be under the circumstances, and he knew his mother would expect him to do what was proper. Maybe he should ask Pastor Hardin about it.

One thing still bothered him. Maggie hadn't come back to church. John yearned to talk to her about it, but he hadn't felt the time was right to bring up the subject. He didn't want to hurt her or push her away with his questions.

✳

Maggie wearied of wearing black. She had been dressed in the depressing color off and on for most of the last year. Although she still grieved over losing both her parents and her brother, she now realized that life must go on.

The next time she went to town, she bought fabric for a new dress. Tiny light blue flowers with dark green leaves scattered in uneven clusters across the deep purple background, making it a good choice for moving away from mourning clothes. In the evening, after taking care of the chores, she worked on the dress.

Things on the farm weren't as bad as she anticipated they would be. In addition to John Collins doing chores in the mornings, several neighbors helped her plant fields of wheat and corn, as well as her kitchen garden. About once a week, one or more of the men came to lend aid as she cared for the crops. Their assistance reinforced Maggie's belief that God hadn't forgotten her.

She started reading her Bible again. One Saturday when Hans and Holly came to help her, they asked if she would accompany them to church. Even though they lived in the opposite direction from town, they offered to pick her up. Probably Holly realized it would be easier for Maggie to return to church if she didn't have to go alone.

The next day as Maggie patted her hair and pushed a hairpin to hold a curl more securely, she heard the buggy approaching. She quickly used a long hat pin to anchor a straw hat on her upswept hairstyle, then pulled on her new white gloves. After picking up her handbag and Bible, she arrived at the door just as Hans knocked.

"Maggie, what a pretty dress. Is it new?" Holly asked when Maggie sat beside her in the buggy.

Maggie nodded. "I made it this week."

"The color really darkens the blue in your eyes."

The trio carried on a lively conversation all the way to town. As they approached the church, Maggie's gaze was drawn toward John Collins, who stood under a tree talking to a farmer. Just looking at him took her breath away.

When John saw her, he walked up to the buggy and extended his hand to help her alight. "You look lovely today, Maggie."

Coming from him, her name sounded like a caress. Warmth rushed to her cheeks.

"Thank you, John." She couldn't keep her voice from sounding husky. Maggie cleared her throat. She hoped he hadn't noticed the blush she felt move up her cheeks.

John accompanied the three of them inside. When they sat, somehow he ended up beside her. Maggie wondered what people thought about her sitting with John. It made them look as if they were a couple. Not that she minded the thought, but it wasn't true.

It felt good to be back in fellowship with other believers. Maggie wondered why she had stayed away so long. The singing warmed her heart and caused a few tears to make their way down her cheeks. Before she could pick up her handbag to search for a handkerchief, John reached into his pocket and retrieved his own. He pressed the white cotton against her palm.

She patted the tears away, enjoying the scent that clung to the pristine white square. John's scent. Woodsy, spicy, masculine. For a moment, all other thoughts fled her mind, and John filled every crevice. When she finished with the hanky, she folded the square and placed it in her handbag. She wanted to wash and iron it before she returned it to him.

After the service, John accompanied her to the Brunsons' buggy.

"Mr. Collins." Holly smiled up at him. "Would you join us for dinner?"

"I wouldn't want to impose, ma'am."

"I have plenty of food. We often ask people to eat Sunday dinner with us, so I prepare extra." Holly put her arm around Maggie's shoulders and pulled her closer. "Maggie is going home with us, too."

John's gaze sought Maggie's. "Then I would be delighted."

All the way to the Brunson farm, Maggie couldn't get John's words out of her mind. What about her delighted him? The warmth in those clear green eyes ignited something deep inside her.

Although she enjoyed the afternoon spent with Holly, Hans, and John, Maggie felt a restlessness she didn't understand. Long into the night, she relived every moment of the day, repeating in her mind every word John said. What was it about the man that touched her so deeply? After she went to bed, it took her a long time to fall asleep.

On Monday Maggie slept later than usual. John had already been to the barn and gone by the time Maggie went out. She sensed the shadow of his presence in the building when she entered, but she missed his substance. She pictured him as he was the last time he was there, muscles rippling under his shirt with the sleeves rolled halfway up his forearms. Maggie wished he would be there every day for the rest of her life.

Father God, why do I feel this way? What am I going to do?

That evening after she fed Rascal and sat down to eat her dinner of cold chicken and biscuits, Maggie heard horses riding up outside the house. It was rather late for company. She peeked out. Two men were dismounting. One was John, and the other one looked a lot like Pastor Hardin. Neither man had ever come to her home this late in the evening. Maggie went to the looking glass and checked her hair. She swept a few stray wisps away from her cheeks and neck and anchored them with hairpins.

When the knock sounded, she paused a few seconds before she moved toward the door. She didn't want them to think she was watching from the window, even if it was true.

"Come in, Pastor, John."

Rascal pushed past Maggie, and John hunkered down to pat him. She offered to make coffee or tea, but the two men declined. After she ushered them to the settee, she sank into the rocking chair and folded her hands in her lap.

Pastor Hardin cleared his throat. "John asked me to accompany him out here tonight. He wanted to talk to you."

Maggie glanced at John. She still didn't understand what was going on. Why did he need to bring someone when he wanted to talk to her?

John stood and shoved his hands into his pockets. He walked closer to where Maggie sat and looked down at her.

"I didn't know what else to do. You don't have a father or brother, so I talked to Martin." John gestured toward the other man. "Pastor Hardin."

Maggie had never seen John so ill at ease. She wondered where this conversation was headed.

John hunkered down by her chair as he had earlier for Rascal. The dog came over and laid his head on John's leg. John absently stroked Rascal, but he kept his attention trained on Maggie's face.

After taking a deep breath, he continued. "Maggie, I want to court you. . .if you'll let me."

Court me? The thought grabbed Maggie's imagination. She looked down at her clasped hands. *Court me.* She hadn't thought about anything like that. She had been too busy. But she wanted to be courted. A strange fluttering sensation started in her stomach.

She raised her eyes to John's face and smiled. "That would be nice."

He looked relieved. He nodded and stood, never taking his eyes from her. A smile lit his face like one of those electric lightbulbs at the hotel. Maggie felt as if the sun was shining on her, even though it was far past sundown.

❧

John whistled as he rode toward the depot. He had gone to do Maggie's chores extra early today. She came to the barn just in time to tell him thank you before he left. Since he had started courting her, John made sure they weren't alone for very long. He didn't want anyone talking about them. Protecting Maggie's reputation was essential to him.

This courtship progressed better than he had dreamed it would. He escorted Maggie to church every Sunday. Often they went to the

Brunsons' for dinner. A time or two, he took her out to eat at the restaurant in the hotel. Once, he and Maggie accompanied Hans and Holly to Minneapolis to see a stage play. Every minute he spent with Maggie made him grow more in love with her. He wanted to be with her and protect her.

Because of all her losses, Maggie had developed depth and strength of character. But John rejoiced that she had been able to move beyond her sorrows. He loved standing beside her at church as they sang hymns. Her rich contralto harmonized with his voice. He wanted to sing with her forever. Each time they parted, it became harder to leave. John yearned to take her in his arms and press his lips against her sweet, bowed mouth and pour all his love for her into the caress. But John knew he couldn't start kissing her. He wasn't sure he would be able to stop.

When he finished work that evening, he and Maggie would take a ride on the *City of St. Louis*. Equipped with electric lights, the boat often floated across the lake in the evening. The day couldn't end soon enough for him. The anticipation of being with Maggie again colored every moment.

Right after he arrived at the depot, his telegraph machine started clicking. He grabbed the pad and pencil and began to decipher the dots and dashes. When the message stopped, John sat back in his chair and smiled. Wait until he told Maggie. He hoped she would share his excitement.

❧

Maggie stood at the railing and watched the huge wheel turn on the side of the boat. With every revolution, the large vessel slid through the tranquil waters of Lake Minnetonka. The day had been windy, but the breeze died down as dusk settled over Maggie and John while they rode in a buggy toward the pier where the *City of St. Louis* waited for passengers. She was glad there wasn't any wind tonight. Even though it was late June, a strong breeze on the lake would have blown chilly air across the deck. Maggie pulled her crocheted shawl higher around her shoulders.

John stepped closer, almost touching her back. "Are you cold?"

All she could do was shake her head no. She forgot everything around them, lost in his nearness. Even the fascinating electric lights paled in comparison to John Collins, the man of her dreams. Noise from a party inside the cabin seeped into the quiet that surrounded them. People talked and laughed while a piano player filled the air with the latest tunes. But out here on the deck, tranquillity prevailed.

Maggie wondered what John would do if she leaned back until she was in his arms. She knew a lady wouldn't do that, but right now she didn't care if she was a lady or not. It was as if John were a magnet and she a piece of iron. It took all her willpower to fight the force that tried to pull their bodies into contact. How Maggie wished her mother were still alive. Did other women feel this way, or was she just wanton?

John shifted to stand beside her and held on to the rail with one hand. "What are you thinking about, Maggie?"

She wondered if he would be shocked if she told him. After a moment of silence, she murmured, "It's beautiful out here on the lake. Thank you for bringing me."

She looked up into green eyes that had deepened in the soft light. Something dark and mysterious called out to her, and for a moment, she thought he was going to kiss her. She wished it were proper for him to do that very thing. Would his lips feel soft or hard like his muscles? She couldn't even imagine what a kiss would feel like, but she really wanted to find out—and soon. Maggie turned back toward the water.

John wanted to pull Maggie into his arms and kiss her. Truthfully, John had never felt this way before. Here he was, twenty-four years old, and he hadn't stolen a kiss from any girl. But every time he looked at Maggie's lips, he desired them above everything else in the world.

He needed to get his mind off that subject. "I received an interesting telegram today, Maggie." How he enjoyed the feel of her name in his mouth.

That caught her interest. "From whom?"

"My father." John still had a hard time believing it. "My parents have never traveled since they had children, but now they're coming to Minnesota to visit me."

Maggie laid her hand on John's arm. "That's wonderful! When are they coming?"

John placed his other hand on top of her fingers, hugging them close. "They'll be here for the Independence Day celebration."

"But that's just next week."

"I know." He gave her hand another squeeze. "They'll arrive on Monday and stay until Friday." John released her fingers and slid one arm around her waist. "I can hardly wait for them to meet you."

Maggie wanted to meet them, too, but she was a little anxious. What if she wasn't what they had in mind for their son? What if his mother could tell what she was thinking? Maggie needed someone to talk to about all that was happening. Maybe Holly could help her.

When Maggie told her best friend what she had been thinking on the boat, Holly laughed. "Oh, Maggie, you're so funny."

The two women sat in the parlor at the Brunson farm. Maggie picked up a decorative pillow from beside her on the sofa. She hugged it close. "I don't see anything funny about it."

Holly got up from the rocking chair and came to sit beside Maggie. "What you're feeling is perfectly natural." She put her arm around Maggie. "That's what a courtship is. Getting to know one another and letting your feelings for each other grow. It wouldn't be natural if you didn't want to touch John and have him touch you."

Maggie smiled. "I really want him to kiss me, even if it wouldn't be proper. On the boat when he put his arm around me, I felt as if I were melting inside. I wanted to stand on tiptoes and kiss him if he wasn't going to kiss me first."

Holly laughed again, even longer this time. "Do you love John?"

"I'm not sure what love for a man is, but I can hardly stand the waiting when we're apart. Even while I'm working around the farm or sewing or taking care of Rascal or the other animals, all I think about is John. The last time we were together. The next time we'll be together. Is that love?"

Holly gave a secret smile. "I know. That's how I felt about Hans. . . before we married."

"And now?"

"Oh, Maggie, that love just grows and grows, and the touching gets better all the time." A blush stained Holly's cheeks. Maggie wondered exactly what she was talking about, and she hoped she would soon find out for herself.

Chapter 6

It had been months since John had last seen his parents. Although he came from a close-knit family, he hadn't realized how much he missed them until he received the message that they were coming to Wayzata. He went to the depot early so he could finish most of his work before they arrived. He planned on taking the rest of the day off so he could show Mom and Dad around town. Not many trains came through on Monday. The eastbound they rode came through about 3:00 p.m. It was the last.

When it was almost time for the train to arrive, John shoved his hands in his pockets and paced the wooden platform that connected the depot to the railroad tracks. The breeze that blew fluffy clouds across the sky brought relief from summer's heat. He wondered what his parents would think about Maggie. He dismissed the question from his mind. How could his family not love the woman he planned to wed?

The next few days would be busy. Tomorrow was the Independence Day celebration, and Wayzata already was decked out in patriotic colors. Bunting hung around buildings and at intervals across the street along the parade route. Not only were Wayzata's citizens planning on participating, but many people from Minneapolis and St. Paul who spent part or all of the summer in cottages on the banks of Lake Minnetonka would be present as well.

The last time John passed the ice cream parlor, he noticed a sign advertising a red, white, and blue sundae made with vanilla ice cream, strawberries, and blueberries. He planned to take Maggie and his parents to get one. Both Maggie and his mother would especially enjoy the frozen treat.

The whistle of the approaching train brought him out of his musings. John moved back and leaned against the wall of the depot, striking a relaxed pose.

The engine chugged into the station accompanied by the squeal of brakes as it slowed to a stop. John scanned the windows, trying to catch a glimpse of his parents. He spotted them in the third passenger car, so he hurried toward that one where the conductor hopped down from the steps. John's father followed the man then turned to offer his hand to John's mother, who stood on the bottom step.

John drank in the beauty of her face. She looked younger than she had the last time he had seen her. When her feet touched the platform, he pulled her into a bear hug and whirled her around. John was glad he was tall like his father instead of being short like his mother.

"John, put me down." Mom whispered into his ear while she held her straw hat on with one hand and hugged him back.

After John settled her on the wooden platform, he shook hands with his dad, then the two men clapped each other on the shoulder.

"Let's get the two of you settled in your hotel room before supper." John picked up the two valises the conductor set on the platform beside them.

❧

John and Maggie ate dinner at the hotel with his parents. It didn't take her long to fall in love with them. His father was as tall and slim as John. Evidently, John had inherited his dark hair. Maggie was sure John would look just as distinguished as his father did when his hair silvered at the temples. John's eyes, though, had come from his mother. Not only were hers the same light green, but they contained a sparkle similar to the one that usually lit his.

Maggie already knew a lot about his parents. How his mother hadn't learned a lot about being a housewife and mother before his parents met. John told her about being a young boy and loving to brush the tangles out of his mother's long strawberry blond curls. She enjoyed letting the children take turns brushing her hair. The woman who sat across the table from Maggie had her hair arranged in a Gibson girl hairdo. The smooth pouf let only a few wisps touch her cheeks and neck. To achieve a style like that, she must have learned how to manage all the curls John talked about.

"John has told us a great deal about you." Mrs. Collins's smile went straight to Maggie's heart. "We're glad he has a good friend like you."

John had told Maggie about his two sisters. Esther was only two years younger than he was, and she had married recently. Miriam was four years younger than John. At ten, their brother, Matthew, was the youngest. The lively conversation around the table contained many references to John's brother and sisters. Maggie imagined that life had been interesting in the Collins's home in North Dakota. She often wished for more brothers and sisters when she was growing up.

"Where are Miriam and Matthew staying?" John asked his mother.

Maggie could tell from the tone of John's voice and the smile on his mother's face that the two of them had a special relationship. She remembered the wonderful relationship Valter had with their mother. Maybe someday she would have a son to love the same way. For a moment, she saw a little boy with dark hair and John's green eyes laughing up at her with love in his expression. It brought the heat of a blush to her cheeks. She hoped no one noticed.

"They're with Esther and Levi. They're the first guests to stay with them in the new house Levi built for Esther before they married." Mrs. Collins straightened the silverware on the table in front of her. "He's such a nice young man. We're glad he and Esther got together."

John's father cleared his throat. "We're sure God put them together, aren't we, Brigit?"

Mrs. Collins turned a loving glance toward her husband and nodded. Then she looked back toward John. "So what are we going to do tomorrow?"

"There's a parade in the morning at eleven o'clock. Then we'll have a picnic. The city has a park down by Lake Minnetonka. That's where most of the activities will take place." John looked at Maggie and paused, giving her a chance to add to what he said.

"There'll be races and games like horseshoes and baseball. I think you can even take a ride on the side-wheeler if you want to. Lake Minnetonka winds around in many directions, and that's the best way to see it."

Mrs. Collins started to say something, but the waitress arrived with their food. After the woman left, John's mother leaned toward Maggie. "It sounds like a lot of fun."

"I'll prepare a picnic basket for us." Maggie looked down at the huge steak sizzling on her plate. She wasn't sure that she would be able to finish it.

"Would you like me to return thanks, son?" John agreed, and his father spoke a few words of blessing over their food.

When John arrived at the farm to pick Maggie up on Tuesday, she had everything prepared for the Independence Day festivities. He went into the house to help her carry the picnic basket. She also handed him a quilt they could spread on the ground under one of the shade trees. Maggie accompanied him to the buggy. Besides her handbag, she carried a large parcel wrapped in brown paper and tied with twine.

"Would you like me to get that for you?"

"No, it's not heavy." Maggie placed the package in the floorboard beside the basket.

"What is it anyway?" John couldn't contain his curiosity.

"You'll see later. It's a surprise."

John placed his hands on Maggie's waist when he helped her up into the vehicle. He liked the feel of her trim waist. "Who is it for? My parents?"

"Aren't you the curious one?" Maggie laughed and didn't give him any more information.

When they arrived at the hotel, John stopped the buggy at the back door and tied the horses to the hitching post. He took the picnic basket in and left it in his parents' room so it would be out of the sun during the parade. Maggie waited in the hotel lobby for him to return with his parents. The proprietor had placed chairs on the boardwalk in front of the building so his customers would have a comfortable place to watch the parade. When the Collins family arrived in the lobby, they accompanied Maggie to choose where they would sit. A canopy over the boardwalk in front of the hotel protected them from the bright sunlight.

Soon after they sat down, the parade started. A band led the procession, playing "Stars and Stripes Forever." Maggie enjoyed the lively march, tapping her toe in tune with the beat. She had read about how John Philip Sousa wrote the march on Christmas Day in 1896 while on an ocean voyage. After his return to the United States, the song became very popular. Now it was a welcome addition to Independence Day celebrations all over the country. The song made Maggie proud to be an American, too. Her parents hadn't been born in the United States, but she and Vally had been.

Soldiers who fought in the Spanish-American War followed the band. Maggie didn't like the idea of war, but this one lasted less than a year. It gave Cuba independence from Spain and made Guam and Puerto Rico part of the United States. It also ended Spanish rule in the Philippines. She understood why the soldiers were proud of the victory they won. As they marched in perfect precision, they often saluted the citizens lining the path of the parade.

Aoooga! Aoooga! Maggie turned her head to look behind the last of the soldiers.

"What is that awful noise?" Mrs. Collins craned her neck as she searched for whatever was causing it.

"It's the horn of a motorcar." John patted his mother's hand.

Maggie watched the mayor of Wayzata as he slowly drove down the street while squeezing the bulb on the horn of his automobile. His wife sat beside him. The open vehicle was painted red with lots of gold accents. "I'm not sure if I really like those things. They make a lot of noise, and my mare shies away from them."

"They cause many of the horses to be restless," John added. "One even ran away with its rider last week. It was the talk of the town for a day or two."

"Thankfully, no one near us has one yet." Mr. Collins frowned as he watched the contraption go down the street away from them.

Following the mayor, several young men rode their bicycles, which they decorated with red, white, and blue streamers. They rang their bells in no particular sequence, but the cacophony wasn't unpleasant. Maggie wondered if it would be hard to ride a bicycle. She liked riding her horse. They were partners in the balancing act, but how could you balance on thin wheels?

Mrs. Collins started laughing at the antics of three clowns who followed the cyclists. One did flips and walked on his hands as he moved down the street; another floated along on tall wooden stilts; and the third rode a unicycle. Maggie had heard about these one-wheeled cycles, but this was the first time she had seen anyone riding one.

With the end of the parade, people started making their way toward the park. John escorted Maggie and his mother to the buggy while his father went to the room to retrieve the basket of food.

When they alighted from the buggy at the park, John led the way to one of the tall trees that spread shade across the lush grass. He chose one on a little rise so they could observe all that went on around them. John noticed that Maggie once again carried the mysterious parcel. However, she set it aside while they had lunch. After they ate their fill of the baked chicken, fresh tomatoes, and chocolate cake, the two women packed all the dishes and utensils back into the basket, and John carried it to the buggy. When he returned, he dropped onto the quilt beside Maggie. His mother was sitting nearby, and his father lay with his head in her lap. Although there were many people in the park, groups were scattered far enough away from each other so it felt almost private.

Maggie looked up at John. "I have a surprise for you." She thrust the parcel into his hands and waited wide-eyed for him to open it.

When he pulled back the brown paper, he uncovered a quilt. "Did you make this for me?"

"My quilt!" His mother leaned close and rubbed her hand gently across the folded cover before she glanced at Maggie. "How did you get my quilt?"

Maggie studied John. "I know you said it was just an old quilt, but when I washed it, I could see that it was special."

"It certainly is!" his mother exclaimed. "I told you all about it in the letter I packed with it when I gave it to you."

John's brows knit in a confused expression. "There wasn't a letter with it."

"I don't understand. I wrote it so you would understand." She gave John a loving pat. "It's all right. You didn't know. I learned to sew while making this quilt using my wedding dress. That's where this green fabric came from." Once again, her hand caressed the coverlet in John's lap.

Mr. Collins sat up and watched them.

"I made my wedding dress, but it fell apart the first time I washed it." She took the quilt from John and spread it out so they could see all the blocks. "This white fabric I used in several blocks. It was the shirt Peter wore for our wedding." She caressed another block with her fingertips. "This was from a gown Mrs. Gladney made for John when he was a baby. She was a member of our church. And this flannel came from one of John's blankets. That's why I gave the quilt to him when he moved."

Maggie had been intently watching John's mother. "I knew the quilt had to be special, but I didn't know how special. It pulled apart in several places after I washed it. My best friend, Holly Brunson, and I restored it. It was actually when we were working on the quilt that my relationship with God was restored, too."

John knew that statement would catch his father's attention.

"Why was your relationship with the Lord damaged?" he asked.

"I pulled away from Him after I lost both my parents and my brother. Holly told me that God could restore my relationship with Him the same way we were mending the quilt. After I had time to think about the idea, I understood what she was talking about. I started going back to church, reading my Bible, and praying. My life completely changed."

John's mother touched his arm. "You haven't told us why Maggie had your quilt in the first place."

"It's kind of a long story." John swallowed a lump in his throat. He felt guilty for not realizing the importance of his mother's gift to him.

"We have plenty of time." John's mother leaned back against the tree and crossed her arms.

John knew she wouldn't leave him alone until she had the whole story, so he told her all about killing Maggie's dog by mistake and taking Rascal to her wrapped in the quilt.

When he finished, Maggie added to the story. "I don't know what I would've done without John's help. . .or without Rascal to love. That puppy filled a void in my life. I'm thankful John brought him to me."

Brigit patted Maggie's arm. "I'm glad he did, too."

Chapter 7

John's mother told him to come by the hotel after he took Maggie home. He figured she would chastise him for not taking care of the quilt. She hadn't told him how important the thing was when she gave it to him. He just remembered it being around the house most of his life. All the way back to town, he rehearsed different ways to apologize to her for what he had done.

His mother answered his knock. "Come in, John."

She didn't look upset. In fact, her bright smile and twinkling eyes warmed his heart. She pulled him into a welcoming hug.

After the embrace ended, John studied his mother. "What did you want to talk to me about?"

"Why, Maggie, of course." The answer contained a lilt of excitement.

John's thoughts jumbled, since he was prepared to apologize and defend his actions but his mother introduced an entirely different subject. "Why do you want to talk about Maggie?"

His father stepped up behind her and placed a hand on her shoulder. "Just what are your intentions toward the young lady?" His eyes also twinkled.

"I'm not trifling with her emotions, if that's what you're asking," John stammered. He wasn't sure what to expect next.

Father shut the door and ushered John to a chair. "We just don't want you to hurt the girl by leading her on. She's very nice, and she deserves more than that."

"I plan on asking her to marry me," John blurted out, almost feeling like the boy he had been when he often got in trouble for all his mischief and had to face his parents.

His mother clapped her hands. "Good! When are you going to do it?"

John felt as if he had stepped into a stage play in the middle of the second act and hadn't seen the script. "I'm not sure. . .uh, soon."

Mother sank into a chair and modestly arranged her skirt. "She doesn't have any family, does she?"

John stood up and paced across the floor, rubbing his hands together. Then he thrust them into his pockets so he could keep them still. He wasn't exactly comfortable talking about this with his parents. "No, but I took Martin. . .uh, Pastor Hardin with me when I asked her if I could court her."

A sweet smile lit Mother's face. "I'm glad you're doing things the proper way. I tried to raise you right."

Father placed a hand on his shoulder. "If you plan on asking her to marry you sometime soon, maybe you could do it while we're here. If she doesn't mind getting married quickly, I could perform the ceremony. It would be a privilege, son."

John felt as if a whirlwind had picked him up and was slinging him around in a dizzy circle. He wished it would deposit him back on the carpet that stretched almost from wall to wall in the room. He needed a firm foundation under his feet so he could think straight. "I'm trying to plan something special for the day I ask her."

That was all Mother needed. He could almost see her creative mind go to work as she jumped up from the chair, reminding John of what she had been like when he was younger. So full of life, meeting every challenge head-on. "Maggie enjoyed the ride on the side-wheeler."

John nodded.

"You could take her tomorrow night." She move closer to John. "If she says yes, we'll telegraph Esther and Levi, telling them how much longer we'll need to stay."

❦

Maggie worked in her garden all morning. She had an abundance of produce, which she didn't want to take the time to can. When John had come to help with the chores that morning, he'd asked if she would like to go on a boat ride after they ate supper with his parents. She looked forward to the evening and didn't want to spend the afternoon slaving over a hot stove. She wanted plenty of time to get ready for the outing.

After lunch, Maggie went into town and delivered all the vegetables to the parsonage. Elizabeth Hardin gladly received the bounty. Then Maggie went to the mercantile to purchase ribbons to match her favorite blue dimity dress. All the way home, she planned the hairstyle she would wear and how she would wind the ribbons through it.

When John arrived to pick her up, Maggie was glad she went to all the trouble. The way his eyes lit up when he saw her made the effort worthwhile.

After supper at the hotel, Mr. and Mrs. Collins accompanied them to the pier where the *City of St. Louis* gently swayed in the water. As the boat moved away from the wooden platform, twilight was falling over the water. Lights along the bank reflected in the ripples, and stars appeared one by one in the sky. Maggie started counting them in her head until there were too many. She and the Collins family stood by the railing and watched the summer night unfold before them accompanied by the gurgle and splash of the water as the wheel lifted it up and poured it out. By the time the boat moved around the first bend in the lake, the inky sky twinkled as though covered with a field of diamonds. A three-quarter moon cast its path across the water, beckoning Maggie to some unknown, enticing place. She knew God had created this spectacular display. Her heart filled with praises.

Before long, people drifted into salons on the boat, where music played and porters served refreshments. Maggie wanted to stay right where she was, beside the man she had come to love with all her heart. John stood so close she could feel the heat radiating from his body, but he didn't touch her. They didn't talk, but instead enjoyed the movement of the boat and the wonder of the night that surrounded them.

When John finally spoke, Maggie turned and noticed that they were alone. Even his parents weren't beside them any longer.

"What are you thinking about, Maggie?"

His quiet voice sounded like a caress. Maggie could only wonder how a real caress from John would feel.

She peered up into his beautiful green eyes, which sparkled in the moonlight. "I was praising God for providing us so much beauty."

A look of disappointment crossed his face for a moment. "Yes. . .it is beautiful." He turned and gazed across the expanse before them.

"And I was thankful that He brought you into my life," Maggie whispered.

John's expression brightened as he turned back toward her. "I am, too, Maggie." His fervent declaration touched her heart.

He moved closer and slipped his arm around her waist. Maggie looked up into his face, studying the lines and planes outlined in the moonlight, all the time aware of the weight and warmth of his arm around her.

"You're lovelier than anything out there." He gestured toward the lake.

Tears pooled in her eyes, and she glanced down at the bright trail across the water. Through her tears, the ripples along the surface looked extra sparkly.

"Maggie, I love you so much my heart feels as if it might burst."

John's words whispered against her hair arrowed to her heart, then she heard him breathe in her scent. She knew what he meant. She felt the same way about him.

"I brought you on this boat ride for a specific purpose."

Maggie didn't know what he meant, but it intrigued her. "And it was. . . ?"

John turned her toward him and gently held her upper arms. "Will you marry me, Maggie Swenson?" His intense gaze almost consumed her. He had spoken the most wonderful words she had ever heard.

"Yes." The syllable slipped out on a whisper. "Yes." This time she made sure John could hear her answer.

He gently cupped her face in his hands and studied her as if memorizing her expression. His eyes stopped their journey on her lips. He slowly lowered his face toward hers but stopped a hairbreadth away.

Maggie slipped her arms around his waist and closed her eyes, lifting her lips willingly to him. When their mouths touched, Maggie couldn't believe the sweetness that enveloped her. The love that poured into her heart and soul was so much greater than she had ever imagined. She became lost in the wonder of it.

※

John could hardly believe how easily the words had poured from him. He didn't know why he worried about it all day. He asked her to marry him, and she said yes. Twice. Her lips tasted better than John had ever imagined. He wasn't sure whether the kiss lasted for a second or an hour. Whichever, it wasn't long enough. A lifetime of kissing Maggie might be long enough, and he was going to find out. He planned to kiss her several times a day for the rest of their lives. The very thought lit a fire deep inside him. A fire he knew would be hard to keep under control. His father's idea of a swift marriage sounded better all the time.

When their lips parted, he gazed into her eyes and read the love there, but she spoke the words anyway. "I love you, John Collins, and I will until the day I die."

He pulled her against him, holding her so that their hearts beat in one accord. She rested her cheek on his chest, and the intimacy of the moment overwhelmed him.

"When, John? When should we get married?"

He pulled back but didn't take his arms from around her waist. "Would it be all right if we get married really soon?"

"How soon?"

John sighed. "I would like to get married before my parents go home. That way my father could perform the ceremony."

Maggie took a deep breath then let it out slowly. "That is soon."

"I'll understand if you want to wait longer. Of course, they can stay a week or two while we make wedding plans." John pulled Maggie's head back against his chest. He loved the feel of her against him. The perfume of her essence filled him with heady anticipation. How he hoped that she would agree to marry quickly.

Maggie took a few minutes to answer, but she didn't pull away. John watched the ripples dancing in the moonlight, feeling as if his heart was dancing right along with them.

"One of us should have family at the wedding. I don't have any left, and it's a long way from North Dakota. I wouldn't ask your parents to return later when there's no real reason the wedding can't take place right away." Maggie smiled up at him. "Do you think it'll be all right with them?"

John leaned his forehead against Maggie's, and their breath mingled. "I told them I planned to ask you to marry me. They thought it was wonderful. It was their idea to stay until the wedding if we get married soon."

⁂

Saturday, July 15, dawned bright and sunny, but a breeze blew welcome relief from the high temperature. Holly spent the night with Maggie, helping her finish making her wedding dress. They had found a bolt of silk the same shade of light green that John's mother wore when she married. They adorned Maggie's dress with an abundance of lace, and Maggie found her mother's lacy veil in one of the trunks. Including the traditions of both mothers in her wedding attire made the day more special.

Holly went out in the late morning and picked wildflowers. With them, she fashioned a bouquet for Maggie to carry. Scraps from the lace they used on the dress surrounded the blossoms.

The wedding was more elaborate than Maggie first thought it would be. All their friends at the church pitched in, planning a wedding supper for after the ceremony. These people provided the food and decorations. Maggie felt blessed to have so many people around her, supporting her.

At four thirty, Pastor Hardin and his wife came to the farm to get Maggie and Holly. White fabric streamers decorated the buggy he drove. He had offered to stand in for Maggie's father and walk her down the aisle. The church was already full when they arrived. John, his father, and Hans waited at the front of the church. John and Maggie had asked Hans and Holly to be their attendants.

All Maggie saw when she walked down the aisle was the face of her beloved. She knew that later she would try to remember every detail, but everything happened so fast. Soon Mr. Collins pronounced them man and wife. *Mr. and Mrs. John Collins.* The fervent kiss John gave her made her blush.

After the new couple exited the church, John's mother came to hug both of them. "Welcome to the family, Maggie. I'm officially making you the keeper of the quilt."

John laughed. "She'll take better care of it than I did."

Once again he kissed his bride, and Maggie welcomed it with all her heart.

Epilogue

By late August, Maggie had settled happily into married life. Sharing a home with John fulfilled many of the dreams Maggie had had as a young girl. She already knew what an honorable man John was, but she never dreamed how much fun he could be. When he came home, he filled the house with laughter and love.

Early in the month, John hired the son of a neighbor to help with the work at the farm. Because he enjoyed being stationmaster and telegrapher, he didn't want to quit his job. But the farm demanded a great deal of time when he got home, and he wanted to spend his evenings with Maggie and Rascal. It was just one more thing for Maggie to love.

One day at noon when he came home for dinner, he carried a package wrapped in brown paper. "I picked up the mail, and this is for you."

Maggie turned from the stove where she stirred gravy. "Who is it from?"

"My mother." John set the parcel on the end of the table. "It's probably a wedding gift."

"Should I open it now?"

"I can't stay long today." John came up behind Maggie and slipped his arms around her, dropping a kiss on her upswept hair. "Open it after we eat. You can show it to me when I get home this evening."

Maggie stepped from his arms, picked up the skillet, and poured the gravy in a waiting bowl. "Okay. Dinner is ready."

Pleasant conversation punctuated the meal, but Maggie couldn't keep her eyes from straying to the package sitting on the other end of the table. After John left, she made herself wash the dishes before she opened it. When she finished, she swiped her hands down the front of her apron before removing it and hanging it on a hook near the sink.

When Maggie unwrapped the brown paper, she found two wrapped bundles. The first parcel contained linens—sheets, pillowcases, and kitchen towels. According to the notes pinned to two pairs of pillowcases decorated with delicate embroidery, Miriam had made one pair and Esther the other. John's mother created a set of pillowcases in cutwork embroidery, outlining the flowers and leaves in many colors. Seven kitchen towels, one for each day of the week, were also decorated with needlework.

Maggie laid them aside and opened the other package. She uncovered a sewing basket. When she opened the top, she found two envelopes on top of the contents. The words READ THIS FIRST were written on one of them. She tore it open.

Dear Maggie,

The time Peter and I spent with you and John was special, and we welcome you into the family. His sisters and I hope you enjoy using these items as much as we enjoyed making them for you.

I must admit I was amazed that John hadn't realized the significance of the quilt, because I wrote him a note explaining it. After I returned home, I searched my sewing basket and found it stuck in the side. It's in the other envelope. I must have neglected to attach it to the quilt when I gave it to John.

My daughters are better seamstresses than I will ever be. They now make my clothing, too. I gave each of the girls her own sewing basket for her birthday when she was twelve years old. Since my sewing basket is lined with some of the same fabric that I used in the quilt, I wanted you to have it.

We hope you and John can come to North Dakota to visit the family soon. The girls are eager to meet you.

Love,
Brigit Streeter Collins

Maggie put the paper down and carefully opened the other envelope.

My dearest son,
This quilt is the story of your family and the love that binds us
together as truly as the threads that hold together these pieces of cloth.
I began this quilt as a new bride. I didn't know any more about
sewing than I did about being a wife, but I knew about love. . . .

As Maggie continued to read the words, tears pooled in her eyes.
Soon they streamed down her face. After she finished reading, she dashed
them from her cheeks with the backs of her hands.

She bowed her head and thanked God for allowing her to become a
part of this wonderful family. Maggie was confident that she, John, and
the wee one she suspected she was carrying would add to the tapestry of
love her mother- and father-in-law had begun.

LENA NELSON DOOLEY lives in Hurst, Texas with her husband, James, and enjoys her two daughters and her grandchildren. Aside from writing, Lena has spoken to women's groups and retreats, as well as written for seminars and conferences. Lena appreciates any opportunity to spread the gospel through missions work and writing. Visit her Web site at www. LenaNelsonDooley.com

The Tie That Binds

by Susan K. Downs

Preface

Between 1854 and 1930 over 200,000 orphaned or abandoned children traveled via orphan trains from the east coast of the United States to points west in hopes of finding new homes. Through this industrious "placing-out" program, as it was referred to in those days, trains carried a company of children to rural communities where people would gather and choose a child. Typically, prior to the train's arrival, a local committee evaluated applicants to determine whether they could provide a good home for a child. However, few committees bothered asking whether those interested in adopting were married or single or why they wanted a child. Despite this loosely structured plan, many children found loving and caring families—thanks to the orphan trains.

Chapter 1

"Well, Miz Watson, I see you still haven't forgiven me for my proposal of marriage," Frank Nance rasped in a futile attempt at a whisper.

Emma swept past Mr. Nance's imposing figure as he held the door open for her. Stepping out of the bright sunlight into the dimly lit interior of Shady Grove's Mercantile and Dry Goods Store, Emma found herself momentarily blinded. The stale, musty air tickled her nose, nearly making her sneeze.

The wind blowing off the prairie was unseasonably hot. But Emma couldn't blame the wind or the afternoon sun for the perspiration now prickling her forehead along her bonnet's brim. The presence of Frank Nance always caused her internal temperature to rise and her stomach to clench in irritation.

"Shush!" Emma responded curtly. "I've not told a soul about your proposal, and the last person I'd want to overhear is Katy Greene!" She scanned the store for a glimpse of the clerk who always made it her business to know everyone else's business. Emma's panic eased just a bit when she caught sight of the town's busybody assisting other customers at the far end of the store.

"Have it your way, ma'am. But the offer I made a year ago still stands. It's a cryin' shame for a pretty lady like yourself to be widowed—alone and childless—at the tender age of twenty-eight. Everyone in the county says we'd make a great lookin' couple. And you could close up that little seamstress shop of yours and be taken care of at home, where a woman belongs. Besides, I could sure use someone like you to help me out on the farm."

Emma gaped in disgust. "How dare you mention my age! Just how on earth did you know it anyway?" Without waiting for a response, Emma rushed, "You certainly have gall to even suggest that my seamstress shop is an inappropriate occupation for a lady!

"And, furthermore. . ." Widow Watson's corset under her starched white shirtwaist dug into her ribs, and she gasped sharply before continuing her tirade. The smirk of amusement on Frank Nance's face only added to her fury. "And furthermore, wheat farming must not be the easy job you boasted it would be when you gave up cattle driving. Otherwise, you wouldn't be so determined to find a wife to take care of the homestead. And you think I should jump at your offer because I need someone to take care of me? Contrary to your obvious opinion, Mr. Nance, I am quite capable of taking care of myself. I do not need you or any other man in my life, for that matter."

Emma punctuated her speech by turning abruptly and stepping to a glass display case, which held an assortment of scissors and knives. Surely, her curt rebuff would end this uncomfortable interchange. But even as she feigned an interest in the nickel-plated pinking shears, she could feel Frank's intense scrutiny. Did he suspect that her words had not been totally honest?

If the truth were known, she had often entertained the idea of remarrying. She didn't look forward to an entire lifetime of widowed loneliness. In fact, since Frank Nance broached the subject a year ago, she found herself imagining what life might be like married to this rugged outdoorsman. He obviously possessed the same adventuresome spirit she had loved in her departed husband, Stanley.

Stanley Watson had always been on the lookout for the next thrill. His death three years ago occurred when he tried to break the bronco dubbed "untamable" by every horse tamer in the county. Stanley took their edict as a challenge to conquer the beast. But the bucking steed threw Stanley within seconds of his mount. Emma could never erase the image of her husband's lifeless body inside the corral fence. His neck snapped as he hit the ground, and her beloved, impulsive husband had died instantly. Still, it would have been the kind of death Stanley would have chosen had he been allowed such a choice.

Oh, but Stanley. Why did you have to go and die so young? Why did you have to leave me alone in this world? Emma struck up this one-sided conversation with her deceased husband as naturally as though he were standing next to her.

Why didn't the good Lord grant us children? I prayed for a child. Your child. If I had borne your child, my grief and incredible longing for you might be just a bit more bearable. How I wish I had more than just my memories of you. If we had been blessed with a child, I wouldn't even listen to the likes of Frank Nance. But it's so lonely without you.

Her thoughts of Stanley caused her to shiver in revulsion at Frank's blatant offer for a loveless marriage. A marriage of convenience. She had known the man only briefly before he proposed. There hadn't been the slightest opportunity for love to grow between them.

Well, Stanley Watson and Frank Nance might have been kindred spirits, but Emma knew, without a doubt, that Stanley had been desperately in love with her—as she had been with him. Frank Nance, with all his good looks and lofty promises of comfort and security, couldn't give her the one thing she longed for most, someone to love, who loved her in return. Besides, unlike Stanley, Frank was a quiet, inexpressive man. Every time she pondered the possibilities of marrying Frank, she remembered the disastrous outcome of her own mother's second marriage to the stone-faced, stern Josiah Trumbull. What if Frank's silent disposition hid a personality as cruel as that hateful man's? Mr. Trumbull had ruined her mother's hopes for a happy life. He had driven Emma away from her mother and her home. Emma would remain single for eternity before she'd enter into the risky union Frank offered. His proposition was simply too full of unknowns.

Still, the persistent Mr. Nance wasn't quite ready to accept Emma's "no" as a final answer to his long-standing proposal. He sidled up to the counter, wedging his way between Emma and the scissors display.

His voice slowly increased in volume as he continued in his attempts to weaken her fierce independence. "It isn't as though you have a passel of eligible men to pick from in these parts." Frank's nervous fidgeting with the suede fringe on his leather vest belied the cockiness of his banter. "'Less'n you consider the undertaker McHenry. He's buried three wives already and has one foot in the grave himself—"

"Mr. Nance, please keep your voice down! And please pay me the courtesy of never addressing this matter again. A marriage for convenience's sake, whether it be your convenience or mine, doesn't interest me in the least. My answer of last year remains my answer today. *No!*"

Emma's final word echoed through the store, and the attentions of Katy Greene and her customers immediately turned to the pair. The rotund store clerk's eyebrows rose in obvious question, but she swallowed her curiosity for the time being and simply said, "Mr. Nance, Miz Watson, I'll be with you directly."

"I imagine Katy Greene is havin' a field day with this orphan train business," Frank said, looking in the shopkeeper's direction. "It's created quite a buzz around town."

Despite her firm rejection of Frank's repeated proposal, Emma was slightly taken aback by his abrupt change in the course of their conversation. Was he, at last, abandoning his idea of marriage? Or did he have a new strategy in mind?

"Excuse me, but I'm afraid that I don't know what you're referring to," she snapped, wishing he would simply do his business and leave.

"No offense, ma'am, but a person would have to be as blind as a post hole not to notice that somethin's goin' on here in Shady Grove. Didn't you see the crowd in front of the *Gazette* office when you walked by?"

Emma glanced out the storefront window to see a dozen or more of the town folk clustered around the newspaper office. Apparently her inability to focus on more than one task at a time had left her, once again, oblivious to her surroundings. Emma's thoughts and energies for the past three days had been consumed with the completion of Lizzy Baxter's wedding gown. Sometimes, especially on days like today, she found it rather surprising that she could even walk and think at the same time.

Attempting to disguise her deficient observation skills, she turned to Frank and calmly replied, "The citizens of Shady Grove are in a constant state of ruckus. What has them stirred up now?"

Stepping up behind Emma, Katy Greene interrupted with her own answer. "Of course, it wouldn't concern you, Miz Watson—what with being a widow and all—but a railcar full of orphans is headed for our little village, straight from New York City. They're looking for folks who will adopt 'em and give 'em a good home. My husband Orville is on the screening committee. He says that several folks have already inquired about adopting these children, and the *Gazette* only posted the notice in Monday's paper. He's hopeful that all fifteen of the orphans will wind up right here in Shady Grove. Why, we might even take one ourselves."

Frank, unobserved by the rambling Mrs. Greene, rolled his eyes at Emma in a look that could only be interpreted as an expressive "Oh brother!"

Despite his irritating ideas, he still possesses a certain boyish charm. The unwelcome thought caught Emma off guard. However, the feelings quickly passed as Frank, eyes twinkling, dashed aside any admiration Emma might have been developing for him.

"Perhaps I'll look into taking one of the boys, too. I've heard tell those orphans make good workers."

Even though his words seemed to be spoken in jest, Emma wondered if his teasing tone was a cover for his ultimate motive. Could this man truly be so coldhearted as to adopt a child for the sake of gaining a helping hand? Emma's ears heated with anger at the very thought. It's bad enough that he would propose a marriage of convenience to a grown woman. . .but only an ogre would adopt an innocent child just for the work he could get out of him. Did Mr. Nance think that adoption was something akin to the purchase of a new pack mule?

She studied his classically handsome features, searching for some answers to her question, but she received none. His mahogany eyes simply reflected his own speculations and appraisals back at her. Under ordinary circumstances, Emma might very well find herself agreeably inclined to Mr. Nance's overtures. Fleetingly, she wondered if she might react differently were the man to at least show some sign of affection for her, some predisposition of falling in love. The thought left her stomach in a disgusting flutter.

An overwhelming urge to run back to the cocoon of her seamstress shop flooded Emma. She didn't want to think about Frank Nance any more today. He flustered her beyond reason, and she refused to stay another moment in this infuriating man's presence.

Emma turned to the shopkeeper and announced, "Mrs. Greene, I really must return to my shop. If you would do me the favor of gathering together the muslin I ordered, along with two dozen shirt buttons and thirty cents worth of seed pearls, I'll be back at four thirty to pick them up." Then she whirled on her heels and clamored out the door, murmuring a perfunctory "good day, sir" as she passed Frank.

Politely picking her way through the townsfolk still clustered in front of the *Gazette* office, Emma managed to position herself in front of the posted news board. The bold WANTED headline seemed more appropriate for a bank robber than adoptive families, but the article that followed tugged at Emma's heartstrings:

WANTED!
HOMES FOR 15 ORPHAN CHILDREN

A company of orphan children under the auspices of the Children's Aid Society of New York will arrive in Shady Grove Thursday afternoon, June 24.

These children are bright, intelligent, and well disciplined, both boys and girls of various ages. A local committee of five prominent Shady Grove citizens has been selected to assist the agents in placing the children. Applications must be made to and endorsed by the local committee, which will convene at the town hall on Thursday, June 24, beginning at 9:00 A.M. Distribution of the children will take place at the opera house on Friday, June 25, at 10:00 A.M.

Come and see the children and hear the address of the child-placing agent.

The engine of Emma's one-track mind began building up steam. As she turned from the signboard and made her way down the street toward her shop and home, her thoughts quickly traveled into uncharted territory.

Why not a widow like me? Emma mentally shot back a response to Katy Greene's earlier statement. Then, as naturally as she drew breath, Emma's thoughts turned into a silent prayer. *Lord, why not a widow like me? One parent would certainly be better than no parent whatsoever. And I would make a great mother! I have a lot of love to give. I could definitely provide a more suitable home for a child than the stone-hearted Mr. Nance.* A spark of self-righteous indignation burst into flame, sending Emma's unspoken prayer to the far recesses of her mind.

The very idea that Frank Nance might even tease about adopting a boy as an extra farmhand. . . Emma's temples began to pound in anger as her thoughts turned, once again, to the infuriating farmer. *Why, if this committee might approve the likes of Frank Nance to adopt a child, surely I can convince them to recommend me!*

Chapter 2

Emma stepped from her spacious porch and across the threshold of her white frame home. Swiftly she rushed through the tastefully decorated parlor and into her workroom, where a worn rolltop desk held her Bible. Emma picked up the Bible and settled into the straight-backed chair that complemented the desk. The room was filled with the necessities of the trade: stacks of fabric in rainbow hues, dressmaker frames, two full-length mirrors, a privacy screen for the customer's convenience, and a trundle sewing machine—Stanley's wedding gift.

With the smell of new fabric surrounding her, she mentally pushed aside thoughts of work and fervently asked God for wisdom. In her typical daily routine of prayer and meditation, she studied her Bible in a systematic fashion. But today, with her thoughts flitting in all different directions like the evening fireflies, she found it impossible to concentrate on one particular Scripture passage. Instead, she thumbed through the yellowed pages of her father's aging Bible, asking God to give her some sort of promise or sign. Did this newborn idea of adoption stem from selfish motivation? Was she simply acting on a desire to prove something to Frank Nance? Or could taking an orphaned child as her own be a part of God's perfect plan?

Instinctively, Emma turned to Psalms—the book of the Bible where she had most often sought and found comfort following Stanley's death. As she skimmed the well-worn pages, her attention rested on a verse just above her right hand. Her index finger pointed to the Sixty-eighth Psalm, and she started reading verses 5 and 6. She must have read this very chapter, these same verses, numerous times: "A father of the fatherless, and a judge of the widows, is God in his holy habitation." Yes. She distinctly remembered pondering the fact that God proved Himself a merciful and loving judge to widows such as herself. But never had the words of Psalm 68:6 leapt out at her as they did now. "God setteth the solitary in families."

Was the Lord showing her a sign? Could it be that a solitary little girl now rode on a train bound for Shady Grove, hoping and praying for someone to love and care for her? Emma knew full well the meaning of the word "solitary." These past three years since Stanley's death she had wallowed in loneliness and solitude. Now her heart ached to think of a mere child facing life without the comfort and security of a home or family.

God setteth the solitary in families. Throughout the remainder of the afternoon the words rang repeatedly through her thoughts until they became a chant. Over the course of the evening, the melodious words turned into song as Emma bathed, washed her hair, and prepared for the next day. *God setteth the solitary in families. God setteth the solitary in families.* Like a soothing lullaby, the psalm soothed Emma to sleep.

When the summer sun's first rays at last broke over the horizon, Emma threw back her bedcovers and sat on the side of her bed. As she glanced across her small, tidy quarters, the psalm still rang through her head. *God setteth the solitary in families.* Once the idea of adopting a little girl had taken root in Emma's mind, her thoughts refused to dwell on anything else. Miss Baxter's wedding dress remained unhemmed. She had even forgotten to return to the mercantile yesterday afternoon to retrieve her order from Katy Greene.

The early morning minutes moved slower than February molasses as Emma waited for the appointed hour that the committee would consider adoption applications. With each loud tick of the mantel clock, her conviction and determination grew. Adopting a child was the right thing to do. Emma pulled up her wavy chestnut hair. Then she stood in her undergarments before the open doors of her wardrobe and riffled through an assortment of dresses. As a seamstress, she didn't lack for clothes. But what would be considered appropriate attire for a widow hoping to adopt a child?

Finally, Emma settled on a dark green taffeta with a white lace collar and black velvet trim. If she were to err, Emma preferred to err on the side of overdressing. Besides, the green cloth brought out the emerald flecks of her otherwise gray eyes. She smiled with smug satisfaction at her mirrored reflection as she buttoned up the bodice to her dress. *They won't turn me down for lack of good looks.* The thought only briefly skittered through her mind, but it was swiftly followed by a rebuff for such self-admiration, lest it border on conceit.

Emma felt like a hostage to time, just waiting for the mantel clock to chime nine o'clock. By the time the clock rang once, announcing 8:15, she was already fumbling with her front door key as she prepared to leave. She couldn't wait one minute more. She really wanted to be among the first in line. Thoughts of tiny arms around her neck, night-night kisses, and playing peekaboo swirled through her mind as her black leather high-top boots clipped a staccato beat on the boardwalk. With certain determination, Emma headed down Main Street toward the town hall.

The swinging doors leading into the meeting room announced her arrival in grating squeaks as she stepped over the threshold. As she had hoped, Emma was apparently the first applicant to arrive. Seated in an intimidating row behind a long table were the two women and three men who composed the recommendation committee. In unison, this team of prominent Shady Grove citizens stopped their busy pursuit of shuffling papers and consulting one another to turn and stare at Emma. The sun's bright rays, spilling in from the high windows, seemed to create a dream-like chasm between Emma and the prospect of adopting a child. Her heart pounding with anticipation, she plunged into the sphere of light as if she were embracing the prospect of adoption all over again. With each of the twenty steps it took her to cross the room, the floorboards creaked in protest, but the noise sounded like nothing less than a sweet melody to Emma. Nothing. . .nothing could dampen her joyful anticipation. . . nothing. . .not even when she suspected the committee's silently scolding, *You're a widow. You're wasting our time.*

Twisting her handkerchief between perspiring palms, Emma cleared her throat and began, "I—I want to adopt a child. A ch–child from the orphan train."

❧

The silver conchos that decorated the outer legs of his tanned leather chaps clinked softly together as Frank Nance hung the protective britches on a peg just inside the kitchen door. Typically, he reserved his chaps for rides out on the range, but today he had worn them as an apron, of sorts, to protect his best wool trousers from getting soiled during his early morning chores. He had no Sunday-go-to-meetin' clothes, so his newest britches would have to suffice. The washtub, which he had pulled into the middle of the kitchen floor last evening, still held the soapy remains of his bath, the clouded water long turned cold.

Crossing from the kitchen to the parlor, Frank stood in front of the room's single adornment, a garishly gilded mirror that hung on the south wall. Only traces of the reflective mercury remained behind the glass, and Frank had to tip his head at just the right angle to catch a glimpse of his reflection. Frank licked his fingers and twirled the ends of his freshly trimmed moustache. Then he ran his hand down his clean-shaven chin and gave his parted and bear-greased hair a final smoothing pat.

"There you are—all citified and sissified," Frank said to his reflection. "But if gettin' gussied up helps me adopt a boy, then gussied up I'll get." However, he hoped and prayed he didn't run into Emma Watson today, looking like he did. She'd for sure think he had gone soft. Or would she? Frank never knew just how that woman would respond. Where the doe-eyed Widow Watson was concerned, or any ladies for that matter, Frank didn't have a notion what to do.

When he had made a proposal of marriage to the young widow, he thought sure she would find his offer hard to resist. He'd been told on more than one occasion that he was a handsome man. He was strong and young and could provide security and stability for a wife.

Frank had never been one to drink or carouse, thanks to his saintly mother, who had raised him to practice good Christian morals and ethics. She had seen to it that he learned right from wrong. Surely those traits held the marks of a good husband. Even though he had not been a particularly religious man of late, he still tried his best to avoid any big sins.

His bachelorhood didn't stem from any odd deficiency or personality quirk. Only his previous profession as a drover along the Chisholm Trail had kept him single and unattached. He knew from watching the married cowhands that life as a cowboy and the duties of a husband don't mix.

After the death of his mother, which left him orphaned at age fourteen, Frank had ridden the range, driving cattle along the Chisholm Trail from Texas through Indian Territory and on into the Kansas plains. Frank learned quickly what it took to survive in the Wild West. Alongside his gun and a good horse, a cowboy needed a gruff exterior and a calloused heart. Frank was an expert at keeping his emotions and opinions to himself.

But the need for cowboys to push longhorns along the trail had grown mighty slim, thanks to the ever-expanding railroad and the fencing in of the plains. Frank had traded his adventurous life as a cowboy for the comparatively mundane existence of a Kansas wheat farmer. Since this drastic change, he found the old familiar loneliness much more difficult to bear. But he found admitting his need for companionship a difficult prospect—even with Widow Watson.

He had hoped beyond hope that Emma would have at least given his marriage proposal last year a glimmer of consideration. The two of them would be a good match. But the Widow Watson made it perfectly clear that she was not interested in even entertaining the idea. Maybe he should have courted her awhile before stating his intentions. He hadn't known her all that well when he first proposed, but Frank was a man who made up his mind quickly, and he didn't see any sense in wasting time. Unfortunately, Emma seemed to think he was much too practical with his straightforward approach.

Despite what the prim and proper widow thought, no other woman interested him. Frank was not just seeking a marriage of convenience. In truth, most of the "conveniences" of his life were cared for by Pedro and

Maria Ramirez, the husband and wife team whom Frank had hired to assist him on the farm. He wanted a life partner. He wanted Emma for his wife. Frank dreaded the thought of facing any more years alone.

When Emma snubbed him again yesterday, Frank determined then and there that he wouldn't wait forever for Emma to change her mind. Ideas of proposing to another woman certainly crossed his mind. Frank had been exposed to more than one coy smile from the collection of young maidens in Shady Grove. However, he had soon dashed aside any notion of marrying another. Thoughts of marrying someone besides Emma Watson simply held no fascination for him—not that he was by any means in love with her. She simply held the maturity and grace that appealed to Frank. Yes, that was it—maturity and grace, nothing more.

So, if he couldn't have the companionship of Widow Watson, he would turn his attentions to other things. The idea of adopting a boy rather appealed to him. While a boy could in no way meet his longing to have Emma for his wife, Frank's desire to be a father would be fulfilled in an adopted son. He and such a boy would be good friends. Best friends.

When Frank had told Emma he might take a boy from the orphan train, he had spoken the words in jest. But the longer he entertained the whim, the more he liked it. After all, he had been orphaned as a child himself. Certainly he could relate to a boy who felt all alone in the world. As a father, Frank would have a lot to offer a son.

Slamming the back door behind him, Frank tromped across the well-worn path that led from the kitchen to the barn. The strong, earthy smell of hay mixed with manure assailed Frank's nostrils as he slid open the barn door. Shadow, the mustang that Frank had lassoed and tamed as a colt, nuzzled up to his arm as he slid the bridle into place. Within seconds after lifting his saddle from the top rail of the horse's stall, Frank had cinched the straps securely and mounted the steed for the short trip to town.

*

Emma's impassioned appeal ultimately convinced the panel members to grant her the coveted and necessary commendation to adopt. The two women on the panel had actually been brought to tears as Emma expressed her deep loneliness since the death of her husband and her desire to relieve the desolation of an orphaned child. The Reverend Barnhart agreed that Emma was faithful in church attendance and would provide well for the spiritual nurture of a young soul. Even the committee's businessmen, mercantile owner Orville Greene and *Gazette* publisher Ben McGowan, nodded their heads in approval when Emma addressed the fact that she could teach her child the art and trade of dressmaking and thus assist the girl in becoming a useful and productive citizen of society. But their approval came with a condition: Emma would be allowed to choose a daughter only if no married couples stepped forward first to claim the child. Clutching the recommendation letter securely in her gloved hand, Emma backed out of the room, nodding her head in appreciation to the committee all the way to the door.

God setteth the solitary in families, Emma's heart sang with joy as she stepped from the meeting chambers into the hallway that extended the length of the town hall. She found the passageway clogged with several applicants nervously queued in pairs. The first couple in line pushed their way past her through the open door, and Emma received little more than a curious glance or two as she zigzagged her way through the small group and into the dust-filled street.

A cacophony of horses, wagons, carriages, and pedestrians met Emma as she closed the door.

"Are my eyes deceivin' me, or did I just catch you coming out of the town hall?" a familiar voice softly spoke in her ear.

Jumping, she turned to stare straight into the right shoulder of the towering man. Lifting her gaze to meet his, her breath caught at the sight of Frank's freshly scrubbed and strikingly handsome face so close to hers. The aroma of strong lye soap still clung to his whiskerless chin. The crow's feet that framed his dark mahogany eyes crinkled as he responded with a grin to her startled response.

"W—why, y—yes. I—I—I. . ." Mad at herself for stammering, Emma's shoulders tensed and her toes curled inside her boots. Why on earth was she reacting to this man like a schoolgirl in the throes of her first crush? Surely the noise and excitement of the morning were wearing on her, for she had never been so challenged in maintaining her composure with

Frank. *Or perhaps you simply want to believe you have never been so affected by him,* a rebellious voice taunted. Emma clamped her teeth in aggravation. *Frank Nance holds no place—absolutely no place whatsoever—in my heart! Period! The very idea is nothing short of lunacy!*

"You didn't by any chance seek a recommendation from the orphan train committee, did you?" The mischief dancing in his dark eyes told Emma that he already knew her answer. But the sparkle quickly disappeared behind a veil of seriousness as he followed the unanswered question with another, more urgent inquiry. "Were your efforts met with success?"

Emma studied the face of this mystifying man. From her previous dealings with Mr. Nance, she had long ago concluded that, despite his dashing good looks, the man was incapable of feeling any deep emotion. Yet, as he stood before her now, his voice took on an almost pleading tone. Why were her adoption plans important to Frank?

Doggedly determined to regain her cool demeanor, Emma raised the coveted recommendation letter for him to see. "Fortunately for me, the committee didn't feel that a widow adopting a child was as absurd an idea as Katy Greene believed it to be. I shall be allowed the opportunity to adopt any young girl that is not claimed by a married couple first." Before Frank could examine the paper further, Emma slid it into her beaded handbag.

"Now, Miz Watson, that's powerful good news," he enthusiastically replied, undaunted by her curt reaction. "After I left the mercantile yesterday, I felt sorry for funnin' around about this orphan train business. Truth be known, I gave the matter considerable ponderin' last night. I'm on my way to meet with the committee myself and see if I can't convince 'em to let me take a boy."

"No, Fran—er, Mr. Nance. You mustn't. . . You can't. . . Why, the very idea of you. . ." An all-too-familiar irritation surfaced as flashes of yesterday's conversation flitted through Emma's mind. Would Frank Nance really adopt a boy just for farm labor?

"And why not, Miz Watson? Why shouldn't I adopt a son? You've made it perfectly clear that you are unwilling to consider my proposal of marriage. Would you have me forever condemned to live a life of loneliness and solitude?"

His sincere words dashed aside all her previous negative thoughts. Never before had the man spoken so openly with Emma. His soul-revealing speech made her squirm uncomfortably against the snug taffeta gown. As she studied his features in hopes of confirming or denying his sincerity, the psalm that had replayed through her thoughts all morning now took on new meaning. *God setteth the solitary in families.* Could this scripture possibly contain a promise for someone like Frank Nance? The idea of his actually needing human companionship had seemed almost preposterous to Emma. Could she have somehow misunderstood this man? If so, was his proposal based on more than he had admitted? Her stomach produced a betraying flutter. *Stop it!* She wanted to scream.

"You're preachin' a double standard, Miz Watson. One that's tipped in your favor, if you ask me." A note of irritation crept into Frank's voice as he continued, waving an arm in front of his face to shoo away a pesky horsefly. "Evidently, you believe adoption to be quite fine and dandy for a widow woman such as yourself but somethin' strange and suspicious for a bachelor like me.

"Don't get me wrong, here, ma'am." Frank fixed his gaze on Emma's face, still whisking at the air to deflect the buzzing bug. "I admire your wantin' a child and your gumption to see this business through. From what I can tell, you have the makin's of a wonderful mama. Just because you aren't inclined to marry again doesn't mean you shouldn't grab at the chance to raise a young'un if such a chance comes along. But I reckon you shouldn't begrudge me the same opportunity."

With the force of a slammed door, a steely glaze hid the soft vulnerability that Emma had glimpsed, ever so briefly, in Frank's eyes. "I'd like to stay and visit with you all day," he said, glancing over his shoulder at the town hall, "but there's important business to tend to."

Tipping his broad-brimmed, gray felt hat, Frank excused himself with an exasperating smirk. "Oh, and Miz Watson," he said, turning to face her once more, "may I say 'thanks' for plowin' the ground ahead of me and plantin' the idea that it's all right for an unmarried person to adopt? If all goes well with me and that committee, I'll see you at the opera house tomorrow."

Chapter 3

The ever-present prairie wind blew down Main Street on Friday morning, swirling the dust into miniature cyclones and whipping at Emma's skirts. She instinctively held a rose-scented handkerchief over her nose to keep from choking on the dry air, heavy with the pungent smell of livestock and working men. She paused before crossing the road and surveyed the collection of people now congregating outside the opera house doors.

Katy Greene's squeaky voice carried above the crowd, prickling Emma's nerves like straight pins jabbing an unthimbled thumb. "Well, Orville wants a boy. But I insist on a girl so I can dress her up like a little doll. There's just not much you can do to fix up a boy, don't you know...."

The mousy woman whom Katy Greene had cornered continued to bob her head in tacit agreement as the vociferous Mrs. Greene droned on. Ignoring the storekeeper's rambling babble, Emma anxiously fingered the blue satin ribbon on the gingham-wrapped parcel she cradled in her right arm. The package contained a china-faced doll with real hair the same chestnut color as her own. A gift for her daughter-to-be. Emma had spent several hours yesterday evening making the doll's frock out of this powder-blue gingham. On her sewing table back home lay another piece of the fabric. She planned to sew her new daughter a dress to match the one the doll now wore. But as she scanned the gathering assembly, doubts now punctured the confident assurance of impending motherhood she had felt just moments before. How many of these couples wanted girls? And exactly how many girls had the orphan train carried into town?

Emma forced these negative contemplations to the back of her mind and, once again, inspected the amassing band of townsfolk. Half a dozen farmers in bib overalls and their plump, plainly dressed wives composed the majority of the prospective parents waiting to enter the opera house. Were they all hoping only to find a new farmhand from among the orphan train riders? Or did they truly want to provide a good home to a child?

Emma had witnessed the area farmers' gab sessions, which took place on the boardwalk in front of the Shady Grove feed store. She knew that a good many ill-conceived ideas came from these weekly meetings. If they discussed adopting for free labor, had Frank been among them?

Until her most recent encounter with him, she strongly would have suspected his being the mastermind behind any self-serving plot, despite the teasing tone he used when he mentioned adopting a boy to help out on the farm. Now she hesitated to charge Frank with certain villainy. For a few unguarded moments, Frank Nance had revealed a different side, a vulnerable side, to Emma. Just those few seconds, when she saw softness and emotion in his eyes, caused her to question her previous conviction that he was totally calloused and cold. Nonetheless, a few doubts still lingered.

But where was he? Just yesterday Frank seemed doggedly determined to follow through on his adoption plan. It was unlikely that he had changed his mind. Emma craned her neck to see if she could spot the one farmer she knew would stand head and shoulders above the rest. Still, he was nowhere to be found. Could it be that his request for a child had been denied?

A whistle sounded from the train station down the road, indicating that the appointed hour had come. Vaguely hoping to catch sight of Frank, Emma crossed the street and nudged her way to the opera house doors. No sooner had the whistle fallen silent than the garishly ornate double doors of the opera house swung open.

"On behalf of the Orphan Train Committee, I welcome you all,"

Reverend Barnhart exclaimed. "Please come in. Those of you who are here in hopes of being matched with a child, we ask that you find a seat among the first few rows of the auditorium. If you are here to simply observe the occasion, please take your seats toward the rear." The dignified and refined minister, bedecked in his black preaching suit, shook the hands of the men and nodded respectfully at the women as they filed past him, instilling an aura of solemnity among the people.

The freshly lit kerosene lanterns that lined the far aisles and front of the stage filled the air with a heavy, sooty smell. The lights' flickering shadows set a mysterious scene for this true-life drama, in which the audience would soon play the lead parts.

Emma discreetly found a seat in the third center row next to the aisle. But once all the couples had taken their seats, an empty place remained beside Emma. Absently, she wondered if some of the couples assumed her spouse would soon arrive. The rest of the seats in the auditorium quickly filled with more than fifty onlookers from Shady Grove's curious citizenry. Seemingly, no one wanted to miss out on the biggest show ever to come to town.

Up on the stage, the rotund publisher of the *Gazette*, Ben McGowan, cleared his throat and shifted from one foot to another as he waited for everyone to find a seat. "Ladies and gentlemen," he began in his deepest bass voice, "we are gathered here today to witness a truly newsworthy and momentous event. For, within a matter of minutes, the young ones who arrived via the orphan train yesterday evening shall be escorted from the Imperial Hotel. Accompanying this band of orphans is the child-placing agent, Mr. E. E. Hill, who shall address this body before the matching of children to parents commences.

"But prior to turning our attentions to the business of the day, may I take just a moment to express my appreciation to the citizens of Shady Grove for the privilege and honor of serving on this select committee. . . ." The verbose newsman continued his pontification, blatantly stalling for time until a chorus of giggles and shushes filtered through the rear doors.

As one body, the crowd's attention turned away from the stage and toward the commotion. Emma shifted in her seat just in time to see none other than Frank Nance, grinning from ear to ear, jauntily striding down the aisle. On Frank's shoulders rode a toddler whose face was hidden under the brim of the ex-cowboy's weathered Stetson. Behind him children of various ages, shapes, sizes, and gender followed in a single line.

Just like the Pied Piper, Emma couldn't help but think, suddenly irritated by Frank's uncharacteristically childish antics. Did she owe her perturbed attitude to a twinge of jealousy? For not once—not even when he had proposed marriage—had Frank shown to her the kind of emotion he so freely displayed with the children. Then again, why should she care? The man meant nothing to her. *Nothing,* she insisted. Wasn't it she who had rejected him? Emma reminded herself that she was not the least bit interested in Frank Nance. However, her mind betrayed her as it insisted on meandering to another question. Was Frank capable of showing that kind of affection for a wife?

Immediately, she squelched any notions she might be developing for the man. *He is not a dedicated Christian,* she firmly told herself. *Even if he is handsome, even if he declares his undying love and devotion, he never darkens the church door!* Emma simply could not involve herself with a man who did not share her passion for the Lord.

When the "orphan parade" reached the stage steps, Frank lifted the tot from atop his shoulders and uncovered the cherub's face as he retrieved his hat. A gentle pat on the young boy's backside sent him scurrying onto the stage to find a seat. Relieved of his charge, Frank turned to search the audience until his gaze rested on Emma and the vacant seat to her left.

Scrunching down in her seat, Emma dug her fingernails into the red velvet armrests, hoping and praying that Frank would find another place to sit. But a quick scan of the lantern-lit room told her there were no other seats as close to the front as the one next to her. Would she ever shake this man?

Bringing up the rear of the orphan processional, a gentleman with an infant in his arms walked to the center of the stage and said, "As he's taking his seat, I'd like to extend my sincere thanks to Mr. Frank Nance for coming to my aid today." Seemingly nonplussed by the hubbub around him, the man intercepted the baby's reach for his glasses while introducing himself as E. E. Hill, the child-placing agent from New York City. While he spoke, he pushed his spectacles back up the bridge of his nose with one thumb before securely clutching the infant's curious fingers in his grasp. His crumpled suit looked as though he had slept in it for several nights.

"Unfortunately, one of the young orphans amongst our party fell ill," Mr. Hill continued. "And my assistant, Mrs. Ima Jean Findlay, found it necessary to remain behind at the Imperial to care for the ailing child. Mr. Nance happened to be eating breakfast at the hotel and observed my single-handed struggles with the children. He graciously volunteered to assist."

Frank, who had already left the stage and was heading for the empty seat next to Emma, paused to respond. Although he spoke softly, the acoustics of the room caused his voice to reverberate throughout the audience. "No need to say thanks, Mr. Hill. I was happy to help out.

"But I don't mind tellin' you. . ." Frank pointed with his hat in the direction of the squirming children. "Herdin' cows is a heap easier than corralin' them kids!" A ripple of lighthearted laughter filtered through the crowd as he came to a stop beside Emma.

"Is it all right with you if I sit there, ma'am?" Frank whispered as he nodded toward the empty seat. Emma sensed, without even lifting her gaze from the package on her lap, that every eye in the building was watching this exchange. Her face heated and the tops of her ears stung with embarrassment over the attention now focused toward her.

Unlike yesterday, when she wanted to wear her best to impress the committee, today Emma had purposefully tried to shrink into the shadows and remain inconspicuous. As the only widow seeking to adopt, she didn't want to endure a morning full of stares. She had even chosen a nondescript brown muslin dress, rather than one made of a finer material or brighter color, for the express purpose of blending in with the crowd. But the boisterous Mr. Nance seemed intent on including her in his spectacle.

What had gotten into him, anyway? Never before had Frank behaved in such a frivolous fashion. Without verbally responding to his request, Emma shifted her skirts to allow him to squeeze past her and occupy the vacant seat. Then, with a flick of her wrist, she opened her whalebone and lace fan and began waving it furiously in front of her face. Despite the early hour, the room already felt uncomfortably stuffy and warm. But then, Frank's presence always seemed to elicit a heated reaction in Emma. In the past she experienced the heat of irritation. But this morning something else was certainly mixed with the irritation, which exasperated her all the more.

"Good mornin', Miz Watson. I reckon you were wonderin' if I was gonna show. Well, here I be. And you'll be happy to know that the committee also approved the likes of me." He waved his approval letter tauntingly in front of her.

A flurry of smart retorts flew through Emma's thoughts. However, when she raised her head to respond, she was struck by the gleam of excitement in Frank's eyes and she held her tongue. The vexation that typically accompanied her every encounter with this man now softened. She didn't want a sour mood to spoil this special day for either of them.

Emma, blinking rapidly, tried to hide the smile of anticipation that bubbled up from within. Frank wasn't the only one excited. The ambiance of the day so swept over Emma that she found herself actually complimenting Mr. Nance.

"You seem to have a real gift for dealing with children. I must confess, I am impressed." The words startled Emma, but not half as much as the spark of admiration that sprang into Frank's eyes. Flustered, she fanned herself all the more fiercely and nodded toward the stage. "We'd best turn our attentions to the platform, or we may miss something."

Forcing herself to stare forward, Emma wondered whatever possessed her to offer such a coquettish response. Now she was nothing short of awkward and uncertain of her every move.

Up on the stage, Mr. Hill handed the baby boy he had been jostling to one of the four older orphan girls seated behind him. He smoothed his coat lapels and cleared his throat before turning to address the crowd. "I realize that many of you are anxiously waiting to be matched with a child, but first we must outline the procedures we will follow and establish a few ground rules. . . ."

Mr. Hill continued with his remarks, but Emma's attentions were compellingly drawn to the children seated behind him. As she focused on the children, Frank's imposing presence seemed to blur. Each of the boys wore new knickers, suit coats, starched white shirts, and neckties. The four girls were outfitted in identical navy blue cotton dresses and stiff white pinafores.

Only four girls, Emma noted with a twinge of disappointment. *O Lord, is one of them to be mine?* She eagerly studied each of their faces as she prayed. They were all a bit older than she had expected them to be—at least nine or ten years old. None shared any obvious physical characteristics with Emma. None reminded Emma of her deceased husband, Stanley. Yet, as they doted and fawned quietly over the baby boy placed temporarily in their care, Emma was favorably impressed with their tenderness and affection toward the child. They appeared polite and well behaved. Certainly Emma could welcome any one of these four girls into her home.

Out of the corner of her eye, Emma caught a glimpse of Frank discreetly waving at the toddler boy whom he had carried "horsey-back" style into the opera house. The youngster scrunched his shoulders and returned Frank's greeting by waving with both hands. Emma simply shook her head in bewilderment at this mystifying man. What had happened to the always logical, practical, emotionless Mr. Nance? If the truth were told, Emma liked the new Frank much better than the old. Still, only time would tell whether the changes were lasting and sincere or just another self-serving scheme.

"In conclusion. . ." Mr. Hill's closing remarks jarred Emma from her daydreams, and she forced herself to focus on his words. "Before we call the first couple to come and select their child, let me emphasize two key points. These boys and girls understand that they are here in hopes of finding a new home. Unfortunately for several of them, their search for a family will not end here—for we have fifteen children among our group, including the one that is ill, and only a dozen homes which have met the standards for committee approval. Despite the unfavorable odds, we will not force any child over age eight to go with a family. The ultimate decision rests with the orphan. If they do not feel comfortable with any of the couples here today, they will board the train with us and travel on to the next town. Our journey west will continue until all of the children have been placed in suitable homes."

Without turning his back on the crowd, the speaker took three steps back and stood between two young boys who were poking at each other. Mr. Hill's close proximity to the youngsters immediately caused them to cease their banter and sit up straight in their chairs.

"Secondly," Mr. Hill continued, "there is a one-year waiting period between child-placement and legal adoption. If, during that period, a family is grievously dissatisfied with the child placed in their care, as has happened on a very rare occasion with our placements, the family should contact us immediately and the child will be removed from the home."

Mr. Hill paused just long enough to pull a large white handkerchief from his back pocket and wipe the perspiration from his brow. "I believe that concludes my remarks. Approved couples will be called in random order as their names are drawn from this hat." He held a black top hat high into the air. "As I call your name, bring your letter of recommendation and join me on the stage. We will meet with our two single candidates for child placement following the matching of all married couples with a child. All right, shall we begin?"

Emma nervously licked her lips and scrutinized the four girls. Would one of them remain for her? She relived that seemingly supernatural assurance that had swept over her when she was approved to adopt. As she looked at the limited number of girls, new doubts assailed her.

The children were instructed to stand and line up across the front of the platform. As soon as the girls stood, they huddled around the oldest one, who held the baby in her arms. The younger boys eagerly jumped from their seats, each trying to shove his way to the front of the line. The older ones took a military stance, their faces solemn and stony. But Emma couldn't help but notice one boy, about ten, who lagged behind, his chin drooping to his chest. His frail body and pale complexion added to the aura of gloom on his face, and he stood a full step behind the others. *Why, what a sad little boy*, Emma fleetingly thought. However, her concentration quickly shifted to Katy and Orville Greene, whose names

Mr. Hill had just called.

Without a moment's deliberation, Katy walked straight toward the four girls. Emma nervously chewed on her fingernails as she tried to guess which girl the annoying Mrs. Greene would chose. To her amazement, Katy reached out and took the dozing baby boy from the arms of his young caregiver. "Oh, Mr. Hill, Orville and I have always wanted a baby boy," Katy gushed. "This is simply a dream come true."

Emma's jaw dropped in amazement. Turning to Frank, she nearly choked on her surprised exclamation. "Why, I distinctly heard Katy say that she had to have a girl!"

Frank rolled his eyes. "That woman's more perplexin' than a two-headed cow!"

Shaking her head, Emma chuckled as Katy carried her new son down the aisle and out the back door while Orville stayed to complete the necessary paperwork.

The next couple called to the platform were strangers to Emma. They appeared shy and withdrawn, obviously the type of folks that preferred to keep to themselves. Straightaway, they walked toward the wan and fragile boy who trailed behind the others. The husband and wife bent to talk with the child, their words inaudible to everyone but him.

"No!" the boy protested, his determined voice ringing out in sharp contrast to his meek demeanor. "I won't go with you. I don't want no new family." Emma leaned forward in her seat, straining to catch the snatches of the ensuing discussion between the boy and Mr. Hill. But she started when Frank nudged her forearm.

"You watch—that boy's gonna be mine," he whispered, beaming like a man who had seen his destiny.

Chapter 4

"What on earth are you talking about?" Emma sputtered. "That boy obviously has more problems than two parents could hope to handle, let alone one. Besides, I thought you wanted an able-bodied worker to help out on the farm." As the sharp words left her mouth, Emma wondered if she should have voiced them. "I mean, he certainly looks too feeble and peaked to assist anyone in that regard. Why would you want to take on such a child? Really, you are full of more surprises than Katy Greene!"

"I know this sounds strange, comin' from the likes of me," he said with a tinge of mockery lacing his words, "but there is no logic or reason behind my hunches. There's just a certain feelin' deep down inside of me. I believe I could really help that boy. And as for being full of surprises, well, I suppose that's true. There's plenty about me you don't know." Frank tugged at the end of his moustache as he continued. "I am not the heartless monster you insist on making me out to be. This isn't the time or the place to discuss the matter, but I believe that a little hard work ain't goin' to hurt a boy. Fact is, a hard-work ethic might be one of the most valuable things a father could pass on to a son."

Her thoughts a mass of confusion, Emma looked at Frank and then back up to the pasty-faced boy. Although Frank's words were spoken almost tenderly, they echoed the stern sentiment she, as a young girl, had heard her harsh and despised stepfather express many times before.

Emma's own father died in battle during the Civil War, and her mother, left nearly destitute, had remarried Josiah Trumbull when Emma was eight-years-old. From that infamous day until the cold March morning when she finally screwed up the courage to run away, Emma had been forced to work like a slave girl in her own home. Although sympathetic, her fearful mother could only cower in submission and resignation to this tyrannical man. Mr. Trumbull's unwieldy insistence that a child be taught the value of a hard day's work robbed Emma of childhood's simple pleasures, and she grew old long before her time.

Would Frank treat this young boy with the same oppression that she had suffered under Mr. Trumbull's authority? Or was he speaking the truth when he pronounced that he was not the heartless monster that she had surmised him to be? Could Frank show true affection for a child? Emma longed to believe that the latter would be true. The poor boy cowering on the stage didn't appear able to withstand much more trauma in his young life. If any child needed a loving, stable home, it was this pathetic specimen of a child.

Emma found herself hoping that Mr. Hill could convince the boy to go with the reserved couple now looking to take him home. Then Frank would be forced to turn his attentions to one of the other orphan boys. But the melodrama now unfolding on the opera house stage continued as Mr. Hill turned his back on the pathetic waif and addressed the mild-mannered pair loud enough for the first few rows of the audience to hear. "If you don't mind my interference, I believe I know the ideal child for you. First, however, I need to ask. Would you consider a girl, or did you have your hearts set on a boy?"

The wife, twisting a handkerchief nervously, looked up to her husband and shrugged her shoulders in submissive deference to his wishes. "We're open to either, Mr. Hill," the balding man replied, running a hand over his smooth head. "Which child did you have in mind?" At this, Mr. Hill led the couple toward the cluster of twittering girls.

"She seems to be the perfect match for them," Frank whispered when the oldest of the orphan girls meekly nodded her assent to Mr. Hill. She stepped between her new parents and waved a timid good-bye to her friends as they walked off the platform.

That leaves only three girls, Emma figured fretfully. *O Lord. Is one of them going to be mine?* Her crumbling assurance that she was going to become a mother on this day dwindled as Mr. Hill proceeded through the list of married couples, for soon there were two girls remaining on stage. Then only one.

Despite her vested interest, Emma couldn't hold back her tears of joy at the sight of Ty and Rebecca Brownstone walking up to the platform and warmly embracing the last orphan girl. The Brownstones' only daughter, Sarah, had drowned two winters ago, after skating onto thin ice. Ty and Rebecca's acceptance of this orphan girl, who strikingly resembled their Sarah, signified their readiness to recover from their grief and lovingly parent once more.

However, hot tears of disappointment supplanted Emma's tears of joy when the Brownstones escorted their new daughter down the aisle. Emma's final hope for a child exited along with the departure of this last orphan girl. She could not begrudge the Brownstones a fresh start. Nor did she resent any of the other couples who had chosen the other three girls. But how could she have so totally misread the will of God? Emma had felt such a peace in her decision to adopt. Hadn't God given her Psalm 68:6 as her own special promise or sign? Had her secret wishes and desires superseded God's plan for her life? Hadn't her motives been pure?

As her mind filled with more unanswered questions and doubts, Emma whisked away any evidence of tears with the back of her gloved hand. Why would God deny her a child? Why? Hadn't she faithfully served Him and sought His will? Emma ground her teeth and forcefully swallowed the knots of anger nearly choking her. Anger toward God for rejecting her request to be a mother. And, however illogical, anger toward Frank Nance, for his earlier premonition about his child appeared likely to come true.

The auditorium began to quickly empty as the final adoptive couple approached the stage. Standing next to Mr. Hill, the pair faced the five remaining orphan boys. After several long moments of contemplation, they moved closer to the anemic, sour-faced boy who had so vehemently refused to go with the first couple. Perhaps the child's clear need for love and attention was tugging at many hearts. With his arms folded across his chest, the pathetic little urchin once again shook his head back and forth in refusal when Mr. Hill asked him if he wanted to go with the nice gentleman and lady to their home.

"Mr. and Mrs. Fletcher," Mr. Hill's voice echoed through the emptying auditorium, "I sincerely regret the obstinate nature of this boy. Rest assured, I shall have a stern word with him about his behavior today. However, you would surely be happier with one of these other fine and well-mannered young men." The placing agent cast a quick scowl in the direction of the offending youngster as he steered the Fletchers toward another boy.

Seemingly content with their newly matched son, this final couple made their way off the stage. As they left the hall, Mr. Hill stood at the edge of the platform and watched them depart. "Andrew Clymer, I'd like to speak with you over here," he said, motioning with his index finger for the skinny, sad-faced boy to join him. The youth stepped away from the other three boys, who seemed resigned that they had not been chosen this round.

As if he were ensnared in the plot of a classic play, Frank leaned forward, his every attention on the child he had declared would be his.

"Andrew, I don't mind telling you—you try my patience!" His stern but gentle voice floated from the stage, despite his attempts to speak confidentially. Placing his arm around the orphan's shoulder, Mr. Hill tenderly chided the child. "Don't you know, you are only hurting yourself and postponing the inevitable? You should have jumped at the chance to have a new family like the Fletchers. Nice folks like them don't come around at every train stop."

The chastised boy clutched the rim of his new hat as he calculated his response. "I ain't goin' nowhere without my sister, Mr. Hill. Not as long as I have any say."

"Er–um." Clearing his throat, Frank gently touched the top of Emma's hand. The brief pressure of his fingers against hers sent an unexpected tremor of tingles racing up her arm. Since Stanley's death, occasions for even the most casual of physical contact with a man were few and far between. But had she reacted so because a man touched her or because Frank touched her? Blinking in confusion, Emma tried to concentrate on his words.

"Excuse me, ma'am, but could you let me by?" Obviously, Frank had no inkling of Emma's response to his touch, for he focused solely on the boy. "I'd like a chance to speak to that boy and Mr. Hill."

"Certainly." Emma's knees began to tremble uncontrollably and fresh tears welled in her eyes as she shifted in her seat, allowing the preoccupied Frank to pass. "I suppose I should be going now, anyway," she muttered, a wave of loneliness washing over her. Not since the months immediately preceding Stanley's death had Emma felt so bereft. And her growing reaction to Frank Nance only heightened her despair and frustration.

She looked around the large hall to see that only a handful of spectators remained. Emma pulled her handbag and the package containing the doll close to her chest in preparation to leave, but the peaks and valleys of emotion she had traversed over the past few days now sapped her strength. Suddenly she didn't trust her trembling limbs enough to stand. She closed her eyes and drew a deep breath as she waited for her strength to return.

In this reflective moment, Emma's mind replayed a sentence just spoken by the boy being chastised on the stage. *I ain't goin' nowhere without my sister. . .not as long as I have any say.* At once, a strong dose of curiosity dashed aside thoughts of leaving. Her eyes popped open in time to watch Frank approach Andrew and Mr. Hill. What did the boy mean when he said he'd go nowhere without his sister? There were no girls left on the stage. Immediately, Emma recalled something she had dismissed earlier. Mr. Hill said an orphan was sick at the hotel. Was the sick child this boy's sister—a girl? A spark of hope ignited in her soul.

Frank knelt on one knee in front of the child. "Listen, I really think you need to come home with me," he said in the usual straightforward manner, which left Emma wincing in memory of his proposal to her.

"Yes, why don't you try and talk some sense into him," Mr. Hill interjected. "I've talked to him 'til I'm blue in the face, but my words seem to fall on deaf ears."

Rising to his full height, Frank towered over Mr. Hill. The child-placing agent took Frank by the arm and ushered him aside.

Emma leaned forward, straining to hear Mr. Hill's words as a new flood of possibilities caused her palms to moisten with anticipation. Once again, the psalm of promise began a slow etching on her mind. *He setteth the solitary in families.*

"The situation is this," Mr. Hill said, his whisper once again audible from Emma's close vantage point. "Andrew's four-year-old sister, Anna, is the one I mentioned earlier as being so sick. She contracted a nasty case of whooping cough, and we couldn't possibly bring her out in public until her health improves."

The words seemed a command for Emma to rise. Still clutching the box containing the doll, she tiptoed toward the stage in hopes of catching his every word. Evidently there was another orphan. A girl. And her name was Anna. *He setteth the solitary in families.* Her heart pounded ferociously as fresh tears stung her eyes.

Anna. My grandmother's name. Emma mouthed the name again silently. *Anna. O Lord. Is this the girl meant for me?* The prayer wove in and out of Emma's soul as Mr. Hill continued.

"Fact of the matter is, we can't proceed with our journey until she gets better. She might not survive another day on the train. You see how thin young Andrew, here, is?" Emma's gaze followed Frank's and Mr. Hill's as they surveyed the boy. "Well, he's plump as a melon compared to little Anna."

Mr. Hill released Frank's arm and approached Andrew, laying a gentle hand on his shoulder again as he spoke. "We don't like to separate family members if we can help it, but so often we must. Certainly, splitting up siblings and placing them in good homes is preferable to the street urchin's life they would lead in New York City.

"I see no other way but to wait 'til Anna's better and then place her with a family farther on down the line." Mr. Hill slowly shook his head from side to side. "But Andrew's luck is going to run out soon. He's passed up several gracious offers from folks willing to give him a good home. There aren't many couples looking to take on a ten-year-old boy as puny as he is. It sure isn't likely that we can find a family to take both him and Anna into their home."

He setteth the solitary in families. He setteth the solitary in families.

"Might I have a word with you, Mr. Hill?" Emma called out, unable to remain silent a moment longer. What had begun as a prayer and a hunch now blossomed into certainty. Little Anna surely was the child God had meant for Emma all along. Her skirts swished beneath her as she scampered up the stairs onto the stage. "I believe I can recommend a reasonable plan."

Emma's boots tapped loudly against the wooden platform as she hurried forward. Due to the quick traverse onto the stage and her nervousness over this hastily conceived plan, she was short of breath. She put her hand to her heart and gasped as she addressed Mr. Hill. "Why not. . .let—let me. . .take Andrew's sister?" She was finally able to fill her lungs sufficiently to finish the sentence without halting. "And place Andrew with Mr. Nance?"

Emma cast a sideways glance at Frank. From his puzzled look, her atypical behavior had left him mystified for a second time within a morning's span. His bewilderment was understandable. Rarely did she act so impulsively.

In all honesty, she should have discussed the matter with Frank first. For, if they each took a sibling, they would surely be forced to face one another with frequency. In light of their current situation, such regular encounters might prove uncomfortable at best. The varying questions flitting across Frank's face reflected Emma's own thoughts.

Have I given this matter sufficient thought? She had been so confident that this was God's plan that she hadn't even paused long enough to breathe a prayer. Well, she couldn't stop now. Emma would smooth things over with Frank later, if need be.

Nervously grinding her boots into the grit on the stage floor, Emma continued pleading her case with Mr. Hill, not daring to look at Frank. "You see, sir, the two of us are acquaintances, and I'm sure we could come up with a suitable visitation arrangement for the children. We've each been approved to take one child."

Emma rummaged through her purse and pulled out her prized paper, hoping that her sweaty palms didn't cause the ink to run. "See, here's my letter from the committee."

"I think you've come up with a satisfactory plan," Mr. Hill said, giving the proffered document a perfunctory skimming. "No doubt Anna's recovery would be hastened under a mother's care. And if you could manage to take her home today, the rest of us could catch tomorrow morning's train for Dodge City. Still, I'm not the one who needs convincing." He tucked his thumbs under his suspender straps as he turned to face Andrew. "What do you think of this nice lady's idea?"

Before Andrew could object, Frank crouched down and looked the young fellow square in the eyes. "The plan seems perfectly logical to me. Don't you agree? It wouldn't bother you none just havin' me as your paw—and no maw, now would it?"

Andrew shook his head slowly from side to side. "No, sir. I wouldn't mind. I'm used to not havin' no womenfolk around, less'n you count Anna." He threw a sheepish glance in Emma's direction as he explained. "You see, my mama died when little Anna was borned. Then, two years ago, our granny that watched after us joined Mama in heaven, too. That left our papa to take care of us kids the best he could.

"Not havin' a mama don't bother me one bit. Truth is, I kinda take to the idea." Emma caught Andrew warily looking at her once again. "B–b–but. . ." The boy hesitated before speaking his mind. "But, my papa always tol' me that if anything ever happen' to him, I was to watch after my little sister and take good care of her. I always promised him I would. Last March, our papa died whilst savin' me and Anna when our apartment buildin' burnt. So, as long as I'm still breathin', the promise I made my papa is a promise I aim to keep.

"Please don't take no offense," Andrew said, bowing his head submissively before the trio of adults. "I'm not meanin' any disrespect. But I don't see how I can watch after li'l Anna if you split us up."

"Take your time and think things through, young man." Emma sandwiched his right hand between her gloved palms. "You and your sister would live close to one another. Mr. Nance's farm, where you would live, is on the outskirts of town. I live right here in Shady Grove—just a block or so down the street.

"I promise you, little Anna would have a loving home and she'd be a real comfort and companion to me. You see, my husband died a few years back and I've been awfully lonely ever since.

"If you go to live with Mr. Nance on his farm, as he's asking you to do, I'm sure he'd allow you to visit Anna frequently. Now, wouldn't you, Frank?"

At the casual use of his given name, Emma shot a glance at Frank to see if he'd noticed her slip. His dancing gaze met hers, obviously enjoying this first crossing of verbal propriety. He briskly nodded as a smile tugged at the corner of his lips. "Certainly, Emma," he replied, seeming to take great pleasure in emphasizing her given name. "You know I'd do anything I could to help the boy keep a solemn vow."

Emma turned her attention quickly back to Andrew before Frank could see the color rising in her warming cheeks. If only the man were more. . .were more affectionate and. . .and dedicated to the Lord. . . .

"I'd love your sister, Andrew, and I'd take good care of her," Emma rushed, intent on sweeping those disturbing thoughts about Frank from her mind. "What do you say? Can we at least give it a try?"

Chapter 5

rank rose from his kneeling position to tower over the boy. He jumped brusquely back into the conversation before Andrew could respond.

"The idea makes good sense to me. Remember, your sister's sick. You don't want her to have to get back on that train again if you can help it, now, do you? And you've no guarantees that a better situation will come along. Might pay you to be reasonable about this. What do you say?"

Frank looked down at his pant legs and began slapping at the dust his knees had gathered while kneeling on the well-traversed stage. "I could sure use a young man such as yourself to help me out on my farm."

Oh, Frank. Hush, will you? Emma wanted to scold him aloud. *Let the boy think things through for himself. Don't you realize that you always push too hard?*

Fresh fears gripped Emma as she watched him talking to the boy. Before her eyes, Frank was rapidly returning to his forever logical and emotionless ways. Perhaps she had acted too hastily in proposing this placing-out plan. For despite the fact that she was gaining a daughter, it also meant that this poor little boy would be going to live with Frank.

In her eagerness to parent his sister, had she sentenced Andrew to a fate worse than orphanage life—a future with a duplicate of her step-father, Mr. Trumbull? Whatever it took, Emma would not allow such a tragedy to occur. Andrew Clymer didn't know it yet, but if the need arose, he had a formidable ally in her. Then she remembered Frank with that toddler. Sighing in resignation, Emma hoped Mr. Nance would disprove her concerns.

The boy's ashen face appeared paler still as he bit his lower lip and contemplated the situation. He stared at the floor for several long moments while the adults waited for his reply. With the toe of a new black leather shoe, he kicked at a loose slat in the wood floor and haltingly began. "W–w–well. . .I suppose we might give it a try. Mrs. Watson seems like a nice lady, and bein' as how she's a widow and lonely and all, I know Anna would keep her in good company." Andrew tossed Emma a weak smile before throwing his head back to look up at Frank.

"Mr. Nance, sounds like you could use a hand on your farm. But you'll have to teach me, sir. I ain't had no experience working in the out-a-doors."

"Now, Andrew," Mr. Hill said, "I believe you have made a wise and mature choice. I'm confident you will be very happy with Mr. Nance. But let me remind you, this agreement works two ways. Mr. Nance may decide to return you to our care if you do not behave yourself in a manner befitting a proper young man. Is that understood? You are not to cause this kind man any trouble. Rather, you are to be a help to him."

Mr. Hill turned to Frank and Emma. "An agent from the state will come by Shady Grove to check on all our orphans in a few weeks. After that, we expect to receive a report concerning the children at least twice a year. If there are problems, you may certainly contact us at any time."

"So, the matter's settled then," Frank stated, reaching for the agent's hand and enthusiastically pumping it up and down. "Where's that contract I'm supposed to sign?"

Mr. Hill turned to retrieve the necessary paperwork from a table set up just off the stage, but Andrew called after him, a fresh note of panic in his voice. "Wait. I can't go with Mr. Nance yet. I've got to tell Anna good-bye."

Instinctively, Emma reached out to offer motherly comfort and assurance to the boy, but she stopped and hastily pulled her arm back to her side. The three remaining boys slumped in wooden folding chairs, awaiting instruction from Mr. Hill. Emma understood the nature of young boys well enough. If she were to hug Andrew in front of his friends, the act would thoroughly embarrass him. Instead, she affirmed him with an assuring wink and turned to Frank.

"Mr. Nance, I know you're itching to get back to your farm. Undoubtedly you've got work to do and I hate to impose. . . ." Her voice trailing, she worried that Frank would think she was overstepping her boundaries by meddling once again. But his nod gave her the courage to go on.

"You'd be doing me a real kindness if you'd allow Andrew to be the one to tell Anna of their separate placements before you leave town. Such news would be better coming from him than from a stranger like me—and he'd have a chance to say his proper farewells."

Andrew nodded his appreciation to Emma for interceding on his behalf. And when both Frank and Mr. Hill agreed to her request, she watched the boy's fretful countenance relax.

As soon as all of Frank's and Emma's child-placement legalities had been tended to, Mr. Hill shoved the official documents into an already bulging leather case and prepared to go. Then the ragtag parade of orphans and adults marched, by twos and threes, down the stage stairs and out the opera house door.

After breathing the fumes of burning kerosene all morning, Emma eagerly filled her lungs with the dry June air as she led the processional toward the Imperial Hotel. Mr. Hill fell into step beside her, followed by Frank and Andrew. The three older orphan boys brought up the rear.

Emma attempted to appear attentive when Mr. Hill launched into a verbose anecdote about a recent adventure on the orphan train. But in actuality, she was straining to catch the conversation between Frank and Andrew as they walked behind her.

Above the squeaks and clatter of passing buggies, Emma could hear Frank answering his new son's rapid volley of questions about life on the farm. By the sound of the boy's interested voice, a transformation was beginning in the sullen child. A smile played at the corners of Emma's lips while she eavesdropped on their amiable conversation. She prayed that all her worries about Frank's coldheartedness were invalid.

This unmarried farmer might very well be the perfect father for the boy after all. Andrew needed someone like Frank—someone to devote undivided attention to him. Emma's smile of pleasure became an inner chuckle as she thought that, perhaps, Andrew might soften Frank's rough edges a bit as well. Surely a ten-year-old could chisel into that granite heart. Teach him how to love. Get him ready for a wife. . . Frank had a long way to go before Emma would reconsider his proposal of marriage, but she'd seen a glimmer of hope in his reaction to Andrew today.

The swinging signboard of the Imperial Hotel came into view, and Emma's pulse pounded in her temples. A marriage of a different sort replaced all thoughts of Frank. For today she and Anna would enter into the union of mother and child. Refusing to succumb to cold feet, Emma had already committed "to have and to hold" Anna as her daughter from this day forward. She had accepted and assumed responsibility for the child—sight unseen.

The anticipated moment of first meeting drew nearer with each clipped step she took down the boardwalk. Soon Emma's dream of a daughter would take on flesh and bone. The group followed Mr. Hill through the Imperial's frosted glass doors, across the lobby, and into the hotel's ornate sitting room. The lavish furnishings and gilded fixtures created an air of opulence that seemed out of place in the prairie town of Shady Grove.

"Miz Watson. . ." Mr. Hill removed his top hat and picked at invisible lint on its brim. "I'd appreciate it if you'd just have a seat for a few minutes and allow me to situate these boys in their rooms. Then I'll accompany Andrew to his sister's bedside as he shares the news of their placement with her. Someone will come to fetch you soon, ma'am, so you can meet little Anna."

Pushing his bent wire-rimmed spectacles up his nose, the agent's sagging shoulders testified to his fatigue as he turned to address Frank. "I appreciate your patience, sir. I know you're anxious to get your boy home. I don't expect this to take long. Please excuse us." Mr. Hill offered a courteous bow to Emma then led Andrew and the other boy out of the room.

From across the lobby, Andrew glanced over his shoulder and waved at Frank. The beaming new father returned the gesture as the boy disappeared up the stairs. "Well," Frank said, turning to face Emma, "there's no use in standin' if we can sit. After you." He motioned to two empty chairs beside the grand piano.

Emma perched on the edge of the overstuffed chair and settled her package and purse on the lamp stand as Frank plopped into the seat next to hers. "I'm glad to see that you aren't upset with me for suggesting that I take Andrew's sister. I wasn't sure just how you would respond."

"I thought your idea was a grand one. Why would I have been upset? Fact is, I'm still hopin' you'll reconsider my proposal of marriage. The way I figure, this new connection we share with Andrew and Anna will increase my chances at changin' your mind." He produced an audacious wink that left Emma with no choice but to reach for her lace and whalebone fan and wave it furiously in front of her face.

"Mr. Nance," she said firmly, "there is no reason for you to continue—"

"No reason, Emma?" he teased.

"Really! Would you please—"

"The facts are, ma'am, either you're warmin' up to me or my name's not Frank Nance."

"My feelings for you in no way—"

"So! You do have feelin's for me?"

"I never said that," she insisted, glancing across the lobby at the distracted hotel clerk.

"Well, regardless of what you care to 'fess up to, my offer does still stand."

"So does my rejection! You need to know, Mr. Nance, I am a woman of deep faith. I could never—absolutely never—marry a man who—"

"Hey! I've got faith!"

"But you never darken a church door!"

"I'll go to church if that'll make you happy." He smiled hopefully.

"I'm terribly sorry, but we seem to be miscommunicating in the most severe manner. I'm talking about—about—what I'm tryin to say is—is. . ." She snapped the fan closed.

"Well, go on."

"I would never marry a man who isn't dedicated to the Lord—with his whole heart. I'm talkin' about more than just a shallow acknowledgment that there is a God."

"I'm not a heathen by no means, Emma," he drawled. "I've been a Christian since my maw led me to the Lord when I was about Andrew's age."

"But is Christ Lord of your life. . .or are you?" The question settled between them, creating a chasm that she knew would never be removed unless Frank could answer in the affirmative.

With the question left unanswered, Emma walked toward the white marble fireplace. Before turning her back to Frank, she caught him watching her with an esteem she had not previously seen on his countenance. Strangely, she sensed that, for the first time, she had somehow gained Mr. Nance's complete respect. How odd that the very issue that separated them would also deepen his regard. Firmly pivoting away from him, she awaited until Mr. Hill returned.

Regard? Did Frank Nance perhaps care for Emma more than he had admitted?

"Are you ready?" A renewed burst of energy seemed to enthuse the agent as he appeared in the arched doorway. "If so, come on with me. Andrew did a fine job of preparing Anna to go with you. She seems excited about meeting her new mother."

Emma skittered lightly across the lush oriental area rug to grab her beaded handbag and the gingham-dressed baby doll. Frank rose from his chair while she gathered her things. His dark eyes reflected the sincerity of his apology as he spoke. "I'm sorry about forever bringin' up my proposal. There wasn't any call for my bein' so selfish while you were waitin' to meet your little girl. I hope all goes well for you upstairs. That's the gospel truth."

"Thanks." She glanced up to see those dark eyes spilling forth with words unspoken. And for the first time, Emma admitted to herself what she had desperately wanted to deny. Despite her attempts to voice her dislike of him, Frank Nance had stirred her pulse for many months.

Nervously excusing herself, she joined Mr. Hill in the hotel lobby and forced all thoughts of Frank's proposal from her mind. A lightning bolt of anticipation seemed to shoot through her, and she shivered with giddy energy. She would have taken the stairs two at a time had no one else been watching.

Mr. Hill led the way down the carpeted hall to the door marked 2-D. Without bothering to knock, he turned the brass doorknob and swung the door open wide, then waited for Emma to enter ahead of him. She stepped past him into the austere room to see a thin woman, dressed in black, sitting in a straight-backed chair next to the room's lone window. The weary woman gave Emma a cursory nod in greeting, making no effort to stand.

At the head of the brass bed, holding on to a post, Andrew stood as though guarding royalty. But the sad-faced child Emma had observed at the opera house was gone, replaced by a grinning ten-year-old. "Here she is, Anna," Andrew bent over the bed and exclaimed. "Your new mama. See, I told you she was pretty."

Nothing could have prepared Emma for the breath-catching moment that followed. A knot of emotion clogged her throat. Goose flesh erupted down her arms. Tears blurred her eyes and spilled onto her cheeks. For eyes the color of roasted chestnuts, big and round as coat buttons, now peeked timidly over the top of crisp white sheets. The flush of fever painted rouge-red circles of color on the child's cheeks. A mass of flaxen ringlets framed her china-doll face.

She's the most beautiful little girl I've ever seen, Emma thought as she approached the bed. *And she's my daughter. My child.* Anna reached out to Emma with twig-thin arms and, in that simple act, erased any of the new mother's misgivings about adoption. Emma rooted her maternal bonds the instant she scooped the child into her arms and held her close. As she buried her hands in Anna's curls, she knew she held the miraculous fulfillment of God's promise. The Lord had answered her prayers.

God setteth the solitary in families. The psalm that had become Emma's constant prayer was now her song of celebration. But another scripture verse joined her chorus of praise. Echoing Hannah of Old Testament days, Emma's heart sang, "For this child I prayed; and the Lord hath given me my petition which I asked of him."

Yes, the Lord had surely heard and answered Emma's prayers.

Thirty minutes later, Emma stepped over the threshold of her daughter's bedroom with Frank and Andrew close behind. "This is your very own room, sweetheart," Emma announced to the flushed, fevered child Frank carried in his arms. "I fixed it up just for you."

Anna's dark eyes grew round with wonderment as she surveyed the room. White Irish lace curtains adorned the windows. A cushioned rocker stood in one corner, ready to soothe both mother and child. On the dressing table sat a lace-trimmed basket, brimming with hand-sewn hair ribbons of every hue. The pearl-handled mirror with matching brush and comb looked too pretty to use.

"I'll just pull back these blankets and we'll tuck you right in." Emma turned back the bedding and vigorously plumped a down-filled pillow before motioning to Frank to lay down the child. She wanted to open the bedroom window and circulate the stifling air, but she feared that a breeze, perhaps filled with dust from the road, would aggravate Anna's croup. As they had prepared to leave the hotel, Anna had suffered a severe coughing spell. Emma wanted to avoid a repeat of that painful episode at all costs. The window remained shut.

Under the watchful eyes of Andrew, Frank gingerly settled the four-year-old between the starched white bed linens. From the end of the bed, Emma shook out a lightweight summer quilt and spread it on top of the sheets. Then, smoothing the covers as she worked her way around the side of the bed, Emma wrapped them snugly around the wisp of a girl so that only her little head poked out.

Beneath the layers of bedclothes, Anna cradled her new doll baby, refusing to relinquish her treasure even momentarily. Emma couldn't resist the urge to brush back the tangled mass of blond curls from Anna's forehead and deposit a feather-light kiss.

Straightening to ease the crick in her back, Emma noticed Andrew standing in the middle of the room, still holding the small parcel of

Anna's things. She walked to the boy and extended her hands to accept the twine-tied package.

The curious boy, relieved of his burden, craned his neck to inspect every inch of Anna's new quarters. "She ain't never had no room of her own before," Andrew said as Emma shook out Anna's new dress and hung it in the cedar wardrobe. "Until we went to the orphanage, she always slept with me."

Emma detected a twinge of jealousy over his little sister's good fortune as Andrew posed a question to Frank. "Uh, Mr. Nance, do I get my own room at your place, too?"

In response, Frank reached over and ruffled Andrew's mousy brown hair. "You can take your pick from several rooms on the second floor of the farmhouse. The folks I bought the farm from had a passel of kids, so they built the place real big.

"But, boy, if you keep on referrin' to me as Mr. Nance, you'll be sleepin' in the barn. What don't you just call me 'Paw'?"

Andrew scratched his head and studied his new shoes. " 'Pahw,' huh?" he said, attempting to mimic Frank's southern twang. "If that's what you want, sir, I'll try."

"Well. . ." Frank hesitated. "You might have to ease into this 'Paw' business. I understand your feelin' awkward and all. Take your time. I won't push you none. And I was just funnin' with you about makin' you sleep in the barn." The laugh lines extending from Frank's eyes creased deeply as he smiled at Andrew.

Watching this bonding interaction between father and son, Emma felt a familiar fire rising in her cheeks and causing her palms to perspire. But the frustration and anger she had once felt in Frank's presence didn't cause this flood of warmth. This heat stemmed from her happy surprise in seeing again—as she had on several occasions throughout the day—a pleasantly different side of Frank. Emma longed for Frank to understand what she was trying to tell him in the hotel lobby.

"All this talk about home reminds me that there's plenty of work waiting for us at the farm," Frank stated, ushering Andrew toward the door. "The cows will be beggin' for milkin' soon. You'd best be tellin' your sister good-bye.

"Emma. . .er. . .Miz Watson. . ." He paused to expose her to humorous scrutiny.

Her cheeks warming, Emma needlessly fussed with Anna's covers.

"Unless there's somethin' else you're needin' from us, we'll see ourselves out."

She glanced up just in time to see Andrew instantly tense at the pronouncement of his imminent separation from Anna. "Wait!" Emma blurted, desperate to ease the boy's fears. "None of us have had a chance to eat lunch yet, and I left a pot of beef stew warming on the stove this morning. I can throw a meal together in a matter of minutes. It's the least I could do since you've been so kind to carry Anna home from the hotel and all."

Frank lifted his head and sniffed at the air. "I've been smellin' your cookin' since I walked in the door. I was hopin' you'd ask us to stay. Andrew, why don't you look after your sister for just a bit while I help Miz Watson set the table for dinner."

"I've got an even better idea," Emma interjected. "Let's prepare meal trays for us all. We can eat right here in Anna's room so she won't need to be left alone."

"Lead the way, ma'am." Frank waved his arm in grandiose fashion, pointing to the open door. "Or would you rather I just follow my nose?"

Preceding Frank into the kitchen, Emma walked straight to the cupboard and began pulling soup bowls from the shelf. As she placed them on the counter next to the potbellied stove, Frank stepped beside her and lifted the lid from the iron soup kettle. A cloud of fragrant steam escaped into the air. Inhaling deeply, he leaned over to Emma and asked, "What can I do to help?"

When he spoke, her hands traitorously quivered as she spooned stew into the bowls. Emma had not been alone in a room with a man these past three years. She was far from prepared for the rush of growing excitement Frank's presence evoked. In the hotel lobby, he expressed his suspicion of her reaction to him, and just knowing that he suspected made her quiver all the more. Emma reminded herself that just two days ago she had stormed out of his presence, hoping never to see him again. But had she really desired to rid her life of Frank?

She handed him the soup ladle, resisting the urge to look into his eyes, lest her renewed resolve disintegrate. "You can take over this chore, if you don't mind. I need to slice up some bread."

In the moments that followed, Emma scurried about the kitchen collecting the makings of an impromptu feast. On one tray, she placed the soup bowls and a crockery pitcher of buttermilk. On another, she precariously piled plates of thick slices of cheese, sourdough bread spread with strawberry jam, and a molasses pie. While she worked, she chattered incessantly, reliving the day's Christmas-like excitement, leaving no opportunity for Frank to comment. At all costs, she couldn't allow him to suspect her vulnerability.

Within half an hour, Frank and Andrew sat on the homemade rag rug in the middle of Anna's room and crisscrossed their legs in preparation for their indoor picnic as Emma arranged the trays next to them. When she announced that she would offer grace, the ten-year-old sheepishly dropped the cheese he held halfway between the plate and his mouth. And although she had a lengthy list of blessings for which she wanted to give thanks to the Lord, she kept her prayer brief. She didn't want to torture the young boy.

Emma watched in amazement as the scrawny Andrew inhaled his meal. Judging by the way he attacked his food, he hadn't eaten his fill in quite a while. Frank protested when the boy grabbed the last piece of bread, but he consoled himself with a generous slice of pie.

"Save some appetite, son," Frank teased the boy. "I'm roastin' you an elephant for supper, and I'll be expectin' you to eat it all." Andrew, whose face was buried behind his bread, stopped eating just long enough to confirm that Frank's words were spoken in jest.

"You keep eating like that and I'll stay busy making you bigger clothes." Emma chuckled.

"You're a good cook, ma'am." Andrew wiped the jam from his mouth with the sleeve of his shirt. "I ain't eaten this good since our granny died."

Unfortunately, Emma's efforts to feed Anna were not met with Andrew's same measure of success. The infirmed child allowed her new mother to spoon-feed her only three bites of stew before she pursed her lips together and refused to eat more.

When the meal had been consumed and Andrew had all but licked the plates dry, Frank stood to his feet. "Andrew and I will carry these trays back to the kitchen for you; then we'd better be gettin' home. The boy's right, though, Emma. You are a great cook."

Despite the pleasure his praise evoked, Emma refused to look directly at Frank for fear of repeating her earlier heart-fluttering reaction. She rose from Anna's bedside and stacked the bowl of barely-touched stew on top of the other dirty dishes. "Perhaps you and Andrew could come for dinner after church a week from Sunday? Lord willing, Anna should be better by then." *And I'll have my emotions back under control*, she added silently.

"Yeah, I be better then." Anna's hoarse whisper floated from the feather bed, soliciting smiles from all the others in the room. But even this brief attempt to contribute to the conversation brought on a fit of barking coughs. Emma hurried to her side and, scooping the child into her arms, began rocking Anna back and forth.

After several long seconds of violent crouping, Anna began gasping for air. Emma looked at Frank for assurance but instead saw genuine concern in his face.

"I'd best be gettin' Doc Gilbert, don't you think?" The rhetorical question needed no answer, for he and Andrew were already headed for the door.

Chapter 6

"P oor little thing is weaker than a kitten, Mrs. Watson. She's so worn out from coughin' that she fell fast asleep in the middle of my examination." Dr. Gilbert softly closed the door to Anna's bedroom and joined the anxious trio of Emma, Frank, and Andrew in the hallway.

"That croup of hers does sound mighty bad. I expect you're gonna fret over every coughin' spell, seein' as you're a new mama and all." Shady Grove's aged physician stroked his bushy gray beard as he spoke. "But listen to me and believe me when I say, I'm sure the child is goin' to pull through, what with your good nursin' and attention.

"There are several things you can do to help her." The doctor's soothing voice took on a serious tone as he rattled off his list of instructions. "First off, soon as I leave I want you to hang a wet sheet near her bed to put moisture into the room. That should help control her cough. And, don't let her lie flat. Keep her propped up so her airways are clear. One good way to do this is to hold her and rock her. You probably wouldn't mind that, now would you?"

The doctor set his black leather bag on the hall runner and stooped to fumble through its contents. "Now, she will likely fight you over it, but you must persist. I want you to give the young'un a teaspoon of this elixir every time she starts a coughin' spell." He pulled the cork stopper and passed the bottle under Emma's nose. "I want you to smell it 'fore

I leave it with you, because most folks think it's ruined when they get their first whiff."

She jerked her head back instantly, her eyes watering at the pungent stench.

"Hey, let me smell," Andrew said, boyish curiosity oozing from him. The doctor obliged his request, and all the adults laughed aloud at his sour face. "Cowboy howdy!" he exclaimed. "I hope I don't never get sick."

The doctor resealed the dark glass container and handed it to Emma. "I know it smells powerful bad. Made it myself from onions, garlic, paregoric, and spirits of camphor mixed in with honey, and I know the potion works. Other than this, the only other medicine I can recommend is time. The cough should run its course in a few days."

Emma stuffed the amber bottle of cough syrup into her apron pocket as the physician picked up his bag and prepared to leave.

"We'll follow you out, Doc," Frank said. "I need to get the boy settled and tend to my chores.

Pinching the crown of his felt hat between his finger and thumb, he politely tipped the headpiece toward Emma before donning it. "Andrew and I will see you a week from Sunday for lunch, if your offer still stands."

"Certainly," she replied. "I'll save you two a place on our pew at church as well. Service begins at ten-thirty."

"Well. . ." His lips formed into a stubborn line. "I'll make certain the boy is there."

So that's it. That's your answer, Emma thought, while gritting her teeth. He had not fully answered her questions about his relationship with the Lord in the Imperial Hotel's lobby. Until now. And the obstinate tilt of his square chin suggested that Frank Nance wouldn't bow at an altar in prayer for any woman.

That's all fine by me, Emma thought as Frank and his son stepped onto her massive porch. *If and when you do decide to give your all to the good Lord, it needs to be something for yourself, not for me.* Nonetheless, the dull ache in Emma's spirit attested to her keen disappointment.

But no sooner had she shut the door on her three visitors than a sole, painful cough rang through the house, dispelling all thoughts of

Frank's infuriating ways. She paused briefly, her back against the door, and took a deep cleansing breath. Emma's prayers had been answered. She was a mother now. But did she have the skills necessary to nurse such a sickly, frail child? Pinpricks of fear stabbed ever so lightly at Emma's euphoria.

Holding her breath against the hope that there would be no new coughs, she peeked around the door into Anna's bedroom. The wisp of a child had awakened and was sitting up in her bed, stroking her doll's hair. Her daughter. This precious little girl with big brown eyes—her daughter. Anna's soft voice would soon call her "Mama." The two of them would share the same family name.

Had only a few hours lapsed since Emma first laid eyes on her? The thought seemed odd as she surveyed this heartwarming scene. Anyone would think, to look at Anna now, that the little princess had always ruled from this quilted throne.

❧

One week later, Frank leaned against the front porch railing and finished his morning cup of coffee as Andrew crossed the barnyard to begin his morning chores. In just a week's time, he had seen tremendous changes in the boy. Thanks to Maria's starchy Mexican dinners and the hours they'd spent together outdoors doing chores, Andrew no longer looked sickly pale and starvation-thin. Emma was sure to be surprised when they showed up for lunch the day after tomorrow. The imagined scene left Frank smiling in amusement. He derived certain pleasure at the prospect of proving to Emma that a few days' work did any boy a good service.

Frank looked forward to Sunday afternoon for other reasons as well. He wanted Andrew to see for himself that Anna was all right. Despite the growing camaraderie he and Andrew shared, Frank knew the boy worried about his sister constantly. Several times throughout the course of a day, Andrew would turn to him and ask how he thought Anna was getting along. Seldom had he witnessed such fierce loyalty in grown men, much less a child. His devotion to his sister constituted more than a deathbed promise made to his father that he was honor-bound to fulfill. Andrew obviously cared deeply for Anna. Yes, for the boy's sake, he was anxious for Sunday to come around.

But Frank wouldn't be honest if he didn't admit that he was eager for Sunday to arrive for his own sake as well. Over the past week, when he'd lain down to sleep, a pleasant memory replayed over and over in his mind. Miz Emma Watson had been nothing short of flustered in his presence since that meeting in the general store. And Frank was beginning to look back on their yearlong acquaintance and suspect that she might have been trying to hide her true feelings for quite some time.

However, a new problem now surfaced with the fair lady. She said she wanted a man who was more committed to the Lord. At first her comments had amused him. Then they had angered him. How dare she be his spiritual judge? But now her words had grown into a recurring mantra in his mind and left him less than comfortable. The truth of the matter was, he knew he could do better by the Lord. Much better. And now that Andrew had come along, the boy deserved the same kind of religious upbringing Frank had been given. But he just wasn't certain he was ready to turn the whole thing over to the Lord. He was nice and comfortable keeping the Lord at arm's length.

Tossing the cold dregs of his coffee into the cracked dry ground next to the porch, he stood and dismissed the disturbing thoughts. *We could sure use some rain,* Frank said to himself as he studied the morning sky. The wispy, streaked clouds didn't hold much promise of breaking this insufferable hot and dry spell. Scanning the horizon, Frank was seized by a strong sense of foreboding, for a peculiar gray haze enveloped the western wheat fields. At once Frank noticed the faint, unpleasant acrid smell that always accompanied a distant fire. His gut twisted in dread. He had heard that a plague of grasshoppers had turned the skies black over Colorado, leaving devastated crops in their wake. But grasshoppers did not produce such a smell. Frank decided to investigate.

Just then, Andrew emerged from the chicken coop and began scattering feed. Frank paused a few moments more to watch his son. The boy's shoes quickly disappeared beneath the brood of bantam chickens as the birds pecked frantically at the seed, their red combs bobbing feverishly. "You've been cornered by chickens, son." Frank laughed with a father's pleasure, and Andrew waved happily to his pa.

Feeding the chickens had become one of Andrew's favorite chores, for when he was done he could hold the cheeping chicks that filled a warming tray just inside the hen house door. Frank had long ago forgotten how much fun such simple pleasures could bring a boy. He had caught himself laughing and smiling more in the past few days than he had in many years. A boy was good for a man's soul.

Suddenly, the gravelly bark of a coonhound in the barnyard shattered the early morning quiet to announce the arrival of a visitor. Frank stepped off the front porch and waved in greeting to a worried-looking man mounted on a sweating, stamping horse. After a brief exchange of words that confirmed Frank's former suspicions, the rider turned his horse, spurring the animal into a full gallop as he rode toward the rising sun.

"Andrew, come here, boy. I need to talk with you." Frank, his stomach clutching ever tighter, didn't wait for the puzzled child to catch up with him. Instead, he hurried into the barn and set about the task of saddling Shadow. Andrew was panting by the time he reached the busy stall.

"Listen, there's a grass fire threatenin' to destroy the Taylor farm, and they're roundin' up as many neighbors as they can to help fight the blaze. I've got to go and see what I can do to help. What with this confounded drought and all, if the Good Lord doesn't help us, them hungry flames will soon spread onto our own land.

"Oh, and Andrew, I realize you don't speak Spanish, and Señor and Señorita Ramirez's English ain't too good. But when they get here, do your best to explain things to them. Draw pictures if you have to, but the smoke should speak for itself. I expect Pedro will come and help us as soon as he gets the word. I don't have time to gab about it. I'll be home just as soon as I can. Maria will watch after you when she arrives. Until then, you are to stay here and tend to your chores, do you hear? I don't need to be worryin' about you on top of everything else."

"Yes, sir. I understand. Don't you fret about me. I'll be just fine."

❧

Andrew watched until Frank rode Shadow over the horizon, then he turned and walked slowly back toward the chicken coop to complete the first of his unfinished chores. The warm prairie wind blew the smell of smoke into the barnyard. A rush of painful memories seized him as, in his mind's eye, he saw his father rushing back into the burning apartment to rescue Anna. Was he to lose another father to the flames? Did some kind of curse follow him?

And what of the fire? Would it spread into town and perhaps burn the Widow Watson's seamstress shop? His father's dying words now haunted him: *Watch after your little sister. Take good care of her.* Yet his new pa's words seemed a direct contradiction to his duty: *You are to stay here and tend to your chores, do you hear? I don't need to be worryin' about you on top of everything else.*

But if he stayed at the farm, Anna might die in the fire. What had he done, allowing a stranger lady to take on his responsibility while he'd headed off to play on the farm? He must check on Anna. Now. When last he'd seen her, Anna had been frightfully sick.

Chapter 7

The fidgeting Anna danced in front of the full-length mirror as Emma attempted to pin a straight hem into her swaying full skirt. "Honey child, please!" she begged, licking a bead of blood from her pinpricked finger. "Hold still for just a minute more."

"But, Mama, I'm pretendin' to be a princess. I can't wait for Andrew to see my new dress." When Emma sat back on the floor, the pinning job sufficiently complete, Anna began twirling around the seamstress shop until the stiff taffeta floated on air.

Anna had surprised them all with her strong will to recover from whooping cough. Each day, she spent more and more time out of bed, and the doctor was calling it nothing short of a miracle. Today only an occasional cough remained. So for the past day, Emma and Anna had been excitedly making plans for Sunday and the child's first public appearance. Their initial item of business had been to make Anna new clothes for the occasion. A remnant piece from Emma's emerald green taffeta dress proved large enough to piece together a matching "coming out" frock for Anna's first time at church.

No doubt, Katy Greene would twitter that such an outfit for a child was frivolous. And, no doubt, Katy's words would be true. Still, there were times that called for more than a little frivolity.

"Hallo, Anna? You in there?" a voice warily called through the opened window.

Emma and Anna paused to exchange a nonplussed stare. "Andrew, is that you?" Emma asked, hurrying toward the window.

"Yes'm," Andrew said, shuffling his feet. His dark eyes brimming with concern, he stuffed his hands into the pockets of his work britches. "I was worried 'bout Anna—"

"Andrew!" Anna squealed from behind.

"Come to the front door," Emma said.

As she opened the door and the boy hesitantly stepped into the parlor, Emma wondered where Frank might be. She scanned the street, bustling with the usual early morning activity, but saw no sign of the boy's father. At once, her heart twisted with a twinge of concern and perhaps a touch of regret at his absence.

Before Emma could interrogate Andrew, Anna ran from across the room and threw her arms around his neck. "Andrew, I'm all better now. And my mama made me a new dress." A slight cough followed her words, and Emma patted the child's back, hoping the excitement over seeing her brother wouldn't instigate a coughing spell.

"That's good news, young'un," Andrew said, tousling her hair. "I was worried about you. That's why I came around." He cast a shamefaced look toward Emma before bowing his head. "I hope you aren't too mad at me, ma'am. I didn't mean to startle you none."

"Where's your pa?" Emma glanced out the door once more to verify Frank's absence as new thoughts whirled through her mind. Had the boy run away because Frank worked him too hard?

"He don't know I'm here. The neighbor's fields were afire and he took off on Shadow to offer his help. That smell of smoke made me want to see Anna somethin' fierce." He drew his sister close to his side. And, despite the boy's attempt at bravado, Emma noticed his bottom lip quivering while he spoke. "I snuck off 'fore Pedro and Maria arrived for work, and if I don't make it back home before Pa gets there, I reckon there'll be grief to pay."

"You're probably right about that, but I'm not about to let you out of my sight. You can't just go traipsing around the countryside—not without your pa knowing your whereabouts and especially if there's a fire.

I don't care if you are all of ten years old." As she looked the boy up and down, she inwardly praised Frank for the healthy changes: the glow of his cheeks, the noticeable weight gain, and his fresh-scrubbed cleanliness. Perhaps Frank Nance was a better father than Emma ever imagined.

His year-old proposal became an undeniable possibility in Emma's spirit as she fussed over starting breakfast for Anna and Andrew. Certainly, if Frank were such a good father, he might easily be a good husband. Her heart palpitated at such a rate that Emma could barely stir the corn bread batter. Her previous concerns that Frank might be like her stepfather began to melt like wax before the fires of respect. Andrew showed no signs of being overworked and underloved—something Emma had readily sensed in a child on more than one occasion. On the contrary, Andrew seemed to be blossoming under the care of his new father.

With all the discretion she could muster, Emma tried to pry more information from the boy as she worked at the stove. She desperately wanted to verify her assumptions as fact. She asked about their daily routine and the chores that he'd been assigned, looking for the slightest hint of Josiah Trumbull tyranny. But young Andrew was full of nothing but praise for his new father. He held Frank Nance in highest esteem. And Emma was certainly beginning to think Frank deserved his son's admiration. Wistfully, she envisioned the four of them as a family.

O Lord, she prayed. *Is there anything I might say to make Frank realize his need of a deeper walk with You?*

All morning Emma prayed that prayer. And by the noon hour, she had certainly begun to pray for other concerns as well. Frank still had not come after Andrew. While she understood that Frank didn't actually know Andrew's location, Emma also figured he would start looking for the boy at her house. Even though the task of fighting a fire was certainly time-consuming, she was beginning to worry about Frank. Andrew had lost one father in a blazing inferno; surely God wouldn't allow him to lose another. Her soul trembled in dread as she tried to stay yet another of Andrew's questions about his father's absence. Instead, she directed the children back to the spacious kitchen to sit at the sturdy oak dining table.

She had no sooner set the plates of beans and corn bread in front of the children than pounding resounded from the front door. She caught her breath, wondering if Frank were the visitor.

"That's probably Pa," Andrew said, his eyes bright with expectation.

"Probably," she said, her heart singing with hope. After removing her apron, she tucked stray strands of hair back into her chignon. The more she encountered Frank, the more Emma fretted with her appearance. Just before opening the door, she pressed her lips together, hoping she wasn't unusually pale after her long days and nights of nursing Anna while trying to keep abreast of her sewing schedule.

But when she opened the door, all concern for her appearance vanished. A gasp slipped from her lips at the sight of the soot-covered man who stood on her spacious porch. If Emma hadn't expected him, she would not have recognized Frank. All the hair had been singed from his face. The lack of eyebrows and lashes added to his wild-eyed look of terror. He held his hands cautiously in front of him, exposing several blistered burns.

"Andrew's missing," he blurted, forgoing salutations as he stepped inside. "He's nowhere to be found at the farm, and Pedro said he's not seen hide nor hair of him. Is he here by chance?" Frank craned his neck to look past Emma. He seemed oblivious to his serious injuries. His only concerns were for his son.

"Yes, he's here. And he's fine," she replied, touching his forearm in concern. "But you don't look as if you are. We must send for Doc Gilbert to care for your burns."

"I'll see the doctor in good time," he said, stepping past her. "I've got more important matters to tend to first. I'd like to take a gander at Andrew, just to set my mind at ease. Then, if you don't mind, I need a private word with you."

Turning, he paused long enough to expose her to a pleading gaze. She caught her breath, wondering exactly what Frank had in mind. She had made her conditions clear in the parlor of the Imperial Hotel. Could it be that Frank had at last understood his need of a total surrender to the Lord? Emma had prayed for exactly that all morning!

Her mind whirling with the implications of the moment, Emma led the way back to the kitchen and watched as Frank crouched slowly and painfully on one knee next to Andrew's chair. For several long moments, he stared intently at the gaping boy. "You had me scared spitless!" Overcome with emotion, Frank closed his eyes tight.

Andrew's lips shook. "I'm sorry, Pa." He flung his arms around Frank's neck. "I know you tol' me not to go, but. . ."

Although Frank winced painfully, he did not discourage the boy's affection. Instead, he gingerly rested his burned hands against Andrew's back.

"The fire!" Andrew continued. "I was worried ta death it was gonna spread to town and kill Anna. And now you. . .you. . .you've been burned up, just like our papa!" Andrew choked on a sob. "Please don't die. . .don't die! I promise. . .I promise, I won't never run off again."

Emma pressed her fingers against her trembling lips and rushed toward Anna, now fretting because of her brother's outburst. She scooped Anna from one of the sturdy oak chairs and held her close. "Don't worry, little one," she crooned. "Everything is fine."

"Andrew's cryin'," she whined. "His pa is all burned up."

"Yes, but he's okay. Everything is fine."

The budding love expressed by father and son dashed aside any remaining doubts that Frank Nance was indeed a wonderful father. . .that he would indeed be an exceptional husband. The man had at last begun to allow Emma to see his true emotions. *O Lord, if only he would let down the barriers with You.* Certainly, Emma realized that these boundaries Frank had erected between himself and others were the very boundaries that were keeping him at a distance with God.

At last, Frank assured Andrew that all would be well and he was indeed fine. After a quarter hour of Frank's calm and assuring words, Andrew finally turned his attention back to the beans and corn bread. Frank grimaced as he rose to face Emma. "Do you think Andrew can look after Anna here in the kitchen for a short spell so you and I can visit in the parlor? There's somethin' I'm needin' to get off my chest."

"Don't you think we should at least put some salve on those burns first?" she asked, settling Anna in front of her noon meal. "I keep a jar right here next to my stove." Chattering nervously, she riffled through the cabinet next to the potbellied stove in search of the illusive ointment. "Seems like I'm constantly splattering grease on myself," she said, barely able to concentrate on the words tumbling from her lips. For all she could think of was Frank, standing so close to her. Despite herself, she began to wonder what it would feel like to have his arms around her. Was he about to restate his proposal? And if he did not profess a renewed love for the Lord, did she have the spiritual strength to refuse him?

As Emma continued in search of the elusive salve, a tense silence settled between them, and she began an internal, heavenward plea. *O Lord, give me the courage to stay with my decision, despite the fact that I. . .that I think I am fall–falling in love with him.*

"The salve can wait a few more minutes," Frank insisted from close behind.

Emma stilled. Her heart pounded. Her palms moistened.

"This is important, and I don't reckon it will take too long."

Swallowing, Emma silently turned from her task and moved toward the parlor, not daring to look into his eyes. A quick glance over her shoulder proved Anna and Andrew were still sufficiently distracted by their meal. All the while she walked toward the parlor, Emma prayed for courage and strength and wisdom. She paused beside the French doors and watched as Frank walked toward the front window, complemented by lace curtains. A tense silence followed, and Emma knew that Frank Nance was deeply troubled.

"Old Man Taylor lost his life today," he said. "And I came close to losin' mine." Frank pivoted to face her. "We had formed a bucket brigade and were attempting to douse the flames of his burning barn when a support beam gave way, sending a portion of the barn roof down on top of us and buryin' Mr. Taylor in flame. I had the wind knocked out of me for a time. As quick as I could, I tried to rescue the old man, but to no avail."

Wearily, he rubbed at his blackened forehead with the back of his wrist. "During those moments everythin' you said to me at the Imperial Hotel started to make a heap of sense. All I could think was that I was really livin' my life for me and. . ." He paused to swallow. "And how far from the Lord I had strayed. . .and just how much I. . .I love you, Emma." His words came out on a broken whisper.

Her eyes filling with tears, Emma laid a trembling hand against her chest.

"And if you want the gospel truth, I think I've been in love with you for a good deal longer than I ever wanted myself to know it." He closed the distance between them and reached to touch her cheek, only to wince with renewed pain.

"We need the doctor—"

"No. Not until I've had my say. I prayed all the way from the farm for two things: that Andrew would be here and that you'd. . .you'd reconsider my proposal. This time, I can promise you, I don't have a single convenience in mind, Miz Watson." His pain-filled eyes produced a mischievous twinkle. "And I can also promise you that the Lord has grabbed my attention and I've done my business with Him." He paused to hold her gaze, his eyes revealing a sincere man. "This isn't any religion of convenience either. The Lord has taken hold of me like He never has before."

Tears trickling from the corners of her eyes, Emma nodded in understanding.

"If only you could find it in your heart to try to love me—"

"Oh, Frank. . ." Emma choked on a sob. "I think I've been on the verge of falling in love with you for months. And all morning I've prayed you'd say just what you've said. I—"

Emma's words were cut off by Frank's whoop of joy and his lips pressed firmly against hers. And in that moment Emma once again understood what it felt like to be madly in love with a man. . .and to have a man madly in love with her.

In the hallway, Andrew, holding his sister's hand, peeked into the parlor to see his pa and Anna's ma kissing. "Yuck!" he whispered. Turning to Anna, he wrinkled his nose.

A soft giggle escaped Anna. "I like your pa."

Dashing aside his aversion to the grown-ups' kiss, Andrew picked up his sister and twirled her around. "Good! 'Cause it looks like he's gonna be your pa, too!"

Epilogue

Crisp autumn air swept off the Kansas prairie and down Church Street as Andrew and Anna clambered up the wooden steps leading into the white frame church. "Whoa. Wait up, you two," Frank called after them. "Give your ol' paw and mama a chance to catch up."

"Anna, did you say hello to the Reverend?" At her father's prompting, the just-turned-five-year-old curtsied politely to the pastor then wiggled her first loose tooth for him to see. In the meantime, Andrew had already escaped inside.

"Mornin', Reverend Barnhart." Frank removed his hat and extended his right hand, still pink and scarred from the June fire. "We've got us a beautiful day to worship!"

"I do believe you'd say the same in the midst of a cyclone, Frank. I hope you never lose your enthusiasm for serving the Lord!"

"Seein' as how He's blessed me, I'd be a lowdown skunk if I didn't give Him praise." Before he could expound any further, Anna reappeared from a brief sojourn into the inner recesses of the sanctuary and grabbed both Frank and Emma by a sleeve.

"Come on, Mama, Pa. Church is gettin' ready to start and Andrew's savin' us a seat right down front." Frank's eyes crinkled in quiet laughter, and he exchanged a look of parental pride with Emma while Anna dragged them down the center aisle.

When the Nance family had situated themselves on the second pew,

Emma gently nudged Frank and nodded for him to look at the children. He turned his head toward Andrew just in time to see the boy playfully stick his tongue out at his little sister. Before Frank could interfere with this sibling squabble, Emma leaned over and whispered into his ear. "Seeing him act like a kid does my heart good; how about you?"

Emma secretly intertwined her fingers in Frank's as he offered to share a hymnal during the opening song. Then Andrew and Anna, Emma and Frank joined their voices in heavenly harmony while the congregation sang:

> *Blest be the tie that binds*
> *Our hearts in Christian love;*
> *The fellowship of kindred minds*
> *Is like to that above.*

Amen.

An Oklahoma native, **Susan K. Downs** is a descendant of Land Run pioneers. But life as a minister's wife has taken her far beyond her roots. While living in Texas, Susan frequently traveled to Russia as an adoption coordinator. Though now settled in Canton, Ohio, this mother of five and grandmother will always be an Okie at heart. Visit her Web site at www.susankdowns.com.

A Heart's Dream

by Birdie L. Etchison

Dedication

Dedicated to my sister, Barbara Ann Rutledge,
though gone from this life, she will continue
to be a source of inspiration for me.
She loved trains.

Chapter 1

June 1900—Creston, Iowa

Charlotte stood at the end of the lane looking back one last time. The house, the only home she'd ever known, now stood empty. Sunshine cast shadows on the old clapboards badly needing paint. Perhaps the new owner would paint it and make it beautiful once again. She bit back the tears.

The furniture, linens, dishes, and pots and pans had been sold at an auction; she'd packed clothing and a few personal belongings in the trunk. Her heart ached with the loss. She'd hoped to find space for Grandfather's favorite painting. It was by a local artist and showed a boy on a riverbank fishing. Done in blues and reds, it had hung in her bedroom since she could remember and was the first thing she saw each morning. It brought a handsome price from a woman who said it had "great depth." Whatever that meant.

Charlotte had needed the money for the train trip. A teaching position awaited her in Traer, Kansas, a small farming town on the Nebraska border. She wanted to stay and teach in Creston. She didn't care that the house looked shabby, the roof leaked, or the fence was leaning. It was home, and she would never forget all that was so dear to her.

The trumpet vine blooming on the side of the house was one memory she would take with her. Just that morning she snipped a bit of vine and tucked it into her carpetbag. She'd put damp shredded paper around it to keep it moist and then wrapped it in a strip of oilcloth. If she watered it often, it might make it all the way to her new home in Kansas. It would take two days—one on the train and one by wagon.

So much change, too fast. First losing Grandmother, then Grandfather, obtaining a teaching certificate, now the journey. Cousin Lily, whom Charlotte had met but once before, had offered to board Charlotte and her brother, Robert, until Charlotte had enough money to find a place of her own. Lily's mother and Charlotte's mother had been sisters.

How could this have happened? Grandfather had not once said he didn't own the land or the house. Even on his deathbed, three months ago, he hadn't revealed that the bank had a lien. He'd either forgotten or simply had no money. She thought of how she'd held his hand when he was dying with a raging fever, his lips parched and bleeding. "Take care of Robert," he'd said. "You're all he has, Charlotte."

Not one word of love. No warning they'd have to move on because neither the house nor the land was his. Mr. Anthony told her that the day after the funeral.

Once again tears threatened, but it wouldn't do to let Robert see her cry. He was only nine and seemingly had not experienced the sadness or loneliness Charlotte felt. He was excited about the adventure of traveling on the train.

"Robert!" she called now. He had hurried to the pasture to see his beloved pony. He was sadder about leaving Brown Beauty than he was about leaving the farm. Brown Beauty was named after the horse in the book *Black Beauty*. Robert was pleased that a nearby farmer had bought the pony for his daughter who was Robert's age. Still, he had said good-bye twice this morning.

She felt an arm on her sleeve. "It's all right, Lottie. We'll like it in Kansas."

He'd caught her wiping her cheeks with the back of her cotton glove. She ruffled his hair and leaned over to kiss his forehead. He was all she had, and she'd do anything to protect him, keep him safe.

"Isn't the wagon supposed to be here now?"

"Soon." Charlotte looked at the freckled face and concentrated on his eagerness, not the hole in his best shoes or his threadbare jacket. "Put your hat back on. You know how easily you get sunburned."

He stuffed the round-brimmed straw hat back on his head and looked up the road. Their dear neighbor, Mr. Farnsworth, had promised to take them to the train station in Creston. If they didn't leave soon, they'd miss the connection.

"I'm sure he's on his way. Don't you fret now," she said more for her own benefit than his.

A relentless sun beat out of a blue sky as she took one last look then turned to the sound of approaching horses and wagon.

Mr. Farnsworth brought the team to a halt and tipped his hat. "Nice morning, isn't it now?"

Charlotte nodded. "It's more than a fair morning, sir!"

"The missus sent a basket for you, something to eat on the trip. I hope you have room in your bag." He held up the small straw basket.

"Oh, thank you very much. It was so kind of her." Charlotte knew there was no room in the bag so she'd have Robert carry the basket aboard the train. Her stomach growled, but she paid it no mind.

"Here, Robert, help me with this trunk," Mr. Farnsworth said.

They took the handles and lifted it high, setting it in the back of the wagon; then Robert climbed in.

Mr. Farnsworth turned to Charlotte. "Let me help you up!" She rode in the seat next to him, the bag, on the floor by her feet, the basket of food in her lap. She'd worn her best calico and the wide-brimmed, navy blue straw hat that had been Grandmother's Sunday-go-to-meeting bonnet. The gloves had a hole in the left palm, but she could hide it.

"It's going to seem mighty strange not to have you living next door."

Charlotte tried to smile. "I will write once I am settled," she said with a lift of her chin. "We are looking forward to this, aren't we, Robert?"

"Oh, yes, Lottie," Robert said in agreement. "I can't wait to ride the train."

Twenty minutes later, when Mr. Farnsworth pulled up to the station, it was not a moment too soon as the train whistle sounded in the distance.

Charlotte took deep breaths and murmured a short prayer. "Yes, we can do this; yes, we can do this; Lord, help us do this."

Robert had already hopped down and stood watching the giant steam engine chug slowly up the track. A big puff of steam rose as it came to a halt mere feet from the wagon. Charlotte watched in dismay, shouting for Robert to stand back.

"The boy is excited," Mr. Farnsworth said from the ground as he held his arm up to Charlotte. "May I help you down?"

Steam still rose from the smokestack, and she wondered how she could have agreed to ride on such a monster.

❧

From the window of the arriving train, Franklin Hill III watched as an older gentleman helped a young, slim woman from a farm wagon. She was pretty, but it was her spunky look that caught his eye. The man now beckoned to a small boy to come help with a trunk. The lad sat his basket down and ran over. It was a large trunk, and Frank sensed it was more than the two could handle. He sat his coat on the train bench and got off the train.

"Could I be of some help?" he asked.

"Yes," the man said, "thank you very much."

The trunk was hoisted onto the baggage car, and Frank, in turn, offered his assistance to the woman with eyes as blue as cornflowers while the lad climbed the steps, shouting, "Where do we sit, Lottie? Where do we sit?"

"Robert! Wait!" But the boy had disappeared inside the train, and her look of distress caused Frank to say, "I'll help you board, Miss."

The frown deepened on her face as their gazes met; then a slight smile turned up at the corners of her mouth.

"I must get on this train," she said.

"I know." Frank grabbed the satchel with one hand and offered his arm. Introductions could come later.

❧

Charlotte had noticed the stranger light from the train and wondered if he would continue on the train, or was this his final destination? Dressed

282

in a bowler hat, white shirt, and dark trousers and jacket, the man had a kind face and dark, warm eyes fringed with long lashes.

"Thank you," she said, her chin trembling. She lifted the skirt of the faded calico and boarded the steps.

"Where do we sit?" Robert asked again, his cheeks all red from the sun because he never kept his hat on.

"I expect anywhere we can find."

"That's one excited boy. Could see that right off." The man tipped his hat. "Name's Franklin Hill."

"And this is Lottie, and I'm Robert." Robert was all smiles, the cowlick sticking up on top of his head. The sight made Charlotte think again of Grandfather. He, too, had had a problem with a cowlick. "Lottie's my sister, and our last name is Lansing," Robert continued.

"Pleased to make your acquaintances," he said. "I'm sitting right across the aisle from you."

"Are you going to Kansas, too, Mr. Hill?" Robert asked.

"Not as far as Kansas. I'm staying in McCook, Nebraska. And please call me Frank."

Charlotte flushed at the sound of his deep voice and withdrew her lace handkerchief. She suddenly felt faint, then remembered she'd been so busy packing the last few items and saying good-bye to the house that she hadn't eaten yet today.

"Are you okay?" Frank was there, standing over her protectively.

"Oh my, yes. The feeling has passed."

"What passed?" Robert was suddenly interested.

"My feeling of dizziness."

"I'll just wager that you didn't eat a proper breakfast this morning," Frank said.

"I, well, it's been such a busy time, getting ready for this trip—"

"And we had to leave the farm and my pony and all our furniture, and—"

"Robert! That's quite enough."

Charlotte rarely chastised him; he looked bewildered.

She fluttered her hanky again. "We're off to stay with dear, dear

283

Cousin Lily, and things are going to work out just fine."

"I have candy to share," Frank said, nodding as he sat back down across the aisle from Charlotte and Robert.

"Oh, goodness, no," Charlotte said. "We have this lovely lunch from Mrs. Farnsworth." She held the basket protectively to her chest.

The train gave a lurch and began rolling forward.

"We're going!" Robert yelled, holding on to his hat.

Charlotte cast him a reproachful look then smiled. "He's been looking forward to this," she said, turning to look shyly at Frank. "We've not been on a train before."

Robert jumped up again. Charlotte wanted it to stop. She wanted more than anything to get right off this train and return home. How could she possibly go to a place she'd never been and teach school? It was almost unthinkable, but there was no turning back. God said in His Word that He would never forsake those He loved, and Charlotte was certain that God loved her. What would she do without God's love and caring spirit?

"I have something for Robert, with your permission, of course." Frank extended a long stick of peppermint candy.

"Oh!" Robert's eyebrows rose. "May I have it, Lottie? Please say yes."

"Well, maybe just this once." Charlotte knew she was far too easy on Robert. How was he to learn discipline when she always let him have his way? He was so lovable.

The train's whistle sounded again as it chugged slowly out of the station, leaving the town behind. The smell of smoke drifted into the open windows, and Charlotte held her hanky to her nose and began praying.

"I'll close the window," Frank offered. "It's open due to the summer heat, but the soot and cinders are bothersome when we first start off."

Charlotte nodded in agreement while Robert brushed off a cinder. "That was hot," he claimed, then looked down at the tiny hole in his jacket.

"Yes, that happens every time I ride the train," Frank said.

Frank was a soothing sort of person, one a person could lean on, and Charlotte was surprised at the sudden fluttering feeling that seemed to take over her being. This feeling had nothing to do with hunger.

"I'm going to make this candy last and last." Robert had licked it to a long point. "I may make it last the whole day!"

A chuckle sounded from across the way. "No need for that, Robert. I have more where that came from." Frank produced a brown bag and opened it for the boy to see. "I never go anywhere without candy. Here, do you want one, Miss Lansing?"

"Oh my, no. But thank you. It's very kind of you." She looked at the basket Mr. Farnsworth had given her earlier. "I have something to eat right here."

Thick, white chunks of bread and slabs of ham and cheese were in one wrapper. Charlotte's stomach lurched. Two apples and cookies, the kind Mrs. Farnsworth was noted for—oatmeal raisin with pecans—were in another.

"Would you like a cookie?" Charlotte said then. "Our neighbor is one of the best cooks in Pottawattamie County."

"Why, thank you very much." He leaned over and took one of the large, round cookies.

His presence seemed to disarm her, and Charlotte wondered why she was feeling this way. A man had never come calling, but at eighteen she wondered what it might be like. Would she ever have a chance now? The last two years had been spent taking care of her sick grandparents. And, of course, Robert. Their mother had died when an influenza epidemic hit their community the year after Robert was born. Their father had left after burying his wife because, in his words, he was "dying of a broken heart."

Charlotte had tugged on his coat, begging him not to leave her and Robert, but he had gone anyway. She remembered the little cloud of dust the horse made as he galloped down the lane and out of sight. The only memento she had was a faded photo of her father as a young man before he'd married her mother. She kept the picture in a locket around her neck.

"This cookie is delicious," Frank said, shaking her out of her reverie.

"I'm glad you like it." She looked over and smiled.

His dark eyes twinkled. "I suppose you bake cookies every bit this good."

"Lottie does," Robert said. "She does all the cookin' and baking." Robert had finished his candy stick and wiped his mouth with the back of his sleeve.

"Robert! You said you were going to savor it."

Frank grinned, as if he remembered what it was like to be a little boy with a candy stick. "Don't scold the lad," he said then. "We'll get more if need be."

The train clickety-clacked over the tracks at a smoother pace, and suddenly Charlotte felt weary. She wanted to forget all that had transpired, forget the worries that crowded her mind though she knew and fully believed that God was in charge. She had said so many prayers this morning, and somehow she knew more would be forthcoming. If only she knew that Cousin Lily would be waiting at the station for them. Her eyelids began to close just as she heard Frank say that he was heading west to be a cowboy.

Chapter 2

Frank had no idea what a cowboy did or why the words slipped out like that. Charlotte suddenly jerked forward and stared at him as if he said he was going to be a thief or a pirate on the high seas or something equally notorious.

He had often thought about going west, but to pursue a career as a cowboy was far-fetched. Only lately had he considered it, since he wasn't sure about continuing in the medical field. If he could just forget what happened back in Ohio. . . .

"You're a *cowboy*?" Robert jumped up and down. "A cowboy ropes cows and rides big, huge bulls and rides on the range all day." He wrinkled his nose. "And what else does he do, huh, Frank?"

Frank couldn't keep from smiling. "You're thinking of a rodeo cowboy, Robert. They rope cows and ride on bucking broncos and other such feats. That's not for me." Frank did not look at Charlotte again. Her disdain was obvious.

Robert wasn't ready to let it go though. "But you could do those things, and it would be fun." Robert twirled his straw hat. "You could give up that hat you got on and have a *real* cowboy hat."

Frank laughed at that image. He certainly was not wearing anything that would fit on the open range. He'd have to add cowboy boots and one of those fancy shirts with a fringed yoke. But he had never thought of being in a rodeo. He just wanted to see what the Wild West was like.

"You do have an imagination," Frank said.

"It's from all the books he reads," Charlotte said with a nod.

At least she was looking his way again, but he knew she was not pleased with the turn their conversation had taken. Why hadn't he just said he was a doctor? Why the sudden cowboy fascination? In his travels of the past, he had discovered that people treated doctors differently. He would be asked all sorts of medical questions and expected to know the answers. Doctors were also expected to be perfect. He was not, nor could he ever be, like that. He was far too impetuous, just like the cowboy remark. Though he had in all honesty entertained the idea, he didn't plan on going through with it. It had been a whim, but now he needed to explain.

"Where are you going?" Robert asked.

"Robert." Charlotte's voice stopped him in the middle of yet another question. "That's enough talk about this going west. Leave Mr. Hill alone now."

Frank didn't want to be left alone. The child was a wonderful diversion, a blessing to be with.

He leaned forward, taking in Charlotte. She was young. Frightened. Alone and going on a train for the first time. Anyone would be scared in those circumstances. Then, too, she had the responsibility of her brother, and it had to be difficult to mother the boy when she was not much over being a child, herself. Offhand, he'd guess her to be nineteen, maybe twenty.

From the first moment he'd laid eyes on her, he knew his being on this train was definitely God's leading. When one prayed each morning for guidance and direction, God was there to help, to lean on. Frank believed that wholeheartedly.

Rest wasn't necessary, but Frank had some thinking to do. He nodded in Robert's direction, took his hat off, placed it carefully on top of his valise, and leaned back.

"Words hastily spoken cannot be taken back," Grandmother Julia had told him. He supposed he was Robert's age then. He'd never forgotten, but his quick tongue had gotten him into trouble more than once.

A trip to the woodshed was often the answer, but on this particular occasion he had to go apologize to his mother for asking why she didn't get out of bed and fix him pancakes for breakfast. Illness meant nothing to him. Dying was a word in a book, something that happened to others but not to Frank. Not until that fateful day six months later when the sheet had been pulled up over his mother's eyes after he'd been summoned in to say good-bye. Could his mother have been saved? The doctor said it was consumption, and most people died from it.

❦

Charlotte did not want to think about what lay ahead. A month ago she'd been secure with a house and a grandfather who was ill, but still someone for her to care for, to love. How dear he had been to her, and even when she discovered the house and farm were no longer hers, she had forgiven him. Whatever happened had happened, and God promised to provide. A verse came to mind, 2 Corinthians 9:8, one of many she had memorized sitting on Grandmother's knee: "And God is able to make all grace abound toward you; that ye, always having all sufficiency in all things, may abound to every good work."

In a dreamlike state, Charlotte thought of the daffodils and hyacinths that sprang to life each spring, the cherry and apple trees that budded and lent shade during the hot summers, bearing fruit in the autumn. She wondered if Cousin Lily lived on the prairies of Kansas, or would there be hills and trees as there had been at home? What would happen when Lily met them? Would they be wanted in this new town, or had Lily sent for them out of duty? Charlotte sighed. Time would tell. By tomorrow morning they would reach their destination and a new life would begin. . . .

Frank's voice stirred her back to the present.

"I rather think cowboys are like farmers," he was saying. "They raise cattle, grow wheat and corn. . .and it's a lot of hard work."

"But if you go west, they just have cattle," Robert said, as if he were the voice of authority.

"That could be," Frank said with a nod. "Guess I've been missing out on the exciting part of it."

"So you really *are* going out west?" Charlotte looked at Frank. He was handsome, his smile pleasant. She thought of her father who had left Iowa and headed west. He too had been handsome and had a nice smile, and he had yearned to be a cowboy. What lured men to that kind of life? Why hadn't he stayed in Iowa or nearby in order to at least see his children? Why had he felt the need to go so far away? No, cowboys were not to be trusted.

"I like traveling," Frank said. "There's lots of country I've never explored."

"Do you know some rope tricks?" Robert looked hopeful.

"Not really. All I know is how to make a monkey out of a handkerchief and make him talk."

"Make him talk?"

Charlotte turned in her seat to stare.

"Yes, I'll show you."

In no time Frank had formed a figure out of the hanky and made it move. Robert stared in fascination at the object, knowing it couldn't talk, then back at Frank. Frank's mouth wasn't moving. Robert's jaw dropped, and Charlotte laughed at the look on his face. Ventriloquism. She'd read about it, but she had never met anyone who could throw his voice.

"That's very good," she said.

Frank turned in her direction, now using a falsetto voice. "You really think so, ma'am?"

Charlotte laughed again. "Yes, I really think so."

"Do it again," Robert begged. "Do it again, Frank."

And so Frank told a story about a man who went on the train and then met a young boy. He spoke with a deep voice as the man and changed it to a younger sounding voice for the boy.

"Are you talking about *me*?" Robert asked.

"Could be," Frank answered in his normal tone. "What do you think?"

"Yes, I'm the boy." Robert held his hand up and tried to make his voice sound different, but it didn't work. "How do you do that?"

"It's something I learned many years ago."

"Do you perform anywhere?" Charlotte asked.

"No. Just do it for my own enjoyment."

"I'm with Robert. I don't see how you can talk and not move your mouth."

"It comes from within." Frank pointed to the back of his tongue. "It takes practice, of course, as all things do."

The conductor came down the aisle, interrupting their conversation as he collected tickets. Frank said something, making it look as if the conductor had said it.

The man turned and stared at Frank, then over at Robert. "That's some trick. Now which one of you did that?"

Robert pointed. "Him."

Chuckling, the conductor shuffled on past, and Charlotte stifled a giggle. It had been so long since she'd had anything to laugh about, and it felt good. Her heart seemed lighter than it had when she first boarded the train back at Creston. Had God brought this man, a cowboy, into their lives for a reason? Even if only for a day, it was a blessing. She believed that one prayed for safety, for an unblemished life, and to be of service to God. Teaching was going to be her service. The schoolchildren would become her children. She might never marry, and that would be all right. She would raise Robert, for he had been entrusted to her care, and he mattered the most right now.

There had been a boy once. Charlotte remembered him watching her at school. He had taken her home, but when he asked to come calling, she had said no. She had no chaperone, as Grandfather was so sick. He moved away shortly after that anyway.

Charlotte leaned back and shut her eyes, resigned to a life without love.

❧

Frank noticed Charlotte's eyes close and hoped she could rest. She was pretty; her blond curls danced from under the wide-brimmed hat. He found himself wishing she'd take it off, wanting to see her hair loose and flying as the breeze came in through a partially opened window. She was probably too young to think of settling down, and he was suddenly thinking seriously about it. He was twenty-seven, after all. Yes, there comes a time when a man should start thinking about a wife, a home. Yes, even doctors needed to be married.

His father had been a pastor, and his grandfather a circuit rider in Arkansas before that, yet Frank had never felt the calling to preach. After his little sister died, he knew he wanted to be a doctor. His father had continued to argue, but he died before Frank entered medical school.

He'd practiced in two towns in Ohio simultaneously and then answered the call from McCook. He wasn't expected for a full month but had felt the need to leave early. His tentative plans were to take the train west, go on to Oregon, and then return to Nebraska. This might allow him enough time to heal from the tragedy back in Ohio. He'd done everything he could, but a young mother had died in childbirth, and he had not been able to save the baby. He could still see the father's face, the anguish in his eyes when Frank told him they were both gone. If only he had been called to the home sooner. If only he had done something different. Try as he might, he had not been able to get that face out of his mind. Perhaps he should have gone into the ministry.

❦

"Frank." Robert tugged on his sleeve. "I like sitting with you."

"And I like having a traveling companion."

"Lottie is sleeping, I think."

"And we need to see that she gets her rest." He put a finger to his mouth. "It's been a hard thing for her to do, moving away like that and going to a new place."

"You mean all that packing and stuff, trying to decide what we had to take and what we *had* to leave behind?"

"Yes, that." *And much more,* Frank wanted to add. More responsibility, too. He couldn't explain his sudden desire to care for and protect the young woman and her brother.

"Will you send me a letter when you get to Oregon?" Robert asked, leaning forward. His feet didn't quite reach the floor, so he had to lean up, which made them barely touch the wooden floorboards.

"I'm not sure of an exact location."

"I hope it's Oregon. And you can follow the Oregon Trail and the covered wagons. I wish I could go in one of them."

"Trains are the main means of transportation these days," Frank said. "I doubt that many go by way of a covered wagon now."

"Do Indians still attack?"

"No, not now. Indians live on reservations and are more peaceful."

And so began a story of a family who had lost everything and eventually their lives except for one child who then had to ride with another family.

"Sorta like me," Robert said. "I only have Lottie, and if something should happen—"

Charlotte sat up at the sound of her name and scolded Robert. "You are being a pest. Now come back here and sit with me."

"He's fine," Frank said, his hand touching the boy's shoulder. "I'd like him for a seat mate, if you don't mind."

Robert's chest puffed out as he beamed.

"If you're sure—"

"Quite sure."

And as the train chugged over the miles, Frank told another story, one his father had told him countless times. It was the story of the lost sheep and about how farmers felt when they lost a sheep.

Soon Robert's head was nodding, and Frank put his coat over Robert's legs. Trains were drafty, and though it was the beginning of summer, the late afternoon breeze could turn chilly. It wouldn't do for the lad to catch cold.

Taking one more glance in Charlotte's direction, Frank was satisfied that she was okay as her head leaned against the dark green cushion. She clutched something, and then he saw it was a Bible. He swallowed hard, remembering his own precious Bible in the bag he'd carried on the train. Did cowboys carry Bibles? He pondered that. If they didn't, they should. Maybe he could be the first, he thought as he allowed the train to lull him to sleep.

Chapter 3

Frank felt something touch him and jerked awake. It was Robert's head resting against his shoulder. The coat had slipped to the floor, yet the little boy slept on. Frank's fatherly instincts gave him a warm, good feeling. Had God entrusted them to his care?

Moving slightly, so as not to disturb Robert, Frank turned to see if Charlotte was still sleeping. Her eyes were closed, and he couldn't help noticing she looked like an angel with the sun streaming in the window, casting shadows on her flushed cheeks. He was glad now he'd accepted the position in McCook. He'd be close to the small school across the border in the growing town of Traer. If she was willing, and the Lord already knew how willing Frank was, he would visit often.

He thought back to his youth and the problems he'd had in school. "Preacher's son," his classmates called him.

"Preacher's son can do no wrong." He bristled at remembering how the words stung. He'd come up fighting with both fists, and that always got him into trouble.

"Troublemaker," one teacher had labeled him. Once a kid had a name, that was it; he was stuck with it.

He thought again of his Bible tucked in the bottom of his bag. The well-worn leather volume had been a gift the Christmas he was eight. He'd carried it ever since. He also thought about how it was assumed he would be a preacher; the last thing his grandfather had said to him was:

"Carry on with the message to God's people, son. There are lots of souls to be saved."

Frank had the last sermon his grandfather had given. There were times he wished he'd carried on with the tradition, but there was also a need for doctors. How would he ever go back to that profession? Would he be able to deliver a child without remembering that last time? For now his major concern was how he was going to reveal the truth to Charlotte and Robert.

The whistle blew three long blasts; the train braked suddenly then lurched to a grinding halt, causing their belongings to slide to the floor.

"Oh my," Charlotte cried out, her eyes wide in a too white face. "What happened?"

Robert had wakened too, lurching to his feet while others scampered out of seats and looked around. Rubbing his eyes, he glanced over at his sister. "Lottie?"

"It's okay, Robert," Frank said. "I think there was something on the track. Probably a cow or a horse." He noted with amusement that Charlotte's hat was askew, and he longed to reach over and straighten it for her.

"Trains don't make smooth stops; it's something they're hoping to change."

Wisps of dirty air floated through the train car, landing on the seats and floor. Charlotte coughed.

"Some day they may have it so it's not so sooty. It helps to cover your mouth," Frank said, covering his face with his hand.

"Are we almost there?" Robert asked, putting his hat back on. "I do hope so."

"Oh no, lad. It'll be several hours before you reach your destination."

One of the passengers had hopped off the train and had come back to report that a hay wagon had overturned on the track. "They said we'd be ready to move in ten minutes or so."

"Hay wagon?" Robert asked. "But what was a hay wagon doing on the track?"

"Might have been pulled by mules," Frank said as he winked at the boy, "and you know how cantankerous an old mule can get."

"But, wouldn't they know they were going to get hit?" Robert persisted.

"Mules don't much care, Robert."

Two people walked through the car: a lady toting a small bag and a gentleman carrying a large box. They sat toward the back of the car.

"Sorry about the unexpected stop," the man said, glancing over at Frank, then Charlotte. "That's Pa's wagon that overturned and caused all the problem."

"Can't be helped sometimes," Frank said. "At least no one was hurt."

The train lurched twice, blew its whistle, and they chugged down the track, trying to pick up steam again. This time Charlotte was prepared as she held the hanky over her nose and mouth. The smoke didn't seem as thick or smell quite as bad, but maybe she was getting used to it. Robert chattered, asking Frank another question. How that boy could talk.

"How long does it take to get to the West?" he asked.

Frank felt a sudden knot lodge in his throat. "I can't rightly say. Probably another four or five days."

"Oh my, that long?" Charlotte looked serious.

"At least."

"I sure wish you were going with us, Frank," Robert broke in. "Are you sure you can't?"

"Robert, mind your manners," Charlotte chided him. "One must not assume, and what a body's got to do, they've got to do."

The trip to Oregon no longer held an interest to Frank. He could arrive at his new office a few weeks early. It was acceptable, as people would think he couldn't wait to get started.

"Do you think I could learn to be a cowboy?" Robert asked, turning in his seat. "I think that's what I'd like to do, too."

"Now, Robert, let's hear no more of this nonsense." And this time Charlotte had a formidable look on her face. "You are going to Kansas with me, and that's that."

"You'll change your mind a hundred times before you grow up," Frank said. "At least I did."

"Did you ever want to be just a plain old farmer?"

"Oh my, yes. I *was* a farmer at your age."

"You were?" Robert bounced up and down in the seat. "And now you're gonna be a cowboy."

"Oh?" The young man who had just boarded the train turned in his seat. "A cowboy?"

Frank's face reddened. "I entertained the idea once, yes." He hoped this discussion would end, as he didn't want to talk about it.

"And he can make sounds that make you think it's someone else talking."

"Oh, one of those ventri—"

"Ventriloquist," Frank finished the word.

Soon Frank was singing a song, making it sound like the voice was Charlotte's. They all laughed and asked him to do it again. Embarrassed, Frank told a story about a young boy and his sister on their first train ride and how much the boy liked it.

The young man shook his head. "Anyone who can throw their voice like that doesn't need to be a farmer or a cowboy."

Robert asked more questions while Frank gave yes or no answers.

Charlotte wondered if all boys Robert's age asked so many questions. She hoped she'd be able to answer them. She knew she would have children of various ages in a one-room schoolhouse, teaching in a place where she knew no one. If she taught in Iowa, she would have known the neighbor children, and it would have been less frightening.

She also pondered about the man who seemed to have all the answers. She gazed out the window, not wanting Frank to see her face. It was embarrassing, but in a dream she'd seen a small child with a toothless grin beaming at her, and his hair was the very color of Frank's. The smile he wore made his dark eyes twinkle. Yet she knew schoolteachers could not marry, so she put the idea out of her mind immediately.

Besides, it was wrong to think about some cowboy who probably had never stepped foot in a church. Then it was as if God was chastising her, whispering to her heart, saying it was that very sort of person He loved the most.

"Oh dear," she said aloud, suddenly realizing how terribly warm it had become inside the car. She undid the carpetbag and looked to see if the trumpet vine was okay. The shreds of paper she'd so carefully wrapped around it that morning were completely dry.

"Is something wrong?" Frank had stood and was bending over her. She nearly jumped.

"It's just that, well, I need some water."

"You're thirsty, of course. I believe I can fetch some for you."

"But it isn't me—it's for my vine."

"Vine?" Frank looked puzzled.

"Yes," Robert answered then. "Lottie brought some of the vine that grows alongside our house. She's got it in that bag."

Charlotte, feeling a bit silly, lifted out the small green slip. It drooped, and she wondered if it really would last until it was once more planted.

"What a wonderful idea. You brought part of your farm with you. So now let's go get some water. What do you say, Robert?"

Charlotte nodded at her brother and watched as the two went up the aisle, the tall man's arm draped around Robert as if he were his own. She swallowed hard. She had to stop thinking about Frank, how she liked it when he looked at her, the way his eyes seemed to smolder. . . *What is wrong with me anyway?*

Her fingers went into the bag, touching the wrapped cookies, but it wasn't food she wanted. Not that kind. She wanted to read her Bible. She needed comforting words about now. She opened her Bible to Matthew 28:20 and read. "And, lo, I am with you always, even unto the end of the world. Amen."

She began humming, ever so lowly, one of her favorite hymns, "Wonderful Words of Life."

"Sing them over again to me, wonderful words of life."

Frank was back, his deep bass voice joining in, singing the words with gusto. Startled, Charlotte looked up into those eyes and trembled. "You know that song?"

"Yep. Sang it in my mother's arms at the little church we attended."

Charlotte took the water to pour around the limp slip of trumpet vine. It was a comforting thought to know that Frank knew hymns and had gone to church.

"Were you just a baby?" Robert asked, always wanting complete details.

"No, not a baby. I couldn't remember from when I was a baby, now could I? No, I was closer to six, maybe seven."

Charlotte had wonderful memories of sitting on her mother's lap; Robert did not. He often asked about his mother. All Charlotte had was one picture in a safe place in the huge trunk and her own recollections to pass on.

"Sing it again," Robert urged. "I like your voice."

I do, too, Charlotte wanted to say, *oh, I do, too,* but she said nothing as Frank's voice filled the car, then another voice joined in and yet another. Last was Charlotte in her high soprano singing the beloved song:

Let me more of their beauty see,
Wonderful words of life
Words of life and beauty,
Teach me faith and duty,
Beautiful words, wonderful words,
Wonderful words of life

The singing was wonderful, and soon tears rolled down Charlotte's cheeks. Other than one or two slipping out of her eyes, she'd held her head high, putting up a brave front—but she could do so no longer. Then Robert was there, putting his arm around her, only making her cry more.

"It's okay, Lottie. We have God who loves us, and it's going to be all right. Just you wait and see."

If only he were right. If only I could be sure. Yet a feeling of fear, of insecurity filled her.

Again, Frank wanted to take Charlotte into his arms to console her, to reassure her that he would take care of her the rest of his life, but he knew it would startle her, make her back away. She needed to regain her composure, so it was better if he looked the other way. He would let her manage it.

"Mr. Hill, it was so kind of you to fetch the water for my trumpet vine."

"You're certainly welcome. And it's Frank, all right?"

"Frank," she murmured, lowering her gaze.

"I know what!" Robert was all smiles again. "When you get back from the West, you can stop by to see us and see just how good this here trumpet vine's a-doing."

Charlotte laughed. It was the second time he'd heard her laugh, and he knew more than anything he wanted to hear that laugh again and again.

God, he prayed, *You've given me quite a task to do. Guess I'd better look in Your Word and get some guidance.*

And as Robert swung his feet out into the middle of the aisle, Frank dug into his satchel for two things: another stick of candy, a lemon one this time, and a worn, loved songbook. It had been his grandmother's. She loved to sing, not only hymns, but also folk songs and especially "I've Been Working on the Railroad." Somewhere from deep within, he was back home, gathered around the warmth of the fire in the living room as his mother played the piano. He'd held on to Mama's hand tightly as they sang one song after another. He began humming the tune under his breath again, and then Robert joined in with his lusty, off-key voice.

> *I've been working on the railroad,*
> *all the livelong day,*
> *I've been working on the railroad,*
> *just to while the time away,*
> *Don't you hear the whistle blowing?*
> *Rise up so early in the morn,*
> *Don't you hear the whistle blowing?*
> *Dinah blow your horn.*

After three more songs, Charlotte brought out the basket of lunch, and they had the crusty bread and ham and cheese. A songfest was the perfect way to end the afternoon.

Chapter 4

The train was quite different from a buggy or hay wagon. The motion kept lulling Charlotte to a sleepy state, but she couldn't quite still the fear in her heart.

They would arrive in McCook soon. As trees and small rolling hills passed by, she thought of how she and Robert would adjust to their new surroundings. What would Cousin Lily's home be like? Did Lily believe in God? Would Charlotte learn to love her new life? And what about Robert? He needed a father. Before he'd had Grandfather, now, no one. He admired Frank. Her heart pounded. She liked Frank, too. He was a nice person, a caring one. Singing the old hymns and songs had been enjoyable. Charlotte could hear his deep bass voice now. Had her father liked singing? She remembered mother playing the piano and singing along. A tight knot filled her throat. How she missed her!

Charlotte knew she must trust God to take care of any problem should it arise. Maybe she could locate work in a hotel or a boarding-house. She was a good cook. At least Grandfather had always said so. Other than teaching, it was the only thing she felt comfortable doing. She had tried sewing, but it didn't come easy, and Grandmother had said once that it took a special knack. She wasn't sure about the teaching. What if she failed? Yet God had promised He cared for her. She opened her Bible to the verse in Matthew: "Behold the fowls of the air: for they sow not, neither do they reap, nor gather into barns; yet your heavenly

Father feedeth them. Are ye not much better than they?"

Charlotte's eyes closed, her hand holding her Bible tight.

Frank was using his ventriloquist trick again, pretending it was Robert talking. Robert also had another candy stick. She couldn't believe he could eat three sticks of candy. She'd wanted to accept when Frank first offered her a candy, but it would not be polite. How could she ever pay him back for all his kindnesses? Maybe he would come through Traer when he returned. *If* he returned. She found herself hoping so.

"Lottie, are you sure we can't go west with Frank?"

She couldn't believe he'd even ask such a thing.

"Young man, maybe you'd better come over here and sit with me."

"Oh, Lottie, I won't ask again." Robert looked crestfallen.

Frank leaned in her direction. "The boy has a natural curiosity."

"I know," she murmured. "I think he needs to sit with me for now."

Robert came over and put his hat over his eyes. He said nothing.

❧

Frank leaned back, thinking about Ohio and how his grandfather had ridden on horseback from town to town, preaching one time in Arkansas, another time in Missouri, and how he had not been there when his child, Frank's father, was born. He also knew his grandmother had been a midwife, bringing hundreds of babies into the world. Another tale he'd heard was that Uncle Peter had fought for the Union while his twin, Paul, had become a rebel. When both her sons died, Grandma took to her bed, never to get up again.

Frank's life had been uncomplicated by contrast. He had never considered marriage until he laid eyes on Charlotte. Something about the stubborn thrust of her chin and the softness behind the fear in her blue, blue eyes had made him care and feel concern. He wanted to protect her. Robert was a bonus. He loved the lad as if he'd known him forever.

He thought about his past community and those patients he'd brought to health. Such stalwart souls! People in Nebraska would be the same. They were farmers with big hearts. He already knew that.

❧

Charlotte relaxed. Robert had to understand that Frank was just passing through. He was a good person, even if he was a cowboy. Not that Charlotte thought that a cowboy was all bad. Probably there were good cowboys. She wished he wasn't going out west. It would be nice to know someone nearby in town, someone she could visit. But he was leaving on the next train, or she assumed so. If only she could calm her fears and just lean on God and His everlasting arms.

She decided to read again. It might help keep her awake.

She fumbled inside the bag on the floor. The trumpet vine was in one corner and looked fine. A lump came to her throat. The vine must live; it had to make it. She opened her Bible again. It was the one treasure she could count on when she felt so bereft. God's Word helped her over the rough spots. It had been hard when Mama was sick, and Charlotte did all she could do to help out. Robert had been her sole charge, and since her mother could not nurse him, Charlotte fed him from a bottle. He reminded her of a little calf with his mouth open and greedy. It had been such a hard time, but she felt empathy for her baby brother since he would never know Mama's sweet face, her endearing smile, or the way it felt when Mama pulled her onto her lap and smoothed the hair back from her hot cheeks. Then Papa left. Charlotte felt a tightness in her now, one that had not been there before. Try as she might, she could not forgive him for leaving like that.

Grandmother died of heart failure, the doctor said, and later Grandpa died. Charlotte knew he was good and strong, but after contracting the influenza, he had died of a broken heart. He missed Grandma too much.

Charlotte had never been alone before. Neighbors and people from church brought food and offered to stay. Charlotte had lifted her chin and said they would manage just fine.

She and Robert had fended for themselves. Then the sky fell in with the news that the farm was no longer theirs. Now she was responsible for getting settled in a new home, finding a church, and attending on a regular basis. She would teach, and Robert would enroll in the third grade. He had not gone to school much the year everyone was ill, so he had fallen behind in his studies. She wished she could have helped him, but there was too much to do and too little time for any of it.

The train whistle blew as it passed through a small town. Robert woke up and asked for permission to sit with Frank again.

Charlotte nodded. "Try not to be a pest."

Soon they were chatting away. Charlotte tried not to listen but then heard Robert's question about Frank's family.

"You didn't have any brothers?" Robert's voice went from low to high-pitched excitement.

"No. I had a sister but no brothers." Frank's smile faded for a moment as he looked away from the searching eyes of the young boy beside him.

"But what happened to her?" Robert probed.

"She's in heaven now, with God. I've never been more sure of anything."

Charlotte's heart skipped a beat. In heaven? Had she heard right? She put a bookmark in her Bible and leaned over to hear better.

"I can be your brother," Robert said, "especially since I don't have a brother. And Lottie can be your sister."

Charlotte's cheeks flamed at the thought.

"Yes, that you could. And I'd be proud to be a big brother to you both."

"Hear that, Lottie?" Robert bounded across the aisle and plopped down beside Charlotte. "Frank's going to be our brother. That means we get to see him again—that is, if he comes back from out west." He turned back to Frank. "Isn't that right?" He ran back and stuck his hand out. "I think we need to shake on it."

Charlotte couldn't stifle the giggle that rose inside her. Robert was so funny at times, and Frank was trying hard not to smirk.

"Yes, we can shake on it." His gaze met Charlotte's over the top of Robert's head. "I'm right proud to be part of your family."

"But you have to shake Lottie's hand, too, or it won't work."

Frank smiled as he clasped her hand.

Charlotte removed her hand, her cheeks flushing a bright red as she looked down at her Bible then back at Frank. "It's a nice thing you've done for my brother."

Frank's gaze never wavered. "It's all my pleasure, Miss Lansing."

"Lottie," Robert said. "You get to call her Lottie now because we're family."

Charlotte smiled. "Yes, we're family now."

"Holdrege is coming up," Frank said, looking at a train schedule he had pulled from his pocket. "We could get out and stretch a bit. I understand we'll be there long enough to get supper."

The picnic lunch eaten earlier had filled the empty space, but Charlotte felt hungry again.

"A lady cooks meals for train passengers, so we could get a bite to eat, or we might buy ice cream at the emporium."

"What's an empor-yum?" Robert asked.

"It's a store that sells lots of items, but the main ones for now are the root beer, a very much sought-after soda pop, and ice cream, which I know you will enjoy."

"It's all right to get off the train?" Charlotte asked. She secretly feared it might leave without them.

"It's fine," Frank said. "The conductor said earlier that there would be several head of cattle to load. It will take at least a half hour."

Robert had grabbed his hat and pushed it down on his head. "I'm for getting off this train; that's for certain. And I want to get one of those root drinks you just talked about."

"Now, Robert, we still have cookies left in the basket from Mrs. Farnsworth." They didn't have money for such tomfoolery, but her mouth watered as she wondered what the treat would taste like. It sounded wonderful.

"But, Lottie, I ain't ever had—"

"Have never had," Charlotte corrected, interrupting him. "That is why you must be enrolled in school, young man. You have much to learn."

"I know." He hung his head just a little. It was a way he had, a sort of pout that made her heart soften. But not this time.

"I'd be happy to buy you both a root beer," Frank said. "It's my gift to my new family."

Charlotte felt the twinge again under her breastbone. Frank was her new "brother," but she didn't want him to be her brother. She felt some-thing different and wondered if it might be this feeling that Mama felt for Papa, lo those twenty years ago. She'd caught Frank looking at her more than once and had trembled when their gazes met.

"We couldn't possibly accept such a gift."

Frank shook his head and stated firmly, "If I can't buy a root beer for my family and friends, then my name isn't Frank Hill."

The whistle blew as the train chugged to a halt. Frank jumped to his feet.

"You have one hour," the conductor said, appearing on the platform as people got off.

"See? We have more time than I thought," Frank said.

Robert bounded down the steps the second the train came to a com-plete stop. Charlotte started down next, but Frank stepped in front of her and held his arm out to help her down.

"Thank you so much, Mr. Hill." She thought of him as Frank, but it didn't seem proper to call him Frank to his face.

The emporium, already crowded, captivated Charlotte. There were barrels with pickles swimming in brine, glass cases full of goodies, color-ful bolts of yardage, and racks of shoes of all sizes.

"Come this way," Frank said, taking her elbow and leading her through the throng of passengers. "I know where we can sit and order our root beers."

Soon each had a tall glass of root beer and a scoop of ice cream in a small dish and were sharing a piece of chocolate cake.

"This is just too much," Charlotte said. "You must save money for your trip to Oregon."

Frank shrugged. "Don't you worry one minute about my trip out west. I have money tucked away in a safe place."

Robert licked his ice cream spoon repeatedly until Charlotte ordered him to stop. His manners were lacking, and she knew it was something else she had failed in. There were so many things she failed at. How could one be a mother and know everything when there was no one to set an example?

"I could buy more ice cream—"

"Absolutely not!" Charlotte's voice shrilled.

"Lottie, can I go look around?" Robert gave his little pouty look that melted her heart once again. She looked at Frank. It was almost as if it was expected that she would rely on him for an answer.

"Do you think it would be all right?"

Frank's eyes twinkled. "I say it would be something a boy needs to do to get the kinks out of his legs."

"You stay right out front then," Charlotte said. "Do you hear me?"

"Yes, Lottie."

Charlotte's ice cream was a melted pool at the bottom of her dish. She had wanted the treat to last forever. It was the first time she'd tasted the cold confection, and here it had melted, but she ate it anyway.

"I think you two were more impressed with the ice cream than the root beer," Frank said, his gaze meeting hers. "I'm glad there was time to get off the train."

Charlotte nodded, taking the last spoonful and letting it stay on the back of her tongue for a long moment.

"I wonder where my little brother went," Frank said.

Alarmed, Charlotte jumped up. "Oh, dear, he isn't where I told him to stay, is he?"

"No, but I can well imagine where he might be. One block over is the livery stable. Don't you think he went to see the horses?"

Just as the word "horses" was out of his mouth, the whistle blew, signaling everyone to get back on the train.

"Oh no! Robert! What am I going to do?" Charlotte ran out the door, holding her skirts high to avoid a mud puddle in the front of the emporium. "I shouldn't have let him go. He just doesn't listen, and now we'll get left behind—"

"We have five minutes," Frank said. "Enough time for me to find him." He put his bowler hat on and commanded Charlotte to board the train in a sharp, no-nonsense tone. "The conductor probably can't hold up the train, but I'll be back as soon as possible. Maybe they can wait for a few minutes."

"Oh, I pray they can!"

Charlotte clutched her reticule and prayed her heart would stop pounding so fiercely as she kept looking down the street. There was no sign yet of Robert or Frank. She hadn't been this scared since the time she'd fallen in the duck pond before she'd learned to swim. "Dear, heavenly Father, please help Frank find Robert, and let the train wait for them," she murmured.

Her knuckles were white as she climbed the steps and went to her seat. "My brother and his, uh, his companion are not here yet," she told the conductor who came through the car.

"We are leaving in three minutes. We cannot wait, ma'am; we must stick to a schedule." His tone was icy, and fear hit her. If they couldn't wait, perhaps she'd better get off. To leave Robert was unthinkable.

Charlotte headed for the door. "I must get off then."

"Ma'am, they can catch the next train."

"Oh my goodness, no. That won't do at all." She started to push past him just as the train began to roll. Charlotte had forgotten her bag with her Bible, the trumpet vine, and her toiletry items. She couldn't leave them, but she couldn't stay on the train either.

A shout sounded, and she saw Frank running with Robert haphazardly carried under one arm as if he were a small pig.

"We're coming! Here!" He half tossed Robert to the conductor who grabbed the small boy and set him on his feet. Robert's hat fell, and Frank stopped to get it, but it went under the wheels.

"Frank!" wailed Robert. "We can't leave Frank!"

"Here!" The conductor held out his hand as Frank ran alongside the slow-moving train. He grabbed the conductor's hand and jumped aboard. Perspiration poured down his face as he breathed in long gulps of air and slumped over onto the first seat by the door. Charlotte, who intended to give Robert a thorough tongue-lashing, stood mute, too scared to speak or scold. Robert flew into her arms, and she held him tight. She caught Frank's glance over the top of her brother's head.

"Are you all right, Mr. Hill? Oh, I do hope so." She turned back to Robert and with no forewarning burst into tears.

"Lottie, I'm sorry." A grimy hand reached up and touched her face. "I had to see the horses, and I didn't mean to be bad."

"Robert, you scared me so!" Her crying, instead of subsiding as she hugged the small body close, became loud, jerking sobs.

❦

Recovered from his frantic race with the train, Frank was at her side, his arms wrapping around her as he pulled both of them close. He felt as if God was telling him: *This is what matters, my son. Not anything else but the lives of people. Think of what you can do, how you can touch someone with your care and concern.*

"You're going to be all right," Frank said. "Sit down. Take long, deep breaths." He finally stepped aside yet still felt the young woman's warmth, the fragrance from her hair, the face that had been so close he could have kissed her. . .

"I'm fine." Charlotte straightened her dress, looking away, not meeting Frank's gaze again. "I was so frightened."

"I know."

"And I'm sorry," Robert repeated. "I won't do anything like that again, Lottie, I promise."

Charlotte nodded. "Yes, but just the same, I think you'd better sit beside me, and we'll read some Scriptures."

Robert didn't argue.

Frank leaned back against the cushioned seat. His heart hadn't slowed down, though he knew it wasn't beating now from the race to catch the train—it was racing from something far more meaningful. He had never felt this way about a woman before, though a young widow from his practice had shown more than a casual interest in him back in Ohio. At one time he proclaimed he would never marry. Some people were meant to marry, but he didn't feel he was one of them. Now his heart was telling him differently. Now he reckoned he knew what people talked about, why they set their feelings to song. He liked the thought of Charlotte in the kitchen preparing breakfast, flashing him one of her warm smiles and taking his hand. How his mind raced on, his thoughts tumbling over one another.

"Frank." A small hand tugged at his arm. "I'm sorry."

"I know you are, and it's okay."

"Lottie says it's not—and perhaps you won't be my brother now."

"I'll be your brother always. A promise is a promise, and one doesn't stop being a brother because of some little problem." He reached out and ruffled Robert's hair. "The very first thing we'll buy in McCook is a new hat. It can be the same color and style as the one you lost."

"You will do that?"

"What are brothers for, anyway?"

"How far now until we get off the train?" Robert asked, clearly eager for another excursion.

Frank looked at his watch. "I'd say a little after daybreak."

"You mean we sleep on the train, too?"

Frank now wished they were on one of the larger trains with a sleeping car so he could offer it to Lottie, but the small trains didn't offer sleeping quarters.

❧

"Lottie, how can I pay for my hat?"

Charlotte had wondered the same thing. She knew one wasn't to be concerned about owing people, that God sent people to help. It was His way of answering prayers. And one especially did not wonder if the person belonged to God, but did Frank belong to God? She wanted to ask but somehow couldn't bring herself to do it.

"Don't you worry now. Having the two of you for friends is all I want. I might come by for a home-cooked supper one night. How does that sound?"

"Oh, Lottie, you can make chicken and dumplings and maybe a fresh gooseberry pie."

"But, Mr. Hill, you are going on to Oregon, isn't that correct?" She felt her cheeks flame as she looked at Frank, hoping they did not betray her.

Frank smiled. "I'll return though. Of this I am sure."

"Oh, that's such good news, isn't it, Lottie?" Robert tugged on her sleeve, but all she could do was nod yes.

Chapter 5

The windows were closed as the sun set and passengers settled in for the night. Frank wondered if one day people might cross the countryside in a matter of hours. The train was much faster than covered wagons had been, so only on rare occasions would someone travel that way now. There had been talk of a vehicle people would drive; a horseless buggy they called it. He just might see one before he died.

Robert sat next to his sister, and the two huddled close to each other. Frank had an extra blanket he often took on the train. He didn't need it. He'd rather give his friends extra cover. The train could be quite drafty at night, even in the summer.

His family. His charges. "Thank You, God, for using me in this way," he murmured as he spread the blanket over them.

While Frank wondered about the cousin the two expected to be waiting at the train station, he thought about the woman at the boardinghouse where he would stay temporarily. She was not expecting him this early. He had planned the side trip to Oregon but knew he could not go now. He would not rest a bit until he knew Charlotte and Robert were in safe surroundings.

He had no idea how late it was when the conductor came through the car carrying a lantern. "Is there a doctor aboard?"

Frank bolted to attention.

"A woman in the next car is in terrible pain. I wondered if someone might help."

Charlotte sat up, but Robert slumped over, his head in her lap. This was one adventure he'd miss out on.

"Is something wrong?" she asked.

In the pale light of the lantern, Frank saw the concern in her eyes. She had faced a lot of sickness and much death for her young years. He explained while the conductor went to the next car.

Frank grabbed his coat and got to his feet.

"Mr. Hill, are you going somewhere?"

"I want to see if she needs my coat. It could be she got a chill from the damp night air."

"You would give her your coat?" Charlotte sounded impressed.

He leaned over and whispered, "Yes, I would." He liked the admiration in her eyes.

Frank walked to the front of the car and opened the door. The night wind rushed through before he could close it. He waited on the platform for the conductor to come back through.

"Alas, there are no doctors aboard."

"I'm a doctor," Frank replied. "I don't have my medicine bag with me, but I'll take a look."

"A doctor?"

Frank nodded. "I had an office in Ohio but haven't practiced for the last few months."

"But I thought you said you were a cowboy. I overheard part of that conversation with the young boy there."

"I know. It was a silly thing to say, and the young lad picked up on it so fast I couldn't get out of it."

"Well, come with me. I hope you can help."

The woman was writhing while her husband held her hand.

Frank bent over her, his insides recoiling as he recognized the problem. How could he do this? "Are you pregnant?" he finally asked.

"She is only into her sixth month," her husband answered as the woman arched again. He lovingly leaned over to kiss her forehead. Frank swallowed. Such tenderness. What a joy it must be to find a loving mate, one who would put his wife's care above his own.

He knew now that he probably couldn't save the premature baby, but he
had to do everything to save the young woman. He didn't want to be here,
but there was no choice.

Frank turned to the conductor. "I'll need your lantern—and another
one if you have it—boiling water, and some clean towels."

"Oh, Lizzie, did you hear that? This doctor is going to help us."

The contractions intensified as she cried out and gripped the sides of
the seat cushion. A makeshift curtain had been set up to allow privacy.

Ten minutes later the baby came. It never took a breath and lay still
in Frank's hands. He wrapped it in a towel, put it in his coat, and turned
back to the woman.

"My baby?"

He leaned over and wiped her forehead. "He didn't make it. I'm so
very sorry."

She cried openly as her husband held her close. Frank's concern was
to stop the hemorrhaging and to make a bed for her to rest. They were
close to McCook, and he prayed that she would survive until then. If the
bleeding stopped, she'd be fine.

The husband crooned to his wife, his gaze not leaving her face except
for an occasional glance at the coat holding his dead son.

"These things happen, and we have no way to stop contractions once
they begin," Frank explained.

"I've never had anything like this happen on my train," the conductor
said.

"And I pray it never happens again."

"We'll have a proper burial in McCook," the young father said.

After checking his patient again, Frank asked the Lord to take care
of Lizzie, then made his way back to his car and found his seat in the
semidarkness.

"Is she going to be all right?" A soft voice came from across the aisle.
Charlotte. He had hoped she might be asleep.

"She is going to be fine because God is with her."

Charlotte leaned closer. "God was part of my grandparents' lives and my mother's, but He didn't heal them."

"He answers prayers always but perhaps not in the way we had hoped."

"How would you know? You being a cowboy and all?"

"And you think cowboys don't know or worship God?"

She sighed. "No, you're right. Of course some probably do. And I guess you're one of them."

Frank pulled his hat over his eyes and hunched up. At least he now knew he could doctor again. The loss of the baby was something that couldn't be helped. He shivered and slunk lower in the seat in an attempt to ward off the early morning chill. What he wouldn't give for a good night's rest in a bed with blankets and a quilt. Grandmother Julia's patchwork would have worked fine.

Charlotte said no more, and Frank was thankful. He slept fitfully for the next hour, slipping down the aisle once to check on the woman. She was asleep, and the bleeding had all but stopped. He was glad to see the first rays of dawn filling the train car.

When Frank reached his seat, Robert jumped up like a spring. "I slept, didn't I?" He grinned as he made his way to the end of the car where the water closet was located.

"Yes, you certainly did," Charlotte said.

She noticed Frank's blanket spread across her legs. She clearly hadn't realized it until now.

"Oh my, you needed this."

"No, I'm fine. Really."

"That was a noble thing to do, giving up your coat and all."

"Yes, well—"

"And you gave me your blanket."

Charlotte put a hand to her hair. "I must look a fright." She took a small mirror from her reticule and gasped. "Oh, I do hope you aren't laughing at me."

Her hat was askew, and he nearly laughed at the sight, but he knew that no gentleman ever laughed at a lady who had not had the benefit of a mirror.

Frank grinned. "Never." He stuck his hat on his head. "I do believe we're all in the same situation."

Robert reappeared, adjusting his coat. "Lottie, do we have any of those cookies left?"

"Of course. Did you wash your hands?"

"Yes."

He grabbed a cookie and began munching. Charlotte offered Frank a cookie, but he shook his head.

"I'd say about two more hours and we will be into McCook."

Robert raised his hands as if to shout for joy that the journey was nearly over, but Charlotte covered his mouth. "No noise, young man. Some people are still sleeping."

The conductor came down the aisle, stopping in front of Frank. "That was a special thing you did for that woman last night. And the prayer helped also. Too bad about the baby though."

Charlotte held her breath. *Praying? Did he say Frank prayed for her? And what about a baby? He didn't mention that. Maybe he is a preaching cowboy; I suppose they have such. Then he has a special calling. Frank has been called from God, and I am more than a bit fortunate to have met him.*

"She was relieved that we had a doctor aboard even if the baby couldn't be saved."

Frank rose. "I'd better go check on her."

A baby died? Charlotte wondered if she'd heard right. *Had the conductor said "doctor"? But how could that be?*

Robert looked puzzled. "I thought you were a cowboy, Frank."

"Oh, he may be one of those, too, but he's going to have a practice in McCook. Isn't that right, sir?" the conductor asked.

Frank nodded. Yes, he was a doctor, and, yes, he had prayed, but it was God who brought wellness to a fellow passenger. But to Charlotte, he was a bold-faced liar. He could not bear to look in her direction, nor did he want to hear what she might say, though he knew he would hear soon enough.

Chapter 6

"You're a *doctor?*" Charlotte said it as if it were a forbidden word.

Frank nodded. Robert stared, looking at the pointy end of his lemon stick.

"Why didn't you tell us?" Charlotte asked.

"I was going to."

"When?"

"When the train pulled out of the station and left me behind—with you and Robert."

Her face flushed at the comment. "So you never *were* a cowboy?"

"Only in my heart. Everyone has wishes, and mine was to go west and be a cowboy. I was considering giving up being a doctor, due to an incident that happened where I blamed myself for the death of a mother and her child."

"Oh my," Charlotte began, but Frank continued.

"I know it was stretching the truth."

Charlotte stared and finally spoke. "But why would you say you were a cowboy? That's the most unlikely part."

"I know what you must think." Frank withdrew his Bible from the valise and brought it over to Charlotte. Psalm 44, verse 21 may plead my case: 'For he knoweth the secrets of the heart.'

"We all dream and wish. You hope for a new life in Kansas as a schoolteacher. I thought of going west because I have a touch of wanderlust.

Robert dreams about riding trains and going to a new school."

Robert made a face. "I'm not looking forward to school."

"I understand." Frank ruffled his hair. "I felt that way, too, when I was your age. All I thought about was my dog and riding my horse out into the hills behind my house."

Robert's ears perked up. "What was your horse's name?"

"Cinnamon, because he was the color of a cinnamon stick."

"I like that name."

"And it's okay for you to wish for a new horse one day."

"Is it, Frank?"

Charlotte looked out the window, staying out of the conversation. Frank hoped she might at least look their way. Anything was better than silence.

"Frank, are you really not going to Oregon?" Robert asked.

"That's right."

"Well, we are going to Traer," Charlotte said.

The train began slowing down, and Charlotte put the small carpetbag on the seat. Robert held the empty picnic basket, and Frank picked up his new, shiny black valise. It had been a gift from a former patient.

❦

Charlotte didn't know what to think. What reasons did Frank have for hiding the fact that he was a doctor? Could she believe what he was saying now? She knew how she felt about him in her heart, yet there was the fact that she had begun falling in love with a man who was a charlatan.

She sat, hands folded in her lap, knowing she could not accept help from Frank. How could she tell Robert to be truthful when someone he admired so much had lied?

Robert, bless his heart, had washed his face earlier, but somehow he had found something sooty and had black smudges on both cheeks. She reached over and rubbed at it with a handkerchief she'd dampened with spittle.

"Lottie, don't." He pulled away.

"Don't you want to look presentable for your cousin Lily?"

"She doesn't care about my face. She'll hug you and talk to you."

"And here you don't even have a hat."

"Frank said he'd buy one for me."

"I'm afraid we cannot accept his gift."

"But, Lottie—"

She reached over, shushing his words, making him swallow them. "We'll have no more of that."

The train came to a full stop, and just as Charlotte rose, it gave one more lurch and she went flying across the aisle, almost into Frank's lap. He caught her, steadied her, and looked into her face. She saw regret in his eyes but chose to ignore it.

Wagons pulled up as workers began unloading trunks and boxes from the baggage area. Charlotte quickly ascended, holding on to Robert. She wasn't about to let him out of her sight. Not ever again. Not even once.

Frank was talking to Lizzie, who had been carried from the train and lifted onto a wagon. Her face looked pale, but it was the bundle in the coat that wrenched his heart.

Her husband shook Frank's hand. "I can never repay you for what you've done. I'll see that your coat is returned."

"Are you from McCook?" Frank asked.

"No. We've come to visit my parents," the young man said.

Frank smiled. "I'll be seeing you around here again. I'd like to check up on your wife in a day or so. I'll be putting my shingle out in a few weeks."

❦

Charlotte stood forlorn, as if lost. Shadowing her face with her hand, she looked down the tracks and by the station, searching the crowd.

"Robert, I do hope the top of your head doesn't get sunburned, what with losing that hat and all. Maybe you'd better go over there in the shade of the station."

"Do you know what your cousin looks like?" asked Frank.

"I have a picture," Charlotte said. "She's blond with a round, plump face."

"She's probably been detained for whatever reason."

He wanted to shelter her, to make things better, but he knew she had lost any feeling she might have had toward him. He waved at one of the boys who had a loaded wagon and was ready to take it to the local hotel.

"Can you get any more on there?"

"Of course, sir."

"The lady, boy, and I will walk; it's not that far. We'll have the bags taken to the boardinghouse." Charlotte started to protest, but Frank wouldn't hear of it.

"I would not be doing you any favor if I left you and Robert out here in the hot sun with no food or water. You must come with me."

Thankfully, Frank had visited McCook earlier to meet the people who were eager to have a town doctor and thus knew his way around the growing town. Charlotte had no choice but to let him help her.

Robert, who had been unusually quiet, suddenly shot ahead of them.

"Really, Mr. Hill, we can fend for ourselves."

Frank was firm. "I'm afraid I can't allow that. A young woman and small boy cannot be left alone on an empty train platform with no people and no place to go."

Robert came back. "Are you going to take us to our cousin's house?"

"Robert! How impertinent of you!"

Frank laughed. "He's saying what's on his mind, and there's nothing wrong with that, no sirree."

"Let's go over to the boardinghouse where travelers stay and a few of the local people live," Frank suggested.

"I cannot pay—"

Frank held up a hand. "I realize that, Charlotte. What I'm thinking is that you can help earn your keep. Mrs. Collins—I met her last time I was here—is a kind woman and seemed shorthanded before."

Charlotte nodded. "Yes, I suppose that is acceptable. I wouldn't have been working right off anyway since school starts in the fall."

The huge, three-story house needed a coat of paint, but the garden of petunias and marigolds out front made Charlotte smile.

Mrs. Collins hugged Charlotte and Robert and insisted they sit right off while she finished cooking breakfast. In a matter of seconds, Frank had explained the situation then left to attend to business.

"I wish I could have gone with Frank," Robert said after downing his glass of orange juice.

Charlotte gave him a cross look, and he sat back down. "You just stay with me. I told you I'm not letting you out of my sight ever again."

He wrinkled his nose. "Not ever?"

"Well, maybe when you're eighteen."

"Ah, Lottie, I won't do that again. 'Sides, we'll never go on a train again."

"And how do you know that? Maybe Lily isn't coming after all, and we may have to go on the next train coming through and head back to Creston."

"We couldn't do that." He raised his eyebrows, his expression stricken.

Charlotte sighed. "I have no idea what we'll do. But in the meantime, we'll accept the food and possibly a place for the night."

Mrs. Collins had brought in coffee for Charlotte, milk for Robert, and a large stack of pancakes when Frank sauntered back in.

"I have unfortunate news," he said, meeting Charlotte's anxious gaze.

"Does it have to do with Lily?"

He nodded. "She sent a wire; it was at the telegraph office."

"What happened?" Charlotte's insides were knotting up. "I must know."

Frank sat across the table and looked back at the two scared faces. "She said she couldn't get away after all to fetch you. Her children are sick, and she can't leave them."

"But, she *will* come?"

"She couldn't promise when."

"Then it's settled. I'll work wherever I can."

"I can help that man with the luggage at the train station," Robert said, puffing out his chest. "I watched, and it's a job I can do."

"Of course you can," Frank said. "I have a better idea. Why don't you two come west with me? We can look it over, and if we don't like it, we'll just head back." His face held no expression.

"Mr. Hill, surely you aren't serious."

Robert stood, his mouth hanging open. When he finally found his voice, he let out a loud whoop, causing others to turn and stare. "That's the best idea yet!"

"It's absurd." Charlotte set down her cup.

"I thought it was a good solution." Frank reached over and took her hand. Charlotte's lips twitched in disdain.

"Don't worry. I was not serious, but what I *am* serious about is getting rooms right here for the night and then worrying about tomorrow when it comes. You need rest. After freshening up, you'll feel like facing the problem."

"I cannot—"

Frank put a hand up. "I know what you're going to say, but please don't. Allow me this one thing. You both have made my trip pleasant, and I want to do this because of the second commandment Jesus gave us: 'Unto one of the least of these my brethren, ye have done it unto me.'"

Charlotte sighed. There was no other answer. She had to accept Frank's offer.

"Can I help out?" Charlotte asked, dabbing at her wet cheeks.

"Mrs. Collins said her other helper left to be with her daughter's family, so she needs someone to do the wash and change the linens."

Charlotte's face brightened. "I can do that." She was proud and did not want to take from someone she didn't know.

A young girl set heaping platters of scrambled eggs and slabs of ham next to the stack of pancakes. "Are you hungry?" she asked.

"Like bears," Frank said. He reached across the table and took both Charlotte's and Robert's hands. "Let's ask the Lord to bless this food."

Frank's loud voice filled the room, and Charlotte suddenly felt safe. Maybe he really had wanted to be a cowboy and had truly intended to go west. Maybe it wasn't an intentional lie to deceive her and Robert. Should she forgive him? Isn't that what God would expect? While she was mulling that over, Robert ate five pancakes, two slices of ham, and a large serving of eggs. Now he was ready to explore. Charlotte relented and let him go with Frank to the stables. She stayed and finished her food, thinking she might as well start right off by washing their dishes.

Mrs. Collins was happy with her work, and after the kitchen was cleaned, she showed Charlotte the room at the top of the stairs.

"From what you've told me about your love for flowers, I think you'll like my new wallpaper."

Charlotte clasped her hands at her throat. Sunshine poured in through a white-curtained window and danced on the pattern of violets and daisies on the walls. A nightstand and large chest filled one corner. It was perfect.

"It's surely God's provision," she murmured.

Mrs. Collins nodded. "Sometimes He sends someone to help."

"Like Frank."

They went back downstairs and found Frank and Robert playing checkers. The sight warmed her heart. Frank looked up, and as their gazes met, she held out her hand. "I've judged you harshly; forgive me."

He took her hand and held it an extra moment. "There is nothing to forgive."

Robert smiled but said nothing. It was as if he had a secret, one he didn't want to share with anyone, at least not yet.

"C'mon, Lottie, show me the room."

Charlotte took her little brother's hand then nodded at Frank as grateful tears filled her eyes. God was making sure she was taken care of. He was fulfilling His promises.

"Mrs. Collins said your room is on the top floor."

As the two went up the stairs, Charlotte began singing: " 'Standing, standing, standing on the promises of God, our Savior. Standing, standing, we're standing on the promises of God.' "

"I love it when you sing," Robert said. "It makes me happy."

"And that's why I sing; it's from a grateful heart."

She imagined God must have looked down and smiled at His children. There was nothing better than voices rejoicing with song.

Chapter 7

Frank was glad to have Robert stay with him for the night. They were not far away should the boy need his sister.

The timing had been perfect. A new church was being built in McCook, and the crew needed helpers. Besides meeting the train, Robert would be the fetch-all kid, bringing water, iced tea, and lemonade to the workers. The first service would be in two weeks, and Frank was looking forward to it. That meant he would get to know the townspeople better. The inside would not be completed for a while, but fancy floors weren't necessary.

"The people are the church," Frank's father had said more than once. "What they meet in to worship is not the most important thing. Coming with a ready heart to serve and praise God is."

God's provision was so evident. When the train came in each morning, Robert would meet and give the passengers directions to the boardinghouse where they would be served a substantial meal. If someone needed help carrying luggage, he would help with that, too.

"I can hardly wait to start," Robert said shortly after they'd come to the room.

"You'll do a fine job," Frank replied. "Charlotte will help Mrs. Collins, who definitely needs an extra pair of hands and steady feet to carry food to the table."

"Will Charlotte still teach school?" Robert asked as he stretched out on the bed. He had changed into his nightshirt and looked up at Frank.

"It depends on whether they still need her in Traer."

"I want to stay here," Robert said. "I like it here."

"And you don't know what to expect in Kansas." Frank finished Robert's thought.

The young boy looked pensive. "I guess I have to go with Charlotte."

Long after the child had fallen asleep, Frank sat with his Bible in hand. He welcomed having a family to care for. He was more than ready for the responsibility of having a wife. If a child came, too, it was an even bigger blessing. If Frank made the decision, Charlotte would become a doctor's wife, not a schoolmarm. He knew now that he wanted that more than anything. His strong feelings had bloomed instantaneously, but he knew that nothing was coincidental, that the Lord had a definite hand in the timing and making sure His children were guided in the right direction.

Frank lowered his head. "Lord God, You have blessed me in so many ways, and I thank You for this town, my friends, and for Charlotte and young Robert. You already know my heart's dream; it's in Your hands now."

Though extremely tired and thankful for a nice room in the boarding-house, Charlotte had a fitful first night. Nightmares caused her to break into a cold sweat. She'd fall asleep, only to dream that Robert was falling from the train. She'd reach out for him, but he'd slip from her grasp. When she woke, her cheeks were wet from tears.

She rose before dawn. Surely Mrs. Collins needed help with breakfast preparations.

Pulling a slightly wrinkled but clean muslin from the trunk, Charlotte dressed and went downstairs.

Mrs. Collins was up and had a huge pot of coffee perking on the old woodstove.

"My goodness, child, I didn't hear you on the stairs." She smiled warmly. "I don't need you yet—"

"I couldn't sleep."

"Was the bed uncomfortable?"

Charlotte shook her head, fighting back tears that suddenly threatened. She'd had no idea that tears were close to the surface. "The bed was what I needed, but my thoughts and fears would not let me sleep."

An arm went around Charlotte's shoulder as the older woman pulled her close. "There, now, you are among friends, and there is to be no fear in your heart. God, in His infinite wisdom, has provided—as He always does, I might add. Ah, lass, you had no way of knowing that I prayed for someone to come off the train yesterday that could help."

Charlotte wiped her tears away with the apron. "You did?"

"I certainly did. And we prayed that our doctor might come early as so many of us are needing medical care."

Charlotte thought back to the train and how Frank had delivered a premature infant and saved the young mother's life. The conversation about Frank going west to be a cowboy seemed unimportant. Would he stay here and be the doctor the town needed, or would he still have the desire to go out west?

"We have a fine young man in Dr. Frank Hill. I knew that the minute I laid eyes on him. And he's certainly what this town needs."

"Yes, he is a fine person."

"He took you and your brother under his wing, and I daresay you two might be the reason he's not continuing on with his trip west."

Charlotte gasped. "You knew about this?"

The older woman nodded. "Told me about it while you did last night's dishes. Said he'd had a change of plans."

Charlotte didn't know what to say, and whenever that happened, she found it worked if she busied herself at some task.

"What can I do first to help?"

"Can you make baking powder biscuits?"

"That I can. My grandmother made the best ones, and I learned from watching her."

Soon biscuits were in the oven and the eggs were scrambled and waiting to be cooked, while thick slabs of ham were frying in two large skillets. A noise from the dining room made Charlotte turn.

"Robert!" she cried, running to her little brother. "You have a hat,

I see, and must be ready to go meet the train."

"Yes, Lottie. Frank bought the hat and gave it to me this morning." His freckled face was scrubbed clean; his eyes looked rested. He hugged Charlotte around the middle.

Charlotte looked beyond the boy, hoping to see Frank in the room. It was empty, and a sudden chill went through her. She hadn't realized until that moment how much she wanted to see him and had hoped he might be there with Robert.

As if reading her mind, Robert answered, "Frank's gone to buy a newspaper."

"Oh."

"Said he'd be back to eat breakfast with us though."

Mrs. Collins pointed to the door. "You've done more than enough, Miss Charlotte. Go with Robert to the train station. Train should be in around seven. Welcome the people who get off; then come back to help serve the food."

"Are you sure you don't mind my leaving?"

"Absolutely."

The morning sun hailed from a full blue sky as the two, arm in arm, trudged down the dusty dirt road to the station.

"I think I can hear it," Robert said, tilting his head toward the east.

"You cannot. I hear nothing but the wind blowing."

"It's coming. We'd better hurry!" Holding his new straw hat on his head with his hand, Robert took off running. Charlotte, laughing, ran after him.

This time when the train rolled into town, stopping with a huff and puff of noise and steam, Charlotte wasn't frightened. She rather liked this steel monster after all.

Faces peered from the windows, and soon people were alighting, waiting for their baggage. Had it only been a day since she and Robert had stood on this platform waiting for Cousin Lily?

Robert went from person to person and found a couple who needed his assistance.

As they went down the street to the boardinghouse where a good meal waited, Charlotte looked up again, thanking God for bringing her here. She had no idea how long she might stay, but she found herself thinking more and more that this was home. This was the place God had destined for her to be. She liked seeing Frank each day, and Robert had blossomed under Frank's tutelage.

She would take it a day at a time, as His answer would be forthcoming.

Chapter 8

I t had been a week since Charlotte, Robert, and Frank arrived in the Nebraska town. The office where Frank would practice had been furnished with medical supplies, and people were stopping by to chat.

Each day Robert and Charlotte met the train, and each morning was a flurry of excitement while she helped Mrs. Collins with the meals.

On Saturday, a man alighted from the train, saying he was looking for a Miss Charlotte Lansing and her brother, Robert.

Charlotte froze.

"I'm Robert, and this is Lottie," her brother said.

The man with craggy eyebrows and a determined look was dressed in pants and a shirt that needed laundering. He stepped forward and held out his hand.

"Lily sent me. Name's Jack Slater."

Charlotte stood, hands at her sides, ignoring his hand. A chill swept over her, and she wanted to turn and run.

He stepped closer. "You really need to come with me. Lily's eager to see you again."

Robert's face blanched.

"I am afraid that is impossible," Charlotte finally said. "My brother and I are quite happy here now, and we both have gainful employment."

Jack scowled, reaching out to take her arm. "I didn't come all this way to be turned aside. . . ."

Charlotte moved back again. "I am terribly sorry, but Mrs. Collins is expecting me back at the boardinghouse to help with the meals. I can perhaps come later."

"Why did you come from that way when Kansas is that way?" Robert had found his voice and stood pointing south.

"I was unavoidably detained on a business trip to Omaha; I insist that you both come with me now."

Charlotte's insides twisted. She didn't want to go to Kansas now. She wanted to stay here and knew Robert did, too. What could she do to convince this horrid man?

Murmuring a prayer under her breath, she started off in the direction of the boardinghouse.

"You *will* come with me." Jack gripped her shoulder, spinning her around. She started to scream, but a hand clamped over her mouth.

Robert yelled and began hitting the man, but he was no match, and Jack shoved him aside. "You can stay here," he said. "It's Charlotte I want."

Charlotte felt faint, and her knees buckled. Her vision blurred, and she feared she might lose consciousness.

Robert bent over his sister, begging her to get up. Jack scooped her into his arms and started to board the train. Nausea gripped her as she struggled to regain her footing and clear her vision.

"Wait a minute!" Robert yelled. "You can't be going to Kansas, because this here train goes out west—that's what Frank said."

"Is that so?"

He pushed past Robert and turned to climb the steps where Charlotte caught a glimpse of a young man standing with his arms folded. And was that the conductor behind him?

Thank You, God, for sending help to my brave little brother. Another wave of nausea assailed Charlotte.

"I know *her*," she heard the conductor say. "She came through with the lad here and a doctor fellow. The good doctor saved a woman's life."

"That's Frank," Robert said proudly, "and he wouldn't want Lottie to go anywhere without his knowing. Besides, we like it here in McCook."

She was half standing, and someone was fanning Charlotte's face, their putrid breath assaulting her nose. She opened her eyes wide and screamed—directly into Jack's filthy face.

"Offhand, I'd say the young lady doesn't want to go with you," the conductor said.

"Well, she must. We're all the family she has."

"I have family," Charlotte said, pushing away from the grimy man. His grip held, and she landed on a small crate. The nausea was subsiding, and her head was beginning to clear at last. "I have friends from church and people in this town. They are all the family I need. Let go of me."

Releasing her, Jack scowled and muttered loud enough for her to hear. "We'll see about this. Lily will not be too happy, I can guarantee you."

"Lily's kids are sick," Robert challenged. "She sent a wire, and Frank read it." He moved protectively to Charlotte's side.

"Sick? Kids?" Jack adjusted his hat and laughed. "Lily just couldn't get away from her job at the bordello."

Charlotte knew she had heard that term before, and if it meant what she thought it did, she was more than happy that Lily had not been able to come.

The train started pulling away from the station. Jack did not get back on but walked toward town. She knew Robert wanted to get Frank, but he was afraid to leave Charlotte alone.

"I need to get back to help serve breakfast." She held on to Robert and reached out to a nearby bench for support, but her legs gave way again.

Once again Frank's mind went to Charlotte as he wondered if he dare say what was in his heart, if he could ask her to come courting. He loved her with all his heart. It had become more apparent with each day since he'd first laid eyes on her. Sometimes he caught her looking at him, and he wondered if she could feel just a smidgeon of the love he felt.

He put his hat on and walked outside as a young man ran up, breathless, and nearly knocked Frank over. "You gotta come quick, Dr. Hill. Miss Charlotte needs help. An awful man tried to force her on the train."

Frank's insides churned. "*Help* Charlotte?"

"Her brother is with her down at the station. She can't seem to move."

Frank took off running, afraid of what he'd find. Charlotte always went with Robert in the morning to greet the train. Sometimes he went along, but not this morning. Now he wished he had.

Charlotte sat on one of the wagons as it headed for town. Robert sat with her, propping her up.

The wagon driver stopped, and Frank jumped aboard. He bent down and pulled Charlotte into his arms. "What happened?"

Robert started to explain, but Frank cut him off halfway. Frank knew about Jack Slater. He'd seen the man once before on a train in Ohio. A professional gambler and thief, he had hoped Slater and his kind would never come to McCook.

"Charlotte, please answer me." He so hoped she wasn't in shock, but it was likely. She'd had a good scare, and if Robert hadn't been there, who knew what might have happened? He checked the pupils of her eyes. They were fine.

"I did not like that man," Robert said, hovering over his sister. "He said he was taking us to Lily. He was going the wrong way, huh, Frank?"

Frank pulled the boy close. "Yes, you're correct. He was going the wrong way."

"The conductor wouldn't let him on the train with Lottie," Robert added.

"Thank goodness for that."

Charlotte opened her eyes and smiled. "You came."

"Of course. Did you ever doubt it?" Concern pulled at Frank's face as he realized more fully what might have happened. "Are you feeling better now?"

"I am now that you're here."

"Let's get you home." He nodded to the young man driving the wagon. "I'm much obliged, Jacob," he said before turning back to Charlotte. "No helping Mrs. Collins today. As your doctor, I insist on complete bed rest."

"I'll be fine. Really, I will."

Robert still hovered. "I can clear the table, Frank, and help with the dishes, too."

Frank nodded. "I know you can. And it's mighty nice of you to offer, but one of the women can also help. I'll see what I can do once I get Charlotte settled."

❧

Charlotte was not at supper that night. Robert waited on the long table, an apron over his pants and shirt. He looked proud to be helping out.

"Is Lottie okay?" Frank asked as he grabbed a carrot stick. He'd been back several times already, and each time Mrs. Collins shook her head. "Says she has a headache."

Frank went up the stairs. He tapped on the door, knowing he dare not go into Charlotte's room, as it wouldn't be proper.

Her voice sounded; then the door opened. If ever there had been a doubt, it vanished the minute their gazes met. "Charlotte," he said, putting an arm around her, "I've been so worried about you."

"I'm going to be fine, Frank." Sudden tears filled her eyes. "He was awful. He wanted us to go and insisted we do so. I just couldn't go with someone I had never met before."

"Jack Slater's up to no good, I'm sure. He left town this afternoon. You're safe now." He wanted to hold her close, to reassure her he would always be there for her. He also wanted to ask her to be his wife and to take Robert as his brother-in-law. Yet the time wasn't right.

"Let me fix up a bit, and I'll come down."

"Have you eaten at all today?"

"Just some soup."

"I could have Robert bring you some of Mrs. Collins's bread pudding."

"No, I want to come down. I'm fine. Having you here has given me strength."

"I'll wait outside the door then."

That evening after the dishes had been cleared and the table set for morning, Mrs. Collins thanked Robert—making a big show of it in Charlotte and Frank's presence—causing the boy to beam with pride.

"You worked hard today, lad. I'll do the washing now. Go on and be with your sister and Frank."

✂

"Charlotte, I don't want you to go to Traer now or ever," Frank said when they walked into the parlor.

"Frank, what are you saying?"

Frank took the handkerchief out of his pocket and formed it into a figure. "Miss Charlotte Lansing, will you be my wife?"

Robert laughed as Charlotte gasped, unable to speak.

"She says 'yes'!" Robert answered, tossing his hat into the air.

Charlotte's face turned crimson, but her eyes gave the answer to Frank's question.

"How soon can you get married?" Mrs. Collins asked from the doorway.

"As soon as a preacher can come," Frank said.

"But the lady hasn't said yes yet."

Frank looked at Charlotte with hope in his eyes. "I have asked our Lord for His blessing and believe He has said yes. Now it's your turn to pray about it."

"Charlotte's prayed about it, and I know what the answer is," Robert said, hugging his sister hard. "It is yes!"

"I have no dowry," Charlotte said.

Frank took her hand and held it tight. "A dowry is not important to me. Don't give it another thought. I just hope you can grow to love me."

"She loves you already," Robert said.

Charlotte looked into Frank's eyes and murmured, "Yes, I do, and that's a fact."

"I'll stand in as a proxy mother," Mrs. Collins said. "And I'll even bake the cake."

Charlotte looked at Frank incredulously and burst into laughter. "Yes, Franklin Hill, I will be honored to marry you."

Epilogue

July 8, 1900

Charlotte wore a simple white lawn dress and new white gloves. A wide-brimmed straw hat was her "something old," and her "something borrowed and something blue" were the borrowed shoes gracing her feet. She was radiant, and Frank never wanted to forget this moment. At his request, she had worn her hair down, letting her loose, blond curls flow from beneath her hat and dance in the gentle breeze.

To please his bride, Frank wore a dark pinstripe suit with a navy blue tie. Now they stood at the train station before the preacher who had arrived on the morning train.

They repeated their marriage vows, gazing into each other's eyes, while Robert, wearing his straw hat and a new pair of trousers, beamed up at them.

When the train chugged out of the station, making its way west, Frank cast a quick glance its way, thinking of when he had wanted to go on an adventure. He no longer needed that adventure, for he had found the wife he needed on the very train that brought him to his new position as the town's only doctor. God had indeed answered more than one prayer in providing Charlotte, his heart's desire. Robert was an added bonus.

Alongside the home that would soon be theirs, the trumpet vine had been transplanted; Frank hoped it would bring a smile to his young bride's face each day as she watered it.

BIRDIE L. ETCHISON lives in Washington State and knows much about the Pacific Northwest, the setting for the majority of her books. She loves to research the colorful history of the United States and uses her research along with family stories to create wonderful novels.

The Bride's Song

by Linda Ford

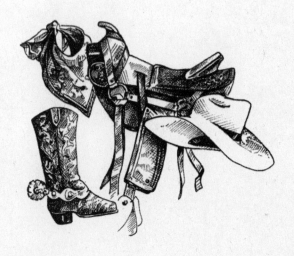

Chapter 1

1898—Freebank, western Canada

A gust of wind swept shiny strands of black hair across Dora Grant's cheek as she hastened across the pleasant, tree-lined street. Lifting her face into the wind, she laughed. At twenty-two she had found the ideal place, and she was supremely happy.

The prosperous town of Freebank was the perfect place for a determined young woman to carve out a life for herself. Situated alongside the Canadian Pacific rail line, which headed west to free land, opportunity, and prosperity, the thriving community boasted of schools, more than twenty stores, six churches, a theater, and an abundant social life.

Climbing the three stairs to Doc Mackenzie's office, Dora stepped inside. She smiled at her reflection as she paused at the hall table to brush her hair back from her face. Her hazel eyes sparkled, revealing her happy state of mind. With deft movements, she tied a crisp white apron over her skirt and blouse. She had changed her mind about wearing her new white lawn blouse this morning, deciding to do the wise thing and save it for a social occasion. Her plain, oft-worn apparel was more appropriate for work.

Dora's footsteps kept pace with the happy tune she hummed as she completed her routine morning chores. Placing freshly boiled instruments on a tray, she covered them with a clean towel.

If Doc Mackenzie doesn't get back soon, he won't have time for his noon meal, she thought when she glanced at the clock over the bookcase. Perhaps she should go into the living quarters and sit with Mrs. Mac until the doctor returned. But before she could cross the room, a buggy rattled into the yard, followed almost immediately by Doc's heavy footfall on the stoop.

Instantly her anxious wonderings eased. Doc would get a chance to eat the simple meal she'd left for Mrs. Mac to serve. Now Dora could relax until their afternoon office hours began.

But the racket of a fast-approaching wagon sent tickling fingers of apprehension up her spine.

"Whoa," a deep voice called out, followed by a frantic inquiry. "Doc. Doc Mackenzie. Are you home?"

Dora hurried to the window, pushing aside the lace curtain. Two heaving and sweating horses stood harnessed to a wagon that still shuddered from its sudden halt. Her gaze followed two men as they jumped down from their seats and reached back into the wagon's bed to lift out a blanket-wrapped body.

The driver gave the reins a quick twist as he leapt to the ground. "Doc," he hollered again. "Injured man here." He hurried to assist the other two.

Dora's heart dipped for an instant before she sprang to the door. Poor Doc would be missing his meal again.

"Bring him in," she instructed the trio of men as they staggered up the steps with their burden. "Doc will be here right away." Dora half extended her hand but quickly pulled it back and stepped out of the way when she saw the extent of the injuries.

"You're sure he's still alive?" At the sound of Doc's familiar voice, her head spun toward the door leading to the living quarters. Doc wiped his mouth on his hanky as he entered the office. Had he grabbed a mouthful of food or only managed a hurried drink? But there was no time to think about Doc's eating requirements.

"He ain't kicking much, but he's still breathing," one man grunted.

"Right here." Dora led the men to an examining table.

Doc flipped aside the blanket and bent over the patient. "A bit battered up, are we?" With deft fingers he lifted the eyelids then bent closer to examine the cut on the forehead. "Dora, give me a hand."

Immediately, she was at the doctor's side. Her breath caught for one fleeting second, but she had worked with Doc long enough to know how to closely observe blood, injuries, pain, and death while still maintaining her composure.

There were a number of bruises on the injured man's face. A head wound oozed over crackled patches of dried blood. The left side of the man's shirt was stained dark red. He was deathly still and pasty white.

The dark spot on his shirt grew.

She shook her head. No telling how much damage was hidden under the torn garment, yet his chest fell and rose with assuring regularity.

"You boys going to tell me what happened?" Doc flashed the trio a glance as Dora unbuttoned the shirt and slipped it from the man's shoulders. Doc probed the kidney area and across the abdomen then pushed the edges of the wound together.

"We found him," the driver answered.

"Thought he was dead," mumbled the younger man as he removed his hat and shuffled his fingers along the rim.

Doc snorted. "Where did you find him?"

"Across the river. About ten miles away." Again it was the driver who supplied the information.

"He was passed out, sittin' in his saddle."

"Just like he was dead." The hat went round and round.

"Shut up, Jack." The third man straightened. "He gonna be okay, Doc?"

"You boys get the sheriff and tell him everything, you hear?" Doc said, casting a glare in their direction. "Now run along so we can take care of him."

Dora smiled. Doc might be getting a little round in the middle and his hair might be gray and thinning, but on occasion he looked and sounded like an army major and received the same instant obedience. She didn't wait for their noisy exit before she filled a basin with warm water. Pulling the tray of instruments close, she began dabbing at the blood.

She worked quietly. Doc didn't care for idle conversation. Her movements coordinated with his as he cleaned and stitched the wounds.

Before the men returned, the patient had been washed and eased into a clean gown. Twice he had moaned and tried to say something before fading back into unconsciousness.

At the sound of shuffling boots, Doc straightened. "They're just in time to help get this young man into bed." He washed and dried his hands before he opened the door to the outer office.

"Come in, Constable." The local Mountie entered, closing the door on the others.

Constable Andrews yanked his hat off as he stared down at the injured man. "He say anything?"

"No. He's a lucky young man to even be alive." Doc lifted the patient's eyelids again. "Can't tell how serious this head wound is." Straightening, he faced the Royal Canadian Mounted Police officer. "There's not much more I can do."

The Mountie nodded. "They brought in his horse and tack." He sighed. "I hoped he'd be able to tell me what happened."

"In good time, my man. In good time." Doc hustled to the door. "Now if you and these gentlemen could give me a wee bit of help, we'll see this lad settled into bed."

Minutes later the patient rested in the sickroom off the office and the room was cleared of nervous men. Doc and Dora stood side by side staring down at the man.

"He's a bonnie young man." Doc lapsed into his Scottish brogue. "He'll be turning heads on many a young lass."

Dora blinked then looked intently at the patient. Dark curls lay flattened across his head. Despite his paleness and bruises, he *was* handsome— in a rugged sort of way.

But his clothing had revealed his occupation. A cowboy. Decisively, Dora shook her head. "Not this lass."

Doc chuckled. "No, my bonnie lassie. You're knowing what you want and how to get it."

She laughed, too. "No wandering cowboy for me."

❧

Office hours over, Dora shooed Doc away for a meal and some much needed rest before dragging a chair to the bedside of her patient. She prepared to keep watch for a few hours.

The injured man tossed and moaned.

In response to his pain, Dora murmured soft, soothing assurances.

His eyes flew open, and she stared into brown eyes so velvety that her breath caught in her throat. The flicker of pain and confusion in those dark orbs quickly reminded her of her duties. "You're at Doc Mackenzie's. You have a cut on your head and another in your side, but you're safe now. If you lay quiet and rest, you'll soon be right as rain."

He flinched.

She offered her most encouraging smile. He could use something for pain, but she didn't dare leave him to fetch Doc. Besides, she knew Doc would be in shortly to check on his patient.

"Can you tell me your name?"

He groaned and his lips moved.

She leaned closer. It sounded like he said, "Rivers." Was he trying to tell her what had happened?

But before she could formulate another question, his eyes closed. She leaned back in her chair, thankful that he hadn't grown more restless. A few minutes later, Doc entered the room.

"Any change?" He bent over the patient as he spoke.

"He opened his eyes for a moment."

Doc nodded, lifting a corner of the dressing on the man's side. "I'm not happy with the looks of this. Could you please get me a clean dressing, Dora?"

She hurried to do as he had asked and quickly returned to his side. Handing him a basin for the soaked bandage, Dora noticed the inflamed edges of the wound.

"Did he say anything?"

"Rivers."

"What does that mean?" Doc stared at her.

She shrugged. "Suppose he was trying to tell us something about where he got hurt."

✵

Dora sat with the patient until late in the evening. The uninterrupted quiet gave her plenty of time to study his features. Doc was right. Many a young woman would throw this man a second look—and a third—while hoping for more. An unsettled feeling surfaced. A familiar feeling. Although she loved her work and where she lived, every once in a while she wished she weren't so alone.

Doc came in. "Dora, you go get your rest now."

"But what about you?" she protested. Doc never got enough rest. When he wasn't caring for patients, he was tending to Mrs. Mac, who had grown weaker with each passing winter month. When hoped-for improvement did not materialize with the arrival of spring, Dora could no longer deny the truth; Mrs. Mac was not going to get stronger. This strange ailment, which had literally eaten the flesh from her frame and left her barely able to function, was not going away.

No wonder Doc looked tired most of the time. She wished she could do more to help this couple who had become as dear as any parents.

But despite Dora's objections, Doc gently pushed her from the room.

"I plan on dozing in the big chair. The laudanum will take effect in a few minutes, and our patient should sleep soundly."

With no other option but to follow the doctor's orders, Dora let herself out and hurried across the street to the little house she called her own. A sense of peace and satisfaction swept over her as she lit the kerosene lamp in the room that served as parlor, kitchen, and dining room. Tacked onto the back of the house was an equally small bedroom.

Would she ever enter this house or cross the street to the doctor's office without experiencing a swell of gratitude for God's wonderful provisions? Knowing she would not, her weariness lifted. A smile played on her lips as she murmured, "Thank You, God."

Her prayer of thanksgiving shifted to one of petition as she quietly spoke to the Lord. ". . .And, dear Father, please bless Doc and Mrs. Mac—and that poor injured man." Breathing a quick "amen," Dora began to hum while she bustled about the kitchen preparing tea and a boiled egg sandwich.

🌿

When Dora arrived for work early the next morning, she found Doc asleep in the chair. Noiselessly, she pulled the patient's door closed and headed for the office to prepare for the day's work. A bit later, upon hearing the murmur of voices, she returned to the sickroom.

Doc glanced up from his examination of the patient's abdominal wound. "Another dressing, please."

As she passed a clean bandage to him, she saw how the lesion oozed.

Doc finished and straightened. "He's conscious now, but I've just given him another dosage of laudanum." He handed the instruments to Dora and dipped his hands in the basin of water. "His name is Josh Rivers."

She smiled at her misunderstanding of the night before.

"He was set upon by two men who robbed him and beat him up, leaving him to die." Doc dried his hands on a fresh white towel. "But he refused to die." He handed the towel to Dora and stood over the patient, his expression serious. "He's got a fight ahead of him yet, I fear. I'll leave him in your care for now. I have house calls to make. Do your best to keep him quiet. I'll leave another dosage of laudanum, should he need it."

Before she could do more than nod her head in agreement, the doctor had gone.

The morning passed slowly. Mr. Rivers stirred several times but settled quickly when she touched him and spoke softly.

Doc returned prior to the afternoon office hours. "I'll manage without you in the office this afternoon." He touched Josh's brow. "I want you to stay by our patient and keep a close eye on him."

Within an hour, Josh was burning with fever.

Dora poured rubbing alcohol into tepid water and sponged him. His life depended on her fighting the fever and keeping him as quiet as possible. She determined to do her very best. As always, she felt a fierce defiance at the illnesses and injuries that attacked her patients.

Doc came in later that afternoon to check the dressing. "Nasty injury," he exclaimed as he pulled the bandage away from the wound. "Let's apply a bread poultice and see if that draws out the infection."

Dora and Doc labored over Josh, his moans tearing at her as they fought the raging fever. Toward morning it abated and the patient fell into a deep sleep.

Dora sank into the chair and let her breath out in a whoosh, tired to the marrow of her bones.

"You run on home and catch some sleep," Doc commanded. She started to argue, but he shooed her from the chair.

"Sleep as long as you need; then come and take over—though I'm hoping the worst is over. If we can keep him quiet a few days, I believe he'll mend."

Dora still hesitated, but Doc had already sunk into the chair, tucking a pillow under his head and stretching out his legs. He waved her away. She stole one more glance at Josh in order to assure herself that he was really and truly better. But she stilled the protective urge to feel his brow one more time before hurrying from the room.

Three hours later she awoke refreshed and, as always, anxious to check on her patient. If she felt a bit more urgency this time, she refused to admit it.

Doc slept in the chair, his head tilted to one side. "Doc," she whispered, "I'll take over." He moaned as he jerked to his feet and wearily plodded from the room.

Josh rested peacefully. She pressed her fingers to his brow and nodded. His fever had not returned. Dora lightly pushed at one brown curl that stubbornly hung over his forehead. The quiet of the house settled around her, and she relaxed into the cushiony softness of the big armchair.

"So you *are* real."

The voice shocked her bolt upright. Dora gaped at her patient, his warm brown eyes on her face, a smile tipping his lips.

"I thought I'd dreamed you." His voice was as deep and slow as a lazy river. She found herself wondering if he always sounded like that or if it was the result of pain and drugs. Then she forced her attentions back to their proper place.

"Welcome back. How are you feeling?" *Certainly his color is improved,* she thought.

In response, he grimaced. "A little like I was run over by a stampede of longhorns."

She smiled. Awake and more alert, his eyes took on a life of their own, darkening with warmth then flashing with pain. She leaned over his bedside. "Can I get you something for the pain? Doc Mackenzie left a powder for you."

He closed his eyes. "The medicine will make me sleep, won't it?"

"Yes."

"But I don't want to sleep." Jaw tightening, eyes flashing, he shot her a determined look. "I have things to do." Dora gasped as he tried to sit up. Instantly, he fell back against the pillow, his face chalk white.

"You must lie still. You have a deep wound in your side that needs time to heal."

He grunted. "Time's one thing I ain't got. Where's my horse?"

"I heard the Mountie say he has your horse and gear."

"What about them rattlers that robbed me?" She shivered at the hard note in his voice.

"They were long gone."

"I gotta get going." He twisted his head from side to side.

"First, you must get better." Dora's lips tightened. If he kept this up, he would start to bleed again. Maybe she should give him the laudanum. What would Doc want?

As if in answer to her question, Doc strode in. "Well, what do we have here? Glad to see you looking alive, young man."

"Doc, I gotta get moving." Again, Josh attempted to sit up.

Doc pressed Josh's shoulders to the bed. "Now, you look here, young fella. You're mighty lucky to be alive. And I intend to see you well. Either you lie quiet until I say otherwise or I'll keep you so doped up you won't have any choice." He glared at Josh.

Josh met Doc's gaze. Neither spoke. Neither flinched.

Dora held her breath. Doc meant every word, and he would not relent. She hoped Josh would see this and save himself a pack of trouble.

Josh suddenly relaxed and smiled. "You're the doctor," he announced almost cheerfully.

Dora grinned. Not only did he have spirit, but this man had brains. He would be a good patient.

Doc relaxed. "There's a good man." He patted Josh's shoulder. "Now let's have a wee look at that wound."

Dora hurried to get fresh bandages as Doc rolled back the dressing. Peering over his shoulder, she saw that the edges of the wound were inflamed but not oozing, an improvement since yesterday.

Doc applied a new dressing. "You must keep still until this heals," he said as he washed his hands. "Dora, get the young man something to eat. Liquids for now." Scowling at Josh, he ordered, "You, young man, are to let Dora feed you. I want you absolutely still. Do you hear?"

Josh grinned. "I hear ya, Doc."

Doc snorted.

Josh's quick flash of humor was a pleasant treat after the many complaining patients she'd had over the winter, and Dora smiled as she headed toward the kitchen.

Mrs. Mac sat at the table toying with her empty teacup.

"How are you today, Mrs. Mac?"

"I'm managing." Her hand shook as she brushed a strand of white hair back. "But I worry about Ian when he works such long hours."

Dora nodded. Doc's hours were long, and doing nursing duty added to them. But there was no other doctor. And Doc would not ignore someone needing medical attention. She tried to put in some time every day helping Mrs. Mac with housework and meals, but Doc had made it clear that her duties as his nurse came first, and she understood it had to be so.

"I'll clean the kitchen while I wait for the water to boil." She quickly put away the food then gathered and washed the dishes. Mixing a spoonful of beef concentrate with hot water in a bowl, she wrinkled her nose at the smell. She'd make some real chicken broth later, but for now this would have to do.

"Thank you, dear," Mrs. Mac said as Dora put away the last dish and prepared the tray.

"You're welcome. I wish I had time to do more, but Doc has ordered me to feed our patient." She checked the tray. Tea, sugar, if he desired, and weak bouillon. Not much for a young man. Imagining how he would feel about his liquid meals, she grimaced.

Yet her lips changed to a smile as she entered the sickroom.

"Good, you're back." Doc stood, pulling his jacket straight. "Keep him on clear fluids today and keep him still. I don't care how. Give him laudanum if necessary."

He made it sound near impossible, but she would not disappoint him. "I understand."

Doc fixed his glare on Josh. "I expect your full cooperation, young man."

"Doc, relax. I'll be a good boy. I promise I won't move a muscle until you say it's safe." He sighed. "I'm sure hoping you don't mean not moving my mouth though. I'd have a hard time keeping it shut for very long."

Doc snorted. "Flap your jaws all you want, sonny. Won't do you any harm." He dipped his head toward Dora. "Might drive your nurse crazy, though."

Dora lifted her chin. " 'Spect he can't be any worse than some of the people I've put up with."

Doc chortled at Josh's groan. He was still chuckling as he left the room.

Ignoring him, she asked Josh, "How about some nourishment?" Then she pushed another pillow behind Josh's head before she pulled the tray close.

He eyed the cup and bowl suspiciously.

She hesitated. "Which would you like first, tea or broth?"

His gaze darted to her face in disbelief. "Does it make a difference?"

"Not to me," she answered cheerily, and lifting the bowl to his chin, she gave him a spoonful of bouillon.

He grimaced. "I've tossed better stuff than that in the fire."

Before he could say more, she fed him another spoonful. "Who says it's supposed to be good? All that matters is it's full of nutrition."

His eyes narrowed. "If it's awful, it must be good for me; is that what you're saying?"

She laughed. "I suppose I am."

He shook his head. "What a dreadful idea." He got a faraway look in his eyes. "Thank goodness life isn't like that. God has given us so much to enjoy. Like nature, friends, and..." He darted a look at the tray. "Good food."

She blinked. He had put into words a sentiment that had been flickering in the back of her mind for a long time. With all her heart she believed life was not *all* pain and disappointment. There was so much good to be enjoyed—gifts from a good and loving God. Like her home, her job, her life here in town. So many of life's unpleasantries were self-inflicted. She clenched her teeth, vowing once again not to make any of the same unwise and devastating choices that her parents had made.

"Ah, sweet Dora, you should not look so sad."

She stifled a gasp. Heat raced up her neck. Such brashness. But she'd heard about wild cowboys.

He held both palms toward her. "Don't get all flustered. I'm not meaning to be bold."

She kept her head bent, unwilling to meet his gaze.

"Some of that tea would be good."

With a guilty start, she realized she had forgotten about feeding him. He downed the last of the broth and drank his tea, then nestled back into his pillow. Filled with an uncomfortable restlessness, she gathered up the utensils and tray and hurried to the kitchen. It was empty, and the house quiet. Doc had undoubtedly gone on his rounds, and Mrs. Mac would be resting.

Dora quickly washed the dishes. Josh's remark about enjoying good things triggered her interest. Obviously, he was a God-fearing man. It might be amusing to get to know him. She bit her bottom lip. Too bad he was a cowboy.

When she returned to the sickroom, Josh lay with his eyes closed. Dora hesitated, but Josh sensed her presence and slowly opened his eyes. "Glad to see you back," he said with a smile. "I thought I might have scared you off and would have to spend the rest of the day staring at the walls." His eyes darkened. "I was thinking about going to find you."

Remembering Doc's orders, she shook her head. "Doc would have my skin if you did."

"I guess that means you have to entertain me then." The smug look on his face made her laugh.

"I'm not sure that's what he meant."

He sighed deep and long. "I feel like I've been hog-tied. All the while, my insides are yearning to move."

Dora made a cluck of sympathy. He had capitulated so completely to Doc's orders that she had failed to realize how much it cost him. Now her heart reached out to ease his restlessness. "What are you so anxious to be doing?"

His eyes brightened. "I'm headed west."

She closed her eyes for a heartbeat. Another fool after land and riches. Chasing an empty bubble. And just when she had decided that he thought the same as she.

"Why are you heading west?" As if she didn't know the answer. The lonely feeling that had surfaced earlier now returned, and she struggled to submerge the emotion. Life was good and pleasant. She would allow nothing to mar her happiness. Not after God had so generously provided.

"I'm going to find me the nicest piece of land ever and start my own little farm." His gaze drifted away, and she knew he was seeing his own dream world.

She shook her head. How often she'd seen that look and heard that tone. Yet, even more often, she had seen the helpless desperation in a child's gaunt face. Her insides coiled, and she pushed away the memories, forcing herself to concentrate on making conversation with her patient—this dreamer headed into the unknown with nothing but a headful of secondhand lies.

"Have you any idea what you're headed for?" She managed to keep her voice smooth and tried to ignore the unreasonable twinge in her heart.

"I've seen it. A few years ago I was trailing a herd to Cochrane Ranch. Prettiest country I ever saw. The air is so pure you can taste yesterday's rain. The moon was so big and golden I was sure it was snagged on a pine tree." He took a deep breath. "I never saw a sky so blue. Seemed like you could reach out and touch it." He turned to Dora with an eager look in his eyes. "You should have seen the flowers. Wild roses so sweet that I dreamed of them at night. Harebells like fine china." He grinned at Dora. "Why, I bet you could hear them ringing if you sat real still."

Not certain what he meant, she stared at him. Then, seeing the twinkle in his eye, she laughed low in her throat. "Indeed?" she replied. "I don't believe I've ever heard the sound of harebells ringing."

He chuckled, beaming at her. "Me neither, but who knows. The country is dandy. So purdy—the land nearly sings." He lay back and stared at the ceiling. "I already knew that I didn't want to be trailing doggies the rest of my life. I made up my mind the minute I saw that little spot of heaven. I would work and save until I had enough to set me up in a nice little place of my own." He heaved a chest-raising sigh. "And just when I figured that the right time had come, I find myself laid up here."

She didn't answer. He made the west country sound like paradise on earth. She could almost hear the music and the bells he described. But she had seen another version of paradise, one with dark corners.

"Perhaps you've been given a warning..." At the sudden change in his expression, she clamped her lips together.

"There you go again. Figuring bad things are good for you."

She wanted to argue. That was not what she had said, nor meant. But he drew his brows together and continued.

"Don't you think I've had plenty of time to think and pray about this?" The fierceness in his expression disappeared as quickly as it had come. "This is a delay. For what purpose, I have no notion. However, my aim is still the same."

Stung by his words, and even more by his judgment, she faced him squarely. "I suppose you know all about farming?"

"I've been keeping my eyes open, and I know enough to run myself a few cows and grow them some feed." He paused. "Besides, I learn quick."

Her annoyance fled as fast as it came. "I'm sorry," Dora offered, shrugging her shoulders. "It's none of my business. Perhaps I've seen too many people lose all they had in the trying."

He chuckled. "Maybe I'm a fool, but I don't see I have much to lose."

Just then, Doc appeared to check on his patient and repeat his order for quiet and rest. A few minutes later, Constable Andrews arrived to ask Josh a few questions and get his description of the two men who had attacked and robbed him. Before the Mountie left, he brought in a pair of saddlebags from the waiting room.

"I have no way of knowing what's missing, but I thought you might like to have your things at hand." He tossed the leather bags on the foot of the bed. "The rest of your tack is at the livery barn. You can pick it up there when you are able to be up and about."

After the Mountie's departure, Dora insisted that her patient rest for a few hours. While he slept, she made a quick trip to the butcher shop and bought a stewing hen, which she put on the stove to simmer. After preparing a meal and dining with the Mackenzies, she helped Doc with his office patients. Despite her busyness, her mind kept returning to the sickroom and her patient. She hoped he was resting quietly and his wounds were healing.

Doc glanced at the door several times as well. "Hope the lad is obeying orders," he murmured under his breath between patients. But another rush of patients prevented either of them from checking on Josh.

"We're done now, lass," Doc said as he closed the door on their last patient. "Go see how our cowboy is getting along."

Doc sat behind his desk and drew his heavy green ledger close. She hurried toward the sickroom, knowing that the doctor would be preoccupied for some time.

Chapter 2

S he brushed a tendril of hair from her face and reached for the knob, then pulled back, not wanting to waken him if he were asleep. Turning the glass knob slowly, she eased the door open and tiptoed into the room.

The afternoon sun filtered through the lace curtains, shooting bright light across the room and making it difficult to distinguish details. Before her eyes adjusted, Josh called out.

"Dora. Thank goodness. I thought no one was coming back." His voice rang with desperation. "Tell me, please. What is that gut-wrenching smell?"

She chuckled. "That would be Lister's spray. A disinfectant that keeps disease from spreading."

"I can believe that. No disease would want to get near such a stench!"

Her eyes had adjusted to the light, and she gasped. "How did you get that stuff?" Items lay scattered across his bedside.

"From my saddlebag." He sounded apprehensive. "I was so bored." He grew defensive. "I barely had to move. Knew exactly where they were. Just had to reach out my toe and drag it close."

She shook her head. It would be a miracle if he hadn't started the wound bleeding again.

"You won't tell Doc will you? I promise I was very careful and didn't pull anything loose. Please, Dora, be a pal."

She looked away from his begging eyes. She knew she shouldn't agree to such a scheme, but she also knew that she would. For the life of her, she couldn't explain why.

"We'd better tidy up." She gathered up the items, surprised when she examined them more closely. Besides several rolled up pairs of socks and a new pair of leather gloves, there was a well-worn leather Bible, its cover as soft as velvet. He retrieved an equally worn book, *The Great Lone Land*, and a picture before she could pack them away.

He watched her, smiling gently. "Thanks a heap."

She straightened and smoothed the crazy-patch quilt, carefully avoiding his gaze—a gaze that somehow compelled her to do things she wouldn't normally agree to do.

Again, his voice softly pleaded. "Could I ask one more favor?" His words made her feel that to refuse him would be mean.

She steeled herself. "You can ask."

He chuckled. "All I want is for you to open those curtains so I can enjoy the sunshine."

His request was so mundane that she had to laugh at her defensiveness as she crossed the floor to do his bidding. Light flooded the room when she pulled back the curtains. Turning back toward Josh, she observed a look of pure pleasure on his face as he lay with his eyes closed. She quickly turned away, for she felt as though she were intruding on someone in the midst of private prayer.

"Does the window open?"

"Certainly." She pushed the sash upward. A refreshing breeze, full of spring warmth and laden with the musky smell of recent winter snow, lifted the lace curtains to brush against her arms. Dora filled her lungs with fresh air.

The room was quiet. A child's voice sounded somewhere in the distance, and a horse clip-clopped down the street. Dora turned to look at Josh. In the bright light, his skin was even more tanned, a stark contrast to the bandage on his forehead. Gold streaks played through his brown curls.

As she studied him, his eyes opened. His expression warm, he said, "Now I can breathe." He smiled. "I've been looking at the picture of my family. See, here they are." He motioned for her to come to his side.

She looked down at the picture, still feeling the lure of the spring breeze.

Then she bent closer. "How many brothers and sisters do you have?" She hadn't meant to sound so startled.

"I'm the oldest of ten." There was no disguising his pride.

"These three," he explained, pointing to the smaller ones, "Ruthie, Tessa, and Mark were born after I left home. Ruthie's nine years old, Tessa's seven, and Mark just turned five."

Dora bent closer. "You're the eldest?" There seemed to be several adults in the photo.

"Firstborn. That's me. This. . ." With his index finger he pointed to a young man who bore a resemblance to Josh. "This is Andy. He's twenty-four. As soon as I saw he was keen on running the mill, unlike myself, I declared I was going to follow my dream. Ten years now I've been working, mostly as a ranch hand or trailing cows." He ran his finger back and forth across the picture. "Good work. Good experience. But I'm ready to settle down and build something for myself. And someday, God willing, for my family."

Dora kept her head bent over the picture. These faces stirred an all-too-familiar feeling within her. The same old dream. The same empty hope she'd seen before. The lure of owning land and creating something for future generations to have and hold. So much hope. So much disappointment and despair. Such a waste. Finally, she lifted her gaze to Josh. "Don't your parents need you at home?"

"There was barely enough of everything to go around. As we grew into adulthood, it seemed there was less."

She narrowed her eyes, amazed that he seemed to feel no bitterness at such a lean existence.

"I go and visit whenever I can." He let his hands drop to his chest. The photo pointed toward the ceiling. "I spent a fortnight with them before I started west. Saying good-bye this time was harder than lassoing a racing bronc, knowing it might be a long while before I see them again." His thumb rubbed the photo. "The little ones will hardly remember me."

She clenched her hands into fists. Her insides screamed to tell him to give up this foolish chase. Instead, she took a deep breath and said, "I put a chicken on the stove to simmer several hours ago. Perhaps you'd like some homemade chicken broth."

He pressed his hands to his chest. "Dora, now I'm certain you're an angel of mercy. Sure you can't add some noodles or potatoes?"

She shook her head. "Not 'til Doc says so." She hesitated at the door. "I'll be back in a few minutes."

In the kitchen, Mrs. Mac stood at the table cutting meat from the chicken carcass.

Dora came up beside her. "Why thank you, Mrs. Mac." She reached out for the knife. "Here, let me finish."

Mrs. Mac nodded and relinquished the knife. "I'm feeling a little better this afternoon."

Dora pulled Mrs. Mac's arm through her own, leading her gently to a chair. "I'm glad."

"I think I'll get stronger with the warmer weather." She leaned heavily on the table as she sat down.

Dora poured tea for her and waited until she grasped the cup and took a sip before she turned back to the counter. She finished the deboning, then peeled potatoes and carrots for a stew for Doc and Mrs. Mac. Straining some broth for Josh's supper, she set aside the remainder and some diced meat. Doc would probably order soft food tomorrow. She would prepare some chicken noodle soup.

As she diced potatoes into the stew, Mrs. Mac asked, "How is your patient this afternoon?"

Dora glanced up and smiled. "He's on the mend, but I think he finds being bedridden difficult." She shook her head. "But he must remain still if he wants that gash in his side to heal."

"Aye, this being idle is not a task to be envied."

Dora dropped the knife and hurried to the older lady's side, bending over to hug her. "Oh Mrs. Mac, you're not idle. You do what you can, and that's all any of us can do."

Mrs. Mac patted Dora's hands and leaned against her shoulder. "Thank you, dearie. You're such a sweet lass. Makes me ashamed of me grumbling."

Before Dora could think of how to respond, Mrs. Mac tipped her face up and flashed blue eyes at her. "My dear, Ian says that your patient is a curly-headed young man handsome enough to melt any woman's heart."

Dora laughed. "Now don't you go getting any ideas. He's much too young for you. Besides, what would Doc say?"

Mrs. Mac smacked Dora's hands gently. "Ach, 'tis for you I'm thinking of him. And don't you go pretending you haven't noticed."

Dora grinned as she returned to dicing the vegetables. "Noticed what? That the edges of the abdominal wound are less reddened? The bruises on his face already fading? And the poor man is starving as we talk." She covered the stew and prepared a tray for the sickroom.

"Aye, that of course." Mrs. Mac turned so she could watch Dora's reactions. "And a whole lot more."

"The dumplings are ready to drop in. Wait about fifteen minutes," she called over her shoulder as she left the room balancing the tray.

Mrs. Mac called, "You got eyes in your head, girl. I know you do." The door clicked, shutting out anything more the older woman would have added.

Dora's grin faded. Certainly she'd noticed some of Josh's more appealing features. But she was no fool. She'd not be letting pretty curls or a handsome face cause her to make choices she'd regret.

Outside the sickroom, she paused to take a deep breath before she shoved open the door.

"That took awhile."

She nodded. "I made stew for Doc and his wife."

"Stew?" He perked up.

"And broth for you."

He groaned.

She pushed another pillow behind him and straightened the covers before setting a bed table across his chest to hold the tray.

He sniffed. "At least it smells like food." And he leaned forward eagerly as she fed him. He had just drained his cup of tea when Doc entered the room. Dora hurried to get a fresh dressing.

Doc lifted the bandage on Josh's forehead first. "Very good," he murmured then turned his attention to the lower wound. "Your injuries are healing well, young man."

"Does that mean I can get up soon?" Josh half pleaded.

"Now don't go undoing everything. You must wait awhile longer yet." Doc patted his shoulders. "You just lay still and enjoy the attention of a pretty young lass."

"I've been doing that, Doc."

Josh's gaze met Dora's. At his teasing grin, heat flooded up her neck and she turned away.

Doc stood. "Josh, Dora's going home to get a good night's sleep, but I'll leave you with a cord that rings a bell in my living quarters. Should you have need of anything, just give it a yank." He turned to Dora. "I'll take the tray to the kitchen. You go on home now, lass."

Dora hesitated.

"Aw, Doc," Josh fussed. "You tell me to enjoy her company and then you send her home."

"I know, laddie. But she needs her rest." He shot a stern look in Dora's direction, but his voice was gentle as he said again, "You go on home. We'll see you in the morning."

She bid them both good night and left the office. As she stepped into her house, she knew Doc had been wise in sending her home. She was bone weary. She made a pot of tea then sank into a big armchair and let her head fall back. Had only two days passed since Josh had been carried into the clinic half alive? It seemed as if she'd known him so much longer. Pushing to her feet, she decided she was more tired than hungry. She headed for bed, blaming her weariness for these thoughts that strayed down useless rabbit trails.

❧

Doc was downing a cup of coffee when she hurried in the side door the next morning.

"Mrs. Mac is still sleeping. Josh is restless and bored. Do your best to keep him quiet." He took another swig of coffee. "He can have soft foods today." He was quiet for a moment. "And let him feed himself. All of his moving around yesterday appears to have done him no harm."

Dora met his flashing gaze. She should have known that they hadn't fooled him.

He set the cup down and grabbed his bag. "I'm off to visit Mrs. Smith. Have a good day." With no further ado, he was gone.

Humming, Dora quickly cleaned up Doc's breakfast and cooked some soft porridge for Josh. She set a place for Mrs. Mac, covering it with a clean towel. Still humming, she pushed open the sickroom door.

"I thought you'd never come back."

She smiled. "I've got your breakfast."

"I'm starving."

"Doc said you could have some real food today." She set up the bed table.

Josh looked at her suspiciously. "I'll bet."

"Really." She glanced at the tray as she set it before him. "Well almost. And Doc says you can feed yourself. Says you didn't do any damage yesterday with your moving about."

He grinned. "Wily old coyote." Without waiting for a response, he grabbed his spoon and, within minutes, polished off everything she'd prepared.

After she removed the tray, she set a basin of water before him. "Why don't you wash up a bit?"

Giving him some privacy, she took the dishes to the kitchen and plunged them into hot water. Her hands idly swirled the suds as she stared out the window humming.

He was done when she returned, and she tidied the room.

"How long before Doc lets me up?"

She could feel his barely contained restlessness and hated to answer. "Probably ten days."

"Ten days." He closed his eyes.

"Perhaps he'll let you sit up in bed in two or three days."

He turned his tortured gaze toward her and whispered hoarsely, "I had hoped to be at my destination by now. Ten days! How can I delay that long?"

She bit her bottom lip. It was going to take a great deal of patience on his part to remain immobile as long as Doc wanted. She would do her best to help. Perhaps she could turn his attention to other things. "What made you take up the life of a cowboy?"

He took a deep breath, and she knew he was trying valiantly to deal with his disappointment. "Horses, I guess. I wanted to be outside riding horses, not bent over machinery, never seeing the sun except on the way to and from the mill." He smiled, and the tautness in her nerves unwound. "I wanted to see the sun cross the sky, breathe air off the damp soil, feel the wind in my face. I wanted the birds to be the song I heard while I worked, not the grind of millstones. I wanted to see the flowers as God created them, not the flour ground by man."

She laughed.

He continued. "Never mind God's goodness in providing the grain." He locked his fingers together under his head, his elbows wide, and grinned at her. "Guess that tells you more than you wanted to know."

Dora had stopped to watch the play of wonder and awe in his expression. Now she quickly bent her head and gave the basin another swipe with the towel. "Not at all." The way he talked made her yearn to see and feel things like he did, with open eagerness. He had accused her of thinking bad was good, which she did not. But neither did she embrace the beauties of life with such trust. She couldn't. She'd learned the hard way to plan her path, testing each step before she took it. She wanted to see where life was leading. She needed some control over the direction. Trusting God meant following carefully the way marked before her, not throwing herself into riotous enjoyment without any regard for the future. No. That wasn't the way for her. She couldn't imagine it being the sensible way for anyone.

She was suddenly aware of his scrutiny and realized she had been quiet for several minutes. Gathering up her thoughts and containing them, she asked, "Didn't your folks mind?"

He nodded. "They minded me going. They didn't mind what I was doing."

"Tell me more about your family."

"We're big and noisy, but I think we're a nice family. How about yours?"

Rather than answer, Dora asked, "You said something about a mill?"

"Yes. My dad and Uncle James own the mill at Morgan's Creek. It's a steady business, but there's not enough income to support us all, even though Uncle James and Aunt Martha have no children." He shrugged. "That's why I was glad when Andy made it plain that he liked working in the mill. I didn't."

"I remember." She grinned. "You wanted to see the sky and taste the dust and smell the ground after a herd of cows had passed."

He laughed then groaned and pressed his hands to his side. "You knew that would hurt, didn't you?"

She tightened her lips. "I didn't know you'd laugh." But she knew her eyes gave her away.

"Right. And I don't know what side of a horse to mount."

She could no longer hide the mirth bubbling inside her, so she turned away.

"Think it's funny, do you?"

She sobered and turned to face him. "Of course not." Laughing at someone's pain would be cruel. She would never do such a thing. But there was no stopping her wide smile.

An answering gleam shone from his eyes—eyes that held her own in a steady gaze. Her heart danced to a song in her head.

"You never did tell me about your family."

She blinked and pulled back, shaken by how quickly her thoughts had spun out of control. "No, I didn't." Pursing her lips, she turned away. Hands wringing, she sought some task to disguise her discomfort. The first thing she saw was the window. Three quick steps took her to stare out at the quiet street, her hands pleating and unpleating the curtains.

"Well?" Although quiet, his voice prodded her. She crushed the pleats in her hands then shrugged and turned.

"There's not much to tell." At least, not much she cared to tell. "There are four children. Two boys and two girls. I'm the oldest girl. My folks have a homestead twenty miles from town."

At the word *homestead*, Josh practically jerked upright. "What's it like? The homestead? How long has your father been there?"

Dora took a deep breath as the questions tumbled out of Josh's mouth. She had no desire to talk about it, but she guessed Josh would plague her now that he knew that much.

"They have a tough life." Dora intended to say no more. "I can't talk now. Doc will have my hide if I don't have the office and waiting room cleaned in time for his patients."

She crossed to the door then paused. She had briefly forgotten that Josh was also her patient. His care came before her own needs and desires. "Is there anything I can do for you before I go?"

Josh groaned behind her, and Dora jerked around. Had he pulled something? But he stared up at the ceiling, his arms crossed over his chest. "I need to be out of here." He raised one hand in protest and grinned. "Don't say it. I already know. Lie quiet. Be patient." He groaned again. "I never realized how hard it is to do nothing." He made a shooing motion with his hand. "Go. I'll be all right."

Her duties called, but Dora hesitated to leave. She wanted to ease Josh's suffering during his stay. "Are you sure?" *I would love to talk with him all day—if only he wouldn't ask me any more questions about my family.*

He nodded.

She didn't hum as she tidied the rooms and prepared them for office hours. Instead, her thoughts circled round and round. It had been four years since she had escaped the homestead. Surely long enough to be able to think about the past without her insides getting brittle. Yet, just an innocent question or two turned her into a quivering mess. She pressed the heels of her hands into her eyes and moaned.

Grabbing the wet cloth, she scrubbed the examining table. Her pounding thoughts kept time with her frantic efforts. There had to be a way of putting aside her memories.

Prayer. That was the answer. She had prayed to be rescued from that situation, and God had wonderfully provided her with this chance. She would never cease to thank Him for it. Her thoughts slowed and she smiled. When Josh asked again about the homestead—and she was certain he would—she would tell him about life in town.

She glanced at the clock and gasped. *Lunch!* Rushing to the kitchen, she barely had time to prepare the chicken noodle soup that she had planned yesterday and take Josh a bowlful before Doc was calling her to the office. His first patients had arrived early.

They were rushed all afternoon. Then she hurried to make supper.

"You've had a busy day," Josh said as she carried in his tray. He waited as she set his meal on the table. "I heard an awful commotion one time."

"That was probably when Mrs. Baker came in with her brood of kids." Besides his Bible and the book he had yesterday, a child's storybook lay on the bed. Little Sam had left the book behind last winter after his recovery from pneumonia. She had planned to return it when she saw his family again. She laughed. "Found some good reading, did you?"

Josh grimaced. "It was the best I could do." He shook his head. "I'm so bored."

"And this helped?" She opened the pages. " 'See Dick run. Run, Dick, run.' " He cradled one arm under his head and looked down his nose at her.

"It made a very interesting study."

"I'll bet." She chortled. "And exactly what did you learn from this 'interesting study'?"

He turned to face her, his eyes dark and unreadable. The laughter died in her throat. Her chest tightened. "I learned how boring recovery can be." His sigh lifted the bedcovers momentarily. Something ticked inside Dora's head, making it impossible for her to speak.

"Boring, boring, boring." Then he grinned. "But now that you're here, I feel much better."

She blinked. It was nice to be appreciated. Josh made it seem even more special by his acknowledgment. "I'll find you some more mature books," she promised. "Unless you prefer this age level."

He grinned. "It's better than nothing. Almost."

"Doc has a collection of books, and I have some as well. You are certainly welcome to borrow them."

Just then Doc entered and stared at the books on the bed. "I trust that you've been obeying orders, young man."

Josh held up his hands. "Best I can, Doc."

Doc waited until Josh finished his meal and Dora removed the tray before he checked the wounds. "You're doing fine." He stood. "Dora, ye go on home, and remember tomorrow's the Sabbath. This young man will manage without nursing care tomorrow. If he needs anything, I'll see to it."

Dora had forgotten what day it was. She turned a startled gaze to Josh and caught the same protesting thought in his eyes. "But—"

"I mean it, Dora. Go home and enjoy a day of rest."

There was no arguing with Doc when he got that stubborn look on his face, so she nodded. "I'll just get him a few of your books to read, if that's all right."

Doc nodded. "Aye. That will help him rest."

She ducked into the office and, skipping the medical texts, chose four adventure books. Doc had a fondness for tales of the north. She had skimmed through several and knew they were full of encounters with wild animals and accounts of fighting the elements, as well as equally unkind residents. These were not the kind of stories she enjoyed, but perhaps Josh would. She delivered the books to his room.

Doc was still there, glowering. She hid a grin. Doc was determined to make sure that his orders were obeyed to the letter.

As she handed the books to Josh, he crooked his finger, indicating she should bend close. When she did, he barely whispered loud enough for her to hear. "Better hurry home. Doc looks like he'd as soon fry an egg on my forehead as have you miss your day of rest."

She choked back a chuckle and straightened slowly, giving herself time to compose her expression.

"I'll be going home now, Doc," she said in her sweetest, most compliant voice. "Say good night to Mrs. Mac for me."

Josh's chuckles followed Dora out of the room. Just before the door closed, she heard Doc growl, "Young whippersnapper." But she didn't know if his words were aimed at her or Josh.

❦

Dora remained in the pew for several minutes following the service, mulling over the points of the sermon. Pastor Luke Daley's favorite topics were faith, love, and forgiveness, and today he had chosen to preach about faith. As usual, his sermon was rich with illustrations and his message clear. Today he had shown how one's choices in daily life revealed the depths of personal faith.

"It takes faith in God's provision," he had said, "to venture into the unknown."

Dora had agreed with him until he used homesteaders as an example of that type of faith. Perhaps, she conceded, for some folks, homesteading was a step of faith. Yet, others were drawn, not by faith, but by an illusion. Of this she was certain.

Dismissing her lingering thoughts, she joined the others as they filed out. Mary, Pastor Luke's wife and Dora's best friend, waited for her at the bottom of the steps.

"Stay until I've spoken to the rest; then we'll talk," Mary whispered as they hugged.

Dora nodded and stepped aside as Mary greeted each of the departing parishioners.

"You'll come for lunch, I hope," Mary said as she joined Dora.

"I was hoping you'd ask." It was a Sunday tradition for them. Even if Mary had invited others, as she often did, Dora was always included.

But today Dora was the only guest. They had barely sat down when Mary leaned toward Dora. "I hear you have a patient."

Dora nodded. "A cowboy who was hurt on the trail."

Mary lifted one eyebrow. "A young cowboy?"

Dora kept her face expressionless, knowing that Mary would read a hundred meanings into anything she imagined she saw. "A handsome young man." Let her guess what that meant.

Mary's mouth made a perfect *O*.

Luke laughed. "She's setting you up, dearest," he warned.

Mary wrinkled her nose at him. "I know that. But I don't care." She turned back to Dora. "How young? How handsome?"

Dora pretended to give her questions a lot of thought. "Let's see." She pressed her finger to her lips. "He said he left home ten years ago. I guess that would make him at least twenty-six. Maybe a few years older."

Mary sighed and leaned back. "Just right for you."

"Why, I'm only twenty-two." Dora did her best to sound shocked.

Mary tsked. "Much too old to be without a husband. Or at least a beau."

"Indeed? Well, I have news for you. I'm quite happy without a man in my life. And much too busy to need one."

"Of course." But Dora knew Mary wasn't agreeing. "And you admit he's handsome?"

"Oh yes." Dora closed her eyes, pretending to be overcome. "Dark curly hair and eyes as warm as—" She sighed rather than finish her sentence.

"Why I declare. I believe you're already half in love with him." Mary practically gloated.

Dora instantly grew serious. "Sorry to disappoint you, but he's headed west to get himself a homestead. Not my kind of man." And she took a mouthful of roast beef.

Luke laughed. "Told you, Mary."

"Some day she'll fall," Mary promised.

"I believe you're right, dearest," he said, turning to speak to Dora. "Someday I expect you'll make the astonishing discovery that some things are worth the risk-taking. Remember, security is not found in a place, position, or possessions, or even in security itself—but in God."

Stung by his assessment of her, Dora stared at him. "Do you really think I'm trusting in something other than God?"

Mary rushed to her defense. "I'm sure he didn't mean that, did you dear?"

"No, of course I didn't. I've seen your faith. But I believe God stretches us all lest we grow complacent." He pushed his chair back. "Now if you girls will excuse me, I am going to my office."

367

After he left, the two young women were quiet a moment.

"I'm sure he didn't mean to criticize you, Dora." Mary kept her face toward her plate.

Dora touched her friend's arm. "I don't feel like he was." But a shiver flickered across her neck. He had warned of change, and she didn't welcome the thought.

Determined to lighten the mood, she asked, "Are you looking forward to the concert?" She spoke of the traveling singing group scheduled to appear ncxt week.

Mary wriggled in her seat. "With great expectation. I can hardly wait. I hear that this is the best group we've had yet."

"You've managed to get some good entertainment." Mary belonged to a committee that arranged a special concert three or four times a year. "After that there's the church picnic, then the debating team."

"Don't forget the ball tournament."

Dora nodded. She enjoyed the crowd and visiting much more than the sport, but Luke was an ardent ball player, so Mary counted ball tournaments high on the list of activities.

Later, at home in her tiny rooms, Dora thought about the day. Let Pastor Luke make his dire predictions; she knew better. It wasn't lack of faith that made her determined to enjoy what God had provided. After all, hadn't she proven her faith when she left home with nothing more than a worn satchel containing a second dress? She had prayed fervently for God to help her find a place to stay, and He had miraculously provided. He made it possible for her to finish her schooling by working after classes in return for her board. And, incredibly, a job in the hotel had opened up for her right after graduation. The job was not one she liked, but again she had prayed and trusted God. Now He had given her this job with Doc Mackenzie. And she loved her job. Perhaps someday she would enter formal nurse's training and improve her skills.

All the talk of Josh had triggered Luke's comments. He and Mary were always nagging her about finding a fellow and getting married.

But, she vowed, she would never allow herself to fall in love with someone like Josh.

She prepared for bed early, eager for the morrow when she could return to work.

❦

The checkerboard lay across Josh's bed. Dora put the checker pieces in place. "I'm going to beat you this time for sure."

Josh lay back, his arms under his head. "You probably could if you paid attention."

"Paid attention, indeed."

"I'll even let you go first."

She narrowed her eyes and studied him. Did letting her go first give him an advantage? Ducking her head to study the board, she admitted she didn't understand strategy. What difference did it make which checker she moved first? Oh, she hated to see him win so easily. Finally, she moved a checker.

"Did I ever tell you about the time a grizzly bear licked my boots?" His attention was riveted on the game board, so she couldn't see his eyes. "Your turn."

She hesitated then moved again. "Is this another of your tall tales?"

His hand to his chest, he drew back. "I swear I didn't make up any of them. Though I couldn't guarantee the same for my friend, Twister. He insisted that he got his name from riding a corkscrew mustang. But I always kinda figgered it was because of the way he twisted the truth. Your turn."

Dora's hand hovered over the game pieces, then she jumped one of his checkers and set it on the edge of the board.

"Anyway, we were taking a break from branding, and I wandered down by the river. The day was nice and sunny, so I sat down by a log and closed my eyes. Your turn.

"All of a sudden, I felt this bump against my foot. I opened my eyes, and there was a grizzly licking my boots. It's your turn again."

Dora squinted at the board. How did he make his plays so fast? She hadn't even followed what he'd done. She reached for one checker but caught herself before she touched it. Moving that one would set up a chain of jumps. She chose a different one.

"It was just a cub, maybe two or three hundred pounds.

"Well, you can bet I figured I was bear breakfast. I gave a quick look around for the mama and saw her about two hundred yards away with a second cub. They were rooting at an old tree stump. Probably eating bugs." He jumped his man across the board and set three of her game pieces on the side. "Your turn.

"I eased away from the cub and, slow as I could, got to my feet. You understand, now I was in a big hurry to leave, but I didn't want to set the cub to crying. All the same, the cub woofed. Old mama bear rose up on her hind feet. Your turn."

His checkers were all over the board, but if she moved one of hers against the edge. . .

"I hightailed it out of there. I could hear that mama bear thudding at my heels. I raced toward the camp." He paused. "Your turn again."

"Josh. For goodness' sake, tell me what happened." She gave the board a quick glance and saw an opening.

"I got ate up."

"Yeah. And came out the other end almost normal."

His smirk changed to a frown; then he laughed. "I guess not. No, I ran and ran. As soon as I saw the men gathered around the fire, I started hollering, 'Bear, bear.' They just stood there gaping at me. I skidded around the cook wagon, wheezing fit to kill. As soon as I could, I looked behind me. And there was nothing." He shrugged. "Guess what I thought was the bear chasing me was really my own heart thudding." He jumped three more of her checkers. "Crown me."

She was staring at Josh, caught in his bear story. She closed her mouth and gave Josh his crowning checker, then moved one of her own men.

"I never did quite live it down. Every so often, when things got boring, one of the men would get all big-eyed and flap his arms in my face and yell, 'Bear.'" He shrugged. "It was kind of funny."

Dora began to chuckle. "I can just see you." She nodded—"Bear, bear"—and laughed harder. "Wish I could have been there."

"Yeah, well, it might not have turned out so good." He crossed his arms over his chest. "By the way, I beat you again."

Sobering instantly, she studied the board and saw he was right. "It's not fair. You distracted me."

He shrugged. "Wasn't much of a challenge."

"Why you!" She flung a handful of checkers at him.

He flipped them away, except for one that he flicked back at her.

She ducked, laughing. "Stop now. You're supposed to be resting."

His deep chuckles made her laugh harder, and just about the time she had it under control, their eyes met and she started again. She couldn't remember when she'd had this much fun.

Chapter 3

Over the next few days, Dora and Josh spent a great deal of time together as she tried to help him while away the hours. They talked about books they'd read and things they enjoyed, and Josh told her more about his family.

She did what she could to make his convalescence pleasant and, in so doing, grew to enjoy his company more and more. He was a good patient, striving to be cheerful and cooperative even when she knew he ached to head west.

Five days later, Doc bent over Josh's dressing. "Young man, you have done very well." He wiped his hands on a towel. "How would ye feel about getting up for a wee while this morning?"

Josh's eyes grew wide then narrowed suspiciously. "You wouldn't be pulling my leg now, would you, Doc?"

Doc beckoned to Dora. "You take one side, lass, and I'll be holding the other." He flipped the covers back and eased Josh's legs over the side of the bed. Dora helped him to sit and steadied him as he swayed.

"Not to worry, son. You'll be a bit shaky at first." Doc kept his fingers on Josh's wrist, checking his pulse. "Sit until the dizziness passes, and then we'll try standing."

Josh hung his head and groaned.

"Take a deep breath and let it out slowly," Dora instructed.

"Ready?" Doc asked after a moment.

Josh nodded, and together they stood. He swayed, his weight pressing against Dora. She watched his face, saw the color slip away and return as he gritted his teeth and steadied himself.

"I'm all right," he grunted.

Dora glanced at Doc. He nodded slightly.

"Let's try a step or two." They shuffled forward as a unit and stopped. "Turn now, lad," Doc said.

With Doc and Dora on each side, he turned and shuffled back to the bed where he collapsed, sweat beading his brow.

"That was fine, laddie. Just fine." Doc checked Josh's pulse and lifted his legs to the bed. "Now you rest a bit, and we'll get you up again later. Dora, get the boy some lunch."

By suppertime, Doc announced that Josh could join them in the kitchen if he felt well enough.

"I'll do it," he eagerly replied. He had insisted on donning his clothes earlier in the afternoon, and now he jerked to his feet.

Dora tightened her lips as Josh, holding himself stiff and upright, walked down the hall to the kitchen.

The next day Doc suggested that Josh might like to sit outside on the veranda and enjoy the warm sunshine. "You'll soon be well enough to be on your way, lad."

Doc's words thumped into the pit of Dora's stomach. Her hands froze in midair.

"I'm glad to hear that." Josh sounded a great distance away.

She took a steadying breath. Had she caught a hesitant note in his voice? She darted a glance at him. A mix of emotions flashed through his expression. She was sure his eagerness was tainted by something sad. Well, what should she expect? He'd never faltered in wishing he could be on his way.

Nevertheless, Dora would be sorry to see him go. He had been a good patient, and she enjoyed his company.

Before Doc could scold her for dillydallying, she hurried outside and moved the wicker rocker into the sun. Josh came out with Doc at his heels. Dora waited until Josh settled into a comfortable position; then she followed Doc inside.

"There's a lad who's through and through nice," Doc said as he folded his stethoscope into his bag and prepared to leave. "You'd do well to have a closer look at him, lassie."

"I—" But not waiting for her reply, Doc grabbed his hat and headed for the door.

Dora stared after him. What a strange comment from Doc. He knew better than anyone how hard she had worked to be where she was.

Pausing on the threshold, Doc glanced over his shoulder at her. "Be sure, lassie, that you don't overlook a prize when you find it." Then, before she could answer, he was gone.

She put the instruments to boil, tidied Doc's desk, and swept the waiting room floor. All the while, her thoughts circled round Doc's comments like a buzzard after a bone.

She would miss Josh something fierce. He had proven himself amusing and entertaining. But his plans hadn't changed. He was headed west to try his hand at farming.

Dora's plans had not altered either. She intended to enjoy what God had provided right here in Freebank.

Her chores done, she checked out the window. Josh sat with his feet up on the rail and a book in his lap, but his gaze was on some distant spot.

A pair of girls passed—Jenny, the storekeeper's daughter, and another she didn't recognize. Jenny's eyes widened as she spied Josh, and she nudged her friend. The two giggled, then Jenny called, "Hello, sir. I trust you are enjoying the sunshine."

Josh slowly lowered his gaze and smiled at the passing pair. "Good morning, ladies. It's a fine day." He seemed oblivious to their adoration and returned to his contemplation of the far horizon.

They hesitated then sauntered past, preening and smiling.

Dora smiled. If they thought to engage him in a flirtation, they had failed. Feeling rather pleased, she headed to the kitchen to make coffee and start lunch. That done, she prepared a tray for Josh and marched down the hall toward the veranda.

At the sound of her footsteps, he looked up, his eyes dark with welcome.

A shock shot through her as her heart responded to his look.

She almost dropped the tray. The rope handles ground into her palm. The coffee scent stung her nose. The bright air was filled with birds' songs and the happy sound of children at play. Her heart leaped for the dazzling sky, and she nearly stumbled.

He attempted to rise as she stepped outside.

"Stay where you are," she ordered, her insides wobbling as she set the tray on the railing. "I thought you might like some coffee."

"You read my mind."

Keeping her face averted, she poured him a cup and offered him a cookie, all the while trying to ignore her tempestuous emotions.

"Aren't you going to join me?"

His words jolted across her nerves, and she jerked to attention. "I have work to do," she muttered. Without so much as a backward glance, Dora raced inside.

Pressing her palms to her tight chest, she leaned against the door waiting for her panic to subside.

She'd promised herself that she would not let this happen. Josh was set on heading west, and she could not—would not—venture into the way of life he had chosen.

She would not allow herself to love such a man. Yet her pulse throbbed at the mere thought of him.

How could she have fallen in love with him? She wanted to cry and shake her hands in his face. Instead, she moaned.

I do not love him. I will not love him. We are headed in opposite directions. All I have to do is keep my distance for a few more days. Doc will surely discharge him, and I can forget I ever met him. Nodding briskly in agreement with her renewed resolve, she hurried off to the kitchen.

Josh came in a short time later and looked around the kitchen.

"Where's Mrs. Mac? I thought I'd keep her company until supper is ready."

She must have heard his voice, for Mrs. Mac scurried in from the front room, her cheeks flushed as if she'd been dozing.

"Ah, Mrs. Mac, I was hoping to see you." He plucked two cups from the cupboard and poured coffee. "I want to hear all about your trip from the Old Country." He ushered her into the front room. Dora heard a chair being moved and knew he was making sure Mrs. Mac was comfortable.

Dora smiled. It hadn't taken him long to discover that the doctor's wife loved to talk about the Old Country and her family back there. Their voices rocked back and forth, one deep and strong, the other soft and reedy.

She tried not to feel annoyance at Josh's preference for Mrs. Mac's company over her own. She gave her head a flick. Things were better this way. The less time she spent with him, the easier it would be to forget him when he left.

Doc returned, and the four of them sat down for their evening meal. Dora jumped up every few minutes to get something from the stove or pantry. If Mrs. Mac wondered why Dora felt an urgency to have jam on the table during supper, she didn't mention it. However, Doc raised his eyebrows when Dora got a second gravy boat and transferred the gravy from one container to the other.

The minute Doc set his fork down, Dora scooped up his plate and started washing dishes.

"Seems we aren't going to linger tonight," Doc commented, his voice dry. "Dora seems anxious to get the place cleaned up."

She felt three pairs of questioning eyes on her but kept her back turned and her hands immersed in soapy water. She hadn't meant to rush them. But she felt a sudden, desperate need to get to her own rooms where she could sort out her thoughts.

"I think I'll run along." She wiped the table. "That is, if I'm not needed for anything more." She hung the towel and wet rag over the towel bar.

"I expect we can manage without you." At Doc's teasing tone, she glanced up and caught him winking at his wife.

A small frown furrowed Mrs. Mac's brow before she turned and smiled at Dora. "Yes, dear, you go on home. You've worked hard all week."

Josh tipped his chair back. "I can certainly take care of myself. Have for years."

Dora lowered her head. She knew she was behaving strangely, but she couldn't stop her insides from twisting and turning. Even so, she knew she had no excuse. She took a steadying breath and looked up. "I'm sorry. I didn't mean to be impolite. I just suddenly realized how much I have to do at home." She let her gaze touch each of them then turned and prepared to leave.

Doc harumphed.

"It's quite all right, dear," Mrs. Mac said. "We do understand."

"You have a good night, Dora." Josh's voice, so filled with kindness, was almost her undoing. Nodding, she hurried out.

By the time she closed the door of her house, she was gasping for breath. She leaned against the wall of the dark room and waited for the pounding in her head to ease. Slowly she relaxed and gained control of her thoughts.

She had gone and done what she promised herself she would *not* do. She had fallen in love with Josh. How foolish to let this bother her so! Josh need never know how he had affected her. He would leave town in a few days, and she would soon forget all about him. In the meantime, she must still serve as his nurse—though there was little she needed to do anymore. She simply had to act normal.

Having thus consoled herself, she prepared for bed.

She overslept the next morning and had to hurry to get ready for church. She was about ready to walk out the door when a knock sounded on the other side. Dora drew her hand to her chest in alarm. Her heart thudding, she pulled open the door.

"Hi," Josh greeted her, his face swathed in a smile. "Doc said it would do me good to go to church. He seemed pretty sure you'd be willing to show me the way."

Dora snorted. The old codger was determined to get the two of them interested in each other. She wondered what he would say if he knew that he didn't have to try on her behalf.

"Certainly," she said to Josh. "You're more than welcome to come with me." Her insides as unsteady as a newborn calf, she faced the room, foolishly relishing every minute spent with him. How could she bear the bittersweet moments of his company while still keeping her secret? And what on earth was Mary going to say?

Filling her lungs and ordering her insides to be quiet, she demurely announced, "I'm ready."

He stepped aside to let her pass then fell into step beside her as they walked the four blocks to church.

"It's a fine morning, is it not?"

Dora's stomach fluttered at the sound of his voice.

"Why, I can hear a half dozen different birds singing in the trees as we pass. Listen. Can you catch the robin's song?"

She cocked her head as though to listen then nodded in agreement. But she hadn't heard the robin's song. The music she heard was the music of her own heart. Dora let the sweet melody swirl through her until she thought she could contain it no longer. Closing her eyes, she took a deep breath.

I must stop. My heart is running away from my head. He'll soon be gone.

She blinked, struggling to settle her emotions. Then a wayward thought surfaced. *All the more reason to enjoy every precious moment we have left to share.*

They'd come to the corner, and he grasped her elbow, gently guiding her across the street.

Her nerves tightened until she feared her heart would burst. She forced herself to stare straight ahead. Surely his behavior was typical, and it was her heightened awareness of him that now made his every word and every touch reverberate with shock waves.

"I hope you don't think I'm presumptuous." He let her arm go as they reached the other side of the street. Suddenly, her legs went weak. To cover her confusion, she paused to smooth her skirt.

"I ordered a picnic lunch," he said. "I was hoping you'd share it with me in the park after the service."

"Why I'd like that very much." Her throat tightened so that her words squeaked. Thankfully they met several others on their way to church and a round of greetings and introductions gave Dora's breathing a chance to slow.

Her senses remained razor-sharp throughout the service. The singing seemed richer and fuller than she remembered as Josh's deep voice blended with hers. The light coming through the windows seemed to have a white quality about it, cleansing those in its path.

Luke spoke of love, and every word dripped honey into Dora's heart.

Afterwards wrapped in a glow, Dora filed down the aisle until she stood before Mary and Luke.

"I'd like you to meet Josh Rivers." She tried to ignore Mary's pleased expression as she made the introductions.

When Mary hugged her, Dora whispered in her ear, "I've agreed to have lunch with Josh. I hope you don't mind."

Mary snorted. "Mind. I guess not. I'm glad you've decided to open your eyes."

"It's not that way." But she knew her protests were wasted as Mary patted her cheek and nodded.

"Dora, I've got eyes, too, and I know what I see."

Dora gave up and said good-bye.

❧

They walked to the hotel where Josh picked up the picnic lunch he had ordered. Then they sauntered to the center of town to the park burgeoning with spring.

"The young preacher delivered a good sermon." Josh spread a blanket on the grass and opened the basket.

"He's a good man." She helped set out the jug of lemonade and glasses. "We're blessed to have him."

Josh passed the plate of sandwiches to her, and she chose egg salad. He chose one with roast beef and leaned his back against a tree. "This seems a real nice little town."

"I think it is. We have all the essentials—school, church, stores—plus lots of nice extras." She went on to tell about the social activities.

"This park is really beautiful." She followed his glance from the little footbridge to the gazebo nestled in the trees and to the winding path along the lake.

"It began as someone's yard. A lady from England. She loved flowers and gardens. Many of the flower gardens were made by her." She pointed out the ones she was certain had been original. "Her husband built the footbridge. When she died, she left the land to the town with the stipulation that it be used as a park." Josh nodded, his eyes warm with interest.

Her tongue grew thick at the look on his face, and she ducked her head to finish her story. "That was Mrs. Free. The town was built on a piece of her husband's land. Hence the name, Freebank."

"Gives the town a right nice feel. I can see why you like this place so much."

He didn't know the half of it. And she couldn't tell him.

Neither of them spoke. Around them filtered the sounds of other people in the park, accompanied by the swelling songs of birds rejoicing in spring and love and building new nests.

Josh cleared his throat, and Dora jerked her gaze to him.

He watched her with a keenness that sent her heart into flight.

"Doc says I'll be able to go in a few more days."

She nodded, her mouth suddenly dry. She knew this moment would come. Perhaps it was best to come sooner rather than later—before her heart led her where she could not go. Nevertheless, her insides plummeted like a rock.

"I need to get going."

Again she nodded, well aware of how much work faced him.

He pushed away from his backrest and leaned toward her. He was so close, she could have touched his face with her trembling fingertips. She squeezed her hands into a tight ball and buried them in her lap.

"Dora." His voice was low and intense. "I haven't known you very long, but it's long enough for me to realize that—er." Josh stumbled on his words. "I—I. . . well, I can't imagine never seeing you again."

Her heart pounded in her throat as, dumbstruck, she stared at him.

"Dora, I've fallen madly and completely in love with you. Just seeing your face and hearing your voice makes my heart sing like these spring-crazed birds around us."

Every word dropped like gentle rain into her heart, adding to the emotion that she had been collecting there—emotion that now threatened to overflow the barriers she had erected.

"Dora, I'm asking you to marry me and go with me to the foothills. We'll find the prettiest spot in all the world and build our own little home, filled with love and laughter."

His words were a song of love—the sweetest sound she'd ever heard. And she almost succumbed. Almost. Then she forced herself to remember the years she'd spent on the farm with her parents. Homesteading held no allure for her. She knew all too well what it meant.

She would never again make herself endure such suffering and hardship.

"Josh, I'm flattered." She avoided his gaze. "But I can't."

She heard him sharply inhale a breath and hated herself for hurting him.

"I guess I read you wrong." His voice sounded strained. "I thought you might care about me."

Her heart shredded. "You weren't wrong," she whispered. "I do care about you." She swallowed hard. "I love you."

His smile flashed, and he leaned forward eagerly.

But she turned away. "But I would never go homesteading."

He jerked back as if she'd slapped him. "Why not?"

Stung by his reaction, she faced him. "I spent two years of sheer torture living without enough of anything and never having one bit of luxury or enjoyment. Homesteading meant nothing but work and deprivation, and I vowed I would never do it again."

The light fled from his eyes, and for a moment she wished she could change her mind. But remembering those years, she stiffened.

"I literally thought I would die." Every nerve in her body ached just remembering. "My dad knew nothing of farming. He made every mistake in the book. We ran out of food the first winter and had to accept charity from some neighbors. My dad and brother built a house, but there wasn't enough money for more than the shell. Snow came through the cracks. I woke up more than once with my toes numb from cold." She choked back tears. "I didn't get warm all winter." Suddenly she couldn't stop. "I outgrew my clothes and had to wear some of my grandmother's old dresses, which made me feel dirt-ugly. Day in and day out, we did nothing but work. There was no church, no school, no nothing." She caught her breath. "I didn't know if we'd starve to death or freeze or simply die of exhaustion." Her voice dropped to a whisper. "I'll never go through such torture again."

Josh stared at her, his eyes round. She turned away, not wanting his pity.

"Oh, Dora, it sounds all horns and rattles. I'm sorry it was so bad." He paused. "But homesteading isn't always that way. I've talked to many—"

"I've heard plenty of lies, too," she hissed. "But I've been there. I know."

He nodded. "How are your folks now?"

"They were fine when I saw them at Christmas." She found it impossible to understand how the rest of her family could now be so content. She wouldn't attempt to offer Josh an explanation.

"Are things any better for them?"

"I suppose." The inside of the house had been finished, the oilcloth placed on the floors, and Mother had been given a new dress. Father talked about spring as if it held all the diamonds in the world.

She felt, rather than saw, Josh nod. "They believed the dream and set out to realize it."

She flung around to face him. "What dream? More like a nightmare, if you ask me." She swept her gaze over the park. "A dream would be beautiful like this—full of pleasure and enjoyment. Not pinched, barely alive torture."

He shrugged and held out his hands in surrender. "I can see you aren't prepared to look at this any other way."

"What other way is there?"

"There's sacrifice in order to achieve a goal. You said your father wasn't a farmer, yet many people have learned because they're willing to learn. That's what I meant when I asked how things are now. Did your father learn how to farm? Did your family have faith? Do they still?"

"Faith?" She fairly spit the word out. "Faith is believing in what God promises, not what the government promises. Faith is using the good sense God gives us, not jumping in front of a train and expecting God to rescue us."

"You're right as far as you go—but faith also includes venturing into the unknown and believing, even when we can't see the end result."

She shook her head. "I guess you can use words any way you want, but it all boils down to one thing. It's madness to try and build something out of nothing."

"Ah, but there's where you're wrong. It isn't, as you say, 'nothing.' God has provided the best land in the world practically free. And I know about cattle and farming. I know how to make something out of the bounty God has offered."

She frowned. "What about grasshoppers, hail, frost? What about sickness? What about all the things over which you have no control?"

He smiled sadly. "None of us can control the future whether we live in town or on a homestead. That's where faith comes in. If you think you can guarantee a safe and predictable future by living in town and refusing to accept love or take risks, then I fear you are in for a dry-bones existence or a very harsh disappointment. Trusting God means leaving the future in His hands."

Rather than answer, Dora gathered up the leftover sandwiches and the untouched cake and returned them to the basket. Josh flung the blanket over his shoulder and scooped up the basket, waiting for Dora to draw abreast. Silently, they headed home, their steps quicker and more determined than they had been earlier. As they crossed Main Street, Josh drew in a sharp breath and ducked down a lane.

Dora stared after him. He hurried to the shadow of a wood shed and pulled close to the building.

"Josh?" She squinted, trying to see his face in the gloom.

"Shush."

Hesitating, she tried to decide if she should follow or wait. Finally, deciding it would be best to join him, she turned into the alley. At the same time, he reappeared from the building's shadows and stepped into the sunlight, his eyes searching behind her. "I'm dead certain that was Slim and Chester."

She wrinkled her brow. "Who?"

"The varmints who stole my money and left me half dead." His eyes darkened and he frowned. "Bet they'd be surprised to see me."

Dora gaped at him.

"In fact, I might just jump out of the shadows and scare the dickens out of them."

Her heart did a strange little flip-flop and her throat seemed suddenly too tight. "Do you suppose they're looking for you?" She had visions of them hunting Josh down and finishing what they'd begun almost two weeks ago.

"I'm guessing they think I'm dead."

A shudder raced up her spine. Josh's steps halted, and she was surprised to see that they had arrived at her house. Her glance jerked from her front door to Josh's face and then past his shoulder. When she saw no approaching figures, she turned her concentration to Josh and what he was saying.

"I wish you'd give my offer more thought. The future is not as frightening as you think—especially when you share it with someone you love."

She shook her head. The present was suddenly frightening enough. Never mind the future. But her anger had disappeared and she regretted saying all those things. "Josh, I really do love you. But I cannot possibly become a homesteader's wife. I'm sorry." Unable to bear the pain in his eyes, she fled indoors.

Chapter 4

Dora peered out from her bedcovers into the darkness and prayed for strength.

She knew what was right for her, but as she reflected on her conversation with Josh, her choices seemed childish and fearful. Hadn't God given her this place and this job? She wasn't about to toss these blessings back in His face.

In time Josh would forget her.

She tossed about, seeking a comfortable position, trying desperately to avoid the truth.

She would never forget him. Not if she lived to be a hundred years old. She tried in vain to ignore the ache in her heart.

Abandoning the hope of sleep, she waited for morning and the moment that she could hurry across the street. Even as her pulse raced at the thought, she wondered how she would face him.

❧

The next morning, she hesitated before she opened the door and entered Doc's house. Doc greeted Dora by saying, "Our young man is out."

"Josh?"

"Aye, Josh. He was dressed and waiting when I got up. Said he was going for a ride. Time to test his strength, he said." Doc shook his head. "Seemed mighty troubled about something in my opinion." He studied Dora with questioning eyes.

In no mood to match wits with Doc, she turned and hastened across the room to fling open the door to the bedroom. The bed was tossed, but Josh and his clothes were missing. She swallowed hard.

Perhaps it was for the best. Then she saw his saddlebags hooked on the post, his books, and the picture of his family lying on the shelf. Relief flooded her.

Doc had followed her, and she said to him, "He must have gone for a ride like you said. See, he's left his things."

"Well, I didn't think he'd leave without saying good-bye," Doc gruffly replied. "I must be on my way."

She nodded. "And I have much to do."

But all the time she cleaned and dusted and prepared meals and helped Doc with patients, her ears were tuned to catch the sound of a horse riding into the yard or boots crossing the veranda.

The day ended without hearing the sounds she strained to catch, and she returned home without seeing him.

Her nerves tight as fence wire under a heavy frost, she paced her rooms for an hour; then, unable to endure the strain any longer, she grabbed a sweater and hurried out the door. Perhaps a visit to Mary would ease her mind.

At the parsonage, Mary drew Dora quickly inside. "I've been longing for some company. Luke's at the church."

Dora hid her relief at the news. Sometimes Luke seemed to see through her with startling clarity. He was often right, a fact which, she admitted wryly, did nothing to make her more comfortable. Smiling at Mary's eagerness, she allowed herself to be led into the kitchen. She could always talk freely with Mary.

"What brings you here so early in the week? I thought you'd be taking a stroll in the park with that handsome young man of yours."

"He's not mine."

"Girl, you must be blind. I saw the way his eyes followed you. If that young man isn't head over heels in love, than I'm—I'm an old fat hen."

Dora grinned, and putting her hands in her armpits, she strutted around the room. "Cluck, cluck," she said, flapping her elbows.

Mary scowled. "You don't fool me. I saw the two of you together." She waited for Dora to return to her chair. "So what's the problem?"

Tossing her head, Dora asked, "Who says there's a problem?"

"Fine. Pretend you didn't come to see me because something's troubling you. We'll simply have ourselves a nice cup of tea." She filled the pot as she spoke. "And we'll talk about something else." She brought the pot to the table and set out two cups. "Did you see the new outfit Mrs. Mellon had on? Where does she get her clothes? There's nothing like that in town, and I certainly didn't see anything that special in the Eaton's catalog. I think it was real fur on the collar of her dress." Mary closed her eyes for a moment. "Don't you think I'd look lovely in such a nice outfit?"

She poured the tea and hurried on. "And where was Abigail? She hasn't been to church for three weeks now. Have you heard if she's ill or away?" She hesitated barely long enough to catch her breath. "No? Well, I was just wondering. And how's Mrs. Mac? She's such a nice lady. I hope she gets stronger now that spring is here. I shudder to think of Doc taking her away. What would we do without him?"

Dora scowled at her friend, annoyed at her silly chatter. She'd come to tell her problems, not listen to a recital of what everyone else said or wore. Mary should know better.

Then, again, Mary had offered to listen, but she had refused. As Mary's incessant prattle continued, Dora felt a chuckle rising from within. Finally, she could contain her laughter no longer. "Enough. Of course I came here to talk. You don't have to make a production out of it."

Mary grinned and leaned back. "So what's the problem?"

"Josh."

"No." Mary pretended shock, covering her mouth with her hand.

Dora shook her head sadly. "I'm afraid so." Suddenly all the silliness was gone. "I love him."

Mary nodded.

"He says he loves me."

Mary clapped her hands. "Lovely."

Dora shook her head again. "Not lovely. He wants me to marry him and go with him to stake out a homestead in the Wild West."

"Yes?" Mary waved her hands impatiently.

"That's just it. I can't go west with him."

"Why ever not?"

"I'm as far west as I plan to go."

Mary shook her head. "I don't understand."

Dora stared at her. "He's a cowboy with a head full of dreams and pockets full of dust. And a gilded tongue to boot. But you, of all people, should know why I can't go."

Her eyes narrowing, Mary studied Dora. "Are you referring to the life you lived out on the farm before you came to town?"

Dora's lips tightened. "I could never live like that again. I won't have people feeling sorry for me."

Mary jerked back. "Sorry? Who feels sorry for you? Or your family? As far as I know, your father is a respected man. He's worked hard and has every right to be proud. What makes you say that?"

Dora shrugged. "It's just that life is so uncertain. Sometimes you get a crop and have money. Other times you don't know how you'll survive. And life is so barren."

Mary smiled. "Enjoyment is a state of mind."

"What's that supposed to mean?"

"Don't you realize that even the most mundane things become events if your heart is happy and whole?"

"It's hard to be happy when life is so uncertain." Dora shook her head, unable to fathom how Mary could be so obtuse when she was generally so agreeable.

Mary continued. "I don't understand. A preacher's life is uncertain. We'll never have much. Some days we don't have enough for the next week. Some would say we depend on other people for our survival. Of course we don't. We depend on God." She drew herself up stiffly. "Do you feel sorry for us?"

Dora sighed. "Of course not. But you're so happy; why would anyone feel sorry for you?"

Mary nodded. "That's it exactly. We're happy anyway. Our circumstances don't dictate how we feel."

Miserable, Dora studied her fingernails. How could she explain how she felt when her emotions were a tangle of fear and reluctance and resolve? She had vowed never to make the kind of mistakes her parents had made—risking everything for a bit of land; facing disaster, failure, and hunger for the right to own one miserable quarter section.

As Dora prepared to leave, Mary looked troubled. "I fear you are clutching too hard to a security that is an illusion. Who can say that life in town will always be so pleasant? Besides, it is always a meaningless sacrifice to forgo love and cling to shallow substitutes."

Dora frowned. It was easy for Mary to talk. From the time she'd seen Luke, she'd known what she wanted.

Mary, having read her expression, hugged her arm. "I don't mean to give you pat answers. I'll pray God will guide your steps."

Dora hurried home. As she rounded the last corner, she strained to catch a glimpse of light coming from the window of Josh's room. Only blackness greeted her. Dora's steps faltered. Even though she had refused his offer, she hadn't expected him to simply disappear.

With heavy feet, she climbed the steps to her house.

The next morning she entered Doc's house as he rushed out. "Our young man has not returned." Doc shook his head. "I don't understand these modern young people."

Dora watched him hurry down the steps then turned her attention to the day's work. She spent a few minutes in Josh's room straightening the bed and rearranging the articles. She barely had time to clean the office before there was a burst of activity. The day was busy with a rash of broken bones and some minor injuries from children recklessly enjoying the freedom of spring.

But despite the busyness, the tightness around Dora's heart intensified with each passing hour. She hurried from the last patient to the kitchen and began supper, cooking a large pot of potatoes and frying an extra steak, all the while refusing to admit that she expected Josh to walk in at any moment.

Mrs. Mac came into the kitchen. "Where is Josh? I haven't seen him all day."

Her voice echoed the impatience of Dora's heart. Poor Mrs. Mac. Josh had brought a ray of sunshine to her life. Now he was gone. Disguising her own disappointment and concern, she answered gently, "He told Doc he was going for a ride. I expect he'll be back soon."

"That was yesterday. He should have been back long ago." She perched on the edge of her chair. "Something must have happened to the poor boy. I know it."

Dora grabbed the back of a chair as pain shot through her. Could he be injured? "Not again," she whispered, remembering his condition such a short while ago.

"Did you say something, lassie?"

"I was only thinking aloud."

"Care to share your thoughts with an old lady?" Mrs. Mac waggled her eyebrows.

Dora smiled. "I don't think you would want to hear my muddled thoughts."

Mrs. Mac snorted, and Dora knew she was waiting for her to say more, but she turned the steaks again and checked the potatoes without adding to her comment.

Doc came into the room and pulled out a chair. They were all waiting for Josh's appearance.

Finally, Doc sighed loudly. "I expect we might as well go ahead without him."

The three of them had little to say as Dora dished up the food.

"Perhaps he's decided he feels well enough to continue his journey," Doc said. "Though I would have thought he would say farewell." He paused then added, "I suppose he will write when he settles and have us send his things."

❦

Doc's words echoed as Dora returned to her house to prepare for choir practice. Josh had left without saying good-bye. It hurt, even though she realized it was for the best.

Choir was one of her greatest pleasures. She loved music, and she found tremendous enjoyment in blending her voice with the others. At least she had until tonight, she thought after she missed another note.

One of the young married women asked the group to her home for refreshments following practice, and Dora agreed despite the ache inside. After all, she reasoned, wasn't social activity one of the reasons she insisted she had to live in town? But the chatter and noise made her head ache, and she slipped away early, pleading tiredness. She returned to her home to spend another troubled night.

※

The next morning, she stepped into Doc's kitchen and blinked. Mrs. Mac was up and dressed, eating toast with her husband.

"Did you notice the Mayday tree?" she asked happily. "It's in blossom."

Dora stopped in her tracks. It had become a tradition to measure the seasons by the trees and flowers. The Mayday tree was their spring marker. When the tree blossomed with its fragrant white flowers, they all agreed spring had officially arrived. Dora had watched for days, hoping to be the first to spot the blooms. She thought she had an advantage, for she passed the tree each morning. But she had walked by this morning without seeing the tree or even noticing the scent. She shook her head. She must have been half asleep.

The day, although busy, passed slowly. Dora tried to tell herself that she had accepted Josh's leaving. But as she rubbed her aching brow, she wished she could convince her heart.

By evening she wanted nothing but to crawl into bed and cover up her head. Still, her thoughts kept sleep at bay.

Since she moved to town, life had been full of enjoyment and peace. Then Josh arrived. Now everything seemed hollow.

She should never have allowed herself to fall in love with him, and she vowed she would dismiss him from her thoughts. But try as she might, she was unable to erase thoughts of him from her mind. Words circled inside her head. *Security. Trust. Risk. Faith.*

What did she want? A safe place free of fear? Fear had been ever present on the farm. Yet deep down she knew that, among her family, only she had felt that gut-wrenching worry about what they'd eat and how they'd live. More than once Mother had assured her, "We don't have a lot, but we'll get by. And things will get better."

But she hadn't stopped agonizing until she got her job with Doc and found this house.

Security is not found in a place, position, or possessions—but in God.

The words bolted into her mind. Where had she heard them? Luke, of course. What else had he said? Something about faith being revealed by one's choices. But did taking risks prove one's faith?

She was certain it did not. Still, she was forced to admit that refusing to take risks didn't reveal faith either. God had provided this situation for her in answer to her prayers. And it was warm and cozy. Like a cocoon.

She bolted upright in bed.

It was true. She was trusting her situation for security. No longer did she cry out to God to meet her needs. She shivered, feeling suddenly lost.

But God hadn't changed. She had. She took a deep breath and lay back down. She was glad of this reminder of what she truly believed. Security was found in God alone.

God, I don't know what's right anymore. I thought I was right to appreciate what You have provided. But I fear that I am finding it too comfortable and not as enjoyable as I once thought. I love Josh and miss him already. Are You leading me into a new adventure? Is my lack of faith keeping me from considering the life of a pioneer wife? God, please bring him back.

She lay quietly for a moment and let her anxiety ease away. A new resolve grew within her. Wherever God led her, she would contentedly go. Even if it meant leaving town, this house, and the job she had come to love.

Her heartbeat quickened, and she pressed her palms to her chest as she admitted that which she had been pushing away: To share a new life with Josh would not require one ounce of sacrifice.

Still, it was too late to think of such a thing. She'd thrown away her chance with Josh. If only she hadn't been so blind. She'd learned her lesson too late. An aching hollowness echoed through her thoughts.

❧

With the dawn of a new day, she crossed the street and headed up the path to Doc's house. A white petal on the ground caught her attention, and she tipped her head to see the Mayday tree in a garment of white, heavy-scented blossoms. But the scent triggered no answering song in her heart. The branches were full of birds exulting in spring, but there was no response in her heart. Spring had lost her song, when only a few days ago creation had rung with music and happiness.

She moaned. Without Josh, life lay before her muted and bland. Turning away, she slowly climbed the steps, her head dipped close to her chest.

Dora entered the sickroom, and she crossed to the bedpost where Josh's saddlebags hung. With trembling fingers she caressed the smooth leather, hungrily breathing in the scent.

Perhaps he would return for his belongings.

❧

The next day, when afternoon office hours were almost over, a young boy clamored in from outside and ran to where his mother sat, waiting to see the doctor. "Mom, guess what? A man just rode up to the sheriff's with two men tied up in ropes. They sure looked mad, too."

Dora smiled at his enthusiasm, knowing that the activity of town was new and exciting for the boy.

Shortly, Dora announced to Doc, "That's the last of today's patients." But before she finished speaking, she heard the clatter of boots on the steps.

Doc groaned. "Not quite, lassie."

The door flung open, and Dora gasped. Josh stood facing them, breathing hard.

Dora knew her mouth hung open, but she couldn't stop staring. Nor could she find her voice.

Josh's gaze held Dora's until she thought she was drowning in something unfamiliar—yet comforting. Doc broke the spell as he spoke. "We thought you had headed west, my boy."

Josh blinked and turned to face the older man. "Sorry about that,

Doc. I hadn't planned to ride away without so much as a good-bye."

Dora couldn't stop looking at Josh. She noted the smudge of dirt along one cheek, the white sun-squint creases that radiated from his eyes, and the way the sun had frosted his eyelashes. And then she was looking into his warm brown eyes again, lost in a thousand sensations that sent her heart rocketing from height to depth. Seeking equilibrium, she tried to tear her gaze away but found she could not. She knew this unsettled state would last until she could explain how she'd changed her mind.

What if Josh has changed his mind as well? The painful thought caused her chest to tighten until she could barely breathe.

"I went out to ride and think, but I soon discovered that I wasn't alone on the road. I caught sight of the two men who had robbed me." Josh continued to watch Dora. "I was near certain that they weren't following me, but I decided to round up the varmints and bring them to justice." He shrugged. "It took longer than I expected to circle round and get the drop on them." At his crooked grin, a tremble raced across Dora's shoulders.

Doc harumphed. "I best go see how Mrs. Mac is doing. She'll be glad to know you're back." He turned on his heel and left the room.

Dora took a deep breath. God had blessed her with another opportunity, and she wasn't going to waste it. But before she could speak, Josh stepped closer.

"I had plenty of time to think while I was gone," he began. Josh's eyes darkened as he studied her face with a hunger that made her cheeks warm. She swallowed hard, hopelessly trying to corral her thoughts. The power of his nearness turned her emotions into a tumult. She held her breath for a moment, trying to slow the quivering of her insides long enough to say the words she'd practiced half the night.

Josh looked down at his hands. The sudden loss of his gaze gave her a rash of goose bumps. Then he looked once more into her eyes, his expression so serious she could feel her pulse under her tongue.

"I don't want to go anywhere without you. Doesn't matter how pretty the country is—without you it is nothing." He paused, and the silence thundered in her ears. "I've decided to get a job in town and live here."

His Adam's apple bobbed. "That is, if you meant it when you said you loved me."

He would give up his dream for her! He was willing to live in town!

She caressed the idea for a moment and found that it gave her no pleasure. God had surely done a work in her heart. A glow began somewhere behind her heart and radiated to her toes, her fingers, her face. It made her want to laugh and cry and shout all at the same time.

"I meant it when I said I love you, Josh." Her voice shook. "But I don't care where we live or what you do." She grinned as his eyes grew round.

"I don't understand."

Her smile widened. "I've had plenty of time to think as well. And I prayed that God would give me another chance to tell you—I will go with you to the farthest mountains if you still want me. . . ."

He didn't wait for her to finish but wrapped her in a hug and swung her off the floor, yelling, "Yahoo." She was gasping when he set her on her feet, his arms still circling her. He dipped his head in order to look into her face. "Are you sure about this?"

"As sure as can be. I realized life in town was a life of quiet desperation if it meant giving up the love of a lifetime." She had learned so much more, and someday she'd tell him. Someday, but not now.

He nodded, still serious. "Even so, I'm willing to live in town. I don't want you to be unhappy."

She shook her head. "That is not necessary." She realized she had turned a corner in her thinking and was no longer afraid to face change or even uncertainty. Excitement replaced her fear.

"I don't want to miss the adventure of a lifetime."

His arms tightened, pressing her to his chest. She rested her face against his dusty shirt, listening to the steady beat of his heart. With warm fingers he tipped her head back.

"Dora Grant, I love you with all my heart. Will you marry me and make my life complete?"

She smiled up at him, listening to the song in her heart. "Josh Rivers, I love you more than anything, and I will marry you and follow you to the ends of the earth. Your love is my song."

He laughed low in his throat. "We'll only go as far as the foothills." Sobering quickly, he added. "I will sing you a love song every day."

She sighed and placed her ear against his chest again so that she could hear his heart. "This is my love song...," she whispered. As was his smile, his voice, his touch. Each new day with Josh would bring a fresh love song.

He caught her chin in his palm and turned her face upward. "I love you so much, Dora." His lips, warm and possessive, found hers. She tangled her fingers in the curls at the back of his neck, letting her kiss say what her heart felt.

He lifted his head. "Ah, my sweet, sweet Dora. I can't imagine life without you." Their gazes sought and held each other for many long moments before he stepped away, catching her hand. "I've something to show you." He drew her to the sickroom and snagged his saddlebags from the end of the bed. Flipping them onto the quilt, he dug into his trousers pocket for a knife. He flicked open the blade and jabbed it into the side of a saddlebag, ripping open the seam.

Dora gasped as a false back opened up and paper money spilled forth.

Josh stood back and grinned, his hands on his hips. "This is what those men were after. There's more in the other bag. More than enough to build a house and start a herd of the best English cows." He sobered, studying her closely. "I thought about what you said—how some people risk everything and sometimes lose it. And you're right. So I propose to put half of this in a bank account as our nest egg. That way, should disaster strike, we'll have enough to start over."

She wanted to say that such a plan wasn't necessary; they could depend on God, but she knew he was right. Her heart was ready to burst. Barely able to speak, she whispered, "You are a very wise man. No wonder I love you."

His lips warm and gentle, he kissed her again. Then he pulled away and grabbed her hand. "Let's go tell Doc and Mrs. Mac."

She laughed, a breathless sound of pure joy. Somehow she didn't think the good doctor and his wife would be surprised to hear how things had turned out.

LINDA FORD draws on her own experiences living on the Canadian prairie and in the Rockies to paint wonderful adventures of romance and faith. She lives in Alberta, Canada, with her family, writing as much as her full-time job of taking care of a paraplegic and four kids at home will allow. Linda says, "I thank God that he has given me a full, productive life and that I'm not bored. I thank Him for placing a little bit of the creative energy revealed in His creation into me, and I pray I might use my writing for His honor and glory." www.lindaford.org

The Barefoot Bride

by Linda Goodnight

Chapter 1

Goodhope, Kansas, 1883

HUSBAND WANTED.
MUST BE GOD-FEARING, HARDWORKING, AND CLEAN.

D r. Matthew Tolivar frowned as he read the carefully lettered sign hanging inside the door of O'Dell's General Store. Removing his battered hat, he swiped a hand through his dark hair, a shaggy reminder of the weeks spent on the road. A second swipe, this one over his square jaw, grated against several days' growth of whiskers.

"What kind of woman would advertise for a husband?" he muttered, half to himself.

"A crazy one."

Matthew turned slowly toward the speaker. The little man stood behind a long, rough-hewn counter, surrounded by an odd assortment of horse tack, yard goods, and canned foods. *Crazy.* His crude answer echoed in Matt's head. *Yes*, he thought, *or desperate.* And Matt Tolivar knew about desperate.

"Name's O'Dell. Jimmy O'Dell. I'm the proprietor here." The store-keeper's woolly tufts of red hair circled his balding head like a fuzzy horseshoe. "You'd be new in town, I'm guessing. Most folks from these parts know all about Emma Russell and her crazy ways."

"So this quest for a husband is just part of her dementia?" Matt let his hat dangle in one hand as he surveyed the store. It reminded him of a hundred other stores he'd visited in his wanderings.

He stifled a weary sigh. He was tired of running. Tired of always being a stranger. Tired of being alone. A situation like his made even a crazy woman's offer sound good.

"No. No," O'Dell answered, "Emma's after a man, all right. That big old farm won't run itself, and she's just a little bit of a woman. Can't do it alone. But her sign's hung there for a year or more, and only the new folks pay it any mind. I just leave it up for conversation. Once in a while some fella takes a notion to head out that direction. Six sections of prime grazing land is a mighty big temptation, you know?"

"Why doesn't she just hire someone?"

"She's touched, I tell you. Young Dan Barton worked for her a bit, and she nearly scared the poor boy to death. 'Possessed,' he said. She was dancing with brooms and talking to the air." He shook his head, foreboding in his expression. "I saw Dan myself, come running into town one day, white as St. Patty's ghost. Since then, the townsfolk keep their distance. No telling what that woman might do."

"Dancing and talking never hurt anyone. Is she dangerous?" Matt was curious. In his days as a physician, the insane had stirred his heart to compassion. Though the common practice was to put them away, Matt had remembered the compassion of Jesus toward the sick in soul and mind. How could a physician do less than try to help them? Sometimes treatments worked; sometimes they didn't. But Matt had always tried.

"You wouldn't be thinking of going out there, would you?"

Was he? Matt didn't know for certain. While he considered the question, a curtain behind the counter parted and a copper-haired woman stepped out, sea green eyes flashing. "Da, are you talking about Emma again?"

"Now, Maureen. . ." O'Dell grinned at Matt. "This avenging angel is my daughter, Maureen. Always she's fighting for those she pities."

Maureen laughed. "An angel, he's calling me. And the two of us always quarreling over something." She came around the counter, pink skirts swaying. "And who might you be, Mr. . . . ?"

"Tolivar," he said. "Matthew Tolivar."

Maureen snitched a peppermint stick from a jar on the counter and aimed it at him. "Well, Mr. Tolivar, don't you go listening to this da of mine. Emma Russell is a gentle woman who's had more suffering than the Lord should allow, and this town has turned its back on her instead of helping out."

"Maureen." Her father scowled at her from behind the cash register. "Don't be getting none of your funny notions. That woman never belonged here in the first place. Old Jeremiah Russell had no business sending off for a mail-order bride. We all told him no good would come of it. Only the demented or desperate would consider such an offer." O'Dell shifted his gaze to Matt. "She was an orphan, you see. And old Jeremiah needed someone to help him care for that big old place of his. Orphans got bad blood, we told him. And we was right." He pursed his lips and gave a knowing jerk of his head. "Now that Jeremiah's dead, we folks in Goodhope have to keep our eyes and ears open lest that crazy widow steal our children or murder us in our sleep."

"Emma would never hurt a soul, Da." Maureen tossed her head, and a red curl bounced down upon one shoulder.

"You're the only one who believes that, girlie. Now you mind what I've told you and stay clear of her, or I'll be tearing a strip off ya."

The harsh warning brought a flush to Maureen's pretty face. Rebellion burned in her eyes, but she gnawed silently on the candy stick.

A tiny seed of compassion sprouted in Matt's chest, both for Maureen and for the Widow Russell. No one knew better than he did about being an outcast, about suffering the sly, speculative glances of his neighbors.

"Where does this widow live?" Matt asked, more curious than ever about the woman. "I could use a day or two of work."

"Just like the sign says." Maureen spoke quickly, casting a defiant glance at her glaring father. "Take the road north out of town about three miles and follow the creek to a stand of cottonwoods. 'Tis the only house for miles."

"Maureen, this young feller can find work somewheres besides there.

Now hush your jabbering and go help your ma with the little 'uns. She's feeling poorly this morning."

From the attached rooms in the back came the noise of playing children. Maureen slanted a glance in that direction then gave a saucy shrug and disappeared around the curtain.

Shaking his head, O'Dell said, "That girl has a heart of gold but doesn't know what's good for her. I 'spect she sneaks off to that crazy woman's house, though I can't catch her at it. Thank the good Lord she's devoted to her mama, or there's no telling what kind of nonsense she'd get into."

"I'm sorry your wife's feeling poorly. I hope her ailment isn't serious." He clamped his teeth together to keep from asking if the woman needed his services. Thankfully, the storekeeper didn't notice.

"Nah, same as always when she's expecting. Sick in the mornings, sleepy all day. After ten of the darlin's, though, she's an old hand at it. Be right as rain in a few months."

A deep ache, worse than the grippe, pulled at Matthew's belly. Visions of Martha rose to haunt him, her body round with his child. Martha, his own wife, the one patient his skilled medical hands couldn't save. He gulped back the wave of guilt and sorrow that was never far away.

"I hope Mrs. O'Dell feels better soon, sir," he said, shifting to safer ground. "Now if you don't mind, I'd like a tin of sardines and a few crackers to take along for my dinner."

The Irishman scuttled around, his boots scraping on the wooden floor, as he gathered up the items and pushed them across the counter.

"Plan on staying in town long, Mr. Tolivar? 'Tis a nice little settlement. Folks are friendly. Plenty of opportunity for a hard worker." He took the coin Matt handed him, testing it between his teeth. Satisfied, he poked at the cash register until the drawer chinged open. "I suppose that Russell woman is the only blight on the whole county, and she knows better than to show her face in town too often. Stay clear of her, and you'll get along fine around here."

Matt didn't appreciate the not-so-subtle warning. He was a man who took care of himself and made his own decisions. Whoever this Russell woman was, she led a hard, solitary life—an existence as lonely and empty as his. That fact alone won her his sympathy.

Matt looked over his shoulder at the faded paper. Suddenly it took on new meaning. The Widow Russell needed a husband and a ranch hand. Matt Tolivar needed a place to hide and a purpose in life. Maybe they could work out a deal.

With his lunch in one hand, he clapped on his hat and headed for his horse.

The people of Goodhope were right. Emma Russell was crazy.

Barefoot, she danced in circles around the early stalks of green corn standing tall in her garden. Her laughter bubbled up and echoed over the vast grasslands surrounding her ranch.

"Thank you!" she called, her voice loud and joyous, though Matt knew for certain she wasn't talking to him. "How can I ever thank you enough?"

As she whirled wildly, her plain calico skirts flapped against the corn-stalks and made a *whap, whap, whapping* noise. "I do declare that's the prettiest sound in all the world. Don't you think so?"

She was turned sideways, talking to the corn or some unseen visitor.

Matt tied his horse to the rough-barked rail running along the front porch of her cabin and waited for her to notice him.

Watching her now, he wondered why he'd bothered to come out here. He'd been warned. But after six years of roaming the frontier, he was too weary to travel on. Besides, he'd long since discovered that a man couldn't outrun his own conscience.

"Ah, would you look at that?" she said to the warm May breeze. "He's back, the little rascal."

For a moment, Matt thought she spoke of him. Then he saw the rabbit hopping toward the garden. To his surprise, instead of flapping her skirts to chase the varmint out of her corn, she pulled a young green stalk and laid it on the ground in the animal's path.

"Now maybe you'll leave the rest alone."

With a smile as pretty as Maureen O'Dell's, the crazy widow hefted the hoe and started toward the cabin, singing and chattering all the way. Halfway there she looked up, spotted him waiting in the cool shade, and stopped to appraise him.

"Lovely day, isn't it?" she asked simply, as though the sight of him standing in her shade was a common one.

"Yes, ma'am," Matt answered in the same matter-of-fact manner; then he stepped forward, removing his hat. He had expected her to be old and ugly as a witch, but she was neither.

"Did you see Noah, then? He's gathering in the animals, two by two."

Her words brought Matt to a halt. He blinked in confusion. Didn't seem to be anyone around but him and her. She *was* crazy. He had to be careful until he knew the extent of her dementia.

"Oh, you have to see him," she insisted. "Come on. I'll show you."

As she crossed the yard, a beatific smile greeted Matthew from beneath honey-colored eyes that matched her hair. Back home in Virginia, women had creamy pale skin, carefully protected from the sun, and their hair was neatly groomed on top of their heads. Emma Russell's skin was as golden brown as freshly baked bread, and she wore no bonnet on the wild, windblown hair that flowed freely over her shoulders and down her back. Her arms and neck were as bare as her feet. She was oddly beautiful in a wild, earthy manner that reminded him of the untamed mustangs he'd seen in his journey across the plains.

As she reached his side, bringing with her the fresh green scent of growing things, she took his hand as easily as if they'd grown up together. Too surprised to pull away, Matt let her lift his arm and point it toward a huge, fluffy configuration of white fair-weather clouds.

"Right there. See?" she said. "It's Noah, I'm certain. See his staff? And that long, flowing beard?"

A chuckle worked its way up inside Matt's chest, but he repressed it. Like a child, the Widow Russell was forming pictures in the clouds. Her insanity was most likely harmless, a return to childlike ways.

"Maybe it's Moses, striking the rock," Matt said, responding to her game. How many years had passed since he'd done such a silly, light-hearted thing?

"You could be right." She dropped his arm and turned to face him with those pale gold eyes. "Are you a God-fearing man, then?"

"Yes, ma'am." The remnants of his faith were all that kept him going, though he'd long since stopped bothering God with his day-to-day worries.

"Good. Good. He wouldn't send any other kind, now, would He?"

Matt blinked at her, baffled. "Who?"

"Why, the Lord, of course."

"Oh. I suppose not." *What is she talking about?*

"He told me you were coming. I just didn't know when." She leaned the hoe against the side of the porch. "Come on in."

"Who told you I was coming?" He followed her across the porch, ducking his head to miss the dangling onions hung in bunches from the rafters. "The Lord?"

Emma turned back, her gaze moving over him as softly as the breeze, which lifted the tendrils of hair from her forehead.

"I've waited two years for you to get here, and now that you've arrived, I can tell you're the right one. God wouldn't send anyone but the best."

She talked crazy, and her behavior was unusual, but her calm, amber eyes looked as sane as any he'd ever held in his gaze.

"Come in. I'll fix us a nice lemonade while we talk."

Matt asked himself again why he didn't just get back on his horse and ride away. But for some strange reason—most likely his medical curiosity—this woman fascinated him.

Or could it actually be the Lord's doing, his being here? Could Emma be right? Did God work that way?

Somewhere from the past he remembered the saying, "God works in mysterious ways, His wonders to perform."

Well, Emma Russell and this bizarre situation were certainly wonders.

He followed her inside, noting how large the cabin was compared to most he'd seen. She led him through a small parlor. A rocking chair and a cradle sat beside the fireplace, and colorful rag rugs covered the plank floor. The place was homey. Pleasant and cozy. The kind of home where a man could put up his feet and relax after a hard day's work. The kind of home that Matt hadn't had in a very long time. As he considered the cleanliness, he thought it unlikely that an insane mind could bring such order. Could the people of Goodhope be wrong about the Widow Russell?

Graceful as a deer, Emma moved about the kitchen, her hair catching the sunlight now streaking in between the yellow curtains. Matt settled at the round oak table to watch and found the experience much more pleasant than he could have imagined. She emanated a gentleness, a peace that stirred him in ways he'd long since forgotten. What was it about her?

"I'm Matthew Tolivar," he said, breaking the silence and his own wayward thoughts. "I saw your sign at the store in town."

"And?" She handed him a cool glass then took one for herself before sitting across from him, as calm and rational as he.

"Why do you want a husband?"

She sighed, a breathy sound that raised the hair on Matt's arm and made him even more aware of Emma Russell's peculiar loveliness. When she began to speak in a low, sweet voice, he set his glass aside and leaned forward, suddenly eager to be convinced, not only of her sanity, but of her need for a husband.

"Two years ago, a blizzard hit this part of Kansas and lasted for weeks."

"The blizzard of '81." Everyone knew about that terrible time when men froze in their saddles and cattle froze in the fields.

"We thought we were safe and snug here in the cabin—my husband, Jeremiah; Lily, our little girl; and me. Jeremiah wasn't a young man, but day after day, he stumbled from the house to the barn, taking care of the stock, bringing in wood. He was so good, so kind. He'd never let me go out there." Absently, Emma drew circles on the table with her glass. "I wasn't surprised when the fever struck him, just scared. Then, soon after, Lily took sick. The wind kept blowing and the snow piled higher. I couldn't go for help." She glanced up. "Goodhope has no doctor, even if I could have gotten out. There was nothing I could do but pray and wait."

A lump formed in Matt's throat. He didn't want to hear this; didn't want to be reminded of his own lost family. He sipped at the tart drink, washing down bitter memories. He'd asked. Now he had to listen.

"Lily was so small, she couldn't fight the sickness. Her little chest closed up so tight that all the mustard plasters in the world couldn't open it up again."

"Pneumonia?" Matt asked quietly, recognizing the strangling symptoms.

Emma nodded, her voice small and distant. "One night I sat beside her bed, listening to the howling wind and counting every breath my baby took. Soon there was only the wind, blowing, blowing, blowing."

The terrible story pulled at Matt. He knew just how hard the loss of a child could hit a parent.

"I'm sorry, Mrs. Russell." As he'd done many times with his patients, Matt reached out and laid his hand over hers. She didn't pull away, and a warmth crept from her small, weathered hand upward to his icy heart.

"I know." She ventured a sad smile. "So am I. Jeremiah died the next day, and there I was, all alone in a cabin with my dead family while the blizzard raged on."

"How long before help came?"

"I don't rightly know, Mr. Tolivar." She shook her head and looked away. "You see, for a while, I lost myself. I know how that sounds. That's why the townsfolk still think I'm crazy to this day. It's hard to explain, and I don't expect you to understand. But my whole world caved in when Jeremiah and Lily died."

Yet Matt did understand. He knew how grief could tear away at the inner man until he was so lost he couldn't find his way back. Hadn't the same thing happened to him in a different way? Hadn't he roamed the plains, searching for something, and all the while that something was within him?

"Grief does strange things," he said kindly.

"In those dark, terrible days after Jeremiah and Lily died, I prayed to die with them. Why should I, with nothing and no reason to live, remain here, when they, who were so good and perfect, were gone? But finally, as I lay on my empty bed one night, the sweetest presence filled that room." She smiled softly, an inner radiance lighting her eyes. "It was Jesus."

Jesus? Matt stiffened, struggling to keep his expression bland. "What did He say?"

"Say?" Emma seemed to come back from a distant place. She tilted her head to the side and shrugged one thin shoulder. "Oh, He didn't say anything. He just stood there, watching me with His wonderful, kind eyes and letting His peace flow around me like a great cleansing river of light. When I woke up the next morning He was gone, but He'd left behind such a strength and joy that I could no longer lie in bed feeling sorry for myself. God had given me life, and Jeremiah had given me this place. I had to do right by both of them."

A dream. That's all. In her grief, she confused a dream with reality. Matt breathed a quiet sigh of relief.

Emma slipped her hand from beneath his and inhaled deeply. "That, Mr. Tolivar, is why I need a husband. Jeremiah left me a fine ranch, but I cannot run it alone. Hired men are either dishonest or afraid of me. They think I'm crazy, you see. Maureen says that some folks in town believe I should be put away and my land sold. A husband can keep that from happening."

Matt set his glass on the table and scooted his chair back, meeting her gaze. "According to the law, Mrs. Russell, a woman's property belongs to her husband. Have you considered that?"

She twisted her hands nervously in her lap. "Yes. I know. That's why I have to find the right person. An honest man who'll do right by me. I've prayed a very long time. And now you've come."

Matt wanted to promise her, then and there, that he'd always take care of her. He didn't know why. The idea didn't make a lick of sense to him. Perhaps her sad story struck a tender chord in his own sick soul. Whatever the reason, he knew he would stay. And he knew he would marry the crazy Widow Russell.

Chapter 2

Matthew awoke to the sound of voices. No, not voices. One voice. A sweet, feminine voice somewhere below.

"Daisy, dear," the voice said. "What would I do without you?"

From his prickly bed in the hayloft, Matt opened one eye and peeked through the missing planks in the barn roof at the first pink-gray hint of morning. Slowly, memory returned to his sleep-fogged mind as he recalled where he was and what he'd agreed to do. Last night, over the best home-cooked meal he'd had in months, he'd consented to marry a woman who, this very moment, was somewhere below him, babbling to herself like a lunatic.

"The Anderson children will appreciate this so much. There are four of them, you know, and children are always hungry." She laughed softly. "But you're taking care of that, aren't you, dear heart?"

Quietly, Matt edged toward the sound until he was lying on his belly peering down at the top of Emma Russell's head. Now he saw what he couldn't see from his bed of hay. She was talking to a sleek, docile Guernsey cow while her small hands rhythmically squirted milk into a gleaming bucket.

"Thank You, Lord, for Daisy." The conversation suddenly switched to prayer, an unsettling habit Matthew had encountered more than once the previous day. "And thank You for sending Matthew Tolivar my way. He's the right one, I know. Though I never expected him to be quite so handsome."

Matthew held his breath, listening. Handsome, was he?

"But I don't mind a bit, Lord, that looking at him is pleasant. Especially since he's sturdy built with shoulders strong enough to do the things around here that I'm too small to do."

A curl of pleasure rose in Matt's belly, warming him like smoke rising from a chimney on a chilly day. She thought he was strong and handsome. For the life of him, he didn't know why her opinion mattered. But it did.

"And his blue eyes, Jesus, as pretty as a summer day, but so full of sadness. You know his secrets. You know what's hurt him. Help him find the peace he needs."

A familiar heaviness descended upon Matthew, erasing all pleasure in Emma's rambling over his good looks. He had come here to hide, to bury himself in hard, mind-numbing work, hoping to blot out all memory of who he was and what he'd once considered his calling in life. By helping the poor widow, he could make amends for his own failure and never have to think of medicine again. That alone was reason enough to marry her. It didn't matter if she thought him as plain as a stick.

Wearily, he rose and thumped back to his bedroll, making enough noise to warn Emma that he was awake. The black medical bag he'd used as a pillow more times than he could remember now mocked him as he rolled it tightly inside the woolen blankets. He stopped, unrolled the bedding, and stashed the bag in the far corner of the loft beneath a pile of hay. He wouldn't need the bag or its contents ever again. He didn't know why he'd kept it so long, except that his selling it might raise questions he didn't want to answer. Someday a traveling peddler would come along, and he'd be rid of the bag for good. For now, he didn't need the reminder of all he'd lost. Today he'd start a new life and leave the old one behind forever.

There was plenty here to keep his body busy and his mind preoccupied. The Widow Russell had done her best to keep things going. He could see that. Even the barn was neatly kept, the hay raked to one side, fresh straw in the stalls. The animals were healthy and well fed, the garden planted and sprouting. But everywhere he'd noticed signs that the job was too big for her to tackle all alone. The barn door sagged to one side. A half-finished row of fence trailed from the barn to nowhere. And the woodpile was woefully low. No doubt, a further inspection would reveal more, and he was glad for that. Glad for the opportunity to hang up his hat and exhaust himself at something worthwhile.

Buttoning his shirt, he descended the ladder. The widow heard him coming and looked over one shoulder.

"Are you ready for some flapjacks?" Emma asked as she spread a clean white cloth over the brimming milk bucket.

"Sounds good." Matt took the pail from her hands. "I'll wash up a bit first, if you don't mind. You did specify 'clean' in your advertisement, didn't you?"

"Did You hear that, Jesus?" With a merry laugh, Emma reclaimed the milk bucket and led them out of the barn, her yellow dress a bright spot in the early morning.

Matt followed behind, shaking his head. Just when he'd decided that only a logical, rational woman could have kept the farm going so long, she talked to a cow or a rabbit or the Lord Himself, raising fresh questions and doubts in his mind.

"How long have you been up?" He stopped to scrub himself at the well where Emma had placed a rag and sliver of soap in anticipation of his needs.

"Awhile. I love the hours before sunrise when the stars are still out and the rest of world is sleeping. You can see things in the darkness that are never around in the daylight." She set the milk on the wooden ledge of the well and drew the water bucket to the top. Pouring a bit of the liquid on a rag, she rinsed her hands and swiped her grass-covered feet. The hem of her gingham dress was dew-drenched, letting him know that she'd been farther than the barn this morning. He couldn't help but wonder where she had gone in the darkness. Did she roam the woods baying at the moon or communing with the devil?

Matt shoved the damp hair back from his forehead and dismissed the ridiculous notions. The conversation with the storekeeper had filled his head with nonsense. He was a man of science, not an ignorant country bumpkin who believed the insane were all devil-possessed. Emma Russell was a Christian woman. Of that he was certain. And with each minute spent in her company, he became more convinced that the town of Goodhope was wrong about her mental state.

Tossing the towel over one shoulder, he hefted the two buckets and followed her to the house. A half dozen red chickens clucked around the front porch, running full speed toward Emma when they saw her coming.

"Not yet, girls. But give me six eggs today, and there will be corn for everyone this evening." To Matt she said, "Just set the milk on the sideboard, please, and sit down. I'll have breakfast ready in no time."

Ignoring her command, Matt strained the milk, set it to cool, and rinsed the bucket, hanging it upside down on a nail by the back door. If he was going to live here, he might as well let her know he wasn't lazy.

Emma opened the cookstove and poked at the fire; then she rubbed an iron skillet with lard before clapping it onto the stovetop. Pancake batter sizzled against the hot skillet, and the smell of sausage set Matt's belly to rumbling. He'd missed this. Missed the familiar warmth and smell of a kitchen and a pretty woman bustling around, preparing a meal.

"Mrs. Russell."

"Might as well call me Emma."

"All right, Emma." He sipped at the coffee she handed him and wondered when he'd last drunk from anything but a tin cup. "I reckon I'll go into town later and fetch the preacher."

Her hands stilled. "You're still agreeable, then?"

"If you'll have me."

"I will." Drawing in a deep breath, she turned toward him, twisting her hands in her apron. "I got no false notions about this, Matthew. You're marrying me for my land. I'm marrying you to hang on to Jeremiah's dreams and the only home I've ever had. A business agreement, pure and simple. That's all I'm asking. I'll look after you and you look after me."

He heard the relief in her voice when she'd gotten the words out, and he understood her meaning. In Virginia, men and women courted, fell in love, and married, though a few still agreed to arranged marriages. Things were different out here. Men ordered wives through the mail or bartered for them when a farmer had more girls than he could feed. Emma was trying to make it clear to him that she wasn't looking for a love match, just a husband to work her farm. That was fine with him. Absolutely fine. There was nothing left inside him to love.

"People marry for worse reasons," he said, half to convince himself. "We'll do all right, if we set our minds to it."

"Thank you." She piled the flapjacks onto a plate and circled them with sausages. "You're a good man."

"How could you possibly know that?"

"I know." She set the steaming breakfast in front of him. "And Jesus knows."

Matt sighed. There she went again. "And I suppose He told you?"

Her innocent amber eyes widened. "How else would I find out?"

How else indeed? But was such a thing possible? Was God the reason that marrying the Widow Russell and resurrecting this farm appealed to him more with each passing moment? Or was it because he could hide here on a farm that other people avoided?

Emma refilled his coffee and placed a jar of molasses next to his elbow. Then she settled into her own chair and plunged into her meal as though she married a stranger every day of the week.

Matthew lifted his fork and looked down at the butter pats on his flapjacks. They were shaped like daisies.

A chunk of ice melted in one corner of Matthew's frozen heart. Emma Russell was fanciful, childlike, utterly fascinating, and certainly in need of a man's protection, but he didn't think she was crazy. The more he knew about her, the more she beguiled him, and the more he wanted to stay.

※

Later that morning, Matt rode away from Goodhope Church, madder than he'd been in years. All the way back to Emma's place, he rehashed the conversation with Reverend Jeffers, trying to come up with a winning argument.

"It's against the laws of God and common sense for the insane to marry, Mr. Tolivar," the parson had said as they stood in the sunlight just outside the church where Matt had found him pounding nails in a rickety step.

"I tell you, Reverend, Mrs. Russell is not insane." Matt leaned against the railing and gazed in frustration at the kneeling man. "Unusual and childlike, yes, but as rational and sound as either you or me."

Laying his hammer aside, Reverend Jeffers stood and dusted his hands down the sides of his trousers. An angular man with hollow cheeks and burning eyes, he pierced Matt with a look. "Mr. Tolivar, how long have you known Mrs. Russell?"

"Long enough." Matt hedged, hesitant to admit he'd agreed to marry a woman less than a day after meeting her. "And in my opinion, Mrs. Russell is perfectly sane."

"I see. And by what authority do you judge her mental state?"

"I. . ." Matt stopped and ground his teeth in frustration. As a doctor, he carried the knowledge and authority to make that judgment, but his profession was part of the past, buried when Martha died. He had no intention of resurrecting it. "I've observed her closely," he finished lamely.

The reverend narrowed his eyes. "Begging your pardon, Mr. Tolivar, but you're a stranger in this town. As the only clergyman for miles around, it's my duty to protect poor Emma from unscrupulous souls who might take advantage of her to gain her land." He held up a bony hand as Matt's expression darkened. "Not that I'm saying you're that kind of man. I don't know you, but I do know Emma. And she has no business making a decision as important as marriage."

"And I'm begging your pardon, Reverend, but this is between Emma and me. All we're asking of you is to perform the ceremony."

"I'm sorry, sir. I cannot, in good conscience, do that. Now if you'll excuse me"—the preacher turned away—"I need to finish this step and get over to the Anderson place."

The dismissal was clear. And so was the message. The Reverend Jeffers would not marry them. Matt crammed his hat onto his head and mounted his horse. The only other preacher was a train ride away, and Matt had no money. He could ask Emma, but most likely all she had was property. Cash was hard to come by.

He stewed over his dilemma the entire three miles back to Emma's place. He thought about praying. Certainly Emma would have. She prayed about everything, talking to God aloud without a bit of embarrassment, then listening with head tilted and expression rapt until Matt was almost sure he could see the Lord whispering in her ear. But that was Emma's way. He was a man, and any man worth his breakfast could find a way without bothering God.

As he rode into the yard, Emma came rushing out the door, amber eyes alight with expectation. When he dismounted and faced her, some of the light faded.

"Parson Jeffers wouldn't come," she said matter-of-factly.

"No." Resisting the urge to ride back into town and drag the minister to the farm, he tethered his horse to the porch. How did he explain that the preacher thought her too unbalanced to marry? "He didn't think it would be right."

"Well." Emma's delicate face registered only momentary disappointment. "We can't blame the parson. He's only following his conscience."

Matt gave her a solemn appraisal. "Are you saying he's right?"

"To his way of thinking, he is." She pushed a tangle of hair behind one ear and tilted her head, looking up at him. "What about you, Matthew? Do you think I'm crazy? Are you certain you want to be married to a woman like me? Shunned by the town, unable to attend church. Is six sections of land worth that much trouble?"

"Is that what you think? That I'm marrying you just for the land?" Anger, all out of proportion to the question, sizzled inside him.

"Why else, then?"

He couldn't honestly answer that question, not if he was to keep his secret, and that bothered him. Even when he'd had little else, he'd kept his honesty. "There are things about me you don't know, Emma. Things that might make you change your mind."

"The Lord sent you. That's all I need to know."

Matt shook his head. Maybe he was the crazy one for considering matrimony with this woman. She talked out loud to Jesus. She accepted a husband she didn't know, and she wouldn't stand up for herself against a town that had badly misjudged her. But then, wasn't that what brought him here in the first place? The crazy widow needed help, and he needed a reason to keep putting one foot in front of the other.

"Then we'll have to go somewhere else to wed."

With a smile she extended a hand and touched his arm. "Don't fret, Matthew. God will provide a way."

Glancing down at her weathered little hand lying against his sleeve, a new determination overtook him. Instantly, he knew how he would get the money. He'd show the town of Goodhope just how little he cared for their opinion. "There's a preacher up in Dodge who can do the job. Though from what I hear, he does more burying than marrying."

Emma laughed. "Then he needs the practice. And I'd love a train ride to the city."

Just like that she accepted the town's rejection and set her sights in a different direction. Without animosity. Without complaint. If that was crazy, Matt wished the whole world would lose its mind.

❧

As Matt guided the team down Goodhope's narrow Main Street, past playing children, chatting ladies, and the occasional horse and rider, he noticed a strange occurrence. Activity stopped each time one of the townspeople caught sight of him and his companion. Not a single person spoke a word of greeting, but all turned to follow their wagon's progress.

A glance at Emma told him that she noticed, too. Head held high, a sweet smile on her lips, she stared straight ahead, but her hands were tightly clenched against her yellow cotton skirt.

Anger surged up in him again. Word must have gotten around that he'd asked the parson to marry them. He yanked the team to a halt in front of the livery and leaped to the ground.

"Emma?" he said, reaching up to her. After a moment's hesitation, she stood and let him swing her down. A woman coming out of the livery gasped, jerked her child against her long skirts, and rushed back inside, voice raised.

"Lucas, hurry. That crazy woman is out here."

A young man, tall, lank, with hands the size of shovels, appeared at the door. "Now, Mama," he said to the woman. "Why don't you and Patsy go on to the house? I'll see to Mrs. Russell. And thank you kindly for the dumplings. They was mighty tasty."

The woman cast another worried look toward Emma then hurried away.

"I'm Luke Winchester." The man wiped his hand down the side of his trousers before offering it to Matthew. "And you must be Matthew Tolivar."

Grimly, Matt inclined his head. "News travels fast."

"Yes, sir, it does. Especially when it concerns Emma."

Matt bristled. "She's not deranged."

The stable owner nodded, his expression sympathetic. "I never said she was. But some folks in this town would disagree."

"So I noticed." Matt scowled at the departing woman and child.

"What can I help you with today, Mr. Tolivar?"

With reluctance, Matt reined in his angry thoughts. No use adding to Emma's embarrassment. "I'll be leaving the team here for a day, maybe a night."

"The bay, too?" Luke asked, indicating Matt's horse tied on behind the wagon.

"He's for sale." Matt jerked a thumb toward the wagon bed. "The saddle, too."

Emma's head shot up, and Matt read the question in her eyes. Why was he selling his horse and saddle?

"A fine piece of horseflesh." Luke walked around the bay, lifting feet, checking teeth. Finally, he named a price.

"You're a fair man, Winchester."

"Yes, sir, I am." He gave Matt the money, counting it into his hand. "I'll take good care of your team, too. You can depend on it."

"Much obliged."

In the distance, a train whistle rent the air. Taking Emma's arm, Matt bid Luke farewell and started toward the depot. With each step down the street, past the barbershop, past the dry goods store, past the apothecary, they were met with the same unfriendly treatment until Matthew felt his blood boil. The storekeeper, O'Dell, had called this a friendly town, but to Matt's way of thinking it was infested with rattlesnakes.

He'd only known Emma two days and they'd known her for years. Yet not one of them, unless it was the liveryman or Maureen, had an ounce of compassion in them. He wondered how they gathered in that church and prayed with a clear conscience.

As they passed the general store where he'd first seen Emma's sign, the shopkeeper's daughter flew out the door and gripped Emma in a fast embrace.

"Emma, I heard. Is Mr. Tolivar the one, then?" Maureen O'Dell's lilting voice talked about him as though he weren't there. "I'd so hoped he was."

Emma took her friend's hands and together they danced in a circle around the boardwalk, drawing scandalized looks from passersby. Emma didn't seem to notice. "The Lord is good, Maureen."

"Aye, He is." The Irish lass tossed her strawberry hair over her shoulder. Her green eyes settled on Matt as she issued a challenge. "And you'd better be the same, Mr. Matthew Tolivar, or you'll be answering to me, you will."

Again, Matt was amazed that news traveled so quickly, but he understood Maureen's concern for her friend. Life hadn't exactly treated Emma well, and if the town's reception today was any indicator, she sorely needed his protection. "You have my word."

" 'Twill have to do, I suppose." Maureen looked none too convinced. "How will you be wed, with the parson so set against it?"

"We're off to Dodge City on the next train." Still gripping Maureen's hands, Emma gazed up at Matt, gratitude in her face. "Matthew sold his horse and saddle for the tickets."

Matt was not surprised that a woman as sensitive as Emma had quickly grasped his reason for selling, but he wasn't prepared for the unexpected rush of pleasure her appreciation gave him.

"Well, God be praised." Maureen looked at Matt anew. "You'll do, Mr. Tolivar. You'll do fine. Now be off with you. That cranky conductor suffers no latecomers, and I've me ma to tend to."

But Emma wouldn't leave without asking, "How is she, Maureen?"

Worry wreathed Maureen's beautiful face. "She's having a hard time of it. Usually by now the sickness is past and she's fair glowing with health. But this baby is different, draining all the life out of her, he is."

Matt's gut clenched at the switch in conversation. A sick pregnant woman again. He couldn't, wouldn't let himself think about it too much. He was a farmer now, not a doctor. Such things no longer concerned him.

"I'll be praying for her."

"You do that, Emma, darlin'." Maureen released Emma's hands and stepped back. "Ask Him to send us a doctor while you're at it. The way this town is growing. . ."

To Matt's relief, her words were interrupted by another blast of the train whistle. "Emma," he said, "we'd better go."

Amid a flurry of hugs and warm wishes, Matt found himself embraced by the exuberant Irishwoman. "I knew you were bringing good the moment I saw you," she whispered.

Puzzling over the curious words, Matt took Emma's elbow and guided her toward the depot. . .and toward a minister who would make them man and wife.

Chapter 3

The preacher wasn't home.

During their delightful train ride, Emma had entertained Matt and two restless children with her songs and stories and frequent exclamations over the marvels outside the train window. Matt's spirits were considerably higher by the time the train pulled into Dodge. Now he sat in the parlor of the Reverend Tobias Jefferson drinking coffee he didn't want and listening to Mrs. Jefferson regale Emma with details of her own wedding thirty years ago in Boston.

". . . And my dress, dear child, it was the loveliest thing. All satin and lace with tiny pearl buttons." She paused, enraptured by the memory. "I still have it, you know, tucked away in a chest upstairs. My daughter wanted to wear it when she married, but Clara's tall, and we couldn't lengthen it."

Emma, perched on the edge of the settee, touched the woman's hand in sympathy. "You must have been so disappointed."

"Yes." Mrs. Jefferson sighed. "I always wanted to see it on another bride, but only a little thing like you or me could ever fit in it." Suddenly she gasped then popped up from the straight-backed chair, her gaze measuring Emma as she walked a circle around Emma's chair. "Emma dear, stand up."

Clearly bewildered, Emma cast a glance at Matt then stood obediently while Mrs. Jefferson continued her assessment. "Yes. . .yes. . .I do believe it would fit. Your waist is every bit as tiny as mine was. And we're almost the same height."

"Oh, Mrs. Jefferson." Emma's hands flew to her cheeks. "You can't possibly mean. . .you couldn't want someone like me to wear your wedding gown."

"And why ever not?"

Emma's eyes found Matt's. In an hour's time, the crazy widow had thoroughly charmed the preacher's wife, and now she didn't know how to react to the woman's kindness. He could see she wanted this. He could read the eagerness in her face. Not that it mattered one whit to him what she wore. After all, this was no love match, and not a soul would care one way or the other if they even got married, but after the ugliness in Goodhope, Matt wasn't about to leave Dodge until Emma was in his legal care. If, while they waited, the young girl within Emma wanted to play dress-up in a thirty-year-old gown, it was fine with him.

"I agree, Emma," he said. "Why ever not?"

His approval seemed to be all she needed. With Emma-like enthusiasm, she embraced the older woman. "I would be so honored to wear your dress."

Mrs. Jefferson clapped her hands in delight. "Oh, wonderful! This will be so much fun. Funerals, funerals. That's all we ever have in this town, with cowboys shooting each other over everything from whose horse is faster to whose daddy was meaner. You'll be so pretty in that dress. And we'll weave a garland for your hair. And pick some flowers for the church." Excitement seemed to emanate from her every pore. Suddenly she whirled around and eyed Matt's shaggy hair and whiskered face. "You could use some sprucing up yourself, young man. It's not every day a woman gets married, and she'd like to see that handsome face of yours, I'm sure."

Surprised by her sudden attack on him, Matt dragged a hand over his prickly jaw. "I suppose I could do with a shave."

"I suppose you could. The barbershop is right down Main Street. You can't miss that red-striped pole." With a flap of her hands, she herded him out the door.

As he settled his hat on his head and started down the street, his insides jangling, Matt wondered how the last hour had gotten so out of hand. This wasn't what he'd bargained for, but then, nothing about the crazy widow had been.

≫

When Matthew returned, his face smooth and stinging from the hot shave, he found Emma in the backyard with the parson's wife and a black-suited man he assumed to be the preacher.

"Now you look more like a bridegroom," Mrs. Jefferson said approvingly. "And your bride is all ready for you."

The shock of seeing Emma dressed in lace with peach blossoms garnishing her long, flowing hair set his heart to thumping. She waited for him beneath the blooming boughs of a peach tree looking much more like a real bride than he'd expected. Martha had looked like this, radiant, hopeful. He squeezed his eyes shut, bowing his head against the torrent of emotion he did not want to feel, and prayed he'd never let Emma down the way he had Martha.

When he opened his eyes again, he noticed what he hadn't seen before, and the sight erased all comparisons to his first wedding. An almost smile threatened his lips. Emma, with her dancing hair and her fancy dress, was barefoot, toes peeking out like a child's, charming him with her sweetness. Peace seeped into him. Taking care of the crazy Widow Russell was the right thing to do. Hat in hand, he went to stand beside his waiting bride.

"Shall we begin?" the pastor asked, opening his Bible.

As the ancient words of faith were spoken, a hush fell over the little gathering, broken only by the hum of insects glorying in the spring. Peach limbs swayed above them, releasing their sweet scent and an occasional shower of blossoms. A pair of robins flitted in and out of the trees tending a nest.

"Will you, Matthew, take this woman. . . ?"

Yes, he would take her as his wife. He would look after Emma and work her land, hiding from his own memories and from the incessant call of medicine on his life. He would promise all that was left of him to Emma Russell, the orphan, the widow, the crazy woman. From this moment on, he'd look forward, not backward.

Gazing down at Emma's upturned face, seeing the hope and trust in her eyes, Matt felt his throat fill and tighten with some unnamed emotion. Swallowing hard, he answered, "I will."

In a whisper that barely reached his ears, Emma repeated her own vows, and while Matt pondered the odd feeling in his chest, the preacher pronounced them husband and wife.

"You may kiss your bride."

Matt and Emma then exchanged equally startled expressions.

At that moment, a yellow butterfly found the flowers in Emma's hair. Matt almost smiled. Emma Russell—he caught himself and nearly smiled again—Emma Tolivar, in satin gown and bare feet, with a butterfly in her hair, had such a strange effect on him. His chest expanded with a sense of satisfaction so profound that he thought he might indeed kiss his bride. But before he could, Emma once again surprised them all as she lifted her clear, sweet voice in a hymn of praise.

When the last pure notes of Emma's song faded away, Mrs. Jefferson dabbed at her eyes with a lace-edged handkerchief. "I felt God smiling down on us the entire time. Truly a match made in heaven."

Matt shoved away the disappointment he'd felt when Emma avoided his kiss. After all, Emma had made it clear that theirs was only a marriage of convenience, and he was certainly in agreement with that. But in the last few years, he'd had few special moments to enjoy, and regardless of the circumstances, the vision of his beautiful barefoot bride would stay with him forever. Mrs. Jefferson was right. God must be smiling. And as he glanced down at his radiant new wife, Matthew Tolivar did the same.

Emma felt the effect of Matt's smile all the way to her bare toes. With blue eyes twinkling above the flash of white teeth, her new husband was a devastatingly handsome man. After a stern reminder that theirs was a marriage of necessity, she commanded her fluttery stomach to still. She knew about marriage. If they were truly blessed, they'd get along, maybe enjoy each other's companionship, and someday they might even share a kindly affection such as she'd shared with Jeremiah. But she had no false notions about love. Still, laughter was good for the soul, and Matthew needed to smile more. Out of gratitude for what he'd done, Emma made up her mind, then and there, to see that he did.

Chapter 4

Spring gave way to a scorching summer as Matt and Emma fell into a comfortable routine. They worked from predawn to nightfall, sometimes side by side, often apart. There was so much to do, so much that had gone undone. Matt felt the constant pressure of time, determined to get as much fence up as possible before the winter. With fencing, he could raise the thousand or more cattle that Jeremiah had left to roam the open range as well as grow plenty of corn and hay to keep them healthy through the fierce Kansas winters. With hard work, he and Emma could have a secure future, and he'd have no time nor need to think about his forsaken medical practice.

When evening came, he sat in the lamplight, exhausted, hot, and filthy while Emma bustled around getting supper on the table. He enjoyed the evenings, enjoyed watching her do the things a woman did—things a man never even thought of doing. And not a day passed that she didn't do something that made him smile.

As though privy to his thoughts, Emma handed Matt his meal. A face stared up at him from the blue-flowered plate. Two slices of tomatoes formed the eyes. A triangle of ham served as the nose. Thick ovals of bread protruded like ears from each side. And a row of fried okra grinned up at him.

"What's this?" he asked, a half grin tugging his lips.

With a saucy smile, she remarked, "That's the look I'd like to see on your face more often, Mr. Tolivar."

"What!" he returned in mock horror. "Red-eyed? With green teeth? Emma, you have a strange taste in men."

Clearly delighted by the joking reply, Emma threw back her mane of hair, her joyous laugh filling the cabin. Some of Matt's weariness lifted as he dug into his whimsical supper.

When he finished his dinner, Emma's work-worn hands quickly removed the empty plate and set a piece of apple pie and glass of milk in front of him. It was too hot to bake, but Emma had perspired over the stove without a murmur of complaint as though she enjoyed preparing the foods he loved.

"Maureen came out today." Settling into a chair with a pan of freshly picked peas, she began the tedious job of shelling them. He saw that her fingers were stained green, the nails chipped and ragged. It wasn't the first time he'd noticed the condition of her hands or seen her futilely rub lard into the cracked, dry skin. "She helped me pick these purple hulls."

"Maureen's a good friend," he said, savoring the taste of cinnamon-rich apples. "I trust she's doing well."

"She is. Her mother's having a very hard time, though." Emma paused, resting her forearms on the edge of the pan. "I just wish there was something I could do. . . ." She tilted her head to one side and smiled as though someone had whispered in her ear. "How silly of me, Jesus. As soon as You send us that doctor, we'll know just what to do for Kathryn, and all of us can breathe a little easier."

Guilt shafted through Matt like a knife. Poor Emma, praying for a doctor, and here one sat. His conscience nearly ate a hole through him.

"Maybe she should rest more, keep her feet up."

Emma glanced at him, eyebrows raised in question. Matt shrugged, purposely nonchalant. "I knew a doctor sometime back. Heard him recommend cutting back on salt and pork and getting plenty of bedrest. She might try that."

"Oh, Matthew, thank you. Maureen will be so relieved, and it certainly wouldn't hurt to try." Emma's ragged little hands resumed their work. "If you're still going into town for supplies tomorrow, I'll send her a letter telling her so."

A measure of relief settled over Matthew as well. He'd helped without revealing his secret, and now maybe he could stop thinking so much about the pregnant woman. *Lord, will the torment never end? Will I never know peace again?*

He swallowed another bite of pie, although the dessert now tasted as bitter as quince. Pushing the plate aside, he leaned his elbows on the table and studied the woman who sat across from him, reviled and scorned, yet filled with serenity. She deserved so much more than public ridicule and a loveless marriage to a man as empty as those pea shells. "Why don't you go into town with me? Visit Maureen awhile. Maybe buy something for yourself."

Her answer was always the same. "No." She shook her head, smiling regretfully. "I wouldn't want to cause trouble."

Though he'd asked her a dozen times, other than the solitary walks she took through the fields and woods under cover of darkness, Emma refused to leave the farm. Having long stopped thinking she was a lunatic crazed by the moon, Matt suspected where she went on those early morning excursions, though she never told him. If he was right, the town's behavior toward Emma was nothing short of hypocrisy.

"Jimmy O'Dell's an ignorant fool," he said gruffly.

"Matthew," she scolded mildly. "He's a good man, doing the best he knows how to take care of his family."

Matt wanted to argue against the people who refused to give Emma a chance, but he knew better. Every time he broached the subject, she sidestepped him, saying something kind. He'd even heard her praying for them, one by one, as she went about her daily tasks. She was a better Christian than he'd ever be. And far better than the residents of Goodhope.

Matt sighed, knowing that he would travel alone tomorrow.

"It's too hot," he complained, drawing a hand down his gritty neck, "and I'm too dirty to sleep."

With a sudden, merry laugh that startled him, Emma plopped the pan of peas onto the table. She jumped up, dropped her apron over the back of a chair, and flung the door wide open.

"Come on, then," she cried. "I have a wonderful idea."

Having no notion of what he'd said to bring on such a reaction, Matt nevertheless pushed himself back from the table and followed her out into the moonlit night. In their short marriage, he'd come to expect such flights of fancy from his bride. And though others might consider her crazy, Matt found release in the joyful way she embraced each moment. He never knew what to expect, and somehow that added spice to each day.

Once he'd found her lying facedown in the backyard and thought she was sick. She shushed him and pulled him down beside her to watch an ant carry a much larger beetle to its hole. Instead of the ant, he'd watched Emma and found the sight of her rapt expression, glowing golden eyes, and smooth tan skin utterly beguiling. He'd even considered kissing her again, but he'd refrained, remembering their wedding day. That night, he'd lain awake puzzled by the feelings she aroused in him and wondering at the odd sensation hammering in his chest.

"Where are we headed?" he asked. Guided only by the moon and stars, Matt followed her flying hair and billowing skirts to the creek. Beating him there, the ever-barefoot Emma plunged into the cool water.

"Come on. It's wonderful."

Tired as he was, the water would refresh and clean him. And Emma's delightful "craziness" would soothe his weary soul.

As he sat on the rocky bank to remove his boots, Emma waded his direction. By the full moon, he could see she was already soaked, dress plastered to her body, hair streaming. She grinned impishly and flicked water at him. The cold drops felt shockingly good against his parched skin, and he barreled into the creek, splashing and flinging water. Emma laughed and returned fire, soaking him in seconds. Like two otters, they frolicked together, forgetting their aching muscles and tired bodies.

"We should do this every night," he said, shaking back his damp, shaggy hair.

"What? This?" From a running start, Emma gave a shove, pushing him backward onto his backside. Her laughter rang over the tree-lined grove.

"You, dear lady, must be taught some manners." As he groped for a handhold to hoist himself up, Matt made contact with something soft and slimy. Feeling like a schoolboy, he gripped the squirming frog and stalked toward Emma. With a squeal, she floundered toward the bank, but Matt's much longer legs caught her. Holding her captive, he dropped the frog down the back of her dress.

Emma danced around the creek squirming and yelping in mock terror. Her antics brought a chuckle to Matt's lips. In another moment, he was laughing. At the sound, Emma yelped and jumped all the more, falling backward into the water, splashing and giggling in delight. Dislodged, the hapless frog croaked and bounded toward safer territory.

Sides aching, Matt slogged over to help Emma up. His courtesy was rewarded with a sharp tug that brought him tumbling down beside her. They sat in the water laughing until they were breathless. When at last the silliness passed, Emma looked up at him, her face golden in the moon shadows.

"Listen, Matthew." The croak of frogs pulsated around them. "Even the frogs are laughing."

"Not the one I dropped down your dress. He's sulking somewhere." The silly answer surprised even him.

With a featherlight touch on his arm, Emma said, "I like to hear you laugh, Matthew. And so does God."

Matthew Tolivar wasn't given to fanciful notions, nor was he one to dance and cavort in the moonlight. The people of Goodhope would most likely think he'd gone as crazy as his bride, but none of that mattered one whit. He felt good—good in a way he hadn't felt in a very long time; a fact that puzzled him no small amount.

The strange sensation in his chest returned, and though he was certain there was no room inside him for love, the feeling stayed with him for days.

✦

Bright and early the next morning, Matt hitched up the wagon, loaded it with Emma's milk, eggs, and vegetables, and headed to town. He'd asked her again to go along, but to his disappointment, she had once again refused.

"The scripture says if something we do offends our brother, we shouldn't do it," Emma had said without rancor. "My presence offends them, Matthew."

"That's their fault," he argued. But in the end, she'd stayed behind, waving him off with her ragged little hands.

During the three-mile drive into town, Matt thought of all the hardship Emma had suffered and determined to try, once more, to make the people of Goodhope see reason. She was the kind of woman who needed people, and though the stubborn townsfolk didn't know it, they needed her zest for life. He was a physician, a trained man of science, who'd lived with Emma for months now. Surely he could convince the people of Goodhope that she posed them no threat. And the best place to start was with her most vocal detractor—the storekeeper, Jimmy O'Dell.

Five minutes into the conversation, Matt knew he was wasting his breath.

"I reckon six sections of land made you an expert on lunatics," Jimmy sneered.

Angered by the insinuation and the man's stubborn refusal to give Emma a chance, Matt was tempted to walk out without the supplies he needed, though it was the only general store for miles. Before he could, Maureen whipped through the curtained door, dragging two redheaded boys by the scruff of their necks.

"Da, it's the woodshed these two are needin' today. Both of 'em running in the house like wild goats, and Patrick here running into Ma and nearly knocking her over."

"I didn't aim to." The accused poked out a defiant lip. "But Danny had a snake!"

Jimmy O'Dell's ruddiness deepened with anger. "You know your ma's not up to such shenanigans from the two of you. Give 'em to me, Maureen. I'll set 'em straight in a hurry if you'll ring up Mr. Tolivar's purchases."

Dragging the recalcitrant boys, the storekeeper banged out the door.

Casting about for a reason to avoid discussing the pregnant woman, Matt spotted a squat white jar on a shelf above Maureen's head. The rose-decorated label read MRS. PARKER'S ROSEWATER OINTMENT. "Is that any good?"

Maureen took down the jar, opened it, and sniffed. "Aye, and it smells heavenly, too. See for yourself."

She stuck it under his nose, and the scent of roses enveloped him.

"Emma's hands. . . ," he started, then stopped, embarrassed. "I'll take it."

Maureen cocked her head to one side and stared at him thoughtfully. Then she pulled a bolt of soft green cotton from the shelf, her golden eyebrows arched in question. "She wouldn't mind a new dress now and again either. This color was made for her, I'm thinking."

Emma loved pretty things, though, unlike the women in his past, she owned so few. Her hands needed tending, and there was no telling when she'd made herself a new dress.

He gave a short, self-conscious nod. "All right, then."

"Don't play coy with me, Mr. Tolivar. You're as transparent as glass." With a twinkle in her eyes, Maureen laid the fabric on the counter, tossing in matching thread and lace. "And it's delighted I am to see it."

While Matt grappled to understand her cryptic comment, a faint call came from the back of the store. "Maureen."

"Coming, Ma, in just a minute." Brow puckering, Maureen shook her red curls and spoke to Matt in an undertone. "Six months gone and she's puffy as one of Danny's toads and weak as water gravy."

The worrisome symptoms filtered through Matt's scientific mind. The woman needed a doctor's care, but it wouldn't be him. He couldn't risk the pain of watching another life slip out of his hands. Not now. Not ever.

His thoughts skittered to a stop when Maureen spoke and he realized he'd been frowning toward the curtained doorway.

"Don't you be fretting now, Mr. Tolivar. The good Lord will provide. With Emma petitioning Him for a doctor, I wouldn't be at all surprised to see one riding into town just any day." Hands and eyes busy with her figuring, she prattled on, unaware of Matt's building anxiety.

Sweat dampened his palms and his heart beat erratically. He needed to get away before he did something irrevocably foolish, like asking to examine the ailing Mrs. O'Dell. Concern for the pregnant woman choking him, Matt managed to gather his purchases, hand over Emma's letter, and make a courteous departure.

"My goodness, you've bought a wagon load," Emma exclaimed, eyeing the bags of flour and meal, the rolls of wire, and the buckets of nails. "I'm certain Mr. O'Dell didn't extend credit for all of this."

"It seems Mr. O'Dell is needing meat for his store, so I bartered a bull calf for this and more. He wants me to supply him all through the winter." If there had been any other place to easily sell the beef, Matt never would have bargained with the likes of Jimmy O'Dell. Theirs had been a grudging agreement, brought on by mutual need.

"Praise be to Jesus." Emma ran her hands over the bags, exploring the wagon like an excited child. When she came upon the plain brown package, Matt had a sudden longing to see her reaction. "Open it," he urged.

Eagerly she released the twine and pulled the paper away. The pale green cloth lay on top.

"Oh, Matt." Her weathered hands caressed the cloth reverently. She lifted the material and held it against her. Maureen was right. The color captured the green flecks in her eyes and turned her hair the shade of ripe wheat.

"Would You look at this, Jesus?" Emma cried, holding the fabric skyward. Suddenly she began to whirl, spinning, spinning until she became a gold and green blur in the summer sunshine. "Matthew, Matthew, Matthew," she chanted, "you're the kindest man on earth."

She was a balm for his weary soul, and he laughed to know he could make her happy with such a small gift. Truly it was more blessed to give than to receive, especially when the recipient reacted like Emma.

Breathlessly she spun to a halt, still clutching the fabric to her chest. Delight shone on her face. Seized by the need to keep it there, Matt said, "There's something else in that package, Mrs. Tolivar."

Back to the wagon she ran, exclaiming over the thread and lace until she came to the jar of Mrs. Parker's Rosewater Ointment. Expression puzzled, she lifted it, turning the bottle in her hands, reading the label, glancing at her mistreated hands.

Seeing her smile disappear, Matt wondered if he'd made a mistake. Was she embarrassed? Insulted? A flicker of anxiety passed over him, but it was short-lived.

Slowly she uncapped the container, releasing the scent of roses. Eyes closed, she sniffed deeply, head tilted back. When at last she looked at him, tears shimmered above an angelic smile. "Never in my life have I owned anything so wonderful." Swallowing convulsively, she whispered, "Thank you," snatched up the green material, and fled into the house.

That night, long after he'd given up and gone to bed, he heard her humming and murmuring to the rhythm of the sewing treadle. He fell asleep with a smile on his lips and the scent of roses in his nostrils.

He dreamed he heard her, far off, praying. "I love him, Jesus," she said. "Now what shall I do about that? Him, who should have a fine lady for a wife, one he could be proud of and take to church on Sundays. And here he is stuck with the village outcast, a worthless orphan. A crazy woman. How can I make up to him for all he's done?"

Straining upward against the dark pull of sleep, Matt wanted to say, "You're the one who's good. You're the one who's given me back a reason to live."

But he didn't, of course. It was, after all, only a dream.

The scents of coffee, bacon, and biscuits drifted into Matt's consciousness, and he rose, chagrined that Emma had once again risen long before him. Darkness still covered the farm, though the rooster was singing his anthem. Bare feet thudding on the wooden plank floor, Matt washed and dressed then stumbled into the kitchen.

"Don't you ever sleep?" he asked blearily, slouching into a chair.

Ever cheerful, she smiled and slid a coffee mug into his hands. "I'm far too excited to sleep."

Then he remembered the cloth and the perfumed ointment. A proud smile twitched at his whiskered face. "Did you sew all night?"

In answer, she left the room, returning momentarily with a green garment that she held up for his inspection. "What do you think?"

To his utter shock, the garment wasn't a dress as he'd expected. It was a carefully crafted man's shirt, as fine as any he'd ever owned.

"But the cloth was for you, for a dress," he protested.

"There's plenty left for that." Brown eyes danced with eagerness.

"Do you like it?"

Fingering the soft cloth, Matt swallowed the lump in his throat. Would she never stop surprising him? Would she never stop thinking of everyone else first?

"Ah, Emma, Emma." He pulled her to him in what he thought was a hug of gratitude. In the next instance, he was kissing her. Her soft, sweet mouth parted in surprise beneath his, and an emotion far stronger than gratitude hammered in Matt's chest. When he pulled back, stunned and breathless, a pair of luminous golden eyes measured him. She pressed trembling fingers to rose-tinted cheeks then did the unexpected once again.

"How would you like your eggs?" she whispered then spun toward the stove, turning her back to him.

Matt blinked, baffled at her response, baffled at the desire to kiss her again, and baffled as to why she was talking of eggs when his insides were twisted in a knot. She cared for him. He was certain. Why had she rejected his kiss?

The answer struck him full in the heart. He hadn't been dreaming when he heard Emma say she loved him. The words had been real. Emma loved him, and she knew he had no love inside to give. Guilt gnawed at him. He'd wanted to heal her brokenness, but he'd only caused her more pain.

Chapter 5

Even though the calendar said September, the prairie summer continued in full fury: hot and dry and unforgiving. Sweat bathed both people and livestock as an urgent need for rain pressed in.

The kiss was not mentioned again, though Matt could think of little else. Now that the blinders were off, he saw Emma's love in everything she did, and the burden of responsibility weighed heavily upon him.

Late in the afternoon, a cloud appeared from nowhere, dark and heavy with rain. As the shade passed over, Matt and Emma glanced up, then at each other.

"Wouldn't that be lovely?" Emma called from her back-bent position.

Before Matt could reply, the sky opened and the blessed cool water gushed over the land. Emma squealed and straightened.

"Rain. Wonderful rain."

As Matt watched, rain pouring off his hat, his wife began to twirl and spin, arms wide, face turned upward to the heavens.

"Dance, Matthew," she called, her voice full of joy and laughter. When he only stood with a smile on his face, she ran to him, gathered his hands into her small rough ones, and stood on his boot tops, dipping and swaying. Matt was caught up in her spontaneous delight, her joy too infectious to ignore. To his utter amazement, he wanted to dance and laugh. Emma grabbed his hand and pulled him, captivated, through the mud puddles, stomping and splashing. She could find more happiness in a mud puddle than most people found in their entire lives.

Drenched to the skin, he pulled Emma close to him and looked into her eyes, the urge to kiss her again welling up inside him like an incoming tide. The rain tumbled from his hat onto her face, and she laughed all the more.

"If the people of Goodhope saw us now, they'd say you've gone as crazy as me," she declared, reaching up to swipe a smear of mud from Matt's face.

The cloudburst passed as quickly as it had come, and a rainbow split the sky in two.

"Let's chase it, Matthew. And find that pot of gold."

"Ah, Emma. Emma, you're a delight. What makes you the way you are? A woman grown who dances in the rain and lies in the grass at night watching falling stars."

Her laugher ceased and a gentle, wistful sweetness settled over her features. "I thought you knew by now, Matthew."

He could see she was serious, so he waited, holding her close, feeling the combined heat and damp transferring from her body to his, smelling the scent of fresh rain against her skin.

She laid a hand against Matt's cheek and tilted her head to one side, eyes glowing.

"When I was a child in the orphanage, there was no frivolity, no laughter. By the time Jeremiah took me in and taught me of Jesus, all the joy in me was gone. And then I had Lily. She could chase a butterfly for hours, clapping her tiny hands, falling, and getting up with a smile on her face." Emma's voice grew soft with longing. "Oh, Matt, she was my joy. So now I dance and laugh and sing and do all those foolish things for Lily." Tears of remembrance filled her wide amber eyes. "I dance in the rain for Lily, because she never will."

With his own heart thudding from the poignant beauty of her admission, he finally recognized the truth. He'd come here thinking he was the healer, the man who could help the poor, crazy widow. But it hadn't been that way at all. It was he who had been healed by Emma's simple faith and her magnificent strength. She had given him back his joy. The truth had been banging at him for weeks, but now he had to tell her.

"I love you, Emma." Feeling her stiffen with shock, he held her all the tighter, kissing away a fat drop of rain clinging to her eyelashes.

"Do you hear me? I love you, Emma," he shouted, laughing anew at the shock on her face that matched the surprise in his heart. "Say you feel the same. I know you do."

And indeed she did. In Emma-like fashion she threw her arms around his neck and kissed him just as the rain began again. Neither of them noticed.

❧

Sunday morning after chores and breakfast, Matthew followed Emma around the cabin, watching her, stealing an occasional kiss, exchanging secret smiles. He was a happy man. Happier than he ever thought possible, and he wanted to be certain Emma was happy, too.

"I'm taking you to church this morning," he declared.

Her hands stilled on the towel she was folding. "Oh, Matthew, I don't think so. But if you want to go. . ."

"You once told me how much you enjoyed worshipping with other believers and how much you missed it after Jeremiah died. I think it's time we went together as man and wife."

"But the people. . ." Her throat convulsed, trepidation in her voice.

"I've made a few friends, Emma, and most of the folks are decent. Jimmy O'Dell's the main one who keeps the trouble stirred up. The others just follow along."

"I don't want to upset anyone."

"Once people see you, get to know you again, they'll realize their mistake." Seeing her misgivings, he pleaded, "Please, Emma. If we're going to live and prosper here, we have to find a way to get along with these folks. Both of us—not just me. You're so brave about everything else. Why won't you face this town and make them stop this nonsense?"

"I don't know. . . ." She gnawed at her lower lip, clearly weakening.

Matt knelt in front of her, grasping her hand. "What if we have a child together? Wouldn't you want him to be accepted?"

Wonderment lit her face at the possibility, and she capitulated. Drawing in a deep breath, she said, "I'll wear my new green dress."

A dozen or so worshippers had already gathered by the time Matt and Emma arrived wearing their matching green. Tipping his hat repeatedly, Matt wove his bride into the church, nodding and smiling, receiving cold looks in return. Beneath his guiding hand, Emma trembled, though she smiled serenely at all she passed.

Matt's pulse thundered. He prayed desperately that he hadn't made a mistake in bringing her here. What else could he do? Somehow he had to give her back her dignity. Searching the gathering for Maureen or Lucas Winchester, he found instead Jimmy O'Dell bearing down on them, his face livid.

"What is that daughter of the devil doing in the house of God?" He shouted so loud, every head in the building turned to stare. Except for a few murmurs of agreement, the place fell quiet.

"I've told you repeatedly, O'Dell, Emma is mentally sound. She has as much right to attend church as you do."

"Mentally sound, you say?" Jimmy whirled toward the crowd. "You hear that, folks? This stranger comes waltzing into town and tries to tell us our business. Well, I think we got something to say about that, don't you?" He

His statement was followed with rumbles of assent. "Yeah. Sure do. You tell 'em, Jimmy."

"Too many people have seen her do crazy things."

"I say she's moonstruck. Barney Adams saw her dancing in a full moon, singing and waving her arms. The next week his good cow died."

Emma stood in the middle, eyes wide, clinging to Matthew's hand. A bearded man in overalls parted the tightening circle.

"She's a witch, if ye ask me." He pointed a finger at Emma. "Seen her myself sneaking around Floyd Anderson's place in the middle of the night just about the time he got hurt. I figure she hexed him."

Matt seethed inside, wanting to tell the real reason for Emma's surreptitious visits to the Anderson place. But when he looked to her for permission, she shook her head in denial. Filled with both frustration and admiration, Matt kept quiet.

The fine churchgoers didn't.

"Mr. Tolivar, you seem to be a good man, hardworking. I've seen the things you're doing to that farm, and I admire you. Your dealings here in town are honest, and we've come to respect you. But when it comes to the widow, you seem blinded, unable to accept that the woman is unbalanced."

"She's evil, all right." This from a squat man with tobacco-stained teeth. "I was there when she chased the undertaker and Parson Jeffers off her place, screaming like a banshee."

"She claimed Jesus came to see her."

"What's wrong with you people?" Matt cried. "Emma was sick with grief then. She'd been locked up in that cabin with her dead husband and child without help. Can't you have a little compassion?"

Some of the women softened and made murmurs of understanding. "Losing a child's a hard thing. Any of us would be sick with grief."

"Yes, and you have other children, other family to comfort you. Emma had no one, nothing left at all."

The church was quiet for a moment, and Matt thought that perhaps he'd convinced them. Surely the folks could see that Emma was no threat to anyone. But Jimmy O'Dell wasn't finished. "I want her out of here before my wife arrives," he cried, shaking his fist at Matt. "She'll mark my unborn child." He turned to the shocked crowd. "And if she does, the fault will belong to all of you for letting such as her live in this town."

Barely controlling his temper, Matt shoved the fist aside. "You'll mark it yourself with your own ignorance."

Wrapping Emma in his protective embrace, Matt shouldered his way out of the church and into the wagon. Fury, hot and dangerous, emanated from every pore as he slapped the horses into motion, leaving the good citizens of Goodhope in his dust.

"Matthew, please don't be so angry. It's all right. Truly it is." Voice husky with emotion, she lay a hand on his stiff forearm. Her obvious pain infuriated him even more.

"You'll never convince me of that, Emma. Someday they'll reap what they've sown, and I, for one, will be glad." As town disappeared behind them, he slowed the team to a walk. Tall, dry buffalo grass waved in the fields beside the road, and yellow sunflowers nodded their giant heads. For once Emma did not exclaim about their beauty. They rode in silence most of the way home, hurt pulsating from her, remorse filling him. The big red barn came into sight, then the chimney, before Emma spoke again.

"What if they're right?" She stared off into the wheat fields, eyes unseeing. A frown creased her brow. "What if there is something basically bad about me?"

"Don't be foolish."

She turned to him, tears glistening on her lashes, and the sight tormented him. Why had he made her go? He'd vowed to protect her, and instead he'd escorted her into the lions' den to be devoured.

"I know nothing about my mother or father, Matthew," she continued sadly. "Perhaps I was born in an insane asylum or to a streetwalker."

"None of that has anything to do with who you are."

Tears trickled down her face as her voice rose in sorrow. "Doesn't it? It's all in the blood, they say. Maybe mine is just bad." A sob broke from her throat. "Bad blood. That's what they call it."

"Emma, no." He'd never seen her like this—weeping, heartbroken. He chastised himself anew for subjecting her to such cruel treatment. Pulling the team to an abrupt stop beside the barn, he turned to her. But before he could draw her sobbing body into his arms, she leaped from the wagon. Chickens squawked in protest as she whipped past, scattering them with her new green skirt as she rushed into the barn. Heart heavy, Matt released the horses and followed after her. He met Emma hobbling out of the barn door, her new skirt drenched in blood.

"Emma!" He rushed to her side. "What happened?"

Her face pale and tearstained, she struggled to regain her composure, but the droplets of moisture on her lip and forehead reflected her intense suffering. "The scythe. I fell."

"Let me see." Behind her thigh, a deep gash bled profusely. "Hold your hand over it. Press hard."

"I've ruined my new dress," she groaned.

"I'll buy you another." Matt scooped her into his arms and charged toward the house, his heart thudding painfully against his ribs. What would he do? How should he handle this? There were no other doctors anywhere around, and Emma needed medical care.

He started for the bedroom.

"Not on the bed. I'll ruin the quilt. The floor is fine."

Relenting, he laid her on the floor in the kitchen. "Now let's look at this better." Pushing away the cloth, he examined the wound. "It needs stitches."

She groaned then set her face in determination. "Many's the time I've stitched a horse or a cow. Once I even stitched up Jeremiah. This is no different. I can do it. Boil a thread and a needle."

Matt did her bidding, all the while fighting an inward battle. His mind fought him, but his heart dictated what must be done. When the supplies were ready, Emma sat up, twisting toward the lacerated skin.

With a resigned sigh, Matt took the needle and thread from her fingers. "You can't reach back here. I'll do it."

Tear-darkened lashes lifted toward him. "Can you sew?"

"Yes," he said tersely. "Now lie down on your belly and let's get this over with."

Bits of hay clung to the torn edges of skin, and he frowned at them, concerned about infection. After a thorough washing with soap and water, he took up the needle, working quickly, efficiently, aware that every needle prick brought her pain. Though she never complained, halfway through the procedure, she twisted her head around and watched him. Six years without practice fell away as he neatly pulled the tissues together and sealed them in a long straight line. His hands remembered what his mind had tried to forget.

"That should do it," Matt said as he clipped the last thread and wiped alcohol across the wound. At her sharp intake of breath, he grimaced, grabbed his hat, and fanned at the row of stitches. "Sorry. We don't want that to get infected."

"It's all right." Not waiting for a bandage, she rolled over and sat up, pulling one of his hands into hers. "Where did you learn to sew like that?"

When he remained silent, she turned his hand over and stroked the fingers. "These aren't a farmer's hands."

"They are now." He pulled away.

Clear amber eyes demanded the truth. "But they haven't always been."

"No." Avoiding her gaze, he began gathering the bloodied supplies, tossing them into the washbasin.

"You're a doctor," she said simply, guessing the truth in her guileless way. "A doctor."

Apprehension flickered through him. He wasn't a doctor. Not anymore. "That's all in the past now."

"If that were true, you wouldn't still be trying to hide the facts. Did something happen? Did you dislike the work?"

Turning his back, he carried the basin to the table and stood staring at the cabin wall, remembering.

"I loved it. And I was good. So good and so confident that I thought I could fix anything and anyone." He pulled one hand wearily down his face. "I was wrong. I couldn't save the two people who mattered most to me in the entire world. My wife and baby."

She wasn't shocked, as he'd expected her to be, just full of compassion and understanding. "And you feel guilty."

"Yes."

"So you've punished yourself by leaving the profession you love. By hiding from God's call on your life."

"No!" But hadn't he? He shrugged. "Perhaps."

"Then it's time to stop, to lay down your guilt. Your skills are needed, desperately needed, right here in this town."

Even if he could lose the guilt and fear that plagued him, he'd never considered practicing medicine in Goodhope. He faced her, incredulous.

"How can you even suggest that I help anyone in that town? After the way they've treated you, they all deserve to suffer."

Emma started awkwardly to her feet, shaking her head. Rushing to assist her, Matt pulled her upright.

"When Jesus came," she said, holding Matt's hand against her heart, "everyone rejected Him. He had reason to hate them, to punish them. Yet He loved them so much—even those who crucified Him—that He prayed for them as He died."

Gripping her shoulders, Matt couldn't decide whether to shake her or hold her. "But they hurt you."

"Yes, they did. But I have you, and I have Jesus. That's all I need to be happy." Arms wrapped around his waist, Emma pressed her head against his heart. "I want you to be happy, too, Matthew. I don't think you ever will be until you can forgive yourself and resume your true life's work."

Dread rose in him like a sickness. He couldn't go back. Another failure would be the end of him.

Matt clasped Emma tightly against him, holding fast to the strength she offered. "I'm a farmer now, Emma. That's enough for me."

But the words rang false even to his own ears.

Chapter 6

A flock of geese winging its way southward caught Matt's attention as he labored in the field north of the house. He tossed a pile of fresh-cut hay into the wagon bed then leaned on the pitchfork, gazing upward. A year ago, he wouldn't have cared about a flock of birds, but now he could enjoy the sight, thanks to Emma. The geese were the very kind of thing she loved. He thought to go and tell her about them, but before he could, the cabin door burst open and Emma rushed out.

"Did you see them, Matthew?" she called, pointing to the heavens. "They're waving at us."

Shading her eyes against the blue-gray glare, Emma hopped up and down, waving back at the honking geese.

With a smile, Matt watched Emma watching the geese. His heart filled with gratitude for this special woman God had sent his way. Her leg had healed well, he thought with relief, in spite of his concerns over infection. That was due in part, he knew, to the care he administered. He'd cleaned and dressed the wound three times a day, finding a measure of satisfaction in the familiar task.

Emma said little else about his abandoned profession, but she watched him with a quiet compassion that was more bothersome than nagging would have been. On the day the stitches came out, she lifted his palms, kissed each one, and said, "God has blessed you with a special gift, Matthew. Healing hands."

He'd not known how to reply. She'd asked for so little. And yet he couldn't give her this one thing she longed for.

"Do you love me, Matthew?" she'd gone on, taking his face in her rough little hands.

"You know I do," he replied almost desperately.

"Yes, you do. But it isn't enough. You'll never be truly happy until you give in to God's calling on your life."

He'd crushed her to him, holding her against his throbbing heart, knowing she was right. The heaviness lay on him even now as the geese disappeared overhead. Emma turned his way, blew him a kiss, and started back to the house.

"Someone's coming," he called, catching sight of a copper-colored head bobbing through the south fields.

"Maureen!" Emma's bare feet churned the ground as she flew toward her friend.

Though her visits were infrequent, Maureen came when she could, bringing bits of town news but, most of all, giving Emma her friendship. While they talked and prayed, their fingers would fly: braiding rugs, piecing a quilt, peeling apples. Matthew liked Maureen as much as he disliked her father.

On his occasional trips to town, Matt was forced to patronize the general store, though he dreaded each encounter. Dreaded the arguments with Jimmy. Dreaded the thought of encountering the pregnant Mrs. O'Dell. Dreaded the longing he felt to practice medicine.

The rest of the town had warmed a bit toward him, though few ever mentioned Emma and none invited the Tolivars to social functions. He knew the other farmers helped one another during harvest. There would be husking bees and threshing parties—none of which the Tolivars would attend. He'd even had a talk with the parson, quite by accident, one day outside the blacksmith shop. Parson Jeffers had apologized for the incident at the church, saying, "The Lord would be displeased if we turn away any who seek Him, Mr. Tolivar. You and your wife are welcome anytime."

Though his anger toward the austere parson had lessened, Matt had no intention of subjecting Emma to another scene like the last.

Matt resumed the task of filling the wagon with hay, glad that the constant toil kept him from thinking too much. Another fork or two, and he'd head to the barn to unload, then start the process all over again. In the distance, beyond the acres and acres of corn and grass yet to be harvested, a spiral of dust rose. Curious, Matt paused in his work again. Two guests in one day?

A horse pounded into the yard, its rider leaping from the saddle and running toward the house.

"Maureen! Maureen! I know you're in there." The panic-stricken voice of one of the O'Dell boys carried all the way out to Matt's hay field.

Maureen came rushing out the door. After a muffled exchange of words that Matt couldn't understand, she mounted the horse behind her brother and the pair raced away, leaving Emma alone in the front yard.

Something had happened. Something bad. Matt's gut knotted with dread. Was there a sickness? An accident? Or was it the pregnant mother?

He hadn't long to wait before the questions were answered. Emma hastened toward him, hair and skirts flying out behind her. Dropping the pitchfork, he rushed to meet her.

"What is it?"

Breathless, her chest rising and falling rapidly, Emma pressed a hand to her heart. The anxiety in Matt's stomach was reflected in her face.

"It's Kathryn O'Dell. Her baby is coming now."

"Babies are born all the time." He wanted to turn away, to run back to Texas or Colorado, anywhere but here with this oppressive sense of duty clawing at him.

"Matthew, please." Emma gripped his arm. "You don't understand. It's too early, and Mrs. O'Dell is so terribly weak."

"No, Emma." Shaking his head, he backed away, knowing what she wanted. "Don't ask this of me."

"I know you, Matthew. You're a good, good man who could never live with himself if something happens to her and you didn't even try."

"How can you say that?" he cried, despairing of making her understand. "My own wife and baby are dead because of my incompetence. Don't you think I tried then? But I couldn't save them. Why do you think this time will be any different?"

"Please. Please, Matthew." Emma slid to her knees before him, the hay stubble crackling under her weight. "I beg of you. Maureen is the only friend I have."

In a posture of pure supplication she knelt before him, ripping his heart in two.

"Stop it, Emma. Get up." He gripped her narrow shoulders, tugging, but she only bowed deeper into the hay. When she began to pray, Matthew almost collapsed beside her.

"Heavenly Father, You know everything. You know why Matthew's wife and baby died. You know how he's suffered over their loss. And You know how desperately Kathryn needs him right now. Please, dear Lord, take the scales from his eyes. Let him recognize the calling on his life to minister to the sick. Give him the strength and courage to fight through this fear of failure and come out victorious. I love him, Jesus. I want him to be happy, to have the peace he lost when Martha died. It means so much to him, and he's fought it for so long. Please, Lord. Open his eyes." And she began to weep.

The gaping wound inside Matthew began to bleed afresh. He'd thought he could lose himself here on the farm with Emma and never have to think of medicine again. Instead, it haunted him, the only unresolved need in his life.

"Emma, I'll go." Bending, Matthew lifted her trembling body and held her close, murmuring against her hair. "If it means that much to you, I'll go. If you'll go with me."

Stiffening, she drew back, regarding him with anxious eyes. Though for different reasons, she was every bit as afraid as he.

"I need you, Emma. I can't do it alone."

Drawing in a deep, shuddering breath, she lifted her chin, aiming it toward Goodhope. "All right, then. I'll pray. You drive."

Drying her eyes, she clambered aboard the loaded hay wagon.

Stomach churning, pulse pounding, Matthew hammered on the back door of Jimmy O'Dell's general store, the portion of the building where the family resided. Emma stood beside him, her face pale, gripping the medical bag he'd dug from its hiding place in the barn.

"What are you doing here?" The disheveled Irishman opened the door. "The store is closed for the day."

"I'm a doctor, Mr. O'Dell. I've come to help your wife."

"A doctor, you say?" His astonished blue gaze went from Matt to the bag in Emma's hands.

"Yes. A doctor. I understand your wife is having the baby."

A muffled cry from the room's interior turned O'Dell around. "Aye. Aye. She's trying." In agitation, he ran a hand over his balding head. " 'Tis a bad time of it she's having, too. Worst I've seen."

"Are you going to let me help her or keep us standing out here while she suffers?"

"You're really a doctor, then?" O'Dell asked, his expression dubious.

"I said I was." Annoyance rapidly replaced Matt's fear. If O'Dell didn't let him in soon, he'd turn around and go home, his conscience clear that he'd tried.

"Da, what's going on?" Maureen's worried face appeared behind her father. "Emma! Matt! Whatever are you doing?"

"Claims he's a doctor. Wants to see your ma."

"For pity's sake, Da. He's the answer to our prayers. Let him in."

"It's little choice I have, but he comes alone. Not with her. I'll not have that crazy woman in my house. We've trouble enough as it is."

Matt's patience snapped. With teeth gritted he leaned toward the storekeeper. "You self-righteous man. After all you've done to hurt her, it was Emma who convinced me to come. Now you can either let us both in, or we'll get back in that wagon and leave you to manage on your own."

"Da, we've prayed and prayed for a doctor, and now that he's here, you're wanting to turn him out? When Ma is needing his help so badly?" Maureen elbowed around her father and grabbed Emma's hand, pulling her inside. Matt followed, feeling the anger of Jimmy O'Dell as he brushed past.

"If anything happens to Kathryn and me babe, I'll have your hide, Matthew Tolivar. And that loony wife of yours will be locked away like she should have been long ago." His venomous tirade was cut short by a cry from the bedroom. In a rush of concern, Matt and Emma left Jimmy to fume and hurried into the bedroom where an older version of Maureen writhed on the bed.

Sweat broke out on Matthew's palms as the image of Martha flashed through his mind. If he failed again, if Kathryn died, he didn't know if he could go on.

Emma, feeling his tension, lay a hand on his. "Guide him, Jesus. Give him wisdom."

The simple prayer lifted him. He wasn't in this alone.

"Mrs. O'Dell," he said, going to her side. "My name is Matthew Tolivar. I'm a doctor. I'm going to help you deliver this baby." He turned to his two assistants. "We'll need boiled string and scissors, lots of towels or rags, and some warmed blankets for the baby."

" 'Tis ready and waiting whenever you say, Doctor."

The title sounded good, stoking his courage. He was a doctor, a trained physician with the skill to do this. Emma and Maureen bustled around the room, doing his bidding, praying out loud, while he examined the patient. To his horror, something was amiss. The baby was there, ready to be born, but even a strong contraction didn't push the infant forward. The mother worried him, too. Except for an occasional moan or the sudden arch of her body, Kathryn was listless. Her eyes were closed, her face pale and moist.

"She's giving out, Doctor. I don't know how she'll manage the strength to finish."

Matt rummaged in the worn medical bag. It had been so long since he'd opened it, but the familiar tools were all inside. Struggling not to think of the last time he'd used them, he handed a pair of forceps to Maureen. "I'll try not to use these, but I want them boiled just in case."

Not every physician agreed that cleanliness was important, but Matt subscribed to Dr. Lister's notion that invisible microbes spread infection. Though he had no carbolic for disinfectant, the boiling water would help. He just wished he had some ether. Taking a baby with forceps was a difficult procedure, but under the circumstances, he was afraid it might be the only choice he'd have. Mrs. O'Dell had given up the battle, and the baby would suffer damage in the birth canal if he waited too long.

Taking out his stethoscope, he listened to Kathryn's chest.

"Her heart is strong," he said with relief. "If she just has the strength to help us a few more times. . ."

Quietly Emma eased to the bedside and grasped Kathryn's pale, puffy hand. "Kathryn, dear, do you remember how you helped me when Lily was born?"

Matt's head whipped around in surprise. She'd never told him that.

Emma's sweet, gentle voice continued. "I couldn't have done it without you. Now I've come to return the favor. You're almost there, my friend. Just a little more and you can hold your sweet, precious babe in your arms."

The pale eyelids fluttered upward.

"That's right. We're going to do it together. Maureen and I will lift your shoulders and Dr. Tolivar will do the rest."

With a flicker of resolve, Kathryn nodded slightly. As the contraction began, Matt reexamined his patient, ready to forcibly deliver the child. What he felt sent a jolt of panic shooting through him.

"Stop!" he cried. "Don't push." Tension knotted his neck and shoulders. His breath grew short and perspiration bathed his face.

The cord was wrapped, not once, but twice around the baby's neck. Any further pushing would strangle the child to death. He remembered this terror all too well. Only extremely skilled hands and the grace of God could save the O'Dell baby. Matt squeezed his eyes shut for a moment.

Please, Jesus, help me to help her.

When he opened his eyes, a strange sense of calm came over him. Moving quickly and efficiently, he worked the tightly wound cord over the slippery little head with one hand while holding back the force of nature with the other. It was difficult, tedious work, and time was against them.

The string of tension in the room bound them all, so that when, at last, the noose was removed, a collective sigh of relief issued from Emma and Maureen. Matt knew better than to relax. At the next contraction, the tiny infant slid into the world, blue and flaccid.

"Oh no," Maureen cried, hands grasping for Emma.

"Breathe, baby girl." Matt ran a finger inside the lax mouth then placed his own lips over the child's and blew gently. The baby gave a shudder then sucked in a chestful of air. Matt swatted her bottom twice and received a mewling cry in return. The wonder of it brought tears to his eyes.

"Thank You, Jesus," Emma whispered. Matthew's heart echoed the sentiment. He rubbed the baby's back, checking her over, waiting until the even breathing and pink hues of health assured him that she was all right. Then he wrapped her in a warmed blanket and handed her to Maureen.

"She's a little thing," he said as he turned back to the exhausted mother. "We'll have to watch her close, keep her good and warm, but I think she'll make it."

"I'll go and tell Da. He's worried sick."

During Maureen's absence, Matt and Emma cared for their patient and were immensely relieved to know that she'd weathered the delivery with no further ill effects. Rest and good food would soon have her well again. Matthew knew a sense of accomplishment he hadn't felt in years.

"I'll be back to check on you first thing tomorrow," Matt promised as he carefully placed the tools of his trade back inside the black bag. "You stay in that bed and let the rest of the family look after you for a while."

"Aye, she'll do that. I'll see to it meself." Jimmy came into the bedroom, cradling the tiny bundle in his arms. He shifted nervously from one foot to the other. "I'm a proud man, Tolivar. Apologies don't come easy. But you've got one coming, so I'm giving it to you. We needed you here today, and you came, knowing I'd fight you tooth and toenail. Still, you came. I'm grateful."

"You can thank Emma for that," Matt said stiffly, not ready to forgive the man who'd caused his wife so much grief.

"Then I do." He turned to Emma, expression sheepish. "Maureen told me how you helped the missus. Thank you."

"I'm the one who's grateful, Mr. O'Dell," she said in her sweetest voice. "Seeing that little girl of yours come into the world was a special privilege."

Jimmy cleared his throat. When he spoke again, his voice was gruff. "If you folks want to come to church on Sunday, I'll stand up for you."

Matthew watched the change come over Emma's face. Unlike Matt, she bore her detractors no animosity, no bitterness, just a Christlike love he still didn't understand. But after today, he wanted to learn.

By the time Emma and Matt arrived at church on Sunday morning, the service was about to begin. As they slipped quietly into a back pew, heads turned to stare. Tensing, ready to take Emma and escape before any trouble began, Matt glared back at the people of Goodhope. A few tentative smiles and a head bob here and there told him that, today, the crowd was friendly. He relaxed, squeezing Emma's cold hand. No one was going to hurt her anymore.

As the organist began to play, the O'Dell family filed in and, seeing the Tolivars, slid onto the bench beside them.

"How's your mother?" Emma whispered.

"Getting stronger. The baby, too," Maureen whispered in return.

Matt leaned forward. "We'll come by after church."

Maureen smiled and nodded as they all quieted, turning their attention to the service. The song master led them in hymns that seemed especially sweet to Matt that morning. His prayers seemed to go straight up to heaven, so thrilled was he to worship freely with other Christians and the woman he loved.

When Pastor Jeffers took the pulpit, his sermon, not surprisingly, was on forgiveness. "Now you folks all know what I'm talking about today," he said toward the end. "We all need forgiveness from the Lord and, at times, from each other. Things have happened this week to wake us up to the fact that we've done wrong by a young couple in our community."

A few dozen pairs of eyes swiveled toward the back pew. Emma sat with head down, an almost holy smile on her lips.

"For months," the reverend went on, "we've prayed for a doctor. Finally, the Lord sees fit to send us one, and we treat his wife so badly, he's not even willing to tell us who he is. We've been stiff-necked, passing judgment on Emma, when who better to judge her mental state than a doctor who spends every day with her? If any of you still have doubts, I believe Floyd Anderson has a word or two to say about it."

Near the front, a man with a noticeable limp stood and hobbled forward. "I wasn't here the last time the Tolivars came to church, or I'd a-told this then." He scratched at his beard and went on. "All of you know the hard time me and the wife had after I busted my leg. I'm a proud man, don't like to ask for help, but if it hadn't been for Emma Tolivar, I reckon we would've starved. All them times someone saw her sneaking over to my house, she was bringing groceries. She didn't want to cause me no embarrassment. That woman's heart is gold, I tell you. She's a pure saint if ever there was one."

With an expression that dared anyone to argue, Floyd clumped back to his pew. Matt was hard-pressed not to smile at the man's feisty attitude even while he was grateful for what was said. Now he knew for certain where Emma went on her early morning walks. No doubt, the Andersons weren't the only recipients of her generosity.

"I got something to say myself, Parson." Jimmy O'Dell rose. "Most of you have already heard about my wife and baby, and how the doctor here and his little wife saved their lives. If it wasn't for them, I'd be in mourning. That's all I got to say." With a self-conscious swipe at his nose, he sat down.

Emma's eyes shone suspiciously as she listened to the total change of public sentiment. More powerful than any medicine, acceptance was a healing balm.

"Dr. Tolivar, this town needs a man of your skills." Parson Jeffers's boots thudded softly on the wooden floor as he came to stand beside Emma and Matt. Every person in the building either stood or turned to watch. "Could the two of you find it in your hearts to forgive us? And, sir, would you consent to be our doctor?"

Pulse pounding, Matt rose to his feet, pulling Emma up beside him. "My wife is the most forgiving person I know. She's never borne you any resentment for the way she was treated. I, on the other hand, have had a bit more difficulty." He gazed fondly at his wife. "Emma here tells me I'll never be content until I let the past go and get back to medicine. Emma's a wise woman." He extended a hand to the preacher. "I'd be proud to serve as Goodhope's physician."

Rousing applause echoed through the room until the organist struck a jarring chord then stood and said, "Thank the good Lord for that. I don't know what we'd do with all the food we cooked if you refused us. You young folks didn't even have a proper shivaree when you was wed, so we figured we'd have us a town celebration in your honor and cover the whole shebang, new doctor, new married couple, and the O'Dell's new baby all in one whack."

The congregation laughed and began to rise, filing slowly out onto the lawn where makeshift tables were set up beneath the trees. As they followed, talking with the well-wishers, the joy on Emma's face was reflected in Matthew's heart. This was what he'd been looking for, what he'd longed for, and the crazy widow of Goodhope had been the answer to his prayers.

Filled with the kind of happiness he'd never thought possible, Matt took Emma's hand and started across the grass. Halfway to the shade trees, right in view of the whole town, Emma stopped. "Wait."

She pulled off her shoes then whirled her husband in a circle, laughing. Matt smiled at his beautiful barefoot wife.

"You think I'm crazy, don't you?" she teased.

"That's not what I think at all."

"What, then?"

"I was thinking of the day I came here, bound by my own guilty past, unable to laugh, a lost and wounded man. And you showed me a better way."

Relishing the brand of freedom she'd taught him, Matt removed his own boots and tossed them high into the air with an exultant shout. A moment of stunned silence settled over the churchyard.

"Well, what are you looking at? Ain't you all got feet?" Jimmy O'Dell plunked himself down on the ground and yanked off his boots so fast the socks came with them. With a cry of delight, Maureen mirrored her father, kicking her shoes into the tree overhead.

The startled looks turned to chuckles. Then, one by one, the people of Goodhope followed suit, discarding boots and slippers, until the whole town was barefoot, and laughing, and dancing. . .and crazy with the joy of the Lord.

LINDA GOODNIGHT and her husband, Gene, live on a farm in their native Oklahoma. They have a blended family of six grown children. An elmentary school teacher for the past sixteen years, Linda is a licensed nurse. You may contact her via e-mail at gnight@brightok.net.

Prairie
Schoolmarm

by JoAnn A. Grote

Dedication

For Vicci and Joey Danens,
two special children who are wonderful
teachers in my own life.
For my relatives who show their commitment to,
and love for, children through teaching:
Jody Kvanli Capehart, Fran Olsen Strommer,
and Heather Adamson Olsen.
And for Sophia (Sophie) Olsen Fletcher.
Welcome to the family, little one!

*I can do all things through Christ
which strengtheneth me.*
PHILIPPIANS 4:13

Chapter 1

May 1871

Marin Nilsson leaned against the ship rail, turned her face into the May winds, and spoke in Swedish to her older sister, Elsbet. "There it is—the United States. I'd begun to think we'd never see it."

Elsbet's gaze rested on the nearing shore, but Marin could see no joy in her sister's blue eyes.

The lack of expression cut into Marin's heart. Would Elsbet's pain last the rest of her life? Two years had passed since her fiancé, Anton, left for America with the promise to send for her when he'd saved enough money for her passage. One year had passed since the news came through friends that he'd married a young woman he'd met in the new land. In the year between, Marin had watched Elsbet's joy and her faith in Anton's love slip slowly into fear—fear he'd been hurt or killed. She rejected speculation from friends and relatives that Anton had abandoned her, as so many men who emigrated had abandoned fiancées, wives, and families in Sweden.

At first, Marin was relieved when news came of Anton's marriage. Perhaps now, she thought, Elsbet would forget him and find someone new. Instead, Elsbet wrapped herself in her pain, in her longing for the love in which she'd believed so strongly. It seemed to Marin that rather than recover from the loss, her sister died a little more each day.

I'll never give a man my heart, Marin promised herself. *Not if I live to be one hundred. When Moder and Fader get old and die, Elsbet and I will take care of each other. Better two old maids than two women with broken hearts.*

Marin had made the same promise almost every day for the last year. Each day her resolve grew greater as the light in Elsbet's eyes failed to return.

"Maybe her heart will heal in America," their mother had said. "Plenty of young Swedish men are there looking for brides."

Marin wasn't so certain America held the remedy.

A young man's wide, smiling face slipped into Marin's view, pushing away her memories. The wind caught at his blond hair as he leaned against the rail on the other side of Elsbet. His gaze met Marin's. "Hello." He addressed the sisters in the lilting language of their homeland. "Exciting, isn't it? Soon we'll walk on American soil."

Elsbet ignored him.

Marin pulled back slightly, dropped an invisible veil over her eyes, and made her voice cool. "Yes, it is exciting." This wasn't the first time Talif Siverson had attempted to start a conversation with her during the crossing. She'd politely rebuffed each effort. It wasn't as though he was a family friend. He wasn't even from the same part of Sweden as the Nilsson family.

She'd noticed him before he approached her the first time, noticed him before they boarded. His handsome face beneath the wide-brimmed, brown felt hat and his gaze filled with excitement at the prospect before him had drawn her attention more than once. *It's natural that a good-looking man should catch a woman's attention,* she assured herself. *It doesn't mean I want to know him better.*

Talif made another attempt. "Maybe we'll see each other in the new land. Where is your family planning to settle?"

"Minnesota," Marin replied, though she was certain Talif already knew the answer. She'd seen him talking with her father and brothers.

"That's where I'll be homesteading. Where in Minnesota is your family headed?"

"Mankato. Our family will stay with another family while Fader looks for land."

Talif's eyes brightened. "That's my plan. My friend, Afton Thomton, says he knows of good land about one hundred miles to the north and west of Mankato, near the Minnesota and Chippewa rivers. We're going to look at it as soon I arrive."

"I hope you find what you want." Marin turned her back to the man and her gaze back to the water. Against all wisdom, her heart insisted on quickening in this man's presence. It was all she could do to keep the welcome from her eyes.

A long pause met her action. She was sorely tempted to shoot a glance back at where he'd stood, but she refrained herself with discipline. Was he still there?

A clearing of his throat finally broke the silence. She heard the pain of her rebuff in his voice. "I'd best be getting my things together. I want everything ready so my time is free to stand up here and watch as we near shore. Good day to you, ladies. I hope to see you in America."

Marin heard his boots smack softly against the deck as he walked away. Her throat burned from holding back her response. She didn't want to see him in America. She didn't want to see any men in America who might threaten her heart.

Chapter 2

Chippewa County, Minnesota—January 1873

Marin heaved a sigh of frustration. "Einer, pay attention," she demanded in Swedish. She glared at her fifteen-year-old brother, who sat across from her at the homemade wooden table in the one-room sod house. Light from the kerosene lantern played across his hair, which was pale brown like their father, Hjalmar's. "I've asked you three times to read the verse from Philippians in English. How do you expect to improve your English if you don't try?"

"What does it matter? We've been in America for a year and a half and never leave the farm or see anyone but other Swedes."

August, twelve and the youngest of the Nilsson family, leaned forward on the barrel he used as a chair. "That's not true. Sometimes you go to town with Fader. You see people who aren't Swedes there."

Einer grunted. "I've gone to town with Fader exactly twice since we moved here last spring."

"More than me," August insisted. "And all our neighbors aren't Swedes. The Andersons are Norwegian. And there's the bachelor on the homestead to the south who came from New York."

"We won't stay so isolated forever," Moder broke in. "New people keep moving into the area."

Marin nodded. "Yes. Besides, we all agreed it's important to learn the language of our new land."

Anger smoldered in Einer's eyes. "None of my friends study English every night." He pushed the family's only copy of the precious Swedish-English translation of the New Testament from in front of him, narrowly missing the kerosene lantern.

"Watch out!" Moder grabbed for the lamp's clear glass base.

"I didn't hit it." Impatience filled Einer's defensive words.

"Einer." Fader's deep voice, low but stern, tumbled through the one-room soddy.

Silence filled the air in the wake of Fader's gentle reproof. Fader never allowed the children to speak with disrespect to Moder.

Einer crossed his arms over his chest and glared at the table.

Marin shifted her weight, uncomfortably aware that everyone was staring at Einer: Moder, who sat beside Marin on the crude log bench; Elsbet, on Marin's other side; August, who sat beside Einer; and Fader, who stood talking in quiet tones with their neighbor, Talif Siverson, beside the large, Dala-painted trunk at the end of Moder and Fader's bed. Normally Fader would be at the table with the rest of the family during the English-learning hour, but he'd excused himself when Talif arrived a quarter hour ago.

Only with difficulty had Marin kept her gaze from Talif and her attention on the lesson. Since he was their nearest neighbor, it wasn't uncommon for Talif to visit with Fader after the day's work was done.

Moder touched Marin's hand. "Marin, let's begin again."

Marin hesitated. No doubt Einer thought he should be visiting with the men instead of sitting with the women and youngest child. Was he embarrassed that Fader reprimanded him in front of Talif?

As the family member who knew English best, Marin led the family's daily English-learning hour. She knew Einer wouldn't dare chance Fader's disapproval by leaving the table, but perhaps she shouldn't insist he read the verse. She cleared her throat and repeated the verse in Swedish from memory before asking, "August, would you read the verse in English?"

The towheaded boy pulled the New Testament near. "Which verse was it again?"

"Philippians, chapter 4, verse 13."

August frowned at the pages before him and read haltingly, " 'I can do all things through Christ which strengtheneth me.' "

The class continued only a few minutes longer. As the four gathered about the table stood up, Moder asked Talif, "Would you care for some bread and coffee before leaving, Mr. Siverson? There's quite a chill in the air tonight."

Marin smiled. A guest never left the Nilsson home without such an offer, regardless of the time of day or the amount of food available or even whether the Nilssons liked the visitor. Hospitality was as much a part of Fader and Moder as their faith.

"*Tack*, Mrs. Nilsson. A little warmth in my belly would be welcome against the cold. Besides, your coffee is always better than mine." He grinned at her and sat down on the barrel Einer had vacated.

As Moder put water in a huge graniteware kettle to heat on the stove, Fader headed to the sod barn to check on the cow and oxen. Einer and August, always glad to leave the dark little house that they considered the womenfolk's place, followed.

Talif reached for the New Testament. "I received one of these from a representative of a Lutheran church in New York when I arrived in America."

"That's where we got this one," Marin told him.

"Your fader tells me your family studies English for an hour each day."

"Yes, it's true, except for *Söndag*. We take turns reading in both Swedish and English. Then we choose a verse to memorize in English."

"That's a good plan. Does your family also speak in English around the house and while they work together each day?"

"We say we will, but it's easy to fall back into Swedish, as you heard tonight."

"Still, it is important to learn English. Those Swedes who know the language best will be able to get along best with Americans in business. Einer knows that. He's just tired."

Marin nodded. "I think he's right about other parents not requiring their children to learn English or even to read and write Swedish, as is required in the homeland."

"It's understandable. Everyone is so busy establishing their fields and homes. It takes all the time and energy available for parents and children alike."

Marin rested her forearms on the table and leaned forward. "But everyone will pay in the end if the children don't learn. How will the parents feel when the children are grown and still unable to communicate easily with the merchants, for instance?"

"I agree with you, but there isn't a school near enough for the children to attend. Chippewa City is the nearest village, and it's too far for the children to walk. The county doesn't have money to build a school here or pay another teacher."

"I know." Deflated, Marin sat back, her shoulders slumping. "For months I've been asking our heavenly Father to provide a school for the children in the area."

"Perhaps you should start one."

"I . . ." Marin stared at him, stunned. "But I'm not a teacher."

Talif shrugged. A smile lit his wide face. "You certainly sounded like one tonight."

"That was only with my family. I've no training to *truly* teach others."

"You've the knowledge that others need, and from your father's comments, I've no doubt you've the ability to share that knowledge with others. What else is required to teach?"

Marin spread her hands. "I don't know, but surely some test must be passed or permission received from the county school superintendent." Still, prickles ran along her skin at the possibility.

"You have a dream, a dream for a school for the Swedish children, and you've asked the Lord to grant this dream. It seems to me the best way for Him to do that is for you to do what you can toward building that dream. If it's to be, He will show you the next step and the next."

"What steps?" As soon as she asked the question, ideas popped into her mind. "Maybe I can talk with Miss Allen, the schoolteacher at Chippewa City. I can ask her what I need to do to become a teacher in this county—whether I need more training or to take a test."

"Yes, that would be a perfect place to start."

"But it won't be possible for me to get more training if I need it."

"Now you're trying to cross a bridge you don't even know needs to be crossed."

"You're right." Another problem loomed. "There's nowhere to hold lessons."

"You teach just fine right here."

"But this is our home. There isn't room for students."

"We hold church services here sometimes, and in other homes, too, some smaller than this."

She couldn't argue the truth of that. Excitement started to build, even as other problems came to mind. "We've no supplies."

"If the Lord can provide the teacher, students, and building, He can certainly provide whatever else is required."

Marin sat quietly for a minute, her mind racing. "Do you truly think it's possible?"

Moder set a cup of coffee on the table in front of Talif. "Didn't we just read tonight that 'all things are possible through Christ'?"

All things. Even a school, with herself as teacher? A thrill of hope ran along Marin's spine.

A minute later, Fader and the boys returned. Moder poured a cup of coffee for Fader and explained Talif's idea. Marin watched her father's face closely, knowing he was good at hiding his true feelings, good at using tact to give a gentle refusal.

"Sounds like a fine idea, Marin. Would you be agreeable to it?"

At Marin's surprised, cautious nod, he continued. "You couldn't give all of your time to it. Moder and Elsbet need your help, too."

Marin nodded again.

Fader glanced up at Moder and smiled. "What do you think, Tekla? Could we share our humble home with the neighbor children a few hours each day?"

"I think we could." Moder's smile lit up Marin's heart.

Marin's gaze darted to Talif, and she caught him grinning back at her like a coconspirator.

"We'll need to rise early tomorrow, Marin," Fader advised, glancing at her over the rim of his pottery cup, "if we're to make it to Chippewa City so you can talk with Miss Allen."

"Yes, Fader." Joy bubbled within Marin's chest. A trip to town, a visit with the teacher, Moder and Fader agreeing to let her use their home as a school, and above all, her parents and Talif's belief in her ability to teach. It seemed too good to be true.

❧

Excitement, ideas, possibilities, and fears churned in Marin's mind, keeping sleep at bay for two hours after the rest of the family fell asleep. Pushing aside the bed curtain, Marin slipped out from under the heavy quilts, careful not to disturb Elsbet, who shared the bed. One of their brothers grunted and rolled over in the bed above Marin and Elsbet's, and Marin held her breath until all was again still.

She trod in stocking feet across the cold dirt floor to the window between the end of her parents' bed and the door, the window by which Fader and Talif had conversed earlier. A cotton curtain hid the bed from view, just like the curtain around the children's bed.

Marin picked up a quilt from the top of the trunk and climbed onto the wide window seat formed by the three-foot-wide blocks of sod. A woven rug of red and blue brightened the sill and warmed the dirt a bit. She pulled her knees up, glad to have her feet off the cold floor, and wrapped the quilt around herself.

The sky was bright with starshine, clear of clouds. *The way the path of my dream appears tonight,* she thought, *bright, guided by starlight, clear.*

Her gaze drifted over the snow-covered prairie. There wasn't much to see, not even one tree. The sod barn, which sheltered the oxen, horse, and cow, stood silhouetted against the night sky. If the hour were earlier, a small point of light would be shining from Talif's window. No light there now. He'd be sleeping, of course. Without the light, his sod house was too far away to see even in the starlit, snow-bright night.

Even so, Marin's gaze searched the prairie where she knew his home stood. Gratitude filled her chest, warming her heart. In all the months they'd lived as neighbors, she'd treated him with a cool politeness. In return, he'd shown her how to reach for her heart's dream: to establish a school for the Swedish children. "Forgive me, Lord," she whispered. "Forgive me, Talif, and tack."

Chapter 3

Marin studied her image in the silver hand mirror Moder had brought from Sweden and patted the blond braids wrapped in a coronet from ear to ear on top of her head. "Do I look proper, Elsbet?"

Elsbet's usually sober face sparkled with laughter. "Like a proper schoolteacher, yes, and beautiful besides. It's time to quit admiring yourself and get ready to greet your students."

"*My* students." Marin handed Elsbet the mirror. Wonder and dismay battled for supremacy. "Do you truly believe I can do this?"

"Of course. You'll be a blessing to your students."

Marin pressed the palms of her hands down the skirt of her best plaid dress, straightened the prim black ribbon bow at the neck, and took a deep, shaky breath. "I hope so."

She pushed back the curtain that divided the beds from the main room, walked to the table, and looked down at her few supplies: the Swedish-English New Testament; the small slate she'd bought at the general store last week when she visited Miss Allen; an old, well-read Mankato newspaper; the few letters they'd received from relatives and friends in Sweden and other parts of America; and the faithful kerosene lamp. The lamp would be needed, for even during the day there wasn't enough light in the sod house by which to read. Marin sighed. "Not much to begin a school with, I'm afraid."

Moder patted Marin's shoulder. "Beginnings are often small."

"Another Swedish proverb, Moder?"

She gave a sweet chuckle. "No, my own."

Marin glanced about the room. Who had ever heard of a schoolroom with the only desk a table on which the family had eaten breakfast an hour before school was scheduled to begin? The odor of corn cakes, ham, and coffee lingered in the air. The stove lent welcome warmth to the room.

August sat on the trunk, his eyes wide with anticipation. Einer leaned against the wall beside the window, trying to look uninterested, but Marin could see his excitement.

Fader entered the room, letting in a blast of chill January wind before he shut the heavy door. His cheeks shone red beneath his fur cap. "Here, Marin. It's time to announce that school will begin in a few minutes." He held out a cowbell. "Every schoolmarm needs a bell to ring."

Marin accepted the cold bell with a laugh and hugged him. "Tack, Fader."

"English, daughter." He shook a finger at her playfully.

Moder placed a thick, gray wool shawl about Marin's shoulders. Marin took a deep breath and opened the front door, bell in hand. A sign Elsbet had tatted hung on the outside of the door: School. Marin smiled, feeling wrapped in her family's love. Each member of the Nilsson family had contributed something to the new school.

The clear sky above the horizon was still bathed in dawn's pale lavender and rose above the snow-swept prairie. At the sight before her, Marin's heart missed a beat. Children waded through the foot-high snow toward the Nilsson house, their jackets, scarves, and hats dark or colorful splashes against the white background. Some of the students were almost to the Nilsson yard. Others were still distant enough that Marin couldn't make out their faces.

With a grin, she closed the door behind her and began to ring the bell. At first, in her excitement, she barely felt the chill. The family's black-and-white dog jumped up on her, barking the news that he saw people coming. "Shush, Sven," she scolded, pushing him down. "It's the schoolchildren. You must be nice to them when they arrive. No jumping on them."

Soon the cold from the air and the metal bell handle seeped into her bones, but she continued ringing the bell until the first group of children arrived at the door. Sven ran circles about them, barking in joyful greeting. Marin recognized the students as the Skarstedt children who lived over two miles to the east.

"God morgon, Eva, Anders, Sture. Stig in, come in."

"God morgon, Marin," ten-year-old Anders and eight-year-old Sture mumbled as they stepped over the threshold.

"God morgon, Miss Nilsson," Eva greeted in her quiet, shy manner.

Marin was torn between the desire to stay outside until all the children arrived and the longing to go in where it was warm. Warmth won. It wouldn't do for the teacher to come down ill on the first day of school. Besides, the other students were on the way and not likely to loiter in the winter morning. She could greet them beside the door inside as well as out.

Ten minutes later, she stood at one end of the table and stared in amazement. Children filled the sod house to bursting. *Students,* she reminded herself, a thrill warming her chest, *not just children, but students. Nineteen of them.*

Marin was glad her plaid skirt hid her knocking knees. She'd longed for this day, and now that it was here, she was terrified. *Don't think about the fear,* she ordered herself. *Just do what you planned. The Lord will take care of the rest.*

"*Velkommen.* Let us begin our first day of school with a prayer of thanksgiving." She clasped her hands and bowed her head. "Our heavenly Father, we thank Thee for granting us a place to gather and learn. Help us to use this opportunity to grow in knowledge and wisdom. Amen."

A murmur of "amens" echoed in the little room.

Marin looked up and smiled brightly. "Now then, we're ready to begin." She immediately faltered once more at the sight of nineteen pairs of eyes concentrated upon her.

The youngest children sat on the beds, their legs dangling over the sides, boots and shoes on the floor. Students' coats and scarves were piled on the quilts behind the children. Elsbet sat on the sod window seat between the bedsteads, keeping watch for the moment over the little ones for Marin. The older boys, including Einer, stood along the wall. Orpha Stenvall and Viola Linder, the oldest girls at thirteen and ten, claimed the top of the Dala-painted immigrant trunk. The in-between-aged children sat at the table. Every child watched her intently.

She swallowed hard, keeping the smile in place. *Just follow your plan,* she reminded herself again. *They're only the children from the church. You know them all. Your family and Talif and the children's parents all believe you can do this.* "We'll begin with the school rules. Each day will begin with a prayer or hymn. In the beginning, we'll speak mostly Swedish, but you'll be required to speak English more as you learn that language. Often I'll say something in Swedish then repeat it in English. That way you'll become accustomed to hearing both languages and perhaps learn English more quickly. There will be no whispering. You will raise your hand and wait for me to call upon you to speak. When I do call upon you, or when you are to recite a lesson, you'll stand. You will address me as Miss Nilsson. Do you understand?"

Most of the students nodded. Jems Stenvall and Knute Linder, two of the older boys, shifted their feet and stared at her without nodding, but they didn't challenge her, either. Marin noticed that the youngest children frowned or looked confused. Was it too much for such little ones to remember at one time? She smiled at Sophia Linder, the tiniest of the students. "Don't worry. If you forget the rules, I'll remind you."

A relieved smile spread across the round face between thick blond braids. "What if I need to go to the necessary?"

Snickers filled the air.

Marin bit back a grin. "You raise your hand and ask permission."

Sophia shook her head, her eyes wide. "I don't like to go alone." She grasped the hand of the seven-year-old girl beside her. "Can my sister, Stina, come with me?"

"Yes."

"Does she have to raise her hand, too, or just me?"

"Just you, Sophia."

Sophia frowned. "I'm thirsty."

"The water pail and dipper are by the wall beside the barrels." Marin pointed to the place. "Students must also raise their hands when they need a drink."

Sophia raised her right hand high.

"Yes, Sophia?"

"I need a drink."

"May I have a drink, Miss Nilsson?"

Sophia shook her head. "I'm not Miss Nilsson. You are."

The other students burst into laughter. Marin swallowed a chuckle. "I meant, the proper way to ask for a drink is, 'May I have a drink, Miss Nilsson?'"

"Oh." Sophia didn't repeat the question. She only looked more confused.

"You may get a drink if you wish, Sophia."

All smiles, Sophia slipped off the bed and headed across the room.

Marin began to relax and turned to the other students. "Your parents were asked to send along with you any books or supplies they had available. Let's see what everyone's brought. Everyone please stand." She looked over at the older boys. "We'll start with you, Jems. Then Knute. Everyone follow in an orderly manner and set your items on the table."

When all the students had passed the table and returned to their seats, Marin's heart sank. The supplies were meager: Marin's small slate, five Swedish-English New Testaments, one well-read and torn Swedish newspaper, and one book of Swedish poetry. She'd known supplies would be limited, but how could she teach so many students with so little?

It wouldn't do to let the students know how discouraged she found their offerings. She forced another smile. "Wonderful. I'm glad to see that each family has a Swedish-English New Testament. That means every student can study reading both languages at home, not only here at school. Now I'm going to talk to the oldest student from each family to find out what education each of you had in Sweden and America. While I do that, my sister, Elsbet, will lead the rest of you in an exercise, memorizing a Bible verse in Swedish and then in English."

The school day went by faster than Marin anticipated. It seemed the day had barely started before the students were filing out the door toward home. Marin stood just inside the door, smiling at the departing children in spite of her exhaustion. *"Vi ses i morgon,"* she repeated again and again. "I'll see you tomorrow."

She leaned down to tighten the ties on little Sophia's red crocheted headband beneath the girl's pointed chin. Sophia smiled her thanks with a charming grin made of little teeth with big spaces in between. "Tack, Teacher."

Marin's heart took a little leap. *Teacher.* *"Ingen orsak*, Sophia. You're welcome."

When the last student had left, Marin leaned back against the door, closed her eyes, and heaved a sigh of relief. The first day was over, and she'd lived through it. She'd been called "Teacher" for the first time. She was living the role she'd asked the Lord to give her. She'd expected it to bring joy, and it did. It also terrified her.

※

Marin was helping Moder and Elsbet clear the dinner dishes from the table when Talif arrived that evening. As usual, he visited with Fader, Einer, and August at the table where light from the kerosene lamp chased away the darkness of the winter evening. All four enjoyed cups of Moder's coffee.

Marin felt her gaze drawn to Talif continually while she worked. Each time she looked in his direction, she saw him watching her, a smiling curiosity in his eyes though he continued chatting about farm topics with Fader. She longed to share with Talif the experiences of her day. After all, he'd helped make the school possible.

"Elsbet and I will do the dishes, Marin," Moder said as she took a large wooden bowl from Marin, "while you prepare tomorrow's lessons."

"Tack, Moder." Marin smiled her gratitude and walked to the immigrant trunk to pick up the New Testament and her slate.

Talif stood, looking contrite. "I should be going. I'm intruding on your English hour again."

Fader pushed himself up from the barrel on which he'd been seated. "No. We've agreed to pass on the family English hour while Marin is teaching. Moder, Elsbet, and I will take time when possible to join Marin's class for our English lessons. Marin doesn't need an extra hour of teaching us each evening in addition to her responsibilities to her students." He reached for his coat hanging on a nail on the wide wooden door frame. "I'd best check on the beasts. Einer, August, come along."

While the brothers put on their coats, Fader lit a lantern. Moder handed him a plate of scraps for the dog. A swirl of cold air entered the warm house when the men left, chasing away a bit of the chicken stew and dumpling odors, and the woodsy smell of heat from the stove. Marin shivered as she sat down across the table from Talif.

Talif smiled at her. "One good thing about sod houses, they keep the cold out."

"*Ja*, that is true when the door isn't open."

"How did your first day of school go?"

"Wonderful!" Marin leaned her forearms against the table's edge, her hands clasped. "And awful." She laughed at the dichotomy.

Talif's grin answered her mirth. "Like most things in life, part good, part not-so-good, huh? Tell me about it."

"I'm afraid I didn't think my plan through well. Including Einer and August, I've nineteen students. Nineteen!"

"That's a roomful, I'd say."

"They're all ages. Sophia Linder is the youngest. She's five. Knute Linder and Einer are the oldest at fifteen. Most of the older students know some math and geography, and how to read and write in Swedish. The youngest students need to learn everything. Some of the students can speak a bit of English, but none of them can read it except my brothers." Marin spread her hands, palms up. "How can I teach so many children who start with such different abilities?"

"With patience," he replied promptly, "and wisdom and ingenuity. The Lord wouldn't have put you in this position if you weren't able to do it."

"I hope you're right." She leaned forward. "We've barely any supplies beyond the Swedish-English New Testaments."

"What supplies do you most need?"

"A blackboard would be wonderful. Slates for each of the children." Marin began ticking items off on her fingertips. "A globe for geography. Math books and readers." She sighed. "Not that it does any good to wish. There's no money for these things."

"Doesn't hurt to make a prayer list for them, does it?"

Marin opened her mouth to protest. It seemed impossible that God could furnish the supplies. The families needed all their money for their homes and fields, yet scripture assured that nothing was impossible with God. "You're right; it won't hurt to ask. After all, the Lord answered my prayer for a school even though it's not what I expected."

Talif laughed. "Things seldom are what we expect. Tell me more about your first day."

She told him of the mixture of excitement and fear with which she'd started the day, of her fear she wouldn't know how to handle the older boys if they chose not to respect her authority, and of Sophia's funny comments. "The best part of the day was when the students left."

"You don't mean it!" Talif raised his blond eyebrows in astonishment.

"Not the way you think," she hastened to assure him. Marin touched the fingertips of her right hand to her throat and swallowed. "When Sophia Linder left, she called me 'Teacher.'" Marin almost whispered the word. "It's the first time anyone's called me that."

Talif met her gaze and smiled into her eyes, a sweet smile that wrapped around her heart.

Marin dropped her gaze to the table, feeling suddenly vulnerable and a bit foolish. "It probably doesn't seem like much, but it is to me. I've always thought teachers such special people, and now. . ."

"Now you are one."

She bit back the words on the tip of her tongue: *If I'm capable of meeting the challenge.* Talif would only repeat that God wouldn't have put her in the position if she wasn't able to meet the duties. Talif was right, of course, but it was going to be more work than she'd ever imagined. Well, she wasn't afraid of hard work. She squared her shoulders and met his gaze. "Yes, now I am one."

Warmth, contentment, and faith spread through her chest as she and Talif shared smiles across the flickering flame from the kerosene lamp.

❧

The joy that shone from Marin's eyes when she proclaimed herself a teacher shone again in Talif's memory an hour and a half later. He stared out the wavy glass in his window, looking across the prairie to where the lights from the Nilsson home gleamed. Marin's happiness stirred his soul.

What an extraordinary woman she was, to take on such a challenge! He'd been attracted to her from the first moment he saw her, but he hadn't known then what a strong, giving person lay hidden by her outer beauty. She'd made it plain from the beginning by her cool attitude that she didn't want him to court her. He'd bided his time, offering only friendship. During that year and a half, his attraction had grown into love. At least lately she acted friendlier toward him. Was he a fool to hope she'd one day return his affection?

He'd encouraged her to believe that with God all things are possible, to believe the Lord would make her dream a reality. Yet Talif didn't quite trust that his own dream of making a home and building a family with Marin would come true. What if the Lord had other plans for her? Even if it was best for them to be together, the Lord allowed people free will. Talif remembered many times seeing people make choices he felt weren't in their best interests.

With a sigh, Talif turned from the window and crawled beneath the heavy quilts on his corn-husk mattress. He slipped his hands beneath his head and stared at the once-white cloth covering the ceiling. Moonlight rested gently on his face, but he didn't notice. His thoughts remained with Marin: *Miss Marin Nilsson, teacher.* A twinge caught at his heart. He envied Miss Nilsson's students, the time spent in her presence.

Chapter 4

Talif laughed at the sight before him as he approached the Nilssons' soddy. Driving his runner-mounted wagon from his place to theirs across the snowbound prairie, he'd wondered what all the people were doing in the yard. Now he knew. Letters and words were carved into the snow. Marin had found an ingenious solution to the lack of a blackboard and slates.

Sunlight bounced off the snow-covered yard and off the young students' red cheeks as they looked up from their work to greet him. Marin glanced up, too, from where she knelt beside Sophia and shot him a quick, small smile before turning her attention back to Sophia's attempts at spelling. *En. Två. Tre.* The little girl was obviously learning to write her Swedish numbers.

His chest constricted in a warm, pleasant way at the sight of Marin so involved with the child. He welcomed the feeling but didn't dwell on it as he directed the horse toward the sod barn.

Talif had barely reached the barn when Mrs. Nilsson came out of the house, carrying the cowbell. Within minutes, laughter drifted through the cold air as children of all ages headed toward home. Boys teased and chased girls and tossed snowballs at each other. Swinging metal lunch pails glinted in the sunshine. Marin stood in the doorway, still in her coat and scarf, watching the students depart.

"Get along there." Talif urged the horse toward the house, stopping only feet from the door. He nodded at Marin. "I apologize for interrupting your class."

"Classes were almost over anyway, as you can see. Are you looking for Fader? He's in the barn."

"*Nej*. I've come bearing gifts." He climbed over the wagon seat and into the wagon bed.

"Gifts? For us?" Curiosity filled Marin's eyes as she walked toward the wagon.

"For your school. For you and your students." Talif's heart picked up speed. Would she like his gifts? All the while he'd worked on them, he'd imagined the pleasure he'd see reflected in her face. Now he doubted the worthiness of his gifts.

He lifted the largest of them and held it up above the side of the wagon for her to see. "Do you know what this is?"

She frowned slightly, studying the gift, and disappointment began to seep into his hope. Then the frown cleared, and her eyes gleamed with excitement. "It's a blackboard. You made us a blackboard."

"Ja. Not a fancy one. It's just boards painted black."

"But it will work, don't you think?"

"Ja. It will work just fine. It won't be as smooth as a real one to write on, of course, though I sanded it down as best I could." He refrained from mentioning the hours and hours he'd spent smoothing the wood with a piece of broken glass.

"Oh, it's a wonderful gift, Talif. The students will be so excited tomorrow when they see it. No more need to write in the snow."

He chuckled as he lowered the blackboard over the side of the wagon bed. "They may not appreciate that part so well. Seemed to me they were enjoying themselves out here."

"It's nice for them to get out of the house. I've tried having them write in the dirt floor, but it's too dark to see well, and Moder doesn't appreciate the way it loosens the dirt. Wherever did you find extra boards for this? Surely you didn't go to the expense of buying them for us?"

"There's an abandoned homesteader's shack, barely larger than a necessary, a couple miles to the west. I took the wood from there. The homesteader headed to the Black Hills after the grasshoppers left. Said he's never coming back. Rather take his chances on finding gold dust than farming. He won't be needing the wood."

Marin's smile blazed. "I never thought I'd be thanking God for the grasshoppers. Imagine the Lord using them to help the school I didn't know last summer would exist now."

"That's our Lord, not one but many steps ahead of us. If we remembered that, we'd trust Him a lot more." Talif leaned down and picked up a small pile of wood from the wagon bed. "Here's some more supplies for your school." He handed them over the side, and Marin took them from him.

Surprise and wonder swept over her face, and a laugh erupted. "You made slates for the students."

"More like tiny blackboards."

"The students will love them. So do I. I'm so grateful for your kindness and the way you've supported this school from the beginning."

Talif shrugged, unexpectedly self-conscious about his offering. "It's little enough compared to the hours you give to the students." He climbed down from the wagon and lifted the large blackboard. "I'll help you get these inside."

Once inside the sod house, he glanced around at the crowded floors and wall space. He hadn't considered the limited space when making the blackboard.

Marin didn't seem to have any misgivings about the cramped conditions. "Set it in front of that curtain at the end of the double bedstead." She flashed a smile at Moder and Elsbet. "Look what Talif brought—a blackboard and slates for the children. He made them himself."

Talif tried to discount the joy and pride that flooded him at her words, but he wasn't successful. He set the board down where she'd said and removed his hat.

Mrs. Nilsson and Elsbet came over to ooh and aah over his work, making him feel foolish but happy. Soon they moved back to the kitchen area to continue preparing the dinner of pork roast and potatoes that was filling the house with mouthwatering odors.

Marin turned her shining blue-eyed gaze on him. "How can I ever thank you for all you've done?"

Talif pushed the hand not holding his hat into his jeans pocket. He'd been waiting for an opportunity to tell her what he wanted. He knew this was the right moment, but it was still hard to say. "There's one thing you can do for me. I'm not a child like your students, but I need to learn how to speak and write English better. If you want to thank me, you can tutor me."

"No!" Shock widened Marin's eyes, and she stepped back, clutching her tan shawl.

Disappointment twisted through Talif. He struggled to keep it from showing.

Marin's gaze darted in one direction and then another. Her refusal to meet his gaze told him she was embarrassed about her sharp and instant refusal. "I—I can't tutor you," she started to explain. "Teaching the students takes all my time." Her words rushed over each other. "I spend every evening planning the lessons for the next day. And I need to help Moder with duties around the house, too."

"Of course." Now it was Talif who looked away. "It was thoughtless of me to think you'd have time. Your obligation is to your students and your family. I understand." He put on his hat and stepped around her toward the door. "I'd best be going. Evening, Mrs. Nilsson, Elsbet."

"I–I'm sorry."

"Don't give it a thought," he reassured Marin, not looking back.

Disappointment cut through him, keen and sharp, as he climbed into the wagon and headed the horse toward home. Marin's excuse was true; he knew that. How she found time to prepare lessons for nineteen students with such a vast difference in needs was beyond his comprehension. He should take her words at face value.

But it wasn't the words that hurt. It was the expression on her face, her first reaction to his request. The horror that spoke of more than a mere lack of time. The repulsion in her eyes and the explosive "No!" said she couldn't bear the thought of spending time that close to him.

"And I can't bear the thought she feels that way," he whispered into the early evening dusk, his gaze on his lonely little sod house on the rise ahead of him, pain tugging at his heart.

❧

Moder stared across the room from her place beside the hot stove, a wooden spoon in one hand. "Marin, how could you be so unkind?"

Marin glanced at her mother, then away. The fingers of one hand twisted her gray woolen skirt while guilt skittered through her. "I wasn't unkind. I haven't time to tutor him. You know better than anyone how much time the teaching takes me."

"You could have been gentler in your refusal. Talif has given so much support to your school, to say nothing of the many ways he's helped your father out of friendship."

The truth in Moder's words deepened Marin's guilt and caused a strange discomfort. She usually got along so well with her mother. They shared ideals and interests and seldom had sharp words for each other. Marin wasn't accustomed to Moder's disapproval. "I didn't mean to speak unkindly. His request seemed so impossible to grant, and—"

"I'm going for a walk." Elsbet stepped toward the door, slipping her coat on. "I won't be long. Don't worry, Moder, I won't go far." She was out the door before Moder or Marin could say good-bye.

Elsbet's actions didn't surprise Marin. Her sister often went for walks in the dusk, before night settled too darkly on the prairie and covered potential dangers such as wolves and coyotes. Marin knew Elsbet liked to spend time away from everyone else in the quiet with her own thoughts. She hated disagreements, also, and that was probably the true reason she'd left now. The knowledge didn't add to Marin's comfort.

Moder's gaze rested on the door. "You don't want to become like Elsbet." Her voice was quiet, filled with sadness.

Marin studied Moder's face. The sadness in her voice shone in her eyes. "Elsbet is a good person. She has such a kind heart. I'd be glad to be more like her." *Elsbet wouldn't have spoken so roughly to Talif. She'd probably have made time to tutor him if she wasn't attracted to him.*

"Elsbet is a lovely person, yes." Moder reached for Marin's hands. "But her heart is closed to love. You don't want to end up like that."

Marin tugged her hands away. "Talif didn't ask me to love him; he asked me to tutor him."

"You said no to him as a man as well as to his request," Moder admonished. "I'm not only a mother but a woman. It is unfortunate that the man Elsbet loved treated her so harshly. My mother's heart aches for her every day. I hate that she was hurt by him, but I hate just as much that she continues to hurt herself."

"How does she do that?"

"By keeping a wall around her heart and refusing to believe that any other man might truly love her. A heart blocked off from love grows cold, Marin. Remember the proverb, 'A life without love is like a year without summer'? I don't want both my daughters to live their lives without love's warmth."

"But I'm not—"

"Talif Siverson cares for you; that's easy to see. He's a good man. Perhaps you truly don't care for him in the way I hope you will one day care for a man, in the way I care for your father, with a love that makes your life larger and better and more beautiful. Yet you could choose to treat Talif more kindly and to entertain the possibility of falling in love with some young man. You've turned down every man who's expressed an interest in courting you."

Marin slipped off her shawl and gave her attention to carefully folding it. "I haven't time for courting. I'm teaching. My first responsibility is to the students."

Moder sighed. "Perhaps it would be best for them to have a teacher who is not only good at English, Swedish, arithmetic, geography, and history, but courageous enough to keep her heart open to love."

"Moder, I—"

Her mother pulled her close in a hug. "I love you just as you are. I only want you to be happy."

"I am happy."

"Then I'll keep my thoughts to myself." Moder loosened her hug and patted Marin on the shoulder. "Why don't you ring that school bell and call the family in to dinner? By the time they get inside and we finish setting the table, the meal will be ready."

The clang of the bell didn't overcome the words whispering in Marin's heart. She'd had no idea Moder knew so clearly how she felt about men and marriage. Her mother's perceptions made Marin feel vulnerable.

Moder was right about Talif, of course. Marin knew the true reason she'd refused to tutor him wasn't lack of time, though her time was filled to overflowing. The true reason she'd refused was that she liked him too much. If she allowed herself to spend as much time with him as tutoring required, she might do exactly as Moder wished and allow her heart to open to him.

"That I will never do," she promised herself, glancing at Talif's house in the distance. Determination hardened like rock inside her chest. "Never."

Chapter 5

Marin looked up from the opening prayer and glanced around at the students stuffed into every corner of the house. Wind and snow whistled around the corners of the sod house and down the stovepipe, though even a winter storm had no power to penetrate the three-foot-thick sod walls.

It always encouraged her to see the students show up in inclement weather. Their dedication to learning gave her strength to work long into the night to plan lessons.

She smiled at the children. "Since you all walked through the stormy weather this morning to get here, I think for our first lesson we'll work together to learn the English expressions regarding weather. I'll say the expression first in Swedish then repeat it in English. After I say it in English, you will all repeat it in English together. Understood?"

The children responded with nods.

"Good. We'll start with a description of today's weather. *Det är kallt.* It is cold."

"It is cold," the class repeated.

"*Det blåser.* It is windy."

"It is windy."

"*Det snöar.* It is snowing."

"It is snowing."

"Good, class. We'll repeat—"

The door opened, and surprise stopped Marin's speech as Talif entered, a windy gust of cold and snow following him inside.

Talif removed his snow-covered, wide-brimmed hat and nodded at her, a polite, challenging smile on his wind-burned face. "God morgon, Miss Nilsson. I'm sorry to be late." He walked to where Einer leaned against one wall. "I'll just take a place here and join the class, if you please."

Marin bit back the response that leaped to her tongue. *If I please? I don't please at all, and you know it.* Anger roiled through her at his presumptuous action, yet she refused to make a scene over it in front of the students. Likely Talif was counting on that. Well, she'd act as if she'd expected him today and tell him after school that under no circumstances was he to return.

The other students stared at Talif and at her, clearly as surprised as she at the presence of a grown man in the classroom. She ignored the fury in her chest and forced a smile. "Of course you may join us, Mr. Siverson. We're learning English terms for weather today." She turned her gaze deliberately away from him. "We'll repeat the phrases all together once more. Then I will write them on the blackboard, and we will break into small groups to memorize the spelling. Tomorrow we will have a quiz on the terms."

A groan erupted from the older boys.

Marin ignored it. "Repeat after me: *Det är stormar*. It is storming." *Storming inside and out,* she raged silently while the students chanted the phrase.

Talif's deep voice made its way through all the others to her ears no matter how many students spoke at the same time. Even when the students broke into groups and she helped the youngest girls with the weather phrases, the sound of Talif studying aloud with the older boys distracted her.

Once Marin caught Elsbet watching her with sympathy in her eyes. The knowledge that Elsbet saw through Marin's defenses only added fuel to her anger. Her mother's comment flashed through her mind: "A heart blocked off from love grows cold." *Better cold than fiery with pain like Elsbet's.*

Little Sophie tugged at Marin's sleeve.

Marin pushed away her uncomfortable thoughts and smiled down at the girl with the blond braids. "Ja?"

"Did I say it right, Teacher?"

Warmth spread over Marin's cheeks. How could she let Talif fill her thoughts to the point she didn't hear her student? "I'm sorry, Sophie. Would you repeat it for me?"

It took a few times for Sophie to learn to drop the *t* that ended the Swedish *kallt* when she said *cold*, but in the end, she said it properly and beamed when Marin praised her.

The day seemed long to Marin and more difficult than usual with her constant awareness of Talif's presence. By the end of the school day, the anger she nursed created an unfamiliar fatigue within her. Still, she stopped Talif as he prepared to leave with the other students. "Mr. Siverson, I'd like to speak with you."

For a moment he hesitated, and she thought he'd refuse, but then he nodded. "Certainly, Miss Nilsson."

As they'd grown to know each other better, they'd fallen into the practice of calling each other by their first names. It sounded strange to hear him address her formally, though she grudgingly appreciated it in front of the students.

She waited uncomfortably while the other students left before turning to him beside the closed door, with a glance at Moder and Elsbet standing by the stove talking while they started dinner. "What do you think you are doing?" Marin kept her voice low and stood closer to him than she liked, hoping to avoid her mother and sister overhearing the conversation, an almost impossible task. She hated the way her voice shook with the anger she'd held inside for hours.

"Two weeks ago I asked you to tutor me." His spoke quietly, evidently as eager as Marin to keep the conversation between the two of them. "You said—"

"I said I hadn't the time, and I don't."

"I realize that. It was inconsiderate of me to ask you when you're so busy with the school."

"If you believe that, why did you barge into my classroom today?"

His gaze met hers evenly. "I came because I want to improve my English, and I don't know how to do that on my own. I figured if I'm just another student in your school, my learning won't make any extra demands on your time."

The guilt she'd originally felt at refusing to tutor him began to creep back. He'd helped her start the school, he wanted to learn, and she'd turned her back on his request for her assistance. Still, that didn't change the fact that she didn't want him around constantly, and she wasn't ready to let go of her anger at him for shoving his way into her class.

She glared at him, tapping one high-top booted toe against the hard-packed dirt floor. "The school is for children, not men."

Something akin to anger flashed in his blue eyes, and his lips pressed together firmly before he spoke. "I thought the purpose of the school was to help people learn. I may be a man, but I'm a student when it comes to learning the language of my new country, and I need help. I plan to attend class and study hard, like any of the other students." He placed his black hat on his head and nodded grimly. "See you tomorrow morning, Miss Nilsson."

She stepped back quickly to get out of his way as he opened the door.

Then he was gone, leaving Marin frustrated. Her head throbbed. She'd meant to insist he not return to her classroom. Wasn't that what she'd done? It had been the intent behind her words, and certainly Talif Siverson knew that. Through the weeks of teaching, she'd grown accustomed to students acquiescing to her demands. It hadn't occurred to her he'd attend class if she made it clear he wasn't welcome.

She looked toward Moder and Elsbet. Elsbet turned quickly back to the stove and dumped the onions she'd just chopped into a hot, cast-iron frying pan, but Moder returned Marin's gaze. Obviously the women knew what Talif and Marin had discussed in spite of their attempts at privacy.

Marin lifted her arms, feeling helpless. "What can I do, Moder?"

"Teach him."

"But he's a man. He doesn't belong in the school."

"Then tutor him."

"You know I haven't time!"

Moder wiped her hands on her apron. "Would you refuse to allow him in class if he were any other man?"

"Of course." In spite of her instant response, the question caught Marin off guard. Would she truly mind if, for instance, Sophie's father wanted to join the class? Honesty made her admit to herself that, rather than be angry, she'd likely be flattered. But then, there was no man whose presence affected her like Talif's.

Moder still watched her intently. Did she again know what Marin was thinking? Marin blushed. "It doesn't matter whether I 'allow' him in class or not. I can hardly force him out if he shows up, and he says he intends to continue attending."

Moder shrugged. "Then there's nothing to do but accept the fact and teach him, is there?" She put a coat over her shoulders. "I'm going to see whether Einer has the cow milked yet. We need some milk for the cooking."

When Moder had left, Marin walked about the room, picking up the small board slates students had used during the day. Another sign of Talif's help with the school. Another reason to feel guilty for not wanting to teach him.

With a sigh, she set the boards on the floor beside the large blackboard then walked over to Elsbet and reached for a paring knife. "Let me help you slice those potatoes."

"Tack."

For a couple of minutes, they worked together in silence, the only sounds the sizzle of the sharp-smelling onions in the frying pan and the crack of burning wood in the cookstove. Marin's thoughts swirled about Talif, his declaration of intent, and her powerlessness to stop him.

"What do you think, Elsbet? I mean about Talif. Do you agree with Moder?"

Elsbet's gaze stayed on the potatoes as she pared. "Do I agree with what? That you should accept the fact that he is going to attend school, and teach him as you do the other students? Or that you would not be upset if it were any man other than Talif?"

If anyone but Elsbet had asked the question, which so directly struck at the heart of the matter, Marin's anger and embarrassment would have increased. But Elsbet's gentle voice and manner made it easier for Marin to accept the probing questions. "You believe, like Moder, that I care for Talif?"

Elsbet shrugged one shoulder, her attention still on her work. "As more than a friend, perhaps. Are you in love with him? Perhaps not. At least, not yet." She lifted her gaze to Marin. A little frown cut between her brows. "Why don't you allow anyone to court you, Marin? Don't you want to be loved, to be married, to have your own family one day?"

Marin looked away. "Because a man wants to court a woman doesn't mean he loves her. All husbands don't love their wives." She refrained from saying that Elsbet, of all people, should know those things. "Some men only want a woman to take care of things like cooking, cleaning, and sewing."

"I think Talif likes you very much. I think he'd court you if you let him and not just to get a housekeeper."

"I don't want to be courted by him, or marry him, or be his house-keeper. I don't need a husband. I'm a teacher. I don't make enough to live on now, but maybe when I have experience and more settlers come here, I can get a teaching job for the county. Then you and I can live together. We'll be just fine, the two of us, without any men."

Elsbet added the sliced potatoes to the onions in the skillet. "You've never been in love. You don't know what it feels like to love someone."

"I don't want to know what love can be like if it can hurt someone as much as it did you."

"Is that why you don't let anyone court you?"

"Maybe." Marin hadn't meant to let Elsbet know how she felt. She took plates out of the cupboard and began setting the table.

"I still think about Anton," Elsbet said quietly from behind Marin.

"I know." *If she didn't think about him,* Marin thought, *Elsbet wouldn't be so sad.*

"Sometimes I think awful things."

"What do you mean?"

"Sometimes I wonder what would happen if Anton's wife died, whether then he'd want me back."

Marin didn't know what to say. The thought of sweet Elsbet having such thoughts stunned her. Is that what loving someone could do to a person? All the more reason not to fall in love.

"I know," Elsbet continued, "it sounds horrible. I don't truly want her to die. I just want Anton back. I know it's not her fault he left me. If he hadn't married her, he would have married someone else. He simply didn't love me as much as I love him."

The emptiness in Elsbet's voice told Marin how much the truth hurt. An old Swedish proverb slipped into Marin's mind. *A wound never heals enough to hide a scar.* "You aren't the only woman whose intended left her behind in Sweden. It happens too often. Men can't be trusted."

"Not all men are like Anton. Some men truly love their wives—men like Fader."

"Yes." Anyone could see how much Fader and Moder loved each other. Marin weighed her words carefully before speaking. "If a woman could be guaranteed a man would love her the way Fader loves Moder, every woman would gladly fall in love. If you believed another man would love you that way, you'd let someone else court you, too, Elsbet."

Elsbet winced. "We're talking about you. You're nineteen, and you haven't started a hope chest."

"I'm too busy teaching." Not for the world would Marin remind Elsbet that her own hope chest, filled with so many hours of loving work, was still under one of the beds, its contents untouched. She linked her arm through Elsbet's. "One day I'll start that hope chest. You and I will need some things when we start our own home."

Elsbet smiled but didn't look convinced.

Time would prove the truth of Marin's intent. For now, she'd just do as Moder said and accept Talif's presence in her classroom. She'd treat him like any other student. Spring was just around the corner. Field work would soon demand Talif's time and require he abandon his plans to attend school. That would be the end of it.

Chapter 6

Teaching had been a heady combination of joy, fear, study, and lack of sleep for Marin before Talif joined the classroom. Now every day challenged her emotions. She was challenged to keep her attention on the other students and their lessons. She was challenged to keep her gaze from darting to Talif whenever she heard his voice or laugh. The greatest challenge came during the part of each day she spent with the older boys on their specific lessons.

Three weeks after Talif began attending class, Marin approached the older boys with dread. Talif, along with Einer, Jems, and Knute, made up the class. Marin kept her gaze carefully away from Talif as she approached them.

"We'll be working on English words with especially difficult spellings and sounds today," she informed them. "We'll start with words that begin with the letter *k*, but the *k* is silent."

Jems, leaning against the wall with his arms crossed, sneered. "Why would a word have a letter that's silent? That's stupid."

"Be that as it may, there are such words." Jems had been challenging her more lately. He'd started school as excited as the other students to learn, but the last week or so his attitude had changed, and she didn't know why. "We'll start with *kniv*, which is spelled *k-n-i-f-e* in English." Marin picked up one of the small board slates, wrote the word, and held the board for the four to see. "It sounds like *nif* with a long *i*."

"So the *e* is silent like the *k*?" Talif asked.

"Yes." She nodded toward Knute. "If you pronounce the word like we do Knute's name, with a *k* sound, you'll be proclaiming your ignorance of the language."

Knute grinned. "That makes it easy for me to remember."

"For all of us," Talif agreed.

Funny how the simple recognition that she'd made learning such a small thing easier for them filled her with pride. "Another word is the English word *know*, which in Swedish is either *veta*, to know something, or *känna*, to know someone."

"The same word is used for both in English?" Talif questioned again.

"Yes." She wrote the word on the board below *knife*.

"It sounds the same as *no*," Jems protested, "the opposite of *ja*. How do we know which form of the word to use?"

"By the way it's used in a sentence," Marin explained, trying to keep her patience. Jems should have known that rule by now. "Why don't you try using each version in a sentence for me right now? Say the entire sentence in English, of course."

"*No*, I won't." Jems grinned. "I don't *know* how to say it."

Knute and Einer laughed, and Marin could see Talif brush his hand over his face to hide a grin. Marin found Jems's play on words rather amusing, too, but the teacher in her wondered whether the action was inappropriate and disrespectful. Best to let it pass, she decided.

"Very good. Now you, Einer."

Einer and Knute each copied Jems by coming up with twists on the two words. The boys' laughs soon drew the other students' attention. "Back to work, everyone," Marin admonished in her most teacherly voice.

Some of the students turned reluctantly away. Others continued to watch, albeit in a less obvious manner. *Oh well*, Marin thought, *at least they may learn something listening*.

Then it was Talif's turn. When he didn't speak at once, Marin glanced at him. He looked like he was struggling to come up with the sentences. She was about to ask if he needed her to clarify something when he said,

"He know she will say no if he asks to court her."

The class erupted into laughter. Marin felt her cheeks grow warm. Was he teasing her? The other students obviously believed he was speaking of himself and her. His eyes glinted with poorly suppressed laughter.

At least his grammar error allowed her to correct him rather than address the meaning of the sentence. "In that use, you would need to add an *s* to the word *know*, Mr. Siverson. 'He knows she will say no.' Please repeat the sentence using the word correctly." Anger cooled her voice.

"He knows she will say no," he repeated, his eyes still laughing, though not his voice.

"Correct." *Let him wonder whether I mean he said it correctly, or whether he's correct in thinking I'd say no,* she thought, triumph overcoming the anger.

She proceeded to explain the way the word *know* changed depending upon singular or plural references, and how *knew*, the past tense of *know*, also had a sound-alike word in *new*. She instructed Talif and the boys to work together using the words in more sentences and practicing pronouncing and spelling the words.

When she finally turned to go back to the younger children and begin an arithmetic class, she gave a sigh of relief.

Talif watched Marin walk away from himself and the older boys and over to a group of younger children. Her shoulders, which inched closer to her ears while talking with his group, lowered back to their normal position.

Did she always feel uncomfortable teaching the older boys? Certainly it couldn't be easy trying to teach her brother Einer. Brothers didn't often like to learn from sisters, especially in front of other boys.

Marin probably worried that Jems and Knute were too close to her in age to respect her knowledge. That would make teaching them tough for her. Lately it seemed Jems was testing her. Not a lot, just pushing a little more than was proper. The situation would bear watching. Talif wasn't about to let Jems or any of the other students cause problems for Marin.

She'd been a good sport about the humorous sentences they'd come up with today. He'd considered using a less volatile sentence, but to subtly tease her had been too tempting in the end. He smiled, remembering how she'd responded with an even subtler jibe. It was the first time he'd experienced her wit.

After his first day at school, he'd more than half expected Marin to recruit her father and insist he demand Talif quit attending the school. Instead, she taught him every day just as if she didn't wish him gone. Of course, her cool reserve and her reference to him as Mr. Siverson instead of Talif told him clearly that she hadn't changed her mind about his attendance.

The clang of the oven door drew his gaze from where Marin bent over young Eva. Mrs. Nilsson was preparing the stove for baking. Her face looked tired in the dim light of the soddy. The realization of how difficult it must be for Marin's family to go about their daily business with the house filled with students jolted through him. There was barely a minute during the day for the Nilssons to relax and spend alone. Not many families would so graciously disrupt their lives for other people's children to have the opportunity to learn.

A memory slipped into his mind: Marin telling him how she hoped to have "a true schoolhouse one day." His gaze slipped back to her. Her earnest expression as she explained an arithmetic problem to Eva caused a little catch in his heartbeat. Marin's dedication to the students never ceased to amaze him.

She deserved that schoolhouse. But how, since neither the county nor the church could afford one?

His heart sent up a prayer. *Dear Lord, please provide the schoolhouse for which Marin longs. If there's any way I can help, please show me. Amen.*

A picture of the homesteader's old shack flashed into his mind. Was that meant as an answer to his prayer? He dismissed the thought. That tumbledown place wasn't fit for skunks, let alone a school, and was nowhere near as large as this little soddy.

An elbow nudging his side caught his attention. "You plan to study these words with us like the teacher said?" A glint in Jems's eyes added sly innuendo to his question.

"Of course. Just remembering something that needs doing." Talif turned back to the group, disgusted at letting himself get caught by a student, especially Jems, watching Marin.

At noon, the students relaxed and talked while they ate the lunches they'd brought from home. Some children had only buttered bread; others had baked potatoes they'd carried hot to school and left on top of the stove to stay warm. The Nilssons waited to eat until the students were done. Then the family sat down at the table while the students went outside for fresh air.

Talif let Eva and Sophie sweet-talk him into playing fox and geese with the younger children. He'd forgotten the joy of simple play in snow under a blue sky, with cold temperatures crisping the air and wood smoke adding a pleasant, warm fragrance.

Marin's ringing of the cowbell brought an end to the games. Talif entered the home-turned-school with the children. Students took advantage during the last minute or two of chatting and laughing together while they removed their coats, mittens, and scarves.

As always, Talif's glance caught sight of Marin. She was picking up the small board slates the ten-year-olds had been using before lunch, nodding and smiling as Sophie regaled her with exaggerated tales of Talif's attempts at fox and geese.

Marin's face changed suddenly from a smile and a pleasantly distracted air to frozen shock. She stared down at the small slate in her hands, the color draining from her cheeks.

Shocked at the sudden change, Talif slipped up behind her and looked over her shoulder at the slate. He was dimly aware of children snickering. "What is it?" he asked, his voice discreetly low.

"Nothing." Marin flipped the board over and stepped briskly away.

But not before he saw it. Someone had drawn a heart, and inside, the words "Teacher + Talif."

He swallowed a groan. This wasn't going to do his cause any good at all.

Chapter 7

One evening two weeks later, Marin rested her elbows on the table, her chin on the palms of her hands, and stared at the open New Testament. She was so weary that the words seemed to swim in the wavering light from the kerosene lamp. The warmth from the stove behind her only made her more tired.

Her gaze slid to the small board slate beside the book. She'd meant to make notes on the slate for tomorrow's lessons, but it remained blank. Her mind refused to follow her intention to plan.

Elsbet sat down opposite her. "You look exhausted. Perhaps you should go to bed."

"No." Marin shook her head. "I haven't planned tomorrow's lessons."

"You'll be too tired to teach if you don't get some sleep. Something will come to you for the lessons tomorrow. It always does."

Does it seem so easy to everyone else, Marin wondered, *to find ways to teach?* "It would be easier if we had proper supplies. I'd like to teach geography, but how, without maps or a globe? I draw maps on the blackboard, but there isn't a way to save them so the students can study them again later. I considered asking the students to write letters to people back in Sweden telling them in English about their new life here. How can they do that on these small board slates? Paper is too precious to expect their parents to allow them to use any for just a lesson."

"Maybe you can have them work on a letter together and write it

499

on the large blackboard."

"But I wanted them to write the words themselves, to practice writing English."

Elsbet's eyebrows lifted in question. "Can't you have a different student write each sentence? Or have them write a sentence on their slates and then you write the sentence on the large board so they can see whether they've written it correctly?"

Marin smiled wearily. "You came up with a solution so easily. I should have asked you for help earlier. Perhaps you should be the teacher."

"Oh no." Elsbet shook her head, smiling. "That's not for me. I can help you with the simple, everyday things children need to learn, but I haven't the head for schooling you've had since you were a wee one. I wish I could be more help to you. I've noticed Talif helping lately."

"Yes. He's quite smart and completed his schooling in Sweden. He only needs help with his English. Since he can spend more time during these winter months away from his farm, he offered to help teach the older boys arithmetic. It's such a help. Knute is usually a conscientious student, but Einer and Jems prefer to tease and cause trouble sometimes. I suppose they're bored or don't like to learn from someone so close to their own age, and a woman at that."

Elsbet casually brushed at a bread crumb that had escaped the after-dinner wipe-down of the table. "So perhaps Talif's insistence on attending school is a blessing in disguise."

Marin's back tensed. "Not such a blessing that it overcomes the difficulties he brings along. At least no more hearts have shown up on students' slates since that awful experience a couple of weeks ago, but I hate the students' sly looks and snickers every time I need to talk with Talif."

"Children are like that. Anything that looks like possible romance amuses them. You know that. It will pass."

"I hope you're right. Teaching isn't nearly as much fun as before the innuendoes began."

"What advice would you give a student in a similar situation, Marin?"

"To ignore it. That to give the teaser a reaction only increases the teasing." Marin laughed, realizing Elsbet's point. "See, you're a natural teacher."

"Only in practical, everyday matters, as I said before." Elsbet stood up as a loud knock interrupted them. "Not in reading, writing, and arithmetic," she said over her shoulder as she hurried to open the door.

Talif entered with the winter cold. Marin was only dimly aware of their greetings as her gaze met Talif's across the room. Annoyance slipped through her veins. Since Talif began attending school, his evening visits with Fader had almost stopped, and from the look in Talif's eyes, he wasn't here to see Fader now.

Marin felt herself tense as Talif removed his hat and gloves and crossed the room to the table. A cylindrical object under one of his arms caught her attention. "*God afton*, Miss Nilsson. I mean, good evening."

"Good evening, Mr. Siverson." Marin straightened her spine and allowed an invisible wall of reserve to slide over her face. "What can I do for you?"

He shifted his weight from one booted foot to the other. "I'd like to do something for you and for the other students." He took the roll of cloth from beneath his arm and handed it to her across the table.

"What is this?" Suspicion made her frown. She accepted the material reluctantly when he didn't respond. Pushing aside the New Testament and slate to make room, she began to unroll the object. It was rectangular in shape and only two-thirds as long as the table's width. The off-white material contrasted sharply with the rough pine boards of the table. Bright-colored embroidered letters began to appear. "A sampler?" When the whole was revealed, she gasped. "Oh!" She covered her cheeks with her fingers.

A picture of a small white cottage with a thatched roof and a barn decorated the top of the sampler. Beneath the picture the Swedish alphabet marched primly, and beside that the English alphabet. Marin ran her fingers lightly across the finely wrought, colorful letters. "It's beautiful. Where did you get it?"

"My sister, Karin, made it for me before I left for America." Talif pointed to the picture at the top. "That's our parents' place in Sweden."

Marin's conscience struggled for supremacy. The sampler would make a wonderful teaching aid, and the school desperately needed such things. Yet. . .

"I can't possibly accept this." Setting her jaw as firmly as her determination, she began rolling the sampler back up. Such mementos from loved ones in the homeland, people who might never again be seen, were precious, even priceless. "A gift from your sister. . ." She shook her head.

Talif reached out and stopped her from continuing to roll the sampler. "Now it's her gift and mine to you and to the students." He glanced at the curtain that hid the beds and behind which Elsbet and Mrs. Nilsson had discreetly disappeared. He leaned closer and lowered his voice. "You give of yourself every day to others who have come to this new land, to help them have a better life. Please, allow me the pleasure of giving to the students also. *Var god.*"

"But it must be so special to you."

"It is." A grin lit his blue eyes. "Isn't that the best kind of gift to give?"

Marin ignored the question. "This sampler is part of your family's heritage now. You should keep it to pass it down to your children and their children."

A strange, almost hurt look filled his eyes for a moment then disappeared behind a thin reserve. "Perhaps by the time I have children of my own, the students will no longer need the sampler." He cleared his throat. "I promise you, my sister will love knowing her sampler is helping students in America."

Marin gently held the sampler against her chest. "Just before you came, I told Elsbet how badly we need supplies for teaching." She tried unsuccessfully to keep tears from welling up in her eyes.

"You keep adding to that prayer list of things you need for the school, and pretty soon there won't be anything left God hasn't provided."

It seemed to Marin that God supplied most of the things through Talif. The thought ran through her mind that perhaps God found it amusing to do so, to keep bringing the one man who attracted her into her life. Had God also brought this man into her life because she was meant to be attracted to Talif? Her heart skittered away from the possibility.

"Thank you, Talif, for your thoughtful gift." She couldn't simply dismiss him after this, couldn't say, "Thank you, and good-bye now." She gestured toward the table. "Let me get you a cup of coffee and a cookie before you go."

"Tack." Talif sat down on one of the upended packing boxes beside the table.

Marin set the sampler down and turned to the stove. She reached for the large graniteware kettle, which still held warm coffee from dinner. Marin poured some for herself and Talif then took from a tin in the homemade pine cupboard some of the eggless cookies Elsbet had made earlier in the day.

When she finally seated herself across from Talif, he said, "I overheard some of the students' parents speaking to you at church last Sunday, telling you that you're doing a good job."

"Yes, it's nice they think so."

"They're right."

His praise pleased her, and she realized it meant more to her than the parents' praise. After all, he saw her teaching every day. None of the parents had visited the school.

The thought of Sunday meetings brought less pleasing recollections of comments by the adults in the congregation. More than one student's mother had asked her whether she and Talif were courting. Of course, Marin denied it in emphatic terms, but the questions made it obvious students and parents alike found Talif's presence in the classroom curious.

"The Linders told me their children are helping them learn English at home," Talif told her. "I suspect the same is happening in the other families. Your teaching is touching lives beyond your classroom."

Marin had never thought of that possibility. She lifted her cup to take a sip of coffee and, looking over the rim, found Talif's blue-eyed gaze intent on her. Suddenly, unexpectedly, she felt shy.

"Moder, Elsbet," she called out, "come see what Talif brought for the school."

The women admired the sampler then sat down to have coffee with

Talif and Marin. The embroidered picture of Talif's home in Sweden stirred the Nilssons' memories, and soon they and Talif were sharing stories of life in the homeland.

While the others talked, Marin discreetly studied Talif. Why hadn't she ever noticed the smattering of freckles on the bridge of his nose, or the way little lines—from laughter or from squinting against the sunshine while working in the fields, or both—fanned out from the corners of his eyes? She'd never considered him a handsome man, but he had a fine, broad, honest face. He'd grown obviously stronger since they met, likely from plowing never-before-plowed land with its tangle of prairie grass roots.

Maybe she'd reacted too strongly to his choice to study with her class. After all, he only wanted to learn to better speak and write English. What was so awful in that? He'd helped her get the school started, made the blackboard and slates, assisted with teaching the other students arithmetic, and now given the school that wonderful alphabet sampler. Surely, if anyone deserved to take part in her class, Talif Siverson did.

After all, just because she wasn't in love with the man was no cause to be unfriendly toward him, was it?

Chapter 8

Talif ran the palm of his hand over the board he'd been smoothing with a piece of broken glass. His lips stretched into a tired smile of satisfaction. No students would end up with slivers in their backsides from this bench seat.

He laid the board on the packed-earth floor and rubbed his right shoulder. Working on that board for hours left its mark on his muscles.

Talif let his gaze wander about his small sod house, lingering on one homemade bench after another. He'd spent hours and hours the last month tearing apart the departed homesteader's shack, hauling the wood home, and cutting and pounding it into small benches for the school. He'd made good progress on his plan for Marin's schoolhouse...or rather, on the plan he believed the Lord had given him for the schoolhouse.

Rain spattered against his only window, in front of which he sat on one of his homemade benches while working, taking advantage of the little sunlight the clouds and rain let in. If this spring storm kept up, the roof would be dripping water and mud soon.

Mud. April's warmth had melted the last of the snow, chased the frost from the ground, and turned solid ground into squishy, boot-sucking mud. Too wet for planting or for building sod houses. When the rains stopped and the ground dried out somewhat, he and the other farmers could get into the fields.

It would be late summer or early fall before the schoolhouse became a reality. Impatience tugged at him as though he were a puppet with annoying strings tied to his limbs. Through each step of preparing for the school, he daydreamed of the expression he'd see on Marin's face when she first viewed the building.

There were still things to do—ordering the window glass and the wood for the window frames and door, for instance. He'd need to do that in Benson, thirty-odd miles across the prairie, the nearest town with a sawmill. There wasn't enough wood left from the homesteader's shack to use for the frames and door, and what was there wasn't good enough quality for such use anyway. No telling when the land would firm up enough for the Benson trip. He'd need to work the trip in after planting. Some things in life couldn't be put off, and planting fields was one of them.

He wished he could put all his energy into building Marin's school, but that wasn't possible. It would all come about in God's timing, of course, but waiting was difficult.

Marin's heart pounded as she looked about the crowded building at the congregation. She could barely believe this day had finally arrived: the first Sunday in May, the day of the school program signifying the end of the school year.

It seemed a good time for the school year to end. Spring heralded an end of the old and beginning of the new. Hadn't the community just celebrated the coming of spring on April 30, with the Swedish Walpurgis Night celebration? Everyone had gathered around bonfires and enjoyed good food while singing and talking about plans for the warm months ahead.

Students would be busy preparing fields and gardens soon. Too busy for schoolwork. The longer, warmer days had already melted the snow cover and left the land so muddy many of the students found it difficult to traverse the prairie to school. Yes, it was time to end the first school year.

The Skarstedt family owned the largest sod house in the area, and they'd graciously offered it for this special Sunday. In spite of its size, parishioners filled it to overflowing. Unlike most of the sod houses, this house had a separate bedroom. There the students gathered after morning church service, waiting for the program to begin.

Marin's gaze wandered over the students, meeting their bright, eager gazes, noting the cheeks red with anticipation, admiring the Sunday-best clothing, and listening to the excited whispers. She knew the importance of the choice of clothing, how it made one feel better about oneself and more capable. She herself wore her best dress, with a new lace collar made by Elsbet especially for this occasion and Moder's precious silver pin, which had been passed down for three generations.

Even Talif wore a suit today. It wasn't new. *My*, Marin thought, *he looks handsome.*

Talif hadn't much part in today's program. She'd thought it might appear improper to the parents or at the very least cause more speculation by adults in the congregation. He'd agreed to help her keep the program running according to plan and take a small part in one skit. To her relief, he seemed satisfied with that.

She lifted an index finger to her lips. "Shhh. It's time for the program to begin. We'll do everything just like we practiced. When others are performing, those of you waiting here are to show them respect and keep quiet. No more whispering. If you've any questions while you wait, ask them of Talif. When it's your turn to perform, don't forget your curtsies and bows." Marin took a deep breath and gave the students a big smile. "I'm so proud of each of you. You will all do wonderfully."

Talif, moving to stand beside her, reaffirmed quietly, "Ja, they will."

Marin glanced at him. The calm certainty in the gaze that met hers spread sweet serenity through her. In spite of her assurance to the students that they would all do wonderfully, her desire for them to make her look good had caused her to worry. Now the knowledge hit her that whatever the students did would be fabulous in their parents' eyes, truly wonderful simply because the students had worked so hard to learn and to put on this program.

Yes, of course everything will go well, she thought. "Now, Eva, Sophia, and Stina, since you're the first to perform, come stand here by the door and wait while I introduce you."

Faces beaming, the girls hurried forward.

Sophia, blue eyes sparkling, put her plump hands over the coiled braids above her ears. "See my ribbons, Teacher? They match the black stripes in my dress."

"The ribbons are very pretty, Sophia, and so is your dress. You look beautiful." Marin smiled at Eva and Stina then turned the smile on the rest of the class. "All the girls look beautiful, and all the boys look handsome." She winked at Sophia and dropped her voice to a whisper. "Be very quiet now while I go tell the parents what you and Eva and Stina are going to do, all right?"

Sophia nodded, her hair ribbons bouncing against her shoulders.

Marin entered the other room, walking over to the square oak table covered with the fine lace cloth. The table served as the altar during the church service. She could smell the comforting scent of the candle that had burned on the altar during the service.

She stood beside the table and faced the congregation, her hands folded primly in front of her green dress with tiny white lace edging the collar. Off to one side sat a special guest, Miss Allen, the teacher from town who had so kindly given Marin advice and encouragement months earlier. She'd made the long trip today to see the students' program. Marin hoped she could return the favor in a couple of weeks when the town students gave their own program.

The parents' faces look as excited and proud as the students', Marin thought. She greeted them in Swedish. "Welcome to the first program of our congregation's school. The students have worked hard over the last months, and each one should be proud of what he or she has learned. They've also worked hard on this program. We hope you'll enjoy it. For our first presentation, Stina and Sophia Linder and Eva Skarstedt will sing a song in English about the days of the week."

The song set the program off to a good start. Marin had written the song with its simple tune. The lyrics told of common housekeeping duties for each day of the week. The students performed actions indicating laundering, baking, and such, which made it apparent to those in the audience who only spoke Swedish which day of the week was represented.

When the ditty was over, the audience burst into applause. At the appreciation, the little girls smiled widely and curtsied again and again, bringing enchanted laughter from their admirers.

Knute Linder, one of the most intelligent of Marin's students, read in Swedish an essay on the beginnings of their new country. The congregation listened wide-eyed and intent while he told of the Stamp Act, the Boston Tea Party, and the Revolutionary War.

The lesson on the United States continued with Orpha Stenvall and Viola Linder, thirteen and ten, reading the Declaration of Independence in Swedish. Marin had spent many long hours, working long into the night by the wavering light of the kerosene lamp, translating the work from English into Swedish. She and Talif had debated whether it should be presented in the new language or the language of the homeland, and Swedish won. Learning to speak English was important, but the adult immigrants—and even Marin's students—hadn't enough knowledge of the language to understand such a long and involved presentation. More important, Marin and Talif decided, was that the audience understood one of its new country's most important documents.

When Orpha and Viola were done, the listeners affirmed Marin and Talif's decision by not only clapping but also cheering. Obviously they agreed with the sentiments of their new country's founders. Marin lifted her gaze above the crowd and searched out Talif where he stood at the bedroom door. His grin and wink made her laugh from the joy of sharing in the wonder of this special moment.

Other students followed with songs and recitations. Finally, it was time for the largest event. Marin introduced it. "Next is a skit. The class wrote it as a joint project, and they did a fine job indeed. It involves situations in which we all find ourselves, simple things like greeting people, asking for directions, and buying things in stores. You'll hear common English phrases, phrases we will all use many times in the years to come. Every student in the class will take part. Talif Siverson will play the part of a store clerk. And now, the Prairie School Players perform for your pleasure."

As Marin walked away, she passed eight-year-old Sture and ten-year-old Anders Skarstedt as they headed to the stage area. She knew her own brothers, Einer and August, were coming from the other direction. The four would begin the first scene, greeting and introducing each other.

"Good morning. How are you, Anders?" Marin heard Einer ask as she reached her place in the back of the room behind the audience.

As she watched, contentment at her students' presentation filled her heart. *Do all teachers feel this incredible sense of satisfaction at their students' accomplishments?* she wondered. Her gaze rested on Miss Allen. She didn't speak Swedish, so she couldn't have understood everything. Yet judging from her expression, she was enjoying the program. Marin hoped this experienced teacher felt the students were doing as well as Marin did.

At the end of the skit, Marin joined the students. They all faced the congregation and recited together Psalm 23 in English. Then Marin invited the audience to join them in reciting the psalm in Swedish.

Before they were done, tears glittered in some of the parents' eyes, and tears blurred Marin's sight as well. Marin thanked the audience for coming and the students for their hard work. She spoke of the things the students had learned during the months of schooling, of how far they'd come, and of the goals she hoped the school could help students achieve in the future. Her own parents' faces gleamed with pride, making Marin feel humble in response.

She was about to dismiss everyone when Talif stepped forward. "Excuse me, Miss Nilsson. There's something I and the other students would like to say."

Surprise kept her from speaking, but she nodded at him and began to step back. Talif touched her elbow, stopping her, then moved his hand away.

"You came today," he said to the audience, "to honor the students for the efforts they've put forth over the last few months and to listen to examples of what they've learned. They deserve your respect, and it's easy to see they've received it. There's someone else here today who deserves your respect and that of the students, as well as all our thanks. Miss Marin Nilsson, one of the finest teachers on the prairie."

The congregation rose as one, clapping and smiling. Calls of "Ja" and "*Många tack*, Miss Nilsson" reached Marin's ears and heart.

Before the ovation died down, Talif faced Marin and continued. "The families wanted you to know how much your devotion to their children means to them, so they've bought you a gift." He looked over at Jems Stenvall. "Jems?"

Her heart lodged in her throat, Marin watched Jems walk over to the stove and pick up from beside it what appeared to be a packing box covered with a woven rug. He brought the box over and held it in front of her. His expression was sober, his eyes serious as he spoke. "Miss Nilsson, all of us students thank you for all you've done for us. We can't truly repay you, but we hope this will show you how grateful we are for your teaching."

Marin covered her lips with her fingers and swallowed twice before she could respond. "Thank you, Jems." She recognized it as an extraordinary speech from the often rebellious student. Who had selected him as the gift giver? The choice was a lovely gesture.

She reached out shaking fingers and lifted the brown-and-tan-striped rug. At the sight of the gift beneath it, she dropped the rug to the floor with a cry.

Jems, Talif, and the other students laughed, and Marin, recognizing their laughter as joy at her response, joined them. She lifted out the gift: a globe of the world. She held it high to show the crowd.

Turning to Talif, she asked, "How did you ever. . . ?"

She didn't need to finish the question. Talif grinned. "All the families contributed to it. Miss Allen sent for it. More than that, she told the county school superintendent about our plan. He decided that since the students' families went to such trouble to start a school, the county could spare a little of their funds to make up for what we hadn't raised in the cost of the globe."

Marin's gaze darted to Miss Allen. The town teacher rose and joined Marin and Talif. "You and the students deserve this gift. You are to be commended, Miss Nilsson. Your dedication to the students is inspiring. I feel privileged to know you."

Marin murmured her thanks as the congregation once again broke into applause.

Marin could barely keep her emotions in control while the parents, one by one, thanked her before leaving, and the female students stopped to give her hugs.

Standing in the background, Talif watched it all, sharing in Marin's happiness from afar. Miss Allen's words rang true: Marin well deserved the praise.

The rest of spring and summer loomed long ahead of him, months without seeing Marin in class every day. But the thought of the surprise gift awaiting her before classes resumed next fall made his heart quick-step. The next school program wouldn't be held in anyone's home but in a school, as was proper. In Marin's school.

He'd spoken with Einer, Knute, and Jems after the program, and they'd agreed to help. Their eyes had shone with excitement at the idea. He knew they'd find time to slip away from their chores and field work to help him when the time came.

Talif leaned back against the wall, arms crossed over his suit front, a smile on his face, joy in his chest, and Marin in his sight and heart.

Chapter 9

Marin knelt in the late August twilight, weeding the garden in the cool of the evening. She was grateful for the light breeze that rustled through the corn and kept the mosquitoes away. Crickets and cicadas sang their songs for her as she worked. Scents of moist earth, green plants, and humid air surrounded her.

Standing up, she stretched, pressing her hands against the small of her back as she lifted her gaze and stared over the land toward Talif's home. His roof was barely visible over the tall prairie grass and her father's field of corn. Grasshoppers had invaded the county again, destroying many crops but for some reason sparing the Nilsson, Siverson, and other nearby fields.

Talif's plowed land lay on the side of his home opposite the Nilsson farm. A small rise hid his fields from her view even in the early spring before the wild grasses and crops grew high. Sometimes on windy days during the spring, she'd seen thin clouds of dirt in the air and known he was working his fields. Now no such signs disclosed his actions.

She hardly dared acknowledge to herself that she missed seeing him every day as she had during the school term, hardly dared acknowledge the ache that tugged at her heart when she remembered all his kind assistance with the school. Last winter, even before school began, Talif had stopped at the house often to visit with Fader. Field work kept all the homesteaders busy during the summer. She knew Talif was no exception.

They all worked late into the evenings. Only when rain kept Talif from the fields did he stop by the house to see Fader now. Talif always greeted Marin pleasantly when he stopped, asking after her, but it wasn't the same as when they worked on his lessons or he helped with the class in some way.

Would he join the class again this fall? He hadn't said, and she wouldn't ask.

Soon she'd need to begin planning lessons again. Likely field work would prevent any but the youngest boys from attending the first fall classes. She expected the parents would allow most of the girls to come to school except during harvest when all female hands were needed to bake and serve the men when they came from the fields.

The black-and-white dog came running out of the cornfield and across the garden rows, eager to greet her. "Sven!" Marin grabbed at the dog. "Come. The garden is no place for you. If Moder sees you among the beans. . ." She let the warning stay unfinished as she urged the dog across the furrows.

"Where've you been, Sven? Did you go with Einer? You're as mysterious as he's been, heading off every night as soon as the evening meal is over, refusing to tell me where he's going. I can't believe Fader lets him go like that."

It wasn't like Fader to let Einer leave that way. The cows needed milking each evening, and Fader and the boys often worked in the fields late. Besides, where could Einer possibly go? They lived too far from town for that to be his destination. She'd asked Fader where Einer went, but he hadn't told her.

Petting Sven's head, she looked out over the prairie then up at the sky where the love star announced the coming of night. Something strange was going on—that was certain.

❧

Talif lifted his hat with one hand and wiped the sweat from his forehead with his opposite forearm. Einer, Knute, and Jems imitated him.

Talif grimaced to hide a grin. Almost nine in the evening and still warm enough that he and the boys broke a sweat working on the building.

514

Of course, cutting prairie sod into three-by-two bricks and laying them up two layers thick to build a house would probably make a man sweat in the midst of a Minnesota winter.

He took a tin dipper of water from the bucket beside him and drank down a refreshing swig. Einer followed suit.

Talif rested his hands on his hips, surveying the building. "You've done a good night's work, boys." Talif studied the cloudless sky. "If the weather holds, we can start the roof tomorrow. Once that's on, we should be able to finish the school by this time next week."

Einer wiped his hands on the back of his jeans and grinned. "Marin's going to be mighty surprised."

"She'd better be." Talif looked from boy to boy. "You've all kept your word? Haven't told anyone but your fathers?"

They all nodded.

"Good. It'd be a crying shame if Miss Nilsson caught wind of what we're doing."

"I haven't told anyone else, but. . ." Knute cleared his throat. "Fader told Moder."

Talif wasn't too surprised. "Well, that's to be expected. Seems men can't keep secrets from their wives no matter how hard they try. Besides, I imagine your mothers insisted on knowing where you boys have been going each evening."

Knute nodded, looking relieved by Talif's response. "Moder wants to help. She's a Dala painter. She thought, if it's all right with you, Talif, she could paint pictures on the door and window lintels."

"Sounds like a great idea. It would sure make the school more attractive. I'll talk with her about it at Sunday service."

Knute leaned over to grab the water dipper, but Talif figured the boy did so more to hide his pride in Talif's response to his mother's offer than because Knute wanted the water.

Soon the boys left for home, leaving Talif alone with the soon-to-be schoolhouse. He walked inside the roofless building, imagining it filled with benches, students, and the most beautiful Swedish teacher on the prairie.

He sighed deeply. "Oh Lord, please let her love it as much I think she will."

❧

Marin sat with her brothers and sisters in the bed of Fader's spring wagon as they bounced across the prairie under the Sunday morning sun. The straw beneath her softened the jolting somewhat but poked through the blanket she sat on and through her stockings, making her calves itch. The back of her head hit the side of the wagon with a thump as the wagon went over a particularly rough bump. "Ouch." She winced and pressed the palm of her hand against the back of her favorite blue sunbonnet. "How much longer before we're there, Fader?"

"Soon. Have patience."

She could hear the laughter in his voice. She wasn't amused. She glanced at Elsbet, who sat beside her, and didn't bother to disguise her disgust. "I don't know why it's such a secret where services will be held today. It's never been a secret before."

Elsbet smiled and patted Marin's calico-covered knee. "May as well enjoy the ride and let Fader enjoy his secret."

They'd passed Talif's home minutes earlier, so obviously the meeting wouldn't be held there. The Linder and Stenvall families lived in the direction they were headed. She hoped the meeting wouldn't be the Stenvall home, which was more cramped than most of the congregation members' houses. Immediately she felt ashamed for her attitude. What could be more crowded than her own home when she taught school?

Marin stretched her neck, trying in vain to see over the wagon's side. The sounds and smells didn't help. The prairie was filled with the scent of earth and the sound of wind rustling through crisping leaves of corn. With a half sigh, half inelegant snort, she gave up and let her mind drift to lesson plans. She mentally listed English words for the everyday lives of her students: *fields, plows, crops, farm, farmer.*

She felt a smile tug at the corners of her mouth. Talif would say this showed she was a God-made teacher. A trickle of sadness slid through her. She missed his presence in her life, missed his encouragement of her teaching. Well, no sense dwelling on that. She forced her mind back to the list. *Trädgård*, garden; *växa*, grow; *grönsaker*, vegetables; *ko*, cow.

Entertained with the list, she didn't notice the wagon slowing and stopping. "Everyone out," Fader called.

Marin stood, looking about. In front of them sat a sod house, one she'd never seen. Rectangular, it had a door in the middle and a window on each side. Someone had cut down the prairie grass in front of the house, and half a dozen horse-drawn wagons stood in the yard. She recognized a number of the teams as belonging to church members.

"Who lives here?" she asked as Fader helped her from the wagon.

"No one."

She opened her mouth to question further, but the twinkle in Fader's eyes told her it would be useless.

The planks making up the door stood unweathered against the prairie winds and still held the smell of newly cut wood. Fader held the door for the family, Marin entering last. She paused a step past the threshold, her gaze wandering over the congregation-filled room as curiosity grew stronger instead of lessening.

The freshly whitewashed walls added light and cheer. The unusual luxury of a window on each end of the building let in additional sunlight and warmth. On the wall facing her hung a painted blackboard like the one Talif had made for the school. Below it, a crate stood on end, three books on the only shelf as though the crate were intended as a bookcase. A metal stove stood square in the middle of the room. Primarily women and children sat on the crude benches facing the far wall. Men and older boys with hats in hands stood along the walls. A small table between the benches and far wall served as an altar. A white cloth with a cross made of Hardanger embroidery covered the table. Two silver candlesticks held candles for the service, and a Bible lay between them. The pleasant scent from the warm candle wax mingled with the odor of fresh earth.

"Good morning, Marin." Talif's whispered greeting came from beside her.

She turned her head to smile at him but didn't think to answer, her mind still attempting to understand where this place came from and why Fader had kept it a secret.

"Come, Marin." Fader's hand against the small of her back urged her forward. She followed her mother and siblings to the front row of benches, which for some reason remained empty in spite of the standing members.

Marin found it difficult to keep her attention on the service and the pastor's words about the Lord bringing all things to a time of harvest. Her gaze and mind kept wandering about the room, noticing every little thing, trying to figure it all out. When the service was over except for the final blessing, the pastor finally mentioned the building.

"The Lord has brought much to harvest in our little congregation this year," he began, "including this wonderful new *kyrka*, church, in which to worship. One day we will have a building of wood or brick, but for the moment, we have a temple filled with love and devotion, and I am sure that makes it a magnificent temple in the eyes and heart of the Lord."

Murmured "amens" and nodding heads showed agreement.

"Our gratitude goes out to the one who conceived the idea for this building, who gave the land for it, and who gave of his own labor and funds to build it. Talif Siverson, please accept our thanks."

Marin whipped her head around in stunned surprise to look at Talif, who still stood beside the door, his face now a ruddy red from the attention and applause of the congregation. Talif had done this, created this place, given it from his own land and labor?

"Every family has contributed something," the pastor continued. "I especially want to honor Einer Nilsson, Knute Linder, and Jems Stenvall, who helped Talif build the church."

Marin's gaze found Einer's face with its pleased but embarrassed expression. This was where he'd disappeared all those evenings!

The pastor lifted his right arm in a sweeping motion. "Mrs. Linder decorated the lintels with Dala painting."

Marin liked the cheer added to the otherwise plain walls by the typical Dala picture elements: a simple, almost childlike style, oversized flowers, bright colors, and people wearing traditional Swedish outfits.

"The Stenvalls contributed a water bucket and dipper," the pastor continued. "Mrs. Nilsson and Elsbet made curtains for the windows, and

Mrs. Skarstedt sewed a curtain for the bookshelf. The women brought their gifts today."

Marin stared in amazement as the women carried the items to the front and laid them reverently on the makeshift altar. When had Elsbet and Moder found time to make the curtains without Marin's knowledge?

After thanking the women, the pastor said, "There are some here who still don't know of this building's complete purpose."

Marin brought her gaze to his and was surprised to find him smiling at her.

"Specifically," he continued, "Miss Marin Nilsson and most of her students. Einer?"

Einer stood and, carrying a rectangular plank, walked to stand beside the pastor. Then he held the plank for everyone to see.

Marin gasped. PRAIRIE CHURCH AND SCHOOL, she read. The words were in script, in two lines, the top in English, the bottom in Swedish. She covered her lips with her fingers. Tears blurred her vision. Through her wonder, she heard the pastor's words. "This building began as a school, a place for our children to learn, a place for our own dedicated Miss Nilsson to teach them."

She missed the rest, the few additional words or phrases, the final blessing. She wanted to turn, to look at Talif, to thank him. How could he possibly have done this marvelous thing? She'd scorned his attentions. In return he'd only given good back to her, encouraged her dream, assisted with teaching ideas, and now built a school.

The wonder of the new school paled beside the other thoughts and feelings flooding her, crumbling the walls she'd built around her heart. Such a man as Talif would never betray a woman as Elsbet's fiancé had betrayed her. A man like Talif would remain devoted to the woman he chose to love.

Marin caught her bottom lip between her teeth. Had she given away any chance of Talif's love? Her chest felt as though squeezed in a vise. She'd hardly seen him the last few months. Had he lost interest in her? But he'd built this school. Had he done so because he loved her or because he also cared deeply for the students? Hope fluttered in her heart. If she received another chance at Talif's love, she wouldn't be so foolish as to refuse it again.

❧

Early the next morning, Marin hurried down the ruts that formed a road between the Nilsson farm and Talif's place. She breathed a sigh of relief as she passed his home apparently undetected and continued along toward the new schoolhouse.

She saw the sign hung above the schoolhouse door long before she reached the building: PRAIRIE CHURCH AND SCHOOL. It sent joy humming through her.

A long piece of carved wood rested on the large flat stone Talif had placed for a doorstep. The sight of the wooden piece brought Marin to a breathless stop six feet from the house. She recognized the piece. Not that specific piece, but the design, like a long, beautiful chisel. Any Swedish woman would recognize the traditional courting request. Bring it inside, and she agreed to be courted by the giver. Leave it on the doorstep, and the giver knew his heart's request was rejected.

Her breath came short and quick as she walked toward it, step by slow step. She stared at it long and hard before kneeling to examine the intricate carving of hearts and flowers with a trembling index finger. It was Talif's work, of course. She lifted the piece and hugged it to her heart, whispering silent thanksgiving to the Lord for the second chance.

Marin carried the courting board inside with her, began to set it down on the desk, then changed her mind. With one hand, she untied her bonnet and laid it on the desk, then began slowly walking around the room, glad to at last be alone to absorb the wonder of this school built for her and her dream.

❧

Talif leaned against the door frame of the open door, watching Marin walking about the room, lost in her own thoughts. He'd known as soon as he saw the courting board gone from the doorstep that she'd accepted his request, but his heart stumbled in joy at the way she clutched it to her. Warmth spread through his chest at the reverence with which she ran her fingers across the simple desk and the back of the barrel chair he'd made her.

Even knowing she welcomed his courting, he felt tentative stepping inside, as if entering new territory. And weren't they? A territory filled with new joys, and new challenges as well. He walked slowly across the packed-dirt floor toward where she stood with her back toward him. "Marin?"

He'd spoken quietly so as not to startle her, but she swung about like a frightened bird, her blue eyes first wide with fright then shining with welcome and something similar to embarrassment. Instinctively he reached to comfort her, his hands on her arms. "I didn't want to frighten you."

"You didn't. I mean, you did, but only for a moment."

His touch made her nervous, he could see. Disappointed, he removed his hands from her arms, reminding himself they were only beginning the move from friendship to courtship.

Marin's lashes hid her eyes from his view as she glanced down at the board she still carried. "I–I'm honored you wish to court me. Thank you for this. It's beautiful."

"You're welcome. I'm honored you agreed."

Her gaze darted about the room. "And this. . .the school. . .everything. I don't know how to begin to thank you."

"By using it for the teaching God created you to do." He took the board from her and set it on the desk. Then gently he brushed the fingers of his right hand over the curve of her cheek, rejoicing when she didn't flinch from his touch. "I wish it could be a wooden building, but I couldn't afford that now, and neither could the congregation."

"That will come in time."

He saw belief in her eyes, and it reinforced his own. Would they help build that school one day together? Would their own children attend it? He swept the thought away. Moving too fast again. She'd only just agreed to court.

Yet unless he was mistaken, there was more than belief in the school to come in her eyes. There was joy at the thought of *them*, of the two of them as a couple. Anticipation? Faith?

His hand slid to the back of her neck, and he leaned close until, an inch away from her lips, he locked her gaze in his and whispered, "May I kiss you, Miss Nilsson?"

"Y—yes."

He touched his lips to hers tenderly, lost in wonder at the gift, the treasure that was Marin, at the hope that she offered him in agreeing to court. One kiss grew to two, gentle, questioning. Then to more, exploring, thanking. Until with a sweet sigh, she leaned against his chest, and his chin rested against her hair. And forgetting all over again not to move too quickly, he said, "I love you, Marin Nilsson. Is that all right?"

Marin shifted her head until he could see the joy shining in her eyes. "It's perfect."

As he drew her into another embrace, he could only agree.

Epilogue

June 1874

The summer breeze tugged playfully at the wildflowers tucked into Marin's coronet braid and tossed the heads of the flowers she carried as she stood outside the church and school, waiting impatiently for the ceremony to begin. Delicate blue, pink, and yellow flowers dotted the prairie grass surrounding the building and growing from the roof.

Marin smiled at Elsbet. "Was any chapel or home ever decorated so beautifully for a wedding?"

Elsbet's gaze held laughter, but she agreed as she smoothed the arms of Marin's dress of dark green silk.

Lovely strains from a violin inside the building reached them, and Marin took a shaky breath. She smiled at Sophia. "Time to begin. Are you scared?"

Wide-eyed, the little girl shook her head no. "Mother says I've the most important job of the whole wedding."

Marin bit back a laugh and avoided looking at Elsbet. "Your mother is right."

Sophia grinned and started toward the church to spread wildflowers from her basket onto Marin's path. At the door stood Fader, waiting to accompany Marin to the altar.

Elsbet slipped her arm about Marin's waist in a quick hug. "I'm so happy for you. Talif is a good man. Seeing his devotion to you. . ." Her voice broke. Marin waited patiently while Elsbet took a deep breath and continued. "Seeing the way he treats you. . .it makes me believe that maybe. . .maybe there's a man somewhere who might love me that way."

Elsbet's hope caught at Marin's heart. She hugged her sister close. "Of course there is," she whispered fiercely. "Can't the Lord do anything? Isn't love His favorite gift?"

Marin saw tears glitter as Elsbet broke away and followed Sophia toward the church.

Moments later, Marin's vision was free from tears as she stood beside the altar and the man who would become, in only minutes, her husband. Seeing the love in Talif's eyes, standing with him before the Lord and her family, and the congregation in the church and school built by Talif's love, she knew her words to Elsbet were true.

That truth sang inside Marin's heart as she and Talif vowed the love they had for each other would continue forever.

JoAnn A. Grote lives in Minnesota, where she grew up. She uses the state for most of her story settings, and like her characters, JoAnn seeks to serve Christ in her work. She believes that readers of novels can receive a message of salvation and encouragement from well-crafted fiction. With over 35 books to her credit, including Heartsong Presents novels, and titles in The American Adventure series for children, she captivates and addresses the deep connection between life and faith. You may contact he via e-mail at jaghi@rconnect.com.

The Provider

by Cathy Marie Hake

Dedication

This book is dedicated to my parents,
Roy and Elvera Smith.
Even when Daddy held no spiritual commitment,
Mom was a steadfast believer.
God used her faithfulness to woo Daddy
until he accepted Christ.
The Lord has blessed them and
used them in mighty ways.
For your example, your love and prayers,
and even for the discipline,
thanks, Mom and Dad.

Chapter 1

I'm sorry, Steven. I tried my best."

Steven Halpern stared at old Doc Willowby and shook his head in mute denial of the terrible truth.

"Jane was too weak. I did all I could, but it wasn't enough." Doc handed him a small bundle and murmured, "It's a girl. She looks to be healthy, but she's a tiny slip of a thing. They are when they come early like this. Keep her warm, and try to feed her watered-down cream with sugar added to it. Do you have any bottles?"

Steven looked blankly at his housekeeper. She nodded, but he didn't even feel a flicker of relief.

"She'll need to be fed every other hour. Give her an ounce each time for the first two days, then two or three ounces after that."

"I can't do this." Steven thrust the baby back, unable to even look at her.

"You have to. She may not make it, but you owe it to Jane to try." Doc gently slid the baby back into his arms. She'd begun to wail. "I'll let you comfort one another."

Doc left, and Steven walked over to the window. Rain pelted the pane. Every last angel in heaven had to be weeping to create such a storm. Stunned as he was, he couldn't even join in. He drew a shattered breath and looked down, ready to hate the child who had cost him his sweet Jane; but she was such a tiny mite, he couldn't dredge up such an ugly emotion. A fluff of dark down covered her head, and her lips puckered. He'd never seen anything as small as her hands. She accidentally found her fingers, sucked on them for an instant, then let out a small mewl of disappointment.

The next morning, the baby gummed the bottle nipple. Her cry was a tiny bleat of woe. Steven stared at her then looked at Mrs. Axelrod. His housekeeper carefully turned the baby around, gently patted her back, and said, "Things are ready. Tom's gathering the hands."

Steven rose from the leather wingback chair and slowly crossed the floor. The planks rang with each step. He had to go out there and lay his wife to rest. Everyone waited while he built up the nerve. Jane had been a dainty woman, a lady of refined taste and delicate sensibilities. Out of respect, Steven scraped the mud off of his boots on the porch steps before heading toward the grave. By the time he reached it, his boots were caked again, but he was too numb to notice.

"Preacher Durley wasn't in town," Mark said, "so we'll all just recite a psalm and Mrs. Axelrod can pray."

Steven kept his eyes trained on the plain pine box and nodded. Jane deserved something far nicer than that pitiful coffin. He'd failed her all around. She'd felt puny since the day she told him he was to become a father, so he hadn't detected any difference in her these last few days. Still, he should have sent for Doc Willowby sooner. Maybe then he might have been able to save her once her laboring began.

"The Lord is my shepherd," the men about him began. He wanted to shout at them. Why did they talk about a shepherd when they were laying his wife to rest on a cattle ranch? "Yea, though I walk through the valley of the shadow of death. . ." No man walked there—he was dragged through, and the ground was covered by millions of jagged stones of memory that caused his soul to bleed.

Steven didn't hear the rest of the recitation, the hymn, or the prayer that followed. He stared at the gaping hole in the dirt and tried to convince himself this wasn't real. Mrs. Axelrod pulled him from his thoughts when she put the baby in his arms. "Go on back into the house," she ordered. "Mark will make sure things are finished up here."

He trudged over to the porch and had to muster courage before going inside. The fragrance of Jane's lavender perfume lingered in the parlor. It sharpened the edge of his grief. Mrs. Axelrod steered him to a chair and pressed another bottle into his hand. "Best try to feed her. She sounds hungry."

Twenty minutes later, Steven said worriedly, "She's only swallowed once, and she choked on it."

"I'll make up another bottle and use blackstrap molasses instead of sugar. Maybe that'll work."

Throughout the day, they tried in vain to get the baby to eat. Her wails grew weaker. Steven raked his hand through his hair and stared out at the new grave. He could not bear to think Jane was there. Even worse, he couldn't imagine failing her by letting the child she'd died to birth falter and die, too. "We have to do something," he rasped.

🌾

Lena Swenson let out a cry of outrage. She ran from the soddy with Lars's old rifle. Sorely tempted to aim true, she paused a second then lifted the muzzle into the air and fired. The rifle recoiled and slammed into her shoulder. It hurt terribly, but not as bad as the sight of the cattle still standing in her cornfield, happily munching away.

She fired once more then took off her apron and paced into the cornfield. Though she whirled the fabric in the air and slapped one of the huge black beasts, Lena reaped no reward for her effort. One cow turned, gave her a baleful glare, and continued to munch on the cornstalk.

Lena smacked the animal again and accomplished nothing more than making her hand sting. She had no choice: She hastily saddled up her old plow horse and rode in. She started herding the strays from her corn when two men rode up. "Your cows are eating my corn!"

"The fence was down," one drawled. He kneed his mount forward and forced another cow into motion.

Lena waved her hand at the trampled crop. "What about my corn?"

The second man knocked his hat backward on his head and swiped his sleeve across his damp forehead. "Hot as it's been, that stunted crop

531

wasn't going to come to much."

"I still counted on it!"

He shrugged. "Your man can come reckon with the boss."

Lena reared back. Her horse danced to the side, and she struggled to handle her mount and emotions. "He is dead."

"No, ma'am. Mr. Halpern ain't dead. It was his wife."

Lena looked back up at them. Her voice shook as she clarified, "I didn't know of that passing. I was speaking of my own Lars."

The man's eyes narrowed. "You mean you're a widow woman? Out here all on your lonesome?"

She sat straighter in the saddle. "No, I am not alone. I have a son."

"We didn't get word of the death or the birth."

Lena looked back at the soddy. "Please get your cows out of here, or I'm not going to have any corn left at all."

"Yes'm."

She lightly tugged on the reins and rode her horse back to the barn. It took very little time to unsaddle him; then she went back to the soddy. Johnny was wailing, so she picked him up and jounced him on her shoulder.

Not having seen another soul in a long time, Lena desperately wanted to visit. She looked about and strained to think of what she could offer as refreshments to the men before they left. She had a few ounces of coffee beans left. Johnny sat on the table as she tossed the beans into the grinder and spun the handle.

"Ma'am?"

"Yes!" Lena scooped Johnny into her arms and stepped back into the bright sunlight. "I was going to make some coffee. You'd like to stay and have a cup, perhaps, *ja*?"

His leathered face creased into an apologetic smile. "Sorry, ma'am. What with us burying Mrs. Halpern this mornin', we don't dare lollygag. That's a mighty fine-lookin' son you've got. Big."

"Thank you." Lena's maternal smile froze as Johnny twisted in her arms and started to nuzzle a button on her bodice.

The cowboy cranked his head away and stared over at the corn. "I'll say something to the boss. Might be a few days before he decides what to do."

"I understand." Lena hastily hoisted her son up to her shoulder. "Thank you for coming to fetch the cows."

"We'll repair the fence."

"Please give Mr. Halpern my condolences."

He turned back, stared at her for a long count, then glanced around. Lena suddenly felt ashamed of her homestead. The crops were pitiful. With the wheat shriveling and corn heat-stunted, she'd be lucky to have enough food to get her through next winter. Last night's downpour, though welcome, wouldn't be enough to turn the tide. Her garden looked bedraggled. Had she even combed her hair today? She couldn't bear to see the pity on the stranger's face, so she dipped her head and busied herself with patting Johnny's back.

"Ma'am, you have my condolences, too."

His raspy tone nearly ripped away the thin veneer of self-control she'd developed over the solitary months. Tears welled up, but she blinked furiously to keep them at bay. Unable to speak for fear of dissolving into a fit of weeping, she bit her lip and nodded.

"I'd best be going."

After he left, she went inside and put away the coffee. There wouldn't be more until next year. No use wasting it on just herself when it was really too hot to enjoy a scalding cup.

Johnny nursed; then she settled him in the wicker basket and carried him out to a shady spot by the barn. "Boris, guard." Her hound lay down, and Lena picked up an axe. She needed to chop firewood for cooking and heat for the approaching winter.

She'd already found a lightning-struck tree and hacked sections of it into manageable pieces so the horse could drag it back to the homestead. Since she wouldn't need to haul water today, this was an opportune time to take care of stocking the woodpile.

The axe was big for her hands, but she'd learned to use its weight to her advantage. Lars could have split the wood into pieces with a single blow, but it took her several. Each swing pulled at her shoulders, each blow jarred her; but she did what she needed to, and with each piece she stacked, she tried to think of another hour of winter warmth for Johnny.

Her thoughts turned toward Mr. Halpern. She knew nothing of him at all other than he was a rich rancher. It was a shame he'd lost his wife. Lena knew firsthand how losing a mate tore at the soul. She looked across the yard to the broken fence and prayed, "Dear Jesus, please comfort Mr. Halpern."

Her gaze fell back on her cornfield. Mr. Halpern's cows had virtually destroyed her crop. She hoped he was a fair man. Maybe he'd simply settle by sending over two barrels of cornmeal and some canning jars of corn.

"Jesus, You taught us to pray for our daily bread. I'm worrying about supplies for winter. I know I'm supposed to trust You to provide, but I'm so scared. The rain was good, and the wheat might still be a fair crop. After harvest, I'll have to leave the farm untended when I take it to the mill. Here I am again, fretting. I don't want to be greedy, Father, but please provide." She lifted the axe and swung yet again.

Mark tapped on the kitchen door and stuck his head inside. "Mrs. Axelrod?"

"What is it now?" She sighed as she stood over the stove.

"Um, well. . ." He shifted from one foot to the other and played with the brim of his hat. He held it in front of himself and seemed to find it inordinately interesting. "A small section of the east fence went down in the storm. Half dozen heifers got into the farmer's corn."

"Mr. Halpern can't be bothered with that tonight," she snapped. "It won't make much difference. He can make restitution in a few months when he's not so troubled."

"I would have thought so, too; but, well, this is different. It's a widow woman over there. Her man died."

"She wouldn't be a widow if her man hadn't died." Mrs. Axelrod wearily wiped her hands on the front of her apron. She used a thick cotton pad to lift the heavy cast-iron skillet. Very carefully, she poured tan-colored creamy liquid into a bottle and muttered worriedly, "Death stalks in threes—but I'm doing my best to be sure the third's not that little babe."

"I never put any store by that old adage."

Mrs. Axelrod sighed. "Tell the woman Mr. Halpern will pay up."

Mark nodded. "From the looks of it, she's gonna need it. She's poor as dirt, and she's got a son, too."

"We can't be bothered right now. In a month or two, when the crop would go to market, she and the boss can settle."

"It wouldn't go to market, ma'am. From the look of things, it would go right to her table."

"Are you telling me she and her boy are going hungry?"

"Can't rightly swear to the fact that she is just now, but I'd reckon she's pert near close to it. She's slender as a willow. On the other hand, her babe is fat as a butchering hog." He watched as Mrs. Axelrod struggled to stretch the ugly black rubber nipple over the glass bottle. "One thing for sure—she may well be struggling at most everything else, but she don't have to mess with none of that kind of gear."

Mrs. Axelrod froze. She turned slowly and asked, "Are you telling me the babe's still a nursling?"

"I believe so." Mark grinned. "Poor woman turned three shades of red when he started rooting on her gown."

"Lord be praised! Go saddle up the boss's horse!"

Chapter 2

Steven heard the ring of the axe before he saw the neighbor woman. He shifted in the saddle and awkwardly clutched his daughter. For such a tiny, lightweight bundle, she was difficult to hold. She'd starve if he didn't get something into her soon. He wanted nothing more than to be left all alone, but the privacy of his grief fell second to providing for the child Jane had wanted so desperately.

As his horse walked past the crops, Steven judged them to be in grave trouble. She'd been on her own, so the widow hadn't plowed and planted much. He figured the corn plot to be only an acre, and the wheat wasn't quite twice as large. The soddy looked like a hovel for beasts instead of a habitation for humans. *How can anyone live like this?*

He spied the woman. He'd never met her—farmers were a blight on the land, and being neighborly with them went against his principles. She was tall and slender, but her shoulders were broad. He'd expected to see her in widow's weeds out of respect for her husband, but she wore faded blue calico. Sweat darkened the back of her bodice and made big rings beneath her arms. Mud caked the bottom ten inches of her gown. He'd never seen such a filthy woman. For an instant, he almost turned to go, but the babe in his arms whimpered and reminded him he couldn't afford to be picky.

The woman stood with her legs spread wide apart and twisted as her arms moved upward in a smooth arc. The axe in her hands almost robbed her of her balance, but she shifted her weight. The axe cut through the air, hit a section of wood, and split it. Both halves fell to the ground. She set down the axe, took up another piece of wood, and positioned it. As she reached for the axe again, a dog growled a warning and started to bark.

The widow woman wheeled around and clutched the axe before her. Her blue eyes were wide in a pale, dirt-streaked face. She stared at him as she sidestepped several yards toward a wicker basket. The dog stood guard over the basket and continued to growl.

"Hello. I am Lena Swenson."

Her voice sounded husky, as if she hadn't spoken in several days. Even with her singsongy Swedish accent, it shook a little, too. Steven stared at her and wondered what she thought she was doing, living alone like this. "I hear you're a widow now."

She recoiled from his blunt words, and Steven knew the sickening grief his words caused. Her lips thinned and she said nothing, but she shifted the axe in front of herself. Her fingers clutched the handle so tightly, the knuckles went white.

Hackles raised, the dog stood beside her. Its growl took on a sinister pitch. "Call off the dog."

She shook her head.

He heard a whimpering sound. She cast a furtive glance at the basket. A wail quavered from it, and the color bled from her face. "I think you'd better leave, mister."

He wanted to. He wanted to ride off and never look back. The last thing he wanted was to place his clean little baby in the arms of this slovenly woman. Most of her silver-blond hair straggled out of an untidy knot on her crown. Jane would have swooned at the thought of such a person ever touching her beloved child. His daughter let out a soft bleat. He had no choice. Either he asked this woman to help, or he'd lose the baby, too.

Steven locked eyes with her, steeled himself with a deep breath, and said, "I heard you might have milk."

She blinked then nodded. "My cow is fresh."

He let out a mirthless bark of a laugh. "Not your cow. You." She didn't react at all, so he flipped back the edge of the blanket. The baby made a pathetic squeak as sunlight hit her tiny face. "My girl is hungry."

Lena's mouth dropped open. She stared at him in shock.

"I heard you had a baby," Steven continued. "From the sounds of it, he's aiming to get some chow. Bluntly put, I want him to share with my daughter."

After a few seconds of silence, he swung down out of the saddle. The bundled baby occupied his left arm. He drew a pistol with his right hand. Lena gasped. "Lady, send that dog off, or I'm going to plug a bullet in him. I won't have him threaten my daughter."

"Ruh," she ordered. *"Sitz."* The dog sat and went silent. The woman studied Steven and said, "Boris will not harm you if you are friendly. Put away the gun."

"I'll holster the gun if you put down the axe."

"You must put the gun in the saddle holster and step away from your horse," she countered.

Steven grew impatient. "Listen, lady—my baby is starving, and you're acting like we're trying to swap horseflesh."

Lena sucked in a deep breath. "Is she sick?"

"No. Hungry."

"Put her in the cradle in the soddy then step back out. I will go in and feed her."

He had no choice. The woman was dirty as a pig, but the baby needed something quick, or she'd dwindle. Her crying was pitifully thin, but constant. He'd give in for this one feeding then find another way to take care of matters. Steven pivoted, strode to the soddy, and went inside.

It was worse than he'd expected. Shafts of late afternoon sun angled through the doorway and illuminated walls made of huge slabs of grassy dirt. An iron bedstead took up a third of the space. Fresh splotches of mud dripped down from the ceiling and plopped onto the red and blue quilt. A rough table and two rickety chairs, a small three-drawer bureau, and a cradle comprised the remainder of the furniture. The tiniest potbellied stove he'd ever seen took up the far corner. Crates and shelves lined one wall. On them sat jars, crocks, sacks, a few bottles and barrels, and candles. Her poverty stunned him. Steven stood still for a moment then did as she asked. He set his daughter into the cradle and paced back out.

She'd lifted her son with one arm. He was old enough to lift his head and look around. His gown slid up, displaying a pair of reassuringly chunky legs. Lena still awkwardly held the axe, and the dog stayed right at her side. "You will wait by the barn," she ordered.

He looked at her grimy hands. "Wash before you touch her."

She skirted around him and disappeared inside.

Steven stood outside and clenched his fists. He was a man who managed everything, but his world was spinning out of control. His heart and soul ached with an emptiness he'd never known. Just the memory of Jane stole the breath from his lungs. He was helpless—as helpless as his baby daughter. Their fate lay in the filthy hands of an ignorant, low-class farmer's wife.

❧

Lena lit the lamp and shut the door. She barred it and didn't care that she was wasting lamp oil when the sun still hung high in the sky. She didn't trust that man. How could he have humiliated her like that? She'd been working all day. Of course she was dirty. He'd asked an incredibly intimate favor then had the unmitigated gall to insult her. If it weren't for the fact that his tiny daughter kept mewling so pitifully, she would have refused him.

Lena hastily stripped out of her clothes, used the water in the bucket by the stove, and washed up. She put on her clean dress then went over to see the baby. The child was a newborn—barely a day or so, and born weeks before her time. Pitifully thin, she barely managed any sound at all. "Dear Jesus, help me to help her!"

Lena gently offered herself to the baby. She was so weak, it took patience, but soon she seemed to get the idea and did passably well at suckling. Lena burped her then laid her in the cradle and picked up Johnny.

A fair bit of time passed—how much, she didn't know. Lena didn't own a timepiece. When both babies were fed and changed, she made sure all of her buttons were closed; then she ran a brush through her hair, plaited it into a thick rope, and left it to hang down her back. With a baby in each arm, she struggled to open the door.

The sunlight was bright after she'd become accustomed to the dim interior of the soddy. By the time she blinked and focused, the man had snatched his baby away. "Well? Did she eat?"

"Yes."

"Your boy is big, so he must have quite an appetite. Did you give her enough?"

Lena's arms curled around Johnny, and she stepped back. "Your baby is small, so she doesn't need much. Since she was very hungry, I fed her first."

"Good."

Good? Not "Thank you," but "Good"? Lena barely held back a shocked retort. She stared at him then said, "You still have a few hours of daylight. If you ride hard, town is south of here. You could get bottles from the general store and milk from the diner for her."

"She doesn't need that now that she has you."

"Mister, I think you'd better get on your horse and leave." She inched from the doorway back into the shadowed interior of her home.

"I can't. Not yet. You managed to satisfy her and quiet her down." He pointed to two half-pint jars on the ground. "I found those in the barn. Doc said she has to eat every other hour. We'll stay 'til you feed her again. You can fill those up, and it'll get us through the night 'til I send someone over for more in the morning."

Lena gawked at him. "I am no milk cow!"

His face took on a thunderous look.

"I don't even know who you are, and you ask this of me?" Her voice cracked. "Do not come back here!" She hurriedly slammed the door shut and bolted it.

"Mrs. Swenson? Mrs. Swenson!" He pounded on her door.

She huddled on the bed. "I have a rifle!"

"You may as well load and use it on both of us. If you don't feed her, she's going to die. As for me—I've already lost my wife. If I lose my baby, I don't want to live, either."

Chapter 3

O nly for a week," she reminded herself as she stepped into Mr. Halpern's house. Lena looked around at the grand home and felt swamped by her inadequacies. She'd tried to wipe her feet, but her worn boots still left small clods and crumbles of dirt on the gleaming wooden floor. Johnny's clean gowns and diapers and her nightgown filled the burlap bag she clutched in a shaky hand. She didn't belong in such a fancy place.

"Mrs. Axelrod," Mr. Halpern ordered, "put Mrs. Swenson in the blue room. She'll stay with us for the next week. Move the cradle in there."

"Yes, sir." The portly woman studied Lena with undisguised curiosity. "Follow me."

Lena carefully balanced a baby in each arm as she went up a flight of stairs. She walked down a hallway, past several closed doors. Mrs. Axelrod opened a door and motioned her inside. "I'm sure you'll find this comfortable."

Lena tentatively shuffled in and looked all around. A blue satin counterpane covered a cherrywood sleigh bed. Wallpaper sprigged with blue columbines gave a dainty, fresh feel to the room. The washstand had a marble top, and the bureau boasted a snowy doily with a porcelain figurine on it. "I've never seen anyplace so beautiful."

The housekeeper nodded. "Mrs. Halpern was very particular. She loved making the house look perfect. You'll have to forgive the boss if he's grumpy these days. He loved her to distraction."

Lena crossed the floor and looked out the window. It was so nice to have real glass panes. She stared out in the direction of her farm and said very quietly, "I understand this kind of pain."

"Yes, I guess you do."

"I will do my best for his daughter. The farm—I cannot leave it even this long. He promised to have someone go tend it for me. After one week, I must go back to my home."

"We'll see."

Lena looked over her shoulder and said in a definitive tone, "One week. It is our agreement. I will not stay longer —I cannot."

Mrs. Axelrod opened the burlap bag and busied herself, putting Johnny's clothes in the second drawer of the bureau. She shook out the nightgown and laid it on the bed. "Did you bring anything else?"

Lena shivered. "My other dress is rolled up behind my saddle. Once the babies are asleep—"

"I'm sure Mr. Halpern will have it brought in."

"It is muddy. I need to wash it."

The woman cast a glance at her and said in a knowing tone, "No wonder, after last night's storm. I'll wash it."

"Oh, but—"

"You are here to see to the baby." The woman plumped the pillow and flicked a nonexistent wrinkle from the bed. "Best you get that straight here and now. Bad enough Miss Jane didn't get through the birthing. Mr. Halpern's going to be a bulldog about the babe. You see to her; I'll see to the laundry."

Lena watched as the woman set her boar bristle brush on the washstand and the Bible on the bedside table. She'd been lucky to grab those last two things—Mr. Halpern had been in such a hurry, she'd barely been able to latch the soddy's door behind them.

The baby girl whimpered. Lena cast an apologetic look at the woman as she set both children on the mattress. It was a shame to mess up the perfectly smooth bed, but there was no chair in the room. Lena stooped, untied her boots, and took them off. She washed her hands and couldn't help noticing how the dainty columbines painted on the edge of the washbowl matched the wallpaper. The linen hand towel was such a fine weave, she felt guilty for using it. She went back to the bed, scooted so her spine rested against the headboard, and dragged a baby to each side.

The housekeeper stayed in the room. She'd gone over to the window, needlessly straightened pale yellow curtains, and then pulled on gold tassels to shut the heavy, blue brocade draperies. She turned back and granted Lena a tight smile. Lena held one hand over the buttons of her bodice and the other on the Halpern child. "I will take good care of her."

The housekeeper nodded. "I'll be back with the cradle."

In the middle of the night, Steven heard a baby. He worried about his daughter. The Swenson woman hadn't come down for supper. Mrs. Axelrod said she'd taken up a tray, and that ought to do. They'd need to feed the woman well so she'd be able to nurse both babies. In truth, she needed more to eat, just for her own sake. He'd lifted her into her saddle, and though she was tall and sturdy through the shoulders, the lean shape of her hips and waist made it clear food wasn't as plentiful on her table as it ought to be. When he sent her back home, he'd be sure to replenish her larder.

Her son was a solid tike—chubby and apple-cheeked. Whatever else she did wrong, one thing was clear—she did well by her child. Would she care for him first and neglect his daughter, though? Steven paced back and forth. A small wail hovered in the air then died out. Should he go check?

Steven fought with himself. He had no business going into the widow's bedchamber; he had every right—his daughter was in there. After fifteen more minutes of grieving over his lost wife and agonizing about how best to see to his daughter's needs, he yielded to temptation. He lightly tapped on the door.

She gave no answer.

Quietly he opened the door. No light shone inside, but she was probably like a mole or a cat—able to navigate in the dark, after living in that disgusting mud hovel. He set the lamp on the hallway floor and tiptoed in.

The top drawer on the dresser was open. The back of a chair sat beneath it for support. Why had she done such an odd thing? The cradle lay empty. His frown deepened and his nose wrinkled. Something stank. Diapers. A wad of them lay in a big bowl. The room was a mess. Jane wouldn't have ever dreamed of letting things get out of place like this.

He stepped closer to the bed. The scene stopped him in his tracks. Lena was asleep. Her hair billowed in a riotous mass all over the pillow. She lay on her back, her left arm bowed out a bit to hold her son close to her side. His hair was the same pale gold, so it was easy to spy above the dark-colored blankets. Steven's daughter lay nestled to Lena's breastbone. A pale flannel blanket covered her, and Lena's big, rough hand held her fast.

Pain laced through him. *Jane wanted this baby so badly. Jane should be holding her. Jane should be cherishing her soft skin and downy hair and fretting over each snuffle and squeak.*

Instead, a stranger, a woman who worked like a man and lived like an animal, held her. The baby made a soft sound. Even in her sleep, Lena tenderly patted his daughter. Obviously accustomed to dealing with the needs of an infant, she murmured soft hushes. A rough hand. An accent to the voice. It was wrong—all wrong.

Steven stumbled out of the room, through the house, into the yard. At his wife's graveside, he stared at the mound of freshly turned earth. Each breath tore at his throat. His chest burned. He leaned against the tree, let his head fall back, and groaned. There were no words for the grief and rage he felt.

❦

Lena woke early and fed her son then settled him into the cradle. He could sit up, so she was afraid to use the drawer as a baby bed for him. As she carefully tucked the Halpern girl into a fresh diaper, she whispered, "I don't know your name, princess. I'll have to ask today."

Lena smiled softly as the wee one made a greedy little sound. It was her first, and it was a good sign. As tiny and tentative as she'd been, that reassurance was welcome.

After a while, Lena turned over and let her finish nursing from the other side. She whispered her morning prayers then started to sleepily drift along. She'd missed out on a lot of sleep, nursing both babies during the night.

Mrs. Axelrod pushed open the door and bustled in with a tray. She took the baby and grinned. "No doubt it's my imagination, but I'd swear she weighs more today than yesterday."

Lena merely smiled and sat up.

Mrs. Axelrod burped the tiny girl and started to change her diaper. "I brought creamed oatmeal with your breakfast. Your son is old enough to be eating regular food."

Lena clutched the blanket to her chest and let out a small sound of distress. "I have enough milk. I am Johnny's mother—"

"Yes, you are. I just figured you'd been giving him rice or barley cereal because he's so stocky." They both glanced over at the cradle. "Your boy is going to grow into a sizable man. It's plain to see, he'll be able to do a man's work earlier than most." She looked down at the newborn. "On the other hand, this one is going to be a dainty little thing. Small as she is, she won't need much milk at all yet. I'm not worried about you having enough for both."

"No one has told me her name."

Mrs. Axelrod pursed her lips. "She doesn't have one yet. I suppose we'll have to ask the boss."

Lena reached over and tenderly caressed the baby's dark hair. "In the Bible there is a girl. Her name is not given. Talitha means 'little girl' and that is all we know her by. For now, I will call her this. When Mr. Halpern decides upon a name, please let me know."

"Talitha?"

"Yes. She was healed. It was a miracle."

"We surely could use a miracle or two around here," the housekeeper mumbled as she headed out the door.

Chapter 4

Originally, Lena agreed to only a week of caring for Talitha; but the baby thrived on breast milk, and she refused to suck from a bottle. Mrs. Axelrod truly tried, but it was to no avail. She lifted her hands in surrender. "I'm afraid you'll just have to keep feeding her. She's still so little."

Lena chewed on her lip and stared out the window. She needed to get back home today. There was so much work to do. . . .

Then, too, there was another problem. This home was like the Garden of Eden. Food was plentiful, and she had companionship. Something about Mrs. Axelrod's friendship after months of isolation drew her. Being able to lie down at night and not fear every strange sound counted for a lot, and she knew Mr. Halpern was more than capable of protecting them all. She felt strong temptation to try to fit in here, but it was wrong for her to relish the creature comforts of this place when she clearly did not belong. The wise thing to do was to leave before she yielded to temptation and tried to wangle her way into a permanent position in the household. Lena squared her shoulders. "I'll take her with me. There's no other way."

"Mr. Halpern won't cotton to that."

Lena carefully positioned her shawl and continued to suckle Johnny. The man who'd been sent to tend the crops couldn't be expected to do women's chores. If she didn't take care of her gardening and canning, she and her son would starve this winter. "Tell Mr. Halpern he has no choice.

I am willing to take her for a time. When she grows bigger, he can have her back."

Mrs. Axelrod pursed her lips and left the room. Lena had barely finished buttoning up her bodice when the door flew open. Steven Halpern filled the doorframe. "You're not going anywhere! What kind of woman are you to abandon a motherless babe?"

She stood, popped Johnny into the cradle, and started to pack her belongings into a sack. "I am not forsaking Talitha. She still needs me, so I am willing to take her along."

In sheer desperation, Steven captured her shoulder. "No one is going anywhere!" He paused as his eyes narrowed. She'd gone perfectly still beneath his touch. The hectic color she'd sported just moments before drained clean out of her cheeks. Very lightly, he rubbed his thumb back and forth across her collarbone. She inhaled sharply and wrenched free. "Did that hurt? Mrs. Axelrod said the rifle bruised your shoulder when you tried to run those cows off your land—"

"It is not fitting to discuss my person, and I am quite well, thank you. Do not touch me again."

He scowled. "What kind of man do you think I am? I loved my wife. I just buried her. You can bet I'm not looking for the likes of you to take her place!"

Lena stood even straighter. She looked at him with wounded dignity then quietly said, "I know of the pain of losing a mate. I have tried to understand the hurt in your heart. When Lars died, my heart was empty. Each day, I wake and know the ache of loneliness. I am sorry for your loss. I did my best. I offered to still feed your daughter, but I must see to my farm, too." She turned and scooped up her son. "If Talitha needs me, you can have someone bring her to me."

Steven gawked at her then shot Mrs. Axelrod a horrified look. "Do something!"

The housekeeper watched as Lena walked off. She grimaced. "We can't make her stay. We'll come up with a schedule for taking Talitha to her."

"Talitha?"

"Mrs. Swenson said it's in the Bible. It means 'little girl.'"

"What business does she have, naming my daughter?"

"It's temporary—'til you decide on something. When she says it, it comes out sounding right pretty."

"Go make a bottle. I don't want that woman touching my daughter again."

❧

Lena was relieved to get home. True to his word, Mr. Halpern had a man there to do the chores. Lena thanked him and sent him on his way. Once he was gone, she took her horse into the barn and noted the cow still hadn't been milked. Her pitiful lowing let Lena know that had to be the first thing she did.

After milking the cow, Lena set the milk pail aside on her way to the house and ducked into the chicken coop. She found only two eggs—the man must have gathered the rest. From the looks of things, he'd done a fair job on the chores. Supposing the eggs were in the soddy, she lifted the pail and headed that direction. As soon as she entered the tiny room, she noticed a bowl full of fresh eggs on the table.

He'd slept in her bed and left it a rumpled mess. She shuddered and set Johnny into the cradle. In a rush of activity, she stripped the feather mattress and set the sheets and quilt to boil.

The ground was still damp, so he hadn't needed to water the crops. He'd visited her garden and staked up a few of the tomato plants. He'd carried the wood she'd chopped and stacked it by the side of the soddy.

She stirred the laundry, hung up the damp things on her line, then wrung out the bedding and hung it up, too. Boris trotted along with her and acted delighted to be in her company.

Lena collected Johnny and sat in the shade to nurse him. It was noon—time for her to make herself some dinner. She wasn't overly hungry, and it would be best for her to skip a meal whenever possible to conserve her supplies. *Jesus, help me not to feel bitter about Mr. Halpern's ingratitude. Please keep Your hand on Talitha and soften her father's heart.*

The ranch hand had left a mess on the table, so Lena scraped the dishes into a slop bucket for the pigs. With water scarce, she took the plates and skillet outside and used sand to scour them. While doing so, she tried to think of a way to make a box of some sort for Johnny. He'd soon be crawling, and she worried that he'd hurt himself while she was busy with chores. Lars would have built something special. He'd made the beautiful cradle. He was so good with his hands. Grief curled in her heart.

Distracted by her sad thoughts, Lena didn't hear the horse until Boris barked. Seconds later, she detected a high-pitched wail as she tucked the dishes into a basket, yet she didn't turn around. *Jesus, please help me act and speak with kindness.*

"What kind of woman are you, Lena Swenson, to leave a motherless baby to starve?" Steven's words stole her breath away. He sat in the saddle glowering at her. He held his daughter as if she were a bale of barbed wire. His eyes were just as sharp.

Lena forced herself to stay silent. The dishes rattled as she put one last cup into the basket and got to her feet. Talitha's wails rose in urgency. Halpern dismounted and headed toward her. "Stop that infernal nonsense and do your duty!"

Lena turned to the side and plucked Johnny from his basket. Without a word, she headed for the soddy. Steven intercepted her. He stood between her and her home. "What," he demanded, "are you doing?"

Her chin jutted forward. "I am doing my duty. My son is wet and hungry."

"So is my daughter."

"Then change her."

"That's a woman's job."

Lena shifted Johnny's weight a bit and stared at her neighbor. "You may think I am cruel, but I will say this, for you must hear it and live by the truth. When your mate dies, there is no such luxury as having men's and women's jobs. Things must be done, and you are the only one who is there to accomplish them. For your daughter's sake, you must learn to care for her. You have no choice."

His face paled. The muscle in his cheek twitched. "Cruel doesn't even begin to cover what I think of you. If there were any other way for my daughter to eat, I'd gladly do it."

Lord, he's so bitter and harsh. Give me a soft word to turn away his wrath. "You brought her. I said if you brought her, I would feed her. Fetch a diaper from your saddlebag. Come inside, and I will teach you how to change her."

He stayed in her path and grimaced.

"Until you decide my home is good enough, I still must see to my own son. Excuse me." She slipped past him and went inside. Lena started to hum as she laid Johnny on the bare mattress and changed his diaper. A huge shadow suddenly blocked out the sunlight spilling from the doorway. She didn't look up. She kept humming a hymn under her breath.

"I didn't bring a diaper."

His confession triggered both pity and concern. How could he plan to keep his daughter when he was so inept? "Go get a diaper off of the clothesline."

He didn't say anything at all. He simply wheeled around and headed off toward the rope where her laundry snapped in the prairie wind. When he reappeared in the doorway, he balanced the laundry basket in one hand and the baby in the other.

"Bring her here." Lena dropped Johnny's wet diaper into a bucket and rinsed her hands in the washbowl. As she dried them, she said in a sad tone, "I am proud of my home. Lars built it for us, and we filled it with love. I know you are used to fancy things, but that is your life. Johnny and I are warm and happy here. If you wish me to help Talitha, you will have to accept me and my home."

"Listen, both of these kids are crying. Can't you feed them first and save your sermon for later?"

Lena stared at him in stunned silence. She went over, turned the rocking chair to face away from the door, and sat down. She pulled a shawl over her shoulder and self-consciously unbuttoned her bodice. A second later, Johnny stopped crying.

"Hey! I thought you said you'd feed my daughter first!"

"She needs to be in a dry diaper and gown."

"Don't tell me Johnny doesn't pee all over you."

550

"Sometimes he does."

"He'll eat everything. You won't have enough left."

"Small babes need very little. God will provide enough."

"Listen to her crying," he said in a nervous tone. "You can feed them both at the same time. Let her eat now, too."

Lena glanced down and readjusted the shawl. "Bring her to me as soon as you are done changing her diaper."

It wasn't long before she heard the ground crunch beneath his feet. He awkwardly changed Talitha then shoved her into Lena's arms and hightailed out of the soddy. After she finished nursing the babes, she went back outside. He turned around, and his haggard look tore at her soul. "Mr. Halpern, I do not mind caring for your daughter, but I must still tend my land."

He nodded curtly. "Nights at my place, days here. She's mine. I want her under my roof and protection at night."

Chapter 5

Lena somberly stepped back into the columbine bedroom. Mrs. Axelrod stood in the doorway and pled, "Please don't be too hard on him. He's grieving for his wife."

Lena cranked her head to the side and swallowed a big lump in her throat. She'd been without Lars for eight months. She'd been terribly alone and afraid. Every day, she suffered the backbreaking farm labor and loneliness. Every night, she fixed supper for only herself. Her grief was still raw.

"I'm not trying to be mean, Lena. You don't understand—"

"I do not understand? I spent eight months in solitude and delivered my son on my own." Her voice broke.

Mrs. Axelrod sucked in a loud breath. "I'm sorry, Lena. Truly I am. You're so good with the babies and keep such a calm spirit, it's hard to remember you're freshly widowed."

"God gives me strength and comfort," Lena whispered.

"Poor Boss. He's shaking his fist at the Almighty for taking his wife. I did the same for a good long while when my Sam passed on. It's a rare person who can endure grief like you have."

Lena settled into the room and confessed, "Each day, I have had to pray for help. It is like being forced to pull a heavy wagon alone when once there was another who shared the yoke. God only gives strength enough for each day, for each step."

Mrs. Axelrod shook her head and pulled Johnny away. "Speaking of strength, you look near worn to a frazzle. If I don't miss my guess, you did three days' work in one morning. You take a rest, and I'll change this one. He's wet as a leaky bucket."

Steven couldn't sleep. He hadn't slept a night through since Jane died. He tossed, punched his pillow, and lay in the darkness. Unable to fill the aching void, he got up and paced out of his room.

Without thinking, he went to Lena's room. Once there, he glanced about and thought how impractical the furniture was. The washstand and sleigh bed were carved alike and useful, but everything else was far too ornate. He hadn't stepped foot in here since the day Jane finished decorating it, and now that he didn't have his wife beside him to distract him, he studied the room and found the whole affair far too fussy. Blue flowers, white lace, and blue ruffles made him want to bolt. Doodads rested on every available surface—little glass bottles, picture frames, porcelain statues.

The dresser top was different. It held only Lena's leather-bound Bible and a hairbrush. The stark simplicity of those two items jarred him. Sturdy. Practical. Like their owner. Ah—and there was a chair there—propping up the top drawer. Still. His scowl deepened as he realized his daughter occupied that makeshift bassinet. He'd get the boy's cradle over here today.

Steven peeked at both babies. They slept like angels. All he could see of Lena was her profile. She'd turned her face away. Her pale hair flowed over the pillows in an unrestrained mass. The sight was a beautiful one—but completely unexpected.

His wife had been proud of her hair. She made a show of taking it down each night, brushing it one hundred strokes, and plaiting it. There was something. . .wanton about a woman who went to bed with her hair unbound and wild. Jane had been far too mannerly and demure to do anything so impulsive. No matter what time of the day or night, she'd been a complete and total lady from the top of her perfectly coifed coronet to her narrow feet. This woman obviously hadn't ever been taught proper conduct. A wry grin twisted his lips. No husband in his right mind would point out that shortcoming and lose such a magnificent vision.

Traversing the room silently was no small feat. Afraid to make any noise or sudden moves, Steven navigated around a marble pedestal with a Grecian statue on it. He practically tripped over the tip of the cradle runner then bumped into the bedside table. He fought the urge to start pitching all of the folderols and knickknacks on it straight out the window. Instead, he breathed a sigh of relief that Lena and both babies were still asleep. He lifted Talitha into his arms, tiptoed out, pulled the door almost shut, and headed for his bedchamber.

Feeling adrift, he paced over to the far side of the room and stared out the window. One work-rough hand cradled the babe to his chest; the other went up and tentatively touched the pane. He could see the tree from here. Jane was buried beneath it. In a grief-heavy whisper he said, "I'm doing the best I can for her, Jane. Her name's Talitha. It's a pretty name. Comes from the Bible." His voice broke. "Oh, sweetheart, I miss you. We need you." He hung his head and finally let his silent tears flow.

A short while later, Steven took a deep breath and dashed away the proof of his raw grief. Sorrow weighted his steps as he went back to his bed. There he curled next to his little blanket-wrapped daughter and finally slowly drifted off to sleep.

❧

Heart in her throat, Lena swept her shawl around her shoulders and ran out into the hallway. Talitha was missing! Lena looked about, unsure of where to go or what to do. She'd never explored the house, but she knew which chamber belonged to Mr. Halpern. Had he taken his daughter? She sped to his door, and though he didn't respond to her knock, she heard Talitha's whimper. Relief flooded her. Lena let out a shaky breath and tapped on the door again.

Her heart nearly broke at the sight that met her when she hesitantly entered the room. Steven Halpern lay curled around a tiny bundle. His big hand cupped it and nestled it close to his heart. How many times had Lena done that with Johnny herself? Snuggled her son to her breast and tried to mute the pain of losing her mate?

Talitha fussed a bit louder. Her father roused a bit and nuzzled her downy hair. Though Lena hated to part them, she tiptoed closer and whispered, "She's hungry."

He opened his eyes and canted up on one elbow. His other hand brushed the edge of the blanket from the baby's face, and he fingered her cheek. "Bring her back when she's done."

Lena did as he asked as soon as Talitha was full. She couldn't deny him that comfort. She slipped his daughter back into his arms. He said nothing, but the pain burning in his eyes and the almost desperate way he accepted his daughter spoke volumes.

Awhile later, Lena woke to find him standing over her. "I think she's hungry again. I changed her already."

She accepted the baby, but to her dismay, Johnny picked that moment to start fussing. "Stay put. I'll change him," Steven said. He lifted her son from the cradle then changed him on the foot of Lena's bed. "He's a fine boy. Robust. Lars must have been proud."

Lena swallowed hard. "Lars never saw his son. You are the first and only man who has ever held Johnny."

"Other than Doc Willowby. . ." His eyes widened as she shook her head negatively. He pulled Johnny up into his strong arms and held him so gently, Lena's heart tripped at the sight. "But, Lena—who? How. . . ?"

She'd assumed Mrs. Axelrod had told him. Obviously he didn't know. "Johnny was born the week before Christmas, during the blizzard. I was alone." Memories assailed her. Fear, pain, loneliness, joy. . . She gave him a sad smile.

"You did it all by yourself," he marveled under his breath. He looked down at Johnny and thought aloud, "Being with child is hard enough on a woman. I can't fathom how you lived alone and managed your chores each day, let alone comprehend handling the birth all on your own. You are a remarkable woman, Lena Swenson. I don't know of another woman who could have done it."

"God gave me strength."

Pain replaced the admiration on his face. "Why," he rasped hoarsely as he put Johnny on the mattress close by her, "why didn't God give Jane strength?"

"I do not know. I am sorry. I do not know why He took Lars, either. Each day, I look at Johnny and try to be thankful for the time I had and the son that his love left me."

"That's not enough. It's not enough for me."

Lena didn't know what to say. He looked awful. His throat worked, and the muscles in his stubbled jaw twitched. The shadows beneath his eyes tattled on how hard grief rode him and robbed him of his rest. She reached out to touch his arm. Wordlessly he jerked away, turned, and left.

Chapter 6

For the next three weeks, Lena rarely saw Steven Halpern other than at night when he snuck Talitha away. They'd come to a tenuous understanding. Lena slept beneath his roof but then took Talitha with her each day when she went home to work her farm. Because of the hours of work she lost by having to travel each day, Steven insisted on having one of his men stay in her barn and work as a hired hand.

From the pretty mahogany and porcelain mantel clock in her bedroom at the Halpern ranch, Lena had learned that tiny little Talitha needed to nurse every hour and a half. Day and night, she had to halt whatever she was doing to take half an hour to feed the newborn. Each day, she looked about the farm and felt more discouraged. No matter how hard she tried, she couldn't keep up. Nursing another baby and traveling back and forth each day robbed her of too much time.

Even with the man helping her water and tend the crops, Lena had plenty to do. Storing and preserving food was a priority. She harvested truck from her garden then canned. It was hot, time-consuming work to boil down the vegetables and sterilize and seal the jars.

Each night, she left a bit later to go to the Halpern place. She'd wear Johnny on her back in a carrier she'd fashioned along the lines of the cradle boards Indians used, and she tucked Talitha in a sash of fabric she wore across her front. Steven insisted she ride his gentlest mare since her old plow horse was too slow to transport her satisfactorily. One night, Mrs.

Axelrod met her on the kitchen porch and snatched Talitha from the sash as she hissed, "Mr. Halpern is in the study. He's fretting, you're so late!"

"I was busy," Lena said dully.

"He was ready to come after you."

"There was no need. I gave my word I would have her here each night, and I keep my promises. The tomatoes—"

"Tomatoes!" The housekeeper glared and warned, "Boss won't listen to flimsy excuses. His daughter always comes first."

Lena took the baby back and headed for the stairs. "Then you can let him know I've gone to my room to suckle her."

Since they were pressuring her to come home by sunset, Lena started rising even earlier. More than once, she dozed off in the saddle while the mare automatically carried her home.

On the rare occasions she saw Mr. Halpern, he was hollow-eyed with grief or occupied running his ranch. Lena prayed for him.

Mrs. Axelrod was far too busy, too. Cooking and cleaning were already a huge job—adding on laundry for another adult and two babies stretched her to the limit. Too tired to do much to help her, Lena tried to rinse and wash the children's clothes and diapers when she could. She insisted upon eating in the kitchen instead of having trays to make things easier on the housekeeper. At supper one night, Mrs. Axelrod asked, "How're things at the farm?"

"Dry. The drought, it is bad," Lena admitted. "That one rain we had, it was not enough."

"We need more," Steven agreed.

After blotting her mouth with a napkin, Lena said, "When there is a need, God can use it as an opportunity to provide." Talitha started to cry, so Lena excused herself from the table.

Behind her, she heard Steven mutter, "God's taking His sweet time, and while we're waiting, her crops languish and my stock suffers." She didn't bother to turn and make a retort. She knew his pain and grief made him angry. With time and prayer, he'd come to understand the truth.

A few days later, Lena got up and yawned as she changed the babies.

Once fed, they both slipped back to sleep. She dressed and plaited her hair then carefully wrapped Johnny into his cradle board and strapped it to her back. Talitha didn't stir at all as Lena lifted her into the sash so she could leave for the farm. Lena held a boot in each hand. Toeing open the door caused it to creak. Johnny let out a wail, and Lena winced.

Steven appeared in his doorway. His hair was rumpled, and his chin looked heavily stubbled. Bare feet stuck out beneath a thick robe. "Lena, what're you doing?"

"I need to go now. Soon the sun will be up."

He padded over, took her boots from her hands, and dropped them on the floor with a loud pair of thuds. In the next instant, he took Talitha from her. "She fussed most of the night. You have to be exhausted."

"I ate cabbage yesterday, and I do not think it agreed with her. I made the rest into sauerkraut, so you do not need to worry. I will not have it again as long as I feed her."

His brow furrowed. "Lena, I'll stock your place when you leave us. Stop preserving food and don't worry about firewood."

In an effort to pacify Johnny since he kept whimpering, she rocked side to side. "Already you have a man doing much good work with my crops. I cannot accept more!"

"Wait here." He walked away and returned a moment later without Talitha. With a few quick tugs, he untied the straps holding Johnny to her back. "He's winding up. Is he hungry?"

"He may be wet again." Steven carried the cradle board into her room and laid it on the bed. She plucked Johnny out and hummed a lullaby under her breath as she deftly changed him.

"You're always so patient with the babies, Lena."

She smiled at the compliment. "It is not easy some days, but they need to be loved, so I try."

When she moved to tuck Johnny back into the cradle board, Steven halted her. He swiped Johnny, slipped him back into his cradle, then turned to her. "I can't let you go back home today, Lena. You're plumb tuckered out. Go back to bed."

She cast a longing look at the bed then decisively shook her head.

"There is much that needs doing."

Strong, lean, tanned fingers captured her jaw. He turned her face ever so slightly toward the window so the first pink rays of dawn illuminated her features. "The dark circles under your eyes tattle, Lena. You're weary beyond imagining. This is ridiculous. If you fall sick, we'll have a real mess on our hands. The babies need you healthy."

"I am not sick."

"You're weaving on your feet!"

A gamine smile tilted her lips. "I am in the habit of rocking. It soothes the children."

"I'll pull a rocking chair in here for you."

"That would be most kind. Thank you."

"For now, you're going to bed." He swept her up and placed her in the center of the bed. Once he settled her there, he cupped her shoulders and gave her a stern look. "You desperately need sleep. Don't even think of getting up 'til noon."

"I am no slugabed!"

"No, Lena, no one could ever rightfully accuse you of sloth. Today, at least, you're going to rest up, though." He turned and paced from the room. Practical, ugly boots in the hallway stopped him. His heart twisted. She'd been tiptoeing out of here and putting on those ugly monstrosities downstairs to keep from awakening him or Mrs. Axelrod. She worked harder than any man he knew, yet she never complained. In fact, he now realized he'd leaned heavily on her, even though she'd suffered a recent loss herself. From all accounts, she and Lars had a strong, happy marriage, yet she handled her grief with a dignity and serenity he could not begin to emulate. He envied her peace of heart.

He picked up the boots and took them back to her room. In the few moments he'd been gone, she'd turned onto her side, curled up, and already fallen fast asleep. In the brief moment he'd lifted her, she'd seemed far too slight. Worried that she might be sickening, he summoned old Doc Willowby.

Doc sat in the parlor that noon. "Her son nurses about every four hours." He paused meaningfully and peered over his glasses. "Your daughter needs feeding every hour and a half."

Steven sucked in a noisy breath. "That was supposed to just be for the first few days."

Doc continued, "Your daughter came a full four weeks early, so she's a wee mite. Her stomach is small and can't hold much, but because she's premature, it takes her longer to suckle. She'll have to eat frequently for a good while yet. Don't get the wrong impression here—Lena didn't complain one bit, even though she's clearly reached the point of total exhaustion."

"Lena never complains." Steven said the words softly. Jane often pouted if she felt put upon, or she lamented little inconveniences. He'd needed to cajole her and placate her with tiny gifts and affection, but he'd figured it was a feminine trait. The realization that he'd made a comparison at all and his beloved wife hadn't been the victor sent pangs of guilt through him.

Doc adjusted his glasses. "You were smart to get Mrs. Swenson to stay in bed, and you are right to be concerned about how thin she's gotten. If she drops any more weight, she'll lose her milk. It's not that she's sick; it's like she's feeding twins, so she needs to eat like a field hand."

Steven groaned and thought of how Lena invariably ate every last morsel off of her plate. Jane always practiced perfect manners and left a few bites, so by comparison, he'd found Lena's manners wanting. Disgusted with himself, he realized aloud, "I've been starving her! Why didn't she say something?"

"I asked. The poor woman had to worry about having enough food on hand, so she never imagined anyone else had much more in the way of supplies. It didn't occur to her that you had more than what was put before her. Every single day has been a struggle for simple survival. On top of that, she's still suffering her own grief. The poor woman was already straining to keep her head above water. Taking on your daughter was the single most selfless act I've ever seen."

"We'll take care of her."

"She can still suckle the babies. In fact, if we take them away, she'll undoubtedly lose her milk in less than two days. Talitha still won't take a bottle, but she's thriving with Lena, so we need to safeguard them both. Food and rest—that's what she needs. Bible-reading time, too. Lena's one of those godly women who needs to nourish her soul to survive. It's undoubtedly what's gotten her through her trials."

"Whatever it takes, she'll have it. Thanks for coming by."

After Doc left, Steven trudged up the stairs. He'd considered Lena a sturdy farm girl until this morning. Wound up in his own sorrow, he'd failed to note how much of a strain he'd put on her. The doctor's words sobered him even more. He had to see her for himself. No noise came from the room, so he tapped lightly on the door.

Mrs. Axelrod opened it. She had Talitha over her shoulder and absently patted her to elicit a tiny burp. He glanced beyond them. Lena lay in bed, her braid once again unwoven so the tresses fanned out in a golden sunburst. Even in sleep, her expression was serene. Doc attributed that to her faith. Steven coveted the peace she had.

Steven stepped closer and intently studied the sleeping woman. Her hands were folded together under her chin as if she'd plummeted into sleep in the middle of a prayer. Deep crescents of fatigue shadowed her eyes. Her neck and hands were impossibly thin. The very thought of her toting buckets of water or chopping wood was completely ludicrous, yet he knew she had. The calluses on her hands were ample proof of that. For the first time, he was glad those were the hands that held and cared for his daughter.

Chapter 7

The morning sun cast a narrow strip of buttery light over the foot of the bed. Steven barely opened the door an inch and let out a sigh of relief. The room was quiet. Lena and the babes were sleeping. A plate had joined Lena's Bible and brush on the dresser. The crust of bread left there bore mute testimony to the fact that Lena had eaten the snack he'd ordered Mrs. Axelrod to take up each night. Steven gently fingered Talitha's blanket then smoothed Johnny's cowlick down before he slipped away. He couldn't set out on a day's work unless he assured himself everyone was faring well.

He saw to a few matters around the ranch then saddled up and headed for town. Folks murmured their condolences, and he accepted them grimly. Some of his old friends invited him to go into the Watering Hole and get rip-roaring drunk with them, but he exercised his self-control and refused. He had more pride and sense than that.

Watts' Mercantile sat between the bank and the diner. Hannah and Thaddeus Watts ran a fair place. They carried the necessities and offered them at a reasonable price. Steven had always gotten his hardware, tools, and essentials here. The store smelled of pickle brine and lemon oil and brand-new leather goods. It always did, and the stability of that fact gave an odd comfort. Hannah stopped dusting off a shelf and gently rested her hand on his arm. "I'm sorry to hear of your loss. How are you and the baby doing?"

He cleared his throat and wished his eyes didn't feel like they had sand blown into them. "I—um, I have Mrs. Swenson there with the baby for the time being."

Hannah's face brightened. "There's a nice arrangement. With Mrs. Axelrod getting on a bit in her years and that great big old house to mind, she simply can't keep up with a baby. Waking up every couple of hours and having to warm bottles would wear her to a frazzle. Lena's young, strong, and has a real sweet way about her. You made a good choice."

Her words about Mrs. Axelrod flummoxed him. Steven had somehow assumed the housekeeper would take on the mothering responsibilities until Talitha reached her schooling years and needed a governess. Now that he pondered on it a moment, cooking, laundry, and cleaning kept Mrs. Axelrod busy morning 'til night. Chasing after a toddler would pose an undue burden on her. As soon as Lena weaned Talitha, he'd need to hire a nanny. Unthinkingly, he asked, "When do women wean their babes?"

Hannah blushed brightly. She dipped her head and murmured, "It's different with each baby."

He shared her embarrassment. Rattled, he blurted out, "I didn't know. Johnny is eight months, so I knew it was at least that long. Talitha is real tiny. She was too weak and small to take a bottle. She came early, you know, and I guess she might, um, need longer. . ." His head dropped back, and he grimaced. Staring at the ceiling, he muttered, "Ma'am, could you do me the great kindness of forgetting this conversation?"

He could feel her lean closer. She whispered, "Mr. Halpern, am I to understand Lena Swenson isn't just minding your baby? That she's wet-nursing her?"

Steven straightened up and rubbed the back of his neck. He stared intently at the woman and wordlessly nodded. *I hope she doesn't gossip this all over the township!*

"Oh," she said in a tiny voice. "Women did that back in Bible times. Poor child! Is she improving at all?"

Paternal pride surged. "She's still a bitty thing, but she's not twig thin anymore. She's holding her head up, too."

Hannah beamed. "How wonderful!"

"Yes, ma'am, it is. I count it close to a miracle. She was so sickly at first, Doc wasn't sure she'd pull through. I owe it all to the very special care she's been given."

She winked. "It'll be our little secret."

He let out a relieved sigh. "Thank you. I appreciate it." Steven paused a moment then lowered his voice even more. "Mrs. Watts, ma'am, truth is, I need to rely on your discretion on another issue, too."

"I assure you, I will hold your confidence." She hastily added, "Save for the fact that I do not keep anything from my husband."

Her addendum was so charmingly honest, it reassured him. Steven leaned a hip against the counter and silently handed her a slip of paper. It was too embarrassing to speak the need aloud, but Lena's clothes were ready for the ragbag, and she used a shawl because she had no robe. He hadn't noticed that last fact until Mrs. Axelrod said something right before he left this morning.

While he waited, Steven selected a few of the smallest baby gowns for Talitha and tossed a pair of the larger ones on the stack for Johnny. His mouth quirked upward. Johnny was an active little guy. A man would be pleased to have a strong son like that to leave his land to. As soon as the thought crossed his mind, he went somber. He'd secretly hoped for a son, and now he'd never have one. He couldn't imagine ever marrying another woman. He'd never be fair to her because he'd cherished Jane, and no other woman could possibly measure up.

"I think we're ready," Mrs. Watts called to him. The bell over the door jangled as she set a small stack of clothing on the counter. "Will there be anything else?"

Steven silently added the baby things and waited for her to wrap it all. He turned and saw two women gossiping furiously behind their hands. One pointed to the counter, and he realized they were gawking at the things he'd bought for Lena.

Lena's cheeks scorched with color when Mrs. Axelrod dumped the contents of the package on the kitchen table. She gave Steven a horrified look. "Mr. Halpern, how could you do this? I cannot accept such fine things!"

"Those gowns cost only two dollars apiece! That's as common as can be." He scowled at the dress she was wearing. "Clearly you need them."

She shook her head. "I am sorry, Mr. Halpern, that you are ashamed of me. I cannot change who I am or what I own. I do not have two dollars to buy a fine lady's church dress to wear so I can go home to clean the chicken coop and muck the stall."

He stared at her in utter silence. Finally, he said, "Lena, I'm not ashamed of you."

"Yes, you are. You had a wife who had soft clothes and softer hands. I never met her, but I am sure you bought her many beautiful two-dollar gowns. I can see how much you cherished her and that you gave her many things. That was lovely, and she was blessed."

"But—"

"But I am a plain woman. My hands get dirty. Even when Lars was alive, we could not afford such luxuries. I did not pine for them. He chose the feed sacks with care because he loved to see me wear blue, and each time I wore my dress, he told me with his eyes and words he was glad I was his wife." She gave Steven a bittersweet smile. "Fancy and expensive things do not suit me. Feed sacks are good enough. I do not need a two-dollar dress to be a happy woman."

He fixed his gaze on her and said slowly, "No, Lena, you don't. I can see you're a woman who finds contentment easily." He then turned to Mrs. Axelrod and silently pled for her to make the poor widow accept his paltry gift.

Mrs. Axelrod obliged. She held up the robe and declared briskly, "Now that we've established that you're not a gold digger, let's face reality. You certainly do need this."

Lena doggedly declared, "My shawl is enough."

Steven bristled. "Woman! Stubbornness better not be a trait passed on in milk, because if it is, Talitha is going to be a handful. Now stop acting so prideful and carry those things up to your chamber!"

Talitha started to cry. Lena lifted a shaking hand to her forehead as if she had a terrible headache. "Please take all of it back. I refuse to wear it and do not want to argue any longer. I need to change and feed the children." Steven realized he'd shouted his last words at her. Her muted response was far more civilized than he'd deserved.

He'd have never let anyone bellow at Jane like that. The woman was stubborn as an old mule and unreasoning as any member of her fair sex. Still, he needed to be careful not to upset her. "Sit down, Lena. Mrs. Axelrod, fix her some chow." He scooped up the clothes and headed for the stairs. "I'll take these things up for you. I'm sure you'll change your mind."

Much later that evening, Lena sought him out. "Could I please have a moment?"

"Sure."

She stared up at him, her eyes glistening. "Mr. Halpern, the sun has set." Her comment seemed ludicrous. "Of course it has."

The corner of her mouth lifted into a wobbly, winsome smile. "The Bible says not to let the sun go down on your anger. I spoke angry words to you. They were honest ones, but I did not temper them as I should have. I know you are hurting in your heart these days, yet you tried to be generous. Please forgive me."

"You're making a barn out of a berry box, Lena. Forget it. I raised my voice, and you got a bit huffy. It's nothing. Just accept the clothes as an expression of my thanks and go to bed."

Steven knew he'd made a grave miscalculation early the next morning. Lena's reaction should have warned him, but he'd been too preoccupied to take the hint. The impact of his actions hit full force when Jane's parents arrived on his doorstep. Amabelle Maxwell swept past him and looked about. "Why didn't your housekeeper answer the door?"

Steven shut the door after Harold Maxwell entered. He swept a hand toward the parlor. "Come on in. Our neighbor's health took a bad turn yesterday, so Mrs. Axelrod went over to help."

The Maxwells didn't bother to go into the parlor. They exchanged a wary look. Amabelle's tone went icy. "Are you telling us you were here, alone, all night with that woman?"

Harold Maxwell didn't even give Steven a chance to answer. He raged, "Even with the gossip in town, we thought to give you a chance. I can see now what they were saying is true. Where there's smoke, there's fire." He grabbed his wife's elbow and started tugging her out the door. "Come, Amabelle."

Amabelle's eyes flooded with tears. "You lecher! Our dear Jane, just buried, and you're already carrying on!"

"Now wait just a minute!" Steven gritted out.

"We're not listening to any of your lies or excuses." Mr. Maxwell pulled his wife outside and stormed, "You can bet we'll take legal measures to get custody of our granddaughter. We won't let you taint her with your wicked example!"

Chapter 8

"Lena, we need to talk."

His heightened color and angry tone made her suck in a deep breath. Lena quietly took a seat and waited for him to speak. *What did I do wrong? Why is he so mad?*

"Jane's parents have petitioned to get Talitha." His eyes blazed as he bit out the words.

"No!"

"Oh yes," he said bitterly. "Her daddy is a retired congressman, and he has some powerful connections. That wily old coot got the whole deal figured out. According to him, I'm an unfit father, so they should rear Talitha."

Lena shook her head. "That makes no sense. It is untrue. You are a good father."

"Oh, they're twisting things around. I'm afraid you're getting dragged into it, and it's dirty."

"Me? How can this be?"

His fist hammered a single, livid blow on the desktop. "The night Mrs. Axelrod went to help Mrs. Brown. They are casting aspersions about you and me being alone here."

Lena felt heat fill her cheeks. "This is silly. I will tell them I only feed Talitha. You and I—we never. . ."

"They won't listen to reason. They've publicly questioned our morals, and half the town is gossiping about how I bought you a robe. A stupid robe!"

"I am sorry. I do not want them to take Talitha from you." She stood. "I will pack and leave right away."

He wearily rubbed his hand down his face a single time. "Sit down, Lena." She complied, and he continued on in a haggard voice, "I don't have much choice. I went to town and talked to Judge Perkins. He said they have grounds for action, and I have call to be concerned. According to him, the only way to solve this is for us to marry." He looked at her and added somberly, "So I'm begging, Lena. Marry me."

His proposal stunned her. Lena couldn't form any coherent words. She silently shook her head.

He came around and towered over her. "I lost my wife. I can't bear to lose my daughter, too. I won't pretend, Lena. I don't love you. I never will. My heart is buried out there with Jane. I won't even lie when we have the judge hitch us. I'll vow to honor and protect and provide for you. You just tell me what you want." His hands fisted. "I'll do whatever you want, buy you anything your heart desires—but you have to marry me so I can keep my baby girl."

Lena's heart twisted. She wet her lips, but before she could utter a word, he blurted, "If you're worrying about your son, you have my word that I'll treat Johnny like my own. When he's a man, he'll get a full share of the ranch just like our other sons. I'll hire a sharecropper if you want to keep the farm going so he can have his father's legacy, too."

The distress on her features cut him to the core. Desperation made him push harder. "Lena, you've been good to Talitha. I know you love her. You do, don't you?" He already knew the answer, but she was honest enough to bob her head in confirmation. "This way, she'll be your daughter, too. You won't ever lose her, either. This way, we can both keep her."

The mantel clock struck the hour. Silence hovered heavily in the room. "I will have to pray about this."

"Pray? Woman, you won't ever be safe living alone. Men will think you're my cast-off mistress. For your sake, and your son's, you don't have any more choice than I do."

Lena slowly rose. Her knees shook so badly, they barely held her up. "I will pray and give you an answer later."

❦

She went to her bedchamber and prayed earnestly. As a clock struck eleven that night, she found Steven out on the veranda. Her voice was subdued as she quietly said, "I will marry you. Thank you for promising to be good to my son."

"You don't have any reason to thank me, Lena. I should have been on my knees, thanking you every day for saving my daughter's life and helping me keep her. Whatever I do for you, it'll never repay you for that. I'll send for Judge Perkins. We'll get married tomorrow." He turned away, went down the steps, and disappeared into the night.

Lena stood there and listened as the sound of his boots on the stairs grew quieter. Doing God's will had never been harder. Over the weeks, she hadn't just fallen in love with Talitha—she'd also come to care very deeply for Steven. The terrible truth was, tomorrow she'd pledge her hand to a man who could never love her back.

❦

The next afternoon, Steven stood in the doorway and watched Lena stab one last pin into her freshly combed hair.

"That dress looks nice on you," he said in a gravelly voice.

She whirled around in surprise then recovered. "A dress so beautiful would make a pig look like a princess."

He continued to stare at her. She wore one of the ordinary, two-buck dresses he'd bought that had gotten them into this fix. It was plain as could be, yet she acted as if a modiste in New York custom-made it for her. She looked like it, too. It wasn't the gown—it was the woman inside it. For the first time, instead of looking common, she looked elegant and refined. His wealth would provide every comfort for her—yet he knew full well she'd been content living in her soddy with Lars. *Because Lars loved her.* Steven knew then that she'd been much better off back then. This was different. Steven asked everything of her, and she'd consented. He did it for Talitha, but he wasn't proud of himself. Lena was a beautiful, warmhearted woman. She deserved a husband who would love her.

Still, she'd accepted his deal, and he was going to hurry her through the ceremony before she changed her mind. "If you're ready, let's go."

Instead of coming directly to him, Lena went to the cradle and lifted Johnny into her arms. "We're ready."

Pale and composed, she stood beside him in the parlor. Steven had summoned the judge to the house instead of standing in the church before Preacher Durley. There were no friends or flowers. He wanted no reminders of what things had been like when he and Jane pledged their everlasting love. Instead of holding his hands for the ceremony, Lena held her son. It was just as well. Mrs. Axelrod stood off to the side and held Talitha. His daughter's nearness gave him strength to get through this sham.

When it came time, Lena took the traditional wifely vows to love and obey. Her voice shook, but she said them. He, on the other hand, had spoken with Judge Perkins and arranged for substitute words. Lena's arms tightened around Johnny's little body, and her gaze dropped as Steven vowed only to provide and protect. Once again, he knew he was cheating her, and he silently promised he'd provide her with all he could to make up for it. When she looked back up at him, her beautiful eyes swam with tears.

The judge sensed he'd best not push his luck and suggest a kiss to seal the deal. Instead, he cleared his throat. "Well, that's that. For what it's worth, I think what you did was right. Those youngsters need two parents. I'll stop off on the way home and make sure Jane's folks know Talitha isn't up for grabs anymore."

Winter was mild. Steven spent most of his time outdoors. When he came in, he made every effort to be cordial to Lena. She saw to the children lovingly, and he found his only happiness in their presence. Johnny crawled about and began to walk by Christmas. Tucked in the corner of the sofa with the support of pillows or held in Lena's arms, Talitha cooed at Johnny's antics. When Steven shucked off his boots and Johnny tried to put them on, he laughed for the first time since Jane died.

Johnny weaned himself and took great glee in spilling his cup down the front of himself. Talitha still nursed, but she'd grown big enough to wake Lena only once or twice a night. Claiming she was well rested, Lena took over more of the household chores.

Out of deference for Lena's feelings, Steven took the tintype of his beloved Jane off the dresser in their bedchamber and put it on a shelf in his den. He couldn't bring himself to hide it away. He walked a tightrope between remembering the love he once had and trying to respect his new bride. Lena never spoke of his struggle, and she never mentioned Lars. It was as if they'd made a pact of silence.

He wordlessly unplaited her hair before they retired and temporarily lost his sadness in the tenderness she gave. In the dark of night, he still knew it was Lena, not Jane; but she was his wife now, and he let his barriers down in those private moments.

Once, she whispered her love in the aftermath of their intimacy. He pressed his fingers to her soft lips and shook his head. "No, Lena. Don't. We care about each other and for each other. That has to be enough. I have nothing else to give you." She'd compressed her lips, grazed his cheek with her fingertips, and turned away. In the light of day, they never acknowledged the fragile bond they shared. Even if he could not cherish her, he hoped she drew strength and comfort from him.

Lena knitted a woolen scarf for him for the winter, and each time he went out, she wrapped it about his neck. She got up early each morning to boil water just so he'd have warm water for shaving. She expertly mended his leather gloves and sewed clothes for the children. He knew she'd accepted her place—and that bothered him even more than if she'd railed against him for cornering her into a loveless marriage. Quietly she cared not just for the children, but for him, too. He didn't deserve it. . .but when he urged her to stay abed or sit and rest, she'd still carry on with the little things that she thought a wife should do. He saw emotions in her eyes that he wanted to ignore—the caring, the need for affection, the sadness; yet Steven also saw the hickory toughness in her, and he hoped time would allow her to adjust to their bargain.

One night he watched Lena finish knotting off a length of thread. She'd kept her head bowed over whatever it was she'd been working on for the past several evenings. "What is that?"

Lena gave him a winsome smile. She held up a charmingly embroidered rag doll. "I thought Talitha needed one of these."

Steven thought of the dolls at the mercantile. They were fragile porcelain. When Talitha got much older, one of those dolls would be a cherished toy; but for a tiny girl who'd drag the doll about and abuse it, a soft, cuddly, homemade cloth doll was far more practical. He smiled. "That's mighty kind of you, Lena. Little Talitha'll probably love the stuffing right out of it."

"I hope so." She set it aside and picked up a piece of muslin and started stitching it.

Her hands were never still unless they held her precious Bible. She read aloud to the babies every evening. It seemed silly at first, but soon Steven made excuses to be present for those stories. Something about that Bible time eased a bit of the ache in his heart. One night when he'd been out with an ailing cow, he came in and caught Lena's quiet voice. He stood in the hallway outside the parlor door. Something held him back from going into the room. He heard her close the Bible.

"So he loved Rachel with all his heart, yet he was married to Leah. Leah tried to be a good wife to him. The very best she could. She gave him many sons, too, but he never grew to love her."

It wasn't just the words. Lena's voice carried a distress he'd rarely heard. Steven quietly tiptoed away before she discovered he'd eavesdropped. Bad enough he'd trapped her into a loveless marriage and cheated her out of all a woman deserved. He could at least let her keep her dignity. He owed her that much.

For Christmas, he ordered new clothes and a beautiful brooch from a catalog for Lena. Lena thanked him sweetly and wore them with grace, but he realized she'd been just as queenly in her ragged feed-sack calico.

She hadn't pitched her old gowns into the ragbag, either. One afternoon he rode in after a few days out on the range to find Lena in her old gown, conscientiously walking one of his mares. "She got colicky. Mark was worried."

Steven took over. "Why didn't Mark walk her?"

Lena gave him a puzzled look. "I am able. Mark is needed for other things." She walked beside him for a while. He finally rested his hand on her shoulder and asked, "Lena, how can you be so calm and have a peaceful heart? You've kept on going in spite of everything."

He stiffened when she slid her arm about his waist, but the horse still needed to stay in motion, so they paced along. Lena quietly said, "If I kept shaking my fist at God, how could I ask Him to hold my hand and lead me on?"

Her words stunned him. He said nothing, and she didn't seem to expect a reply. They continued walking in total silence; then she gave him a light squeeze. "I'll see you at supper."

"Fine."

"And, Steven?" She let go and gave him a tender smile. "It is not easy, but you are not alone. God wants to comfort you and lead you on. Just as you want only good things for our children, God wants good things for you. Think on that."

Chapter 9

Spring passed, and summer scorched the land. Since winter had been mild, the water table was low. Heat shimmered on the land. Prairie grasses were dangerously dry. Steven worried over having sufficient water for the stock; Lena fretted over saving every last drop for her garden.

Johnny ran about and had taken to calling Steven "Daddy." Talitha now crawled and mouthed a few sounds. She had a specific one for Lena, "Mamama." They'd become a family, simply by virtue of the love they shared for the children. Though she hadn't given birth to Talitha, Lena knew the little girl was truly her own daughter. She also knew Steven thoroughly loved her son. Even if he didn't love her, she couldn't help loving him. He'd kept his vows and provided well. He'd given her the protection of his name. He didn't flaunt his wealth, but he was generous to a fault. His spiritual struggle hadn't grown any easier, so she faithfully placed him in God's keeping.

Late one morning, Lena glanced out the window and narrowed her eyes. The heat of the day was already brutal, and she'd started to pull the curtains to keep out the harsh sunlight, but an ugly gray-black on the horizon captured her attention. Mrs. Axelrod had gone to her sister's for a few days, so Lena was alone with the kids. Her mouth went dry. She had no help, and she knew what that darkness meant: *Fire.*

Both children were napping. She ran to the barn and hitched the wagon herself. Quickly she drove it right to the veranda steps. With a glance over her shoulder, she checked the progress of the prairie fire. Lena knew she had precious little time. She pulled the drawer from Steven's desk that held all of his bookkeeping for the ranch. She put it in the wagon along with his money box then ran upstairs. In a matter of moments, she dumped the children's clothing on quilts, tied the corners, and threw the bundles down the stairs. In her haste, she made one more bundle and included her Bible, then grabbed both children from their cribs and raced outside. Praying ardently, she put the children in the wagon, climbed in, and set the wagon careening for safety.

❧

"Fire!"

Steven squinted and caught his breath. Prairie fires moved lightning fast, and this one was no exception. He raced for his horse, vaulted into the saddle, and headed for home. Lena and the children were alone. *Dear God, keep them safe!* he prayed.

Every hoofbeat, every heartbeat drummed home his worry. Cattle stampeded and every beast of the prairie bolted in panic. Animals knew to run, but would Lena? Even if she realized the danger, she'd never be able to handle the children. Big as they'd grown, she couldn't carry them both. How could she possibly get away? The wind shifted and picked up. It swept embers and flames directly toward his home. Steven knew the creek lay in the path of the fire, but it wasn't wide enough to stop the flames. *God, please, please at least let it buy me a few more minutes to get to them!*

He coughed from the acrid smoke, leaned closer to his horse, and urged it on. His family needed him. Nothing else mattered—not the cattle, not the barn or house or machinery. Danger roared toward his wife and sweet babies. They must be so very afraid. . . .

Terror and relief mingled as he reached the edge of his yard. Steven rode straight up to the house and tied his antsy mount to the kitchen railing. "Lena! Lena!"

He burst through the kitchen and into the hallway. "Lena!"

No one answered. He hastily searched the house, yelling; but when he found the cribs rumpled and empty, he knew she'd taken the babies and fled. Steven ran back to his horse and spied the wagon tracks in the dirt out in front of the house. He followed them.

"Lena!" he called, but she didn't hear him. He watched as she veered off the road because the wind had shifted yet again. She'd exercised common sense and instinct to plot a course to safety. Steven closed the distance between them and jumped from his gelding onto the wagon seat then took the reins from her. She let out a cry of gladness then scrambled into the back to hold tightly to the children. He drove the wagon over the bridge and finally pulled it to a stop in a safe place on the other side of the river. Once he set the brake, he twisted around. "Are you all right?"

Lena gave him a quick nod. Both children clung to her. He didn't blame them in the least. He felt a mite shaky himself. He joined them in the wagon bed and pulled all three of them into his arms. "Jesus, thank You for keeping them safe!"

"He did keep us. I prayed, too," Lena whispered into his smoky shirt. "He took care of all of us."

For a while, no one moved. They all huddled together in a knot. When Talitha started to fuss, Steven scooted to the side a bit. Lena lifted her and crooned softly. Something stabbed Steven in the hip. "What is this?"

Lena wouldn't meet his eyes. "I didn't have much time. I couldn't save much. Clothes, guns, your books and money box."

Essentials. Lena had been so very practical. He could scarcely credit that she'd hitched the wagon and made an escape at all—but she'd even had the foresight to grab a few of the most basic things. His respect for her mushroomed. . .until he bumped a quilt and his desk drawer came into view. She'd not only brought his books—Lena had grabbed the tintype of Jane he treasured.

Steven stared at it and looked back at her. She turned away and busied herself by giving Talitha the rag dolly to gnaw on. "Lena, why? Of everything in the house, why did you save this?"

She shrugged, but from the tension singing through her body, he knew the gesture was not a casual one. "You love her. It was a little thing, but I knew you and Talitha would want it."

He cupped her chin and lifted her face. "Lena, I loved Jane. She was the wife of my youth." Pain streaked across her features. He hastened to add, "Young men grow up, Lena. Today I discovered I've been in love with you for a long while."

She pulled away and dumbly shook her head.

"No, Lena. Please hear me out. I don't need a decorative little woman. I need a wife. I need a helpmate, a partner in life. You are that woman. Jane wouldn't have left the house. She'd have sat in the parlor and wrung her hands. She'd have collected her pretty clothes and treasures and waited there. You are wise and capable. You acted and saved the children and yourself. Things can be replaced; a family cannot. You'll never know the terror I endured trying to reach you."

He raked his hand through his hair and continued on. "Now I know the truth. God was never far from me. Even when He took Jane, He was good enough to provide you so we could carry on. In my ignorance, I raged at Him; but He never abandoned me, and He gave you and Johnny to me as a gift. In my times of sorrow and strife, God blessed me with a woman and two babies to love. He was never far away, Lena. He was faithful, and He was there."

"Yes, He was," she agreed.

The reserve in her voice tore at him. Steven knew why it was there. He got to his knees and settled his hands on her shoulders. Gently he ran his thumbs up the beating pulse in her neck and lifted her chin. "I was a fool, Lena. I let you feel like Leah, an unwanted wife. Hear me now: You aren't Leah; you're like Ruth. She was a widow, too. God gave her to a man she barely knew, but they found grace and love. Let me be that kind of husband to you. Believe me, sweetheart. I couldn't say it months ago because I refused to lie—now I say it freely: I love you."

For weeks he'd ignored the love light in her eyes, and she'd finally banked it. She went about, filling their home with her special warmth and tenderness; but he caught the quiet hurt in her eyes and carried terrible guilt in knowing he put it there. Even now, wariness painted her features.

"Lena, you once said every need gave God an opportunity to provide and bless us. You didn't tell me the other part."

"What other part?" The words barely whispered between her lips.

"With every sorrow, God takes the opportunity to comfort and draw us close to Him. He did that through you, Lena. God used you to console me and teach me to risk loving again. That lesson came hard. It cost you every bit as much as it cost me. Please, sweetheart—let's both be whole again and of one accord as He wants us to be."

Tears sparkled in her eyes. "Is this what you truly want, Steven?"

"With all my heart."

He'd just finished kissing her soundly when Mark rode up. He was covered in soot. "Glad to see your family's fine, Boss, but the rest of the news ain't good." He grimaced. "Your place burned flat to the ground."

Steven cradled Lena close. "I have all I need, and God will provide."

Epilogue

From the ashes of their ranch house, Steven and Lena worked together to rebuild a home. During those months, their love blossomed and Steven found the serenity he'd been lacking. They filled the rooms of their new home with laughter and soon gave Johnny and Talitha a baby brother.

"He's a hefty little man," Steven said as he admired his newborn son. He tenderly tucked a damp curl behind Lena's ear. "I can only pray this one is half as smart and strong as our Johnny-boy."

"Ja, that would be a blessing." Lena gave him a weary smile.

Warmth filled his soul. Steven knew the Lord had blessed them with a deep and abiding love. God had been faithful.

CATHY MARIE HAKE is a Southern California native who loves her work as a nurse and Lamaze teacher. She and her husband have a daughter, a son, and a dog, so life is never dull or quiet. Cathy Marie considers herself a sentimental packrat, collecting antiques and Hummel figurines. She otherwise keeps busy with reading, writing, baking, and being a prayer warrior. "I am easily distracted during prayer, so I devote certain tasks and chores to specific requests or persons so I can keep faithful in my prayer life."

Freedom's Ring

by Judith McCoy Miller

Dedication

June Coombs
Ann Dunn
Jesse Grant
Ramona Kelly
Barbara Langham
Connie Long
Betty Marshall
Letty Meek

The friends who have prayed me through good times, bad times, and looming deadlines. The Thursday evening Women's Care Group, Maranatha Baptist Fellowship, Topeka, Kansas.

Chapter 1

November 1, 1840

Hannah Falcrest stood at the railing of the *Republic* and stared into the blackness of the water below. Flickering light danced from a mast lantern, and the resulting play of eerie shadows on the ship's deck sent chills rushing down Hannah's spine.

Hannah had fervently prayed. She prayed as she prepared for her family's departure from their hamlet on the outskirts of Yorkshire. . .and during the journey to Liverpool. . .and while waiting three days in a boardinghouse for their ship to sail. As much as she loved her English homeland, she had been willing to forsake kith and kin if, by immigrating to America, there was a possibility of Edward finding contentment. Then, perhaps, his happiness would overflow and spill out to include their marriage. *Oh Lord, make it so,* she had constantly, silently pleaded.

Now her journey to America neared an end. No longer must she cook her meals and brew her tea at the communal fire supplied to steerage passengers. No longer need she worry about her provisions running low, the distant, raging storms, or the dreaded seasickness. And no longer need she pray for a change in her marriage.

After forty-eight days at sea, and within four days of their scheduled arrival, the vessel dropped anchor in a New Orleans port. Everything seemed to be going according to plan. Everything—except for the fact that Hannah was no longer the wife of Edward Falcrest and mother of two children. Instead, she was a widow. Her husband and young son lost at sea. All that remained as evidence of her marriage was her eight-month-old daughter, Elizabeth, and the small gold wedding band on her finger. With a surprising determination, she twisted the thin circle of metal from her hand and watched as the ring dropped silently into the water below.

"Not thinking of jumping overboard, I hope."

Hannah hastily turned and moved away from the railing.

"I'm sorry, Mrs. Falcrest. I didn't mean to frighten you."

"Mr. Winslow?"

"Yes," he replied, moving forward so that the lamplight illuminated his broad-shouldered frame. "I grew concerned when I didn't see you below with the other women. Mrs. Iverson said you'd ask her to look after your daughter."

Hannah moved a step closer to him. The lantern glow mingled with the red-orange hue of an autumn moon to highlight William Winslow's well-chiseled features and send luminescent streaks of vermilion and gold through his ebony hair.

"Since my husband's death, I don't enjoy keeping company with the other women."

"They aren't helpful?" he inquired, a look of concern crossing his face.

"They are very nice. But—" She hesitated momentarily, gathering her thoughts. "But the women expect me to grieve the loss of my husband.

"I don't wish to speak ill of the dead, Mr. Winslow. However, I have no tears for Edward. The only tears I shed are for my son, Frederick. Does that shock you?" she quickly added, lifting her head and allowing her gaze to meet his velvet-gray eyes. His gentle countenance astonished her.

"Few things surprise me, Mrs. Falcrest. Indeed, I realize there are many unhappy marriages—I'm just not sure what causes them," he tenderly replied.

"From my experience, it would be beneficial if the betrothed parties loved each other, or at least liked one another, prior to the marriage."

"I would have to agree, ma'am. Am I to conclude, then, that your marriage to Mr. Falcrest was a loveless one?"

"Our marriage was nothing more than a business transaction—arranged to settle my father's gambling debts with Edward. But God blessed the union with two lovely children. For me, that proved sufficient compensation for the cruelties imposed by my late husband." Hannah's shoulders sagged with the weight of regret as she spoke. "Now Edward is no longer alive. But neither is my precious Frederick." Her voice wavered at the mention of the boy, and she turned her gaze back toward the murky water that was gently slapping the sides of the ship.

"Tell me," Mr. Winslow asked, his voice once again filled with the quiet tenderness she had earlier detected, "what are your plans?"

"I've come on deck to get a much-needed breath of fresh air and to seek counsel in the matter," she replied, giving him a reticent smile.

"Ah. And whose counsel might you be seeking?"

She watched as he glanced about, as if expecting to find someone lurking in the nearby darkness. "God's," she responded simply.

"And has He supplied your answers?"

"Not all. But at least the most urgent ones."

"I wish I could say that God answers *my* questions so directly."

"Perhaps you're just not listening," she suggested. "Or perhaps you don't like the answer and choose to pretend the answer is not from God."

His eyes seemed to twinkle in response to her comment. "You may be correct, Mrs. Falcrest. May I inquire as to when you and your baby will be returning to England?"

"I shall remain in America," she firmly replied, straightening to her full height with an air of stubborn determination.

"Would it be fair to assume that this is one of those answers from God that *you* would rather ignore?"

A small smile tugged at the corners of her full, pink lips as she glanced toward the beckoning lights of New Orleans in the distance. "I suppose that would be a fair assumption."

He threw his head back and gave a deep, resonant laugh that filled the night air. "You are truthful to a fault, my dear lady."

"I would certainly like to think so," Hannah responded.

"Forgive my laughter, but I find your forthright answers refreshing."

"That's an interesting comment, Mr. Winslow. I like to think that truthful, forthright conversation is a common practice. You speak as though the opposite were true."

"Perhaps I've spent too much time associating with the wrong people. I'll need to see if I can change that," he replied.

"A week or so after we set sail from England, I believe my husband mentioned he had visited with you."

As Mr. Winslow's face broke into a smile, Hannah attempted to recollect what Edward had told her about him. She raised her eyebrows in question and asked, "Didn't he tell me that you've previously visited the United States?"

"That would be correct," he replied cordially.

She had hoped that Mr. Winslow would elaborate without being quizzed. Hannah lacked the skill of engaging in small talk, especially with gentlemen, but she felt a desperate need for knowledge about this new country that would soon become her home. "Are you planning to settle in America?" she ventured.

"My dear lady, I've already made my home in the United States. I was back in England only briefly in order to meet with some business associates."

"So you've found them agreeable?" she inquired.

"Found what agreeable?"

"The United States."

"Yes, of course. Quite agreeable."

"And where do you reside, if I may be so bold as to inquire?"

"We've settled in New Orleans," he answered.

"We?"

"My mother lives with me."

Although she waited for what seemed an inordinate period of time, he said nothing further. Hannah could restrain herself no longer. "Mr. Winslow, only minutes ago, you told me that you appreciate forthright and truthful conversation. Is that not correct?"

"Yes, I did."

"Then why do you persist in giving me only the most meager of answers to my questions? Is it not obvious that I desire information about the United States and what I may expect in this new land?"

"I apologize, Mrs. Falcrest. But something tells me that once I provide you with the answers you desire, you'll scurry back below deck and I'll not see you again. I found myself mostly alone throughout the course of our journey, and I much prefer your company, even if I must gain this pleasure by devious means.

"However, I must confess you have succeeded in making me feel remorseful. Please, ask me your questions, and I shall answer them as fully as possible. But with one provision," he quickly added. "You must agree to accept my assistance once we land."

Hannah chose to ignore his final remark. She needed information—information that Mr. Winslow could provide.

Before they embarked on their journey, Hannah's husband had not been lax in gathering facts about America. Quite the contrary. In truth, many folks had scoffed at Edward's determination to investigate all aspects of this venture before leaving England. But although her husband had shared some of his newly acquired knowledge with Hannah, she knew that they would encounter unexpected circumstances at every turn. Edward's death had not been among the unforeseen situations she had considered. That event seemed to magnify every uncertainty the two of them had weighed only days before their sojourn.

"Prior to our departure, my husband was in correspondence with several people living in the United States. He decided that our best opportunity to start a new home was in a place called Illinois," Hannah explained. "We sailed to New Orleans, rather than one of the eastern ports, in order to avoid crossing the Allegheny Mountains, for Edward felt that such a trip would cause undue hardship with the children and our belongings. Someone suggested that we sail to New Orleans and then take a steamer up the Mississippi River, where we could board a boat at St. Louis to traverse the Illinois River."

Mr. Winslow nodded his head in agreement. "Sounds like a good plan. What was to be your final destination?"

"Edward learned of good land to be homesteaded not far from Pike's Ferry, near the Big Blue Creek. Are you familiar with that area?" she asked, her deep blue eyes alight with anticipation as she waited for his answer.

"No, I can't say that I am. I've traveled the Mississippi to St. Louis and farther north, but I've not sailed the Illinois River or been to Pike's Ferry. So your husband was a farmer, planning to homestead?"

"We planned to homestead, although my husband had little farming experience. We were told that a person who was not afraid of hard work could succeed. My husband wanted to own a piece of land and make his way in the world. That opportunity was not possible in England."

"Please don't think me unfeeling, but surely you don't intend to follow your husband's previous plan."

"What else can I do? We have already invested considerable money in the land, and I can ill afford to throw it away. Besides, I have no family left in England. At least I own land in America."

"Your husband purchased land sight unseen?" Mr. Winslow inquired with a note of disbelief in his voice.

"Edward had been writing to Mr. Henry Martin, who lives on the adjoining property. The land came highly recommended by him—eighty acres of improved land with sugar maples and some of the acreage broken up for sowing wheat, and another portion ready to be sown with Indian corn and oats. Of course, I'll want a vegetable garden near the house and perhaps a small flower garden."

"I don't mean to discourage you, ma'am, but I still don't see how you're going to farm the land, what with only you and the baby left. Why don't you see if you can find a buyer and plan to settle in the city? You won't be able to plant and harvest the crops by yourself. It's hard enough to eke out a living with both husband and wife working the land."

"Who do you think is going to buy the land, Mr. Winslow? As you already stated, land is rarely purchased sight unseen. The only person expecting our arrival is Mr. Martin, and the only place I have to call my home is this land in Illinois. Unless my situation changes, I see no other recourse but to continue my journey. I find little pleasure to think of leaving this ship and the few people who have befriended me throughout this voyage. They represent my last link to England."

"Since you earlier agreed to accept my assistance, let me make a—"

"You misinterpreted my silence for agreement, Mr. Winslow. I agreed to nothing," Hannah interrupted.

"William," he replied.

"Excuse me?"

"My name is William. Why don't you call me William? If we are to be friends, I think it would be acceptable to address each other by our given names. What is your first name?"

Hannah stared back at him, her earlier argument forgotten with this latest suggestion. "My name is Hannah, but—"

"Well, Hannah, as I was saying, why don't you let me do a bit of checking to see if I can find someone to purchase the land? You could then remain in New Orleans—or return to England, as the Lord so directs," he added.

She shook her head. "I firmly believe that I'm to go to the farmstead, Mr. Winslow."

"William," he corrected.

"William or Mr. Winslow—makes no difference—I believe I am to make my home in Illinois, not New Orleans, and not England."

"You certainly are privy to explicit directions, aren't you?"

"Not always."

"But this time you're absolutely certain that God has said, 'Hannah Falcrest, I want you to go to Pike's Ferry and live on that eighty acres of land.'" A tone of amusement edged his voice.

"God didn't actually say the words, Mr. Win—William. I just *feel* it, in here," she said, pointing to her heart.

"I see. Well, do you feel in there," he asked while pointing toward her heart, "exactly *how* you're supposed to care for yourself and Elizabeth on that land? Or do you expect to receive that information on another day or in some other way?"

"Are you intending to shock me by your blasphemous questions, sir?"

"They're not meant to be blasphemous. I am a God-fearing man, Hannah. But I need you to clarify this matter. I believe God intends us to use the brains He has given us, as well as clear logic, to figure out what to do in situations such as this. And to be honest, your decision defies logic."

"So you think me to be an irrational woman incapable of making a sound decision?"

"I beg to differ with you! I never said that," William retorted. "You've twisted my words. I merely stated that given the circumstances at hand—"

"It seems I have made an irrational decision," she said, completing his sentence for him.

"Think this through, Hannah. How do you think you'll be able to survive in the wilderness? How will you plow the land, plant and harvest crops, care for a home, and take care of an infant? Even if you had spent your lifetime on a farm, it would be impossible. You don't even have experience growing flowers. Tell me how you plan to succeed," he persisted.

"God will provide a way," she answered calmly. "I know this is what I'm supposed to do."

There was an assurance in her voice and a set to her jaw that seemed to signal the end of the argument. Hannah knew that she would make the journey to Pike's Ferry. And she wouldn't tell William Winslow how frightened she was, no matter how many times he forced her to confirm that decision.

"If that's your final word on the matter, I beg you to make one small concession," he requested.

"If I am able."

"Permit me to accompany you. Once you've seen the land, you can make your final determination, but I feel it would be unwise for you to travel into uncharted territory by yourself."

"But it isn't uncharted territory, William. Mr. Martin lives but ten miles away, and I'm sure that there are other neighbors."

"Did Mr. Martin mention other settlers?"

"Not that I can recall, but I'm sure there are others nearby."

"I don't want to appear argumentative, Hannah, but I must once again disagree. There are probably very few settlers in that area, which will make it even more difficult for you to survive. Will you permit this one compromise?"

Hannah remained silent for several minutes, allowing the impact of William's words to take hold. The company of another person would give her great comfort—even a person she had known for such a short time. And no doubt, Mr. Winslow could be of great assistance. On the other hand, how could she possibly travel in the company of a man who was not her husband? How could he remain with her once they reached Illinois? There would be no impropriety on her part, but such behavior would certainly set tongues to wagging. And, she reasoned, that was no way to begin a new life.

"What do you say about my proposal, Hannah?" he asked when she delayed her response.

"I realize that I have no control over your comings and goings, William. However, I believe such an arrangement would be improper. And what of your business? Surely it would be impossible for you to trek off on a sojourn into the wilderness and leave your employment."

"Being away from my business is the least of my concerns, dear lady. I am in a joint venture with several other gentlemen from Liverpool who now live in New Orleans. Believe me, my presence is not required until such time as an occasional document needs my signature. Otherwise, I wouldn't be sailing with you right now," he explained. "As to the impropriety of the situation, I'm merely offering my assistance. There's nothing improper about that."

"I see. But I still don't think it would be prudent," she quietly replied. "Now I must go below and check on Elizabeth. I'm sure she is sleeping soundly, but I don't want to take advantage of Mrs. Iverson's kindness."

William remained on deck long after Hannah had gone below. What about this particular woman made him feel that he must throw a cloak of protection around her? He had certainly courted women of higher title and greater beauty. But there was something about her that begged his attention—perhaps the fact that she seemed unwilling to accept his assistance. No matter the reason, an undeniable urge to come to her aid now welled deep within his being.

Perhaps God is speaking to me, he pondered for a fleeting moment. Then, just as quickly, he brushed the thought from his mind.

"Are you all right, Mr. Winslow?" the captain inquired as he walked toward William.

"Yes, just enjoying the night breeze. I am glad to be back in port," William replied.

"Aye, as am I. In all likelihood, we will disembark at first light. But I could get one of my men to row you ashore now if you're anxious to get back on land," the captain offered.

"Thank you. That's very kind, but I'll wait until morning like the rest of the passengers."

"As you wish. Did I see you speaking with the Widow Falcrest earlier?" the captain inquired.

"Yes, you did."

"Poor woman—such a tragedy. I had not lost a passenger on my last five voyages, and then to lose both Mr. Falcrest and the little boy. Terrible!"

"You had no control over the situation, Captain. Mrs. Falcrest holds no one to blame."

"I know, I know." The captain shook his head slowly back and forth. "Still, what a waste of human life—the boy so young and all...," he said, his voice trailing off with uncertainty.

"Right. Well, storms are uncertain things, and with the little boy already asleep on the bowsprit, little could have been done to save him, although his father mounted a valiant try."

"I'm not so sure Mr. Falcrest wouldn't have done better by his family had he not tried quite so hard. Don't misunderstand. I applaud his efforts. But his death makes things doubly hard on Mrs. Falcrest, what with losing her husband *and* son."

"That's true. However, I'm sure her husband was thinking of nothing but saving the boy from the unforgiving depths of the ocean."

"Now those waters are the resting place for the both of them," the captain concluded.

William nodded in agreement. There was nothing left to say. The event had struck fear in every one of the passengers, most of the parents now guarding their children with renewed vigor, while husbands and wives gave thanks that it had not been their mates who had perished.

"Is she returning to England?" the captain inquired, disturbing William's thoughts.

"No. She says that she'll carry on with the plans she and Mr. Falcrest made before leaving home."

The captain appeared dumbfounded by William's reply. "What? Can she not afford passage for her return?"

"I doubt she has enough for passage, but that isn't the issue. She tells me that she's had a word with God about her situation and He intends for her to carry on as planned," William confided.

"Do you think she's gone bleary-headed, what with her husband and the boy dyin'? Such things happen—grief causing a person to go insane."

William gave the captain a hearty laugh. "She's not insane. In fact, she is probably more sane than most of the people I know, Captain. At best, I'd say she's a woman determined to follow God's leading; at worst, I'd say she's pigheaded."

The captain appeared unconvinced of William's assessment concerning Mrs. Falcrest's mental stability, but he questioned the matter no further. "New Orleans is a far cry from a country home in England. She probably won't take long to change her mind and return to the homeland," the captain surmised.

"Ah, but she's not planning on remaining in New Orleans. Mr. and Mrs. Falcrest had made arrangements to homestead eighty acres of land in Illinois, and she intends on following through with those plans—alone."

"You're pulling my leg!" the captain replied as he slapped William on the back. "That's a good one, all right."

"I am not joking. She fully intends to establish a homestead near a place called Pike's Ferry."

"Off the Big Blue Creek?" the captain inquired.

"Yes. Do you know the area?"

"That I do. My sister and her husband homestead near Springfield. I travel that direction when I visit them. Pretty desolate country around Pike's Ferry. Not many settlers. For her own good, she ought to consider living nearer to Springfield."

"Unfortunately, that isn't an option." Concern etching his face, William shook his head slowly from side to side. "Ever heard of a Mr. Martin? Evidently Mr. Falcrest had been in correspondence with a man named Martin and sent him money toward the purchase of land near Pike's Ferry."

"No. Don't believe I've heard the name. But I could make some inquiries the next time I'm heading that direction," the captain offered.

"No, that's not necessary," William replied.

"I've got a few things to finish up before I turn in for the night, so I'd best be moving along. Have a pleasant evening, Mr. Winslow."

"Thank you, Captain, and you do the same," William absently answered as he stared off toward the blinking lights of New Orleans, again wondering why he felt compelled to help this woman and her child.

Chapter 2

H annah bit her lower lip, hoping to hold back the tears now threatening to spill over their banks. Bidding farewell to her beleaguered fellow travelers would prove difficult. Many of them had become friends. They had shared their hopes and anxieties about moving to a new land, laughed and cried together, cooked together and shared meals—and they had held a fitting memorial service for her husband and dear son after their drownings at sea. Most important, they had shared her grief at the boy's death. She prayed that leaving her fellow passengers wouldn't rekindle the deep aching within her.

Earlier the passengers had listened as the captain announced that the customhouse officers would be delayed in their examination of the ship and its contents. Explaining that more ships than normal had arrived within the last week and that the officials had fallen behind schedule, he encouraged the passengers to be patient for just a little longer.

The bleak pronouncements were met with groans of dismay and more than a few angry words. The already-weary immigrants were anxious to leave their floating habitation, and several of the men quickly blamed the captain for the delay. But William was at Hannah's side before the ship's officer finished relaying the ill tidings.

"You have nothing upon which a duty can be levied, and the captain signed a document on your behalf for the inspectors. The captain knows me and knows that I am a man of honesty. We've had previous business

597

dealings, and I merely requested his assistance. The matter is as simple as that. Now please let me help you," William urged.

"I feel like a traitor leaving the other passengers on board. Besides, the captain said that the inspectors wouldn't be here for several days," Hannah argued.

"This document will be given to a customs official who will meet us at the dock. And you mustn't think you are a traitor, Hannah. If any of the other passengers were given an opportunity to leave, they certainly would do so," William quietly explained.

Hannah turned and met William's gaze. His tone was soft, his eyes filled with tenderness. He seemed to sense her agony. "Please," he gently added, "let me carry the baby."

The kindness overwhelmed her, and now the tears rolled freely as she handed him the tiny child. Without a word, he pulled a linen handkerchief from his breast pocket and tenderly wiped her cheeks. She failed miserably in her endeavor to return his smile, but somehow she knew that he understood and that no words were necessary.

Once they had reached the dock, Hannah allowed William to take charge. "Wait here. I'll hail a carriage and arrange for storage of your belongings. If you have money that you wish to have exchanged for American dollars, I can do that for you," he offered.

Hannah hesitated only a moment and then reached into her reticule. She pulled out her money, all in English sovereigns, and handed the cash to William.

"You can wait over there while I speak to the inspectors," he said, pointing toward a bench not far from the dock. Hannah watched as he entered a small building and then, a few moments later, returned to the dock. After briefly talking to a lanky man wearing a bright bandanna around his neck, William beckoned for her to join him. In less than an hour, they were in a carriage moving slowly away from the waterfront.

"I thought today was Sunday. I must have gotten my days confused," Hannah remarked, peering at the vendors who hawked their wares along the muddy street. She shuddered at the sight of several black men shackled together as they were prodded along toward a large open area where many people were gathered.

"It *is* Sunday," William replied. "I'm afraid you'll find that the general population of New Orleans doesn't hold the Lord's Day in much reverence. Don't misunderstand—there are those who are attempting to correct the situation. My mother staunchly supports reform."

"What's going on over there?" she questioned, unable to look away from the unfolding scene.

"Slave auction," he replied without further comment.

"And you, William, do you support reform?"

He hesitated for a moment. "I must admit I am not as adamant as my mother. I'm not quite as offended with the 'business as usual' attitude."

There seemed to be a note of caution in his reply. "Does that mean you observe the Lord's Day but have little concern for the eternal salvation of others, Mr. Winslow?" Hannah asked.

"Ah, I see I've struck a chord."

"What makes you say that?" she inquired while shifting positions, her chin jutting forward just a fraction.

"You addressed me as Mr. Winslow rather than William," he replied with a slight smile playing at the corner of his lips.

"I suppose I did," she thoughtfully answered.

"Your religious convictions haven't gone unnoticed, Hannah. I'd be a total fool not to realize that a woman who looks for divine intervention in her decision making would disapprove of the New Orleans lifestyle—and working conditions," he quickly added.

"There's no denying that I believe Sunday is a day that should be dedicated to worship and rest. But there are those, even in England, who don't share my belief. Apparently, however, many of the people of New Orleans have taken liberties far beyond what I would have imagined possible."

He nodded. "For many, it's not because they want to work on Sunday. Undoubtedly, a great number of these folks would prefer to be at a worship service. But they have been forced to make a choice—earn a living or attend church. With families to feed and immigrants arriving daily who would gladly take their jobs, the choice soon seems simple enough."

"Perhaps they've placed their faith in the wrong things," Hannah quietly replied.

"Easily enough said," William replied as the carriage came to a halt in front of a two-story home on the outskirts of the city. He stepped out of the carriage, took the baby into one arm, and lifted the other to assist Hannah down.

Hannah quickly observed the house and surrounding area. From outward appearances, William and his mother must be comfortable but not overly wealthy. The house boasted a large front porch that wrapped around the house and a small sitting porch on the second floor that overlooked a flower garden. Hannah decided the sitting porch was attached to the master bedroom.

A tall, thin black man graciously greeted them at the front door as if it were a commonplace event for William to arrive home with a strange woman and her baby in tow.

"My mother?" William inquired, stepping into the foyer.

"At church," the man simply replied. "Have you eaten? I'll have breakfast prepared," he offered.

"Please," William replied. "Let me show you upstairs where you can freshen up and see to the baby," he said, turning to Hannah.

They ascended the wooden staircase and turned down a hallway. A narrow strip of worn floral carpet was centered down the hall; bare wooden floorboards peeked out from each side.

"I hope you'll find the accommodations bearable. This house leaves much to be desired," William said, pushing the door open to permit her entry.

Hannah stared about the room. A small sitting area led into a larger bedroom, which overlooked the flower garden she had admired earlier. Beyond the garden and grassy lawn, there were several run-down outbuildings and what appeared to be a vegetable patch.

"What are those?" Hannah asked, pointing out the window.

"At one time, they were slave quarters."

"Were?"

"The previous owner of this house was engaged in slave trading. He housed slaves in those buildings until they were sold," William replied.

"And what of your slaves, sir? Don't they also reside in those buildings?"

"We own no slaves, Hannah," William simply replied.

"Really? What of the man who answered the door? And who is cooking our breakfast?"

"I employ servants, Hannah. They are not slaves. I don't own them, and they are paid for their labor," he replied, immediately turning to leave. "Come down and have something to eat when you are ready. I'll see to a cradle for Elizabeth."

"William—I'm sorry. My comments were rude and inconsiderate. I have no right to question the manner in which you run your household. Please forgive me," she begged, though her tone sounded more like an urgent plea than she intended.

"There's nothing to forgive," he said while giving her a quick smile. "I'll be downstairs. Take your time."

She had just begun to chastise herself for her boorish behavior when Elizabeth's cries demanded her attentions. With experienced hands, she quickly replaced the baby's wet nappy with a dry one, tightly wrapped her in a blanket, and gently lifted the child to her breast. Elizabeth's eyes fluttered between wakefulness and sleep until her tiny belly was filled; then Hannah carefully placed her sleeping child on the bed.

Discovering a towel and washcloth on the commode, Hannah poured water into the basin and dipped the cloth into its depths. She held the cloth to her face and inhaled the cool dampness. The air seemed hard to breathe, a stifling humidity lingering in the air. She had heard stories of the difficult climate and yellow fever that seemed to plague New Orleans and the surrounding countryside, but she hadn't been prepared for the permeating heavy air. Her dress seemed oppressive as she slowly descended the stairs and entered the dining room a short time later.

William was seated at a highly polished mahogany table; behind him, a gleaming silver coffee service graced a buffet along the wall. A kind-faced woman rapidly waved a fan back and forth in front of herself, and she appeared to cling to William's every word.

"And here she is now," William said, rising from his chair. A smile spread across the woman's round face as Hannah entered the room.

"Mother, this is Hannah Falcrest. Hannah, my mother, Mrs. Julia Winslow."

Hannah offered her hand in greeting. "So nice to meet you, Mrs. Winslow."

"Address me as Julia, please, and the pleasure is mine. William has been filling me in on the details of your journey. My deepest sympathies, dear child."

"Thank you," Hannah replied softly. "And has your son mentioned his many acts of kindness to me? I don't know how I would have managed had he not come to my aid."

"William doesn't tell me much about himself—he speaks only of others," she remarked as she gave her son a knowing look. "William tells me that you hold a deep faith in God. I admire that."

"Sometimes my faith isn't as strong as it should be, I'm afraid. But I attempt to seek God's will for my life, and I pray for opportunities to share my beliefs."

"The Lord apparently has heard your prayers," Mrs. Winslow commented.

"What do you mean?"

"He sent you to New Orleans. If ever there was a city that needed God's hand at work, it is New Orleans. Personally, I can't wait to shake the dust of this wicked city from my shoes, but it seems that there is always something holding me back," the older woman replied.

"Oh, I'm not remaining in New Orleans. This isn't where God intends me to be at all. I am going to Illinois. But with the humidity in this region, I doubt that you'd ever encounter any dust to shake off your shoes," Hannah said with a gentle chuckle.

Mrs. Winslow gave her a halfhearted smile, although William laughed aloud at Hannah's wit.

"William tells me you plan to homestead. Quite an undertaking for a single woman with an infant. Have you considered that you might want to give that decision a little more thought? Perhaps talk to some people who have homesteaded—hear about the hardships and adversities they were forced to endure while living in the wilderness?"

"Such conversations might prove helpful," Hannah answered, "but they wouldn't change my decision."

William smiled at his mother. "Hannah has prayed about this venture, and God has told her that she is to settle in Illinois."

"You needn't make me sound like a raving lunatic, William. I did not set sail from England without any knowledge or planning for my future. My husband and I had—"

"Yes, William told me that your husband had purchased land in Illinois." Several minutes passed as the older woman unfolded and then carefully refolded a lace handkerchief that lay in her lap. "Don't misunderstand, Hannah, for I share your belief that God has a plan for our lives. But sometimes in our haste to hear from Him, we—how shall I put this?—misinterpret what we think are divine answers."

Hannah thoughtfully nodded her head and pushed away the half-eaten plate of food. Carefully wiping the corners of her mouth with an embroidered linen napkin, she met Mrs. Winslow's gaze. "I understand and respect your opinion, Julia. However, you cannot dissuade me from what I know I must do."

"I didn't expect that I could, but I felt the need to test your reaction. Apparently you and William are in for quite an adventure," she responded.

"Well, I don't think William. . .that is to say, traveling together. . . homesteading. . .wouldn't be proper for the two of us. . .unmarried. . .and all," she stammered.

"Quite so," Mrs. Winslow mused. "However, when the Almighty has a plan, nothing is impossible," she quickly added with a glimmer in her eyes.

"If you'll excuse me, I must check on Elizabeth," Hannah said, rising from the table. "I won't be long."

"Bring her down if she's awake. It has been too long since I've held a baby. No matter how often I nag at this son of mine, he ignores my pleas for a grandchild," she said, now directing her eyes toward William.

Hannah didn't know how to answer the comment, so she quickly exited the room, glad to remove herself from a discussion between Mrs. Winslow and William—at least any discussion that had to do with his producing grandchildren for the older woman.

❧

"Really, Mother! That remark was uncalled for," William chided. "You're certainly lacking in manners today."

"I spoke only the truth. If it makes you uncomfortable, so be it. I like that young woman. She has backbone—and the courage of her convictions. She's pretty, too," Julia added, almost as an afterthought.

"I've pursued prettier," William replied. "But I agree. There is something special about her. Perhaps it's her diminutive figure or the subtle appearance of golden streaks in her cinnamon-colored hair."

"Or her quick smile and upturned nose," his mother said with a laugh. "I'll tell you one thing, William—you may have courted woman who were a trifle more comely, but never one with half the gumption of Hannah Falcrest. She makes all the others appear fainthearted. Besides, I'm certain you've never courted a woman with her deep belief in God."

"That goes without saying. In fact, I don't believe I've ever known, much less courted, a woman her age with such beliefs."

"I'd say that a rare opportunity is knocking, Son. Don't rush her, of course. She's still in mourning for her husband. In due time. In due time."

"She mourns for her child, Mother, but not her husband. From what she told me, her marriage was an arranged one. Her father used her to pay off a gambling debt, so to speak."

"Surely not! Why, the poor dear, she can't be more than nineteen or twenty years old. How old was her son?"

"He was four," Hannah answered, walking into the room with Elizabeth in her arms. "And I am twenty-four."

"Only two years younger than William," Julia said, her cheeks flushing pink.

"No need to be embarrassed, Mother," William teased. "I'm sure that Hannah grew accustomed to people meddling in her affairs on board the ship. Didn't you, Hannah?" William asked, hoping to put his mother in her place.

"She's not meddling, William, and her curiosity isn't ill placed. Your mother is most gracious. I would want the same information if the situation was reversed and strangers were residing in my home. Feel free to ask me anything, Mrs. Winslow," Hannah offered.

"Only if you promise to tell me when I'm being intrusive," Julia replied, giving William a gleeful look.

"Does that offer go for me as well?" William asked.

"Of course not, Mr. Winslow—I fear your inquiries might be most unacceptable," Hannah replied. "I don't think your mother will ask me any objectionable questions."

William leaned back in his chair and snorted boisterously. "Obviously you don't know my mother, Hannah."

"That will do, young man," his mother cautioned from across the table. "Now keep your voice down. You will frighten the baby. Hand her here," Julia ordered as she stretched forth her arms to receive the child. "Oh, just look at her. What a sweet little darling. We're going to become great friends," she cooed at the infant. "William, why don't you take Hannah out to see the garden? I'll look after Elizabeth."

Hannah glanced first at Julia and then at William, trying to interpret the silent communication taking place between mother and son. "I'm sure Hannah would rather stay indoors," William answered, choosing to ignore the look his mother threw him. He knew what she wanted. Julia had used those looks as her silent form of communication throughout his life.

"Of course she wouldn't. She'd like to see the garden. Wouldn't you, Hannah?"

"If William would like to show me the garden, that would be lovely," she replied, obviously unsure what answer she should give.

"Certainly. This way," he said, rising from his chair and motioning toward a door at the side of the house.

Once outside, William led her through the garden to a small, shaded pavilion graced by two small fountains.

"You didn't want to show me the garden, did you?" Hannah finally asked.

"Oh, it's not that. I'm twenty-six years old, so I tend to resent my mother's attempts to direct my life. I am pleased to spend time with you, Hannah. But I had planned to attend to several other matters this afternoon. My mother doesn't approve of my Sunday activities," he answered.

"And what are your Sunday activities, if I may be so bold as to inquire?"

"Sometimes I handle business that can't wait. Today I was planning to check on the schedule of steamships heading up the Mississippi."

"Certainly that can wait until tomorrow," she calmly answered.

"But will you feel that way if I miss the opportunity to book passage on a steamer because I waited an extra day?"

"Of course. I would never want to be the cause of someone conducting business on the Lord's Day, William. However, if you desire to go into town, don't let my presence stop you."

"So if I were able to make the arrangements today, that would be acceptable?"

"You're putting words in my mouth. If the only reason that you are going into town is to conduct business concerning my passage up the Mississippi, I would prefer that it wait until tomorrow. Does that clarify the matter?"

"It's as clear as the sky above me," he replied. "Now since we have the balance of the day, would you care to see the vegetable garden?"

Hannah chuckled. Obviously William found it difficult to spend time at home.

Chapter 3

W hat do you mean, book passage for four?" William asked. "Hannah isn't even convinced that she wants me to accompany her." For the love of heaven, what had gotten into his mother? In her midfifties, she thought she was ready to embark on some grand adventure.

"Exactly my point," Julia responded. "Don't you see the impropriety of the situation? We've discussed it."

"You've discussed it?"

"Yes, Hannah and I. She believes that even though you are well intentioned, it would be improper to travel together. And then there would be settling the land. You couldn't live together. Such brashness would ruin her reputation. Surely you can see that, William?"

She was acting as though he were a complete ninny. "Do you think I haven't given considerable thought to the situation?" he asked. It took everything he had to hold his temper in check.

"Honestly? No, I didn't think you'd give the issue much thought whatsoever. Men don't think about such things."

"Mother, please don't generalize. Perhaps there are men who don't think about such things, but there are a few of us who give some thought to these matters. I know Hannah is a righteous young woman, and I wouldn't want to jeopardize her reputation. I would never want to do anything to cause her harm. Is that so difficult for you to believe?"

"No, of course not. But if you've given this matter your attention, then what, pray tell, is your solution?"

As usual, his mother had managed to put him on the defensive. He had given the situation some thought, although truth be known, he hadn't dwelled upon the matter for long. Obviously, social impropriety fell further to the bottom of his list than that of his mother. Now she was giving him one of those motherly looks that said, *I've caught you in a lie, young man*. Why didn't he just admit that his mother was right? It would be much easier, and it certainly would put a smile on her face.

"Well?" she questioned, breaking into his thoughts.

He shifted to his left foot, clasped his hands behind his back, and met his mother's unrelenting gaze. "We're going to be married," he blurted out.

"What? Married? Why, you never said. . .Hannah never mentioned. . ."

"We've known each other such a short time that she thought you would disapprove. I wanted to honor Hannah's wishes," he continued.

"When is the wedding to take place? You said you were planning to book passage right away. But you've not left the house long enough to make any arrangements for a marriage," Julia countered.

He could see his mother's mind at work. If he didn't get out of her presence soon, he was going to be caught in his own web of deceit. "You're absolutely right, Mother. I was going to stop at the church and talk with the preacher on my way to book passage. Remember, Mother, we're talking about a simple exchange of vows, not an elaborate wedding."

"Wedding? Who's getting married?" Hannah inquired as she walked into the room while cradling Elizabeth in her arms.

"Family friends," William quickly replied.

"Sit down, dear," Julia offered, leading Hannah toward the brocade settee. "You know, Hannah, I think you are a lovely young woman. And Elizabeth—well, it goes without saying that she is a delight."

"Mother!" William warned from between clenched teeth.

His mother gave him a syrupy sweet smile as she lifted Elizabeth into her arms. "Don't you need to go and make your arrangements, William?"

"I think they can wait a few minutes," he replied, dropping down beside Hannah on the settee.

"What do you think of your mother's suggestion?" Hannah inquired. "You have told him, haven't you?" Hannah asked, shifting her gaze toward Julia.

"Of course I've told him," Julia responded. "I don't think he's particularly fond of my idea. Are you, William?"

"It's not that I don't want you to come along, Mother. It's just that it will be a difficult journey, and there's really no need for you to—"

"She was thinking of my reputation. How selfish of me—I didn't give any thought to your health and well-being, Julia," Hannah apologized.

"Humph! My health is just fine, and I daresay that I could probably work longer and harder than either of you. I was looking forward to the adventure! As I told you earlier, Hannah, I would love to get away from New Orleans. But William tells me—"

"I hope you'll forgive me, Hannah, but I told Mother that we are to be married," William interrupted as he grabbed Hannah around the waist and pulled her into a deliberate embrace.

"You told your mother what?"

Hannah's voice pulsated between a croak and a shriek. William pulled her closer, hoping to silence her. His fingers tightened firmly around her rib cage. With his free hand, he took hold of her chin and turned her head toward him. Forcing his lips into a frozen smile, he furrowed his brow, met Hannah's questioning gaze, and threw her what he hoped was a look of warning.

"The announcement was necessary, my dear," William continued while still holding her chin, his steely gray eyes demanding that she not turn away. "You see, Mother told me the two of you had been discussing the impropriety of our traveling arrangements. I realize that you didn't want Mother to know of our marriage plans, but in light of the circumstances, well, I felt it necessary to tell her. After all, I wouldn't want Mother to make a trip into the wilderness thinking she needed to save your reputation when your reputation was already protected."

Hannah looked so pitifully bewildered that he wanted to pull her into his arms, kiss away her concerns, and tell her everything was going to be fine. He wanted to assure her that he would take care of her forever—that he loved her and would protect her.

Forcing himself to clear his head, William leaned down and whispered into her ear, "Play along with me, Hannah. I'll explain later." He hoped his mother would view the gesture as a show of affection.

Hannah's head moved ever so slightly, and her eyes seemed to register understanding. Inch by inch, William allowed his fingers to loosen around her waist until he had completely released his grip. Dropping his hand from her chin, he waited momentarily, not sure what she would do.

Hannah kept her gaze directed at him. He thought he detected a tiny glimmer in her eyes.

"I do understand, my dear. It was rude not to include everyone in the marriage plans. However, since your mother desires to go along, I can think of nothing more delightful than having her join us. Why, what a wonderful opportunity for us to get better acquainted. Don't you think so?" Hannah generously inquired.

She was giving him an ever-so-sweet smile, and her eyes seemed to dance with delight. "We'll discuss the matter further—in private," he replied hastily.

"Why, thank you, Hannah. I knew I liked you from the moment we met. Didn't I say that, William?" his mother asked as she affectionately ran her fingers through Baby Elizabeth's curly blond hair.

Without comment, William rose from the settee and moved toward the windows that overlooked the garden. *Those two must certainly be collaborating.* They had to be! How could this have happened otherwise? Only a short time earlier, he was a carefree bachelor. Now he found himself propelled into marriage, fatherhood, and a journey into the wilderness of Illinois. An excursion that would, of all things, include his mother. Unthinkable!

"Didn't I, William?" his mother insisted.

"What? Oh yes, I suppose you did," he muttered, still trying to gather his thoughts.

"Is something wrong, William?" Hannah inquired.

Her voice seemed to vibrate with merriment. "Nothing that can't be attended to right now," he replied. "Mother, will you see to Elizabeth while Hannah and I take a stroll in the garden?"

"Of course, of course. You two lovebirds take some time for yourselves. In fact, why don't you both walk to the church and visit with Reverend Milrose about your wedding plans? No time like the present, I always say," Julia replied, a smile sweeping across her face.

"Right," William answered as he took Hannah's arm and led her toward the front door. "We won't be long."

"No, not long at all," Hannah added. "I'll need to feed Elizabeth soon."

"You just fed Elizabeth before you walked into the parlor and wreaked havoc," William replied, tightening his grip as they reached the street.

"I wreaked havoc? Surely you jest, Mr. Winslow. You are responsible for telling your mother those preposterous lies, sir."

She had turned to face him, her intense blue eyes appearing almost black. A tinge of crimson highlighted her cheeks, and her bottom lip seemed to quiver as she stood before him. Once again he felt the undeniable urge to enfold her in his arms, cover her lips with his own, and promise her that everything would be fine. He lifted his finger and softly ran it down the side of her flushed cheek.

"You are so lovely," he murmured.

"And you, sir, are a—"

"Don't say anything you will regret," he admonished, his finger coming to rest on her lips.

"I never regret the truth," she sputtered around the index finger that he continued to press gently against her mouth.

"Why don't we stroll over to the park, and I'll explain this whole situation. I think our dilemma can be easily rectified."

"I don't appear to have much choice," Hannah answered.

"You certainly aren't the frail little thing I first thought," he said, surprised by her strength as she attempted to free her arm from his grasp. "Please don't be angry, Hannah, but when my mother told me the two of you were making plans for the journey, I had to think of something in a hurry."

"And a big lie was the best you could do."

"Well, she caught me off guard. I hadn't planned to deceive her, but the thought of my mother traveling with us to Illinois—well, the idea was more than I wanted to even consider. Besides, our marrying isn't such a bad idea."

"Not such a bad idea? You truly think we should get married?"

He couldn't help himself. He laughed. A long, boisterous guffaw that caused passersby to stop and stare.

"Would you please stop? People will think you crazy. Or worse yet," Hannah argued, "they'll think I'm crazy for being in the company of someone like you." Finally, she stomped her foot. "Stop, William. Stop right now!"

Her tone warned that she would brook no nonsense. William immediately sobered and gazed deeply into her smoldering eyes. He knew that she was filled with anger, but her strong emotion made her only more beautiful. More desirable. More delightful. More the woman he had dreamed of all his life.

"Oh yes, Hannah. I truly know that we should marry. And the sooner the better," he whispered, his voice husky with emotion.

"What has come over you, William? You make no sense whatsoever. Your mother has agreed to accompany us. Surely you find that more tolerable than entering into a marriage charade," she replied.

He continued to hold her gaze. He felt frozen in place; not a muscle twitched, not a sound penetrated his hearing except for the sweet sound of her voice.

"But don't you see? Our marriage wouldn't be a charade, Hannah. I want to marry you, to be your husband, to be Elizabeth's father. Do you find that so hard to believe?"

Now Hannah burst into laughter, clapping her hands together as she exclaimed, "Oh, that was excellent, William. You should take up a career on the stage. Why, even your mother would have believed that little speech—I know I almost did," she continued, dabbing at her eyes with a linen handkerchief as she began to regain her composure.

"You think my words were all for show—a performance? That I was merely concocting a speech to impress you with my acting ability?"

"Or ability to deceive, if you prefer," she answered. "In any event, there's no need for this foolishness to go any further. Your mother wants to accompany us, and that takes care of any impropriety in our travel arrangements. That is, if you still intend to accompany me."

"Of course I intend to accompany you. But my mother traveling with us doesn't take care of everything. I told her we plan to be married, and she expects a wedding to occur. I know you don't want to disappoint her. She has grown so fond of you and Elizabeth," he continued.

"Please don't exaggerate, William. She's only known us two days."

"Perhaps, but you must admit that she dotes on Elizabeth, and she's told me she thinks you're remarkable—and quite beautiful. We're in agreement over those facts," he added with a smile.

She hesitated momentarily and then met his gaze, her eyes serious. "William, even if I were to believe the things you've said, which I don't, you must realize that after one arranged marriage, I'd be a fool to jump into another. Do you remember that night on board ship when you approached me and asked if I was contemplating jumping overboard?"

He nodded. "I remember."

"Just before you spoke to me, I had removed my wedding band and dropped it into the water alongside the ship. My fervent hope was that it would wash into the very depths of the ocean. I wanted nothing that symbolized my loveless marriage; I was arriving in a free land where I had the right to prayerfully make my own decisions. Freedom! You can't possibly understand what that word means to me, William. You've never been bound in cruelty to another."

"But, Hannah, this is completely different. It was your father who made the arrangements with that heinous Edward Falcrest. Surely you don't place me in the same category as your dead husband! I'm a good man, Hannah, although I must admit you're probably hard-pressed to believe that since I've seen fit to show you my worst characteristics in the past two days."

"So telling—"

"Stretching the truth," he interrupted.

"I see. So stretching the truth is your worst vice, William?"

"Well, I'm not in the habit of stretching the truth. That seems to have come upon me in full measure only since I've made your acquaintance. However, I'm not sure how the good Lord categorizes vices. I tend to believe that a vice is a vice, and He frowns upon all of them. But I'd like to think that most of my habits are pleasing to God."

"I believe you're a good man, William. Otherwise, you wouldn't have been so kind to Elizabeth and me. And I genuinely appreciate all you've done for us. But marriage. . ."

"Don't say anything just yet, Hannah. Would you at least just think about my proposal? Better yet, would you pray about becoming my wife?"

"We'd better be getting back. I'm sure your mother has grown tired of being a nursemaid to Elizabeth."

"Hannah?"

"Yes, William, I promise I'll think about it—and I'll pray about it, too," she added.

They were silent as they returned to the house, each deep in thought, each unsure what the other was thinking, each afraid to break the silence.

"Here comes your mother," Julia cooed to Elizabeth as the couple walked into the parlor.

"Has she been crying?" Hannah inquired.

"Not a peep. She's been good as gold for her granny," Julia replied, kissing the baby's plump cheek. "She loves her granny, don't you 'Lizabeth?"

William and Hannah exchanged a quick look as Hannah reached for the infant.

"Well, what did Reverend Milrose have to say? When's the wedding?" Julia questioned.

"He wasn't. . . ," William faltered.

"We didn't talk with him, Julia. William and I had some matters that we needed to discuss privately. We didn't make it to the church. I hope you're not upset," Hannah interrupted.

"Of course not. There's ample time to take care of details. After all, it's not as though we're on a tight schedule. There are steamers up and down the Mississippi all the time. I'll see to dinner," she replied. "You two go ahead and continue your plans," she added as she walked toward the kitchen.

"You see, William? The truth wasn't so difficult, was it?" Hannah whispered as Julia proceeded down the hallway.

"No, not so difficult," he answered, his thoughts returning to the words he'd spoken earlier. Words of truth that expressed his deepest longing to make her his wife. Words of truth that she had chosen to believe were lies. He had to find a way to make Hannah his wife. She was made for him, and in his heart he knew it. All that remained was to convince her. Perhaps he was the one who needed to pray.

Chapter 4

Hannah gathered Elizabeth to her breast and stroked the baby's cheek as she nursed. This had been a long day, and Hannah was weary. Weary of trying to sort out the occurrences of the days since her arrival and weary of attempting to plan an uncertain future. Her thoughts wandered back to William and her earlier promise to pray about his marriage proposal. Did he really want to marry her? How could he? They barely knew each other. Yet when he had looked at her this afternoon, his eyes alight with what appeared to be desire, she had felt an urging deep within her, a longing to believe that what he said was true, to believe that he would protect her, to—dare she think it?—love her. He could have any woman in New Orleans. His mother had as much as told her so. Why would he want to saddle himself with a widow and baby? Especially one who was determined to settle in the wilderness! Nothing seemed to make any sense.

Placing Elizabeth in the wooden cradle that William had thoughtfully brought to her room only yesterday, Hannah covered the baby and then knelt beside her bed. "Give me wisdom, oh Lord. Show me what I am to do. I come seeking Your divine guidance, Father, and because You are always faithful, I know You will answer. You know my confusion, so I pray You will make Your answer crystal clear. I thank You for all Your blessings, Father," she whispered, her head now resting on the side of the bed. Forcing herself to rise, Hannah slipped under the covers and immediately fell into a sound sleep.

"Who is it?" Hannah called out as she rubbed her eyes. Sun was shining through the curtains, and Elizabeth was awake, babbling softly and playing with her toes.

"It's Julia. Are you ill?"

"No, come in."

"I was getting worried when you didn't come down for breakfast. William left hours ago, and I didn't know whether to waken you or not."

"I'm fine, Julia. I'll join you as soon as I've fed Elizabeth and dressed."

"Good. We need to talk," she replied.

The older woman seemed distracted as Hannah entered the parlor a short time later with Elizabeth in her arms. "Here we are—finally," Hannah announced.

"Sit down, Hannah. I've something to tell you," Julia replied, patting the seat beside her. Reaching out, she took Hannah's hand in her own. "I don't know how to tell you this. I feel just terrible about it," she said while fiddling with a small brooch fastened to the collar of her dress.

"What is it, Julia? You look distraught. Surely nothing so terrible could have happened since last evening."

"Oh, but it has. We received word early this morning that my sister is very ill back in England. She's asked that I return to see her before she. . ."

"Julia, I'm so sorry," Hannah said, embracing the older woman as she wept. "Of course you need to go and be with her."

"But don't you see? I promised to go with you to Illinois, and now I can't go along." Once again she broke into unrelenting sobs. "I've let you down," she wailed.

"You haven't let me down. Everything is going to be fine."

"Of course it is," William agreed as he strode into the room, his hands filled with a sheaf of papers.

"What's all that?" Julia inquired.

"Shipping invoices, a purchase order for goods, steamer tickets, and an appointment to see Reverend Milrose," he said, waving one of the papers in the air. "We're to be married this afternoon at four o'clock—that way you'll be able to attend, Mother." Without missing a beat, he turned toward Hannah and added, "Mother's ship sails tomorrow morning, and our steamer departs midafternoon."

"We need to talk, William," Hannah said, nodding toward the other room.

"You're right; we do. Mother, would you look after Elizabeth for a few minutes?" Before his mother had an opportunity to answer, William grabbed Hannah's hand and led her to the garden.

"I believe God's answered our prayers," William began.

"Our prayers?"

"You did pray, didn't you? After all, you promised, Hannah."

"Well, yes, I. . ."

A smile crossed his face and he kissed her hand. "I know you did— don't look so serious. After all, we've already received an answer. The answer I prayed for, I might add."

"So you believe that your aunt's imminent death is an answer to our prayers?" an astonished Hannah questioned.

"Of course not. My aunt has sent for my mother three times in the last several years. She gets lonely and each time sends word that she's dying. Mother rushes back to England and they have a nice long visit, which seems to miraculously cure Aunt Birdie for six months or so."

"Hasn't your mother caught on to this ploy?"

"Yes, of course, but there's always the fear that this time it might be true. If she doesn't go and something should happen to Birdie, Mother would never forgive herself. It seems to me that we are meant to be married, Hannah. Don't you agree?"

She couldn't even sort out her thoughts, let alone make an intelligent decision. It was all happening so fast, yet she knew there wasn't time to delay. "I'm not sure. It would appear that all other doors have closed."

"Except the church door," William hastened to add. "I'm sorry. I couldn't resist." He grinned.

"We may as well remain lighthearted about the situation. Otherwise, I think I would dissolve into tears," she replied as she turned toward the parlor.

"Wait, Hannah. On a more serious note, there is one other thing I want to discuss with you."

She returned and faced him. What else could he possibly have up his sleeve?

"I purchased a wedding ring for you this morning." He reached into his weskit and pulled out a wide gold band. "You see, it has a heart engraved in the center," he said, tracing his finger around the delicately etched outline. "Quite unique, don't you think?"

"Yes, it's beautiful," she replied. "I didn't expect—I mean, you didn't need to—"

"You must have a ring, Hannah. It signifies to the world that you are a married woman. But this ring will also have a special significance to the two of us. When we are married, I will place the ring on your finger with the pointed end turned toward your heart. Until such time as you turn the ring and place the point outward, toward my heart, you will be my wife in name only. I shall not force myself upon you."

"William, I don't know what to say. That's most kind of you."

"I pray that it won't be long. But I give you my solemn oath that I will wait until you choose to be my wife."

"Thank you," she whispered, unable to immediately comprehend such loving generosity.

Hannah settled herself beside William as the steamer chugged its way up the Mississippi. "What do you think of the country so far, Mrs. Winslow?" William inquired of his new bride as he took Elizabeth and placed her upon his lap.

"I believe this scenery could make anyone forget her homeland. The landscape is too beautiful for words—except for that," she said, pointing toward a cluster of black workers cultivating land on one of the many plantations they had passed. "I thought this was a land of freedom," she murmured.

"For some but, unfortunately, not for all," William replied.

She nodded at his comment, but her gaze remained focused in the direction of the slaves until long after they had disappeared from sight.

Day after day they moved up the river, stopping frequently to obtain timber with which to fuel the steamer. After two days on board the boat, the three of them began going ashore at each stop, enjoying the brief respites to once again walk on firm ground and spend a few moments by themselves. The plantations soon gave way to more uncultivated land, and majestic forests replaced the date and plantain trees. Hannah marveled at the untamed beauty of it all until, twelve days and thirteen hundred miles later, the paddleboat hissed and shook its way into port at St. Louis.

"This isn't what I expected," Hannah told William as she attempted to gain a better view of the city. "I thought it would be much grander, with buildings of stone instead of wood. But still, it will be enjoyable to see what sights St. Louis has to offer and sleep in a decent bed for the night."

No sooner had Hannah uttered those words than a crewman called to William. "Best hurry, Mr. Winslow. The packet headed for Pike's Ferry is leaving soon."

"We must leave immediately? And we're traveling on that? I had hoped to visit St. Louis," Hannah complained as William led her toward a worn and unkempt boat.

"We've only a hundred more miles. Take heart, my dear. We'll soon be home."

Home? She returned his smile, but the less-than-adequate accommodations and chilly November air caused her to wonder what she had gotten them into. Wrapping another blanket around Elizabeth, Hannah once again gave thanks for the child's sweet disposition.

❧

About nightfall the next day, the packet came to a halt, and a small boat was lowered into the water. "You folks need to collect your luggage and get into that boat," the captain explained.

"Excuse me? Why would we want to do that?" Hannah inquired.

"That's Pike's Ferry over there. My man will row you over and come back to get the rest of your belongings. Careful as you go, missus," he continued while pushing Hannah toward the boat.

"There's been a mistake," Hannah said, pulling away from the captain.

"This can't be the place. There's nothing in sight but woods."

"No mistake, missus. That there is Pike's Ferry. Step lively now. We need to keep moving."

"Come along, Hannah. Let me take Elizabeth," William offered. "Let the captain help you down."

"William! We can't go ashore here. It's nightfall, and there's not a dwelling in sight."

"This is where God told you to come, my dear. Remember?" he whispered in her ear.

"Yes, William, I remember," she replied, pasting a smile on her face as she tripped and fell into the boat.

"Careful, missus. You don't want to get wet. You'll catch your death, what with this frosty night air," the captain warned.

"Thank you so much for your concern, Captain," Hannah replied.

"Was there a note of insincerity in that 'thank you'?" William inquired as the boat cut slowly through the water toward shore.

"Perhaps just the tiniest bit," Hannah replied with a giggle.

By the time the small family and their belongings had finally been deposited at Pike's Ferry, Hannah's laughter had subsided. In fact, she was now attempting to hold back a floodgate of tears. She chewed upon her lower lip, but it didn't work. The tears rolled freely down her cheeks as dusk gave way to twinkling stars bursting through the darkening sky and the chill of a damp frost invaded the countryside.

"There's nothing in sight, William, not a sign of habitation. What are we going to do?"

"First of all, we're going to remain calm. The owner of the ferry must live nearby. We will probably find a homestead clearing just beyond these woods. I want you and Elizabeth to remain here. I'll go and see if I can find someone. Everything will be fine—you'll see," he said, placing a comforting arm around her shoulder and pulling her close.

The warmth of his body radiated through her like the warmth of a glowing ember. She pressed tightly against him, drawing from his body heat and attempting to ward off the chill of fear that now attacked her very soul.

"Please, William. You can't leave us. What if something happens to you out there? What would we do? We'd never survive."

"Of course you would. Besides, nothing is going to happen. Remember who brought us here, Hannah. While I'm gone, perhaps you could ask for some divine guidance."

"Yes, William, of course. I'm being foolish. I'll be in prayer while you look for help. You're right. Everything is going to be wonderful."

"Now don't put words in my mouth, Hannah. I never said everything was going to be wonderful," he said as he gave her a smile. "I'd best be on my way before it gets any darker. You stay right here, no matter what. You understand?"

She nodded her head in agreement as he turned to go.

"William, wait!"

Without further thought, she rushed to him, pulled his head down to hers, and firmly kissed his lips. "Hurry back," she begged, her heart pounding so loudly that she could barely hear her own words as she spoke.

His eyes filled with a profound passion that ignited a spark of love deep inside her very being. Pulling her into his arms, he held her tightly, his mouth covering hers with kisses as he murmured her name over and over again. Her knees felt as though they would capsize beneath her. She clung to him, hungry for his touch and craving his love with a raw emotion that she had never before felt.

Without warning, he pulled away from her. "I must leave now. Otherwise, I'm going to break my promise. I'll be back soon," he called over his shoulder.

Hannah dropped onto one of the trunks, her legs now unable to hold her upright. Her body was trembling, but not from the cool night air. What was happening? Was this the love God created for man and wife? Was it possible that she had fallen in love with her husband?

Dropping to her knees on the bare, cold ground, Hannah looked upward. "Oh Father, I don't know why You want me in this place, but I'm trying my best to follow Your direction. I come now to thank You for sending William. I pray that You will protect him as he seeks help for us. I think I may be in love with him, and for that I'm eternally grateful. Show us Your will for our lives and what You would have us do in this place called Pike's Ferry, for it certainly escapes my humble knowledge, Lord. Thank You for Your provision thus far. Amen."

Pulling a quilt from one of her trunks, Hannah tightly tucked it around the soundly sleeping Elizabeth. The star-filled canopy of heaven hung overhead, while the deep, silent river ran in front of her and dark woods stood looming to the rear. There was no place to go, nothing to do—nothing but to trust in God. It seemed as though hours passed, but she had no way of knowing for sure. The sky grew darker. More stars hovered above. And the moon shone brighter and larger than when they had first arrived.

The sound of barking dogs in the distance caused Hannah to snatch up Elizabeth. As the sounds grew louder, she clutched the child all the more tightly, wondering where she could possibly hide should the wild dogs seek them out and attempt an attack. She certainly couldn't go into the river. And running into the woods wasn't practical. The dogs would hunt them down in no time.

Cradling the baby, she rocked back and forth, fear rippling through her body as the barking continued—growing louder and more incessant with each passing moment. Then she heard it, the breaking of nearby branches as the animals approached. She could hear them panting and see their eyes glistening in the moonlight as they coursed toward her with long, calculated strides. The first one arrived, closely followed by three others, forming a semicircle around her and Elizabeth as they howled to their master that they had found their prey.

"Back off, you dogs," a deep voice bellowed in the distance. "Get back afore you scare the poor woman to death," he hollered at the dogs as they chased back and forth between the approaching wagon and a tearful Hannah, guarding her daughter.

"Hannah! It's me, William. The dogs will do you no harm," he called out while racing toward her. "Are you all right?" he asked as he reached the small clearing where she stood cradling Elizabeth in one arm while holding a large stick in her opposite hand.

"Oh, William! I was so frightened. I thought they were wild dogs. I see you found someone," she panted, unable to gain control of her emotions as she stared toward the unkempt-looking man sitting atop a mule-drawn wagon.

"I did. This, my dear, is Mr. Henry Martin," William announced.

"It is? I mean, how do you do, Mr. Martin? It's a pleasure to meet you. My late husband was in correspondence with you. That is to say, we purchased land from you," she stammered.

"So your present husband says," the man dryly remarked as he spit a stream of tobacco juice from between his front teeth. "You planning to spend the night out here jawing, or you want to load up and get back to my place?"

"He's certainly rude," Hannah whispered to William.

"So I've noticed," William replied.

"We appreciate your invitation, Mr. Martin," she called out as the man jumped down and began tossing their belongings onto the wagon. "We'll do that, Mr. Martin. Some of my dishes are in those barrels."

"Ain't no need for fancy dinnerware in this part of the country. Couple of tin pans and some iron cooking pots will serve you better," he replied with a snort as he continued loading the wagon.

"I'll load those things, Mr. Martin. Why don't you see to your dogs, and then I'd appreciate your help with the heavier pieces," William diplomatically suggested.

"Yeah, guess I better get them dogs in tow, or they'll be off and chasing after raccoons all night." Jumping down from the back of the wagon, he began hollering and calling the dogs, with his temper reaching fever pitch by the time he'd gotten them under control.

Hannah was thankful that few items remained unloaded by the time Mr. Martin returned to the wagon with the animals. He helped William lift the last of the heavy furniture and ordered Hannah to take the baby and be seated in the rear. She did as she was told without a word. Obviously Mr. Martin's manners matched his appearance, and she was too tired to argue.

After a few unseemly words and the crack of his whip, the team of mules finally moved forward. The wagon creaked under its burden as they lumbered down an overgrown cattle track. When they finally came to a halt, Hannah stared in utter disbelief. She had seen the large plantation homes and even the slaves' quarters as they had traversed the Mississippi, but she had seen nothing quite like the dwelling that stood before her. The house, made of hewn logs, squared and notched to each other with gaping spaces between the timbers, defied any architectural structure she had ever seen.

The front door opened, and a small-framed woman came out to greet them. Her wispy gray hair appeared to shoot about in every direction, and a trail of smoke circled above her head as she puffed on a pipe held between tightly clenched teeth.

"Whatever have I gotten us into?" Hannah whispered as William helped her out of the wagon.

"I'm not sure, my dear, but I think we both should keep praying!"

Chapter 5

"Get on in here," the sprightly little woman commanded. "It's too cold to hold this door open much longer."

"Then close it! I can open it myself when I'm ready to come in," Mr. Martin hollered back at her. "I never asked you to open it in the first place!"

It seemed to Hannah that the woman found great delight in slamming the door. Meanwhile, Mr. Martin continued to unhitch the mules as though nothing were amiss.

"Do you think this is their normal exchange of conversation?" Hannah whispered to William.

"As far as I've observed, it seems to be. They're a strange couple," he advised in a quiet voice.

"You may as well go inside while I finish tending to the animals. We'll leave your belongings on the wagon unless there's something you need tonight."

"No, this one small trunk and the baby's cradle are all we need," William replied. "Come along, Hannah. Let's get you and Elizabeth by the fire. Don't expect much. The inside of the house isn't any more attractive than the outside," he quietly warned as he banged on the door.

"Let yourself in," Mrs. Martin called from inside.

William pushed open the door and stepped aside, permitting Hannah to enter. She knew she was staring, but the interior of the cabin was so unsightly, so contrary to what she had anticipated, that she couldn't help herself. She could sense Mrs. Martin watching her, probably thinking her completely ill mannered and rude.

"I know what you must be feeling," Mrs. Martin said, breaking the silence.

"You do?" Hannah questioned, knowing that she must now apologize.

" 'Course I do. You're looking around here wondering just how long it's gonna take afore you and your mister have a place as fine as this. Well, I can tell you it's taken us nigh onto three years to get this place looking this good."

"Three years?" Hannah gasped.

"I know, I know. You just can't imagine having anything like this in a mere three years. Your place may take a mite longer, but if you work hard, you'll make it," she encouraged.

Hannah sat down on the rough wood bench and surveyed the room. A few boards had been nailed together in the form of a table and were attached by leather hinges to the timber walls of the cabin. Mrs. Martin proudly called it her "sideboard." In the center of the room stood another small table. This one, covered with a piece of coarse brown calico, appeared to be the dining table. The most respectable furniture was a set of four chairs with seats of plaited hickory bark. In addition to the chairs, there were two stools and the bench upon which Hannah was now seated. Along the entire end of the house, there was a grotesque stone chimney.

"Your chimney," Hannah said but then faltered.

"It's a beauty, ain't it? All them stones was gathered off our land."

"I see," Hannah replied while trying to understand the woman's pride in such a crudely assembled object. "And what is it that you've used to hold the stones in place? It certainly doesn't appear that it's cement."

" 'Course not. It's a mixture of clay and mud. Same thing we use between the timbers of the house. We haven't finished that just yet."

"So I see," Hannah remarked while observing a clumsily fashioned candlestick made from an ear of Indian corn, two or three warped trenchers, and a few battered tin drinking vessels sitting on the hearth. In the far corner stood farm tools, made with the same poor workmanship as was evident in everything else in the house. Suspended from the roof were a variety of herbs alongside several smoked hams and sides of bacon, and a rifle hung over the fireplace.

"Oh, and wait 'til you see this. Put the baby down and come in here," she ordered. Hannah followed the woman into the adjoining room, where Mrs. Martin pulled four large earthenware pots of honey from beneath the bed. "This here's a real treasure. Ain't nothing like coffee with a spoonful of honey. And this is my hand loom, but I guess you knew that," she continued, pointing toward the weaving machine. "Come along and I'll show you the cellar," she proudly insisted while taking the candle from the hearth and leading the way downward. "We growed this tobacco ourselves," she announced as she pointed to a pungent mound of the product that appeared sufficient to serve an ordinary smoker for a lifetime. "We'll have an even bigger crop next year."

Hannah gave a weak smile. "Lard?" she inquired, motioning toward two rough-hewn tubs filled with the solid whitish substance.

"Right you are, missus," the woman replied as she continued pointing to an assortment of dried vegetables and meat stored in the dark room.

Hannah attempted to appear dutifully impressed with the stockpile, but the pretense was growing more difficult by the moment. When Mrs. Martin was finally convinced there was nothing else that she could show Hannah, the two women returned to the main room, where Mr. Martin and William were deep in discussion. William appeared to look displeased, but why shouldn't he be? Hannah wasn't overly delighted, either. The Martins were certainly not the genteel people her deceased husband had described to her back in England, nor was the homestead what he had depicted.

"Come sit down, Hannah," William said, looking toward her and indicating the chair beside him. "I know you are weary. I think we all are," he said, glancing about the table.

"That's a fact," Mr. Martin agreed. "We can finish our business come morning. You folks can make a pallet in front of the fire. Get some blankets, woman," he ordered his wife.

"Already done it," Mrs. Martin replied, indicating a worn quilt and a woolen blanket piled near the hearth. "Best I got to offer," she said. "No extra charge."

Hannah laughed. "Thank you. I'm sure we'll put them to good use. The night air coming through these walls—"

"If you don't like what we got to offer, you're free to go elsewhere," Mr. Martin interrupted.

"No, no. I only meant that we would use the blankets and appreciate your hospitality. I certainly didn't mean to offend you or your wife," Hannah quickly apologized.

The man nodded his head. "In that case, no offense taken. We'll be turning in for the night," he said, motioning his wife toward the bedroom.

Hannah and William waited until the Martins left the room, and then William unfolded the blankets on the floor, being careful to spread them far enough from the fireplace to avoid any embers that might escape.

"We need to talk," William whispered a short time later.

"Is something wrong?"

"Mr. Martin insists that Edward never sent any money for the land."

"That's a lie, William!"

"Keep your voice down. They'll hear us," William warned.

Hannah nodded, but in truth, she wanted to rush into the other room and confront Mr. Martin at that very moment. How dare he say such a thing!

"Did you ask him how we knew about this place?"

"Of course. He doesn't deny that he corresponded with Edward. He claims that the two of them had reached a final agreement, all except for the payment of the money. Now he says he'll sell us the land for the same price that he negotiated with Edward."

"Oh, the gall of that man!"

"I did gain one concession that I think will please you," William said with a mischievous smile.

"And what might that be?"

"Since tomorrow is Sunday, I inquired if we might ride along with the Martins to church."

"That does please me. I don't mean to sound judgmental, William, but Mr. Martin doesn't seem to be much of a Christian."

"Well, I don't know whether he professes to be a Christian or not, but he doesn't attend church."

"Then how are we supposed to go with them?" Hannah asked while trying to hide her exasperation.

"He gave me instructions on how to get to the church, and he said we could use his wagon and mules—for a price, that is."

Hannah shook her head. "That man has no conscience, William. Unfortunately, there is no way I can prove that Edward paid for the land. Why would God want me to come all the way to this place to be made a fool of by Henry Martin?"

"I doubt that was God's intention, Hannah. I'd say it's time we did some more praying about this situation. Perhaps you'll have another revelation," he responded and kissed her lightly on the cheek. "I think we'd do well to follow Elizabeth's example and get some sleep. Morning will come soon enough."

❧

"I can't go to church looking like this," Hannah mumbled as she attempted to straighten the wrinkles out of the rumpled dress she had worn for several days.

"Don't you have another in the trunk?" William inquired, motioning toward the small chest he'd brought in the night before.

"Yes, of course," Hannah replied, brightening.

"And you can use our bedroom to dress yourself and the baby. I'll fetch some water so you can wash yourself," Mrs. Martin graciously offered, much to Hannah's surprise.

"Why, thank you. That's very kind," Hannah replied.

"I think I may have misjudged her," Hannah told William a few moments later when Mrs. Martin was out of earshot.

"Don't be too sure," William said with a smile. "While you finish dressing, I'll go and make sure that Mr. Martin hasn't forgotten our arrangement to use the wagon."

"Here we are," Mrs. Martin said as she entered the house, carrying a bucket of water. "I'll just heat some of this water while you're feeding the baby. That's a lovely dress you've got there."

Mrs. Martin seemed like a different person this morning. Perhaps it was because her husband was out of the house and she could act more natural, more like herself. *That must be it,* Hannah decided as she nursed the baby.

"Here you are, heated spring water," Mrs. Martin announced as she poured warm water into the pitcher for Hannah. "You better get yourself dressed. Would you like me to hold the baby?"

"Thank you. That's very kind," Hannah said once again as she handed over Elizabeth. *The change is truly amazing,* Hannah decided, giving the older woman a warm smile.

Mrs. Martin smiled back through her tobacco-stained teeth and nodded her head. "Church starts at ten o'clock, and the trip takes nigh unto an hour from here. You'll need to leave soon."

Working as rapidly as she could, Hannah washed, combed, and rearranged her chestnut brown hair. Carefully she stepped into the muslin petticoats and then pulled her dark green silk dress over her head. She placed a white embroidered collar around her neck and donned a matching bonnet with dark green ribbons. She had hoped to wear her black leather dress slippers, but the scuffed brown walking shoes would have to do. If she was careful, her dress would keep the shabby footwear hidden.

"My, ain't you just the sight," Mrs. Martin exclaimed as Hannah walked out of the bedroom. "That's just about the prettiest dress I ever seen."

"And just about the prettiest woman I've ever seen that's wearing it," William agreed as he entered the house with Mr. Martin.

Hannah could feel her cheeks flush at his remark. "I think we're just about ready. Mrs. Martin's been looking after Elizabeth. Her assistance certainly made it easier to get dressed."

"We do appreciate that," William said, giving the woman an appreciative smile.

"My pleasure. I just added it to your bill. By the time you folks leave here, I should have enough money to buy me a couple of them fancy dresses—matching bonnets, too," she added.

"Our bill?" Hannah stammered. "What are you talking about?"

"Surely you didn't think we was putting you folks up out of the goodness of our hearts, did you?" she asked with a greedy glint in her eyes.

"You mean—you're charging us to sleep here?" Hannah asked, horrified at the thought.

"Sleep, eat, tote your water, fetch wood for your fire, watch after your baby, tour my house and cellar. . ."

"Surely you're jesting. That's preposterous!"

"I don't know what that word means, but I can tell you this is no joke. You'll be paying and paying dearly for all we've done."

"That's enough, wife. They understand how things are," Mr. Martin said. "I'll be expecting you back here with my mules and wagon by midafternoon, no later," he said to William. "I don't want to turn you in as a thief."

William nodded as he helped Hannah onto the wagon seat and then handed Elizabeth up to her. "Don't worry. We'll be back," he replied as he hoisted himself onto the wagon seat and slapped the reins, setting the mules into motion.

"The nerve of those people. Can you believe them?" Hannah stormed.

"No need to get yourself all worked up. Your anger won't change anything, and it'll just ruin your time worshipping the Lord."

Hannah turned on the seat and scrutinized him.

"What?" William queried as she stared at him. "Well, am I wrong? Anger will ruin our worship, won't it?"

"I suppose it will," she agreed with a dainty smile.

"That's better," he replied. "Why don't you move a little closer? That way people will think you like me just a little. After all, we wouldn't want to make a bad impression the first time we meet these folks," he continued while giving her a wink.

Hannah felt her stomach flip-flop and her cheeks flush when he winked. This was, after all, the first time in her life that she had been courted, and she liked it! Inching closer, she turned, met William's gaze, and smiled as he held the reins with one hand while taking her left hand into his own.

"Your hands are cold. You should be wearing gloves," he said with a note of concern.

"I didn't realize the weather would be quite so cold. I probably should have worn my lined bonnet instead of this one."

"But you look absolutely beautiful in it. Besides, we'll be there soon. In the meantime, I'll be pleased to help keep you warm."

"You are such a gentleman, William. You would make your mother very proud," Hannah replied, a smile playing at the corners of her mouth.

"There you go again. Do I detect a hint of insincerity in your words?" he asked with laughter in his voice.

"You are a gentleman, William. Even though I was jesting only moments ago, I truly realize and admire what a gentleman you are. I don't think anyone else in this world would have been so good to me, done all that you have—and with such merciful kindness," she added, her voice now soft and serious.

"Thank you for those sweet words, my dear. If I've been merciful or kind, it's because of the mercy and kindness you've shown me. I admire your relationship with God, Hannah, and just being around you has caused me to realize that I need to depend on Him for everything. I'm seeking His guidance before I make decisions, which means I spend a lot more time in prayer. I've even found it much easier to overlook others' shortcomings than I did only a few weeks ago. Perhaps that's because God has been making me aware of my own imperfections as each day passes."

Hannah smiled. "Evidently your faith has grown stronger while mine has grown weaker," she replied in a sad voice.

"I think we both need this worship service," William said as they neared the church.

"Perhaps you're right. I haven't attended church since leaving England. Those Sundays when I could worship God and fellowship with other believers helped make my life with Edward bearable, and I'm certain it will improve my disposition toward the Martins."

"Good morning and welcome," a middle-aged man greeted as they entered the church. "I'm John Keating, the pastor. You folks must be new to the area. Where are you homesteading?"

"We thought we had purchased the eighty acres adjoining Henry Martin's place. But apparently the payment for our land never reached him, so we're not sure what the future holds," William answered as he shook Reverend Keating's hand.

"Ah, I see," the pastor said, nodding his head. "Henry Martin's sold that same eighty acres to a couple of families—seems he never does get the money."

"You mean he's done this to others?" Hannah asked, anger beginning to bubble up inside.

The pastor nodded. "I think you'd be about the third family."

"What happened to the others?" William inquired.

"One family returned to St. Louis. I'm told the other one, a single man, was so disheartened by the situation that he took his own life."

"Oh my!" Hannah exclaimed.

"Now, now, Hannah, things aren't so dire that we need think about anything like that. If we can't resolve the matter, we'll merely return to New Orleans."

"Before you plan to leave, let me introduce you to Millie Sutherford. She's from England, too," the pastor added. "The Sutherfords were one of the first families to homestead this area. They settled here about fifteen years ago. Millie has a lovely little farmstead not far from here, and—well, I'll have her talk to you. I'm not sure if she's arrived yet, but I'll be sure to introduce you after church."

"Thank you," Hannah replied, uncertain exactly how meeting Millie Sutherford was going to help.

Chapter 6

S o you see why I believe you're an answer to my prayers?" Millie asked William and Hannah as the three of them sat around Millie's kitchen table drinking steaming mugs of tea. Their stomachs were full from a midday meal of ham, boiled turnips, and thick slices of warm bread slathered with freshly churned butter.

William was silent for a moment. "What if I can't keep the place running? I've never farmed before, ma'am, and I wouldn't want to let you down," William replied.

"You were planning on farming your own land, and if I'm any judge of character, you'll not let me down. Besides, you'll find that most folks will help out. I couldn't have made it these five months since my husband's death if it hadn't been for my church family. They've come and worked, helping me with everything from tending the animals to harvesting my crops. They'll do the same for you, if you need," Millie assured.

"You're sure this is what you want to do?" William asked again.

"Sure as I can be. I can't run this farm on my own, and I've been praying that God would send just the right family to take over the place. I want to return to England, spend time with my few remaining relatives, and visit the places where my husband and I first met. I'm not sure if I'll stay in England or return to America. But if I do return, I want to live in one of those big cities back east that I hear folks talk about, not out here in the country. Would you feel easier about making a decision if you took some time to pray about it?"

The woman's gentle sincerity spoke to Hannah's heart. "Could we go into the other room to talk and pray?" Hannah inquired.

"Of course. And while you do, would you permit me to look after this sweet child?" she offered. "I promise not to charge a penny," Millie quickly added with a soft chuckle.

The newlyweds had taken Mrs. Sutherford into their confidence, relating the events that had occurred since their arrival at the Martin homestead. The older woman had nodded knowingly, disclosing that she had been praying for the Martins ever since their arrival at Pike's Ferry. Millie longed to be God's instrument in helping to turn the lives of Mr. and Mrs. Martin toward Him. But, she lamented, thus far her prayers had gone unanswered. With chagrin she noted that, unfortunately, the Martins were as mean-spirited today as they were the day they first arrived in Illinois.

A short time later, William and Hannah returned to the living area where Millie sat playing with Elizabeth. "We've decided to accept your offer," William announced. "Provided you'll give me time to arrange for the funds."

"Of course. And I want you to move in here immediately. I can't bear the thought of your staying with the Martins another minute. Besides, just think how wonderful it will be to have someone to talk to—especially you," she said, hugging Elizabeth close and placing a kiss on the baby's cheek.

William looked at his pocket watch. "I need to get the wagon back to Mr. Martin, or he'll soon be turning me in for stealing and will be claiming our belongings as his own."

"Why don't you unload those things before you return the wagon? Hannah and the baby can stay here with me while you're gone. Just tie my mare to the wagon and ride her back."

"That would be grand," Hannah agreed enthusiastically. "But we'd better hurry."

"You can take the bed and other furniture to the shed out back," Millie suggested.

The three of them worked at a fever pitch, and when they had finally accomplished the task, the two women bid William good-bye, with Millie promising a savory stew and dumplings upon his return.

Thankfully, the mules moved along at a steady pace as William turned at the road in front of the church and continued onward toward the Martins' place. Soon the distinct odor of smoke began to permeate the air and the stubborn mules became skittish. When the mare began pulling at the rope that tethered her to the rear of the wagon, William, now growing increasingly troubled by the smoke, resolutely determined that he could prod the mules no further. Jumping down from the wagon, he tied the team to a nearby tree, still hoping that he could walk the remaining distance to the Martin homestead before midafternoon.

As he grew nearer, a thickening wall of smoke caused his eyes to water, and his breathing became more difficult. Pulling a handkerchief from his pocket, he covered his nose and mouth, knotting the folded triangle behind his head. Moving forward, he squinted his eyes while waving his arm in a futile attempt to clear away the thick haze.

"Who's that?" a raspy voice called out. "I see ya out there."

"Mr. Martin? It's me, William Winslow. What's happened?"

"Step forward and let me see your face," the older man commanded.

William moved carefully through the dense smoke, Henry Martin's voice guiding him as he attempted to discern the looming remains of what had been the Martin home only hours earlier.

"Are you injured? Where's your wife?" William asked as he endeavored to make some sense of the ruin that suddenly lay before him.

"Over there," Mr. Martin answered, pointing toward the weather-worn woman, who sat rocking back and forth on the ground, weeping. "She's beside herself—won't quit that bawling. It's her fault this happened and she knows it," he said a little more loudly, obviously wanting Mrs. Martin to hear his accusation.

If she heard, she gave no sign, so William looked back toward the man. "I've got your mules and wagon down the road a piece." He didn't know what else to say. Words couldn't bring back the loss of their farmstead, and he certainly didn't know how to lend comfort to the wailing

Mrs. Martin. He now wished that Hannah had come along. At that moment, as he thought of Hannah, he knew what he should do. He bowed his head and prayed—he prayed more fervently than he'd ever prayed before, seeking wisdom, guidance, mercy, and God's blessing upon the Martins. When he finished, he lifted his head and met Mr. Martin's awestruck stare.

"You and your wife come with me. We'll take your wagon and return to Mrs. Sutherford's place," William said, taking command of the situation.

"I thought you went to church. What were you doing over at Sutherford's?"

"I'll explain on the way. You think you can get your wife settled enough to walk to the wagon?"

"Why are you helping us? You thinking you'll be able to write off what you owe me by showing us a bit of kindness? 'Cause if that's what you're up to, it won't work. I know exactly how much you owe."

"No, Mr. Martin, I'm merely trying to extend a helping hand. I don't know what Widow Sutherford will think about the fact that I've invited you to her home, but I believe she'll treat you much better than you may deserve. Now why don't you assist your wife, and let's be on our way. There's nothing to be done here."

William's tone left no doubt that the conversation had come to an end. Mr. Martin pulled his wife to her feet and half dragged, half carried her alongside him until they reached the wagon.

"Where's your belongings?" Mr. Martin queried, eyeing the empty buckboard. "And whose horse is that?"

"I said I'd explain on the way," William replied. "Help your wife into the back. You drive—I hope these mules will move for you. At least we'll be heading away from the smoke."

When they were finally back on the crude path and Mrs. Martin's sobbing had subsided, William told Mr. Martin of his plans to take over the Sutherford homestead, adding that he had no intention of purchasing the land that Hannah's husband had secured.

"Even if Mrs. Sutherford hadn't made us this offer, after observing your conduct and the condition of the land, I wouldn't consider doing business with you, sir," William said as he concluded his explanation of the afternoon's occurrences.

Mr. Martin said nothing but gave his wife a menacing glare when she began to speak.

"You can park the wagon over there," William instructed, pointing toward a spot near the shed.

"William! We were beginning to worry," Hannah called while opening the front door. As soon as the words were spoken, she came to a halt, her mouth opened wide in obvious disbelief.

"I'm fine, Hannah. Would you ask Millie to step out here? I need to have a word with her," William asked.

A few moments later, Millie met William in front of the house. "I hope I haven't overstepped my bounds," he said, nodding toward the Martins.

"What happened? And what's that I smell? Smoke?"

"Their place caught fire while we were at church. They are burned out. With the weather turning cold, I thought maybe...well, I didn't want to..." He stammered, hoping to find the words.

"They need a place to stay and you offered your home. Is that what you're trying to say, William?"

"I offered your home, Millie."

"It's not mine anymore. You agreed to purchase it, or have you forgotten so soon?"

"No, of course I haven't forgotten, but I won't think of it as our home until I've paid for it," William answered.

"Well, if it were my home, I would have no objection. In fact, I'd say you have done what would be pleasing to the Lord."

William smiled and took her tiny hand in his own. "Thank you, Millie."

"No, thank you, William. You may have given me the opportunity I've prayed for all these years. I'll go talk to Mr. and Mrs. Martin; I think you'd better go visit with Hannah. She seems a bit perplexed."

"No doubt," he said as he ran toward the house.

"What are they doing here?" Hannah asked just as William bounded through the door.

"Sit down and let me explain," he replied, first swooping Elizabeth from her cradle and kissing her along the chubby folds of her neck until she giggled in delight.

Hannah wiped her hands on the flowered cambric apron tied around her waist, tucked a wisp of unruly hair behind her ear, and sat down at the dining table. "So explain," she said, giving him her full attention as he placed Elizabeth back in her cradle.

"Have I ever told you what beautiful eyes you have?" William asked, wishing that he could stare into her very soul through their ocean blue depths. He seated himself close to her on the straight-backed wooden bench. "And how I love the shape of your nose and your high cheek-bones, the creamy texture of your skin, and the softness of your lips?" he continued. He lifted her fingers to his lips and then gently stroked the back of her hand. Suddenly his eyes dropped to her fingers and then rose again sharply to meet her eyes.

A tender smile played at the corners of her mouth as his gaze returned to her hand. "When did you do that? How could I have gone without noticing?"

"You mean the ring?" she innocently inquired.

"You know I mean the ring. Are you going to become shy now that I've noticed? Because if that's the case, you need not," he said as he pulled her into his arms. His lips brushed hers with a wispy tenderness as he ran his finger along the side of her face. "How I've longed for this moment," he murmured. He felt her shiver beneath his embrace and pulled her more closely to him, meeting her lips in a lingering, passion-ate kiss.

"Oh, William," she whispered.

A muffled cough from the doorway caused them to scoot apart. "I hope we're not interrupting anything," Millie said with a broad grin on her face as she led the Martins into the house.

"As a matter of fact, you are," William replied. "But I imagine it's get-ting too cold to ask you to remain outdoors," he joked.

"Well, what do you think, Hannah? I told the Martins that this would have to be a matter we all agreed upon," Millie said, rubbing her hands as she moved toward the fire.

"We were, uh. . .discussing another matter, Millie. I haven't had a chance to explain the Martins' circumstances just yet," William interjected.

"Ah. I could see you were in the midst of a deep discussion about something when I walked in," she responded with a crisp laugh. "In that case, why don't we let Mr. Martin explain while I finish getting supper ready? I'm sure that everybody will be ready for a bite to eat. Mrs. Martin, would you care to clean up in the bedroom? You will find water and fresh towels on the bureau," Millie offered.

William observed Mrs. Martin look toward Hannah as she rose from her chair. Hannah smiled and nodded as if to add her agreement to the overture. He wondered if Mrs. Martin was thinking of her own miserly attitude earlier that very day.

"You want me to tell you about it, missus?" Mr. Martin asked as his wife moved off toward the bedroom.

"Yes, please," Hannah replied, giving him her full attention.

"Well, to start with, it's all her fault," he said, gesturing toward the bedroom. "You got something I can spit in?" he asked, tapping his tobacco-filled cheek with a dirty finger.

"We don't smoke or chew in this house, Mr. Martin. And you can rid yourself of that tobacco outside," Millie answered from the hearth.

He didn't argue but returned to the table a few moments later, the puffiness gone from his cheek. "See, here's how it happened. You might recall the missus was washing clothes when you left for church?" he said in a questioning tone.

"How could I forget?" Hannah replied, remembering how she had tried to encourage Mrs. Martin to observe the Lord's Day by waiting until Monday, when she would help.

"Well, she thought she could get the clothes to dry faster if she hung them inside. I told her it wasn't that cold outside—that they'd eventually dry. But no. She refused to listen. So she commenced to stringing up a rope in front of the fireplace and draping the clothes across it."

Hannah nodded. She'd done the same thing back in England on damp winter days.

"Only it seems she's forgotten how to tie a knot. While she's out puttering around—"

"I was collecting eggs!" Mrs. Martin yelled from the bedroom.

"You keep out of this, woman; I'm telling this tale!" Mr. Martin hollered back.

"Then tell it right! Don't make it sound like I was out having me a good time, and I left the house to burn to the ground. I was working, just like you."

He ignored her remarks and continued in a lowered voice. "As I was saying, the missus is out and about somewheres, and the knot in her rope gives way. The clothes caught fire, the house caught fire, and the rest is history. We're wiped out."

"Well, you still have your land—and ours," Hannah added, glancing at William and giving him a faint smile.

"That's true enough, but with winter coming on, I won't be able to rebuild until spring. Winters around here are long and cold. When your husband made his kind offer, I have to admit I was surprised, but I thought it was provision sent from above."

"I see. So you believe in God?" Hannah inquired.

"Well, of course I believe there's a God."

"That's not what she's asking, Mr. Martin," Millie interrupted. "She wants to know if you've accepted Jesus Christ as your Lord and Savior and invited Him into your heart. Do you know Him, or do you believe merely that He's up there just floating around in the clouds? I'm asking because it's your own eternal salvation that's at stake. You might want to give some serious thought and prayer to the matter—and your wife, too," she added, looking toward the bedroom door.

"She don't mince words, does she?" Mr. Martin whispered to William.

"Not about something this serious. Did you know that she's been praying for you and your wife since you moved to Pike's Ferry?" William asked.

"Why would she do such a thing? I never asked her to pray for me."

"Because she's a woman who wants others to have the same peace that she's found. Spend some time talking with her, Henry—both of you. I don't think you'll be sorry," he advised. "I think Hannah and I need to discuss things further, so if you'll excuse us for a few moments, I think we'll step outside," William added as he reached for Hannah's heavy woolen shawl.

"What do you think?" William tentatively inquired once they were on the porch.

"I know it's the Christian thing to do, William. My heart says yes, but my mind says no. A part of me wants to treat them as badly as they treated us, but I won't do that. Millie has no objection, and apparently you think we should help them."

"If it makes it any easier, Millie tells me that the old cabin she and her husband built when they first moved here sits back behind the tree line. With some cleaning and a little repair, she thinks it will be quite usable for the Martins until they rebuild. They wouldn't be living in the same house with us for long."

"Perhaps long enough that God will stir their hearts. How could I object?"

"You're sure? I don't want this to cause a problem between us, especially since. . ."

"Since I've turned the ring?"

"Especially since you've turned the ring," he agreed. "And you never did answer me. How long did it take me to notice?"

"Not long," she replied.

"Will you tell me—what made you decide?" he asked.

"Many things. Your kindness, your gentle ways with Elizabeth, your tenderness toward me, but primarily the fact that you permitted me the time I needed to fall in love with you.

"I must admit I didn't believe you would be patient. Deep in my heart, I thought you would grow weary of my hesitation and force yourself upon me. Instead, with each day that passed, you grew more unselfish, more caring. How could I resist such compassion and love? I now know that you never intended me to feel obligated or bound to you out of necessity. This ring is a symbol of freedom, not bondage or servitude. You wanted me to come to you freely, to stand beside you as your helpmate, your lover, and your friend. I'm ready to do all of those things, William," she whispered as he pulled her into a fervent embrace.

JUDITH MCCOY MILLER makes her home in Kansas with her family. Intrigued by the law, Judy is a certified legal assistant currently employed as a public service administrator in the Legal Section of the Department of Administration for the State of Kansas. After ignoring an 'urge' to write for approximately two years, Judy quit thinking about what she had to say and began writing it and then was and has been extremely blessed! Her first two books earned her the honor of being selected Heartsong's favorite new author in 1997. You may contact her via e-mail at jamauthor@aol.com.

Returning Amanda

by Kathleen Paul

Chapter 1

S heriff Jake Moore carefully rolled the week-old St. Louis paper into a tight baton. He eased his shoulders away from the wooden slats of his office chair and swung his paper bat down against the heavy desk. *Whack!*

"Forty-three," he said, satisfied.

He flicked the fly carcass onto the floor, propped his boot heels back on the desktop, and unrolled the paper. Scanning the page, he found the article he'd been reading. Fool paper said those mechanical carriages would one day take over private transportation.

"Humph," grunted the sheriff. A scowl momentarily brought thick brown eyebrows down over his hazel eyes.

Jake picked up the bandanna lying over his lap and made another swipe across his face, wiping sweat from his strong, square jaw. A bristly stubble darkened his chin.

When had he shaved? About seven that morning. The four o'clock eastbound hadn't even blown its whistle at the crossing yet, and here his face already felt like sandpaper. Fortunately, the Wednesday night church social didn't require him to spruce up. If it were a town meeting, he'd make the effort, but not for the ladies of the church. It wasn't as if there was someone there he wanted to impress. He'd go for the good eats, and maybe he'd corner Elder Kotchkis and get him going on predestination. Kotchkis was always open for a good debate.

Jake ran his hand over the stubble he did not intend to shave. It'd be better, he decided, if all those women thought the sheriff was too unkempt to take home for keeps. He was tired of being viewed as potential husband material for every single female in the county. How was it that this town had so many widows and unmarried gals anyway? He'd made it twenty-six years without a female's coddling; he could make it a few more.

A fly buzzed around his head, and Sheriff Moore watched it as he once again rolled the St. Louis paper into a weapon. His lean frame tensed as the fly landed on the Kansas map hanging on the wall behind him. It would be a stretch, but he had long arms to match his tall, angular body. Jake tipped his chair back another inch, pressed his lips together in concentration, and slowed his breathing. Waiting for just the right moment, he struck. *Whack!*

The chair slipped off the two back legs. Jake crashed to the floor. "Ouch!"

He rolled out of his sturdy throne, feeling just exactly where the wooden arm had refused to flatten under the small of his back. He rubbed the spot with a strong hand. A small black speck lay a foot from his elbow.

"Forty-four," he muttered.

A soft knock sounded from the front door of the jailhouse.

Jake wrinkled his brow. Nobody knocked at his door—they just came tromping in with all sorts of complaints and problems. Twenty-eight dollars and fifty cents, plus room and board at Maggie's, paid Sheriff Jake Moore to worry about the citizens of Lawrence, Kansas, and their difficulties.

The knock sounded politely again.

Jake unwound himself, placed his hands on the edge of his desk, and rose up to see what matter of business had intruded on his formerly peaceful afternoon.

He looked out and saw no one; then his gaze drifted down from where he had expected to see a face. A small girl stood on the boardwalk porch just outside his door. Corn-silk hair in tight curls billowed out of the bonnet topping the pudgy, frowning face. The bonnet matched the blue dress covered with tiny yellow flowers and petite green vines. She carried a doll under her arm and a small square basket by its handle.

"Are you the sheriff?" she asked. Her scowl lightened to a small smile as she took in the image of the man behind the desk.

"Yes, ma'am." Jake stood and righted his chair. He looked over the diminutive figure in his doorway. Her clothes looked expensive. Her speech was refined. Her face held an expression of intelligence. In a few years she'd be breaking hearts. Now she looked hot and tired. Jake didn't recognize her as one of the town children.

He sighed, relieved that his visitor wasn't one of the older girls in town, one of the pesky females dogging his bachelor steps. Whoever this was, she most likely wouldn't carry the tale of his falling out of his office chair to wagging tongues.

"What can I do for you?" he asked the small stranger.

"I've come to report a robbery." Her hard black button-up shoes tapped on the wooden floor as she stepped into the room and crossed to stand in front of his desk. Her smile wavered, and her forehead creased with worry. The proud little chin quivered slightly. She blinked deep chocolate eyes hard, pushing back tears.

Where did this filly come from? Jake took pity on the little mite. He pulled up the only other chair in the room and offered it to his guest.

"I don't believe I know you," said Jake.

She put down the basket to climb into the chair. With her knee in the oversized seat, she hoisted her chubby body up and twisted her backside into place. Plump legs encased in white stockings stuck straight out in front of her. She smoothed her skirts around them. She looked kind of cute in all her finery.

"I'm Sheriff Moore," Jake said. He winked at her the way he did with the small girls at church. He didn't mind flirting with the little ones. It was the bigger ones, the ones who dreamed about marriage. Those he avoided.

"I'm Amanda Greer of St. Louis, Missouri." She supplied the information with crisp, polite formality.

"And you've had some property stolen?" Jake sat down in his chair, steepled his fingers, and leaned his elbows on the table. One tender elbow told him he must have slammed it on the way down. He leaned back.

The little face scrunched into a frown again.

"Not prop-er-ty," she said.

Jake suppressed a smile. With all her self-assurance, he found it humorous to see her puzzle over the unfamiliar word.

"Can you tell me what was stolen?"

Her lips snapped into an angry line, and she scowled at him.

Whoa, thought Jake, *she's got a temper.*

"Of course I can," she answered smartly. But the flare of temper fizzled. The fierce pride on the chubby face melted. The little mouth softened, and the chin quivered. The dark eyes batted. Amanda Greer took a deep breath and let it out with the merest suggestion of a sob. She pursed her lips, breathed again, and spoke hurriedly, getting the two words out as quickly as possible.

"My sister."

Jake sat up and leaned forward.

"Where are your parents?" he asked.

"In New York City, New York." Her head bobbed as she said the words, and the profusion of golden curls bounced.

"Do you know who took your sister? Did you see it happen?"

She nodded, the curls again springing into action.

"Who?" he asked.

Tears pooled in the soulful eyes and spilled down her cheeks.

"The train." The words came out in a whimper, and Jake thought for a moment he must have misunderstood.

"The train?" Then it dawned on him—Amanda had been left behind when the train had pulled out of the station. She and her sister must've been traveling west together.

The curls bounced again. Amanda Greer pulled the doll into a tight embrace and buried her face in its cloth head. Jake froze, immobilized by the muffled wails punctuated with loud sniffs. The chubby little blond with an extra helping of dignity rocked back and forth with her dolly, her abject misery piercing the heart of one confirmed bachelor.

"Now don't cry," Jake said, desperation shaking his usually solid baritone. "Your sister will realize that you've been left behind, and she'll probably get off at the next stop and come right back for you." He abruptly stood and paced to the door, away from the distressed child. He looked out at the dusty street, squinting into the glare.

Henry Bladcomb swept the stoop before his jewelry shop. Gladys Sence gabbed with Miriam Halley in front of the mercantile. The Jones kids laid ambush to the Whitcombs beside the livery. Was there any help for him among these fine citizens of Lawrence?

Jake looked up the street to the station. A pile of luggage blocked his view of the telegraph office.

"Miss Amanda," said the sheriff, swiveling back to his weeping visitor, "we'll go right now to the telegraph office and send a telegram. That's what we'll do. That telegram will be waiting for your sister when they make the stop at Big Springs."

Jake jammed his hat on his head and grabbed the little girl's square basket.

"Come on, now," he urged. "Let's do something about this predicament. No use crying when we can do something."

Amanda bravely lifted her head, sniffing loudly. She delved into a side pocket of her dress and pulled out a white hankie edged in elegant green crochet. With a honk that certainly didn't fit her diminutive size, she blew her nose. Replacing the hankie, she gathered up her doll and hopped out of the chair.

"Sheriff?" she asked, tilting up her chin to look him in the eye. "I'm tired."

Jake didn't quite know how to talk to a yard-high person. He crouched down, almost sitting on his heels. The tears had left tracks on her cheeks. Her little shoulders sagged, and all the sparkle had washed out of her eyes.

"Let's go out to the pump and wash your face before we go," he suggested.

Amanda reached out a small hand and took his large calloused one.

How he came to be carrying the mite, he didn't know. But there he was walking down Main Street with a chubby bundle of feminine sweetness. Not only did she ride in his arms, but she'd put her head down on his shoulder, and her soft breath tickled his neck.

Jake kept his eyes trained on his destination, giving only curt nods to those who tried to speak to him.

"Hello, Samuel," he said as soon as he reached the telegrapher's open window.

Samuel jumped. The balding man ruffled like a hen at the interruption. He scooted his small frame around on his wooden stool and lowered his glasses from where they rested over the top of his head to their proper position on his nose.

"Sheriff," he clucked, "you startled me. Need to send a telegram?"

"Yes, Samuel." Sheriff Moore nodded at the child relaxed against his shoulder. "This is Amanda Greer. She was accidentally left when the westbound went through."

"Oh," said Samuel, alarmed. "I'll have to get the stationmaster. Oh, he's not going to like this. Left, you say." Samuel tutted, starting up from his chair.

"Wait, Samuel," ordered Jake. "Before you go get Blake, send off the telegram. We may be able to catch the girl's sister at Big Springs."

Samuel plopped back down on his chair, shaking his head.

"Oh no, I don't think so," he muttered. "No, no, it's too late."

"Too late?" asked Jake. He tried to shift the deadweight in his arms and was rewarded with a delicate snore in his ear. He set the square basket on the wide sill that served as a counter and leaned against the frame with the shoulder that did not hold the sleeping beauty.

"Samuel, I need to find Miss Amanda's sister."

"Yes, yes, of course," agreed the telegrapher, pushing his glasses back up a fraction of an inch. "But don't you see that the westbound went through around noon? That was almost four hours ago. The eastbound is due any minute. The westbound passed Big Springs, made Topeka, had a layover, and has left already for San Francisco."

"Samuel"—Jake ground out the name—"wire Big Springs and see if a Miss Greer got off the train there and is taking the eastbound back."

"Yes, sir." Samuel turned back to his apparatus.

Just then the eastbound blew its whistle at the outskirts of town. Sheriff Moore abandoned Samuel and crossed the wooden platform. Maybe the telegram would be unnecessary. He peered anxiously down the tracks. A cloud of smoke puffed over the trees just before the four o'clock rounded the bend. It came huffing and hissing to a stop at the station.

A conductor jumped down and placed a step beside the metal stairs at the end of a passenger car. Jake held his breath. The conductor doffed his hat and offered a gloved hand to a matron as she negotiated the descent. A sprightly young lady with golden hair caught up under a wide-brimmed hat came next. Jake started forward, but a clean-shaven man hopped off behind her and, with a possessive air, tucked her hand in the crook of his arm, escorting her to claim their luggage.

Harold Smithridge got off. Jake hadn't known the banker was out of town. Two young men who Jake assumed were students at the University of Kansas hopped off and strutted toward town. Orville and Margaret Cullen got off, back from visiting their grandchildren. A man with all the earmarks of an elixir peddler got off, carrying a big black case. Jake hoped whatever he was selling wouldn't make people sick. The peddler was the last passenger off. Jake waited a moment, watching until he was satisfied Amanda Greer's sister was not on the train.

Discouraged and still carrying his increasingly heavy burden, Jake returned to Samuel's window.

"Oh my, oh my, broken foot," said Samuel, wagging his head from side to side.

Jake pinned him with an impatient look and waited for the man to clarify his statement.

"Miss Greer got off at Big Springs in a panic about her sister and broke her foot. Dear, dear, oh my! Doctor says she can't travel for a week. A week! Mr. Blake says to put the little girl on the westbound tomorrow, no charge. Can you imagine, no charge from Mr. Blake?"

"What am I supposed to do with her tonight?" asked Jake, more to himself than to the distraught Samuel.

"Can't put her in jail, Sheriff." The man offered serious advice.

"I know that," snapped the sheriff.

"Better feed her and find some woman to take her in." Samuel nodded earnestly, and his glasses slipped down on his nose.

Jake grinned, thinking of the church social and all those eager females.

"Thanks, Samuel," he said. "I'll do that."

Chapter 2

"Am I arrested?" Amanda's indignant question roused Jake from his paperwork. He studied the plump, disheveled figure sitting up on one of the padded cots in the first cell. The bonnet sat crookedly on her head. Maybe he should have taken it off of her when he laid her down.

"If you were arrested," Jake told her, "the door would be shut and locked."

"I'm hungry," she complained. She tugged at her bonnet, trying to straighten it.

"We're going to a church social tonight. There'll be lots of good food there."

"You said you'd get my sister back," she accused. Her hands left off fidgeting with the crooked bonnet and rested in her lap. She cast him a squinty-eyed glare with her lower lip stuck out to demonstrate her disapproval.

"She's waiting for you in Big Springs. You can get on the train tomorrow and join her."

"By myself?" she asked, obviously doubting him.

"The conductor will be sure you get there just fine."

She sat for a minute thinking this over. Jake watched her anxiously. He didn't relish the idea of another bout of tears.

"All right," she said and kicked the towel off her legs. An hour and a half earlier, Jake had covered her with the only clean thing he could find. Amanda slid off the cot, gathered her doll and basket, and tapped across the floor in her ankle-high shoes. Maybe he should have taken those things off, too, when he laid her down. They looked mighty hot and uncomfortable.

The scorching summer afternoon had stilled into an oppressive swelter. Clouds gathered in the west. Rain would be welcome, as long as it came gently, good for the crops, not torrents to tear down the fields.

Amanda stood looking at him with solemn dark eyes.

"I have to go," she said.

"It's out back."

She stared at him.

"I'm not going with you," he said. "Go out that door." Jake pointed to the only door in sight. "Go around the building. You can't miss it." He looked back at the papers spread out on his desk, avoiding her eyes and hoping she'd go by herself. He heard the distinctive tapping of those awful shoes and breathed a sigh of relief.

❧

"Well, well," said Mel Kotchkis as he put down another stack of plates next to his daughter. She worked busily preparing the long table in the fellowship hall for the social. "Seems Sheriff Moore has finally come to a church social with a pretty gal on his arm."

Mel bit his mustached lip to keep from laughing as he watched his daughter, Pamela, react to his statement. Her spine stiffened and her hands ceased the rapid arrangement of cutlery on the table. Slowly she reached for the stack of plates and moved them one inch farther from the edge of the table. Her capable long, tapered fingers returned to fussing over the forks, precisely lining them up in a staggered formation.

Pamela sidled her trim figure down the table, carefully keeping her back to the commotion going on at the front door. Mel put his hand over his quivering lips and stroked his work-worn fingers through his full salt-and-pepper beard.

"She's darling," said Mrs. Sence, her chirping voice carrying across the hall.

"Look at those precious curls," said Ruth Bladcomb in a stage whisper to her husband. The older couple stood at the far end of the table, mixing the punch in large glass pitchers. "I declare, did you ever see such fine clothes? She must be from the city. Wherever did Jake Moore come up with a little beauty like that?"

Pamela Kotchkis skittered back to the corner of the table, rounded it neatly, grabbed the box of knives, and shuffled them out onto the table-cloth. When the first row lay precisely as she wanted them, her blue eyes lifted, obviously drawn to the spectacle at the front door.

Mel watched his favorite daughter's stone face soften into a warm smile. That expression, so like his Maddie's, gladdened his old heart. What was it Maddie used to say when he was rocking one of their young'uns? Something about when a rough-and-tumble man cradled a wee child. . . it could wrench the tender heart of any woman. The sight of rugged Jake Moore with the mysterious little girl in his arms had no doubt pierced the armor his headstrong Pamela kept around her heart. Mel sent up a fervent, though silent, *Praise the Lord!*

The old farmer watched his daughter lift a hand to the tawny curl dangling at her temple and tuck it back off her face behind her delicate ear. His Maddie had used the same nervous gesture. He loved this daughter and all the sweet recollections she brought to his mind, but it was time for her to make new connections. Pamela was twenty! She couldn't be Papa's girl for the rest of her life.

Maddie would be proud of this last gal. Of course, Mel was properly proud of all five. But the first four had married city men. His baby was the only one left on the farm. All grown up now and ready to find her husband.

Mel prayed that it would be a man willing to take over after him. His life's work had established Kotchkis Kansas Corn. Mel was proud of it. He wanted to know his grandchildren would grow up on the piece of land he and Maddie had claimed.

Just Pamela remained. Pamela, the last of Maddie's brood, Mel's last chance to bring a young man into the harness of a mighty fine farm. Pamela, stubborn and beautiful, prideful and charming, deeply fascinated by the handsome sheriff, and rigidly determined not to give in to her attraction.

Well, Lord, said Mel in a comfortable silent conversation with his God and Savior, *I've been praying for ten years. I watched each of our girls grow, fall like so many silly geese in love, and leave. Now I'm satisfied with what You've done. You lead them well. I thank You. But here's Pamela, denying she longs to take that young man's interest. To my way of thinking, Jake Moore is just the right suitor for our gal. He's a strong man, got a good handle on You being the God of the universe and all, understands Your gospel, and is living under Your authority. I'd be mighty grateful if You'd give these young folks a nudge. In Your time, of course. But I reckon You know I'm getting a tad impatient. Amen.*

With a concerted effort, Mel Kotchkis managed to snag the sheriff and get him and his pretty little charge seated at a table with himself and Pamela. It had been no easy task with those nosy, matchmaking women intent on cornering the poor bachelor. Sheriff Moore's face had flashed desperation as he'd been surrounded, and Mel thought of himself as the man's rescuer. Mel wished Maddie were still with him to enjoy life's little comedies. She'd been a woman who could laugh.

"Would you like butter on your roll?" Mel asked Jake's small companion.

"Yes, Mr. Kottis." Amanda nodded. "Thank you."

Mel grinned at her prim and proper mispronunciation of his name, took up her roll, split it, and spread the butter, replacing it on her plate.

Pamela turned to Sheriff Moore, her curiosity getting the better of her. She'd heard bits and pieces of the story from the other ladies as they worked together.

"How old is she?" she asked.

"Hmm?" Jake chewed on the large helping of beans he had just spooned into his mouth.

"Amanda," clarified Miss Kotchkis, "how old is she?"

Jake swallowed. "I don't know."

"You didn't ask her?"

"No."

"Oh."

Pamela pushed the peas around on her plate. She ate a couple of bites of the potato salad. Mrs. Sence had made it. She must get the recipe from Mrs. Sence.

"Why did she get off the train?" she asked.

Jake chewed and cast an anxious look at Kotchkis's daughter.

He swallowed, reached for his punch, and took a swig.

"She didn't say," he finally answered.

"You didn't ask?" A merry chortle escaped with her question.

Jake grinned. The deep dimples on each side of his mouth danced in his cheeks. "Guess I'm not much good at interrogating the young and innocent. Now if she'd been a mean hombre with a marked resemblance to one of the posters on my wall, I might have gotten more information out of her."

Their eyes caught, sharing the good humor of their conversation. Pamela watched the twinkle in his hazel eyes change subtly to a gleam of admiration. She noticed how the green irises held flecks of brown and a dark rim clarified the odd color. They were fine eyes, eyes she would enjoy looking into over the dinner table in the bright kitchen at home. . . .

Suddenly Pamela felt uncomfortable and pulled her attention away. She turned quickly and interrupted the conversation between her father and Amanda.

"Amanda," she said rather breathlessly, "Sheriff Moore doesn't know how old you are."

"I'm four, Miss Kottis." Amanda's cultured tones sounded so out of place coming from her round and adorable baby face that Pamela smiled.

"Does your mommy call you Mandy?" asked Pamela.

"No, that's not my proper name. Mother calls me by my proper name."

"Oh," said Pamela.

"What is your proper name, Miss Kottis?" Amanda asked earnestly.

"Pamela."

"That's very pretty."

"Thank you," said Pamela. Amanda Greer sounded like one of the old ladies around the quilting frame. This pert little girl had the same intonations of a dowager who had come into town visiting a relative. Pamela could just picture the little girl sitting with the matrons, replying to their inquiries with only the politest and tritest information.

"Is Pamela a family name?" asked Amanda.

"Well," said Pamela, "my parents wanted to name a son after my father. His name is Mel. My mother had all girls, and I was the last, so they named me Pamela because Mel is in the middle of it."

Amanda nodded politely. "My name is a family name. I have an older sister named Amelia and an Aunt Amelia. My oldest sister is Althea and my mother's name is Althea. My other sister is Augusta, which isn't a family name, but she was supposed to be born in August, and my father thought it fitting. Augusta came on the last day of July. Father said he wouldn't give in to her willfulness and named her Augusta anyway."

Pamela heard a snort that sounded suspiciously like a laugh cut short. It came from the sheriff, proving he had eavesdropped on their conversation. She chose to ignore him.

"And do you have an Aunt Amanda?" asked Pamela.

Amanda nodded. "Deceased," she explained.

"Oh, I'm sorry."

Amanda nodded again and turned her attention back to the chicken on her plate.

"Remind me," said Jake in a low voice, "to bring you to the jail next time I've got an outlaw. You've pretty much got her family history."

"Hush," scolded Pamela and turned back to find Amanda scowling at her. The wrinkled brow and puckered lips looked adorable. Pamela fought the urge to scoop her up and give her a big hug to drive away that crosspatch glower.

Pamela carefully took a bite of peas instead. After a moment, Amanda politely asked for another helping of potato salad.

"This is quite good," she said. "I don't believe I've ever had potatoes fixed in this manner."

Pamela again felt as if a little old lady occupied the seat next to her instead of a four-year-old—as if a very short adult dominated that pudgy body. Pamela wanted to talk to the child.

"I grew up with four sisters," said Pamela. "It's fun to have a house full of girls to play with." Pamela gave Amanda a friendly smile, hoping the little girl would abandon her grown-up demeanor and chatter away like her nieces or the little girls she taught in Sunday school.

Amanda frowned again, thinking.

"My sisters do not play. They aren't girls," she explained after a moment of consideration. "They are grown-up women."

"Oh," said Pamela.

"I am a twilight child," Amanda explained further and picked up the basket of rolls beside her plate. She took one and offered the basket to Pamela. Pamela took it in a daze and offered it to Jake Moore. Their eyes met again, and this time the look they shared held no humor. Pamela's eyes shone with sorrow as she imagined a little girl's life in a house full of adults who did not play.

❦

After the meal, the men moved back the tables and rearranged the chairs so everyone could enjoy the music for the evening. The ladies made short work of the cleaning up. Mel Kotchkis and Pamela sat in the seats to the side where they usually sat on social evenings like this. Several of the women Jake had ignored earlier noticed that Sheriff Moore and his little girl visitor had decided to sit with them.

"Who is going to take care of her tonight?" asked Pamela, referring to Amanda.

"I think I'll take her back to Maggie's with me," answered Jake. "Maggie will put her up." He'd changed his mind once he'd arrived and seen how the women carried on and fussed over the child. Amanda was much too sensitive a girl for such silliness. He would just keep her himself.

"I heard Mrs. Jones offer to take her," observed Pamela.

"Her kids are too rowdy. They'd scare Miss Amanda."

"And Mrs. Whitcomb?" said Pamela.

"Same thing," answered the sheriff without batting an eye.

"Surely Mrs. Dobson and Mrs. Roper wouldn't scare her. The sisters are gentle and genteel."

"Too old," said Jake.

"Old?"

"What if something should happen? They're too old to take care of an emergency."

Pamela nodded her head at the sheriff, but one little dimple peeked out at the corner of her mouth. Jake watched that dimple quiver in and out of existence like a twinkling star—for some reason the sight of it reassured him. Pamela Kotchkis was a sensible woman, and she understood a child's needs.

She might laugh at him for being possessive with the little mite, but she understood. It didn't seem right to foist Amanda onto another family when she'd already been through so much today. Miss Amanda trusted him. He'd take care of her until tomorrow and put her on the train himself. Jake smiled back at Pamela Kotchkis, enjoying the laughter in her eyes and the gentle glow of happiness about her.

Beyond Pamela sat Amanda. Her eyes glowed as she listened to the spirituals and hymns. She'd crawled up into Mel's lap, or had he picked her up? They looked natural together. Mel had a lot of experience with girls, first his own and now his grandchildren. Jake admired him for the ease with which he held the little girl.

Jake turned his attention to the Burkett family. They'd gone to the front to sing a special together. The Burketts all looked alike with bushy blond hair and wide grins.

Jake noted the room full of families. That was the way it always was. He was the only single man in the bunch. There was nothing wrong with being single, he reminded himself. Being single had its advantages.

"Are you getting tired, sweetie?" Pamela asked Amanda in a soft voice that warmed Jake's heart.

"No, Miss Kottis," Amanda replied. "I had a nap in the jail."

"You slept in the jail?" asked Pamela.

"Yes, ma'am. In Sheriff Moore's jail cell."

Pamela turned scandalized eyes to the handsome sheriff. He could see the gleam of mischief in her look.

"Sheriff, really!" she said, mocking horror, "that is not the proper place for a young lady to sleep."

"No, it isn't," he agreed. He feasted his eyes on her. Pamela Kotchkis would make a fine mother. She had a head full of tawny gold hair and blue eyes rimmed with dark lashes.

Would all her children look alike in the same way the Burketts resembled one another? Would they all look happy like Pamela did tonight? Or would they all be reserved, as she'd always been with him before this night?

The only thing he'd noticed about Pamela Kotchkis before was that she had good sense. The good sense not to bump into him "by accident." The good sense not to casually walk up and join in a conversation that had nothing to do with her. The good sense not to giggle and flirt.

Pamela Kotchkis turned and smiled at something her father said. *She's a pretty woman,* Jake thought, *a calm, serene, gracious woman. She's got dignity, but not too much. She has a pretty smile. And that dimple. . .*

No doubt her children would play and laugh and know they were loved. Her husband would hurry home, assured that her warm sense of humor and gentle ways would welcome him. He looked at that tiny dimple that flashed so intriguingly at the corner of her mouth. Her lips were pink. They looked soft.

Jake heard the huge yawn and shifted his eyes reluctantly to the little girl who claimed she was not sleepy.

Amanda shook her head wearily. "That wasn't a proper place for me to sleep."

Jake had to think. What wasn't? Oh, the jail. His mind must have wandered.

Chapter 3

"I need a nightgown," Amanda Greer announced stubbornly and not for the first time.

"Miss Amanda, I don't have a little nightgown," said Jake between clenched teeth. He bit back other more impatient words. "I don't have any nightgown, big or little. You are just going to have to sleep in your shift."

"It is not proper for a young lady to sleep in her shift. A young lady needs a nightgown." Amanda crossed her chubby arms across her chest, stuck out her lower lip, and frowned the fiercest frown she could summon.

Jake cast a look at Maggie. His eyes held equal measures of exasperation and desperation. Draped in her habitual black sagging gown, Maggie leaned squarely against her parlor door. She raised a scrawny shoulder in an expression of indifference.

Jake counted off with self-righteous indignation the number of times Miss Maggie Hardmore had made it clear she didn't appreciate his bringing the tired little girl to her boardinghouse. *There isn't an ounce of compassion in the woman's bony breast.* Obviously he'd get no help from her quarter.

"I'll be right back," said Jake, and he bolted from the room, taking the narrow stairs two at a time. In a minute he thundered down the same stairs and burst back into the parlor. He held a creamy yellow shirt of soft material. He offered it to the midget minx who had remained like a stubborn statue anchored to the parlor room rug.

"This is my dancing shirt."

From her position by the door, Maggie rolled her eyes.

"Shirts do not dance," said Amanda.

"No!" barked Sheriff Moore. He took a cooling breath. "No," he repeated in a milder tone underscored by a heavy black line of forced patience. "It is the shirt I wear to dances." He knelt down and held the shirt out for the girl to feel. "It's soft. The ladies like it."

Maggie made a strangled chortling noise behind him. "Since when do you go out of your way to attract the ladies, Jake Moore?"

"Maggie, if you are not going to help, be quiet," said the sheriff.

Amanda touched the fabric with chubby fingers. Sighing in resignation, she took it.

"It's not a nightgown." She made one last protest.

"It's a nightshirt," conceded Jake.

The furrows deepened on Amanda's brow. "Father wears a nightshirt," she said. "I've seen it on the laundry line."

"Then you know"—Jake spoke quickly before her mature little mind could reason out further objections—"he'd think it more proper for you to wear a nightshirt than a shift."

Amanda nodded.

"Fine," said Jake, unfolding his body and stretching to his full height. He looked at Maggie, daring her to abandon him. He spoke to Amanda. "Go with Mrs. Hardmore and change for bed."

Maggie stretched out a hand hardened by years of housekeeping. Amanda crossed reluctantly, took it, and followed the old crow out of the room without looking back.

Jake took the stack of sheets and blankets, provided under protest by Maggie, from the chair in the corner and began making a bed for Amanda on the parlor sofa. Finished, he collapsed in the big overstuffed chair.

"Where am I going to sleep?" asked Amanda, standing at his elbow.

Realizing he must have dozed off, he looked her over with groggy eyes. She was dressed in the pale yellow shirt. The rolled-up sleeves came to her elbows. The hem dragged on the floor.

Maggie Hardmore had brushed the unruly curls and wrestled them into two short braids. Amanda held her doll tightly against her side with a grip around its neck that would have strangled any living creature. In the other hand she carried the square basket.

Jake leaned forward in the overstuffed chair. It had been a long day, and his own bed called to him. He rubbed a hand across his scratchy face and stretched.

"On the sofa," he answered.

"In the parlor?"

Jake didn't like the way Amanda had said the word "parlor." Somehow it sounded as though he was about to have trouble, and the trouble would be with a strong-minded little girl.

"It's a very nice sofa. Mrs. Hardmore is very proud of her company parlor and the furnishings therein. The sofa came from St. Louis."

Amanda took a couple of small steps across the dim room on silent bare feet. She stood next to the sofa and examined it thoroughly. Sad eyes traveled from one brocade-covered arm to the other. Her solemn face showed her disapproval.

Finally, she shook her head. The short braids swung and thumped her on the cheeks.

"It's not proper for a young lady to sleep in the parlor," she said in a low, calm voice. "It's not proper for a young lady to sleep on a sofa. I want a bed. I want my room. I want Miss Kottis."

She turned mournful eyes brimming with tears and faced down the sheriff.

"Miss Kottis?" Jake was surprised. "I mean, Kotchkis? Miss Pamela? She went home. She's miles away in a farmhouse outside of town."

"Miss Kottis knows what's proper for a young lady." Amanda hung her head and sniffed.

"This is just for one night, Miss Amanda," assured Jake. He pulled himself out of the chair and dropped to his knees. He put an arm around the stubborn, stiff shoulders of his little guest. "You must be a brave little girl and crawl into bed with your doll. At lunchtime tomorrow the train will come, and you can climb aboard and go to your sister in Big Springs."

Jake pulled the blanket back in an invitation to the little girl to climb in. She looked at him with pity in her eyes and sighed. Shaking her head over his ignorance, she put her doll and the basket on the sofa and knelt beside it. She seemed to be waiting for him, so Jake hobbled on his knees closer beside her.

"Heavenly Father," said Amanda with her eyes firmly shut and her hands clenched in prayer, "thank You for this lovely day. Please take care of Althea's broken foot. Please take care of Mother and Father as they travel to New York City, New York. Please take care of Amelia and her suitable husband, Mr. Beasley, and all the little beastly Beasleys. Please take care of Augusta and her ne'er-do-well husband, Mr. Jenkins, and my scoundrel cousins, James, John, Jordon, and Jacob. Thank You for the nice dinner and the sheriff and Miss Kottis. Keep me safe this night in this awful parlor and this awful sofa. Amen."

Amanda rose to her feet and took up the doll and basket once more. She stood in quiet misery, staring at the sofa while big tears coursed down her round cheeks.

"It's not that bad, Miss Amanda," whispered Jake, strangely moved by the silent tears.

"Do you have a bed?" she whispered in return.

"Yes, but I have slept on the ground outside on more than one occasion."

Amanda transferred the basket to the same hand that held the doll. She rested her free hand on the sheriff's shoulder and gave it a consoling pat. Clearly sleeping on the ground was worse than sleeping on the awful sofa. Jake put his arm around the tiny figure, and she melted against his chest, burying her face against his shoulder.

"Please, Sheriff Moore," she sobbed, "find me a real bed, not in a parlor."

✹

Jake rode Dancer at a sedate pace through the muggy night air. Completely limp, the little figure sitting before him in his yellow dancing shirt sagged against him. He took the handle of the square basket from her fingers before she dropped it. They hadn't been a mile out of town before she relaxed, not two miles before her head lolled to one side and her mouth drooped with a whispered snore.

Now why, he wondered, was it not proper for a young lady to sleep in a parlor on a perfectly comfortable sofa, but it was perfectly proper to ride out of town in the middle of the night wearing his good shirt? Of course, he didn't point out the quirkiness of this reasoning to the mite sleeping before him.

Back in Maggie's parlor, overwhelmed by the child's tears, Jake had proposed taking her to Miss Kottis, who knew what was "proper for a young lady." When Miss Amanda agreed, he scooped her up with the doll and basket and made for the livery stable as fast as his long legs would carry him. She clung to him with those fat little arms, and he found himself holding her tighter as if to assure her that everything was going to be all right.

And everything was going to be all right. It wasn't really the middle of the night. The church social had ended around eight thirty. He'd wasted a little under an hour trying to get Miss Amanda to bed at the boardinghouse. It would be around ten o'clock when he reached the Kotchkis place. If he were coming calling, ten o'clock would be improper. But this wasn't a social call.

What did he care about what was proper and improper? He was just doing his duty, seeing that the little mite got a good night's sleep before her journey tomorrow. He'd sent a prayer up to God for an answer to his dilemma. Then he firmly put aside any thoughts about why the first face that came into his mind had a tempting dimple right at the corner of lips it would be improper to kiss.

When Sheriff Moore turned into the long drive between two rows of white oak, a few windows of the Kotchkis farmhouse still glowed with yellow lamplight. A couple of dogs barked a greeting. He reined in Dancer at the front porch. Carefully hoisting Miss Amanda up against his shoulder, he slid out of the saddle. He spoke softly to his horse as he looped the reins over the hitching post.

"This won't take but a minute, Dancer."

His boots clomped on the wooden steps, and the door opened before he had a chance to knock.

Mel Kotchkis walked out onto the porch and clapped Jake on the shoulder as if this were not only an expected visit but one with nothing unusual about it, not the hour of the night, nor the pudgy, miniature proper miss draped over the sheriff's shoulder.

"She wouldn't sleep at Maggie's," said Jake.

"Hmm? Gave you some trouble?" Kotchkis grinned amiably. "Little girls are like that. Pamela will know what to do."

Pamela, in a robe thrown over her nightgown, came rushing down the stairs.

She'd heard the exchange at the door.

"Carry her on up the stairs, Sheriff Moore," she spoke softly. "We'll try to put her down without waking her."

Jake followed, but Mel went to the kitchen table. His big Bible lay open to the book of Matthew, and he patted the pages as he sat down.

"Yes, Jesus," he breathed the words with a grateful sigh. "Just the right suitor for our gal."

❦

"In here, Sheriff." Pamela pushed the door wide open as she scurried into a room ahead of him. A lantern sat on a bedside table. A book lay open, facedown beside it. The covers were turned back and pillows were stacked against the headboard.

Pamela grabbed the top pillow and pushed it to the other side of the double bed. She smoothed the sheet and pulled the covers back a bit more then stood aside for Sheriff Moore to gently put down his burden.

Amanda groaned, and he patted her back, speaking soothing words. When she settled, he stepped away. Pamela tucked the little girl in and turned down the lamp.

Pamela's tawny curls caught the glimmer of the soft light and surrounded her face like a halo. Jake smelled the clean fragrance of soap and rosewater on her skin. The soul-shaking thought that he was in Pamela's bedroom, next to the bed she must have hopped out of when she heard him at the door, enjoying the sight, the smell of her, and even relishing the sound of her breathing, nearly sent him racing from the house in panic.

He stopped in the hall, trying to think of a time when his heart had last raced like that. When Tommy Blake holed up in the livery, and he had to talk the outlaw out so he could arrest him without bloodshed? No, this was different. This was a whole lot different.

"Sheriff Moore?" Pamela came out into the upstairs hallway and closed the door softly behind her. "Where are her clothes?"

"What?"

"Her clothes."

"Maggie has them." He turned to look at her—which was his first mistake. She was close and sweet and looking up at him with puzzlement in her eyes. The little furrow across her brow was just at the right height for him to kiss. If she tilted her chin just a mite, her lips. . . He couldn't kiss her! *You don't kiss a woman in her nightgown and robe unless you're married to her.* Where was Mel Kotchkis? His daughter was up here with a. . .a. . .

Jake stumbled on the first step but caught himself and hurried down the stairs. About halfway down he remembered he was supposed to be quiet or he'd wake Amanda. At the bottom, in the foyer's bright light, he felt like a fool for running from her. Pamela's slow and steady footsteps descended the stairs he'd just plummeted down.

"Thank you, Miss Pamela," he croaked. Jake cleared his throat and began again. "Thank you, Miss Pamela. Her train leaves at noon. If you don't mind, I'll come by at eleven to pick her up. I'll bring her clothes with me then."

"That will be fine, Sheriff."

"Evening." Staring at her radiance, he reached for the doorknob, missed, dragged his gaze away from that angel face surrounded by the halo of soft gold hair, and focused on the cold, round doorknob.

"Much obliged," he muttered.

Sheriff Jake Moore strode out the door, flew down the steps, and vaulted into the saddle. A kid's trick, but he wasn't trying to impress the woman. He was trying to escape.

Chapter 4

Nothing pressing came up to keep Sheriff Moore in town. He'd swept out his jail cells, strolled down Main Street, and checked with Widow Harper on whether Daniel Frigby had turned up to do the work the judge had sentenced him to do as punishment for public drunkenness. Going out to collect Miss Amanda happened to be next on his list of things to do. The clock said nine instead of eleven, but there was no reason to put off a chore just because the night before he'd thought he wouldn't get around to it until later in the morning.

Jake whistled "All Creatures of Our God and King," and when he got to the alleluias, he lifted his baritone voice to fill the gloomy, heavy morning air with his praise. As Jake turned his horse down the lane to the Kotchkis farm, he noted the sky's angry countenance. Black clouds churned overhead and fits of wind spurted across his path, swirling the dust across the road in hectic dust devils.

Jake looked over the vast field of corn. The crops needed rain. A gentle, all-day rain would do.

Miss Pamela sat on the front porch in a rocker, a sewing basket beside her, and something pink in her hands. Miss Amanda scurried around the yard, dressed more like a young girl than the day before. She raised a hand to wave at him and went back to her present interest, chasing the chickens. She had a small bag Jake guessed was feed. Instead of standing still and throwing out the grain, the city girl cornered the hens and gave them their breakfast. From the saddle, Jake watched Amanda as she tried to force-feed the hens. With a chuckle, Jake dismounted and looped his reins over the hitching rail. Digging in his saddlebag, he produced the tightly wadded bundle containing Amanda's dress, shift, stockings, shoes, and bonnet. He walked up the wooden porch steps and presented it to Miss Pamela.

She shook her head over the compressed and crumpled clothing. Glancing at Jake with laughter bubbling in her voice, she proclaimed, "She won't wear these clothes in this wrinkled condition, you know."

Jake plunked down in the opposite rocker and removed his hat. None of the previous night's awkwardness remained. He gazed over the white railing surrounding the porch, watching Amanda's fruitless endeavors to corner a hen.

"Where did she get those clothes?" he asked.

"We have an attic full of little girl clothes, Sheriff Moore," answered Pamela. "Remember, I am one of five sisters."

Jake tossed her a charming smile with both dimples showing in his broad masculine cheeks.

"Miss Amanda," he called, standing up and walking down the steps to his little friend. "You must entice the chicken to come to you." He stooped to talk to Amanda, putting his arm around the chubby shoulders covered with a plain brown smock dress. "Here, stand very still and sprinkle the grain over the ground around you. The hens have very small brains and will soon forget you've been trying to catch them. Look, see how they're eyeing your bag of grain? They'll come up and peck the feed right at your feet."

The fat hens soothed down their ruffled feathers and scuttled closer to the feed. Jake eased himself to a stand and backed off, returning to his seat beside Miss Pamela.

"You're not a town boy after all," she said.

Jake smiled easily at her, taking in the way little wisps of hair curled around her forehead with the moist heat of the day.

"No, I spent ten years on a farm in Indiana." He leaned back in the rocker, and his eyes moved to admire the field of corn just beyond the barn. "It was my uncle Will's place. I went to live there after my folks died. We raised corn but nothing as fine as this strain your father has developed."

"He'd like hearing that. He has a lot of pride in Kotchkis Kansas Corn."

"Rightly so," Jake said.

"So you didn't like farming and looked for a town job?" Pamela asked.

"Not exactly," said Jake, rubbing his hand across his chin. "Uncle Will never made a secret of the fact the farm was for his boys. He has two, Bill and George. They had ten years on me and always carried fifty to a hundred pounds more muscle."

Pamela let the pink apron she was hemming rest in her lap. Jake's voice held a note of regret. She studied his profile while he peered out over her father's latest test field. The hybrid flourished with strong green stalks and heavy, full ears sporting golden tassels.

"So you liked farming?" she prompted.

Sheriff Moore nodded. "Funny thing was that of the three of us, Bill, George, and skinny Jake, I was the one who took to the fields. I liked the smell of the dirt, the sight of the seedlings popping up in rows along a furrow."

"But you left the farm?"

"I left the farm." He nodded toward the field. "Your father and I talk about the corn. It brings up the old ache inside me. I get him talking about predestination so I don't have to think about it." Jake tossed the farmer's daughter a mischievous grin.

Pamela laughed and plied her needle once more. Jake watched her. It was a comforting sight, the pretty young woman doing something domestic, calmly rocking on the front porch. At Uncle Will's there had been no woman's touch since Uncle Will's wife had died some years earlier. A hired woman came in and did the laundry and some other chores twice a week.

In those bleak days, Jake had escaped to the fields to relish the beauty of tender shoots breaking through the dark soil and swaying in the gentle breeze. Out there he talked to God as his mother had done before her death. Out there he felt the presence of a loving Father who delighted in a young boy's company. In Jake's early childhood, his father had lifted him onto muscled shoulders and carried him down rows of fully grown corn. Even on top of his pa's broad shoulders, only Jake's head peeked over the crop.

Living with Uncle Will had been a dry time. Young Jake Moore received his nourishment in the fields. There, memories of his past and the comfort of his Lord watered his thirsty soul.

A sudden gust of wind brought a spattering of mammoth plops of rain. Pamela jumped to her feet, throwing the apron into the empty rocker. Jake grabbed his hat as the wind shuffled it across the wooden porch. Pamela's skirts brushed past him as she hurried out into the yard. He looked up to see her gather Amanda into her arms. Amanda dug her fists into her eyes. Wind whipped dirt up into the air and it swirled against the little girl. She cried that it was stinging her skin and hurting her eyes. Pamela wrapped her body around the child, sheltering her from the bluster.

Jake took two steps down the wooden stairs and heard the distant roar of a train. For a split second he froze, knowing that no train ran close enough to the Kotchkis place to be heard. Then it dawned on him—a tornado.

Dancer reared, his high-pitched whinny shrieking with fear. Jake sprang into action, and with difficulty, he stripped away the saddle and dropped it to the ground. He worked against the nervous horse to remove the bridle and halter. Once free, Dancer rose up on his hind legs and beat the air with his hooves. With one last roll of panicked eyes, he charged out of the yard down the lane, removing himself from danger. The wind had beaten Pamela and Amanda into a ball huddled against the ground. Jake fought against the brutal strength of the wind's onslaught and the flotsam flying with deadly velocity. Holding his arms up to block the debris, he managed to fall to his knees beside Pamela. He put strong arms around her, using his body to shield her, and pressed his face against her hair.

"Storm shelter?" he yelled.

She nodded and tried to rise. Jake scooped up Amanda, and she clung to him with her arms around his neck, her face buried in his chest, and her legs wrapped around his waist. Pamela pressed against his other side. He had a strong arm around each female, but the force of the wind threatened to tear them from his grasp. A branch hurled across the yard and assaulted them. Jake and Pamela beat the whipping limbs off. The wind caught it and carried it away.

Stooped against the aggressive force, the three pushed around the side of the building where two slanted doors covered steps into the basement. Jake handed Amanda to Pamela and wrestled the door open. Turning back, he took hold of Pamela's arm to guide her down the stone steps. Just as he had the two far enough down to be out of the most severe gusts, a blast against the wooden door heaved it against Jake. He catapulted down the stairs. His head whacked a beam, and his unconscious body smashed against Amanda and Pamela, slamming them to the dirt floor of the cellar.

The roar of the tornado above did not diminish in the recesses of the cellar. Instead, the sound of the wooden structure swaying added to the horrible cacophony. Pamela covered her ears and prayed, "Lord, help us!"

She squirmed out from under the heavy sheriff and managed to roll him over onto his back. Amanda scrambled into Pamela's lap and threw her arms around her neck. Pamela could feel her shaking and knew the words of comfort she mumbled into her little ear could not be heard.

The impact of some flying object jarred the house. The wood above them squealed, straining.

The house is going to go, thought Pamela. *What should I do? Oh Lord, what should I do? Where is the safest place?*

Pamela searched the dark recesses of the cellar. *We've got to be against the wall,* she thought. *Which wall, Father?* she asked in prayer. The darkest corner where only a child's mattress stood against the wall beckoned her.

Pamela forced Amanda to let go of her. Then, pushing her arms under Jake's shoulders and grabbing what she could of his shirt, Pamela began to drag Jake toward the corner of the cellar room.

Amanda took hold of Jake's belt and began to tug as well. Pamela realized with surprise the little girl was helping move the man to safety. With the winds howling, fear gave Pamela strength, and she soon dragged Jake across the dirt floor. She put Amanda right against the stone corner and then positioned her body in front of the child's. She pulled on Jake until she had his upper body in her lap, his head against her chest. Then she prayed.

The crescendo of the storm pounded on their senses. The house shuddered; the noise peaked. Amanda covered her ears and curled into a tighter ball. Pamela squeezed Jake in her arms and fought the terror by repeating a single sentence. *Lord, help!* She couldn't make her brain function any further to provide details. It seemed enough to just hold on to that lifeline to the heavenly Father.

The timbre of the roar changed. Pamela raised her head to listen. The clamor receded and the drone of torrential rain dominated. She turned slightly and gathered Amanda in her arms.

"We're safe," she said.

Amanda hugged her fiercely and whimpered softly against Pamela's side.

"It'll be all right now. Those kinds of storms only go in one direction. It won't turn around to batter us again. We're safe." Pamela kept up the flow of soothing words until the rain slackened. "We've got to see to the sheriff," Pamela told Amanda. She gently pushed the child away from her.

"Sheriff Jake." Pamela bent over the form still draped across her legs. She gently shook his shoulder. No response. She put her trembling hand behind his head and drew back when she touched something warm and sticky. "Oh, you're bleeding." She shifted him to one side, trying to see the wound.

"He's hurt bad," said Amanda in a small voice.

"Maybe not," said Pamela. "It's a head wound, and cuts on the scalp bleed a lot, even when it isn't serious. I need to stop the bleeding."

"He needs a bandage?"

"Yes," said Pamela. "Here, Amanda, you hold his head in your lap, and

I'll try to find something clean to press against the wound."

Pamela managed to shift Jake's heavy body, laying just his head in the little girl's lap. Then she crawled directly to a stack of trunks. Finding the one she wanted, she opened it and rummaged through the contents. She came back with an old tablecloth, tore a strip off using her teeth to get it started, then folded the strip into a pad. She pressed it against the sticky place on the back of Jake's head.

"Is it going to rain forever?" asked Amanda.

"No, honey," answered Pamela.

"Will someone come help us?"

For the first time Pamela thought of her father. He'd been out in the south field. Had he found shelter?

"Let's pray," said Pamela. "Let's pray for all the people who were out in that storm."

Amanda obediently folded her little hands, resting them on Jake's face. His head still lay in her lap.

"Dear Lord, that was a scary wind, and it's raining awful hard," Amanda said. "We thank You that we're safe and ask that You help Sheriff Moore wake up from sleeping because of his head wound and that his scalp will quit bleeding all over the place. And for the chickens to be safe because they haven't finished eating their breakfast yet, and for me and Miss Kottis to wait patiently while You do all the things You have to do to undo all the things that the scary wind did, and please make it stop raining soon so we can get out of this dark place without getting all wet. Amen."

"Father in heaven," said Pamela, "thank You for keeping us safe, and I ask that You take care of my father and all the other people in the path of the tornado. Amen."

Slowly the sound of the heavy rain abated to a drizzle.

Jake groaned and lifted his head only to let it drop again. Amanda patted his face.

"You are going to be all right," she said. "We prayed."

Pamela changed the pad pressed against his bleeding scalp. His eyes flickered open.

"You hit your head when we fell into the cellar," she explained.

"Help me sit up," said Jake.

"Maybe you should just lie still for a while," suggested Pamela.

"No, there are people out there who need help. My head's hard. I can make it."

Both Pamela and Amanda helped the sheriff sit. Once up, he had to rest against Pamela as the room swayed and darkness threatened to engulf him once more.

As soon as his head quit swimming, he tried to stand.

"Wait," said Pamela. "Move over closer to the steps where it's lighter. I'll bind a bandage to that thick skull, and then you can try to get up."

Jake obediently crawled across the dirt floor of the cellar and collapsed against the wooden boxes next to the steps. A fine mist from the still falling rain blew in. Everything was wet and debris covered the steps.

While Pamela affixed a fresh pad to the oozing wound and wrapped a narrow strip of the tablecloth around Jake's head to tie it on, Amanda began pulling bits and pieces of wood, tree limbs, hay, and shredded plants off the lowest steps.

Just as Pamela tied off the ends of the cloth, Amanda stopped and dug around in the clutter.

"Look," she said, holding up her find, "a china teacup."

Amanda held it out to Pamela. She sat back on her heels and took it carefully in her hands. Pamela examined the blue forget-me-nots decorating one side and the fluted handle with a thin line of blue accenting the curve. The small bone china cup had not a nick or crack.

"Gladys Sence," she said. "This belongs to Gladys Sence."

The picture of Gladys Sence proudly pouring out tea from the matching teapot sprang into Pamela's mind. The Sunday school teachers met once a month in Gladys's homey little kitchen. The cup in Pamela's hand proved with a certainty that the Sence home had been shattered by the tornado.

She put the cup on a wooden crate so her shaking hands wouldn't drop it. Then she stared at the unharmed cup and imagined the wind ripping through her friend's home and carrying it here. She shuddered, wrapping her arms around her waist and bending forward to ward off the horror. She began to sob.

Jake's strong arms gathered her up. He rocked her and spoke words of comfort just as she had rocked and soothed Amanda almost an hour before.

Amanda put down the limb she used as a little broom to knock things off the step. She settled down beside the two adults and leaned against them. With one chubby, grubby hand, she stroked Pamela's arm.

"We should pray again," Amanda said, looking up at Jake's pale face.

He nodded, and his soothing baritone filled the dim and dank cellar with hope.

Chapter 5

"Pamela! Pamela!" Mel Kotchkis's voice boomed across the empty farmyard.

Pamela jerked out of Jake's arms and scrambled to the steps. She peered up at the opening, disregarding the light rain misting over her upturned face.

"Here, Pa," she called. "We're in here."

Mel appeared at the top, his scratched and dirty face beaming relief with a wide grin.

"Jake is hurt," she called.

Mel's smile disappeared, and he plunged down the steps, pushing branches and debris out of his way.

The older man knelt beside the sheriff.

"It's nothing but a knock on the head, Mel," reassured Jake. "How is it out there?"

Mel leaned back and inspected the sheriff with a knowing eye. Satisfied that the young man didn't seem to be seriously hurt, he turned his mind to what he'd seen, and his huge work-hardened hand went up to his forehead. He made a swipe downward across his face as if to wipe the memory away.

"It's bad," he said. "Let's get you up into the house." He reached to support Jake as he stood. "Our house has some broken windows, and there's a huge sycamore standing upside down, leaning against the back.

But the roof is still on, and even the porch doesn't look like it's suffered much. I want to get over to the barn and see to the animals now that I know my Pamela and our little guest are all right."

They struggled up the steps.

"Do you know which way it went?" asked Jake.

"I don't think it hit town, but I'd say the railroad track is gone."

"Why is that?"

"My south field is riveted with railroad ties stuck in the ground like so many toothpicks. When I crawled out of the ditch and saw those heavy ties poked in the ground, some buried two or three feet by the force the tornado hurled them at the ground. . ." Mel paused and shook his head, still in a daze by the power in that awful wind. He shook his head again and cleared his throat. "Well, I praised God for protection and then high-tailed it back to the house. I had to see if Pamela was all right." He laid a hand on Amanda's curly head. "And our Miss Amanda."

She beamed at him with the smile of a little girl who'd fallen in love with a grandpa. She took his hand, and they went around the house to the front porch. One rocker out of the three still stood. The flowerpots filled with marigolds were gone. A bedraggled set of long johns dangled from the eaves.

Mel chortled as they passed the red underwear. "I sure hope those were hanging on somebody's clothesline this morning and not on one of my neighbors' skinny hides."

Inside the house they found water standing on the floor where rain had blown in through the broken windows.

Amanda let go of Pamela's hand and raced upstairs. A moment later she came down carrying her doll and the square basket.

"I won't go to Big Springs today, will I?" She cast a worried glance at Sheriff Moore.

Jake squatted to put a hand on her shoulder and look her directly in the eyes.

"I'm sorry, Amanda," he said. "I can't return you to your family today. I can't put you on the train as we planned, and I can't take you myself. I need to go help some people."

She patted his arm. "That's all right. I need to help Miss Kottis clean up this mess."

Impulsively Jake gathered the dirty little mite into his arms and gave her a big hug. Amanda returned the hug full force.

"I was scared," she whispered in his ear.

"I was, too," he admitted. He leaned back from their embrace and looked into the solemn little face. "Right now Mr. Kotchkis and I have to go see if there are some other scared people who need our help."

She gave him a serious nod and released him. Jake stood up and looked at Pamela. He stood transfixed by the beauty of her eyes. What was it the Bible said? In Genesis, wasn't it? "And the Lord God said, It is not good that the man should be alone; I will make him an help meet for him." Never before had Jake felt those words were for him. Now as he looked into the clear blue gaze of Pamela Kotchkis, he felt the terrible aloneness God never meant for His children to endure. He suppressed the urge to take her in his arms with the same ease he had gathered up the little girl. He knew that to give and receive comfort from Mel Kotchkis's daughter was not his privilege. He'd held her in the cellar, and it had felt right. Now he had to turn away and get busy with the things God had set before him to do this day.

Mel cleared his throat. "Before we go out," he said, "let's take a minute to pray."

❧

Amanda and Pamela spent the next hour cleaning. That included bathing and changing clothes. They sat down to dinner alone, but before they'd finished, homeless neighbors began to arrive. Her pa and the sheriff were directing people to their door. By supper, the Kotchkis farmhouse sheltered women and children from three houses torn apart by the tornado.

Amanda bustled about the house as a born hostess, making sure the visitors had drink and food and a comfortable place to rest. Never shy, she addressed adults and children alike and carried messages to Pamela, who worked in the kitchen.

"We're going to have a dance," Amanda announced as she brought in an empty plate from the parlor.

"A dance?" Pamela put the hot pan of muffins down on the kitchen table. "When?"

"Saturday night," said Amanda, crawling up into the chair beside the table and watching as Pamela carefully plucked out the fresh muffins.

Pamela sank into the chair beside her and leaned on her elbows.

"I can't imagine why people are talking of a dance," Pamela said. She poured a glass of milk for herself and a smaller one for Amanda and put a muffin before the child. "It seems a mighty poor time for frivolity."

"People are going to bring things for the people who lost everything. The dance will be a place to collect and dis. . .distri. . ."

"Distribute?" Pamela supplied a word.

Amanda nodded, her blond curls bouncing.

"I suppose that's a good idea." Pamela took her glass of milk and went to the window over the sink. She looked out toward the road. Another family limped toward the house. It was Gladys Sence and her children.

"Why are you smiling?" asked Amanda.

"I see the lady who owns the teacup coming down the lane," answered Pamela.

"I thought you saw Sheriff Moore coming."

Pamela turned to look at Amanda with a puzzled frown wrinkling her brow. "Why would you think that?"

"My sister Augusta smiles when she sees her husband, Mr. Jenkins, coming. Mr. Jenkins is a ne'er-do-well," said Amanda before taking a bigger-than-polite bite of muffin. Pamela grinned. Amanda's city manners were dropping away. Perhaps the softer, more comfortable clothes allowed the little girl to be less stiff. Perhaps just being surrounded by more casual adults made the difference.

"Do you like Mr. Jenkins?" asked Pamela.

Amanda's head jerked up, and she studied Pamela's friendly face. After a moment she nodded cautiously, still examining Pamela's expression. The little girl chewed slowly and swallowed before making any comment.

"Mr. Jenkins tells stories," she said, the tone of her voice condemning such a practice.

Again Pamela felt her face wrinkle as she tried to decipher the statement. "He tells lies?" she asked.

Amanda vigorously shook her head, sending the curls wildly dancing. "No, real stories," she explained. "About fairies."

"Where do the Jenkinses live, Amanda?"

"In St. Louis, Kansas," answered Amanda. "They don't live on the right side of the river."

"The Missouri side is the right side?" Pamela raised her eyebrows at this petty prejudice.

Amanda nodded. "We live on the Missouri side."

"Of course," observed Pamela, trying to remember that Amanda was merely repeating what she'd been told.

Gladys Sence bustled into the room, coming directly over to Pamela and giving her a hearty hug. She then sank into a table chair and removed her bonnet.

"Such a day!" she exclaimed. "Such a day! What wonders I have seen. Pamela, three of your silly-looking banty chickens are sitting at the very top of the post oak tree down by the river. Probably scared to death, never been up so high in their lives. Certainly didn't fly up there."

"Oh dear, my Banties," moaned Pamela.

"Well, don't carry on," admonished Gladys, her usual smile brightening her face. "That father of yours and the sheriff are trying to get them down. All the work that needs to be done and they're taking time out to fool with some plaything chickens."

Pamela laughed at Gladys's good-natured fussing. No one in all of Lawrence had a bigger heart than Gladys. Her face sobered as she remembered the teacup.

"Gladys, was your house hit?" she asked.

Gladys nodded her head in amazement. "That twister aimed for my house, and that's God's own truth. But God did like He did to Job and said, 'Go ahead and take those boards, every pillar and post, but you can't have my servant Gladys Sence!'" Gladys clapped her hands together. "Fred hadn't even gone out to the fields yet 'cause he was working on the old plow harness that needed repairing. He came charging in the house, gathered us all up, and rushed us out to the banks of the river. I wanted to go down into the cellar, and he said, 'No!' And he can't tell me why he knew to go to the river instead of down in the cellar, but it's a good thing. What pieces of our house that didn't scatter all over the fields fell into the cellar."

"Oh, Gladys, praise God," Pamela whispered, and her hand moved to her throat as she realized what a close call it had been for her neighbors.

"You're right about that, Pamela," answered the older woman. "And I'm thanking Him that Fred is such a put-it-off-till-tomorrow man."

Pamela nodded and then giggled at the look of pure mischief in Gladys's eyes.

"If he had built that extra bedroom like I've been after him to do for two years, I would have been vexed to see it blown up like that." She shrugged. "Now he'll be building a whole house, and it can't be too much trouble to put in another bedroom for my girls."

They laughed together. Gladys jumped to her feet.

"Well, Pamela, tell me what you want me to do." She gestured toward the other room where people gathered to talk. "You'll be feeding that whole crew tonight, and probably tomorrow. Do you want me to mix up some biscuits?"

While the women worked together, Gladys told all the bits of news she had gathered, whose farms had been hit and what people had been injured. She talked of who was out helping people and where the injured had been taken.

❦

Pamela vacillated between the blue dress that brought out the blue in her eyes and her favorite yellow dress. When she tried the yellow dress on for Amanda and did a twirl in her bedroom, Amanda clapped her hands with enthusiasm over the way the skirt swung out.

"That one's the prettiest," she said, "and it matches Sheriff Moore's dancing shirt."

The two young ladies dug around in the attic trunks and found another party dress for Amanda to wear.

Mel escorted them to the dance on Saturday night and then left them to their own devices as he took up his fiddle and helped provide the music.

Pamela politely asked Amanda for the first dance, remembering when her older sisters would partner her at the community dances. Pamela guided her little friend over to the square where adults and children laughed together. Amanda curtsied with skill but then just stood there as if she knew none of the steps. Everyone in the square took pleasure in helping her through the formations. Three dances passed before Pamela insisted they go get some punch.

The refreshment table sat under a huge sweet gum tree. Amanda drank her punch quickly, leaving a red mustache across her upper lip. Pamela laughed as she watched the little girl scurry off to join some other children playing nearby.

Pamela took her cup of punch and sat on one of the wooden benches along the outside wall of the town meeting hall, away from the small crowd around the refreshment table. She picked up one of the large star-shaped leaves of the sweet gum tree and gently crushed it between her fingers. It released the pleasant fragrance that gave it the "sweet" part of its name. Pamela inhaled deeply, enjoying the essence of the beautiful night.

A breeze riffled the leaves above her, and she saw stars peeking through the branches of the tree. A three-quarter moon gave some silvery light, adding to the golden glow shining from the windows of the well-lit hall. The magical night hummed with the life of people coming together to help one another. Pamela thanked God for the farmers and townspeople willing to give of themselves in a time of need. The tornado had reminded her how generous her neighbors could be.

Pamela leaned back against the building, her head resting against the boards but her foot tapping on the dirt. She could feel the wood vibrate with the strong beat of the hoedown and the rhythmic movement of the dancers within. She imagined the building itself would like to join the dancing, just as her feet couldn't seem to keep still.

Amanda skipped back to her side and proudly displayed a ribbon one of the older girls had fastened in her hair.

"Do you like it, Miss Kottis?" she asked breathlessly.

"Yes, it's very pretty."

"I got it from my friends." Amanda's eyes glowed with excitement, and she rushed back to join the square they were forming to dance under the trees.

"What are you doing out here?" asked a familiar low voice from the shadows.

Jake's voice made her heart leap, and she felt her face flood with an expectant blush. She'd always been so careful to keep from falling under the sheriff's spell. She'd kept her distance and thereby kept her dignity. She'd always felt contempt for those girls in town who blatantly flirted around Jake Moore. Now she hoped she could at least behave with some decorum, because her heart wanted to betray how she felt.

Smiling cautiously, Pamela turned to greet the sheriff as he sat on the bench beside her.

"We were hot, so we came outside." Pamela nodded toward Amanda, who had joined hands with the other children and moved as the circle rotated with the music. "Amanda is playing. I didn't want to leave her out here alone."

"She's not quite the stuffy little city miss she was four days ago." Pamela studied him as he watched the children. The girls in town made a point of being available as he finished each dance. She couldn't blame them. He seemed to find pleasure when he danced with the homely, awkward gals as well as with the pretty ones. And he danced as easily as he walked. The joy and fun he expressed as he whirled one partner after another around the hardwood floor caused many a girl to swoon over him.

She'd noted that where he carefully avoided the women when at church, he had no problem dancing with every female in sight at the community dances. He'd even taken the preacher's wife to the floor and danced with the elderly sisters Mrs. Dobson and Mrs. Roper, both widows in their sixties.

Pamela had never been his partner. Her careful adherence to the code of dignity had cost her that privilege. Pamela sighed, and the mournful sound on the night air caught his attention.

Jake turned to see the soft light of the moon bathing her gentle face. She smiled at him, and he spotted the dimple that had on occasion bewitched him. The dance inside had ended, and the violin played the first notes of the next, more sedate tune.

"Miss Pamela," said Sheriff Moore, "may I have this dance?"

Pamela nodded, and he took her hand. They stood and faced each other in the golden light spilling out of the open window. She put her hand on his shoulder. He put his on her waist, and they waltzed under the trees. Neither noticed the children pairing off to do an ungainly imitation of the dance. Pamela only knew she danced with the most wonderful man she'd ever met. Jake felt his heart surrender.

Chapter 6

The railroad crews settled into work, but a train wouldn't run for at least a week. The telegraph lines still lay on the ground, but riders carried messages to the neighboring towns. Most folks had started their repairs or the clearing away of the debris for their new houses. Monday morning had brought enough regularity to the community that Jake felt he could now leave to return Miss Amanda to her sister in Big Springs.

As he'd talked over his plans with Mel Kotchkis after church the day before, the farmer had offered his surrey for the trip.

"It's a fine rig," he explained. "Got it for the girls when there were so many of them at home, always getting rigged up and prettified for the church socials and community shindigs. It has genuine leather seats, silly little fringe dangling off the roof, and yeller wheels. Miss Amanda will feel right comfortable in that fancy wagon." Mel grinned at the mention of it. "And if you wouldn't be opposed to it, my daughter Grace lives in Big Springs; you could take Pamela along to help you with Miss Amanda, and it'd give Pamela a chance to visit her big sister."

Jake, who at first had thought the surrey sounded like more trouble than putting Amanda across the front of his saddle on Dancer, suddenly took a hankering to driving the fancy rig and two charming ladies to Big Springs.

Jake rode past the Kotchkis cornfields, headed once more for the farmhouse. This morning the sun kissed the corn, urging the battered plants to stand straight. The blue of the sky sparkled its hue over the meadow to one side of the road. Milking cows lumbered without hurry over the lush green grass. A warm, light breeze ruffled the hair on Jake's neck, and he pulled his new hat firmly down to keep it from blowing off.

Jake lifted his hearty baritone voice, singing "Sunshine in My Soul." With each verse his voice grew stronger, and when he reined Dancer to a halt before the Kotchkis hitching post, he heard Mel's tenor and Pamela's soprano join him in the chorus.

Amanda danced out onto the porch, laughing at the grown-ups' happy song.

When they ended on a ringing chord, Mel standing in the door of the barn, Pamela on the porch, and Jake still sitting on his horse, the little girl doubled over with mirth.

"I want to sing the words," she chirped as soon as the laughter left her throat. "Teach me!"

"We will," said Jake, "on the way to Big Springs."

"We have a picnic basket," Amanda squealed. "With tarts! I helped make them. Miss Kottis says we have to watch you because the knave of hearts steals the tarts!" She jumped up and down in her excitement.

Jake leveled his gaze at his accuser. "So I am the knave of hearts."

"Yes, yes." Amanda clapped her hands. "But Miss Kottis is not the queen."

"She's not?"

"No, 'cause she doesn't want to be married to the king, who beat the knave full sore."

"Ah!" said Jake as he swung down from Dancer's back. "She's too softhearted."

"Yes," answered Amanda. "Do you want to know what kind of tarts they are?"

Jake came up the porch steps and swept Miss Amanda up in his arms for a big hug.

"What kind?" he asked.

"I won't tell," said Amanda. "You have to wait for our picnic."

"You're a tease, Miss Amanda," Jake protested, laughing.

She giggled and squeezed his neck in a tight hug. "Let's go. We're ready. Miss Kottis and I packed two bags, one for her and one for me, and a big picnic basket."

"Whoa," said Jake. "We're going to have so much to tote, we won't have room for one little girl, and if we don't take the little girl, we don't need to go."

Amanda laughed and squirmed to get down. She raced past Pamela and into the house.

"Are you ready to go, too?" Jake asked Pamela, his hat in his hand, his eyes taking in the fresh beauty of her as she stood on the porch.

She nodded, smiling with only a hint of her joy getting past the shyness that suddenly enveloped her.

"I'll get our things," she said. "Pa's coming with the surrey."

In a manner of minutes, Jake had turned Dancer out into the near pasture and had swung his saddlebags into the back of the surrey, putting them on the floor in front of the second seat. Two bay horses were harnessed to the rig, and they stamped their feet, seemingly as anxious to get started as Amanda. Amanda had set the bag of clothing Pamela had given her and her little square basket on the floor beside the saddlebags. She clutched her doll, waiting for the adults to finish with their goodbyes. In the end, she gave Mr. Kotchkis one more big hug as he lifted her into the front seat.

"You write me a letter," he admonished her. "And when your sister's foot gets better, you talk her into coming to visit us."

Amanda waved until they turned the corner, out of the farm lane and onto the main road heading west.

"How long before we get there?" was her first question.

Pamela laughed. "We just started. We won't get there until late afternoon."

"Does Althea know I'm coming?"

"She knows you're coming this week," said Jake. "I sent a letter with a fellow who was riding that way. But I sent it Saturday, before I knew just which day I'd be able to get away. She'll be surprised to see you so soon."

Amanda chattered for a while and then remembered the hymn Jake had been singing when he arrived at the farmhouse. They spent an hour going over the words, and toward the end Pamela and Jake harmonized, making Amanda clap her hands with enthusiasm.

When they took their first break to let the horses rest, Pamela took Amanda behind some bushes and introduced her to the reality of life without a privy. Amanda stamped back into the clearing, scowling as she marched up to where Jake sat on a log. She stood before him with her hands on her hips.

"What's the matter, little mite?" asked Jake.

"I like traveling on a train better than this," she said.

Jake raised an eyebrow at her. "You do?"

She nodded vigorously. "Except I do like the horses."

"Uh-huh," agreed Jake.

"And the surrey is pretty," she added.

"Uh-huh," agreed Jake again. He caught the glimmer in Pamela's eye and had to look away to keep from laughing.

"And I like it better being with you, Sheriff Moore, and with Miss Kottis." She smiled at her friends. "And, of course, I like the picnic."

Jake nodded with a solemn air.

"And the surrey bumps and rocks you, and I like that 'cause the train jiggles and jostles and jambers your nerves."

"Jambers?" asked Jake.

Amanda nodded hard twice, making her curls bounce.

Pamela came from behind her and sat on the log with Jake.

"Why did you get off the train, Amanda?" Pamela asked.

Amanda's face went red. She looked over at the bushes and then back at her friends. Her face reflected a war between telling and not. Finally, she giggled and climbed into Pamela's lap.

"I was looking for a fresh privy," she said. "The one on the train smelled."

Pamela admirably did not show any amusement at this confession. Jake took a sudden interest in a hawk flying over the field.

"Where was your sister?" asked Pamela.

"Sleeping."

"And did you find a privy?" asked Pamela.

Amanda nodded. "There was one at the station, but it wasn't much better, and when I came out, the train was going away with my sister on it."

"And so began," said Jake in a deep, dramatic voice, "the adventures of Miss Amanda Greer of St. Louis, Missouri."

Amanda laughed and wiggled out of Pamela's lap and into his. As the child passed from one set of arms to the other, the looped crocheted edging on Pamela's cuff snagged on the sheriff's gun belt.

"I'm stuck," said Pamela.

"Hop down, Miss Amanda," said Jake.

Amanda looked on as Jake carefully disengaged the delicate threads from the belt at his waist. She didn't notice how quiet her two friends became. She didn't see the flush spread to Pamela's face. She certainly didn't understand why the sheriff held Miss Kottis's hand carefully in his after he succeeded in freeing her sleeve.

❧

As they went farther down the road, Jake told stories about going to school in Indiana with his cousins, Bill and George. His cousins had been larger than he was and twice as ornery. Jake had had to use his wits to survive. Amanda listened attentively and laughed when Jake got the better of his cousins in their childhood pranks.

"Sheriff Moore," she asked, "didn't you go to a country school?"

"Yes," he answered. "Remember, I said there were four grades in one room and four grades in the other. I never could get away from those rapscallion cousins."

"Rap-skal-yun," echoed Amanda, letting the unfamiliar word roll over her tongue.

"Mischief makers," explained Jake.

Amanda nodded. "Father is going to send me to a first-class private school for girls of refined civility in St. Louis." Amanda looked puzzled.

"Father says that you can't learn to talk right, or act right, in the common schools."

Jake and Pamela exchanged a look over the head of their passenger.

"You talk proper," said Amanda to Jake with a sigh.

"Actually," said Pamela, "I've noticed that, too. You do speak with more precision than most farmers."

"Well," said Jake, "I always knew that I wouldn't be on the farm when I grew up. So I took pains in my studies at school and visited with the two schoolmasters, Mr. Ted Bishop and Mr. Edward Bishop, after school and sometimes on Sunday afternoon for extra tutoring. They were brothers and had more books than a library. They gave me odd jobs to do around their place. I cut their wood and such—neither one of the brothers was very strong. And I ended up with good grades and came to Lawrence to go to the university."

"You didn't!" exclaimed Pamela.

He looked sharply at her. "You don't believe I'm smart enough?"

"No, that's. . .that's not it," Pamela stuttered in confusion. "I just. . .I didn't think. . ." She broke off and looked at him. "Did you finish?"

"No, I took a job as a deputy because I was studying law," he explained. "Then I discovered I liked arresting the criminals better than defending them."

"Jake Moore, I'm impressed," said Pamela.

"Because I went to the university?"

"Well, that," she admitted, "but more because you did what you wanted to do. You went to school when you wanted to, and I'm sure you had to work to make the grades and work to make the money. Then you had the gumption to take another course when the first one didn't turn out to be what you expected. Some people just decide to do things and even when they know it's not what they wanted, they just plow ahead."

Jake grinned at her. "Well, I'm glad I told you. Next time I get to thinking I'm not as good as I should be 'cause I dropped out of college, I'll remember that you think I made the right choice."

"Well, I do!" she exclaimed. "God wants us to enjoy this life He's given us, and that means doing a life work that gives us pleasure. He's just as delighted with a shoemaker who makes a good boot and enjoys his trade as He is with the president of the United States."

Jake laughed out loud. "Sometimes I'm sure He's more delighted with a shoemaker, especially if the lowly man is walking in the Light."

"Walking in the Light?" asked Amanda, her face turned to Jake's and a furrow on her brow.

"It means following Jesus," he explained.

Amanda shook her head. "You can't follow Jesus. He doesn't go anywhere."

Jake grinned at her. "Following Jesus means finding out what He wants from reading your Bible and praying. His Holy Spirit helps us to understand what we read and guides us in our decisions."

"I have a Bible," said Amanda.

"You do?" said Pamela.

The little girl nodded her head, causing her silvery blond curls to bounce. "In my basket," she explained. "Pastor Jarmin talked about journeys the Sunday before Althea and I left on our trip. He said God would protect our steps so we wouldn't get lost. I packed my Bible and carried it with me so Althea and I wouldn't have troubles." She sighed. "It didn't work. I got lost from Althea, Althea got hurt, and the tornado nearly swooped me away."

" 'Order my steps in thy word: and let not any iniquity have dominion over me,' " quoted Pamela. "Psalm 119:133."

Jake looked at Pamela and shrugged. He didn't have any inspiration, so he willingly let her handle it.

"Amanda," said Pamela, "that text and many like it tell us to choose to do things that God has told us are good. The Bible tells us how God thinks about things, which things are good and which are bad. When a person chooses to do bad, then the bad things get control of him, and he can be very unhappy. This is important. God says it often in the Bible, so He must think it is very important. You must follow the paths that He has labeled to be good. If you do that, then you will be a happy person, and you will know God is helping you."

"But I still have troubles," lamented Amanda.

"Yes, but you have God watching over you. Carrying the Bible doesn't make Him closer to you," Pamela explained. "You have to carry Him in your heart. You have to love Him. Being a Christian isn't something you can pack in your basket. It's your attitude toward your heavenly Father."

"You started out on a journey," said Jake, "thinking the Bible in your basket was going to keep you safe. If you had left that Bible on the train, God still would have led you to my office. He still would have given you shelter during the tornado. He still would have put people in Big Springs to take care of your sister. The things that happen aren't dependent upon your having the Bible; they're dependent on God. You can't put God in a basket or leave Him behind on a train."

"Yes," said Pamela, "and that is so much better, because no matter what happens, you know He is there with you."

"So my journey can have bad things happen, but I still have God," said Amanda.

"Right," said Jake. "And the Bible also tells us that all things work together for good for those who love Jesus. I know that's true because even though getting left by the train was a bad thing, look how much good came from it."

"I have new friends," said Amanda.

"Yes," agreed Pamela.

"And I get to ride in a surrey," she continued.

"Yes," said both adults.

"And you and you get to go on a trip with me." Amanda clapped her hands together.

Jake turned a smile filled with admiration and charm to his female companions. His gaze rested on Pamela, and she blushed under the warmth of it.

They stopped for lunch under willow trees by a stream. Amanda proudly displayed her peach tarts, and Jake ate his dessert first, which made both of his female companions laugh.

"I won't eat my tart first," said Amanda in her old stuffy voice. "It isn't proper."

"Being proper isn't necessary on a picnic," said Pamela as she took a huge bite of tart to prove it.

Amanda gasped and then giggled. She ate her tart first as well.

After cold, fried chicken and baked potatoes filled with cheese, Pamela and Jake rested, leaning against the trunk of the tree. Amanda played for a while with her doll.

"I need to go freshen up," she announced to Pamela.

Pamela started to get up.

"I can go by myself," said Amanda. "I'll go wash my hands in the stream and then go over there for the other." She pointed to some bushes not ten feet away.

Pamela looked at the gentle brook, debating whether it was safe to let the girl go alone. It was deep enough to be dangerous.

Jake took hold of Pamela's arm so she couldn't rise.

"All right, Amanda," he said to the child while tenderly keeping Pamela by his side. "Miss Kotchkis will sit with me, and you can call if you need anything."

Amanda thrust her doll into Pamela's arms and skipped off to the water's edge.

"Don't worry," said Jake. "We can see her from here if she falls in, and nothing is going to happen to her in the bushes."

They fell into conversation again. Pamela kept an eye on the little girl as she dawdled by the water, more playing than washing.

By the time Amanda skipped over to the bushes, Pamela had relaxed again against the tree trunk, listening to Jake tell of one of his classes at the university.

"What did she say?" asked Pamela abruptly.

"She's talking to herself," answered Jake. "If she was in trouble, she'd yell."

"She's talking to someone," insisted Pamela.

"An imaginary friend," said Jake, but he cocked his ear toward the bushes.

"Here, kitty, kitty," he heard Amanda call. He started to rise.

Pamela had heard her, too.

"Don't touch a stray kitten, Pamela," she called. "It may not be friendly."

"Come see him, Miss Kottis. He's pretty," said Amanda. "He's all fluffy and very little. I think he's lost. Here, kitty, kitty."

Jake put out a hand to help Amanda stand. They started toward the bushes.

"Oh! Nasty kitty!" cried Amanda.

Jake and Pamela quickened their steps, but they knew before they rounded the bushes what kind of cat Amanda had found. Amanda held tight to the small black-and-white critter even as the air took on a most horrendous odor.

"Put the baby down and let him go back to his mother," said Jake.

Amanda bent and released the "kitty" as she was told, but tears filled her eyes. The skunk scurried into the underbrush and disappeared.

Chapter 7

W e can't return her to her sister like this." Pamela crossed the little clearing to stand next to poor Amanda, but she couldn't bring herself to embrace the sniffling child.

"You've got a suitcase," said Jake. "Doesn't she have something else to wear?"

"That's not going to solve the problem," snapped Pamela. "She'll still stink."

Amanda gave up trying to be brave and started crying.

"Oh dear," said Pamela, crouching down beside her. "I'm sorry, Amanda. I'm not mad at you. I know you're miserable, and Sheriff Moore and I will think of something."

"We can rinse her off in the creek," suggested Jake.

"Yes, that will help some," agreed Pamela. "Don't cry so, Amanda. We'll take off this dress, and Jake can bury it."

She started untying the pinafore and glanced up at Jake, who seemed to have frozen on the spot.

"Sheriff, do you have any soap in your saddlebags?" Pamela asked.

"I have a cake of shaving soap."

"That will have to do," said Pamela.

Amanda took a couple of big sniffs. "I have pretty soap," she said.

"You do?" asked Pamela.

Amanda nodded. "In my basket. A lady takes her own soap so she doesn't have to use the soap in the common washroom."

"Well, then," said Pamela, "we'll use Sheriff Moore's soap first, because it is probably stronger, and then we'll use your pretty soap because it probably smells nicer."

Amanda sniffed and nodded again. Jake went off to find the soaps and the clothes.

Pamela removed her own shoes, socks, and skirt. That left her clothed decently enough, she decided, with her shirtwaist, shift, and bloomers. She coaxed Amanda into the stream.

The water was warm from the hot summer days. Pamela held both of Amanda's hands as they waded deeper into the gently flowing water. Once it was up to the little girl's waist, Amanda began to treat her stream bath as an adventure. She let go of Pamela's hands.

"Look, I can dog paddle." Amanda demonstrated her splashy technique.

"Very good," said Pamela. "But let's take off that smelly shift."

"All right." Amanda put her feet back down on the sandy bottom and tugged at the wet shift, trying to get it over her head.

"Let me help," offered Pamela. She took a step forward, and at that moment the shift slid over Amanda's head and slapped Pamela in the face. Pamela sputtered and fell. She landed on the bottom of the streambed, sitting with her head and shoulders above the water. Amanda grinned and slapped the water to splash her friend.

"Amanda, stop it," said Pamela, grabbing Amanda playfully. "We've got to get that smell off of you."

"I've got the soap." Jake's voice startled Pamela. He stood, looking tall and handsome, at the edge of the stream with the two suitcases at his feet. Pamela looked down to make sure the murky water covered her.

"I can't come get it," she answered.

"I'll toss it to you," said Jake and swung his arm back to pitch the first cake of soap.

"No," she squealed. "I'll drop it in the stream."

"Then I'll just have to bring it to you." Jake sat down and began pulling off his boots.

"Sheriff Moore," protested Pamela, "this isn't proper."

Amanda bubbled over with giggles. "Sheriff Moore doesn't know what's proper, Miss Kottis." She hopped up and down in the water. "He can't take a bath with us, but he can come swimming. I've gone swimming with my cousins, James, John, Jordon, and Jacob, and even their father, Mr. Jenkins, and my sister Augusta."

Jake threw down his last sock and stood up.

"Here I come," he warned.

"Splash him! Splash him!" squealed Amanda, and she did her best to scoop up the water and send it flying across to the advancing sheriff. Her efforts weren't very threatening until Pamela joined the onslaught.

Jake laughed and plunged on. He put the cakes of soap in his shirt pockets. Then, with his hands free, he shoveled water fast and efficiently, sending it showering over Pamela and Amanda.

The ladies shrieked and splashed all the harder as he came near. The fun continued even after Jake brought out the soap. Amanda wiggled as the two adults soaped her from head to toe, twice with Jake's shaving soap and twice with her perfumed soap from the finest mercantile in St. Louis.

"Now you must go up to the horses," said Pamela.

Jake laughed at her with a roguish twinkle in his eye and the two dimples deeply set in his smiling face.

"Why?" he asked.

"Because," Pamela said, her own face beaming with the joy of his teasing, "Miss Amanda and I want to get out of the stream and into some dry clothes."

"You have to go, Sheriff Moore," insisted Amanda. "Miss Kottis and I are proper ladies."

Jake leaned back in the shallow water and let his body float. "I'm not finished with my swim," he said.

With one swift movement, Pamela reached over and dunked the sheriff's head under the water. While he sputtered, she grabbed Amanda and plodded through the shallow water and up the bank. She put Amanda down and snatched the suitcases, hustling her little charge into the bushes.

Jake trudged to the bank and came out dripping. He grabbed up his boots and socks, but he couldn't resist rattling the bushes as he went by.

The girls squealed and he chortled. Without stopping, he made his way back to their picnic site.

"You're no gentleman, Jake Moore," Pamela called after him.

Jake turned on his heel and walked backward a few steps as he answered, "Never said I was, ma'am."

He stretched out on the blanket in the sun, hoping to dry some while he waited. He closed his eyes and felt the warmth of the sun on his face. He couldn't imagine a more perfect afternoon, smelly skunk and all. *Dear Jesus, You have awakened a desire in my heart this past week. I find myself thinking, dreaming of this woman. I watch her every move, knowing I'm letting myself get drawn in closer and closer to that sacred state of matrimony. I don't want to hurt her or do anything that will shame You. I'm expecting You to give me a peace about this decision. I don't want to be guilty of taking this holy covenant of marriage lightly. Guide me. When I listen to her speak, may I hear words of encouragement from You. Amen.*

Jake wrinkled his nose as Amanda approached.

"Sit here in the sun next to the sheriff, and I'll comb out your hair," said Pamela.

Amanda plopped down on the blanket. Pamela sat behind her and started gently working the brush through the tangled wet locks.

"Where's my own clothes?" asked Amanda with a pout.

"Remember? They blew away with the tornado," answered Jake. "They might have flown right back to St. Louis, Missouri. They might have landed right in your very own backyard and hung themselves up on that laundry line you spoke of, right next to your father's nightshirt."

"I don't think so." Amanda squirmed under Pamela's brushing and yawned. "Althea isn't going to like this dress. Althea has good taste. She's very par-tic-u-lar about her attire."

"I think," said Pamela, "Althea is going to be so glad to see you're safe that she won't fuss about what you are wearing."

Amanda leaned sideways against Pamela's lap, and her head sank down on her folded arms.

"Augusta says Althea can fuss better than a flock of hens. She says Althea has taken fussing seriously as if it were an art form."

"And what does Althea say about that?" asked Jake.

Amanda yawned again. "Althea says, 'What can you expect from a woman who lets her husband call her Gussie?'"

Finally, the tangles were out, but Pamela continued to stroke the brush through Amanda's curls.

"She's asleep," whispered Jake.

"It's been a long day for her, and she usually takes a nap," answered Pamela. She put down the brush and smoothed the curls back from the sleeping child's face. "Isn't she adorable? She bounces back and forth from acting like a little old lady to the little girl she is. I would love to keep her and give her the chance to get dirty more often."

"As long as it's dirty and not smelly," said Jake.

Pamela giggled. "She does have rather an air about her still."

"Should we load up the sleeping beauty and get back on the road?" asked Jake.

"Oh no," said Pamela, looking off toward the stream. "I've spread our wet things on the bushes to dry, and you could use some time to dry as well."

"We're going to be late getting into Big Springs."

"Does it matter?" asked Pamela. "Amanda's sister isn't expecting us today, so she won't be worried. My sister isn't expecting us, either. I'd rather stay here." She didn't say that she wanted the day together to last as long as possible, but she looked back at Jake stretched out on the blanket, and her eyes took on the softness of thorough contentment.

Jake gazed at her for a minute and then shook himself as if trying to awaken from a dream.

"We'd better move her out of the sun, then, or she'll get a burn." He quickly rose, and with Pamela clutching the blanket on one side and he the other, they moved it under the shade of the willow again. Settling down on each side of the sleeping child, they spoke quietly.

"All of your sisters have moved to cities, haven't they?" asked Jake.

Pamela nodded. She leaned back on the blanket and studied the trailing limbs of the willow that nearly surrounded them as a leafy bower.

"Do you want to leave the farm, too?" asked Jake.

Pamela's head jerked around to look at him. "No, not at all. I'm the youngest, and I think I missed the worst hardships during the early years when Pa was building up the farm. I've heard the stories about how grueling it was, and my older sisters relish the comparative ease of living in town. But by the time I was old enough to take note of things, Pa's farm was well established. It's still a hardworking life, but not nearly what it once was. Now he's doing well enough to have hired help.

"I love the farm. I love gardening and my chickens and the excitement of harvesttime. I want to stay."

Jake nodded. "It is hard work, but it's good work. It would be my first choice." He shrugged and gave her a wistful smile. "Maybe someday I'll figure out just exactly what it is God wants me to do with my life. At first I thought it was farming because I took to it so natural. Then when Uncle Will's constant reminders that the farm was going to his boys finally sunk in, I thought it was being a lawyer. I thought maybe I'd be a lawyer for the Grange Movement, or the Farmers' Alliance, but God didn't seem to be directing me that way either. I'm twenty-six years old, Pamela, and still living day by day with no vision of what the Lord wants me to do with my life."

"Patience, waiting, longsuffering," said Pamela. "I think that's the hardest thing God asks us to do."

Jake nodded.

"But it'll come, Jake." She smiled at him. "I know you've been faithful with the small things, living the day-to-day life of a Christian without any fanfare. Someday God will lay a purpose on your heart, and you'll be ready."

Jake could only nod in her direction. He didn't have all the words he wanted to say to tell her how grateful he was that she understood. He didn't think he could explain how, through her words, she had just answered a prayer.

He leaned back and folded his arms behind his neck, looking up into the branches of the tree. He spotted a squirrel jerking its bushy tail and eyeing them. He pointed the saucy animal out to Pamela.

During the comfortable quiet that followed, Jake turned over the conversation in his mind. Pamela Kotchkis understood his frustration and didn't condemn him for having no goal in life. She was right that he had to wait on God's leading instead of forging ahead on his own. God had made him the sheriff, and he would be a good sheriff until another door opened up.

Jake rolled on his side to speak to her but saw she was asleep. She had turned on her side, facing Amanda. The breeze lifted the small curls on Pamela's forehead. The cinnamon brown lashes of her eyes lay in a fringed semicircle across each cheek.

"Pamela," Jake whispered. She didn't stir. "Pamela," he whispered again, just because he liked the sound of it. She'd called him Jake instead of Sheriff, and he'd forgotten the formality of Miss Kotchkis, or even Miss Pamela. He felt comfortable with Miss Pamela Kotchkis, and as soon as they returned Amanda to her family, he intended to court the lady in a proper fashion.

A smile hovered on Pamela's lips as if she dreamed of something pleasant. The dimple flashed. Jake moved to his knees and leaned carefully over Amanda so as not to disturb her sleep. With great care, he stretched an arm over to prop himself. Slowly, not wanting to disturb either sleeper, he moved in and laid a gentle kiss on Pamela's lips. She responded slightly to the kiss, and Jake jerked back. He searched her face, thinking he must have awakened her. She didn't move. He sighed and leaned back on his heels. A small giggle caught him off guard, and he looked down into Amanda's laughing eyes.

"Shh!" He put a finger to his lips.

"You kissed Miss Kottis," whispered Amanda.

"Her name is Miss Kotchkis," said Jake.

"Kost-sis," repeated Amanda.

"No," said Jake patiently, "Kotch-kis."

"Kot-kis,"

"No, Amanda. Think about playing a game of tag. If I was it and I chased you and caught you, I would say, 'Caught cha.' Can you say, 'Caught cha'?"

Amanda nodded. "Caught cha."

"That's good. Now say 'caught cha' real fast and leave off the 'uh' at the end. Like this: caughtch."

"Caughtch," she repeated perfectly.

Jake grinned. "Now just add 'kiss'. Caughtch-kiss."

"Caughtch-kiss," said Amanda and clapped her hands, delighted with her success.

"It sounds like you two are having a sneezing fit," said Pamela as she sat up.

"Miss Kotchkis! Miss Kotchkis!" Amanda turned and threw her arms around her friend. "I learned to say your name. Sheriff Moore taught me 'cause I caught him kissing you. Kotchkis, Kotchkis, I caught cha kissing Miss Kotchkis."

She bounced out of Pamela's lap and tackled Jake, knocking him over so they rolled on the ground. He tickled her, telling her not to tell secrets. Pamela crossed her arms over her chest and watched them. When they settled down a bit, she addressed the child.

"Amanda, would you please go see if our clothes are dry and pack them in the luggage? I need to talk to Sheriff Moore."

Amanda scrambled to her feet and started for the bushes.

Jake sat up and reached for his hat. He concentrated on putting it on, smoothing his hair, setting it in place, taking it off, and replacing it a tad farther back on his head.

He finally looked at Pamela.

"Well?" she asked with an eyebrow raised.

He blushed and started to rise. "Perhaps I'd better help Miss Amanda. We don't want her picking up any more country kitties."

Pamela put a hand on his arm and stopped him.

"Why did you kiss me?" she asked quietly.

Her voice had a bubble of enjoyment in it, and Jake looked directly into her eyes, trying to decipher its meaning. The irrepressible dimple hovered at the corner of her lips, and her eyes twinkled with amusement over his discomfort.

"It was your fault," he said.

"Mine!"

"You've got this dimple that invites me to kiss you," said Jake with a certain amount of phony priggishness. "I've done my best to resist temptation, but when you start winking that dimple at me even when you're asleep. . .what's a man suppose to do?"

Pamela's mouth dropped open in outrage, and she snatched his new hat right off his head. With mock anger, she bludgeoned him with it. He raised his arms to ward off the attack, and when he saw an opening, he reached past the flailing hat and grabbed her around the waist. With a twist, he had her pinned to the blanket. She laughed so hard he had no trouble reclaiming his hat. With one hand, he jammed it on top of her head, still keeping her arms captured.

"You have no right to be battering an officer of the law that way, Miss Kotchkis."

"It was you who trespassed against me while sleeping." Pamela laughed and continued, "I have a confession to make, Sheriff."

"Yes?"

"I wasn't asleep."

She laughed again at the expression on his face.

"Miss Kotchkis, I fear you must be punished by the law for your trickery."

"Oh dear," she sighed. "What is my punishment?"

He didn't answer but lowered his head to touch his lips again to hers. The tender kiss led to another. That one led to one less tender and more urgent. Somehow her arms escaped, and she wrapped them around his shoulders. He leaned back and gazed into the dreamy expression in her eyes. He shifted his weight to free her and pulled on her arms so that she sat beside him.

Just then Amanda came struggling through the bushes, dragging a suitcase. She stopped and looked at the happy couple.

"I caught cha kissing again, didn't I, Miss Kotchkis?"

Jake stood in one swift movement and easily lifted Pamela to stand beside him. He wrapped an arm around her waist and addressed Amanda.

"I've decided I must change her name, Miss Amanda."

Pamela looked up at him with suspicion in her eyes.

"If she'll have me, I'm going to marry her so her name will be Moore and not Kotchkis anymore. I'd hate to think she was going around all over Kansas being caught kissing." He turned to look again at the smiling face he adored. He cleared his throat. "Unless it was me she was kissing."

Pamela shook her head slightly. "That may cause us more problems, Sheriff," she said.

He frowned.

"I might become demanding," she explained. She stretched up on tip-toe and kissed him quickly on the lips. "I might start demanding Moore, Moore, Moore." She punctuated each pronunciation of his name with a kiss.

"Are you going to marry the sheriff?" asked Amanda.

"Oh yes, most definitely," answered Pamela.

"Can we go to Big Springs first? I want to tell Althea about the tornado and the china cup and feeding the banty hens and dancing and the skunk. She'll never believe it all."

"I think she'll believe the skunk, Miss Amanda," said Jake as he bent to pick up the blanket and fold it.

Amanda pouted.

"Never mind him, Amanda," said Pamela. "Right now he's pretty full of himself. Let's gather up the rest of our things and pack up the surrey. We still have a fine bit of traveling to do to get to Big Springs tonight."

Amanda nodded. The curls were dry and bounced a happy rhythm around her face.

"Yes," she said. "We can't forget to do our duty just because we're having a grand time."

Jake looked at her, puzzled. "I guess I've been having too grand a time, Miss Amanda. Just what is our duty today?"

Amanda placed her hands on her hips and announced loud and clear: "Returning Amanda!"

KATHLEEN PAUL teaches spelling, creative writing, and first-grade part-time in a home school supplementary academy. Kate's desire to write inspirational romance came about several years ago when her daughter wanted to read "grown-up" books about love. She decided to write something romantic that wouldn't "pollute her heart, mind, and soul." Her daughter is now living her own Christian romance, leaving Kate with her mom, son, two dogs, and dust bunnies in a Colorado Springs household recovering from wedding shock.

Only Believe

by Janet Spaeth

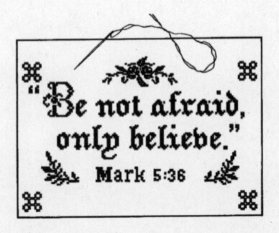

"Be not afraid,
only believe."
Mark 5:36

Chapter 1

Dakota Territory, 1879

Catherine stared at the heap of metal and leather. This was probably the equipment she needed to harvest Andrew's fields. Then again, it might just be what he used to plant. Or maybe it was all the same gear.

She sighed. She had no idea.

From the nearby stall, a horse whinnied a greeting, and Catherine turned to see the huge animal's velvety gray nose nudging the low slats of the gate.

Catherine laughed. "The worst part of all this is that you probably know exactly what this is and how it goes together. But you don't speak English, and I, my equine friend, do not speak Horse."

She moved to the stable gate and stroked the soft nose. The horse whickered again, and Catherine tried an experimental whinny in return. Was it her imagination, or did the horse perk up his ears?

She tried again. Yes, definitely the beast was responding. She whinnied once more and waited, almost expecting to hear a response.

"Ma'am?"

She jumped.

The silhouette of a man stood outlined against the late afternoon sun. Dust from the straw on the barn floor drifted in the hot August air, surrounding him with a slowly moving aura of glistening bits.

She was frozen in place. Her heart had stopped beating entirely, she was sure. He was here to—well, she didn't exactly know what he was here for, but it had to be bad. Men didn't just appear out of nowhere with good intentions.

He moved into the barn, out of the direct sunlight, and walked straight toward her.

The horse nickered, and Catherine stared as the man went directly to the stall, murmuring the name Orion, and holding out an apple he'd taken from his pocket.

The horse bobbed his head up and down in recognition as the man spoke quietly to him.

"You know him?" Catherine wasn't sure how she managed to speak, nor was she sure if she was talking to the horse or to the man.

The man turned, and in the half light of the dim barn, she could see his face at last.

His was a face shaped by weather—and by laughter. The lines that were carved in it were premature. He couldn't be much past thirty.

He studied her with eyes as dark as chocolate drops, and then his cheeks crinkled into a smile. "I didn't mean to startle you," he said, extending his hand. "I'm Micah Dunford. I have the next claim over."

Micah Dunford. She knew the name. Her brother had said it before he lapsed back into the deep sleep of a coma.

"I'm glad to meet you." She took the hand and shook it. His grasp was firm and warm, and she could feel the blisters on his palm, evidence of hard work. "Andrew spoke of you."

"You must be Catherine." His fingers gripped hers even tighter. "Andrew talked about you often, about how much he missed you and how much he wished you were here. And now you are. This is wonderful."

She forced her lips into a bad imitation of a smile. "I wish the circumstances were different."

"Of course, of course," he agreed, his words tinged with sadness. "How is Andrew, by the way?"

"When I saw him, he was doing as well as could be expected." She swallowed over the lump that ached in her throat.

"Has he regained consciousness?"

She nodded, fighting the tears that threatened to overwhelm her. "Only for a moment. Just a moment."

The memory of his eyes fluttering open, the way his hand weakly but distinctly squeezed her fingers, the single word that tore from his lips, then a too-rapid drop back into that deep sleep—it was too much for her to think about right now.

Micah's forehead furrowed with concern. "I wish him a rapid recovery. Do the doctors have a better picture of his prognosis?"

Catherine blinked back the tight dryness of unshed tears. "They weren't overly worried about the coma. They said it gives his body time to heal. He should be home by late September." She had to clear her throat. "At least that's the hope."

"You know he's in good hands," Micah said softly.

"The doctors at the hospital are the best in the region," she admitted.

"Of course. But I was referring to a more powerful healer."

Catherine stared at him. "There's someone better?" She pulled on his sleeve urgently. "Tell me who he is so I can send him to Andrew!"

"He's already with Him." Micah removed her hand from his arm and grasped it tightly. "I mean God."

"Well, of course." Catherine pulled her hand away, trying to push away the sense of betrayal. "I thought you meant a doctor. That kind of healer."

"God is the worker of miracles." Micah's dark eyes held hers intently.

"Andrew doesn't need a miracle," she said defiantly. "He just needs sleep."

"Don't you believe?" he asked. "I know Andrew does."

"Of course I believe." She was ready to end this conversation. "My whole family believes. We know who made us, who made this world."

"Do you trust Him?"

Catherine paused. Did she? Resolutely she shook away the nagging thought. "Naturally." Her answer was brisk and no-nonsense, suppressing the doubt that rose in her chest like bile. "I pray to Him that He will heal Andrew."

Micah nodded as the dust motes danced around his head like an angel's blessing. "I pray that, too."

He touched the pile of harness gear with the booted toe of his foot. "This is Andrew's equipment," he said almost absently. "It's somewhat of a mess right now because we were sorting through it together. We were—"

"I can do it." She moved closer to the tangled pile almost possessively. "It's my responsibility now. Until Andrew comes home and takes over, I'll see to the care of this claim."

Micah tilted his head and studied her. "I'm glad to help. Andrew and I were going to work together anyway."

"It's my responsibility," she repeated. "I'll do it myself."

He lifted an oddly shaped iron bar with his toe and let it drop back into place. "You know how to set this up?" he asked, so quietly that it seemed to Catherine that he was talking to himself.

"I don't, but I can figure it out."

She felt tiny in the barn, overshadowed by the giant horse and the giant man who stood beside her, a half smile on his face. "Well, I'd best be getting back to my place," he said at last. "I have some things in my barn I need to tend to."

Micah pulled his cap back onto his head and, with a jaunty wave, vanished from the barn.

Catherine watched him walk away, a dark silhouette against the setting sun.

So that was Micah Dunford.

※

From the small wooden box on the table, she took out the sampler she had begun stitching during the train trip from Massachusetts. The challenge of the pattern and the clean rhythm of the needle sliding through the cloth calmed her nervous fingers. . .and her equally nervous mind.

She picked up the scrap of material that had been folded and refolded many times in the past week. Smoothing it out on her knees, she could begin to make out the beginning letters of the verse: " 'Be not afraid, only believe.' Mark 5:36."

She picked up her needle and, as she had done so many times, concentrated as the even flow of the thin silver wove in and out of the cloth. Then she switched to a spring green strand and began to form yet another letter.

"Be not afraid."

She'd chosen the verse at random. No, that wasn't true. She'd chosen it because it had reminded her of Andrew. She'd heard him recite the verse often enough.

"Be not afraid."

For years she had lived in his reflected glory, a pale shadow of a girl; too shy to speak, yet always adoring the older brother who had raised her when influenza claimed their parents.

And now she had the chance to repay him for all he'd done. She had to do the job herself. She owed her brother a debt of honor.

But a dreadful debt. If only Andrew had stayed in Massachusetts, he would still be safe. The wanderlust in him, that enthusiastic embracing of the challenges of life, had called him out here to this dreadful land, where a simple fall off a wagon had put him in the deathlike sleep of a coma.

Dakota Territory. Even the name sounded cold and forbidding.

She glanced out the window as the last bits of daylight left the tiny house. She would have to light the lamp soon.

Yet on the seemingly endless, infinite horizon, a glorious array spread over the land. The sky burst into brilliant pinks and purples and oranges and reds, turning the amber fields a fiery crimson.

Catherine's breath caught in her throat. She'd never seen such a sunset.

Still, even a magnificent sunset could not draw her to this place. Nothing, absolutely nothing would convince her to stay in Dakota once Andrew was healthy again.

Given the first chance, she'd talk him into coming back to Massachusetts with her, back to a life that was normal and predictable, where his livelihood didn't depend upon a tangled pile of leather and metal.

Well, all this musing would do nothing but make her crazy. She rose and stood on her tiptoes to take a lamp from the shelf.

A piece of paper fluttered down, and she picked it up curiously.

It was a letter to her in Andrew's handwriting, dated the day of his accident. Eagerly she scanned the page, relishing the sound of his written voice as he relayed the daily workings of the claim.

The words at the end brought her up short.

"I want you to come out here," he'd written. "I have already told you about Micah Dunford, and the more I see of him, the more impressed I am. I want you to be happy, Catherine. I want to see you with children around you. I want to see you smiling at your husband as he comes home from the fields."

Her eyes clouded with tears as she read. "Micah is a safe man. A kind man, a good man, a Christian man. He is the kind of man you should love. Give this some thought, Catherine. Pray about it. I hope you do not think me too forward to suggest this so boldly, but I have prayed about how to broach the subject, and I feel that God would want me to say my piece straightforward."

Her breath caught at the next words. "I have spoken to him about all this and he says that he has prayed for a helpmeet to join him here. Catherine, might it be—" And the letter ended.

She sat down in the chair, the unlit lamp beside her.

Micah thought she was the answer to his prayer?

"Oh my," she said aloud. "Oh my."

Across the summer prairie, a beam of light stretched from an open window and spilled onto the ground beyond the small house. The glow from the single lamp conquered the surrounding darkness, illuminating a man bent over a well-worn book.

He read carefully, sometimes frowning, sometimes smiling.

At last he shut the book and closed his eyes. He missed his prayer partner, but there were some prayers that needed to be private.

"My Father, she is here. I prayed for her and now she is here. I sense that she is not here to answer the need in me, perhaps, but to fill the need in herself. You sent her here for a purpose—a purpose which may be clear to You but, at the moment, is not clear to me. She is special, Lord. This woman is truly special."

Chapter 2

"Be not afraid,
only believe."
Mark 5:36

The shadows fell around Catherine as she sat in the chair, the letter in her hand and the still-unlit lamp at her side. She knew she should rise and place a match's flame to the wick and bring the darkness into light, but she could not.

Marriage!

Throughout her childhood, she had dreamed of having a husband and a child of her own, but so far she had experienced only the vaguest flickerings of interest from the young men around her.

And the mirror reminded her daily she wasn't getting any younger. At this stage, she'd pretty much resigned herself to a lifetime of being alone.

Marriage!

There was, at the word, a stirring of that young girl, so many years ago, who had rocked her doll under the careful eye of her brother, and who had dreamed of someday holding a real-life baby while her husband gazed at her.

A baby is still a possibility, she reminded herself practically, *but not without a husband.* That much she did know.

Her fingers traced the words of Andrew's letter. The idea that her brother wanted her married and settled wasn't all that odd. He'd always taken his responsibility quite seriously. It was only natural that he'd want to see her happily wedded.

No, the strange part was that Andrew had chosen Micah.

Clearly there's a dearth of eligible bachelors on the prairie, she told herself.

But even so, the image of Micah's deep brown eyes, as soft as warmed chocolate, the laugh lines etched much too early in his face, the open concern for her brother's welfare—all these were signs that Andrew was right in his assessment of Micah.

Catherine laughed aloud. Yes, she knew so much about this man. She'd talked to him for all of five minutes and had him well summed up.

She laid the letter on the table beside her chair and stood up. Dusk had deepened into absolute night, and she found the matches only with the aid of the starlight that flooded through the undraped window.

She paused before striking the match and gazed out the window. The prairie glowed with the light of the stars and the full moon overhead. As far as she could see, the nighttime prairie stretched ahead of her. A vast expanse of dark land-sea, nearly ripened wheat nodding in waves before the wind that rippled the top-heavy stalks.

But this was an empty land. As far as her eyes could see, the only visible structures were the small house and barn on Andrew's claim—and whatever buildings Micah had on his.

Across the shadowy distance, a light twinkled, and she wondered if it might not be Micah's claim. She had no idea how far away he lived. All she knew was that Andrew had mentioned that Micah's place was "near," but here on the prairie, "near" seemed a relative term. Nothing was near.

Catherine turned from the window and lit the lamp at last. The light poured into the room, making it seem like a haven against the darkness that pressed against the outer walls.

She picked up the embroidery that she'd laid aside.

The piece was destined to be a welcome-home gift for Andrew. She'd worked on it all the way from Massachusetts, taking solace from the even flash of the silver needle through the textured Hardanger cloth. Each slice of the needle through the cloth had marked her progress one stitch closer to Andrew and then, after realizing that, one stitch closer to Dakota.

The rhythm of the cross-stitch had echoed the pulse of the train's wheels on the rails, and now, as she began her stitching again, she could almost feel the subtle swaying of the train car as it had lumbered through the forests and into the plains.

The piece, when finished, would be a surprise for her brother. It was meant for Andrew, but she recognized that she was also making it for herself. Always shy and tending to hide behind Andrew's exuberant exterior, she had selected the verse for her as well as for him. "Be not afraid, only believe."

The task ahead of her was great.

She'd realized that fact as soon as she'd seen the tangle of implements on the barn floor. A part of her wanted to run away from this spot and go back to her safe life in Massachusetts.

Andrew would understand. He had always understood. He hadn't expected much of his timid little sister. But this time, she mustn't let him down.

This was her chance to prove to him—and to herself—that she could do something besides her usual day-to-day activities in Massachusetts at the dressmaker's. She had insulated herself from challenge, but that was going to change. Starting with the mess on the floor of the barn.

She laid the embroidery aside and stood up resolutely. She would go to the barn and take another look at the heap of leather straps and metal pieces and see if she couldn't at least sort through them a bit.

She wrapped her shawl around her shoulders. There was a hint of rain in the thick August night air.

Then, with the lantern in hand, she made her way to the barn.

Barn swallows swooped at her head, and she swatted them away. They were vehemently protecting their nests, she knew, but they were such a bother.

The barn seemed cavernous at night. Her lamp's light barely pierced the dark corners.

Orion whinnied a soft greeting from his stall and tossed his head at her.

She'd forgotten to bring him a snack, but she noticed an apple on the shelf by the door. She hadn't put it there. It must be something Micah had left.

She fed it to the horse, trying not to cringe as the big horse's mouth opened and closed around the apple she held in her fingers.

But he was gentle and good, this horse, and didn't even nip her as he took the apple from her.

She rubbed his soft nose and spoke to him before turning to the business at hand: sorting out the knotted bindings and their associated metal pieces.

She nudged the pile with her toe and considered her next step. *What I need to do,* she decided, *is untangle it.* She knelt beside the pile and began the tedious task of separating it into smaller parts.

She was actually beginning to enjoy the chore. *This feels like real progress,* she decided as she laid one entire section aside neatly. Once she got this figured out, the rest would be no problem at all.

"Show yourself!"

The words from the entrance to the barn brought her to her feet quickly. Her heart pounded its way into her throat, and she snatched the lantern and held it high so she could see who the intruder was.

It was Micah, and she could see from his face that he was as terrified as she was.

They both spoke at once, their words falling over the other's.

"You scared me to death!"

"I thought you were a robber!"

"Don't *ever* do that again!"

"Don't *you* ever do that again!"

"You scared the wits out of me!"

"Me? You!"

They stared at each other and then broke into the laughter that comes with relief.

"I thought you were someone breaking into Andrew's barn," Micah said.

"And I—well, I don't know what I thought, if I thought at all. I was suddenly overcome with an awful panic." She paused as a dreadful realization struck home. She was quite alone in that small house, with nothing but the vast prairie around her.

As if he could read her thoughts, Micah smiled gently but seriously. The lamplight cast golden sparks in his deep brown eyes. "There is a natural cause for worry, Catherine. The prairie has dangers of its own, and there are certainly those who would take advantage of anyone here alone."

Her fear must have shown in her face, because his look deepened. "You are not alone, though, not really. Don't forget that there is a Creator who watches over you every minute."

"Yes, of course. But the Creator who made me also made the wolf."

He nodded. "You do have a gun?"

The last was more a question than a statement.

"Yes, I suppose I do." Catherine realized that he was referring to the rifle hung over a window in the house.

"Do you know how to use it?"

"If need be," she hedged. In fact, she had never once found such a need. There was some way to put bullets in it and, yes, pull the trigger. That much she knew. It wasn't enough, but she was absolutely not going to experiment to find out how to shoot a gun.

Micah nodded. "I see. Well, if you don't mind, I will stop by and check on you each night."

She could feel her chin rising defiantly. "You don't have to check on me."

"It's no problem. I check on my stock—the cattle, the horses, and the pigs—anyway, and I'll simply add you to the list."

"Your *stock*? I'm not some kind of farm animal, sir!" She realized too late that he was teasing her.

He was laughing as he turned to leave. "You know, Miss Cooper, I think you're going to be an interesting neighbor. I never guessed that Andrew had such a delightful sister."

And as quickly as he had filled the barn with life and warmth, he was gone.

She crossed her arms over her chest and shivered involuntarily, despite the heavy summer heat. The claim seemed so empty without his shielding presence.

The words from Andrew's unmailed letter came back to her. *"Micah is a safe man. A kind man, a good man, a Christian man."* Andrew had trusted him, and so should she. At this stage, unsure as she was on the frontier, she needed to rely on him for certain things.

As she left the barn, she stumbled over the edge of the harvesting gear.

She would *not* rely on him to save Andrew's claim. That was her duty, her self-assigned task. If she could do that, it would settle, once and for all, the debt she felt toward her brother.

She hurried across the short distance between the barn and the house, grateful for the sanctuary of the small house at last.

Her thoughts still centered on Micah, and at the core of them all was the fact that she liked having him near her. He made her feel safe and confident and welcome.

He was all those things Andrew had said.

But as she was getting ready to blow out the lamp and retire for the night, the next sentence in her brother's letter leaped into her mind.

"He is the kind of man you should love."

The night wrapped the prairie in a blanket of black, illuminated only by starlight.

The man was exhausted, but for him, prayer was as necessary as sleep. He took the time to talk to his Lord.

He smiled as he prayed. "You invented laughter, Lord, and You know I've needed some in my life lately. She has a certain way of smiling that makes my heart laugh. You are blessing me in a strange way, Lord."

Chapter 3

"Be not afraid,
only believe."
Mark 5:36

Catherine awoke the next morning tired and out of sorts, feeling as if she'd tossed and turned all night long—but then again, that was precisely what she had done. Images of Micah had flown in and out of her mind like the swallows that swooped at her whenever she entered the barn, relentlessly diving and plunging at her head.

If only I hadn't found Andrew's letter, she told herself as she splashed cold water on her face, *things would be fine.* Micah would simply be a neighbor, a friend of her brother. She would never have studied those tiny laugh lines that the sun had etched around his eyes. Nor would she have noticed those golden glints that sparkled in his deep brown eyes. And she certainly never would have paid any attention to the way her heart seemed to smile when she saw him.

I'm probably lonely, she decided as she dried off her face. What she needed to do was to get her mind off this entire situation by getting to work.

And there was plenty of work to do. The garden needed quite a bit of work. It had become overgrown and, according to her quick survey, quite a feast for the rabbits.

She was no gardener, but she could do some harvesting of the yellow squash that the rabbits had left alone, and the carrots, which were safely underground. She tried to drive down the voice that challenged her to know a ripe squash from an unripe one. Hadn't she purchased squash in the market just two weeks ago?

Squash that tasted dry and awful, the little voice persisted in her ear.

She dismissed the nagging words with the reminder that she would be the one to eat the food, and if it were unripe or overripe, she would not find it much different than that which she bought in the city.

The air was hot and clear as she shrugged into her lightest dress. She planned to finish the garden today then move toward harvesting the fields. They looked quite ripe to her, but the tiny voice roared, *You don't know a head of wheat from a thistle seed!* The nagging thought was only a slight exaggeration.

She should probably talk to Micah a bit and learn everything he could tell her about harvesting.

She realized she was smiling and tried to stop.

But there was something—something very special about Micah Dunford.

The garden was an untamed tangle of weeds and vegetables, but she realized that her task ahead was not as major as she'd feared. The squash were recognizable by the fortunate fact that they grew aboveground. All she had to do was pick the familiar shapes. The carrots, although underground, had distinguishing leafy tops that clearly identified them. The carrots she'd purchased in Massachusetts came attached to the same feathery greens.

As she moved through the garden, lifting a mass of leaves here and pulling a recalcitrant root there, she let her mind drift to the strange circumstances that had brought her here, to the strange land that was the Dakota Territory.

She'd almost pushed the worry about Andrew out of her mind, afraid of coming too close to it. The thought of losing him was so incredibly painful that even the briefest flicker of that image pressed on her soul with an unimaginable anguish.

It was easier to focus on other things, like the sampler she was stitching, or the puzzle of the harvesting equipment in the barn, or the incredible sweetness of Micah's smile.

A sharp prick brought her back to reality. She looked down and realized that she had grasped a thistle rather than a carrot top. Her fingers and palms were filled with the nearly invisible spikes.

The stinging was intense, and before she could stop herself, she stuck her fingers in her mouth, trying to pull out the tiny needles with her teeth.

"Were you planning on serving that tonight?" Micah asked as he came up behind her. He moved the offending plant off the pile of freshly pulled carrots and threw it into the rubbish heap. "We'll burn that later. It's the only way to get rid of those nasty things. In the meantime, let me see your hands."

He took hold of her hands and, with a skillful gentleness that surprised her, studied the situation. "Amazing. You used both hands, too. What a mess. Let's move into the full sunshine and I'll see what I can do."

One by one, he took out the thistle's spikes, and as he did, Catherine had the chance to study him. How old was he? He couldn't be much past thirty, but the sun had done its aging on him. He seemed so much a part of the Dakota Territory, every bit the image of the hearty homesteader; still, there were other parts of him that she wanted to tap.

Of course, she'd known him for only a day. There were all sorts of hidden possibilities. Just because her brother had suggested that he might be her husband. . .

He looked at her suddenly, and she had the horrible thought that she must have said something or made a sound. But he smiled. "All through."

He stood up and wiped his hands on his shirt. "Your hands might sting a bit tonight, but other than that, there shouldn't be any lasting effects."

"Good, because I have some work to do. I'd like to finish the garden today."

He glanced at the two piles she'd made on the ground, one of vegetables and the other of weeds, and then at the garden plot. "Looks like you've already finished the garden."

From the way he said it, the laughter just under the surface of his words, she knew she'd bungled the task. Perhaps not totally—that much was obvious from the pile that included the carrots—but in her weed heap must be some plants that were edible.

She shrugged. Whatever they were, she probably didn't want to eat them. If she couldn't see them, they couldn't be worth much, except for the carrots.

"Dig under here and you'll probably find potatoes." Micah pointed to one of the sections that she'd stripped the greenery from. "That was very clever of you to clear the tops so digging would be easier."

Catherine tried to act as if that had indeed been her plan, but she knew—and he knew—that she'd had no idea that beneath those viny plants grew potatoes.

"I came over here, actually, for another reason," Micah said, suddenly changing the subject. "When do you want to start bringing in the wheat?"

"I was going to put the equipment together this afternoon." She was sure she saw the corner of his mouth twitch, as if he were trying to suppress a smile. She drew herself up straighter. "I can do this myself, you know."

"I don't doubt that for a moment, but you should be aware that Dakotans, well, we watch out for each other. It may not look like the neighborhoods that you're used to, but on the prairie, that's exactly what it is—a neighborhood. And we help out when we can, even when we can't. We've got to. That's the way we survive."

Catherine looked out over the prairie, now so rich with unharvested wheat, but in her mind, she pictured the land covered over with snow. Instead of undulating in subtle waves, almost as if they were breathing, the fields of wheat would too soon transform to fields of snow. A frozen paradise? Hardly.

Whatever feelings for Micah that might have been budding in her withered and died. He was a man committed to life in the Dakota Territory, and she wanted nothing more than to see Andrew healthy and safe—away from this land that had injured him.

The only way she could see to do that was to get the crop in, sell it, then use the money to pay the doctors and buy them both train tickets bound for Massachusetts.

"I'm sure that's true," she told him, amazed at the backbone she suddenly felt, "but I have a commitment here to take care of this myself. I can do it." She swallowed. "I have to do it."

He moved a bit closer to her, and she realized that he was not angry at her words. His true concern radiated from him. "Please remember that I am always ready to help you. If there is anything at all that I can do, I'm just over there." He pointed at a spot on the distant horizon, and in spite of herself, Catherine laughed.

"Just over there? So if I need a cup of sugar, I can just stop in." She shook her head. "This place is very strange. My next-door neighbor is more than a mile away."

"Speaking of borrowing a cup of sugar, there is one thing I do need to get from you. Andrew had ordered a hoe blade that's due to come in, and since I'm going into Fargo anyway, I can pick it up if it's there. I'll need his receipt, though."

"You're welcome to come in," she said, "although I have no idea where it might be."

He smiled, his even white teeth flashing in the sunlight. "I know exactly where he kept them. Andrew stuck everything of importance in his Bible."

As they entered the house, Micah looked around admiringly. "Andrew put a lot into this house. He didn't have anyone special yet—he said he was waiting to get established before he'd find himself a wife—but he did say that he wanted to bring his wife home to a good house, one that would make them both proud."

"What is your house like?" she asked, and as soon as the words were out of her mouth, she realized how they must sound. Her face flooded with warmth.

But he didn't seem to notice. "It's about the same size as this one, but not quite as finished. I still have a board floor and everything needs paint."

He reached for the Bible. "Andrew always kept this in the same place." He ran his hand over the leather cover. "Sometimes we'd sit in the summer sunshine, having worked in the fields all day, and we'd try to outdo each other in a Bible verse game. Andrew would quote a verse, and I'd have to identify it, or at least give its context. And then it'd be my turn. I hardly ever beat him at it."

"Just like men," Catherine said, blinking back the tears at the image of her brother healthy and whole. "Always competitive, even with the Bible!"

Micah shrugged. "The game helped us learn the Word. Out here, occasionally a circuit-rider minister might come through, but pretty much we're on our own for religious education. So we do the best we can."

He picked up the sampler she had laid aside. "'Be not afraid, only believe.' That's Andrew's favorite verse. He said it was what sustained him."

Micah looked away, and Catherine saw that he was blinking rapidly. *He's crying!*

Of course. Why hadn't she realized it before? They were best friends, Andrew and Micah. Now Micah was alone, just as she was.

Her heart softened, and she reached to touch his arm in reassurance.

As she did, Micah turned and a piece of paper fluttered out of the Bible he held. He leaned over to pick it up. "This must be the receipt—," he began, but Catherine noticed the handwriting and snatched it away from him.

It was the letter from Andrew, the one in which he asked Catherine to consider Micah as a husband.

Had he seen the words? His expression hadn't changed, so he must not have.

She took the Bible from him and, trying to cover her confusion, leafed through it until she found the receipt.

"Remember, if you ever need help, let me know. I'll be over every day to check on things here," he said as he took the paper from her. He touched the Bible she held. "And don't forget the Friend. You are never alone here."

He left, and she sank into the chair with a sigh of relief.

She liked Micah—liked him quite a bit—but she kept seeing him as a potential husband, thanks to Andrew's letter.

Thankfully, he hadn't read her brother's letter. What would he think if—

She sat up straight. She was so dumb sometimes. Of course he knew. The letter said he'd discussed it with Andrew.

All along, he'd known.

After seeing her, was that still his intention?

Her heart answered with a fervent wish that surprised her: *Yes.*

�֍

His mind finally closed around the bit of information he'd been pushing away: the letter from Andrew in the Bible. He hadn't read it—the words weren't meant for him—but he wondered what it said. The way she had snatched the page away made him wonder if Andrew had mentioned their plan to her.

It wasn't something he was proud of. In fact, he was downright ashamed. He seemed no better than those desperate men who got mail-order brides to live with them out here.

She deserved better. Much better.

"Dearest Father, take away that thought from me and let me start fresh with Catherine. I see in her everything I have wanted in a wife, but my affection grows too soon. Help me guard my words, guard my eyes, guard my thoughts. She is a woman I could love. . . ."

Chapter 4

"Be not afraid, only believe."
Mark 5:36

What she needed to do was quit mooning around like she was a young girl. It was pointless, and besides, she had work to do.

Resolutely Catherine strode out to the barn, prepared to do battle with the equipment that still lay in a huddle on the packed-earth floor.

The straps and metal bits seemed to have intertwined themselves even more since her last visit here. She sighed and dropped to a sitting position to begin the laborious process of untangling them.

It was a nearly automatic process, wrapping this strap around that, moving the darkened silver of the metal loops here, pulling the harness pieces free.

There was something familiar about it, and at last Catherine understood.

The motion mirrored that of her sewing, the same in and out, over and through, of her needle flashing through the cloth. And in the end, both efforts would be pleasing to her brother.

Knowing that, she approached her task at hand with renewed enthusiasm, taking pleasure from the rhythmic unweaving of the snarled pile.

At last she laid the final leather strip into place and leaned back with satisfaction. An immediate pain in the small of her back ran up her spine and reminded her that she had been sitting in one position entirely too long.

Sunset had begun to fall without her even realizing it. Long shadows cast the barn's interior into pools of scattered darkness. She stood up slowly and painfully as the kinks worked themselves out of her back and hobbled back into the house.

What she needed was a good cup of tea and a soak in a warm bath. She built up the fire and put two large kettles on to heat.

She glanced longingly at her embroidery. A part of her wanted to pick it up and stitch some more, but the ache in her arms stopped her. And whenever she shut her eyes, even for a moment, all she saw was a hodgepodge of straps, and the image swam in front of her eyes as she ran her fingers over the silky floss.

Catherine shuddered. The dye on the leather had stained her fingertips black. She wouldn't be able to embroider anyway. Not without the risk of getting the cloth and thread stained.

It was a pity, but her important duty was to the harvest—and to her brother.

Orion whinnied and shook his head. The horse's mane shimmered in the early morning light. Someone—Micah, probably—had been here grooming Orion, she realized guiltily. She'd basically been ignoring the beast, except for feeding him and turning him loose in the enclosed paddock area for some exercise.

"You're a good boy," she cooed, stroking the gray velvet nose. When he had calmed down, she led him from the stall into the bright sunshine outside.

Orion stamped his feet nervously as she approached him with the first bit of equipment that she felt sure was the harness, but the horse let her slip the straps onto his massive neck and body.

She stood back, inordinately pleased at how well this initial step had gone.

But the rest was not nearly so easy. Two hours later, sweaty and frustrated, she was unbuckling Orion from the harness when Micah rode up.

She would have felt considerably better if he hadn't burst into laughter at what she had done.

He leaped off his horse and raced to Orion. As he rearranged the system of straps, buckles, and rings, he spoke to the horse softly. Catherine was sure she heard her name mentioned repeatedly as he chuckled occasionally in the horse's ear.

What she had unsuccessfully struggled to do, for the better part of the morning, he did easily in little more than a matter of minutes.

As he hooked up the equipment to the harness, he told her the purpose of each part.

"And then you have to hook it up to the binder," he finished.

"The binder. All right. It's in here, right?" She rummaged through the odd bits that were left after she'd assembled the harness.

He was trying not to laugh. She could see that.

"No," he answered slowly, and he rubbed his hand over his mouth in a futile attempt to hide his smile. "Come with me."

He led her into the barn. "It's back here."

She hadn't noticed the contraption before, mainly because she had not explored the shadowed corners of the huge barn, but she felt dense and stupid not to have noticed it.

It was a big contraption, larger than she'd ever expected. It looked somewhat like a paddle wheel, but with thinner blades.

Her mind spun with the words as he tried to explain the process. "It'll gather the grain into bundles, and then we'll put those bundles together into shocks, and then it'll all go through a threshing machine."

She nodded, but it didn't make any sense.

"You really do need more than one horse for this," he warned. "Usually people use four horses, but Andrew and I scaled this down to make it work with ours. We'd planned for both of our horses to pull the binder."

If she had to stand in place of one of the horses and pull the plow herself, she would. She would not accept anyone's help.

"Let me show you how this works," he said, leading Orion to the edge of the field.

He led Orion, and she wondered if he was pulling the binder, too, to lighten the load.

It looked so easy as she watched them, man and horse, working together to harvest the wheat. They moved as one, both used to the rhythm of the field work. There would be no problem for her to finish this herself, and she told him so.

For a moment, Micah looked at her, studying her face. "You really want to do this"—he motioned toward the vast field—"all by yourself?"

"Yes, yes," she said impatiently, anxious to get on with the task while she still had the image of how it worked in her mind.

He held the reins, as if weighing something in his mind, and at last he nodded and handed them to her.

"I'll be in my own fields today," he said, "but don't hesitate to come over if you'd like some help."

"I…don't…want…any…help," she said with deliberate slowness. "Now go and tend to your own work. I'll be fine here. Come along, Orion."

And without a further look backward, she stepped into the field and began the harvest on her own.

※

Catherine sat in the middle of the downed wheat and buried her face in her hands. All around her was the day's work, and the result was nothing more than total destruction.

The job had looked so easy when Micah had done it. He had simply walked through the field, leading Orion, and the wheat had fallen neatly.

And then he'd said something about a machine that would finish the work.

Or that's what she thought he'd said.

She raised her head and looked around her. The wheat was strewn here and there. The kernels had already fallen off most of it, and the blackbirds had quickly discovered what a delightful treat she'd provided for them.

No machine invented by man could come through here and repair the damage she'd done. She had ruined this section entirely.

Orion stamped his hooves impatiently, and she got to her feet. "I know, I know," she told the horse, "I don't quite have the touch yet."

The awful truth was that she didn't have the touch at all. Orion had been nervous throughout her attempts to harvest the wheat, clearly recognizing her inexperience.

The horse wasn't that way with Micah, she thought somewhat grumpily.

She unhooked Orion from the equipment, leaving it lying in the field, and walked him back to the barn, ignoring the wide swaths of clumsily mowed wheat that lay behind her like accusatory wounds on her brother's land.

After getting Orion cleaned up and fed, she trudged back into the house and cleaned and fed herself.

There was more to this harvest thing than she'd allowed herself to admit. Why had the plow worked so well for Micah and not for her?

She put her head back and shut her eyes. She visualized the equipment, pictured it working. And then she knew what she had done wrong.

Quickly she jumped up and ran to the fields through the gathering darkness. Mosquitoes surrounded her like a biting cloud, but she ignored them.

She leaned over and examined the rig where it lay on the ground. And then she stood up with a sigh of satisfaction. She'd been right. A piece had come unhooked.

With a lighter heart, she walked back to the small house. Things were looking better already.

The next evening, Catherine looked over a somewhat erratically harvested section of the field. It was uneven, to be sure, but the work was done.

And in that she felt a measure of satisfaction that was almost overwhelming in its intensity.

The next day she worked, and the next, and the next, and each day the rhythm got easier, and she and Orion wove through the field with the same cadence of her silver needle shooting through the cloth on the sampler.

The rhythm is all the same, she thought. She simply had to tackle the task and do it to the best of her ability. All along, she had been embroidering it: "Only believe."

The field, when harvested, might not look as neat and tidy as Micah's undoubtedly did, but to her it was quickly becoming a thing of beauty, as sure as her colorful sampler inside.

Catherine smiled at the full moon that shone over the decimated part of the field. "I can do this," she said aloud. "I really can do it."

🌱

The sun had just come up on the prairie. *The early morning walk will do me good,* he told himself. The long pace after the short start-stop rhythm of the early harvest was good exercise for a man.

He didn't have as much time as he would have liked to come by and check on her progress, so if his morning walk took him by her fields, all the better.

It had been difficult, just watching and not being able to help as she tried repeatedly to get the binder to work.

But she had accomplished the feat.

He felt as proud as if he'd done it himself.

Lord, every day is a delight with You. You are the sun on the fields, the rain from the heavens, the nourishment of the soil. May this harvest and all who work it be a blessing to You.

Chapter 5

"Be not afraid,
only believe."
Mark 5:36

She could hear his horse's hooves on the ground even before she saw him. Sound carried with an astonishing intensity on the prairie.

Something was driving him onward. He'd never ridden that fast or that furious.

His horse had barely stopped before Micah swung his legs over the saddle and leaped off in a seamless dismount.

In his hand he held a piece of paper.

"This. . .came. . . ." He was clearly winded.

She took the note from him without wiping the rich valley soil from her hands. It was a telegram.

Her eyes scanned it quickly. There were only a few words, but they were powerful ones.

"Andrew is—?"

Micah shook his head. "He's alive, but his condition is worsening, Catherine. They're. . .they're concerned."

"Concerned?" She realized too late that she was shouting. "I'm sorry. I didn't mean to yell at you. But he's going to be all right, isn't he?"

She wanted to see him smile. She wanted to hear his laugh as he told her it was all a joke. But the look on his face told her that this was all grimly real.

She looked again at the telegram. The words swam in front of her. Something about swelling in his brain. . .

"I have to go to St. Paul," she said. "I have to see him."

"I don't think they'll let you," he responded gently. "He needs absolute quiet right now. He's in a deep coma, and even if he could move, he shouldn't. The brain does swell from trauma, and—"

"How do you know all this? Are you a prairie doctor?" she asked.

He shook his head. "Son of a doctor. Until he retired, my father practiced at St. Elizabeth's, the hospital where Andrew is."

"Why did the message come to you rather than to me?" she asked.

"I didn't know that you were coming. I could only hope that you were. So I used my name as the contact person. I got this wire because I went into Fargo to pick up the harness bit that your brother ordered."

Catherine looked at the wire. It was dated four days earlier. "Look at this! By now he could be d—" She couldn't bring herself to say the word.

"He's not dead. I sent a follow-up wire and waited for the response. It said simply, 'No change.' I did ask that if—*when*—Andrew awakens, that he's told you are near. We can be there in a day, if we ride the horses hard."

She ran her hand across her forehead, aware that she was probably wiping a streak of dirt across her sweat-soaked forehead but not caring. "Let's go now."

"We can't. We couldn't do anything anyway. We can best serve Andrew by bringing in his crop. Knowing that his crop is safe will speed him to recovery more than anything when he comes out of the coma."

He moved toward her. "Let me help you, Catherine."

She shook her head. "No. This is something I have to do myself. And right now, Micah—" Her voice faltered, and she paused before continuing. "Right now I think I need to be by myself."

He nodded. "I understand. If it's all right with you, I'll stop back by tonight to see if there's anything you need."

She looked at him sadly. "The only thing I need is my brother with me, whole again."

"Have you taken this to the Lord?" he asked.

Catherine shook her head mutely.

"He made the blind see and the deaf hear," Micah said. "You might ask Him to help Andrew."

She could only nod numbly before running into the house.

The tears would not come. She would not allow that. That would be a sign of weakness, and she could not permit herself even a moment of weakness.

Catherine paced the perimeter of the small house, picking up this and studying that.

This was Andrew's, all Andrew's. She was the caretaker, custodian of everything he owned.

The house was small, but it was more than most people had on the prairie. She knew that. If the crop didn't come in, if the money from it wasn't realized, everything would be lost. The house, which she was sure had been built with borrowed money, would go back to the bank. The land would go back to the government.

And Andrew would come back to her.

How long she stood in that spot, she had no idea. Micah must have taken Orion in, curried him, and fed him, because she heard his soft whinny from the barn in response to the early evening hoot of an owl.

The August days here in Dakota were long, providing an astonishing number of hours of daylight. But twilight, when its time did arrive, fell quickly on the summer prairie, and darkness raced across the flat land.

She moved to light the lamp, and as she did, her glance fell upon the sampler, long forgotten as she'd focused on bringing in the harvest.

She picked it up and, after moving the lamp closer to her elbow, began the stitching again.

"Be not afraid, only believe."

Her needle moved in and out of the cloth, pulling this time an orchid thread the same hue as the last traces of the prairie sunset.

I'll finish this one word, she told herself, *and then I'll lie down and try to sleep.* She needed sleep to finish the harvest. And Micah was right—having the harvest done would be a powerful medicine for her brother.

Over and down, across and up. Over and down, across and up. The words her grandmother had taught her so long ago came back to her. They were the pattern of cross-stitch.

The orchid was a beautiful color in the skein, but it paled as a single thread on the off-white background. But, she reminded herself, other colors would come in that would work together. No one would even notice that the orchid thread was there. Instead, there would be a glorious display of purples and golds and greens, all blending together as completely as a sunset.

There. She had finished the first part of the word. Andrew would be proud of her work.

She buried her face in the sampler. Andrew. She wanted him to live more than anything. He had to live. He simply had to.

She could not cry, especially into the sampler. She smoothed it over her knee, forcing herself to check the stitching on the letters.

The pale thread caught the lamplight and seemed to make the word she'd just stitched glow: "Believe."

Believe? In what? That he would live?

Or that he would die?

She couldn't bear the thought. She arose, snatched her shawl from the post by the door, and walked outside.

Autumn was coming on the wind. She could smell it. She could hear it. The sharp edge of the yet-warm wind whipped her skirt around her ankles. Winter would soon follow, carried on the crisp promise of icy crystals.

The harvest couldn't wait. No matter what was happening with Andrew in St. Paul, she had to bring in the crop.

She walked out into the partially harvested field, remembering her early flippancy about getting the crop in. She had stood here, at the edge of this very field, and asked herself, "How hard can it be?"

Now she knew.

The night wind carried the sound of hoofbeats. Micah was coming. She recognized his approaching figure in the bright moonlight.

He was at her side quickly. "Are you all right?"

She nodded. "It's so warm, and yet I can't stop shivering."

"Winter will be here before we know it," he said, and she glanced at him in surprise.

"How odd. I was just thinking about that," she said.

"You're becoming one of us." His dark eyes twinkled.

"One of you? In what way?"

"A farmer is always thinking about the weather."

She laughed, grateful to have her thoughts shifted away from her troubles. "I don't think that I will ever be a farmer."

"A farmer's wife, perhaps?"

She whirled to face him. "Excuse me?"

"I wondered if you'd be a farmer's wife someday." His voice was bland.

"Why do you ask?" Her voice sounded shaky and high-pitched to her ears.

"I simply asked to ask, that's all."

Her heart was racing as fast as the prairie wind. "Then I will answer to answer. I will marry the man I love, and if he is a greengrocer, then I am a greengrocer's wife. If he is a carpenter, then I am a carpenter's wife. And if he is a farmer, then I am a farmer's wife."

He didn't respond, and Catherine knew she may have said exactly the wrong thing, but she didn't know what else she could have said.

She took a deep breath. "I think I will go inside now. I would like an early start tomorrow."

He caught her arm as she turned to leave. "Catherine, would you do me a favor?"

"What?" she responded numbly.

He probably wanted to borrow a tool or perhaps have her mend a torn seam in his jacket. This was an odd time to make such a request.

But she was not ready for his response.

"Pray with me."

A thousand questions collided and shoved their way around her bruised and battered heart. Pray to God? Why? What had God done for Andrew? Injured him and then put him in a faraway hospital to die?

Why should she pray to this God who did such terrible things to

744

good people? Andrew hadn't deserved this fate. He was a man who loved his Lord, who tithed not only his money but his time in devotion.

It seemed to Catherine that God had allowed someone as caring and kind and gentle as Andrew to suffer. She wasn't inclined to offer Him her prayers.

But Andrew would be so inclined if the situation were reversed, she heard her heart say.

Suddenly all her resolve, all her opposition, melted away with a flood of tears.

She opened herself to what was true and real. She could no longer avoid the truth.

The raw wounds on her soul were nothing compared to those of her Lord. Jesus had died for her. He had borne her sins and promised her life eternal.

With a force more powerful than she had imagined possible, she understood about this God whom Andrew and Micah worshipped.

The words she had been stitching on cloth were now embroidered onto her heart: "Be not afraid, only believe."

Her worries were His, and He could shoulder them when her endurance was taxed to the limit.

She just had to ask. The solution was that simple.

"I am Yours, God," she said, and with those words of surrender, she became a new being.

Micah's arms were waiting for her, and together they dropped to their knees.

There, in the field amid half-harvested wheat, with the warmth of summer and the promise of autumn around them, the two offered to God their most fervent prayers for Andrew's healing and recovery.

As the words flowed from their hearts and lips, Catherine felt a release such as she'd never known before. What they said didn't seem to matter as much as what they felt, and the power around them was so strong that she was sure it could be felt in St. Paul.

There was a special warmth in Micah's touch as he helped her to her feet, and although neither said much of consequence before he left, much had indeed been said between them.

God was with them both. And yes, she could be a farmer's wife.

※

Both he and his horse were thirsty, and the creek ran clear and cold. He swung off the saddle, and both horse and man drank deeply from the refreshing stream.

The horse was content to graze a bit, so he sat under the lone cottonwood and looked out over his prairie, for that was how he thought of it.

His prairie. It was as if he and the rich soil, the blue sky, the astonishingly white clouds, were all one.

It was good.

It lacked only one thing. Someone to share it with. And now Catherine was here. Was she the one?

His prayer was short: "Lord, am I seeing only what I want, and not what I need?"

Chapter 6

"Be not afraid, only believe."
Mark 5:36

Nothing seemed to ease Catherine's mind except focusing solely on the harvest. Daily she strained to finish the reaping, always reminding herself to take it slowly and carefully.

The ruined section lay as a mute testimony to her earlier rashness. It looked to her, for all the world, like a bad haircut—stalks left standing here, others leveled to the ground there.

Two weeks later, she stood at the house, her noonday meal in hand, admiring the work she'd done. She could see the improvement in the way the stalks lay neatly, ready for sheaving. That would be the next step.

The news from St. Paul was patchy, at best. Updates had arrived, and the news was not good. Andrew's condition was worsening.

Once the crop was in safely, once the harvest was done, she would go to St. Paul and see him.

It might be her last chance to see him alive.

Stated so baldly, the realization was terrifying, but she'd thought the words often enough to blister over them. She centered on the word "alive" rather than "last."

Jesus had brought the dead to life; that was true. But she did not expect such a miracle. If only Andrew lived—that would be a true miracle for her.

She sat on the step by the door and stared at the midday sun contemplatively. Her life had changed so much. Not just by coming here to the Dakota Territory, but because of what she had found. Micah, with his compassion. Her inner strength, which had probably always been there, but buried. And most of all, the real living God, the ever-present author of compassion.

Her eyes shut in prayer as she thanked God for all she had discovered out here; then she asked for His guidance concerning Andrew.

Her prayer was interrupted by the sound of Micah's arrival. She opened her eyes and was surprised to see that he had brought a thresher.

"Catherine, there's a storm coming. We have to hurry." The urgency in his voice was clear. "It looks bad."

"What kind of a storm?"

He brushed off her question. "We've got to move quickly or we'll lose the crop."

"I can do it." She laid her meal aside. "I'll go now."

"No, Catherine, *we* will do it. I've brought my own—"

"You don't understand," she said. "I have to do this—myself."

"Listen," he said, taking her arm, "I don't know why you feel this need to do all of the work by yourself; however, I respect that. I wouldn't have given you a plug nickel's chance at first, but you've done it and done it alone. Now I'm going to make this quick because we don't have time to waste. If we do this together, we can do it faster and better."

"But—," she began.

He waved away her objection. "No. Andrew and I had always planned to jointly harvest our fields, and I intend to see it through. I will not let your private battles, whatever they may be, ruin this for Andrew."

"How long do we have?"

"Probably two hours."

She didn't have time for thought. There was no choice in her decision. She must now choose for Andrew and not for her.

And she knew her decision was right.

She nodded. "Let's do it."

As they headed out into the final section together, Catherine put her whole body and mind into the task at hand. This was her final test.

The rows had never seemed this long, nor had Orion ever moved so slowly.

She couldn't see the storm yet, but she could feel the electricity of its approach. Apparently Orion could, too. He neighed uneasily, and she tried to calm him as she urged him on.

The mosquitoes clung to her arms and bit mercilessly, but she didn't take the time to shoo them away. As quickly as she could, she gathered the bundles and shocked them.

Her hands were sliced and bleeding. She should have worn gloves, but going back to the house now would mean sacrificing minutes they didn't have.

Bundle after bundle. Shock after shock.

Still she persevered. Somewhere on this expansive field Micah was working; she didn't know where. She didn't have time to lift her head and look.

She mopped the sweat from her forehead. Every muscle in her body ached. Still she could not stop.

Tears of frustration sprang to her eyes, and she wiped them away. There was no time to cry.

But her efforts were futile.

They were losing to the storm. She knew it. The fact was as clear as the endless rows before her.

What she had left to finish would require a good four days' work. Even with their combined efforts. Even with Micah's skill. There was no way they could beat the weather that would soon bear down on them.

There was no time to stop. She prayed as she drove Orion onward. What she prayed, what syllables she used, what requests she made, she had no idea. Her prayer was a wordless petition, springing from intense need.

Oh God. Dear God. My God. Please, God. God. God. God.

"Look!" Micah's shout called her attention to his side of the field.

From the distance, slowly but surely, more wagons, more horses, more threshers, and more people headed for Andrew's fields.

"What are they doing?" she shouted back at him. The wind was beginning to whip up, snatching the words from her lips.

"They're your neighbors. They're coming to help."

There was no time to ask questions. The newcomers fell quickly to work, efficiently and collectively shocking the bundles, taking the bundles to the threshers now stationed around the field, and beginning the process of threshing the wheat.

She didn't know these people. Maybe they were Micah's friends or Andrew's friends. She had no idea.

But they came, and even more followed them. Despite the gathering storm, which she could now see on the horizon, they continued to stream across the prairie, risking their own lives, and possibly their own crops, to save hers.

The field seemed to swarm with strangers and their machinery. Some had sophisticated engines that worked quickly and efficiently. Others had self-created mechanisms, similar to what Andrew and Micah had, that worked slowly but surely.

Together they toiled, each an individual but working as one.

Suddenly she realized that Micah was at her side. "Let's yoke our horses together," he shouted over the gathering wind. "We can do it even faster."

She knew he was at her side. She felt his strong male presence, a bulwark against the storm, and she was pleased.

Together they worked the fields, until at last, as the first hailstones pelted her arms, Catherine realized that they were done.

The others were already leaving, rushing to the safety of their own homes, and she tried to thank them. But there were too many, and they were too hurried. She would have to tell them of her appreciation later.

"Unhook the horses!" Micah shouted, and Catherine automatically obeyed the command. The hailstones were coming rapidly now, larger and faster.

They ran to the barn with the horses, and from the safety of the barn, they watched the last figures on the horizon as they headed for home.

"Will they be safe?" she asked as she brushed Orion's coat. He had worked so hard that he was dripping with sweat. She had to move quickly before he got chilled.

He nodded. "The horses can take refuge under a tree—"

"A tree?" she interrupted, laughing. "Where would you find a tree here?"

He grinned in wry agreement. "Good point. There are a few, and trust me, these folks know every one. They can tie their horses under one of those trees, and they can take cover under the wagons. This isn't going to be a long storm, just a nasty one. After the storm passes, I'll go out and take care of their equipment."

"We'll go out," she corrected him, and she was rewarded with a smile. "Who are they?"

"They're your neighbors, all good people. Most of them join together when they can to worship with us."

"Where? I don't see a church around here."

"Andrew and I were going to take part of our profits this year and build one. But that's your call now, at least until Andrew returns. We were going to break ground on it after the harvest." His voice was guarded, and he ducked his head behind his horse's broad back as he curried it.

Catherine paused and thought about his words.

Money. The crop was in and, to her eyes at least, it looked good. It should sell for a nice profit.

Initially she'd planned to use it to bring Andrew home, to Massachusetts.

Now she couldn't imagine going back there. Her soul, in less than one month, had found its home in Dakota.

"The money should be used as Andrew wants it used. There will be hospital bills, of course, but if it is possible, yes, I would like for some of the profit to go toward building a church."

Micah's head popped up over the side of his horse, and she almost laughed at the open delight apparent in his face.

"You would, of course, be consulted until Andrew is able to make his own decisions," Micah said.

"I trust you." The words were true, and merely speaking them brought rest to her worn heart.

There was another question in Micah's eyes, one she would have liked to answer, but it was too soon. When Andrew's condition was stabilized, when she had asked and answered all the questions in her own heart, when all was secure, then and only then would she answer.

Would he wait?

She didn't have to respond.

She trusted, and she believed. And there was no more fear.

❦

The sun never shines as brightly as it does after a storm, he thought while cleaning the threshers the neighbors had left. He would return them the next day when the ground had dried.

The hailstones were melting quickly in the August sun, and he pitched one across the harvested field. They'd be gone within the hour.

The birds had come out of their refuges, and the insects buzzed hungrily around his head.

All creation was back to normal.

A rainbow was poised over the horizon, a shimmering vision of God's promise.

He stopped in midaction as he realized that the rainbow came after the rain, and not before it. There was a farmer's explanation for this: Trust in the Lord, but bring your harvest in before the storm.

God didn't want him to be foolish, just to trust Him as a working partner.

"Lord, I want a partner here on earth, someone with whom I can share my love of the land and for You. Someone who will work with me and laugh with me and worship with me. Someone who will love me and love You. Someone, dear Father, like Catherine."

Chapter 7

"Be not afraid,
only believe."
Mark 5:36

The hospital was cooler than Catherine had expected. A heat wave made the city shimmer through the tall paned windows as she and Micah walked down the long, high-ceilinged hallway toward Andrew.

Andrew, who had regained consciousness two days earlier.

Automatically she reached for Micah's hand. It was the first time they had touched so purposely. His fingers wrapped around hers securely, and she thought she felt a slight telltale tremble in his own hand. He was worried more than he let on.

The nurse led them onward, her heavily starched dress moving above her feet like a white bell.

She swung sharply into a large room with four beds, two on each side.

And, at last, Catherine was at her brother's bedside.

She thought she had prepared herself for what she might see, steadied her nerves so she'd show nothing except joy, but when she saw her brother's pallid face under the snowy bandages, she crumpled against Micah.

He moved to support her, and he began to say something, but the words died on his lips when Andrew's eyes fluttered open.

"Did I miss the wedding?" Andrew's words were careful, spoken from parched lips that had difficulty forming the syllables. Immediately the nurse was at his side, helping him take a sip of water.

Micah laughed. "Hello, Andrew."

Andrew focused on him. "I've forgotten, so you'll have to remind me again. How many children do you two have?"

Catherine smoothed the lines in his too-pale forehead. "We don't have any children. We're not married?"

Her brother became agitated. "You're not getting married?"

"I didn't say that," she soothed, easing him back onto the fluffy pillow. "I didn't say that at all."

Andrew smiled. "That's good, because you belong together. I know." His words faded out, and his eyes slowly shut. He was asleep.

The nurse straightened Andrew's sheets. "He is still exhausted from this. He needs a good deal of sleep. You might as well leave. He'll sleep for a couple of hours, I suspect."

She led them back to the waiting room of St. Elizabeth's. "You are certainly welcome to stay here. If you're hungry, there's a fine eating establishment two blocks away. I'll check back here when he's awake again."

The nurse left them alone in the black-and-white-tiled room. Catherine reached into her bag and pulled out her embroidery.

"Are you hungry?" Micah asked.

She shook her head. "I couldn't eat right now."

"Me either," he agreed.

"Micah, he's so pale!" The tears she'd held back so long finally started to flow, and he took her in his arms.

"There, there," he hushed her as his work-roughened fingers stroked her hair.

"He's so thin, and so weak."

"But he's getting better," he soothed. "The doctor told us he would be back with us, probably within six weeks, perhaps a month."

"I know," she said, sniffling, "but I wish there were something more I could do."

"We can pray," he offered simply.

There in the starkly tiled room, they bent their heads and silently asked the Lord to visit His presence and His healing hand upon Andrew.

Their fingers knit together, and their heads almost touched as they joined their hearts in love for her brother.

❦

The thread slipped through the cloth easily, this time pulling a golden strand as luminous as the morning sun.

"You've been working on that since we left St. Paul," Micah said. "May I see it?"

"It's not finished," she said, but she handed it to him.

"It's beautiful. 'Be not afraid, only believe.' He is going to treasure this, you know." Micah studied it. "You stitch very well. I've been watching you. You do this with a confidence that astonishes me. If I were to do this, I'd be all thumbs and toes and my thread would be knotted immediately."

She laughed as she took the sampler back from him. "I've had some practice with this. It's not unlike when I watched you start the harvest, and then I made my clumsy attempts. If you want to learn to embroider—"

"Oh no!" He waved her offer away. "These hands are meant for horses and wheat, not for fine stitchery."

The train jolted them along, and they passed the time in friendly companionship, he reading a newspaper, she embroidering, until, at last, he laid his paper aside.

"I'm going to stretch my legs," he said, standing up. "I'll be back shortly."

He walked away, and Catherine laid the cloth she was embroidering on her lap and rubbed her eyes. She usually didn't stitch this long, and her eyes were tired.

She held her hands against her eyes, hoping the darkness would soothe the irritation.

Images began to flash before her. Andrew in the hospital bed, so waxen against the white sheets. The limpness of his hand as she touched him. The words that came so slowly and painfully from swollen lips.

She'd been taking things day by day, never looking forward and certainly never looking back.

But now she remembered standing in Andrew's house for the first time. The cold, empty house was so clearly Andrew's, but yet an Andrew she didn't know. She had always held tightly to their closeness. So the sudden, awful awareness that this untamed prairie was a part of him, yet did not belong to her, staggered her.

She had moved on. Always looking forward and never back.

Everything, everything had been for Andrew. What if the doctors were wrong? What if he never returned?

She couldn't stop the sobs that broke free from her heart. She kept her hands over her eyes and wept as though there was nothing else in the world.

She was only faintly aware that strong arms wrapped around her shoulders and gathered her in, and that a familiar voice comforted her: " 'Be not afraid. Only believe.' "

Micah.

"Shh, shh, shh," he said, his lips pressed against her hair. "Cry it out."

At last the tears ran themselves dry, and with one last shuddering sob, she was through. "I'm so sorry," she said to him, her voice muffled against the handkerchief he'd handed her. "I let myself succumb to weakness for a moment."

"Don't apologize. You needed to do that. I suspect you've needed to do that for a long, long time."

"Probably," she admitted, "but I hadn't intended to do so on a train."

He laughed.

The crying had made her tired, and she was glad of Micah's offer of his rolled-up coat as a pillow.

As she drifted off to sleep, she glanced out the window and watched the landscape go by. They were still in the rolling hills of Minnesota, and she was suddenly, desperately, homesick—but not for Massachusetts. She wanted to be home—in Dakota.

❧

Micah deposited her traveling bag inside the living room.

They were back on Andrew's claim, and she busied herself with lighting a fire to take the chill out of the room.

"Brrr," she said, rubbing her arms and moving closer to the fledgling fire. "There's a special coldness in a house where no one's been. This fire should take that edge off. Come on over and warm up."

He joined her. "I was glad to see Andrew. It did my soul good to see him move, to hear him talk."

"He's so pale and so weak." Catherine cringed at the image.

"He's had a major head injury," Micah said. "It takes time."

"Well, it's that," she said, "and more. Micah, tell me the truth. Is he going to be, well, totally all right?"

"What do you mean?" Micah frowned.

"He did have a head injury, and that's where his brain is."

"Yes," he agreed.

"Will it affect his thinking?" She took a deep breath and blurted it out. "He speaks so slowly, and he seems, well, confused. Micah, he doesn't seem to be quite right in his mind."

"Because he said we were getting married?" Micah's voice was only a whisper in her ear.

She pulled away and wiped furiously at her eyes. "Oh, Micah, I've known about that all along. It was a foolish idea he had and—"

The sudden hurt in Micah's eyes told her everything she had wanted to know.

"Micah," she said gently, touching his face, "is it really what you want? Please tell me."

He took her hand from his cheek and held it tightly. "From the first time Andrew spoke about you, I began to imagine what you must be like. And from that grew a dream, a foolish dream, that someday you might be my wife."

Foolish dream? Catherine's heart suspended beating. It was as she had feared—he didn't want her after all.

"But then," he continued, "you came out here, and I realized that my dream had been just that—a dream—but you were real, flesh and blood."

"You didn't want me." There. She had said the words he was afraid to say. He began to speak, but she waved his words away. "No, no. I know I'm no beauty. You can't hurt me with that. I know it's a fact."

"That's not it at all." He held her hand even tighter. "You were better and so perfect that I had to abandon the dream. And I realized that you wouldn't want to stay here with me, a wheat farmer in Dakota...."

Her heart began to beat again.

"What are your plans when your brother comes home?" he asked, his voice husky.

She hadn't planned for it to happen this way. She had wanted to tell him in her own way, in her own time, once she had figured it all out herself.

But she went to her bag and took out the sampler. "It's done," she said, and she handed it to him.

He didn't speak, and for a moment she was afraid he didn't understand what she was trying to say.

"Does this mean—?" His chocolate-drop eyes asked her the question, too.

She ran her finger along the edge. "I added this on the way home."

There was a new border. An amber wheat field in full grain against a vivid Dakota sunset ran around the edge.

"You did all this on the way home?"

"It goes quickly when the heart is in it."

"It means—?"

"It means I think I will stay. Andrew will need me."

"Yes, he will," Micah agreed.

It seemed as if neither one of them breathed for a long while.

Then, at last, Micah broke the silence. "You answered that question. Will you answer another?"

It was moving so quickly, this thing that she had wanted and was yet so afraid of.

She bent her head and could not speak.

He spoke for her. "Catherine, I know this is very sudden, but would you consider being my wife?"

Her heart answered first.

"Yes, Micah, I will—consider it. I cannot agree to marry you until Andrew is back and healthy once again. If, by the time a year has come and gone, another crop planted and harvested, you still want me and I still want you, then yes, I will marry you."

"Walk with me in the moonlight," Micah said suddenly.

They went as one into the fields, now cleared of grain. The harvest was in, but the greatest one was yet to come. There was no reason for fear, only belief, for those who loved each other and their Lord.

꽃

The prairie was warm that night, and the sky was aglow with starlight. He could feel it so clearly: All creation was happy.

His prayer was simple and heartfelt. "Thank You for the chance to love. It is enough."

Epilogue

They walked down the road together. They were going slowly because the little boy alternately begged to be carried and to be allowed to walk on his own. A soft July breeze sent a strand of the woman's hair across her face, and the man smoothed it back behind her ear.

The church's bell began to toll, the call to worship ringing across the prairie, and the three hastened their footsteps.

"We don't want to be late, Cooper," Catherine said to her son.

He looked at her with eyes as dark as his father's. "No. Up." His chubby arms were lifted to her, and she swung him up to balance him on her waist. She never tired of this, nor did he.

Micah looked at his wife and child, and his heart flooded with warmth. Four years ago, he had prayed for love, and now he had it not once, but twofold.

A man could not be happier, he thought.

A shout from the converging road told them that Andrew and his new wife, Ardette, were late this morning, too.

Catherine's brother now walked without any hesitation at all. The only sign of his injury was a faint scar along his hairline.

The five walked to church together, hurrying their footsteps to arrive before the first hymn began.

As she slid into the pew next to her husband, their son nestled between them, half on her lap and half on his, she let herself look at the picture on the wall beside the altar.

There, bordered by a frame that Andrew had carved during his rehabilitation, was her stitchery. The letters caught the gentle Sunday sunshine and seemed to glow with the message: "Be not afraid, only believe."

She realized that Micah was watching her, and she smiled.

There was no fear in her heart; there was only love, for now she believed.

For as long as she can remember, **JANET SPAETH** has loved to read, and romances were always a favorite. Today she is delighted to be able to write romances based upon the greatest love story of all, that of our Lord for us. When she isn't writing, Janet spends her time reading a romance or a cozy mystery, baking chocolate chip cookies, or spending precious hours with her family in North Dakota.

If you enjoyed

THE PRAIRIE ROMANCE
COLLECTION

then read

WILD PRAIRIE ROSES

A Daughter's Quest by Lena Nelson Dooley
Tara's Gold by Lisa Harris
Better Than Gold by Laurie Alice Eakes

If you enjoyed

THE PRAIRIE ROMANCE
COLLECTION

then read

BLUE RIDGE BRIDES

THREE-IN-ONE COLLECTION

Journey to Love by Lauralee Bliss
Corduroy Road to Love by Lynn A. Coleman
The Music of Home by Tamela Hancock Murray
